Vancouver

Vancouver

A Novel

David Cruise and Alison Griffiths

HarperCollins*Publishers*Ltd

www.harpercanada.com

HarperCollins books may be purchased for
educational, business, or sales promotional use.
For information please write:

Special Markets Department

HarperCollins Canada

2 Bloor Street East, 20th Floor

Toronto, Ontario, Canada M4W 1A8

First edition

National Library of Canada Cataloguing in
Publication

Cruise, David, 1950–
Vancouver : a novel / David Cruise and Alison
Griffiths.

ISBN 0-00-200658-8

I. Griffiths, Alison, 1953– II. Title.

PS8555.R83V36 2003   C813'.6
C2003-900498-8
PR9199.4.C7V36 2003

HCNY 9 8 7 6 5 4 3 2 1

Printed and bound in the United States

To dearest Claudia: our firstborn, out on her own.
May your life be as rich as ours has been.

Contents

PART I

Manto

and

Inish

1

＊

13,477 B.C.

Utqiagvik, Northern Alaska

A dozen pairs of small, round, black eyes stared greedily into the tall man's black face. The children scarcely breathed, so intent was their concentration. His words floated over and around them like a warm breath—deep, sonorous, enriching.

"The Mountain carried the child people in her belly. She lifted up her face to the sky and spoke to One Spirit, asking, 'Is it time to send my children to walk the earth?'

"One Spirit answered, 'No, it is too cold. They are fragile. They will freeze to death.' The sun came and went many times. The moon bared its face and hid many times. Again and again Sopka, the Mountain, asked One Spirit the same question. Again and again One Spirit replied, 'Too cold. Too wet. Too dark.'"

The children, packed shoulder to shoulder on rugs of skin, blinked raptly as Tall Man acted out each part of his tale, speaking with two distinctly different female voices to represent One Spirit and Sopka.

"Finally, Sopka became impatient. She came to believe that One Spirit did not want to share the world, and the people in her belly would die if they did not feel sun on their faces. She felt her children move inside her and thought of releasing them without One Spirit's permission. But she worried that One Spirit might kill them in anger."

"No! No! Save them!" the children called out.

"Yes, little seals, save them. That is what Sopka wanted. And soooo," he drew the word out in a slow, low growl, "Sopka did a terrible thing."

"What did she do?" the children asked, barely able to form the words in their excitement.

"She made a bargain with the most powerful *kelet* of all, the changeling maker of storms. She agreed to let the changeling command all the land that could be seen from her highest peak if it would create a storm strong enough to carry away One Spirit."

Tall Man stood up as high as he could in the *qargi,* the communal snow shelter, waving his arms furiously, hooting and howling as the voice of the storm. He grabbed a child's hood of tuttu caribou fur that lay across her back and quickly pulled it over her face.

"And all was gone!" he boomed. The children shrieked in fear and glee.

"It blew and roared as the *kelet* called winds and snow from all the world. Rocks bigger than the largest whales were lifted up and carried off. Every tree was sucked off the edge of the world."

"Trees," the children breathed.

"Yes, show me what trees were, before the *kelet* took them away," instructed Tall Man.

A boy awkwardly made the trade sign for tree that Tall Man had shown him, elbow of one arm resting on the back of his other hand and fingers of the upraised arm wiggling, to symbolize branches moving in the wind. The sign had to be taught, as no trees grew in the land of the Yupik, the ice people of far northern Alaska.

"The storms blew away all color, leaving only white behind."

The children chanted, "Color! Color! Color!"

Theirs was a world of limited palette, though great differences lay within that palette for those who knew where to look. To the Yupik the white surrounding them had a hundred shadings, each with its own portent and name. The yellow white *mauyaq,* fooling snow, which masked rotten ice below; the purply cast of snow bridges spanning dangerous crevasses; the almost colorless white of *pilik,* ice crystals in the air before a storm; brownish-tinged *aunniq,* breaking-up ice.

"One Spirit hung on and hung on against the powerful winds until . . ."

Tall Man leaned forward, fists clenched in front of him, gripping an invisible object, face contorted in an incredible effort of fighting against an unseen force. The children's eyes moved as one to his long fingers. First one finger, then all failed.

". . . until suddenly she could hang on no longer!" His hands flew apart and the children's heads snapped back. "Ooooo!"

"And she was gone."

The Tall Man paused for a moment to let a vision of the events form in their young minds.

"Sopka was happy. Her children could be born at last. In her excitement she lifted her head and cried out her joy to the sky and called forth her children. Out they came from her belly in clouds of steam."

"*Sopka akimaruq!*" the children clapped their approval. "Sopka won!"

Tall Man shook his head in sadness. "She won and lost. Sopka was too happy, too full with pride. She showed no humility in her victory. Fire and steam and rock flew out of her belly. Too much! Her people fell everywhere. Rolling down the mountain, falling down cliffs, plunging into the river and behind chased rock that melted as it met the earth. Sopka's joy made the river boil and the lakes turn to fire. Children were killed from falling, from fire, from drowning. Sopka tried to stop it but she could not."

Tall Man's head dropped to his knees with the tragedy. The children rushed to him, patting him all over, soothing his pain.

"Sopka began to cry," he whispered, holding out his hand, and in his palm were small, milky-green, nearly oval objects. "Her tears froze and lay everywhere."

The children touched the smooth-faced things. They rolled about Tall Man's cracked palm, clicking softly against one another. Beqat, the bold boy who was first to make the tree sign, picked one up and rubbed its soft skin against his lips.

"Babies inside?"

"No," answered Tall Man, "only sorrow."

Beqat placed the green bead against his cheek, where a tear might lie.

"Sopka wanted to die," Tall Man explained softly.

The children nodded their understanding. Death was preferable to life without children, for children, they were taught, were the sustenance of life. No children, no life.

"Who will save Sopka?" asked Tall Man.

"One Spirit and Black Bird!" the children shouted joyfully.

Tall Man smiled. "Yes, One Spirit was not dead. As the storm blew her away, Black Bird plucked her from the wind. His wings were as large as a whale's tail and twice as strong. Black Bird brought One Spirit back to Sopka. One Spirit knew that she must accept blame for the death of Sopka's children, for it was true, she did not really want to share the earth.

"So One Spirit asked Black Bird to bring more children. He flew off and was gone for many seasons. When he returned he opened his mouth . . .'" Tall Man stretched his mouth wide and stuck his tongue out. The children all did the same.

". . . and out walked children. Black like the bird, black like rock deep within Sopka." He leaned forward urgently, "And where did they come from?"

"Kahnamut!" the children threw up their hands.

"Yes. Yes. This is the story of the Nush-da and how they came from Kahnamut to live in Sopka's valley."

✳

"First people. Black people."

Tall Man smiled. "Yes, black with the earth in their bodies. My people. The Nush-da were the first people. As time passed, more people were made, but there wasn't enough color to go around. Each new tribe became paler and paler."

Tall Man reached out and sunk a finger into Beqat's round, soft, smiling cheek. "Pale like the little seal here." The boy giggled, pleased to be singled out.

"It is said that somewhere there are people more white than *nanuq*, the ice bear."

The children laughed, their tawny faces flushed with pink from the warm air inside the shelter. How awful. How would you see them against the snow?

Tall Man's eyes sought those of his own in the group inside the snow shelter. Manto. The boy's long limbs folded against him, he looked like a young caribou asleep on the snow. Tooke, Tall Man, had four children and eleven grandchildren, all of them shortened and lightened by Yupik blood—except Manto. When the first of Tooke's children was borne by the warmhearted wife of another man, Tooke felt as if his people had disappeared. No trace of the Nush-da, the Tall Man's birth people, could be seen in the baby boy's light-brown skin and pebble-small nose, nor in those that followed. The Nush-da may well have been the first people, Tooke thought gloomily when the first of the grandchildren began arriving, but our blood has not left the slaughter field of the Nush-da valley. The valley lay deep within the Siberian peninsula of Kamchatka, seamed by volcanic ridges and capped by a broad expanse of rocky tundra. Everywhere the land defied survival except in the valley, where a microclimate protected and nurtured it. It was there that the Paleolithic black-skinned people settled, having made their way from the African continent in the sudden warming trend of thirty-five thousand years ago, when modern deserts blossomed and the hunters of Africa followed their prey from one opening landscape to another. In eastern Europe and Russia they clashed with the Neanderthal survivors—light-skinned, flat-faced, and stocky. The two peoples drew apart, one to the plains of the Dnestr, Don, and Dnepr, and the other, the

Nush-da, followed the path of the woolly mammoth, musk-ox, and woolly rhinoceros on their trek toward Beringia.

It was Sopka, as Tooke told it, who drew the Nush-da away from Beringia and south into the lush valley of the Kamchatka. It was Sopka who gathered her children to her when enemies from the north and the flooding of angry seas changed the earth once again as it warmed to turn back the glaciers of the last ice age. And it was a furiously erupting Sopka who nearly killed them all.

I have long left Sopka, Tooke often contemplated. All that remains of my people is the color of my skin and the green tears Sopka shed over us. Then came Manto. Long-limbed, curly-haired, and thick-lipped, with a broad, fleshy nose twice the size of his Yupik playmates', he was the image of *Pi* Tooke, his grandfather.

✳

Eighteen years before the birth of Manto, Yat, the walrus hunter, found Tooke embracing death on the Alaskan side of dying Beringia, the deteriorating ice bridge between Siberia and the high arctic of North America. The nearly frozen creature, heart barely beating, emaciated body curled inside a thick, ragged cape decorated with unusual objects and elaborate braiding, could not walk or even open his eyes. Yat hurried back to his village, fourteen domed *aputyaq* of identical size and shape made from perfectly carved blocks of hard snow, each with a tunnel entrance. Yat had little time, as winter was losing strength and the ice devils were already beginning to wake. Their cracking and groaning could be heard at great distances as they stretched and yawned deep inside the ice. Soon it would not be safe to travel.

How strange that Yat should be in that place, should find that man, the villagers later pondered. Why had he strayed so far from his usual hunting area? Normally neither he nor any of the other Yupik ventured near the Lonely Sisters at that time of year. Yat himself could provide no answer.

"I set my feet toward the walrus place," he told the other hunters as they chewed dried fat. "But I found they would not do as I told them."

"Maybe one of the Sisters called you," teased one. "Maybe they'd like to try a man."

Yat laughed. It was as good an explanation as any.

The Lonely Sisters, two nubs of land facing each other—one in Siberia, the other in Alaska, across the Bering Sea—had sinned. As people, they preferred each other's bodies to those of their husbands. They were banished forever to live on either side of the narrow sea, touching only briefly in the

coldest months, while the ice devils slept. As the weather warmed fraction-
ally during the months when the sun shone, the bridge tore at itself, leaving
gaping caverns, treacherous crevasses, and a thin skim of snow, hiding a
certain plunge to death for any foolish enough to venture across.

This was fit punishment, to the Yupik's way of thinking. Though kind and
trusting by nature, they judged harshly those who strayed outside established
ways. The sisters had sinned and now they suffered. That was as it should be.

✳

"Where did this long, black creature come from," they marveled as they
dragged Tooke back to their snow houses. "Is it a man?" Some said yes.
Some said no.

Matti, Yat's wife, took one look at the nearly frozen creature and said,
in her practical way, "Let us make it live again, then we will ask."

Matti directed them to bring Tooke into one of the shelters and lay him
upon a snow bench, which was lined with fur. It was very awkward, as the black
being was extraordinarily heavy, despite its emaciated condition. Long limbs
left little room to maneuver through the low entrance. Inside, a small stone vat
of blubber burned, blackening the icy walls with smoke. Matti stripped off her
three layers of clothing, sealskin outer layer, wapiti next, and finally otter, which
lay against her skin fur-side in, for the most warmth. She peeled the tough walrus *mookuks,* packed with rare goat wool, off her feet. Then, with her giggling
sisters, she set to pulling off the black thing's clothing. After the battered leggings came off, she scurried to the opening and stuck her head out.

"A man!" she called to the curious throng, making a penis shape with
her hand at her crotch. "It is a man."

"Ahhh!" they responded in approval, clapping their hands in triumph
as if they had personally created him.

For three days Matti lay with Tooke, whom they called Takko, or Tall
Man. Later, at his insistence, it became Takko Tooke. Hour by hour, her
thick body warmed his, and by the second day she could feel his heart
regaining vigor. Yat visited her often and they talked about what to do with
him should he ever wake up. Matti left the bed only to relieve herself in a
stiff, skin pan, which one of her sisters emptied twice a day.

"I brought you liver. It is still warm." Yat handed over the small, slippery organ from the bird he had painstakingly stalked earlier that morning,
the third day. Matti, resting on one elbow, chewed it appreciatively. Yat
squinted into Tall Man's face.

"This one may be wrong in the head," he suggested.

"Why do you say that?" asked Matti, licking her fingers, wishing Yat had killed two birds.

"To walk so far without a sun finger is not the act of a normal man," he stated. "If he wakes he will be *illuktuq*, snow-blind. I am certain."

The Yupik never traveled anywhere without a sun finger. Thin strands of gut woven on a semi-circular bone frame formed a visor, which they wore on their heads. It acted as a hand with fingers slightly splayed to deflect the piercing rays that bounced cruelly off the permanent ice. During the light months the sun remained just above the horizon for hours on end, blinding anyone foolish enough to walk without protection.

"Where did he come from?" pondered Yat.

"He must have come from the dying sun. All people came from there and walked into the morning sun, did they not?"

"But he does not look like us nor like those who live closer to the dying sun. Nor any others we have ever heard of."

Matti nodded. The Yupik knew that other people of the ice lived to the west of the Lonely Sisters, though they had not been seen in several generations. They too were fishermen and hunters. Stories from generations ago told of the two arctic people on either side of Beringia, the ice bridge created by the sisters joining hands, hunting mammoth together. For a few brief weeks the wasteland lived with grass and gnarly heather, which grew in pockets of soil and gravel left behind as the polar glacier retreated. The great creatures moved slowly across from one continent to another, fattening on the fleeting delicacy. But since Matti and Yat's great-grandparents were young, the going had become too treacherous and the herds of mammoth shifted their summer foraging to the tundra of the permanent continents.

✳

"He moves!"

Yat jumped to his feet excitedly, nearly hitting his head on the low roof of ice.

Tooke's lids pulled themselves ajar and instantly tears flooded from his eyes. Burning pain. Stabbing shards right into his brain. His fingers dug into his eyeballs seeking to alleviate the torment. Yat pressed a handful of snow onto the man's sore eyes, then scrabbled out of the tunnel to summon the others. The shelter, with two snow sleeping-shelves, comfortably held four people, six if some were young children. Within minutes, twelve bodies crammed inside with as many more outside eagerly waiting their turn.

Matti dressed as best she could and squeezed past them.

"It is good to walk again," she said to her sister who hugged her out-side. "He will live, I am sure, but his eyes are very bad. He may not see. Yat thinks he is wrong in his head."

"Should we send him back?"

"Back where?"

Her sister pointed to the weak glow on the western horizon. Matti shook her head and tapped her finger to her chest.

"I do not believe he came from there."

"But all people came from there."

"Not any who look like that," she emphasized. "I believe he is the seal that took off his flippers and tail."

"Yes, of course, there is a story of such a man," the sister said, remember-ing. A seal, hunting fish for his family, was blown far from his home by a terri-ble storm. He became trapped and confused by the endless narrow fjords that poked deep into the land, ice rising tall on either side, each one looking much like the last. Desperate, the seal decided to go overland, so he took off his flip-pers and tail and became a man. He never found his home, walking forever in search of it. This must be that seal for, like the seal, he was long and black.

✳

Tooke intended to stay with the Yupik only until he became strong enough to travel again. Through pantomime, snow-drawing, and arranging the precious store of pebbles Yat kept inside his shelter, Tooke made it clear he would leave one day, but the Yupik knew better. Matti poulticed his eyes with fat, and eventually he was able to discern objects and faces at short distances, but the Yupik doubted that he could ever again navigate for him-self in the open country. His eyes pained him constantly and he was not blessed with the Yupik's innate ability to find their way even in the very worst conditions. The following year, when his eyes improved as much as they ever would, Tooke ventured out on his own.

"Your nose is too big!" laughed Yat, who eventually found him and led him back.

"What do you mean?" Tooke demanded crossly, feeling like a child whose mother had yanked him back from danger. Yat laughed again at his annoyance but also at Tooke's deep voice mangling the choppy words of the Yupik tongue.

"We do not look for our way, we smell it. But your nose is far too big. It takes in too much. You are confused."

"Smell your way? What nonsense! There is nothing to smell!"

Yat thought for a moment. How could he describe something that just was to someone who had no experience of it. His mind went round and round the puzzle as he led the tall man back.

"I know!" he said, stopping so suddenly that Tooke bumped into him. "I will close my eyes while we walk home and I will describe what I do as we go."

"You can find your way back without seeing?" Tooke asked dubiously.

"Of course."

Tooke kept a careful watch on Yat to make sure he wasn't cheating, a notion that never entered Yat's mind. They walked in silence for some time.

"Here!" Yat finally shouted triumphantly.

"Where?"

"We are back."

Tooke could see nothing but a low ridge of snow.

"On the other side of that *aniuvak*," Yat said without opening his eyes.

Tooke carefully walked to the top of the ridge and, sure enough, could just make out the humps of the *aputyaq* roofs.

"But you said nothing the whole way!" he protested to Yat.

Yat shrugged. "There was nothing to say."

✳

By the end of his second year with the Yupik, Tooke was much stronger but his resolve to find the legendary Kahnamut had weakened. He thought often about the Nush-da story of that place, and wondered where his days would end—here or there. Time seemed full among the Yupik; these were good people. He would wait until the next season of long sun. He would go south to find Kahnamut then. But the long suns came and went and Tooke never left.

Yat offered to share Matti, who happily bore Tooke two children, with one more each from her younger sisters. All were ruddy-skinned, flat-faced, and straight-haired.

Tooke's sight was too poor to allow him to hunt. His teeth were not strong enough to work gut and skin into rope, and his fingers were too damaged from frostbite to help make the bone skeletons of the travois that the Yupik used to haul their catch. There was little stone available to make blades and weapon points—the specialty of his family in Kamchatka. He could not even participate in the throat-singing ceremonies at the beginning of each new moon, as his tongue, which had swelled badly from thirst during his trek, did not have the nimbleness of the Yupik. What earned Tooke an honored place among the Yupik were his stories. In time, their languages melted together, as languages do, and he was able to add layer upon layer to his tales of the Nush-da, their destruction at the hands of treacherous traders from the north, his three-year walk from the valley in the shadow of Sopka, and his near death on the eastern side of deteriorating Beringia. Always he told them of Kahnamut, the mythical land that held the secrets of the Nush-da's origins. The Yupik dissected the stories of Kahnamut at length, wondering about the portent of Black Bird and curious about what a river of fresh-water entirely free from ice might be like.

Tooke told them of Elkit, the ancient woman who claimed to have traveled from the valley of Sopka on Kamchatka all the way to the Lonely Sisters, across the narrow sea, down through mountains, a long valley corridor, and into a land of a color none of them had ever seen. Green, like the tears, but more. His story told of one man left there while the others returned the same way, a voyage taking so long a caribou or even mammoth would have lived out its life.

The Yupik were entranced by his descriptions of Kahnamut and awed by the notion of trees. But none felt the slightest desire to go there—wherever "there" was. They already lived in a perfect land, their kingdom of ice and snow. And they were quietly amused by his contention that black people walked the land long before the Yupik. But no hint of their feelings ever leaked out. They were happy to allow Tall Man that vanity; it did no harm.

By the time the story ended, light had almost disappeared inside the shelter and Tooke could barely make out the faces of the contented children. He took hold of Manto's hand.

"Come, it is late. Your mother will be angry at me."

Manto chortled at the idea. The Yupik were rarely angry, though there had been a terrible scene early in the winter when two young brothers had shouted at each other over a broken harpoon tip. Each blamed the other, and their argument came to blows, with one boy suffering a cut that scarred him from eye to jaw. There was tension in the air for days afterward. The unusual flare-up caused a wound on the body of the Yupik that needed more time to heal than the damage to the boy's face.

At seven, Manto was as tall as his mother and almost as tall as his father. Tooke looked at him proudly.

"Are there really more who look like us?" the boy turned his face to his grandfather, his breath puffing steamy clouds with every word.

"I am not sure," confessed Tooke. "An ancient woman of my time, Elkit, told me many times how the Nush-da came from Kahnamut as I described it to you. She also said that our people went back to that place and brought news of it to the Nush-da valley."

Manto hopped up and down, eager to finish the story. "Yes! Yes! And the one left behind was a bad man who could never see the beautiful world."

His words made Tooke shiver. Often, as he looked at the world around him through his watery, weak eyes, he felt like the man in the story, the man who could not see. The man who had been left behind in Kahnamut to claim it for the others.

Elkit's words came to him. "The land was bountiful, and all manner of creatures offered themselves up. Soon he stopped hunting and fishing for himself. He ignored One Spirit and told her he did not need her any longer. He lived in the land of plenty and had all a man could want. Angered, One Spirit summoned Black Bird, who had saved her, and bade it to embrace the man in his great, black wings. When Black Bird released him, he looked around him and saw nothing—though it was all still there. And that was his punishment. To be surrounded by plenty, to know it was there, but to see nothing."

"Is this *my* punishment?" he wondered. "Perhaps I am in Kahnamut but can't see it. Only white and gray and shapes in the distance."

"*I* will go to Kahnamut," Manto was saying, stamping his feet in emphasis. "I have told Iko, my mother, that I will go when I am fifteen and a man. I will go and bring back more like me and your green stuff that lies on the ground. *Pi!* Grandfather! I swear! You will sleep on it warm and comfortable."

Tooke barely remembered the feel of broad blades of summer grass beneath his feet but he easily conjured up the rich, green color of the Nush-da valley in the short summer and futilely tried to describe it to Manto and the Yupik.

By the time Tooke died at the tremendous age of forty-three, Manto was on fire with the quest.

2

*

"You must have hit your head when you slipped out of your mother," Arqat, grandson of Yat, scoffed when seventeen-year-old Manto announced his decision to seek the origins of his grandfather's people in the big river land of green-on-the-ground and trees.

"Ha!" retorted Manto. "And who cannot find his way from one *aputyaq* to another?" Arqat took the jibe in good humor. Despite the Yupik's extraordinary skill in navigating the featureless terrain, as a child, Arqat had become lost going the short distance from his mother's snow shelter to his aunt's. Fourteen years later he was still teased about it.

Manto grew serious. "I want to see Kahnamut. I want to know if other black skins exist. And trees! Do you think they are as wondrous as *Pi* Tooke said?"

No one in Manto's world had ever seen one. Arqat doubted whether any such thing existed. Before Tooke arrived, there had been no word in Yupik for something that grew like a giant stem of tundra grass and had many arms, like a man, with bunches of green where the fingers would be.

"The ice will surely end long before you reach Tall Man's origins as he told it," Arqat stated emphatically. "And where there is no ice there is no world. It just is. How can you find what is not there?"

"What you say has reason," Manto admitted. "But I must go. I promised *Pi* Tooke that I would find Kahnamut." This wasn't strictly true.

As Tooke neared the end of his span, he became unable to distinguish between the Kamchatka valley of his birth and the legend passed on to him by Elkit. He became confused about Elkit, the elder, and in his last few years Tooke described her as a spirit helper of Sopka, who lived in Sopka's volcanic, black-sand skirt.

Manto was filled with sorrow when his grandfather's storytelling started to flounder; the words seemed to dry up on themselves, and each recitation ended sooner than the last. Tooke even forgot he himself had been trying to reach Kahnamut after his people had been slaughtered, and when Manto vowed to take up his quest, Tooke smiled benignly and wondered what he was talking about.

To the Yupik, promises were like spiritual currency. Breaking them left one poorer. So Manto had presented his own growing obsession as a vow to his grandfather, which, of course, must be carried out without question. Then there were the green tears. Now carried in a small sack suspended around his neck, the beautiful stones proved the truth of Tooke's stories in Manto's mind. He had no doubt of what they were. And if the tears of a great mountain in a far-off land to the west of the dying sun existed, then Kahnamut must also.

When he left on the first day of endless sun, there was no grieving, celebration, or prayers. Manto's departure was a simple act of promise-keeping. His mother, father, brothers, sisters, and the rest of the extended family expected that he would make an attempt to fulfill his promise, then return, honor intact, long before the sun grew weary and headed for its long sleep.

As Manto traveled south, the ice accompanied him. Initially he kept the tormented coastline in sight even as it began jutting west, pushed there by the immense range of mountains that erupted above the tree line. Along the edge of land and sea, death lay in every footstep. Like a restless spirit, the earth shifted constantly and the longer the days the more the turmoil. Massive flows, urged forward by the North Pacific drift as it melded into the Alaskan current, locked themselves with the land as if trying to climb out of the sea. Cracks in shriveling ice gave Manto gravelly shelter in their cavelike folds but made walking and climbing extremely difficult as he pushed onward. He remembered Tooke's directions to the big river land with green-on-the-ground, directions he said came from the old spirit woman born of those who had been there.

"Warm this side as the sun wakes," Tooke touched Manto's left cheek in a moment of clarity about his grandson's quest, "and warm that side as it walks toward sleep," he laid his finger on the boy's right cheek. "In that way Kahnamut will always be before you."

When Manto adjusted his course to move with the sun, he bypassed, without realizing it, the great Alaskan landmass bulging out toward Siberia. By the time he reached the banks of what later became known as the Yukon River, late in the summer, he was sure he must have completed his grandfather's quest. He had moved from tundra to coniferous forest in just a few moon cycles, and the sudden change in vegetation and animal life awed him. The shrubby arctic birch and willows gave way to jack pine—tall, straight trees with a sharp, pointed froth of green at their tips. He chewed the needles, enjoying their bitter taste and sharp aroma, and he found the sap marvelous for repairing cracks in the small bone bowl made out of a mammoth skull, which he used for drinking.

Manto grew lean and hard in his months of travel. The rich darkness of his skin stretched glowingly over his body. Before he departed, his father gave him two sun fingers, sternly warning him never to move across the land without one strapped to his forehead. But in this oasis, at the elbow of the river, with the most northerly range of Alaska at his back and the southerly mountains far in the distance to the south, he did not need the fingers, for the permanent ice had left him. The Yupik were obviously wrong, for the earth did continue after the ice was left behind.

This certainly seemed like *Pi* Tooke's descriptions of Kahnamut, Manto concluded. The sun warmed the skin enough to put aside furs at the high point of the day. And there was plenty to eat. Tasty purple berries grew fat on bushes lining the river, and he saw animal spoor everywhere. As he considered the situation, he cut a shaft from the whippy bushes growing near the mouth of a creek intercepting the river and easily speared two fat silver fish with humped backs.

Manto spent several days savoring the rich smells of the forest and the mouthwatering taste of fresh game before starting to explore. Altering his direction slightly every day, he walked the maximum distance that would allow him to return to the camp each night. At first he set out in high spirits, but as the days passed, his step became heavier and his resolve weakened. This was a place of perfection, just as Tooke had spoken, but there was no one like him here. No one at all, in fact. No track, no spoor, no hint there had ever been. As the story had been told, the arrogant Nush-da who had been blinded by the wings of Black Bird, had sired many children with the beasts that served him. And the offspring all took human form to populate the rich land. But there was no one here. If he had reached Kahnamut, what now?

Curiosity drove Manto on this journey, but he had given no thought to what he would do when he arrived. "You are *heetit,* curious," his friends had said as the child Manto shifted one rock after another just to see what lay beneath. *Heetit.* The word didn't have an altogether positive connotation to the Yupik.

As the sun dwindled more quickly each day, Manto contemplated, for the first time in his life, the future beyond his quest. He could certainly stay. There seemed to be plenty to keep a man alive. But there were no people, specifically no women. The Yupik blood in him demanded children. What would be the point of staying in this marvelous place if he was alone? To die without ever mating was unthinkable!

In ten thousand years' time, the fourteen hundred miles stretching south from Manto's shelter on the banks of the Yukon River to the mouth of the Columbia River where it splits the Cascade Mountains would be home to the second most diverse collection of languages on earth. Eleven language groups with nearly forty tribal tongues would make Europe seem a banal linguistic landscape in comparison, with its single Indo-European family encompassing every language, except Turkish, in the straight line from Dover to the Bosporus, roughly the same distance as from the Yukon to the Columbia.

But on that day, more than thirteen thousand years before the birth of Christ, Manto, son of Iko and Maku, grandson of Tooke and Matti, appeared to be the only human being in existence. Perhaps *Pi* Tooke's story was only partly right, his grandson thought as he worried over his isolation. Perhaps the arrogant one who had taken One Spirit for granted was here but could not see or be seen.

"I am here but no other," he spoke aloud. His Yupik words were spiced by the low trill of Nush-da intonation assimilated from Tooke.

Something else bothered him—the great Black Bird so prominent in Tooke's stories, and recently in Manto's dreams, with wings as long as a man's body. It held the secret of the Nush-da. Tooke assured Manto that it would appear, yet there'd been no sign of it.

"If I see it, will it make more who look like me?" Manto often queried. "Does it carry our people in its mouth, like the green tears you carry always?"

"Yes, little Manto!" Tooke had clapped his hands together. "That is it!"

"Then I will search for that bird," the boy said solemnly, "and bring the color back to our home. I will make my brothers and sisters as dark as me." When he told this to his family, they roared in delight and rubbed his skin hard with their hands to see if the glowing black of the child's skin would slip onto their own.

These thoughts carried Manto through the nights. Days he spent fishing, gathering sumptuous berries, and improving the shelter he'd fashioned with three stripped poles lashed to a tree, forming a roof skeleton that he covered with many layers of branches. As the days of the long sun rapidly dwindled, the air grew crisp, sharpened by a wind that shifted from west to north and became more powerful every day.

It was a punishing wind destined to be famous. Nineteenth-century northern sailors and explorers dubbed it Retribution as it hurtled off the Arctic Ocean, powering its way along the lowlands of the Yukon River. In Manto's time, the faces of retreating glaciers hanging chalky and raddled off the mountains on either side cooled the air, lending energy to the blast. It hit Manto the way he had once seen a sea bear rise full-force out of the water and strike a man flat.

Long before dawn on the day that Retribution struck in earnest, Manto's shelter was pummeled to kindling. He had never felt colder nor more desolate in his life. He tried to think. This could not be Kahnamut. There were no people, no Black Bird, and now it was cold and he felt the snows coming. He must not have traveled far enough. That must be the answer. If he had found this place, as briefly kind as it was, perhaps Kahnamut yet waited for him.

The mountains, sharp and hard with the virility of youth, implacably stared as he trudged along the narrowing valley of the Tanana, which broke from the Yukon and flowed south. Within a month, he had reached the mountains to be called St. Elias, which stunned him with the immensity of their long, white march along the western horizon. Each day he moved, the land became more rugged, as if whatever spirits had created this scape were in constant argument. But the valleys remained broad, as the great floods of the next millennium had yet to swell rivers, lakes, and oceans, and claim back land once covered by the glaciers. The valley of the Tanana was also quite flat, which made it easy to press southward. As more storms overtook him, he tunneled out snow caves to wait till their fury passed. With plenty of food dried from the summer catch, he snugly weathered the worst storms. In this way he traveled the whole winter, his Yupik heritage making it possible to stay on a southern course despite the days of darkness.

Early the following spring Manto spotted the two-legged creatures. After watching them for a time, he surmised they were people of a sort, though stones grew from their bodies, and their faces had no eyes, noses, or mouths, just holes without definition. Fear quickly replaced *heetit*, as the walking beings began killing—not animals but each other.

Manto had never seen humans fight, though his grandfather had spo-

ken of it often. Yupik boys and girls played like bear cubs, robustly rolling
and tumbling but never hurting intentionally. He clutched the pouch that
lay against his skin just inside his hip. The Pale Tears, Sopka's tears, the
seeds of the Nush-da, passed to him by Tooke just before his death.

Faceless things, they flailed away furiously with stone clubs, sharpened
poles, and what looked like long knives on the end of short sticks, which
they thrust at each other with screaming grunts.

✻

He must get as far away from these creatures as possible. Manto was convinced they were *ircinrraqs,* or their forest equivalent: mischievous but
sometimes vicious people of the ice and summer tundra who woke in
spring. In Yupik stories, they danced and played on the rivers breaking up
in summer, but they also were contentious and fought each other at night.
In this place they must also fight during the day. Manto turned to run.

The death howl stopped him. There had been five. Three battling two.
When one of the two fell, three attackers hacked at its head, finally hauling
it from the body with jubilant shouts. The other being was on its knees,
jabbing desperately with a double-pointed stick to fend off the attackers.
The taller of the group of three swung a stone club over its head and Manto
could hear a cracking thud as bone shattered. The victors urinated on the
bodies, then, drunk with triumph, they swaggered off, pushing and shoving
each other like boys at play.

For nearly an hour Manto crouched motionless, waiting to see if the
ircinrraq spirit maker returned to make the slain ones whole again. Finally
the *heetit,* curious one, could bear it no longer; he crept forward. They
bled! Their bodies were covered in skin! Paler than his, but skin indeed.
They were people! The faceless heads were actually wooden masks carved
with eye and mouth holes.

Their clothing particularly intrigued Manto. He poked tentatively at
one lifeless form to ensure he wouldn't come alive. Across his chest was a
leather plate of tough, thick hide covered with wooden slats. Manto marveled at the evenly fashioned pieces of wood, each as thick as a finger and as
wide as a man's shoulders. Smaller slats were woven together, covering the
upper thighs. The wooden armwear was jointed at the elbow to give the
being full range of motion. Stones had been somehow fastened to the chest
armor to repel blades. How they remained stuck there Manto had no idea.

The thing's head cover was tall, like a flat-topped cone. Manto assumed it had been made from skin but he ran his hand cautiously across the surface—wood! Around the tower of the hat, daggerlike teeth were painted, and at the crown, leering lips split apart. What skill they had, to make such things and decorate them so exotically! The art of the Yupik lay not in their hands but upon their tongues. They wove stories as other peoples wove cloth. But these people were capable of extraordinary craft.

Manto knelt on all fours to examine the hat more closely. It was held on the being's head with straps of hide, which were inserted into the base of the hat through carefully carved slits. The hide pieces were then attached to the shoulder garment. Manto wanted it. It was the most ingenious, beautiful object he had ever seen. With trembling fingers he reached forward to remove it. The head lolled grotesquely. One strap untied, then another, six in all.

"*Aaayuk! Untuuk!*" a voice shrieked.

Manto leapt to his feet with a cry of fright. Then his eyes widened in amazement. Before him stood a tiny human, squat, bowlegged, possibly female. Her teeth bared in an animal snarl as she poked at him with a sharpened stick. At her waist hung a club with a stone head, a smaller version of the ones the fighters used.

✳

Inish was more than a little surprised herself. She had seen the end of the battle from a bluff above the river where she had been gathering firewood. Certain the fallen were from the family that owned her, she hurried down the cliff path, losing sight of the bodies as she ran. Two families had been feuding for many seasons. Already each had lost four members. Should two more be killed from her own family, there would certainly be war on a larger scale, with other alliances called upon to bolster their numbers. She was almost on top of the dead warriors before she saw the incredibly long man—he looked more or less human—bending over one of the dead. When he jumped up to confront her she almost dropped her spear stick. The whites of his eyes shone from an earth-dark face. It was not paint, she was sure of that. And he wore a headdress of black moss.

She bellowed, then lunged forward, the point of her stick grazing his ribs. Manto grunted in shock, grabbing his side. Blood gushed out through his fingers.

"Ooomph!" he staggered back, staring at her in disbelief as she moved to strike him again.

Wako, the low wolf, saved Manto's life. With short legs and broad body the wolverine looked ungainly but there was hardly a creature living which could match it for short bursts of speed. And pound for pound, there is no more ferocious animal than the low wolf. Even the great ice bear avoided it whenever possible.

As Manto and Inish faced each other, *wako* crept between them. A barking snarl drew the pair's attention. A wolverine never retreats when it has the opportunity to fight. With no more warning it flew at Inish who was closest. Short legs belied the animal's tremendous jumping ability. It caught her ankle but also the stick. She screamed and tried to wrench the shaft free of the animal's powerful jaws.

If a single intelligent notion had sped through Manto's brain, he would have run, leaving the ugly one to its fate. Instead, he snatched up a river boulder and, with the skill learned from many seasons of stunning fish, he smashed the rock down upon the wolverine's head as it wrestled with the stick for a better grasp of Inish's ankle. A perfectly aimed, fatal blow.

"Oh, Seeriq, save me please!" pleaded Inish in her own language as she fell to the ground. "Let him use me but let me live. Seeriq, I will sacrifice double to you. Please, Seeriq. Hear me!"

"That must have been the devil in the Hungry Moon," Manto responded shakily in Yupik to Inish's back. "You have terrible devils here. I have heard of the Hungry Moon's anger when the season of less comes upon it," he babbled. "But I have never seen it. No, never! I hope to never again," he went on, his voice breathy from the fright now past. "Did it hurt you?" he reached over and touched Inish's back.

"Nooo!" Inish shrieked, flipping over and crab-walking backward on her hands and feet. "I beg you, Seeriq! Stand with me. Stand with me," she burbled.

Manto bent over her, his large hand, cracked and pinky-brown on the palm, splayed over her face. Inish sucked in her breath and shut her eyes, cursing the Seeriq spirit that had never done her a moment of good in her wretched life, for all the precious sacrifices she made to it.

Suddenly she was upright, as if blown to her feet by a gentle wind. And then she was sitting again, cradled in the lap of the black thing, her bitten leg grasped between his hands. He drew her injured ankle to his mouth.

"Tulgut!" she moaned. "The Black One is an eater." Strength fled from her body and she sagged against the cannibal. On the edge of conscious-ness, she became aware of a warm sensation as the cannibal licked the blood from her wound. Then a sharp pain as the black thing took a first bite, and she fell senseless.

"It is important not to leave tooth marks in your body," he explained in a soft voice to the senseless form. "Its spirit will get inside you where it will live. You will die." Manto nibbled at the torn flesh until he pared the ragged skin, leaving a clean-edged wound. The Yupik would have seared blubber and packed it into the wound. But Manto had finished off his last chunk long ago.

Manto considered what to do with the body in his lap. It was clearly a female: he could see small but womanly breasts through a gap in her covering. But she was ugly and smelled terrible. When he looked at the wolverine's nearby corpse, he remembered his mother's ministrations to women in childbirth. The blood should be as fresh as possible. Eel fish was best, but . . .

He leaped up after setting the little figure to one side. He took his bone knife, far superior to the clumsy things the fighters were stabbing at each other, and sliced into *wako*'s chest. The heart still had the spongy elasticity of life. He quickly cut it out of the body. Kneeling, he squeezed blood from the heart, drop by drop, on the woman's torn ankle.

Through slitted eyes, Inish watched the long, black man. She was intensely pragmatic. Caught in a life with little advantage, she took it where she could. Manto turned and caught her scrutinizing him. He smiled tentatively. The woman was not appealing, but she was human. Her people seemed very dangerous, like walrus in mating season—but they were people. He had begun to think he was alone in this land. Knowing he was not gave him renewed vitality and hope.

✳

That night, as meat from an animal the Tlingit called *dzisk'w*, moose, roasted on hot rocks set in a fire pit, Inish, with permission from her owners, spoke of the encounter with the attackers and the low wolf. They would own the story once it left her mouth, but she had the honor of presenting it first. Though it was her first time in the center of the circle, Inish spun the tale as if wealth was her heritage and she owned stories and songs in abundance. Her stubby arms waved energetically as she hopped on her uninjured leg around and around the circle of people, emphasizing one point or another. Her gestures were so broad and her miming skills so evocative, Manto understood most of the re-creation of the battle.

"There were ten of that family," Inish exclaimed, holding up both hands. "They trapped our brave *x'igaa káa*, soldiers, and demanded ransom. The *x'igaa káa* refused. 'We are rich and the owners of many songs! They scorned the enemy! Your family is poor and has few songs. We two shall sing longer than you ten. If we do not then you may fight us if you dare and take ransom if you win.'"

Inish hobbled back and forth, naming the songs the soldiers sang. Naming them was permissible but no more; the songs belonged to others. "Our *x'igaa káa* sang and sang until the ten could not match them. I heard something! There were birds in every tree! They added their joy to our soldiers and drowned out the voices of the ten."

She dropped her chin down into her short, thick neck for emphasis. "We triumphed but the ten were furious. They refused to honor the victory. The ten attacked, cutting the brave *x'igaa káa* down. Ten cowards, with spirits of rabbits!" Inish's voice rang out as the gathering joined her in raucous condemnation.

She swung around, both arms outstretched and hands clasped, the Tlingit sign to acknowledge nobility or greatness. She pointed toward Manto. "The birds could not help against club and knife and treachery so they brought us the giant Black with moss for hair and skin like earth."

"*T'ooch' káa*. Black! Black!" The assemblage bellowed approval.

"He floated from the trees and the ten were so terrified they ran away."

"Cowards!" the throng growled.

Manto, squatting silently in the warm bath of the fire, blinked. He got the gist of the story as Inish was telling it, but it didn't match his recall. For one thing, there were only five involved. Yet the woman held up both hands.

"*Wako*," called out Nama, her owner, for Inish had already described the attack of the low wolf to him. "Tell us again of *wako*."

Inish set her lips eagerly; this was the best part. "One of the ten summoned up the low wolf, who only helps liars and cheats."

Her audience murmured agreement. This was true.

"It attacked without warning!" Inish hopped around to provide a view of her wounds. "Then Black picked up a rock it would take five men to lift," she said, stretching her arms as wide as she could. "With one hand he threw it into the air and commanded it to find the head of low wolf."

She demonstrated the dramatic moment with a stone she scooped up from the ground and flung it into the fire, causing an impressive eruption of sparks.

"Ahhhhh!"

Her voice slid into a growly whisper. "I was near death, as low wolf had sucked out my blood. Black," she pointed again at Manto, who hoped she was saying something good, "swept me up and lay his mouth water over the broken flesh. I live! I walk!" Inish slumped to the ground, exhausted by the performance.

Dancing went on for hours inside the palisaded fort built by the Tlingit on a precipice over the floodplain of the river Taku in the northernmost reaches of what would be British Columbia. The location of the fort intrigued Manto. The Yupik situated themselves either where protection from the elements was favorable or, in summer, for easy access to migration corridors of reindeer, mammoth, and wild horses.

The Tlingit's enclosure was permanent and sited for entirely different reasons, with sharpened posts planted at a forty-five-degree angle to impale any who tried to rush the fortress. Logs were strategically stacked around the walls, the bottom ones attached to a long hide rope, which, when yanked, upset the top logs and sent them tumbling down on intruders. The location of the village meant a difficult walk—treacherous, Manto suspected, in the rain or snow—to get water or food. The Tlingit's waste pits were also inside the walls, something that would have appalled the Yupik. It didn't make any sense to Manto.

Manto intended to stay just long enough to replenish his dried-food stores and acquire sufficient skins to protect him in the winter ahead. But as the weeks went by, the Tlingit pestered him to remain. Conversation grew easier as Manto happily detected words similar to the language of the Yupik. He already had a grasp of more than one tongue, as Tooke had taught him songs and stories the way the Nush-da told them. The words of a third language came easy, once he opened his ears, stopped struggling to understand, and let the phrases embed themselves in him.

"No one travels in the snows," they said over and over, not believing his part-pantomimed, part-spoken stories of the great distances covered by the Yupik in winter, when the ice was safer and snow bridges strong.

The Tlingit called him Essaht, seeker, when he managed to explain that the pale green rocks he carried were the seeds of his own people, which were shed by a great mountain as tears. The story was in high demand and he told it again and again, improving it each time as his tongue became more comfortable with the rounder edges of Tlingit.

For the rest of that summer and long into the winter he watched the Tlingit prepare for war to avenge the death of the two *x'igaa káa*.

"More of your people will surely die," he stated to Nama, the owner of Inish. "How can that be good?"

"If we do not fight then we are useless," shrugged Nama, amused that Black, for all his size, did not seem anxious to join in the fighting.

"But what use are you if you are dead?"

"Not dead!" scoffed Nama. "Removed. The strength of the one whose walking spirit has gone away is given back to his people. It's like this," Nama said, motioning to two of his children to join them. "Pass me stones!" he ordered. He placed one small one in Manto's palm. "You are born with a small heart, small spirit. If there is no courage in your people, the heart and spirit remains as it is born." He took more stones from his children who shoved at each other in their eagerness to be the one to hand them over.

"But when your family defends itself and its tribe, their strength becomes yours." He added more stones to Manto's palm. "If they take from others and build their wealth, you grow stronger. And when your time comes to be a man, then you begin to gather your own stones and your heart and spirit swell with your deeds."

Manto glanced at the pile in his hand. "How many stones do you carry?"

Nama puffed his chest. "So many I had to turn them into a mountain!" he said, pointing to a snow-capped peak in the distance. The children giggled and strutted, proud of the boast. Manto smiled.

"To vanquish the ten cowards you too must have a mountain," conceded Nama, "though not as large as mine!"

Manto silently eyed the stones. According to the Tlingit thinking, he thought, my heart would be little more than a pebble.

The early days of the warming sun were auspicious for war. The Tlingit were ready. Manto was not. He had been revisited by the old dream planted in his head by his grandfather. He woke, certain Tooke had just spoken in his ear, urging him on. Manto was rested and well provisioned. He would never admit to his pugnacious hosts that he had no desire to see their blood spilled. The day before Nama was to go into seclusion to discuss with his spirit the tactics of attack, Manto announced his departure.

Nama was disappointed. He would have liked to see just how this long, black man handled himself in a real fight. Still, he could not let him leave without gifts, as the story of the two against ten now belonged to him, thanks to Manto. He would be diminished if he did not at least match the offering.

"Here," Nama pushed Inish toward Manto as he gathered his few possessions and a store of food lashed to a pack. The travois of the ice lands would not work on this rugged terrain. "Not much to look at," Nama said, ritually belittling the gift. "And she bears no children, but she will carry for you and keep you warm at night."

Shocked, Manto held out his hand to ward her off. "I could not take a person as a gift!" he protested.

Nama pushed her at him again and said with finality: "I have no need of her! You will take her."

A cheer rose up from the group of Tlingit gathered to watch Manto's departure. Manto made as if to refuse again but Inish's terrified look and Nama's gathering scowl convinced him otherwise. For all their good humor and hospitality, these were not people to anger lightly.

Without another word he turned and strode off, not looking to see if the woman followed.

3

✳

"Kwakwaka me," Inish declared as they sat on a fallen log savoring the last of a brown hare she'd deftly snared. "My mother was chiefly rank."

Kwakwaka. Yet another of the peoples who lived on and near the coast far south of the ice lands. When permanent ice ended on Manto's journey to Kahnamut, people started springing up like seals on *sarri,* ice packs, at spring mating. The Kwakwaka tribe lived to the south and west of the Tlingit stronghold and spoke a kindred language. In time they would evolve into the most feared of coastal warriors, the Kwakiutl.

Manto was surprised by her words. They had been traveling south from the Tlingit settlement at the very southwestern edge of Alaska for several moons. At first he hadn't known what to do with her. When they stopped the first night, she gathered wood and built a compact fire in minutes. In the morning she silently carried more than half of Manto's possessions. While they walked she introduced Manto to the lore of the forest. His life had been snow and ice, not tree and rock. Finding game in the woods and, more important, killing it, identifying edible plants and in general finding his way about, were utter mysteries. As the forest grew denser, he couldn't see the stars at night or even the sun at rise and set, which made it impossible to orient himself. Inish taught him how to read the moss that grew always on the same side of trees, though sometimes it was only a subtle shading on the bark. It was as reliable as the sun, or the large night star, for setting direction.

From the first, she scouted far ahead, finding the easiest path. Try as he might he could not keep up, though she carried more than half the weight. Finally he asked her secret.

"One must know long and short walking," she explained. "I doubt that you can do it," she added.

"I am Manto, grandson of Tooke of the Great Walk," he stated.

"You walk like a fish," she countered.

✳

The long walk consisted of a limber, exaggerated stride, which quickly covered the ground when the going was easy and flat. "Make yourself like a forest creature," she instructed, "if you want to be as fast as me." Once Tooke got into the rhythm he was able to keep pace; short walking was another matter. He never mastered the small-stepping, slightly hunched, buttocks-tucked technique needed for scrambling over boulders, hopping over deadfalls, wading streams, and scudding down slopes.

Aside from those few words of instruction, in their entire time together Inish said little until the day they sat on the log pulling the meat off a hare.

Manto assumed Inish was a Tlingit who had done something to shame herself into what they called *goox*, slavery. Nama, her owner, had tried to explain *goox* to Manto, but the concept was foreign to his Yupik heritage, though Tooke had told stories of his people owning slaves—flat-faced, light-skinned captives from northern Siberia.

Nothing about Inish suggested chiefly rank. She wore no labrets—decorative stone, bone, or wood plugs in her lips, cheeks, or ears. All Tlingit men wore lip labrets, but Manto understood that the highest-born Tlingit and Kwakwaka women had them also, usually in their cheeks. Inish saw him looking at her face.

"We were taken during the grease wars," she stated matter-of-factly, with none of the flourishes she used to embellish the story of their attack. "My two brothers and self. The slits had not yet been cut, I was too young." She traced a stubby finger across one cheek. "My mother was sick. Coughing all the time with blood coming. They took the four of us, but my mother could not walk fast enough, so they killed her."

She spoke the words with glacial calm.

"Your brothers live?"

"One. He was sold to the Haida Gwaii, people from across waters. Became *goox*." Manto had heard of the Gwaii warriors who lived "across waters," in the sleeping sun. They traveled in enormous boats carrying as many as twenty. Their lives were on the deep salt water, whereas the Tlingit and Kwakwaka, with a treacherous coastline, turned to the land and river. No one knew where the Haida Gwaii came from. It was said that the Gwaii conjured up enormous sea creatures from the deep, which lifted their boats above water so they could mate and sleep. When the Gwaii boats appeared, terror reigned, but it had not always been so.

"My grandmother told me a story, which came from her grand-mother," Inish related. "It was of the time before the Tlingit took me. Among our people it is women who tell and men who dance," she added.

"Haida Gwaii came seeking an alliance. They brought their canoes up the river my grandfather's family owned for summer fishing. My grand-mother said they were tall, like you, and very dark but not black. Their faces were long too, like yours, but their hair was straight."

"An alliance?" Manto queried.

"They asked our people to help them take a Tlingit village, which was very rich. This village was also powerful, with two strong houses that they boasted no one could penetrate."

Inish slid from the log and settled in with her back against a thick branch. Manto moved to sit beside her.

"That was the beginning of the grease wars."

As Manto squatted next to Inish, eager for the story, he ran his hand over the rough skin of the tree being. He would like to see one fall. It must be an extraordinary sight. If he lived to be as ancient as his grandfather Tooke, he would never look at a tree without amazement. He wished he could carry one north. He would like to see the faces of his Yupik family as he placed a giant tree in front of them. They would have to invent a word for it then!

"Why fight over grease?"

Yupik shared their oil, which came from the blubber of seal and wal-rus. Grease in the south came from small fish, Inish told him, about as long as a man's hand. The fish swam thickly in certain streams of the Kwakwaka and Tlingit territory. It was so rich in oil it could be dried, set on fire, then stuck into the ground to serve as a torch. The Tlingit called it *oolachon*, the Kwakwaka *hollikan*, and the Haida Gwaii used a word that meant "to save," because the fish became plentiful in the dying of winter when most gath-ered food was gone.

Frowning, Inish held up her hand at his impatience for the story to unfold. Though permissible for the Yupik to ask questions, or even intro-duce a tangent during a story, the Tlingit and Kwakwaka considered such behavior a gross rudeness.

"Haida Gwaii wanted ownership of a grease trail, a stream where the *hollikan* ran. They paid for my grandfather's help with their origin story, four exceptional *goox*, and a long boat filled with whale bones." Manto nodded his appreciation at the magnitude of the gift. Origin stories were rarely traded among these people.

"But Haida were treacherous," Inish continued. "They had already linked arms with Tsimish, from over the mountains."

Tsimish! Another people. Supposedly of Tlingit descent, the Tsimish, who had been driven over the mountains eons ago, longed to return to the coast lands. Manto had heard of this during his time with the Tlingit.

✳

"While my grandfather feasted the Haida, Tsimish moved near at night and attacked. It was a terrible battle, beset from within and without, but my grandfather escaped with others from different families. Haida took our grease trail. We were very poor for many years."

"I thought the agreement had been made? How could they break it? What shame!"

"You cannot trust Haida, Tsimish, or Tlingit."

"How did your family get wealth and chiefly rank back again?"

"Before I was born we lived in cliff caves. While the grease war ran up and down the coast, we retreated there. There were great runs in those years, and everyone grew rich, which made them want to steal the grease trails of others. As my grandfather told it, Haida and Tsimish fell out, then Kwakwaka and Tlingit took back some of the trails. Families within people fought each other, and some tribes were reduced to a few people."

"Families fought each other!" Manto gaped.

"My grandfather and father took back a small grease trail and were living there to protect it, when Tlingit came and destroyed our village and killed my mother. My father tried to get us back. He offered the grease trail and everything else in his possession, but Tlingit laughed at him."

Inish bowed her head.

"Then the Tlingit sent a runner to my father. They would accept his offer if he filled a bowl with the blood of his own."

"But there were only two left who were free!"

"Yes. So, my grandfather decided it would be he. My father protested but the decision was made. They came to Tlingit village, and before all, my father cut my grandfather." Inish pressed her finger across her throat.

"Blood gushed. Everyone cheered. But my father could not capture all the blood."

"Did he fill the bowl?"

"It was a very large bowl." Manto had his answer.

"Tlingit killed my father. They said he had tricked them by telling my grandfather's spirit to take the blood with it when it left."

Inish sat quietly. A blue armored beetle hopped in front of her, and she reached out her open hand slowly, until it hovered just above the fat bug. Then she moved so quickly the bug was snared almost before Manto saw her move. Inish offered it to him and he swallowed it.

"They threw my father's body off the cliffs into the water, where it pounds day and night. Tlingit never bury enemies or dead *goox*," she added.

Inish collected firewood for Nama's family, matching the loads of the male slaves of other families. Tasks like freshening the pits where tribal members relieved themselves, a daily job of layering aromatic needles on top of the waste to keep away flies and reduce odor, earned her an extra chunk of fish or meat. If Inish displeased Nama or a family member, she was beaten. Thanks to her plainness, she was rarely bothered sexually.

That was the last time Inish spoke of her people or her life with the Tlingit.

"No other stories are mine," she explained with finality when Manto urged her to tell him more.

✳

Manto's skills as a hunter left much to be desired, though as a fisherman he was unparalleled thanks to the skill of fine string-making and hook-carving—both of which he showed to Inish. He also taught her the Yupik art of slinging, which conserved harpoon tips during the salmon runs, when the fish were dense. So far north, the river broke for only a few weeks each year, so it was important to catch as many fish as possible. The women and young boys waited on the riverbanks for fish to surge forward. As they did, the men, with a quick wrist flick, launched stone missiles into their hard-charging midst, often stunning two or three fish at once. Women and children quickly scooped them up in baskets made from pliant young seal bones woven with gut.

Inish and Manto moved into a dry, narrow valley, which pointed them south like a beckoning finger. Initially they crossed many shallow rivers, which teemed with fish, but in the last two moon cycles the rivers had become far deeper and barren of fish. With little oil left, Inish wondered how she would feed the embers she carried when it was all gone. Manto's invaluable string allowed her to feed the embers gradually by dipping several strings braided together into the oil and then laying them across the ember bed. Inish carried the ember sack, a stiff leather pouch with ventilation holes. A carved-out stone sat inside, cradling the embers, which smoldered for hours as they traveled. When they stopped, she kindled a fire with the embers and a handful of tiny dead branches, blowing and feeding it until it burned hot and strong.

✻

Their first winter, Manto and Inish sheltered on a rock beach near the edge of a tiny lake. It was a well protected site and at first there was plenty of game and lots of fish. Then the lake froze and the game disappeared. Even the giant rabbit no longer left its prints in the snow around their camp. As the snow accumulated, cold set in and their food was consumed.

"Do not lose your spirit, little plug," Manto said. "I go now to catch fish through the ice. I waited until the ice was thick enough to walk on."

Others in her tribe had derided her stature. Even Manto teased her about it. "Get off your knees," he would order her when she stretched to her full height of four feet. In the time Manto lived with Nama he would often see her returning to her rough shelter next to Nama's fine house built of log and stone. He noticed bruises on her body from blows landed by irate women when she didn't do her work quickly enough. One day he whispered to her: "Stand tall, little plug!"

"It is forbidden," Inish shrieked. "Fish sleep in this time! No one may catch them. We will be cursed if you disturb them," Inish wailed. "And they would be poison to eat."

"How do you know they sleep?" he asked, astonished at her reaction. "How do you know they are poison in this time?" Manto retorted. "My people catch fish every winter. In just this way."

"My people know!" sputtered Inish, anxious to distract him from this foolish plan. "Even the Tlingit know."

"Perhaps your people simply don't know how to catch fish," Manto snorted.

"No one eats winter fish. No one!"

"We have no meat. How will we live?"

"We can go back."

"Go back?" Manto said incredulously. This was a side of Inish he had never seen before. Always she had been willing to push forward. Kahnamut was his destiny. A destiny passed to him. Of course, it would be hers as well.

Inish quaked when Manto set out onto the ice. They were near starving.

Manto took some embers and branches for a fire. Once it was burning, he built a tiny shelter on the lake with their last skins and tended the choking, smoky fire until the ice was soft enough to drive a pole through. That day he landed the first fish on a bone hook, baited with their last morsels of meat. When Manto brought the fish, fat and blue, to show Inish, she cowered away from it.

Manto cavorted in a circle around her, offering the fish to the heavens, caressing it lovingly, beating himself across the chest with it. Inish shrank farther away.

"I am a man, oh fish, oh fish! I am a man!" he yelled in great puffs of icy breath.

By the time he had finished his celebration dance, the fish was beginning to freeze. He dropped to his knees in the snow, pulled his fine blade from his belt, and swiftly peeled off skin and scale to preserve them. Then he sliced off a thick, juicy fillet and cut away the liver. He scooted into the hut on hands and knees.

"The fish came to me, Inish. Look!" Grinning, Manto proffered the choice meat.

"Aieeee! Get away! You are a fool! We will die if we eat the fish!"

"We will die if we don't," he countered.

No amount of coaxing could persuade the frightened Inish to take a bite. Finally, on her fourth day without food, she was so weak Manto was able to dribble some fish blood into her mouth. By dusk she was gulping the remaining fish down with both hands. No more was ever said about the poison of winter fish.

✳

Inish held her hand up to the sun, positioning her four fingers horizontally, with her baby finger lying along the horizon to judge the time remaining to sun-lying-down. The light lay behind her middle finger. Solstice was not far off. She did not know what to expect from winter in this place. The climate had recently changed from dry and cold to wet and cold.

✳

They neared the time of the Hungry Moon and Short Sun. It would be their second winter. The bitter wind seemed pulled down from the north by a powerful hand that unleashed the force of every blow on top of Inish and Manto. They crept south, day by day, growing gaunt yet strong. The trees grew taller, thicker, and more numerous. At times they blocked the sky for days as the two travelers threaded their way through narrow valleys and along rocky tributaries. The underbrush was denser too, with fat, green leaves wetly smacking at their legs, or gray, hard needles hiding vicious thorns that ripped flesh more easily than the sharpest knife. Some days Manto's legs streamed blood, yet Inish rarely suffered a scratch. The sun lived longer now than in the Tlingit lands but still weakened with every day. And now the sound.

Manto felt it up through the soles of his feet. It vibrated in his belly and sent a finger of sensation into the back of his throat. Inish crept up beside him. Manto looked down on the top of her head.

"I feel it too," she whispered, holding her hand over her stomach. "Does Kahnamut have such a voice?"

"*Pi* Tooke said it has the sound of a great black bird. He calls to the one who sees him and leads the Nush-da to the land of our beginnings. I am Nush-da through *Pi* Tooke. I believe the great Black Bird will call to me."

"This does not sound like a bird of a size to make this noise."

"No," agreed Manto.

He looked off into the distant south, where blue-gray caps of ice shrouded the shoulders and peaks of a long range that had followed them almost since Manto left the Tlingit with Inish in his wake. Manto knew Inish doubted the existence of Kahnamut and that every day she expected the ground to end suddenly beneath their feet. Still she came, keeping her fear hidden. She was a very practical woman. Born to rank, she'd lived with fewer rights than a dog. Yet she had adapted to that life as she would adapt to this one.

The rumble rose and fell rhythmically.

"It is water," said Inish.

"Of course," agreed Manto.

"But a great water."

"Perhaps it is the belly of the earth itself," Manto breathed, biting back his excitement. "Kahnamut."

Inish shut her eyes. They'd traveled nearly nine hundred excruciatingly hard miles, most of it along an inland corridor running between the glacier-capped peaks of the Rocky Mountain chain to the east and the mostly ice-bound coast to the west. The corridor possessed a unique microclimate, a magic pathway, drier and warmer than the surrounding ice-bound country.

They did not know it, but if they'd chosen to follow the coast they would have been long dead. The last of the massive ice sheets were drawing back. The process had been under way for nearly two thousand years and would continue for another millennium, but what would be Alaska's and British Columbia's western boundaries was beginning to reveal itself. Shelves of ice sheared off without notice, natural bridges collapsed in tons of rubble, crevasses suddenly opened to reveal the young bays and inland waterways. But in their protected inland corridor, Inish and Manto found adequate game and a route they could travel in relative safety.

※

Manto gurgled in his throat following the rumble in the distance.

"We move on and find what makes this sound." He looked over his shoulder. "A brown bear has followed us for two nights."

"Four," Inish corrected, holding up that number of fingers.

"Four?"

"Four."

"Why did you not tell me?"

"The bear has brought me child," Inish said shyly. A rare smile split her long, drooping face. She folded her stubby fingers across her stomach.

"The bear is watching to make sure she has placed the baby in a worthy body."

"A child?" Manto said stupidly.

For nearly two years they'd had no contact with another soul. Manto had become accustomed to her thin breasts and her squat limbs, which folded inside his so easily for warmth. Their bodies had joined, sometimes in fear, sometimes in despair, and occasionally in joy. Though she always accepted him, it had never occurred to Manto that her unfortunate physique could give him children.

"A child?" His hand went to a thin packet of fine soft leather he wore slung across his chest. The side next to his skin was worn to a gloss from the oil and sweat of his body. He fingered the shiny stones of rich yet palest green, twelve in all, the same number his grandfather had when he'd left the valley of the Nush-da.

"A child."

"We move on," said Inish.

※

The forest had grown impossibly thick in just a few days. No obvious route led toward the rumbling that shook the earth. Together they picked their way cautiously over rocks strewn across the path and down steep slopes. The rocks were black, sharp, and slippery with moss.

Now Manto walked ahead, ranging widely, searching for easier routes. Inish trod deliberately, slowly, guarding her cargo.

One moment it was a belly-felt rumble, the next a reverberating wave. Manto stumbled back, gasping at the power of the noise.

Wet, black canyon walls plunged straight down to a roiling mass of water. Spray coated everything, and a permanent mist hung above the riverbed. Huge rapids clashed with rock and exhausted themselves in furious white whirlpools. Manto and Inish had seen and heard a young glacier peel away from the parent ice with crack and thunder. They had felt the earth shudder with the storms that ushered in the boreal lights. They had once watched in terror as the moon mated with the sun and the gods, angry at this unnatural joining, sucked light from the day.

But this noise, this power. Nothing matched it! Manto grew dizzy. He stepped to the edge; sound rolled up, filling him like a feast. He moved closer to feel the booming caress.

"Manto! Come back!"

Inish's hand at his belt dragged him back. "What are you doing!" she shrieked, fear whitening her cheeks.

"I . . . I don't know. For a moment the water became me. That was what I was."

"We must move on," she urged. "It is too wet to stay here. The fire will not take."

For three days they struggled through a jungle so tangled and slippery that every few steps brought them to their knees. The sound of the river gradually receded.

"That was the mouth of death," breathed Inish. "What do your legends tell of it?"

"Nothing," replied Manto dully, confused at the sudden change of terrain and weather and sickening from the cold and wet.

It rained and rained. It rained so hard the downpour seemed to move the horizon. Try as they might, neither could tell where the sun rose or set. The world retreated, leaving them in a hollow pocket of their bodies and wearying feet moving slowly through the sodden forest. They thought they were moving south but could not be sure; rain obscured everything.

"The embers are dead," Inish said one night as they lay huddled between two tree roots that rose like bent knees out of the mossy earth. They had battled to find a crossing or an easier path that might lead them away from the river. This giant, angry snake could not be the wide placid river of Tooke's Kahnamut. Even the sun fled from the terrible noise.

But the river, from the time of its birth between two young volcanic ranges near the fifty-fourth parallel to its maturation in the wake of three major glacial scourings, was a watercourse of many conflicting characters. Sections of it are like discordant family members, tied together unwillingly, always at war.

"Kwakwaka say the coast runs to the whale winter grounds where sun and moon and water and land become one," Inish muttered, pointing to the west. "That is not your Kahnamut, but it is somewhere. I will find the coast toward the setting sun but stay away from the accursed river, which is running that way," she motioned southward.

"You talk again of returning!" spat Manto angrily, before dissolving in a racking, phlegmy cough. Since they'd moved out of the dry, cold valley into the dense, damp forest, the harsh coughing spells attacked him more and more. Inish thought of her mother, who had weakened in the same way.

"You are tired. We must try to stay dry. Tomorrow I will look for spark rocks and kindle the embers. Then we can begin again. See," she said, pointing into the darkening sky at the quick scudding clouds. "It will be dry when the sun wakes again."

That night Inish lay awake listening to the rattle in Manto's chest. When his breathing finally settled and deep sleep claimed him, she inched herself away. Earlier in the day she'd found some nuts and cones, which yielded several handfuls of seed meat. She took these with her, along with Manto's broad hat and an ancient cape that had been repaired many times. Covering him with layers of evergreen boughs, Inish backed out of the crude shelter, sprinkling needles and balls of pungent resin as she went, to obscure their scent. She prayed the animals would not find him before she returned.

She would go west and find a route away from the river. The way south held nothing but danger—of that she was certain.

4
*

Inish strode briskly, the morning sun warming the back of her head. The mad river was moving south but she knew that all normal rivers flowed west, into the dying sun—that was her experience. Where the sun died was the big water that tasted bitter on the tongue. The Tlingit and Kwakwaka believed that a great creature waited in the deep beneath the ice flows for the summer rivers to empty themselves into the bitter water. The creature sucked back the now poisoned river, cleaned it, then returned it to the streams on land. Where the river waters gave themselves up promised good fishing.

The Kwakwaka, her birth people, also believed the river was Toogu káa, the mother spirit. They spent every moment, from first spring melting to the new snows, at river mouths provisioning themselves with fish for the winter. When the fish slept, the Kwakwaka moved upriver, where the narrow valley enticed game and sheltered pockets of plants and herbs. Also, on the banks grew smaller trees with flexible branches, remarkably useful for making baskets. Rivers were *kusti*—life. But Inish wanted nothing to do with the terrifying power of this mad one. In the thousand-mile journey from her homeland, nothing had frightened her as much, not even Manto's ice fishing, but the child within her belly made her determined to survive.

After a few hours of long walking, the rain stopped, and despite the heavy gray clouds Inish knew she was heading for the sun's resting place. There she would find the bitter waters and perhaps, just perhaps, signs of people. There had been no indication of people for so long Inish was certain they must be nearing the end of the world.

The sun was just reaching its apex when she felt a soft drumming underfoot. Then a low hum. The sound traveled up her legs, prickling with terror. She knew right away it was the mad river. It had looped around and caught her. She turned and ran, tripping over slippery roots and sliding on the thick, slimy carpet of leaves.

An hour, a day—Inish didn't know how long or how far she ran. Trees grabbed her with clinging tendrils, the sky darkened, thorny underbrush leaped out at her until her legs and arms were raw. Three times she changed direction, three times the sound caught her, surrounding her like an eel enclosing its prey. The thrum of water against rock beckoned. "Come to my arms, Inish. Come behold me, Inish. Lay your body in my embrace. Inish. Inish. Inish. Inish."

Her tears stopped. Her legs were heavy and languid. She could fight it no more. She was lost here in a dank land ruled by an evil river.

"Inish. Inish. Inish," it whispered.

She walked toward the sound, anticipating the explosion of boiling fury once the river had her in sight. She had not eaten since early the previous day. Her head felt light, as if it would float away from her body if she didn't hold on to it.

Her feet found the edge before her eyes warned her. Inish grabbed a branch and barely saved herself from falling over the precipice. On closer inspection, it wasn't nearly as steep as the cliffs that guarded the narrow cauldron upstream. She took a deep, slow breath and, willing herself to be brave, peered over the edge. Another breath. Sharp and shallow this time.

Before Inish lay the mad river, transformed—broad, green-blue, and gentle, it napped against a group of large rocks in its midst, later cascading over a series of gentle rapids. Lingering mist clung to the area where she crouched, but through it she could see, bathed in sun, a wider, kinder river with a low bank meeting grassy hillocks, which were rising to the point where she stood. She spotted a herd of tiny deer scenting the wind before nimbly picking their way down to drink. At the limit of her vision, the plume of a waterfall rose into the air. That was what she had heard and felt earlier. The shoreline in front of her was very narrow but flat. It promised shelter and food.

Inish gazed in wonder.

"*Makuiq ar Kahnamut?*" she breathed.

It took Inish all day to make her way back to Manto. This time she followed the river as best she could even as the trees closed in, the banks grew high, and the rocks dark and wet. Seeing the river's gentler side stoked Inish's confidence. Now the growing tumult reassured her. She sang to it as she moved along, the thudding crash singing back, guiding her to Manto. She found a plentiful supply of mushrooms and devoured them so hungrily her chin and hands were stained black from the spores.

Some hours later, Inish heard something making its way awkwardly through the woods.

"Inish! I am here!" Manto croaked. Inish flung herself at him. "I have found what we need!"

"Is it Kahnamut of the Nush-da?"

"I don't know what Kahnamut is except in your head. But I have found what will be our place. There is game, fish, I am sure, and shelter."

"Are there faces in the trees?"

"No," she replied flatly.

"Did you see Black Bird?"

"No, but . . ."

Manto raised his hand to silence her. "That is not my vision. It is not the story of *Pi* Tooke. We must seek another route."

"Another route?" Inish gaped at him. "We will have food! The land welcomes us there."

"In Kahnamut the trees rise to the sky and hold the faces of my ancestors. That is the belly of the earth."

"Manto!" she said, almost growling. "My belly tells me this is the place. I came back for you. I will go there and no farther." Inish grabbed at his arm. It felt flaccid under her strong, stubby fingers. The life seemed drained from him.

"Come with me!" she pleaded. "We will have a child. Please!"

He looked into her pouchy face sunk into neckless shoulders.

"Manto!" she urged. "We must go!" Manto turned away and began to chant the Yupik song of farewell.

Quietly Inish gathered her few belongings—the stone ember bowl and its pouch; a smooth, elongated rock with a bulbous end, which had many purposes, from grinding seed to smearing fat over skin that was being cured to stunning freshly caught fish. Then, from the things they shared, she carefully selected two spear tips, four lengths of string, one burin blade finely finished and one still rough, which could be fashioned into either a blade or a scraper. She took the clothing on her back; a loose cape of otter, which repelled the rain; a skirt that had once fallen below her knees but now was so shredded it resembled loincloth; leggings; and a cone-shaped hat of woven fiber that she also used to gather roots and berries. They had two tightly wrapped bundles of foot skins, which they strapped around their feet for travel on the snow and ice. She tied one bundle to her back with a length of gut.

Inish fingered the two hooks Manto had made for ice fishing but put them back. She picked up the flat packet that cradled the twelve wonderfully smooth, pale-green objects. Tears of a great mountain, seeds of his people.

Inish had mixed feelings about the stones. Her people's gods were more practical, inhabiting the whale, fish, and seal. They fed, punished, and sheltered the Kwakwaka and gave them children, but she doubted any gods would have created something so exquisite with no obvious purpose. She had followed the man, not his stories or his stones. Still, she hoped that the sight of the sacred tears might rouse him from his torpor.

"Manto," she said softly, tinkling the stones from the pouch into his lap.

He stared resolutely away from her. Inish sadly laid the pouch on top of the lovely array. "*Héen, dáx náx, káa,*" she said as she left. "River, we come, my child and I."

The rain began again. Not so much rain as thickening sheets of moisture coating her hair and face in a sweaty sheen. Inish would return to the spot where the river opened its true heart to her. There her child would be born. The two of them would be the first, and likely the last, to tread that land. There were worse ways to spend what remained of a woman's life.

Darkness was beginning to fall when Inish sought shelter in a jumble of rocks. Heaped against each other, they would provide protection from any deluge. It was also close to where she'd found the mushrooms, and her belly was already gnawing at itself.

✳

"Stand tall, little plug!" a voice boomed. Inish started and for the second time in a year her lips stretched earward.

"You thought you could steal from me!" barked Manto, ragged but regal.

"I stole nothing."

"You took my best burin!"

"Those you gave me when we joined."

"You took my string!"

"I made that string with your instruction."

"You took my spirit rocks! The tears of *my* mountain."

Inish pointed at his chest. "They lie against your chest."

"And what of the ember pot!"

"It is my own."

"You run away with *our* child!"

"Unborn, she belongs to Nnarlik." Nnarlik was a god with a very short attention span, so her parents gave her possession of all children but only until they breathed air.

"And born," Inish continued firmly, "she belongs to me."

"And to her father!" Among the Yupik, children were viewed as developing in both woman and man equally. When their wives went into labor, men would seclude themselves and suffer sympathetic agonies of birth. No woman could leave her mate when she was with child, for it would be akin to stealing.

Manto reached for Inish and glared down at her.

"Go. I follow."

✳

The rain pounded on. Manto thrashed in Inish's wake. He felt so weary. Each step drained him a little bit more. Inish seemed to be moving so quickly. Why was she running like that? Lifting his head, he saw her standing, waiting. He crouched down, held his knees, and coughed until a thick bloody wad filled his mouth. Inish waited patiently for him to stand upright. Water streamed across her face. She felt no chill from the weather, but a cold knot lodged inside her.

"Come, Manto, come," she urged. "We will find the green banks and the warm sun and you will be better."

They descended to the narrow, gentler shoreline Inish had discovered. She could easily feed Manto here. He hadn't eaten much in days.

"I will fish with my string," he said weakly, struggling to untie the sodden skin bag strapped to his back.

"No," said Inish. "I will go. I do not need your hook and string. From up there," she pointed to the high bank where she had gazed over the river's new self, "I'm sure I could see the fish. All I will need is this." She held up a sturdy forked stick used to trap the fish in the shallows.

That night, struggling against the gusting torrent of rain, they attached their tattered canopy of skins to a massive tree fallen near the water's edge. Even in the dim, water-washed light, Inish marveled at the glow of its thick white skin, which curled back onto itself up and down the main trunk. The tree was a majestic birch of the type that, in those times, grew only in the warmer valley of the Fraser River. A hundred feet tall, with branches spreading outward like opened arms, measuring two feet at their base. It was the biggest tree of its kind Inish had ever seen.

Inish nestled against Manto under the skins, which did not keep them dry but at least stopped the worst of the deluge from soaking them further. Manto's lungs labored with every breath, the rattle almost matching the downpour in volume. Finally Inish descended into sleep only to waken a few hours later as her face slipped into a pool of water.

The river, friendly no longer, had swamped them. Manto lay as if dead, yet he was still breathing.

"Manto!" Inish poked and shook him, shouting in his ear. "Manto, wake. The river rises!" He groaned but did not move, so Inish grabbed his arms and tried to pull him away from the water. Manto was many hand-widths taller than she, and heavier by half again. Her hands slipped use-lessly off his skin.

Inish scurried out from the skin canopy. There was water everywhere she had walked the day before. It was already nearly hip deep. Even as she stood, it inched up to her growing belly. The stream where she'd caught a fish fed into the river but it too was gone, overwhelmed by the flood rising up like a living thing. Soon it would cover everything in its path. As strong as she was, she could not drag Manto off the tree, much less to higher ground. A jab of lightning illuminated the downed birch, which now seemed ghostly and dangerous. She felt the giant tree shudder and lift itself. The river was taking it away!

✳

Most of their belongings had floated away, but scrambling around in the water, she found two lengths of gut cord and some thrice-braided string, which Manto had made in anticipation of landing larger fish. Frantically she bound his body to two crossing branches, quaking as the river rose around her and the great tree moaned against the beach. Just as she fin-ished, Inish felt the tree rise gently and roll to one side. Toogu káa, the mother spirit, smiled! The tree's roll lifted them clear of the water instead of submerging them. Inish clasped one branch tightly, her legs wrapped around another. She couldn't see Manto, or hear him. As she called his name, the tree broke free. Slowly it sidled out into the river until the tumult caught it up and it began to move. Fast. Faster.

Only the spirits saw the giant tree careening down the river, two tiny peo-ple high in its branches. The rippling thunder might have been laughter.

Luckily Inish couldn't see the rocks racing toward her. Earlier the river had flowed softly around them, now they lay in wait beneath the quickening water. She felt for Manto with her foot. As her toes touched him, the rock struck, slamming into the top of the tree, spinning it around, rolling it over. The river snatched away the broken branches. The impact nearly jarred Inish from her precarious perch. As she clung desperately, the jagged arm of a splitting branch, torn from the main trunk, bucked up into Inish's jaw. She felt the sudden pain of teeth in her tongue and felt the warm blood. Then nothing.

The tree, shorn of half its branches and much of its bark, eventually dug into the muddy bottom at the river's mouth, turned in a lazy circle, then came to a gentle halt. It had been nearly a full day and night since Inish lashed Manto to the big branch. Concussed, she drifted in and out of consciousness.

Saturated clouds climbed the peaks of the island Captain George Vancouver would some day call Vancouver's Island, raced eastward across the strait separating the mainland and the island, and collided with the colder coastal mountains lining the ocean shore far to the north of the river. The warm air mass from the water and the cold mass hanging over the mountains released a deluge that lasted all night and well into the day. The surging water overwhelmed the land for miles to the north and south, eclipsed dozens of small islands, and climbed halfway up the orange-skinned arbutus trees, which tilted like spectators over the bank.

At its height, the flood covered five hundred thousand acres, submerging most of the narrow valley on either side. The flood was life-giving and life-taking. The brown waters carried alluvial loam to settle on the valley floor, but as it receded, corpses of drowned deer, fox, rabbits, and possums littered the land or floated in the soupy waters, their bloated bellies bobbing grotesquely.

As Inish fought for consciousness, life returned to the swollen river. Birds with legs as long as her own and loopy necks minced their way along the new shoreline, posing immobile as stone when they found their spot. Dart! Gray feathers lifted slightly as one speared a fish. On the far bank, low-slung animals with fat tails and black masks assiduously washed a fish before tearing it apart.

Tall, yellow grass, with seed heads so plump she could see them easily, struggled against the water. The sodden shore, filthy with sludge, eventually gave way to a thick, green swathe rolling off into the watery distance.

"Manto!" Inish whispered groggily. Her eyes were swollen almost shut. "Manto," her voice gained strength. Her eyes stung painfully as she squinted at the sky, a blue so thick with color she felt she could touch it and come away with the glorious hue on her fingers.

"Manto!"

Pain shot through every joint of her body as she tried to move. Inish slowly realized that her legs were jammed tightly into a tree crotch while her arms held the trunk in a death grip. Gingerly pulling herself free, she flopped into the water, startling a school of striped fish.

No Manto. The only sign of him were broken pieces of gut dangling from a limb. Inish took a deep breath, which made her head pound as though stone was banging against her skull. She slipped under the water and pulled herself along, trying to feel for him. She forced her eyes open but could see nothing in the murkiness that tasted faintly of brine.

Inish searched under the tree for an hour, stopping frequently to rest and ease her aching head. No sign. No tears had ever stained her face. Not even when the Tlingit forced her to watch her father kill his father and in turn be killed himself. But as she fruitlessly groped in the chill water, salty tears flooded down her cheeks, joining the river.

"Caw'ah! Caw'ah!"

✳

So loud, the bird seemed at her shoulder. Inish swiveled her throbbing head and saw it perched on one of the few remaining stretches of white bark. The creature's iridescent blackness was so lustrous the sun bounced off its back in a dozen dark shades, giving it a purplish hue. The contrast between the pale tree and the dark feathers was startling. Clenching and unclenching its claws, the bird cocked its head, staring the whole time at Inish.

The bird's scrutiny and boldness frightened her, but she recalled Manto's stories. Could this be his bird: the large, deep-bodied bird with the shiny beak that encased the selfish Nush-da in its wings? This bird didn't seem nearly large enough for such a feat, but many spirits could change their size at will.

Disconcertingly, the bird appeared to be smiling at her.

Inish gathered her courage. "You are as Manto described," she said, addressing the bird, which opened its yellow mouth wide.

"Caw'ah! Caw'ah! Caw'ah!" the bird responded raucously, dipping and weaving on the branch.

Inish picked herself up and waded to the shore, which steamed in the sun, as strong now as it had been weak before.

She stood in a muddy bay. Judging from the long-legged birds wading far out into the water, it must remain shallow for a long way out. To her right was a prow of land, high and thickly treed. There appeared to be a rim of beach at the foot of sandy cliffs. To her left was a delta, shimmering in the flood waters. There were few trees on it but she could make out hundreds of shrubs. In the northern distance the skyline was a rim of white. Not the gray-white of the aging glaciers near the Tlingit forts but an eye-stabbing white, pure and stark against the sky.

Ahead lay the sea. A terrifying expanse of flat, shimmering water. Inish had never seen so much water before. The Tlingit kept to the shelter of the high rocky fjords. And only the strongest men of the Kwakwaka ventured close to the endless waters for the seals during mating season. The boats of both people were strong enough to navigate the rivers, but only a mad person, or the fearsome Haida Gwaii, ventured out into the sea.

✳

"*Caw'ah!*" The bird sounded close to her ear.

"Do you know where Manto is?" she asked urgently.

"*Caw eee'ah!*"

The bird flew upstream. "*Caw'ah'ah!*"

Inish stumbled after it, tripping on bits of wood and other flood debris.

She thought she'd lost sight of the bird when it sang out again and she spied it perched on a white log at the shore.

"*Aw! Aw!*" the bird urged.

Come! Come! Inish imagined it saying.

Fearfully she edged nearer. As she drew closer, Inish realized it wasn't a log at all but an enormous piece of the birch-tree skin, which had peeled off in its pell-mell race down the river. The bark, already drying in the sun, had curled into a hollow log.

The bird pounded its beak on the bark as if grubbing for insects.

"*Caw eeeee!*"

This time the creature's cry sounded distinctly like laughter.

A black object poked out of the curled bark. Emboldened, Inish moved closer. It was a hand, twitching. Inish dove onto the white skin, prying it open. Manto lay there, his long black body naked, his arms wrapped around one drawn-up knee, the pouch with the pale-green stones clutched in his fist.

"Stand tall, little plug," Manto mumbled through cracked lips.

Inish's joy pushed up from the soles of her feet and exploded into her mouth. "The bird! The bird brought me here! The stories are true!"

She tore away at the edges of the bark, opening it fully. When she looked down at Manto, seeing his body clearly now, the laughter came. Mud caked his nose, wiry hair, and skin. Blood from scratches had congealed in brown-red scabs. His manhood hung limply over one thigh, it too crusted with dirt. She laughed and laughed. It was the funniest thing she'd ever seen. The only funny thing she'd ever seen.

"*Caw'ah!*" Black Bird joined her.

"That is Black Bird of Kahnamut?" Manto asked, peering at it a little doubtfully. "It is not large!"

Inish, still laughing, nodded.

"Are the faces of my ancestors carved in the trees?"

Inish shook her head. Manto frowned in disappointment.

Inish bent toward him, a broad smile still wrapped around her features. Manto puzzled over the transformation in her face. Inish laid a stubby hand across his cheek.

"This is Kahnamut," Inish declared with surety. She patted her bulging belly for emphasis. "And the faces. You must fashion them for yourself. Then your ancestors will be here with us."

PART II

Gitsula

5

✳

212 A.D.

Kahnamut, Mouth of the

North Fork of the Fraser River

Fifteen millennia have passed since Manto and Inish landed at the mouth of the big river in the land of Kahnamut. Manto kept alive legends of the Nush-da and Yupik, while Inish contributed the spirit tales and taboos of the Kwakwaka and Tlingit. Manto also brought remnants of the technology nurtured in the Kamchatka valley, which in turn had been introduced into Siberia by Paleolithic travelers from Olduvai. The skills of Inish's people had been enhanced by northern Asian peoples of different heritage who had ventured across Beringia long before the notion ever entered Tooke's head.

As Manto and Inish's three children grew to adulthood, the Cordilleran ice sheet that once covered the river that saved them was in full retreat. Climate and sea levels were beginning to stabilize. The warm, dry inland corridor cleaving a north-south passage on the western side of the newly formed Rocky Mountains, Manto and Inish's route to Kahnamut, had begun its reversion. Temperate winters and semi-arid summers changed to short, hot summers and winters marked by heavy, often wet snows. Four millennia before Inish and Manto nearly drowned, Kahnamut too had been dry but also cold, with the seas locked by year-round ice and the coastal mountains and valleys covered by a glacial blanket hundreds of feet deep. The ice sheet blanketing what are now Vancouver, Seattle, and hundreds of islands in between, was nearly a mile thick. The debris left as it retreated, and the valleys and bays the ice carved became the nursery for what followed.

The coastal climate warmed as the interior corridor cooled. With the warming came rains that swelled rivers, encouraging new forms of life. The forests that overwhelmed Manto and Inish were mere pockets of trees compared to the growth in the centuries after their deaths, when immense woodlands of towering fir, spruce, and cedar crowded down to every shoreline. Grassland near the river became rare, confined mainly to a few sandy shores, areas where beaver ponds overflowed, constantly spilling into low-lying deltas south of the big river, which the flooding seas drowned again and again in a briny bath. The occasional meadow was created by fires from lightning strikes.

The beginnings of the great forests provided Manto and Inish with softer woods for carving and building. The sturdiness of their shelters and the abundant food allowed the descendants of the tall, black man and the squat, chiefly born woman leisure to be creative with their hands and minds. Leisure meant time for the embellishment of stories, for argument and discord. Discord came naturally, as the blood of Manto and Inish's people was an international melting pot. Though there were no other people in their immediate vicinity, Manto and Inish were wrong in their thinking that they were the first to arrive at the end of the world (her thought) or the belly of the earth (his belief).

The remains of the Clovis people of European descent who first populated the central and north American plains had sought shelter in the west four thousand years before Tooke was born. Most were wiped out by the same climactic catastrophes that took the Ice Age mammals. But a few survived to cross the ice fields of the Rockies and become the Pueblos, Hopi, Chumash, Tillamook, and Makah of the southwest and Pacific Coast. Their blood did not remain pure. Long before the Nush-da, the single surviving line of Paleolithic Africans in eastern Asia, was wiped out, leaving only Tooke—and long before the Yupik of northern Alaska found Tooke near death—the tougher people of the northern Asian tundra and steppes had followed game into northern America. They were better bred for the conditions than the ancestors of the Nush-da or the Europeans. In time their blood dominated what was left of the Clovis in America.

Inish teased Manto about the strange imprint his teeth made on skin and soft wood. His incisors marked with a single, almost straight line, while hers left a triangular impression, three strong edges instead of just one. Her teeth had evolved from the much harsher climate of northern Asia, requiring teeth that could tear and cut, along with great jaw strength. Manto owed his straighter teeth to the Nush-da, who lived an easier life in their Kamchatka oasis, eating more plants and seafood. It was the sinodonty, or dental structure, of Inish's heritage combined with the migration of northern Asians who'd come before that dominated in all the native people of the Americas. But today, every now and then, archaeologists unearth teeth and a jaw structure on the North American continent that resembles Manto's African ancestors.

By the time Manto and Inish's children grew to adulthood, the small family had made numerous excursions up the big river, to be named Stahlo then Stó:lō by the Indians and Fraser by the whites. They ventured north and across what would be Burrard Inlet to the majestic coastal mountains and farther south, exploring the tributaries of the river's floodplain. They found the Stó:lō, the river people; the Muthkweyum people of the delta grasses; the Skwamus of the northern shores; and eventually the mysterious Tsleil'waututh, also of the northern shores but farther inland, along a dark and rainy inlet surrounded by fog-shrouded hills. Intermarriage happened readily, when the instinctual need for new blood in the close family groupings coupled with the desire to obtain skills possessed by others.

The Stó:lō held sway over the dip fishing grounds near the first of the river's canyons. They eventually traded access to it for permission to take advantage of the early salmon run farther down river, those rights owned by Manto and Inish's descendants who called themselves the Kahnamut, the chosen ones. The Muthkweyum were exceptional weavers and reed-basket makers, as over sixty varieties of grasses were available to them. They offered both material and technique in return for otter and lynx caught in abundance by the Kahnamut in the forests north of the big river. But always the tribe of Manto and Inish returned to the fecund shoreline of the big river, where they had everything they could possibly want.

In addition to nine species of salmon, seventy-one other kinds of fish lived in the river, from the tiniest *tsaianuk,* no bigger than a child's finger, to the sturgeon, the ancient twenty-foot-long devil fish, which guarded the bottom of the world. Nowhere else did birds of prey winter over so far north. Nowhere else did rich river silt support so many varieties of shellfish, from minute cockles to drooping geoduck clams so large it took two grown people to carry a single one from the shore to the village.

Fifteen millennia after Manto coughed the river's debris out of his mouth, more than a hundred thousand people had spread over Stahlo's valley, the northern shore, and the delta lands. They had also settled west, in the many islands off the coast, and south, in the deep sounds of what would be Washington state. Their three distinct language groups spawned dozens of dialects. The descendants of Manto and Inish spoke Kalakun. Thousands of years had not entirely erased the faint connections to the ancient Mongolian tongue that had given rise to Inish's language and to the guttural clicks and pops of the Paleolithic peoples of Olduvai. They under-stood well enough the Hunguminum of their closest neighbors and the Muthkweyum of the delta, as well as the language spoken by the Skwamus.

The Kahnamut grew to number in the thousands, spreading through marriage and disagreement to different areas along the river; around the point of the peninsula, which jutted out into the strait; and even across the inlet to the mountainous north shore. But the main village in 212 A.D. sat a stone's throw from where Manto and Inish's birch tree grounded. In that village dwelled eleven families—153 people—connected through three kinship lines. In spring, summer, and most of the fall they lived in sturdy houses on the Stahlo's banks facing a small group of bird-rich islands at the river's mouth. In winter they overlanded due north to live beside the more sheltered sandy beaches of a saltwater bay facing the snow-peaked moun-tains. There they caught winter seals in sea pens, hunted elk, and trapped muskrat and beaver.

The clan of the Eagle Moon numbered thirty-two people. They lived in a 52-foot longhouse, modest compared to the 125-foot-long by 30-foot-wide residence of the Kahnamut chief, which was home to fifty-five women, men, and children. The chief also had a subhouse, the only one in the village, reserved for special visitors and honored guests of the pot-latch—a competitive gift-giving festival, an event both better and worse than war as honor was bestowed or stripped in the subtle dance of giving and getting.

Birth determined status, but there was room between the birth and the becoming for a person to win, buy, or marry into an important name. More exalted spirits allied themselves with the better names, but even that had a degree of fluidity. A disappointed or crossed spirit might choose to take up residence with a family possessing a lesser name, so all behavior was carefully scrutinized to determine whether such an event was under way or if the individual was attempting to leap, like the spawning salmon, from the still pool of lower status into the rushing torrent of importance.

✴

Gitsula squeezed her eyes tightly shut. Spots swam in the blackness and a soft ringing enveloped her ears. She stretched one limb at a time to its lim-its. Then, with a sigh, she flipped over to her stomach and buried her hands in her belly, balled fists pushing her buttocks against the wool dog blanket that lay between her and the scratchy deer pelt on top. The cedar mat beneath shifted as she wiggled on the wooden shelf that had been her bed for eleven round seasons. Gitsula was thirteen round seasons old.

Young Gitsula faithfully pressed a painted thumbprint into the wood of her bed shelf as each part of the round season, or year, was welcomed with dance, drink, songs, stories, and worship. White for summer was the very first print at the top of the circle. Reddish brown for autumn, the color of abundance, came next at the left corner. A bluish purple marked winter and lay to the right, beside its cousin summer.

Raven black, restless black, was last. The color of spring.

Spring. When the land shivered, crept quietly, then bounded raucously out of dim days. Spring. When the smell of blood running in the warming trees excited all creatures. It was the time when spirits could be fooled as they drank the elixir running with the air over the sentry mountains to the north.

Spring. Danger and beauty. Madness and calm. When frogs shed their skins and salmon walked. Spring. When important clans sought unions for their young. The joining was not just flesh with flesh; it melded season and spirit, and always politics and necessity.

Spring was a time of opposition when rain and chill shouldered against sun and fire. A time of confusion between the was and will, *llolo* and *llokete*. The joining of young eased the transition, pulled the land out of winter and pushed it toward summer.

Soon-to-be-married-Gitsula sat up, pulled the cedar mat back, and peered at the eleven series of thumbprints. The white ones jumped out in the gloomy light, the dark ones hiding themselves in the grain of the wood. With her little finger she traced the impressions of the first round season spent on her own away from her mother's body. Even that finger was too big. How could she have been so small? She who was soon to be married and bear her own children.

Her birth nearly killed her mother, who was, everyone agreed, far too old at twenty-three to have children. Most first births were attended by a birth wife, though thereafter women found a spot in the woods and squatted until the baby appeared sufficiently to be pulled from her body by her own hands.

As the birth woman applied a poultice of fat leaves pounded to a paste with fish oil against the tears between Anawa's legs, stanching the blood, she chastised her for allowing her husband to enter her without proper regard for the position of the moon, thus risking pregnancy.

"We will stand you in the river before sundown to ward off another baby," she sternly instructed. "And you must bury the birth sack at ebb tide tomorrow. That will help dry you inside."

The woman held up the bag of *slowi,* the inner bark of cedar beaten until it was soft as duck down.

"Shall we wrap it or plug it?" she asked matter-of-factly.

Wanted babies were swaddled in it. Unwanted ones, usually girls in a family too full of them, had a gag of it stuffed into their mouths as the mother pinched their nostrils shut. It was rare to "pinch out" an only child even if it was a girl, but it was the birth woman's job to ask.

"Wrap!" Anawa said loudly and firmly despite her birth fatigue. The woman bent to her task.

Anawa smiled weakly, only half-listening to the chatter of the others who had gathered. The light in the longhouse had departed with the sun and she could barely make out the snub-nosed baby lying on her chest. Anawa savored the smell of sweet blood and fluid from her body. The baby would not be washed for hours yet, for to clean her prematurely was to deny the child protection from the Birdfish, a tortured creature that sought young girls.

"*Uhh up uhh!*" chanted the birth woman. "*Te méle.* A son." She chanted the words over and over to fool the Birdfish in case it listened.

Birdfish flew in the air but ate underwater. It had been born in human form as three living children, an exceedingly rare event. The mother of the triplets begged the raven and the salmon to grant her a third breast in order to feed her hungry babies, but she was denied.

Her breasts shriveled and dried from the demands of the three. In desperation she took the last-born, a girl, away from the other two who lay sleeping. Along with the baby, the mother carried a wooden oil box and a bone needle. Setting the child gently down upon a rock, she plunged the needle into the baby's neck. Blood pulsed down the needle and into the box positioned to catch the precious drops. The woman wept, her tears mingling with the baby's blood.

The two firstborn, both boys, thrived on their sister's blood, growing to be superior in all things. Season after season the honor of taking the first salmon fell to one or the other. When time came for union, a highly favorable match with two daughters of the Cap'eeno tribe was arranged. The mother was ecstatic, for such marriage ensured the longevity of her own clan. Cap'eeno were distantly related to the Kahnamut but had long lived in relative isolation high up in a rocky canyon enclave cut deeply into the northern mountains. The river that flowed out of the canyon emptied calmly, as the twin arms of the Fraser did, into the sea but not before a turbulent journey of rock, rapid, and fall.

Only the Cap'eeno could negotiate the river on its angry journey to the sea. This they did every year when the salmon ran. They camped on the pebble beach at the river's mouth for two months. Only then did they have contact with other tribes as they traded pelts of mountain sheep and chunks of a very hard rock found high up in the canyon for baskets, boats, dried lowland berries, and shells.

The twins' marriages were celebrated with a potlatch, which lasted nine days before the food ran out and the men of the Kahnamut and Cap'eeno fell into a stuporous sleep. As they slept, the women of both tribes prepared the marriage beds and garments for the ceremony.

But when the women entered the brothers' house to rouse them, they were greeted by a horrific scene. Joined like two chunks of ice melting together, the twins, who shared one bed, were transforming into a creature with the head of a bird and the body of a fish. It was, all later agreed, punishment for drinking the lifeblood of their dead sister. Once fully formed, the Birdfish chased the terrified women out of the house, then disappeared with a thunderous clap of its scaly wings. The Birdfish, cursed to eternal life, thereafter spent its days and nights searching for the sacrificed sister to complete the trinity and allow them to return to their human form. Invariably, the death of a baby girl was attributed to the Birdfish.

The story of the Birdfish didn't frighten Anawa as it did the others, though she carefully followed the taboos and rituals to protect her new baby from the creature. She believed the story was one of sacrifice, love, and creation—not, as the storytellers always interpreted it, revenge and destruction.

As Gitsula grew, Anawa often rocked her to sleep crooning the tale of the seeking Birdfish. She told of its sadness, its eternal search for completion, always adding a chant of her own creation about the dead sister and how she too wandered forever, caught between earth and sky, unable to find her two brothers.

"Where is sister?" she crooned. "Where is sister?"

"Sister there?" little Gitsula would ask, pointing to an object before calling out its name, her baby tongue stumbling over the cadences and sounds of her forming language. Often they played the game during the day, while Anawa, a weaver, harvested cedar bark, which she soaked in saltwater and pounded until malleable and soft, then used it for braiding and weaving into blankets, capes, and garments.

"Who before?" Anawa asked, pointing to a stone, a moss patch, or a tree. She would kneel down and let the child, wrapped on her back, touch the object. "Who before? Is it sister?"

Solemnly Gitsula leaned forward over her mother's shoulder and placed her hands upon the thing. "No sister," she'd say after a suitable pause. "Too bad, no sister." The burbling giggle inevitably followed.

The Kahnamut believed all were claimed after death by the spirits and transformed into something else. The speed of transformation was completely dependent on the worth, wealth, and deeds of the individual during his or her time on earth. Anawa was a weaver, which allowed her to speak the language of the tree, asking permission before she hacked and peeled away the deep-ridged layers of bark. The spirit of the ancestor residing in the tree would claim her when the time was right.

Men and women alike discussed the ideas and possibilities of transformation, particularly during the most important time of year, the coming of the thirteenth moon. In the time of the darkest days, Sis'et, the elder moon, appeared, encouraging the Kahnamut to gather and converse. Parents and grandparents were expected to instruct their young about the passages of time and their obligations to those before.

Gitsula loved those days of flickering light and the warmth of her mother's body and the endless conversation that made sense of everything. Day and night melted together as she played near the fire with her older cousins. Knowledge filled the air, they breathed it in effortlessly, unknowingly.

6

*

Uunutu, Gitsula's father, was a quiet man, small of stature, soft-spoken and slow-moving. Within the village he had acquired a second name, as many did to describe their deeds, character, or appearance. Kweekulates, he was called, one who leaves no footprint. Uunutu's face was squarer than most and his eyes rounder. His forehead was unfortunately high, giving way to an unusually domed crown. His mother had been lazy, preferring hours of gossip at the wash river to time spent carefully wrapping her children's heads to compress them into a more appealing and high-status shallow forehead, sloping sharply back to a slightly conical point.

Uunutu's Eagle Moon clan were makers of knives and netting and gatherers of stones used for milling and nutting. Family stories depicted Eagle Moon ancestors as the high-status makers of harpoon points and sturgeon spears. Killing the twenty-foot-long, fifteen-hundred-pound fish demanded a spear fifty feet or more in length, made with extraordinary strength in the shaft. It must not be too heavy, or the several men needed to carry it couldn't accurately launch it into the fish. Once the wicked barb in the point was lodged in the sturgeon, the wooden shaft bobbed along, tiring the giant fish, while marking its route until it died and could be towed to the nearest beach landing. The task of making sturgeon spears and harpoon points had long ago been taken by others and now resided in Eagle Moon clan stories only.

During the four feasts of the four seasons, Uunutu had the right to bring forward these stories as his mother and grandfather had proudly done. The ownership of stories passed from man to woman to man. It was his turn, but Uunutu suspected that some of the villagers had begun to doubt the tales. He'd heard whispers contending that the stories had been borrowed or stolen and did not belong to the Eagle Moon clan at all.

He didn't mind allowing those stories to sleep, because he had a more important role as the hereditary custodian of the Green Tears, oblong beadlike objects slightly less than the length of a child's small finger and about as big around. They were soft, yet hard, smooth, yet when you rubbed a Tear across your teeth there was a slight drag, as if the surface was rough. Each one weighed less than a stone of the same size yet more than an equal piece of wood.

*

Though he respected the story of the Tears' origins, it was clear to Uunutu's experienced eye that they had been worked and molded by hand or perhaps by the force of some spirit. Even the finest stone chisel Uunutu could fashion wasn't capable of making the intricate indentation around the girth of each one. He often wondered if the shiny metal knives, rumored to be possessed by certain tribes, could etch those marks. He'd never seen such knives, nor had anyone else as far as he knew. On the basis of the stories, he once tried to create a small blade out of gold. He was able to make it incredibly sharp, but it failed to hold its edge after a single pass on a hard object.

*

Uunutu wanted to make a ceremonial blade from copper, but he had none. Among the nobles of coastal nations copper was the most valued possession. It was fashioned into plaques by pounding it thin, with edges so sharp, if they weren't slightly rounded and bent back they could cut a person's finger to the bone. The surfaces of the plaques were etched and embossed with family crests and depictions of animal spirits. The very rich gave them away at potlatches, enhanced their daughters' dowries, or gained great status by destroying them before an enemy tribe. All people valued them, even the whaling Nuu-chah-nulth of the big island across the strait to be named Georgia, and the warrior Haida Gwaii preferred a single one to the spoils of an entire plundered village.

Uunutu would never be wealthy enough to possess a copper, but he wouldn't give up his stewardship of the Green Tears for any number of them. In his palm the Tears felt cool and warm at the same time. This was part of their magic. When he rolled them gently back and forth they touched each other, click, click, click.

All adults had a song that explained their place on earth and their vision quest and connected them with their transformation spirit. Such songs were not created or crafted, they emerged from within. These songs were sung at potlatches and other celebrations. They might even be sung to welcome the sun or moon on a day that felt either blessed or dangerous. In Uunutu's song he attempted to reproduce the clicking sound of the Green Tears. The Kahnamut were adept at using breath, throat, and tongue to create a wondrous variety of sounds, often mimicking animals, birds, leaves rustling, and the imagined sounds of fish conversing. But Uunutu could never quite capture the delicate click, click of the Tears as they kissed each other.

When Anawa of the Sea Frogs, an allied family of Kahnamut living in a village a short distance away, named Uunutu as her preferred mate, he was obligated to tell her that he had been chosen by his clan to protect the Tears until his death.

"I do not mind," she shrugged.

"There is no one of rank in our stories."

"You mean you are *tsas,* a commoner!" Anawa imbued her voice with mock surprise.

Uunutu bowed his head. She would not want him now. Then he heard her characteristic chuckle.

"I too."

"Yes, but it is known you have *siiam,* chief connection, in your clan."

"It is true," chirped Anawa gaily.

"And a house board with the mark of the raven."

"That is true too."

Uunutu had never set foot in Anawa's longhouse, even though the two villages cooperated during the salmon run and the annual whale hunt in the sea inlet. Her family's house boasted a front board at the entrance, with the image of a raven, a powerful symbol.

"But the board is often faced down," Anawa revealed. "Whenever the chief hunts poorly or his wives anger him, he blames us, the Sea Frogs. The last time his fourth wife bore him another daughter he pulled our house board down, broke a piece off, and buried it!" Anawa shrugged. "So how powerful can our raven be?"

The Sea Frogs were a respected family, once of rank. Generations before, one of the men went fishing with the chief's two sons in the whale waters of the salt inlet bordered by the north shore mountains. When they were set upon by a war boat of the Sqwamus, the Sea Frog clansman dove overboard, leaving the boys to fend for themselves. One died, the other eventually made it back to the village where he denounced the Sea Frog, who produced a passionate counterstory.

The Sea Frog man could have been killed for cowardice but the council, after much debate, concluded that they could not know which version was correct. They noted, however, that one boy was dead. That was not in dispute. He had been the Sea Frog's responsibility. That was also not in dispute. The Sea Frog was stripped of rank and banned from the three secret societies to which he belonged. As a concession, because of the ambiguity of the situation, he was allowed to keep the raven image on his house board.

"If you become part of the Eagle Moon," Uunutu warned, "you must understand that your husband will never advance himself."

"My husband, my husband," teased Anawa. "Do you mean you?"

Uunutu was a little miffed by her bantering. Referring to himself in the third person was the proper way to broach this serious subject. Instead of responding in the same vein, the woman mocked him.

"The Green Tears are important, so the one taking care of them must not be," explained Uunutu overearnestly. "My father and grandfather both had opportunities to advance. They chose not to. Wisely! It is certain the *sulu,* the council of women, would have removed the Tears from our family."

"I would like to see them."

Uunutu couldn't hold back a little gasp of surprise. She was so bold! It was rude to probe a story and to ask to see the sacred Tears without waiting for the offer to be made. Uunutu had sufficient reason to leave. Other men would have.

Uunutu thought for a moment. He felt the gaze of Anawa's narrow, dark eyes boring into him. A more modest woman would not stare so openly. A prickling in his chest and his dampened hands made him uncomfortable. Failing to rebuff her for the initial inappropriate questions somehow made it harder for him to leave now. Uunutu stared at the top of Anawa's beautifully coned head, which sloped back sharply almost from her eyebrows. His hand twitched. He would like to touch her hair where she had wrapped it and mudded it to emphasize the point of her head.

"Eagle Moon has kept the Tears since ice slept in the valley," Uunutu said, letting the rudeness pass. "A house pole was carved long ago to represent the spirit of those who keep the Tears. What is left of it protects our winter house."

"What images are there?"

This was an acceptable question. "Beaver and clam," responded Uunutu.

Anawa nodded approvingly. Beaver meant steadfastness and the clam symbolized caution.

Oddly, despite the ritual associated with them, the Green Tears had no value as such within the village. They could not be sold nor traded. They couldn't be exchanged within the clan for anything, nor could the caretaking right be bartered for something of worth. They were, quite simply, an insurance for the future.

Exactly why Uunutu's family was first chosen *ahsqqik,* keepers, wasn't explained in the clan's own stories or those belonging to the larger tribe. But all agreed that the Tears were safe in the hands of Uunutu's family. Despite the strictures, a greedy man might sell the Tears to another tribe. An ambitious man might barter them for a noble alliance with a son or daughter of a rich chief. A seeking man might give them back to the gods in return for magical powers. A boastful man might show them off to a visiting tribe during a potlatch, tempting a raid. Uunutu's line were none of those things.

It was a wonderful irony that the very reason the tribe felt secure with the Tears under the stewardship of Uunutu's clan was the same reason the Eagle Moon weren't greatly respected.

✳

Uunutu ducked inside the entrance to Anawa's longhouse. He carried a hank of her hair, his permission to enter. Four days and nights he squatted in the corner of the longhouse by the entrance. Uunutu huddled under his blanket, trying to ignore the ache in his limbs and the dryness of his throat. No one spoke to him, fed him, or offered water. Bringing food or drink into the house reflected badly on supplicants. He had a small quantity of mint leaves, which he chewed slowly to diminish his appetite and moisten his mouth. In all, he reflected, he was decently treated. It wasn't unknown for the brothers of a prospective bride to urinate on a candidate who displeased them.

Anawa was sequestered the entire time in a nearby clan's house. At the end of the vigil her family stoked their fire hot and bright and sat to consider Uunutu's request. He heard laughter, scoffing, and argument. Finally a neighbor who attended the proceedings to act as communicator approached him in the dim corner. She held out a side of blackfish skin still redolent with fat. Uunutu breathed deeply in relief. He had been accepted.

"You will not need a welcome stick to prepare for him," a granddaughter of the chief mocked after the announcement was made. "Uunutu is Kweekulatuuk, the insignificant one who leaves no footprint. I'm sure his manhood will make the same impression on you!"

These and similar comments provoked torrents of knowing laughter from the *stoles*, the already wives. Though Anawa was popular, many thought her too sunny and optimistic to be taken seriously. Her father suffered also for accepting for his daughter a man who had no hope of becoming *smelah*, worthy.

That night, after Uunutu left her longhouse, Anawa went into seclusion to prepare for the day. The married women of the family dug a shoulder-high pit. Over it they made a roof of boughs collected from an area of the forests that had never been cut or harvested. The pit was just big enough for Anawa to lie down in comfortably. She brought with her some basketry to complete while she fasted and cleansed herself in order to present her husband with as pure a spirit as possible.

The witch wife sat outside the pit instructing Anawa in her responsibilities and warning of taboos. Ah'we'tan had been the witch wife as long as anyone could remember. Every young bride sitting in the darkness of her pit heard the cautionary tale about the woman who, out of fear of the pain, initially refused to let her husband lie with her. The spirits cursed her to bear large numbers of monstrous children, each larger and more hideously formed, until finally a birth split her in two.

During her seclusion Anawa diligently used the welcome stick—a smooth, rounded pole greased with a special mix of fish oil and soothing herbs that Ah'we'tan gave to prospective brides. Every day they plunged it a little farther into themselves in order to strengthen the passage, ensuring protection for the baby they were soon to carry. Anawa found herself enjoying the ritual, stroking and teasing herself with the stick before she pressed it eagerly into the tight darkness between her legs.

The morning of their wedding Anawa waited for Uunutu to come to her. This was the final opportunity for either to change their mind, no reasons required and no consequences suffered. If both still agreed to proceed, they boasted of what they would contribute to enrich each other and their families. And they both proclaimed the results of their individual vision quests, discussing their portents for the future.

Uunutu slept poorly during Anawa's seclusion. He dreaded this meeting but he decided to speak his mind.

"Many think I am weak," he confessed. The word sounded appalling on his lips.

"How can that be?" his cheery bride-to-be replied, though she knew full well.

"I do not advance myself and take opportunities when they arise." He looked at her, wanting her outraged denial of such a point of view.

"But you are the keeper of the Tears! It is not required or expected. Isn't that true?"

"Yes, but I could pass on the Tears to another house. The chief builds a new sweat lodge. It is much larger and will hold more men. I could seek a place."

"The Tears are your duty," Anawa responded. "Duty is more important than opportunity."

Uunutu smiled broadly. This was the response he hoped for.

✳

K'we'tan, sister of Ah'we'tan, helped them paint their bodies ruddy with special pigments. She left them a stone bowl containing a milky dye. They used a rabbit's foot dipped in the bowl to stroke circles representing the sun, thick upright lines representing fertility, and horizontal dashes and curves for the spirits, over each other's naked bodies. Chanting and praying for wisdom and guidance, they rocked back and forth. Hours passed while they painted. Finally they collapsed, exhausted, in each other's arms. Night was far advanced when they awoke, clinging hungrily together.

Kneeling upright, Uunutu grasped Anawa's thighs, drawing her close. Strong and erect, he eased himself into his eager wife. Anawa gasped with pleasure. She was oiled by the women of her own family to make the act easier but she had no need of it, the joy of her body flowed out of her.

The fertility feast came the second day of the marriage. It was also a time when barren wives could take other men to their bed and men without children could take other women. Both sought to prove that having no children was the fault of the other.

The feast began with the chief's presentation of bear entrails, a rare delicacy sufficient for all people of both villages. Uunutu and Anawa ate their fill of the nearly black gut before launching into their stories.

"I am stone and horn!" Uunutu proclaimed, shaking his elaborate headdress, a fully racked elk's head.

"We come from the wilderness of little light."

"Dark! Night!" chanted the crowd.

"Where snow spirit lives both summer and winter!"

The crowd clasped their blankets close and howled.

"We," Uunutu pounded around the circle, "fought the Bear People."

On and on the story went. The Kahnamut fought Bear People who ate dogs for meat, lived in ice caves, hunted creatures as big as a longhouse, and had hair covering their faces and bodies for warmth.

When they finally arrived at the welcome land, the important spirits, the salmon, the raven, the wolf, and the whale, met with the eldest moon and her consort, the eagle, to decide if the Kahnamut could remain or should be driven back among the fighting people in the north.

As the elder spirits debated in their enclave on the northern shore mountains, they were attacked by Akka'a, an eagle of the consort's clan, jealous that she was not included in the important discussion. Akka'a ripped the belly out of the consort, killing him instantly. Her rage ran rampant. Soon the salmon, raven, wolf, and whale were lying mortally wounded.

"You can see them," Anawa joined in pointing toward four humps along the skyline of the northern mountains. "That is what is left of their souls."

Anawa glided into the center of the circle, "cooking" her breasts in wide caressing circles with her hands to encourage milk for the baby to come.

"Akka'a turned to Sis'et, the elder moon. Tearing at her yellow face, Akka'a dealt death blow after death blow until the moon's light began to fade. Flickering its last, the moon called out!"

"Manuuto!" shrieked the frenzied crowd.

"Yes! Yes! Manuuto heard Sis'et cry and seized an ax he was making."

Uunutu snatched up one he had specially made for the occasion. The obsidian face was round and rough on one side to represent the unfinished ax head, and straight on the other. It was attached to a fine handle made from the heart of a fir tree.

"Into the sky he flung it, catching Akka'a on the neck!" Uunutu bellowed. Anawa fell to her knees grasping her neck.

"So sharp was the blade, so well balanced the handle that Akka'a's head cleaved right off. The evil bird fell into the sea strait between our winter village and the mountain land. Where Akka'a's head fell lies the sacred forest."

Anawa traced the outline of a chunk of land, nearly an island, that would one day be Vancouver's Stanley Park. She filled in the outline with feathers to represent the trees, poured water for its eyes, and lay down a large diving-duck bill for the beak.

The Kahnamut rounded the rocky shores of the thousand acres near the island, every year, to enter the inlet for the whale hunt. But they never set foot on the land itself lest Akka'a be awakened to fly again.

"And Sis'et?" called out the voices. "What of her?"

The grateful Sis'et granted the people the right of fishing and hunting over all the land seen by the thirteenth moon, including the delta to the south, the big river, the mountains to the north, and the islands in the sea to the west.

"Aaaah!" cried the crowd as they leaped to their feet in celebration of their own strength, bravery, and skill. The dancing went long into the night.

7

✳

Anawa was born with far more curiosity than was seemly for a woman of her time. For that reason alone she was delighted with her marriage to Uunutu. Few men were as patient and kind as he. Fewer still would tolerate her playful, questioning nature that often veered across the line of respect.

It was near the third moon after their wedding when she took Uunutu's hand and placed it across her belly. "A child, I am certain."

Whooping, Uunutu clutched her tightly. "So soon?"

Anawa giggled at his joy. "Of course," she answered haughtily. "You may be plain, ordinary, and powerless but I . . . I am the daughter of a goddess so powerful that just looking at her shrivels the wolf. I knew before we met. I knew before we married. I knew before your sleeping giant," she gestured toward his flaccid penis, "awoke and came to me."

Uunutu chortled. He had been horribly shy when they first slept together, but now he felt as comfortable with Anawa as if she were a part of his own body. He buried his face in her soft belly and sunk his fingers deep in the cleft between her buttocks.

"*Is inaqwa,*" she breathed, arching her hips toward him. His fingers found her wetness and his manhood ached. For her he would do anything.

✳

Four pregnancies, four deaths in a rush of blood and tissue early in the second trimester.

"It will be your death, if you get with child again," Ah'we'tan, the witch woman, concluded somberly after the third.

But Anawa would not be stilled. A fourth pregnancy, a fourth loss, then no more pregnancies. Grimness replaced her smiles and the laughter. Even Anawa's babble of talk dried up as she became obsessed with her weaving, often working long into the night when all light was doused, feeling her way with her fingertips. She strove to create ever more complex patterns in the cedar fiber cloth, while introducing more color and texture than had ever been seen before in a Kahnamut cape or blanket. Anawa's creativity caught the chief's eye. He gave her two wool dogs to make him a cape festooned with horn buttons and feathers. She even crafted a collar of fur from twenty mink tails stitched together.

Uunutu was irritated by the chief's largesse. It was a slight to him, he felt. Two wool dogs were worth far more than Anawa's most beautiful garment. But then something so unexpected and so dramatic happened, it drove out all thought of the chief, even making Anawa forget, for a time, her empty body.

Each spring a member of the village was chosen to take the first salmon. That year, for the third time, the chief picked his brother 'Xan for the honor. It was a careful honor, a political honor. Power was fluid among the Kahnamut. If his people didn't agree with the chief's decision they simply ignored it. If they ignored enough decisions he would no longer be chief. Accordingly the chief weighed each decision exceedingly carefully. The only real challenger to him in the village was his own brother 'Xan, whose wealth, the key marker of power and prestige, was increasing rapidly.

'Xan's wife owned a large herd of wool dogs, the only ones in the village aside from those owned by the chief and the two given to Anawa, both unbred bitches. The fur of the small, curly-coated animals, fashioned into hats and coverings, was valued for its ability to retain warmth even when wet. Some believed 'Xan was actually wealthier than his older brother, although, because he was abrasive and arrogant, no one wished to demand that the two brothers compare their possessions. If it was deemed 'Xan was truly wealthier then he would automatically have the right to challenge his brother for the position of chief.

"It may come in time," K'we'tan, Ah'we'tan's sister, the interpreter of dreams, counseled, "for wealth has its own spirit, which will not lie abed indefinitely. But we shall wait and let his possessions speak for him."

In the meantime, the chief placated 'Xan by granting him privileges and honors, such as the right to take the first fish of the season. A second, and much desired benefit of taking first fish was that the chosen's children became the bone carriers. After a day of prayers to the salmon asking permission to borrow its flesh, the first salmon was caught and respectfully consumed. The honored children returned the bones to the river, giving the fish back to its kind. If the bones were not handled with dignity and promptly set into the river, its flesh would not grow back, and many seasons would pass with poor fishing.

'Xan's three children, all boys, were entrusted with the bones, which had been carefully anointed with oil and wrapped in leaves. Often dried cranberries or blueberries were included in the parcel to give the salmon sustenance for its journey back from the spirit world. On this day summer pushed spring aside, driving the damp out of the ground. Flowers scented the air, making the bees giddy.

The children skipped away from the summer dwelling on the banks of the most northerly finger of the Stahlo near where it joined the sea. It was the ideal spot for the coming of the salmon; elaborate weirs, drying racks, and smoke pits to catch and preserve the fish lined the banks and extended into the river. The fishing grounds were one of the tribe's most valued possessions. Farther downriver, toward open water, another related tribe fished. It was a less desirable location, lacking protection from the winds, and it had wide channels within the river, which made it difficult to anchor weirs. Their catch was inevitably poorer.

When the children reached the river they saw the poles of the neighboring tribe's weirs apparently untended.

"I don't see anyone," said Ee'Xan, the oldest boy. "Let's look."

They set the bones on an exposed rock, cautiously making their way toward the poles. An old man slept in the bush at river's edge but there was no one guarding the weirs.

"Stay here," Ee'Xan whispered to his two brothers, who quivered with excitement. "I will return with a prize that will make father proud." Stealing within the tribe was forbidden; however, theft from other tribes was acceptable, especially if the victim had done something to offend. Besides, nothing could be taken if it was attended to properly.

Ee'Xan slipped through the shallows, walking in the water so any stones dislodged would make no sound. What a prize! Two beautifully woven baskets sat unattended, attached to a long stick. Inside were aromatic leaves used to flavor the smoking fish. Even better! Inside one of the baskets was a wooden oil box.

Fish oil derived from the thin, bony eulachon fish was valuable currency for all tribes. The Kahnamut traded it to the inland people for pelts and to the whale people, the Nuu'chal'nuth, far across the water, for whale blubber and walrus hides. It could take several hundred fish to produce oil enough to fill one box. Ee'Xan snatched up the baskets and hurried back to his brothers, who had crept closer to the shore where they could watch.

When the three returned to the rock, the bones were gone! Not only that, but so were the protective leaves, which, as part of the ritual, they were required to take back to the camp and burn. Though they were young, the boys had a clear sense of impending disaster. Next year the salmon might not come to them at all. Worse, one of the salmon people might appear in human form to seek revenge.

It was well known that if some aspect of the annual salmon hunt displeased them, a salmon person visited villages by borrowing the body of a strong, handsome young man. The only hint that he was not of the walking ones was that a part of his body would not be perfectly formed, or would be missing altogether. It could be something as small as an earlobe, a deformed toe, or a finger half-grown. If he had a split lip and spoke with slurred words, it was clear he was one of the most powerful of the salmon and thus could not entirely shed his form. Such ones were to be feared.

A salmon person might request the hand of the most beautiful girl in the village, whose father was also the wealthiest and whose mother's status was evident in her fine basket work, sewing, or weaving. Usually the young girl simply disappeared, never to be seen again.

The boys quaked, their bravado gone.

"You will tell father!" the oldest boy commanded, grabbing his baby brother by the hair. "You will fall down and apologize for your mistake."

"Nooo!" squeaked the terrified child who was no more than five. "Nooo!"

"Yes, you will!" snarled Ee'Xan, strong now with a solution. "You will tell him we gave you the honor and you ran ahead, fell down, got scared, and lost the bones and the leaf wrap. You will tell him that!"

"Why me? Oh please, why me?" The boy wept, trying to wiggle out of his brother's iron grasp.

"Because you are doubly unlucky! You are the last born. And you are the third boy. Everyone knows the third boy will be unlucky unless he is blessed by an animal spirit."

"I too got a spirit," the boy protested, a little of his spunk returning. "Mother says I have the look of a goat. She is sure it is in me."

"You have more the look of a warty toad to me!" scoffed his brother.

He shoved his brother hard. The middle boy, a squat child with strangely short arms and stubby fingers and toes moved over to stand at his older brother's shoulder, siding with him against the child.

"Go!"

"Uh, uh, uh," the boy hiccuped in terror.

"If you don't, toad face," the boy leaned in, his mealy breath bathing the younger child's face, "I will wake up the worms inside."

This was the scariest threat in Ee'Xan's arsenal. The wrath of 'Xan, the disgust of the chief, the anger and fear of the tribe did not compare to this threatened invasion of his chubby little body by worms. His brother had long terrorized him by claiming the power to summon worms that could find their way to his heart through his nostrils, mouth, or ears. Even more painfully, they could enter through the boy's pee pipe.

One morning, not so long ago, he woke to find two shriveled, brown carcasses in his bed. Shrieking, he fell to the floor as his mother laughed and gathered him into her arms. Later, Ee'Xan told him the finger-length bits of skin were what was left behind when the worms shed their outer selves, before they entered a body.

"If you forever do what I say, the worms will sleep within you," his brother warned. "But if you displease me, I shall summon them to wake, and your pee pole will fall off." He paused and glanced meaningfully at his brother's groin. "That'll hurt, you bet. And then you'll pee like a girl."

The child looked to his middle brother for support but the boy carefully avoided his eyes.

"Which will it be?" demanded Ee'Xan. "Do what I say or the worms?"

The child was shunned by the entire tribe. Only when the salmon ran again would he know if he was forgiven. Ee'Xan might have ameliorated things for his brother by offering his baskets to the chief, but he decided there was no point in wasting such valuable property.

The fish did return, and in reasonable numbers, though many evaded the nets and weirs, leaping high in the water, their laughter heard at night. That winter too had been harsh. A rare blizzard followed by freezing rain caught three children in its grasp and ended their lives. Eventually the elders allowed the boy back into the fold, reasoning that he was young and had not intentionally harmed the tribe.

✳

"There is opportunity in this!" Uunutu's father's sister said eagerly of the flux created by the embarrassment to 'Xan's family. "You must seek 'Xan's place in the chief's longhouse."

The six families who lived in Uunutu's lodge advocated the bid. None were nobility; it would raise the status of all.

"It is a chance," father's sister repeated urgently. "You must do it. But be quick. I have heard others speak of the same thing."

"They would have a better chance than me," Uunutu demurred, squatting to warm his face by the fire.

The older woman impatiently pulled her rough cape over her head.

"No!" she said angrily. "You must listen to our wishes. You are the keeper of the Tears, the chief should hear you first. That would be your right."

The others gathered around. "*Ukel y Ukel!*" Challenge! You must challenge!" One after another they urged, "*Ukel y Ukel!*"

The woman came so close Uunutu could see the brown cracks in her few remaining teeth, and smell the stale odor of her old, old body. "It is your duty to leap ahead like the salmon. To gain respect and wealth for us."

"The Tears earn me respect!" Uunutu bridled.

The woman spat hard on the floor. Several others followed suit. They were angry now. Such an opportunity would not come again.

"You have the spirit of a rabbit!" she hissed. The others growled their agreement.

"The Tears cannot match the importance of a place in the sweat house," his brother argued. "Give them up. *Y Ukel.*"

Uunutu squirmed but said nothing more.

✳

That night, as they banked their fire to preserve the embers, Uunutu whispered to Anawa: "The others wish it. It is rare that a *tsas*, a commoner like myself, could push aside one as powerful as 'Xan."

"There are others to keep the Tears," Anawa murmured.

He had not expected the comment. He felt a stab of anger, but when Anawa gently laid her hand upon his smoothly muscled chest, his rancor melted.

"The Tears are my duty," Uunutu stated, his voice taking on a pleading edge. "They have been with my family since all beginning."

For the first time in their lives together, Anawa felt a prick of annoyance at his worship of the Tears. The objects had no function and would not until they were needed. They had never become a vital part of ceremony, worship, or feast. They just were. She tried another tack.

"Perhaps if you pass on the Tears you will be accepted into the sweat lodge," Anawa took a deep breath at the thought. She had never coveted anything beyond what she had. But as she accepted her barrenness, her feelings began to change. If her husband won a place beside the chief she would also be entitled to favors. She could take the child of a lower family to work for her or possibly demand a male wool dog to start her own herd.

"Perhaps even you would be blessed with the chief's spirit and we would have live children."

"Shame!" Uunutu shouted suddenly, jumping up and shaking his fist, his face suffused with rage. "You fault me? I am the one to give you children. It is your body that kills them."

Anawa tilted her head in submission. "I meant no offense," she whispered, shocked to the core.

The evening noises inside the lodge stilled suddenly and the ceaseless fall of raindrops as big as pebbles could be heard hitting the roof planks. The families of Eagle Moon had been tending their fires, stretching skin on frames, stacking baskets, and crushing nuts. Beside Uunutu and Anawa lived a family of tanners. The women and girls had been applying curing oil to otter hides. Thwap, thwap, thwap. The willow tanning whisks beat against the scraped skin. For a moment, these were the only sounds in the lodge, then the whisks too fell silent. Even the children were quiet in those seconds. Uunutu's fury reverberated in the long, smoky building like a clap of thunder.

Two men, cousins of Uunutu three fires over, repaired round nets used to scoop salmon out of the weirs. They were so startled by Uunutu's outburst that one let go of his hold on the wooden circle, which formed the frame of the net. It sprang apart, smacking him in the face. The other's raucous laughter broke the silence as the tears poured down the injured man's face. Others in the lodge joined in. Uunutu was forgotten.

Even before the laughter died down, Anawa picked up the roof pole, a long, slender poplar sapling, and began adjusting the roof planks as if nothing had happened. To an unknowing eye, the roofs of the longhouses looked like helter-skelter piles of planks sitting on the massive support beams. In fact they were clever arrangements that protected from the rain, channeling it away, while at the same time allowing smoke from the fires to escape. Keeping wind, water, and smoke in balance required frequent adjustments. A woman who couldn't keep her roof planks properly aligned was not admired.

When there were disagreements among families, the opposing women sometimes adjusted the planks so that the runoff poured into another's fire. The closer to the middle of the longhouse, the more desirable the location, because there was less runoff to deal with and less risk from neighbors.

Uunutu sought the wisdom of K'we'tan, the interpreter of dreams, who fasted for a day to clear her body and mind, then drank a potion so that she might enter his thoughts. She saw dreams of boats, long tall ones, like those of the whalers or the warrior Haida.

"Does it mean we shall be attacked?"

"No, no," the woman puzzled. "I do not think so. But I am bothered. I do not see the Tears in your dreams, nor do I see your spirit form. And the boats do not speak to me."

Later, while she bathed with her family, K'we'tan took the opportunity to preempt any criticism of her inability to read Uunutu's dream. "He is weak," she stated. "Strong, clear dreams come from strong, clear men. Uunutu is like a child inside, soft and unformed."

The others nodded and clucked in agreement. This much was well known about Uunutu.

In truth, Uunutu had no wish to usurp 'Xan's position. He loved the Tears more than anything, except Anawa. He made up his mind. He couldn't disappoint her. He would do as she wished. The time of challenge drew close, the waning of the harvest moon. He would prepare, he would gather gifts and wealth to support his cause.

"Ssshhh," Anawa said as he began to tell her. "Come."

They left the longhouse, Anawa moving quickly, ignoring the annoyed protests as she pushed past other families. She fairly ran to the beach over-looking the saltwater bay and the mountains. Winter had come early to the hills, and their shoulders were startling white. She walked along the shore-line where the water had left the sand damp. With each step she leaned down to press her fist into the sand beside the impression of her foot. Uunutu stared at her wondering what had taken her mind.

"Do you understand nothing?" she called out gaily, her voice like a girl's.

"I see what you are doing but I don't know why."

"Look!" she waved him closer. "Look at that." She pointed to the dents in the sand. Uunutu studied the marks. She laughed at his concentration.

"The footprints of our child." She held her belly. "This one will live."

✳

"Take me too! Take me too!" seven-year-old Gitsula begged her father to let her help him move the Tears to their new seasonal resting place.

"Never!" Uunutu declared sternly, teasing.

"I will be a good girl," she wheedled.

"Never!" Uunutu repeated.

"I will weave you a warm blanket."

"Never!"

"I will ask the Sun to bring you a copper."

"I have no interest in wealth!"

"I will marry and bear ten sons with the strength of bears."

Uunutu held her narrow, black-eyed gaze with his.

"Promise?"

"Yes, father! I promise!"

"Did she promise?" Uunutu asked Anawa.

"I was not listening. I cannot say," she shrugged.

"I promised! I promised!" squealed Gitsula jumping up and down with impatience.

"Does she mean it?" Uunutu asked his wife.

"Who can tell?" she replied blandly.

"Perhaps it was the Trickster speaking, not my daughter."

"That could be," agreed Anawa. "The Trickster can enter the bodies of the unwary."

"Yes," Uunutu said solemnly. "I had best go alone. I do not want the Trickster to know the Green Tears' resting place."

"Oh please," Gitsula begged, worried now that he meant to leave her behind. "There is no Trickster. See?" She danced and cavorted. "What Trickster can dance like this? And look!"

She thrust her face at her parents and stuck out her tongue. "Does not the Trickster make the tongue grow in two or fall back on itself? Look at my tongue."

Anawa and Uunutu peered dutifully into their daughter's gaping mouth. "For a fact, your tongue is a little long," Uunutu concluded. With one quick motion he swept her up and held her tightly to him. "I shall squeeze the Trickster out!"

His coarse hand cradled her glossy head, fragrant with butter extracted from seeds. Women pounded seeds into a paste, then mixed them with spring water. After gentle heating over a fire, the oils pooled on the surface and could be skimmed off with a flat wooden ladle. Mothers applied the butter to their daughters' hair to bring them fertility, as the seeds reproduced themselves year after year. Uunutu rubbed his lips across his daughter's brow. He loved the smell.

"Come now. We have work to do. It is time to tend to the Tears."

With Gitsula's birth, Anawa's grim face disappeared as if it had never been.

✳

In the morning, incapable of movement without chant or song, Anawa tended bread for breakfast, smearing it with pungent eulachon fat while carrying on a long conversation in verse with the spirit of the fish that gave them fat and the seed of the grain ground to make a coarse bread.

Uunutu leaned over Gitsula's shelf and whispered: "Your mother sings, you must rise and eat or she'll get louder and louder until the walls fall down."

Gitsula crowed and leaped from her mat, landing with a thud on the floor. Anawa, well aware of the joke shared between father and daughter, abruptly fell silent. She continued her work, trying hard not to smile or acknowledge either of them. They began one of her favorite songs, pretending to stumble forgetfully over the words, hoping to entice her to join in. She continued working sternly and silently. Gitsula cavorted, pulled her nose back, blew out her lips, anything to break her mother's silence. Finally tears dampened Anawa's face with the effort of not laughing and the greater effort of not talking.

Because she would be the next keeper, by age ten Gitsula knew the story of the Green Tears that had been entrusted to her family since time began and fish walked.

"In that age," Anawa instructed Gitsula, "all things talked to one another. The orca understood the howl of the wolf, the wolf the chatter of the raven, and all could interpret the rustle of the trees. We have pieces left. In my past life I could converse with the trees whose bark I borrow." She shook her head sadly. "But now I can only sense the spirit within."

"And father?" prodded Gitsula.

"Ahh, your father once spoke to the stones, which is why today he is able to coax out of them the blades and points he makes so finely."

✳

Uunutu looked forward to the day when his spirit would rise out of his body and he would ride the owl's back, gazing down as Gitsula hung the soft pouch sheltering the Tears between her breasts and carried them season after season to their new resting place.

"You must not worry about wealth," he counseled Gitsula when he caught her enviously gazing at a stunning wedding garment being created for the daughter of the chief's first wife. Its beauty lay in its decoration of sculpted bone and shells available only from southern tribes. The mother had traded a small boat full of otter skins and sturgeon bladders for the bluish shells rimmed with pink.

"Would you prefer that dress, which one day will rot and return to the earth, or would you prefer to have the Tears in our family for all eternity?"

Gitsula quickly summoned up the correct answer. "I would rather have the Tears, Father!"

"Your eyes tell me otherwise," he said severely. "You wish the dress now but it is only your earthly self who wants it. Desires are like blossoms on the fruit-giving trees, whose lives are short. But one's spirit lives long, like the tree itself. A spirit has many lives. It may return as the bear or wolf," he teased, "and then what would you do with such a dress?"

Gitsula laughed at the thought. A child such as she, born into a family such as hers, would never be transformed after death into something so powerful as a bear or wolf. But she liked the idea. She also liked the dress.

8

*

As the gloom lightened, Gitsula pondered her approaching marriage. A new beginning, just as each of the thumbprints on her bed shelf marked the birth of a new season. She traced the childish marks with her baby finger, remembering events, big and small, from each season. Who was born, who died, the first time Uunutu let her touch the Green Tears, and the first time she finished an entire basket. She smiled at that memory. The basket was lopsided and oversized. Anawa patiently unpicked the tight-packed strands of cured and pounded cedar bark, then guided Gitsula's hands as she rewove it. When she finished, it was the most beautiful thing she'd ever seen. It was intended as a berry basket, but when she showed it to Uunutu, he disappeared into the area of the longhouse where each family stored seasonal items. Without letting Gitsula see, he placed something in the basket.

"What is it? Can I see?"

"Yes, you can see, but first you must retell your promise."

Anawa laughed. "And how is she supposed to remember which of the many she has made?"

"I will help her remember."

Uunutu's feet shuffled slowly in the splay-footed steps of the seal dance, which families danced when their children joined in marriage, hoping to bring fertility to the union.

Gitsula nodded eagerly. "Yes! Ten babies! I will have ten babies, all boys and strong as bears!"

Uunutu squatted down on his heels, satisfied.

"And who will weave cloth to keep these bears warm?" scoffed Anawa. "And tend fire and extract fish oil to make their coats glossy? And who will decorate their ceremonial capes and who," she paused significantly, "will catch and prepare the food these ten bears shall eat?"

"I will have a girl too," agreed Gitsula.

"And that is all you will need," declared Anawa triumphantly. "One girl can do the work of ten bears!" She paused pointedly. "And many more men."

A small stone figurine lay in the basket. Its eyes took up half the face, and large, pouty lips the other half. Dangling from the lower lip were ten tiny bone circles representing ten children.

"It is so beautiful," breathed Gitsula, rubbing her thumb over the figurine's large belly and touching each of the circles.

"This will be your dowry basket and in it is your first blessing," Uunutu proclaimed.

Gitsula hugged the figurine. "Gitsula's babies. I will name them all."

Six years later, Gitsula-soon-to-be-married enjoyed the memory and whispered the names she gave to her imaginary children.

"Tciatmuq for father's animal spirit, the owl; Siatlmeq to honor the rain; Tsukai for the sockeye salmon; Uthkay for the long black seal who once walked as a man; Nushqwa for the . . ."

Gitsula felt a hand on her foot. Startled, she sat up quickly.

"Sssshh," breathed Uunutu in her ear. "Come, something terrible has happened!"

Gitsula scrambled to the ground. Two old women stooped at the far end of the longhouse kindling their morning fires, but most others, including Anawa, were still asleep. Uunutu wore the cone-shaped hat of his people, but this morning two flat beaver tails hung over each ear. It was the giving symbol. During feasts or potlatches one wore a beaver tail somewhere on his body to encourage the gifts being offered to return to the giver as the beaver returned to its elaborate dam year after year. Gitsula noticed the addition to his hat but gave no thought to it as her heart thumped with excitement to discover what her father had found that was so terrible.

During the last waning moon Gitsula had woven branches into a triangular shape about knee high and set it outside the longhouse entrance. Beneath it she'd placed her dowry basket half-filled with the objects she had accumulated. An intricately carved ceremonial ladle, bone fish hooks carefully bound together with fine string that had many purposes, a tiny hat carved from white cedar—a replica of the conical basket hats both men and women wore, polished otter ribs to decorate her hair, and an assortment of Uunutu's best knives and chisels.

Before marriage, anyone in the village could add items to the basket. If a girl was popular, it soon overflowed. If not, its contents rarely increased. And if she had wronged someone, that person, after consultation with the *siu,* medicine woman, had the right to take something from the basket, which discharged the wrong and helped the bride cleanse herself.

"Something has been in your basket," said Uunutu sadly, blocking her view of it.

"Not the fox!" Gitsula felt the sting of tears. The basket of a girl with a lazy or careless heart might be visited by the fox, who stole to point out inattentiveness and sloth.

"Oh, please, not the fox!"

Uunutu stepped gravely aside. Gitsula dropped to her knees, her small breasts trembling with the impact. On top of the basket lay a large, round object with a hole about the size of Gitsula's index finger in the middle. It was thin and black and its shiny surface was completely covered in etched pictures. A spindle whorl.

Uunutu had presented a similar one to Anawa before they married. She thought it was a decoration to be suspended from her lip plug, though it was rather large for that purpose. She was amazed when Uunutu told her he had spent most of one winter considering the problem of how to keep the wool from slipping down the spindle.

"I watched my mother and sister weave and I saw you too trying to hold the wool on with one hand while the other worked the spindle."

The spindle whorl worked wonderfully. It held the wool in place and, being round, it spun with the spindle. As an added benefit, it created a bit of a drag on the spindle, keeping the wool from feeding out too quickly. By the time Gitsula was born, several other women in the village had started using the invention, including the chief's wives. That Uunutu could conjure up something so clever made Anawa all the more certain that she had chosen her mate wisely.

But the wives of 'Xan scorned the spindle. They stubbornly stuck to the old way, while maintaining, out of earshot of the chief's wives, that the spindle whorl was for lazy weavers. They claimed the cloth made with its assistance was inferior. The individual lines of yarn did not lie as well against one another, they all agreed, because the weaver using a spindle whorl moved too quickly from one end of the loom to another.

Gitsula picked up the elegantly crafted whorl. Around the perimeter her father had etched the symbols of the Eagle Moon tribe. Encircling the whole was an elongated salmon. Out of its mouth rose little bubbles, which

Uunutu expanded into symbols of fertility and safety. Just above the salmon's tail he'd carved the eyes and beak of the owl.

"It is wonderful!" Gitsula clasped the object to her. "What cloth I shall weave! Thank you, Father!" She hugged him hard and Uunutu's heart swelled.

One more dowry item was yet to come. A bentwood box. Steamed and bent at three corners, with the fourth laced tightly together, good ones were a marvel of workmanship and patience. Uunutu would fit the bottom so perfectly that not a drop of water would seep out. The box was his great secret. Gitsula would never expect such a gift from her father. The box shell and bottom alone took many weeks to bend and shape. Almost as much time again could be spent carving decorations on it, scraping and sanding the surface, oiling it to a luster, and finally rubbing various pigments on it to highlight the carvings. A bent box was far more than a beautifully and skillfully made object. It was a statement that the giver had sufficient wealth to obtain the raw materials and the leisure to create it.

Uunutu had neither, so he stole time to work on the box in the predawn hours and late at night, while other men gathered before sleep to talk of the next salmon run, boast of some deed, or listen to tales spun by the storyteller. While they drifted toward sleep, Uunutu toiled away at Gitsula's box.

The perfect board took ages to find. It had to be meticulously wedged from the larger log, because the box board had to be flawless—exactly even in width from top to bottom and of equal thickness along its length. Considerable time could be wasted honing the board to size, so precision-cutting at this stage saved work later. After the board was sized, it was soaked, then steamed, softening it for the initial bending. Each day the wood was checked for pliability. The coarse fibers of the cedar made it admirable for bending but if it soaked too long, the grain separated.

Several weeks into the process, when Uunutu pulled the board from its bath, his inspecting fingers came across a mushy spot. He frowned and probed further. A few fibers pulled away, leaving a faint indentation. He might be able to save it. If he bent the wood to keep the flaw on the inside, careful sanding and oiling would hide it from view. He contemplated the board. Everything had a purpose. If you knew the purpose of a thing and allowed it to express itself then the object would repay you with years of use. Was this wood meant to be a box for his daughter's dowry?

Uunutu thought of the cost of the board, ten otter skins. He was not a trapper, so he had to trade for those as well. The price was so high, he had to include the promise of two not-yet-started knives, an unusual move which ensured that Uunutu would have to work extra hard in the coming season. He had to make this board work. First, he marked the corner points and carefully scored the wood, scraping it again and again along the angle of the bend, removing excess wood to allow the board to fold sufficiently to create the corner.

After soaking, he began to steam the wood. This part required careful monitoring. The wood was wrapped in wet leaves, but if the fire became too hot the leaves flared, scorching the wood—too cool and the board wouldn't bend properly. Uunutu steamed the board for a week and then searched out rocks for the bending. The rock had to be heavy and square. Uunutu heated it until his hand, passed over it, could feel the warmth. Then, wrapping his hands with wet deer hide rags, he took the board and began to bend it around the rock for the first corner. He loved this part. It was when the character of the tree offered itself up to become something else. Transformation. As with people and animals, so too with rocks and trees and water. He could hardly wait to see Gitsula's face when he gave her the box.

In that moment of pleasant dreaming he heard it. Not a crack or a pop indicating the wood had still not absorbed sufficient water to soften it for the bending process, nor a sign that he was too hasty in coaxing the wood to give in to the rock. It was a faint groan, the tiniest creak. The board was separating at the fault. Peering closely, Uunutu could just make out the hair-thin split beginning on either side of the flaw. The box was as surely ruined as if it had been chopped to splinters. His stomach turned on itself and he wanted to scream.

Despair overcame him. He had been a fool to buy the board so hastily. He'd paid too dearly. He'd been cheated—of that he was now certain. What craftsman would not know such a weak point existed as he took the board off the mother log? What was he going to do?

Uunutu had been working on the beach, for the light and privacy. The late winter air hung thick with moisture, though it did not rain. This was the feel of winter dying. The watery sun threw a weak, gray glaze across the bay. A long stretch of sand, known as Kahnamut's Blanket, cupped the bay, extending into the big creek that ended in a tiny rivulet, then hooking around the near island of land his people called Kwayuukway.

"I have failed," Uunutu muttered despondently, throwing the box board into the fire. He walked past the low beach grasses into the fir forest to sit and think. Perfectly grained boards, expertly wedged, split, and properly dried, were expensive. The damaged one had already been more than he could afford. For three years he had been accumulating furs, knives, bone hooks and needles, and tanned skins, both to pay for Gitsula's wedding potlatch and for the dowry he would present to the family of Gitsula's husband. He had nothing left.

Removing anything from either cache would be a disgrace and bad luck. Gitsula was to marry within the tribe, a boy of the second longhouse. Though his family were *tsas* also, the men were house-pole finders and the women made pigments for paint. Both tasks gave the men entry into the secret totem-dance society and occasionally garnered them an invitation into the chief's sweat lodge. They would advance themselves, of that Uunutu was sure. Sklau of the Beaver, Gitsula's husband-to-be, was a stout young man with broad shoulders and big, deft hands. He was apprenticed to one of the totem carvers. Though likely always a commoner, one day he would rank above his father. It was a good match.

Uunutu sighed heavily. He could forget the box, but it was an important possession for a young woman to take into marriage. He could seek out a tree and cut his own board, but that would anger the fallers and wedgers of the tribe and, besides, he did not have sufficient time. It took weeks to find the right tree and receive its permission to be taken, much less felling it and wedging off the boards. Bringing down a tree was a huge job requiring a team of experienced men.

Uunutu stewed for several days, casting a glowering shadow over the area in the longhouse where his family lived. Finally he concluded his only hope was to throw himself on the mercy of the chief. He must have the box for his daughter, for his wife, and for himself.

✳

Uunutu found the chief's third wife working in a small clearing to the side of the longhouse. The chief fondly called her Enee'qua Enu, meaning "enchanted," though she was a sour-faced child. Behind her, Uunutu could see into a sizable hut filled with racks of dried fish and the precious eulachon oil stored inside the fleshy tubes of giant bull-kelp hung from the rafters—a small part of the chief's great wealth.

"He sees no one," she sniffed. She was tiny, looking ten round seasons old despite the fact that her belly was enormous with new life and her breasts were taut with milk awaiting the chief's fourth child—her first. Her posture and demeanor were condescending. Her every gesture was a slight. But to get to the chief, Uunutu must first pass through this girl and her pretensions. Enchanted Child couldn't grant an audience herself, but she could provide an introduction to the chief's senior wives.

"Her time is very soon," Uunutu thought to himself, staring at the whitish beads of first milk accumulating at her tiny nipples. The girl stared back at him implacably. It was rude for a man to eye the belly of a woman with child, but her breasts held no such taboo. In fact, she was proud of how they had swelled from mere bumps on her chest to these fountains of life. Periodically she squeezed droplets from her nipples so they lay shining against her brown flesh, a boast of her fecundity.

"I have an urgent request."

"He sees no one while he prepares," she stated portentously.

At the cusp of the season's change, the chief sequestered himself to dance and sing songs to the coming season. When he emerged, the tribe feasted and he gave gifts to all the villagers to demonstrate his wealth and power and bring them luck for the salmon catch.

The first wife and, to a lesser extent the second, had rights of access to the chief that no one else did. Occasionally the second wife, at a chief's whim, was "raised" to the status of the first and had equal rights. The chief's first two wives were sisters who looked so much alike and behaved so similarly they were as one despite being five years apart in age. The chief, before he moved up to take his uncle's place as leader, married them at the same time. The first was called Naw and the second Seyek.

Messages to the chief, especially during ceremonial times or when he was in seclusion, could be carried by either of the sisters. But it would have been disrespectful for Uunutu to speak directly to either wife. Unless there was some emergency, he properly should approach another member of the house, as he had done, who would then take the message to the senior wives. If they deemed the request important or timely, they'd take it to the chief.

"I am the keeper of the Tears," Uunutu stated. This child was born lower than he. How she'd managed to marry the chief mystified him. There must be powerful medicine in her family, which made the chief believe the alliance would enrich him in spirit and possessions.

She rounded her little lips pensively as if considering the situation carefully. Her lip plug stood straight out from her face. "Is it a matter of the Tears?"

Uunutu hesitated. He was tempted to lie. It was his right as the keeper to address the chief about anything pertaining to his stewardship of the Tears. Anyone with a ceremonial or spiritual role, from the head shaman down to the lowliest commoner such as Uunutu, had the right to address the chief on those matters.

One of the families in Uunutu's longhouse were keepers of the hunt stories. Both men and women of the family nurtured tales of the annual hunts for bear and deer. The Kahnamut were not great hunters, but these events were important to usher boys out of boyhood, acquire bear fat for smearing on their bodies for warmth in winter and, most important, to confirm their claim to the land they resided on.

Recently two of the hunt tellers had approached the chief because the story of a bear who ate a boy and became a boy himself had become "twisted." One of the tellers had "recaptured" in a dream some words the bear had spoken to the boy before eating him. She added those words to the story and her cousin, also a teller, queried them. For days the issue of whether the words belonged to the story or not was discussed in great detail at night by the adults in the longhouse while the children, fascinated by a story under such minute examination, crowded around to listen. With no resolution, the chief had to be consulted. Though it was already winter's fourth moon and the chief was readying himself to participate in the salmon blessing prior to the arrival of the fish, he put everything aside to seclude himself with the tellers.

After consulting K'we'tan, the dream reader, the chief proclaimed that the dream had been falsely placed in the teller's head by the wolf spirit, which, being a jealous sort, often tried to insinuate himself into ceremonies and stories. The teller who'd had the dream accepted the interpretation. She returned to the longhouse to cast out the words by burning cedar needles and singing the appropriate words.

"I have something important to discuss," Uunutu said with a heavy sigh. "But it is not about the Tears."

"Then I cannot approach him!" the girl said haughtily. "How could you ask such a thing?"

"It is important to my family," Uunutu responded weakly.

The girl ignored him. She squatted down, her belly almost touching the dirt, to attend to the charcoal sticks lying in the fire. Soon she would scrap the scorched wood and mix it to a paste with berry juice, creating a dye that adhered well to skin. Next day the chief would begin to decorate his body with it to bless the salmon. Uunutu didn't move. The girl raised her eyes and disdainfully spoke to his crotch.

"Go away," she said rising and turning her back.

A thrill of rage imbedded itself in Uunutu's gut. The feeling was so unfamiliar he thought for a moment he was suffering an acute bellyache. First the faulty board and now this!

He looked around. It was early afternoon, a time when women were at their food caches or gathering roots. Most of the men were collecting branches to repair broken weirs or at the beach assisting in the carving of a new canoe, the largest one the village had ever made. It was being built to welcome the fierce whale hunters of the Nuu'chah'nulth people. They had passed a visit message from their land on the rugged, storm-swept west coast of the big island, through their relatives the Opetchesaht, who then crossed the sea strait to the upper finger of the Stahlo's mouth and passed it on to the Kahnamut. There were seven Kahnamut villages but Uunutu's chief won the right to host the visitors.

The whalers would come. With them, in their massive canoes twice the length of those the Kahnamut built, they would bring whale skin, blubber, cook oil, and bone for trade. Never before had people of the big waves come to the Kahnamut's land. They had traded with them through other tribes but never directly. When Uunutu was a young boy he'd heard that the whalers had come to the Sqwamus of the northern shore but they had not ventured farther south to his own people.

The village was busy preparing for the momentous occasion, which was to happen within the next five days, the beginning of spring, the most propitious time for potlatches and the hatching of new enterprises. Gitsula's marriage paled in importance to the arrival of the whalers, but it had already been agreed upon when the whale people issued their visit declaration. Joy coursed through Gitsula when she heard of the impending arrival, for it would add luster to her wedding.

'Xan was angry when his brother refused his demand to move Gitsula's wedding to the summer season. Though Uunutu never challenged 'Xan during his family's time of embarrassment, the fact that he didn't infuriated 'Xan. Uunutu's inaction implied the clan of 'Xan was not worth the effort. He'd hated the "man who leaves no footprint" ever since.

"How can you let this rabbit's daughter gain status by marrying during the potlatch?" 'Xan complained to his brother.

"How can I stop it?" the chief asked reasonably. "I gave my permission long before we knew the whalers were coming."

✳

With effort Uunutu stifled his building anger. Icy resolve took its place.

"I will pay well if you present me to the first wife," he said evenly.

"Pay?" the girl replied with sudden interest.

"I have many things which have not yet been taken to the dowry," Uunutu lied.

The girl narrowed her eyes. Uunutu was poor but she knew his mate was a masterful weaver. Perhaps he had one of her special feather blankets, which had not yet been officially deposited in the dowry. She coveted a feather blanket. She'd happily take a message to Naw or Seyek, risking their ire, for a chance at such a treasure.

"A feather blanket?"

"If that is what you wish."

"It is what I demand."

It was a staggering demand in return for such a small request. But Uunutu had no choice.

"Bring it to me," the girl commanded. "Then I will take you to the wives."

Bring it to me! Bring it to me! Bring it to me! The words burned through Uunutu's brain.

For this insolent child to demand payment before service was the final affront. Uunutu embraced the fury that would not be repressed. He grabbed Enchanted Child roughly from behind, pinning her arms.

"You will do as I wish!" he hissed, shoving her to the floor, thrilling at his power.

The girl was shocked, but it didn't occur to her that Uunutu might harm her. She laughed at him harshly, her mirth cut short when he hauled her to her feet then pushed her into one of the drying racks.

"I will give you the two-headed baby!"

Uunutu grabbed a handful of *slowi* and stuffed it into her mouth. The girl doubled over from the retching. Uunutu wrenched her head around to look at him.

"Eeeoooo!" she keened behind the gag. Uunutu's hand circled his erection, hard and menacing. It thrust itself forward the second he laid hands on her. To have sex with a woman so near her time was forbidden. The baby could be born with two heads and the man might never father another child. That he was prepared to violate the taboo and risk so much now terrified her. She squirmed frantically as Uunutu forced her to the floor. To enter her from behind was the only feasible way with such a belly. Her reed skirt separated and her buttocks, soft and not yet wide with the bearing of children, parted for him. Uunutu panted with lust.

He would teach her! He would teach them all! His hands were sticky with milk spurting from the frightened girl's breasts. Head back, teeth bared—he yanked aside the deer skin flap across his groin, then plunged ferociously into her narrow passage. His roar of triumph and her howl of pain melded.

As he drew back to drive into her a second time, the image of Gitsula appeared behind his clenched eyes. He cried out her name and suddenly the enormity of his actions flooded over him. Pulling quickly out of the girl he staggered back. If he released his seed all would be lost. She fell to her side sobbing, hands buried between her legs.

Uunutu sucked in a shuddering breath. He looked around. None had witnessed his moment of shame. Perhaps he could salvage something.

"I have marked you!" he sneered, trying to control the tremor in his voice. "You will do what I say or I will finish what I started. Then you will have the two-headed baby."

He punctuated the threat by giving her a disdainful push in the belly with his foot.

She lay on the floor completely cowed. Something evil had possessed this man. Could it return to harm her unborn child? Would he carry out his threat?

"You will do as I wish or I will return," he repeated. "No one will believe you if you say anything. Am I not Uunutu who leaves no footprint?"

9

*

The chief was a powerful man, with thick, hunched shoulders and a deep chest. Still in his early middle years, his face had the deeply etched lines of an older man. His legs, though heavily muscled, had been severely bowed by childhood illness. Over his shoulders the chief wore a cape of perfectly matched eagle feathers and a headdress adorned with ten bear snouts. To commoners and most nobility the chief spoke slowly and deliberately. It was an act of kindness. His power was so great he must moderate the force of his words so as not to make the listener dizzy and weak.

"I beg your forgiveness," Uunutu said humbly.

"How can your request be more important than my preparation to welcome the whalers?"

"It is not."

"And the feast of the salmon moon? We must prepare for that as well. It is not long off."

"It matters nothing compared to that."

"But still you stand here, owl spirit upon your shoulder."

Uunutu had dressed carefully for the audience, arranging a small cape with an owl wing across one shoulder. If ever he needed his guardian spirit it was now.

The chief had positioned himself so that his back was to the longhouse fire. The low morning sun shot through the gaps in the planks, haloing him. If Uunutu dared look at his chief's face he would have seen only a swirl of smoke stabbed through with blinding rays. As it was, the effect from the shoulders down was mesmerizing, fearsome.

The chief glanced over at Enchanted Child. His young wife sat quietly in a dark corner. She was motionless, but the chief sensed her fright. Something was amiss. Why else would she come directly to him, risking the wrath of his senior wives?

The chief liked to keep ahead of events; it helped him seem wise. He had spies in every longhouse, even his own, who reported on conversations, disagreements, and alliances. But often the best information came if he just bided his time and observed. So far nothing he'd seen provided any insight into Enu's strange behavior. He'd keep her close until he had answers.

"I come about Gitsula's dowry."

"It is finished?"

"No."

"It is promised?" the chief asked. To speak about the richness of a daughter's dowry was to boast, and a boast was the same as issuing a challenge. If the box did not appear, Uunutu would be derided and others might demur from contributing.

"Promised," sighed Uunutu. He could not help himself; he had spoken of the box to many in his pride.

"She marries at the next moon?" the chief asked, knowing perfectly well that the girl was to take her husband when the whalers arrived.

Uunutu launched into the story of his desire to provide an oil box as dowry, of the board and its flaws, and the impossibility of securing another perfect board in time to make the box. He lamented the bad faith of the man who sold him the wood.

"Why not take these fine knives that you have given me for this audience and trade them for a board?" The chief knew that none of the wedgers in the village would sell Uunutu a board for that price, especially knowing how desperately he needed it.

"It's too late!" Uunutu groaned. "I have no time for the bending."

How could he ask the question that needed to be asked? What could he offer?

The chief blew loudly through his nostrils but said nothing. He had seen the great moose snort in such a way. It frightened him. It would frighten this one. The silence dragged on.

"I must have a box," Uunutu pleaded, opening his hands upward in the sign of supplication.

"I have a box," the chief exhaled loudly through his nostrils again. He owned fourteen boxes of different sizes, so many that they were not required for any purpose. Only the wealthiest had possessions that were not used.

"Yes," said Uunutu, holding his breath.

"But you have no possession valuable enough to trade for one of them."

Enchanted Child smothered a gasp. The chief smiled grimly to himself. She thought he was turning Uunutu down. Why did she care? What hold did this little man have over her?

The chief adored his third wife. Though she was greedy and probably counted the fox prominently among her spirit ancestors, he worshiped her elfin body and face, and had since he'd laid eyes on her. The Kahnamut were forbidden to lie with a child. Some had been put to death for breaking the taboo. But at eleven, with tiny breasts, thin legs, gaunt frame, and hairless pubis, she'd excited the chief like no other. Unable to wait, he took her as wife against the recommendation of the shaman, the senior wives, and Ah'we'tan. Even so, he carefully abided by the taboo. He spent hours caressing the child, inflaming his passion, and then accepting relief from her hands. But he forbore entering her until she was of age, a year of painful waiting. He ensured the village was aware of his virtue by summoning Ah'we'tan to act as chaperone each time his urge for the child's flesh became overpowering.

"I will pledge anything!" begged Uunutu, his dignity in tatters.

The chief pondered the matter. He saw no particular reason to grant the man's request. As his daughter was marrying another of similar station, the dowry need not be lavish. Though a finely crafted oil box was a highly desirable item, to be without it would not change her position. Having one did give her the opportunity to advance herself, perhaps buy her husband's way into one of the lesser dance societies. In any case, the family was one which had never before demonstrated the least ambition. The chief well remembered Uunutu's decision not to challenge 'Xan.

However, Uunutu was the keeper of the Tears. He'd never requested a favor before, so he should not be dismissed lightly. It might reflect badly on the chief. It might even annoy Raven, the black bird who'd once held the Tears in his beak. As the chief gazed past Uunutu's averted head and down the length of the longhouse, a shaft of dust-filled light danced in front of his breath. He peered at it. A shape. He stopped breathing and waited. The cluster of dust stretched, becoming pointed at one end, the point rising high and curving slightly outward. A boat. It was not of the Kahnamut, for the prow rose far beyond their boats' prows. What was the shape trying to tell him?

The chief exhaled suddenly and the shape dissolved. A boat, yes. But a boat from the west. It was a whaler. A Nuu'chah'nulth whaler. Suddenly he saw the way. This man had been sent to solve a problem. Once more he trumpeted through his nose.

"I grant your request."

Uunutu almost shouted with joy but he controlled himself, standing as still as he could.

"And I have one in return. You may take whichever box you desire but when the sun rises again you must return to hear my request."

✳

Anawa laughed as Uunutu wrapped his arm around her, pulling her close; she could feel his hardness press against the crack of her buttocks. His desire held the excitement of youth. Gitsula suddenly felt shy in the presence of their display. She bent her head quickly to her work—a catch basket for holding fish scooped from a weir. Her head was full of thoughts of her husband-to-be. She'd seen him only three times since winter set in, and then only in passing or from a distance. Until the day before the wedding they were forbidden to speak.

A few days earlier, when Gitsula had lain down to sleep, something jabbed her. She felt around and came up with a thin object. The boards of the longhouse let in just enough moonlight to see it. A bone hair decoration. Slightly curved, carved, and polished, it was a pretty little thing. She lay down smiling, the gift—from her betrothed she was sure—clutched in her hand. He should not have entered her families' longhouse, let alone approached her sleeping place. The thought of his daring hand pushing the gift beneath her blanket made her shiver.

Uunutu intended to wait until Gitsula's wedding day to present the box, but could not. The next morning, before he dressed to meet the chief, he gave it to her. His daughter's eyes shone as she turned it over and over in her hands. Her skin was caked with white mud to ward off disease and protect her from the biting insects that swarmed to the Stahlo at this time of year. Dark rivulets streaked her cheeks as joyous tears slowly tracked down her face.

Anawa was almost speechless.

"It is worth it to see my wife without words," he joked. "I must go and meet the chief."

Anawa looked up, amazed. As far as she knew, Uunutu had never before even spoken to the chief. Now twice in two days he had been invited into the chief's longhouse. It could only mean good things to come.

✳

Uunutu's euphoria disappeared with the force of a thunderclap. Panic clutched at his throat, a grip as strong as ten men. He felt the air leave his body and his head grow faint. His eyes tried to focus. Heat. Unbearable heat rising up his back and into his head.

What a fool he'd been to make an open-ended promise to the chief. A man didn't get to such a position by failing to snatch up opportunities, then squeezing every last advantage out of them. But how could he have guessed what the chief wanted? The chief watched curiously as dread invaded Uunutu's body.

In his distress, Uunutu's eyes jumped to the face of the man standing before him. Black, hard, shiny orbs bored into him. The bear snouts crowning the chief's head mocked him. The chief raised his arms slowly and beat them back and forth, rippling the cape heavy with feathers, sending waves of cedar-scented air at Uunutu. It was a terrifying sight. Thunderbird. He would be swallowed, consumed.

"Bring her," the chief commanded.

Uunutu had no memory of stumbling out of the longhouse, of the search in the village for Anawa and Gitsula, of the odd looks given him by the old women squatting on rocks and stitching coarse fabric together for the mat walls of their summer houses. Nor did his feet recall the interminable walk along the deer path leading away from the beach to a tiny lake fed by a thin, seasonal creek. He found them bent over, pulling moss from the massive trees hovering over the lake. The song of the moss echoed absurdly in his head.

Take an arm, leave an arm,
Take a leg, leave a leg,
Feed the head and next I come,
The body will grow back again.

✳

Anawa gently smeared an unguent on the tree after removing the moss, carefully leaving a portion of each patch unharvested. The sour-smelling substance encouraged growth, repaying the moss for permitting the harvest.

Anawa saw him first. Gitsula was oblivious, her mind far away, daydreaming of her wedding feast. But she heard her mother's grunt, heard the pain in the utterance, then a piercing scream—as a wolf, only human.

Uunutu disappeared immediately after telling Gitsula she must appear before the chief. Anawa seemed to be folded in on herself and would tell her nothing but bade her search out Ah'we'tan to accompany her to the chief's longhouse.

Ah'we'tan said little when the shaking girl made her request, merely narrowed her eyes before limping off, the girl hurrying behind.

"Oh, please, please, great wise one, please tell me why I am called."

Ah'we'tan frowned and shook her head, which only made Gitsula more anxious.

"What will I say?"

Ah'we'tan's fleshy lips pulled down.

"Tell me what you know, old one! Please tell me, if you know!"

Ah'we'tan stopped suddenly, and Gitsula almost plowed into her. Ah'we'tan eyed the girl, noting the sweat on her breasts. Too bad she was so poor. Weakness was the best source of wealth and an even better source of power if you knew how to manipulate it. And Ah'we'tan knew better than most. She pointed to the bone hair decoration.

"My husband gave it to me," stammered Gitsula.

"Aaaha!" chuckled Ah'we'tan. "Do you not want to know?"

Gitsula choked on the saliva that suddenly filled her mouth and she clutched her stomach to stop the heaving. Perhaps her husband was dead. But no, if he were dead she would even now hear the moaning of the women of the village who would have brought some token of his body to her to break the news. Men had nothing to do with the dead until the bodies were cold and the person's name spirit had time to leave.

Not dead. What then? Perhaps worse. Perhaps disgraced. He may have shamed his name through cowardice or thievery. She must know something to prepare her. A trembling hand touched the bone decoration held in her thick luxuriant hair made oily and redolent by the finest fish oil. Gitsula rationalized that she was trading the precious thing for both of them. If she stood before the chief in terror-stricken idiocy, it would reflect badly on her husband-to-be. And perhaps the chief would impart good news. A little charge of hope ran through her.

Ah'we'tan grunted, holding out her shriveled hand.

The chief's most recent wife might have requested a maid. That person could be Gitsula! It would be a hard life, as the girl was notoriously lazy and unskilled. But the honor would be great. As a result, Gitsula's children-to-be might apprentice with the tribe's boat builders, a sought-after position in the village. Or they might become fallers, an equally important skill. A good faller saved the village much labor by bringing down perfect trees near water and in such a way that few were broken.

Gitsula smiled, pulled the bone from her hair, and handed it to the old woman, who took it so quickly it seemed to disappear.

"Do not cry aloud. Cry into your spirit," Ah'we'tan counseled. "Open your mouth." She placed on Gitsula's tongue a rubbery strip cut from the lung tissue of deer. Then she took a needle-sharp piece of antler and sliced it across her tongue. The blood welled quickly.

"Shut it," she barked at the startled girl. "Encourage the blood. This will take you into a dream and your spirit will not be bold before the chief. That will please him. Concentrate on the blood. Feel it. Swallow it. When you return home, take the lung piece and bury it. It will absorb the strength of the chief's power and you will not sicken."

She told her nothing more.

✳

Gitsula stood before the chief in terror. The salt of the blood on her tongue sharpened rather than dulled her senses as Ah'we'tan said it would. His smell. Unlike boys who cleansed themselves regularly to please the spirits in hopes that their vision quest would be successful and a spirit would swiftly enter their body, the chief avoided washing to cultivate his power and repel evil usurpers. Gitsula inhaled the earthy tang of his body, an intense odor of man and authority.

"We join with the people of the whale," he spoke in a sonorous, slow voice. Gitsula caught a glimpse of Ah'we'tan by the fire in the center of the longhouse.

What has this to do with me? Gitsula wondered, her head beginning to spin with the heat and smoke from a small aromatic fire by the chief. Blood. Fire. Salt on her tongue. Then him. He stood beside her. With a start she realized that the frighteningly powerful chief was in reality quite short.

He barely passes my shoulder, Gitsula said to herself. Even in her fear of the unknown, she found herself suppressing a giggle. The great Thunderbird is shorter than me.

"Whale. Eagle Moon of Kahnamut." The chief chanted the words softly, slowly, over and over. The haze grew thicker.

"Whale bride. Bride of Kahnamut. Whale bride. You will be the whaler's bride."

Gitsula's knees buckled but somehow she did not fall. The chief tenderly guided her body to the enveloping skins. Only then did Gitsula notice a group of elders sitting stonelike in a half circle. One of them, bent in half by age, scuttled to the chief, clutching a fan of feathers. The cape was taken from his shoulders. It isn't real, Gitsula convinced herself. I cannot marry a whaler. I am not in the chief's longhouse. None of it is real.

She watched Ah'we'tan tease the chief's groin with the feather fan. She did the same to Gitsula, tickling her with the scratchy feather tips. Gitsula wanted to laugh. The chief's body was hard and squat, his belly only just beginning to show his age. He knelt between her legs, which had been pulled apart by the old woman. No part of him touched her except his organ, which he smeared with some substance before meeting her body.

An hour, a day, a week could have passed before Ah'we'tan led Gitsula to the seclusion hut where she would be pampered and washed and decorated prior to her marriage to a man of the Nuu'chah'nulth, the whale people. The chief's final words rang in her head:

"I join to you as you will join our people to the spirit of the whale."

"His seed ensures your safety among the whale people," explained Ah'we'tan. "It will live inside you forever and your children will bear the rank of his children in the new land. It is a great honor," she breathed into the girl's ear.

✳

"It is an important honor," Ah'we'tan told the distraught Anawa. "And if we do not make this connection, the Sqwamus will, and allied to the whalers they will take our summer place on the river."

After Ah'we'tan led Gitsula away, the chief celebrated with the elder men who ruled the sweat lodge society. They, along with the women of Ah'we'tan's circle, were the powers of the village.

"We have searched long for the correct gift," one of the men said grudgingly. He was annoyed that his own suggestions had not been taken. They had all spoken of a bride who would bind the Nuu'chah'nulth to the Kahnamut. The problem had been in finding one. The chief's own children weren't yet of age, and his brother 'Xan had no daughters. In fact, at that moment there wasn't a single female of marriageable age in the whole tribe who wasn't addled, lazy, or ugly. Except Gitsula, who was already promised.

To complicate matters, there was always the possibility that the Nuu'chah'nulth were thinking in the same direction. They might bring

along a bride-gift of their own. The whalers were notoriously testy. If the
Kahnamut didn't adequately reciprocate, a commercial union was unlikely.
And conflict was always a possibility. They were legendary fighters of
extraordinary bravery, whose boats were larger and faster than any others.

Then the foolish little rabbit put himself in the chief's power. Though
not high born, Gitsula was comely and there was a special way about her
that promised much. Her rare, ebony skin color also set Gitsula apart, giving
her a hint of nobility. Hopefully this would appeal to the Nuu'chah'nulth,
who were said to be partial to the color of the black-and-white orca whale.

"She is the one!" the chief said to his inner circle. "Her face came to me
in a dream." Only among them did the chief assume a normal tone and
speed of speaking. They were men who had proven themselves in great
deeds and brave feats and their guiding spirits would not be overwhelmed
by the chief's.

"That's not the only thing that came to you," leered 'Xan.

"I gave her my seed for the good of the tribe," the chief protested.

The men shouted their appreciation. To solve the problem of a gift for
the whalers so simply and cheaply, a daughter for a bent box, showed
remarkable skill.

"Perhaps you should sleep with Anawa too," proposed one slyly. "It is
through the mother that you know the daughter."

The chief had always liked the look of Anawa's rounded, happy form.

"Yes, I see the advantage in that," the chief agreed. "I might take her to be
my fourth wife. With Uunutu as her husband, she will be hardly used at all."

"And this came to you in a dream also?" asked another.

"It did," he replied solemnly.

The lewd guffaws that followed eased the men into a pleasurable few
hours of banter about the women they'd known in their youth and the
ones yet to know. The chief sat on a hummock of skins watching, listening,
considering the possibilities of an enriching alliance between two nations.
The Kahnamut people of the mainland coast and the whale warriors of the
island coast. Caretakers of the inland waters and caretakers of the waters
beyond.

His eyes closed. He could hear the paddles, slip, whoosh, slip, whoosh.
He could feel the thunk of swells against the boats. He could smell the
whale stacked in yellow squares.

"The Nuu'chah'nulth come," he breathed to himself.

✳

10

"Do not anger them," warned Makal, the wife of Anawa's uncle.

"How do I anger them?" retorted Anawa, tossing her head toward the chief's senior wives. "I have done nothing."

"Haiii!" answered her friend. "Nothing is the problem. You must embrace the union."

"I have followed what my spirit demands," Anawa countered. "I laid offerings at the feet of my trees and asked the gulls to watch over my Gitsula."

"That is the world beyond," Makal frowned at her friend's obstinacy. "You must also do what is demanded in this world."

Anawa sighed heavily. She knew what was expected. She must pay an appreciation gift, an acknowledgment that the wives had played a part in this honor, though in all likelihood they'd had nothing to do with it. But the fact that the foundation for such an important prospective union was laid in their lodge gave them the right to claim responsibility.

"I must pay them for taking away my daughter!" Anawa said bitterly.

"You must. But do not let it hold such a weight upon you. You are lucky." Makal turned her back and continued washing. "Uunutu has unwittingly given you an opportunity."

Anawa bristled. She despised her husband for his pride and poor judgment. "A bent box is not worth a daughter," she snapped.

Makal was achingly jealous of Anawa's unexpected good fortune and even more annoyed that she wouldn't take advantage of it. Her own two daughters were equally worthy, more so, she thought, yet they had no such luck. One was already wed and one not yet of age. Anawa's unhappiness irked her. It was shortsighted. "The chief has presented no gift to you?"

"He has given me nothing." In her distress, the thought hadn't even occurred to Anawa.

"You have the right of asking," Makal emphasized. "Uunutu got his box. Losing your daughter means you also lose her children who would care for you in old age. This is understood. Take something back."

"I want nothing," Anawa sighed, reluctant to even think of the matter.

Makal shook her head in frustration. Life was a series of arrangements and barters. Anawa never approached things with this in mind. And that was one reason Eagle Moon clan remained at the bottom of the village society. Then Makal had an inspiration.

"What is it we played at when we were children? What is it that you wanted then?"

Despite her gloom Anawa smiled at the memory. She'd always played the role of healer, an exalted position that never went to one from a *tsas* family or clan. Though she enjoyed being a weaver—an occupation chosen for her as it had been for her mother and grandmother—it was herbs, fungus, and wild plants that spoke most forcefully to her. She was sure they would give up their healing secrets if she had the opportunity. For the first time in days Anawa thought of something other than Gitsula. Makal was right. If she requested the role of healer, she would be brought into the circle led by Ah'we'tan and her sister and move to a more favorable place in her own longhouse. Even more important, she could demand several children to collect for her. They could be slave children or even children born of lower-status women in the village. Perhaps a boy and a girl.

Anawa was not greedy. She would never have married Uunutu otherwise. But the light Makal shone on her dreadful situation awakened a powerful desire within her. Anawa stared at the beak of her friend's nose and her narrow, low forehead. Truly she was not an attractive woman. Her teeth fit poorly, jutting her lower jaw over her upper, and her legs were too thin for the broad, strong body. But Makal was determined and smart and a canny scavenger. She could turn any discarded object into something valuable. As a result she had suitors long before marriageable age. It didn't surprise Anawa that her old friend could see a way to salvage a good result out of the sudden chaos of her life. Makal read her friend's emotions and her thoughts.

"First go to the wives," she advised. "Present them with your thanks. Then think of what I have said. But don't wait long! The chief will only be obligated as long as Gitsula remains with us."

✳

Gitsula lay motionless in the seclusion pit, prolonging the last gentle fingers of sleep cradling her body and mind. Eyes shut, she saw hard bodies straining. Somewhere among them was a man—her husband. The new one. Her betrothed had vanished when he'd heard the news. Anawa heard that he had gone west along the beach to the tip of the peninsula of land that reached out into the Kahnamut Sea. There, amidst relatives of the chief, he would find a wife. In another month the salmon would run, and his path would cross that of his home tribe as hundreds converged on the river to fish. But she would not see him.

Half awake, Gitsula heard the chatter and working noises of men toiling on the water. She shot upright, heart hammering. The shouts, the grunts of nearly simultaneous exertion—dip, stroke, pull. This was no dream.

"They come! They come!" The calls grew louder.

"*Nuu'chah'nulth ki!*" The whale people come!

Excited, babbling children, laughing women, and pounding feet. The caroling cry of the first greeters filtered up from the beach. The chief and his wives, the shaman and his two assistants, and the *sqomten* and *siu*, medicine man and woman, stood at the water's edge surrounded by the council of elders. Gitsula thought she heard the beginning words of the welcoming chant, faintly filtering through the breeze. She yearned to join the throng heading to the water, but she was not to be seen by the whalers until she was presented to them.

Villagers hurriedly set out large fiber mats to display the first gifts; these would not be the prime feast offerings, only welcoming tokens. Everyone was expected to donate, and while no one was forced to give beyond their means, those who outdid themselves were noticed.

Anawa shouldered two large pack baskets. They were flat on one side, to sit comfortably against the hip or lay across the back for heavier loads. Many women made such baskets, but they were often lumpy and irregular, as they indiscriminately used the entire branch, from thin tip to thicker stalk, in order to make the work go more quickly.

Anawa chose only the most uniform of slender cedar branches to keep the weaving perfectly even. She carefully staggered the join where one branch ended and another began, so an inverted V-shape was evident when one looked at the front of the pack basket. She also ensured that the gaps between the branches were equal by inserting spacers while weaving the green cedar. Only when the basket was thoroughly dried did she remove them. Spacing was important, since the baskets were used to carry mussels, clams, and crabs from the beach back to the village. While the women walked, sand and water fell out as the shellfish clicked against each other.

Anawa also shaped the top of her basket into a steep angle, leaving even more gaps between the branches. When it rained, she hung the baskets, allowing the water to further clean the catch. Her baskets took far longer to make than other women's, but they rarely needed repair. These particular baskets, she thought, were her best ever. She had another gift for the feast, an exquisite cape with a spectacular rainbow design in tiny shells applied to the back. It had taken her months to make it out of sight of the women who competed with each other to craft the most exquisite and valuable items for the giving.

The chief's words echoed in her head as Anawa hurried to greet the whalers. Surrounded by his wives, he'd admitted her the night before even though he was busy preparing for his visitors. Her request was simply spoken, her justifications given. Anawa was surprised by how calm she felt addressing the man who could make the trees bow down with the power of his voice. In the silence that followed her request she waited with her gaze averted until an object was pressed into her hands. A bowl. In it an oblong pounding stone.

"*Suquotiu*," the chief whispered. "Healer."

The angry face of the second wife came to her as she approached the beach. Her clan, the Sun Frog, had been healers for generations. Now that role would pass through the Eagle Moon. Anawa smiled triumphantly. She was surprised at how much she enjoyed taking what had never been hers.

Chants filled the late-morning air, lifting and swelling with the mist. Joy, excitement, yet also suspicion, curiosity, and fear. Children tugged at one another, pointing out the hazy outlines of the boats as they entered the bay after their long journey from the west coast of the big island, around its southern tip, past Swift Waters, and into the Kahnamut Sea. Anawa searched through the throng for Uunutu but saw no sign of him.

For a moment all was quiet as the first thrusting prows of the canoes came clearly into sight.

"Yaaaahhhhh!" a cry of awe went up.

It was the villagers' first contact with the people of the fierce coast. As the early centuries of the new millennium ground on in terror, darkness, and horror in Europe, the Kahnamut lived in abundance and safety. Skirmishes among them were few and they traveled out of curiosity and for sport rather than need. Occasionally men from several Kahnamut villages ventured across the sea to trade with distantly related tribes that had settled on the rocky southern tip of the big island—the Malahat, Saanich, and Esquimalt.

Only a few of the oldest in the village had ever seen a Haida Gwaii, the fierce people who owned the islands far to the north of the big island, or the Tsimshian who occupied sections of the northern mainland coast, or the Tlingit who lived in a cold, hard land of snow and rock even farther north. But the Kahnamut knew of their ways from stories told by their immediate northern neighbors, the Kwakwaka, who had evolved into far-ranging warrior-traders. Their boats, it was told, had traveled so far into the setting sun they once landed in a place of constant heat, massive insects, bizarre trees with no branches, and broad, brown people of enormous strength who spoke a songlike language.

In a tremendous display of trading acumen, the Kahnamut chief had exchanged two precious copper crests the size of an adult's torso, each pounded thin and elaborately etched, for a Kwakwaka pole carved in the likeness of that tree without branches. The bark of the tree lay like roof shingles along the length of the pole, and its fernlike leaves adorned the top of a straight trunk, much as a feathered headdress might. Near the base of the pole the skilled Kwakwaka carvers had fashioned a wreath of spirit forms held up by a whale, its tail folded back on itself. Midway up the trunk four coppers hugged the pole, symbolizing the wealth of the man who owned it and the boat that made the great trek.

The pole was not large, two men's height at most. It guarded the chief's sleeping area and had been openly coveted by 'Xan for as long as anyone could remember.

The pole was slyly referred to in private as "'Xan's desire."

The pole was brought to the beach and planted prominently for the arrival of the whalers. It would underscore the chief's importance, worldliness, and wealth.

Normally the Nuu'chah'nulth, aloof and suspicious, had no reason to venture south around the big island and east to the mainland across the difficult waters of the strait. But word had passed of the Kahnamut's protected bay, their superior fishing grounds on the Stahlo, and their ready access to deer and bear in the gentle, treed lands immediately adjacent to the winter village. They would either be worthy trade partners or, if the stories proved untrue, valuable slaves. Should the visitors be disappointed, they would leave after burning all the gifts to disgrace their hosts. When time was right, they would return to capture the village and avenge their disappointment.

Anawa cried out in admiration as the lead boat emerged dramatically from a mist so thick it obscured all but the nearest water in the bay and most of the mountains on the north shore. The boat, a cedar dugout at least eighty feet long, with an immense Thunderbird mounted menacingly on the prow, stopped a few hundred feet offshore, where it was silently joined by six more, one after another. The boats lined up a paddle-length apart, facing the beach. Anawa counted eleven men at the paddles of each boat, a leader in the bow, and a stroke caller at the stern. Huge piles of cargo were heaped in the middle. The men howled their greeting, long, loud, and harsh. The Kahnamut replied with their own chorus of welcome, the volume rising and rising as each tried to outdo the other.

At a gesture from the chief, the Kahnamut fell silent. The whalers followed suit. Then, with the high, screaming cry of the eagle, the whalers' leader signaled and all seven boats surged forward, paddlers digging deep and fast in a fury of motion. On and on, they came straight to the beach. For all the visitors knew, it could have been hull tearing, jagged rock, but the Nuu'chah'nulth demonstrated their bravery by not slowing or flinching as they powered toward the shore. They developed such extraordinary speed that the boats mounted the sand and did not stop until the hulls were almost completely free of the water. Just as the boats began to teeter on their slightly rounded bottoms, the men slammed their paddles down to the beach to steady it.

A collective whoosh of exhaled breath hummed in the watching crowd. An impressive arrival. The chief grinned and laughed, clapping at the show.

While the whalers basked in the approval, the Kahnamut chief barked a brisk series of commands, and floods of villagers—men, women, and older children—dashed to the boats. They lifted them straight in the air, men, loads, and all, and carried them far up onto the beach. It was all the astonished whalers could do to maintain their composure in the face of this grand display of élan.

"Come!" urged Makal, who was bold about such things. "Let's get closer. I want to see what they are made of."

"Skin and blood and bone and spirit breath, just like you and me," Anawa said, eyes also wide with curiosity.

"Nooo, I hear their men are so large they mate with she-bears!"

Anawa giggled. "All right. Here," she fingered a tooth fall attached to her ear. Made from dog teeth, the largest at the top running down to the small front teeth at the bottom, the tooth falls made pretty ear ornaments, which clattered with every movement of a woman's head.

"If they are so big then you may have this. See how perfect I made the holes to string them together, and you," she thought for a moment, "you must give me . . ."

"A spoon!"

"No."

"A fur collar."

"No."

"Leggings for your husband."

"No."

"Then what?" Makal said with pretend testiness.

"Your next born!"

"Done!"

As children, they had bet many times on the outcome of games, and as adolescents on the likelihood of a parent doing one thing or another. Anawa reckoned that Makal owed her an entire village full of children, based on her losing bets about who in the longhouse would audibly pass wind first, scratch their buttocks, or yawn.

Anawa was impressed. The men were tall and lean, with round faces accented by prominent cheekbones and large eyes. Their mouths were also round, whereas those of her people were wide and fleshy. And their noses, pierced with feathers, appeared flat and broad. Their thighs were straight and lean compared to the squatter limbs of the Kahnamut. They wore long blankets over their shoulders, and their knees were wrapped with some kind of padding to protect the skin as they half-knelt and paddled. Their chief was fully clothed in hide leggings, a war vest of bones tightly lashed together with hide, and a towering headpiece in the shape of a whale. The slaves, three to a boat, were naked except for knee pads and braided belts on which were tied the talismans of their owners.

"Chinook!" breathed Makal.

The Chinook lived to the south on the edge of a bay, in time to be known as Puget Sound, that pushed deep into a glacier-capped mountain range, which would, one day, be called the Olympics. They also occupied large tracts of land around the mouth of the Columbia River. The Chinook were expert middlemen, shuttling along the coast, often serving as the only contact between antagonistic nations. Their most valuable currency was their ability to move large quantities of dentalia shells, furs, oil, and slaves, between villages and nations. Their presence on the Nuu'chah'nulth boats flaunted the wealth of these visitors, who could take such valuable captives—skilled linguists and traders—and use them as common labor.

"How can you tell?" asked Anawa.

"Their heads, see? They are flat."

Chinook spent much of their infancy strapped to wooden cradles, rounded at the bottom and topped with a flat piece of plank at the top. They were held snugly on a soft bed of dried moss and covered with soft cedar fiber blankets with their heads resting against the flat top. As they grew, the soft bones of their heads pushed against the cradle tops, flattening and widening. The flatter the head the more beautiful the child and the more likely that the mother was of a noble line, a woman with slaves and the time to make the constant adjustments necessary to ensure an even flattening of the head.

After the whalers disembarked, they sang to the mountains on the north shore, thanking them for protection from the killing winds. High tones, like a bird, and low barking croons melted together, lifting in the winds. Anawa's spirits rose with the song as she stared at the men's hard backs. She could see the effects of their tremendous voyage. Their bellies were like rock, but their ribs showed clearly and their cheeks were sunken beneath the jutting bones of their faces. Large shells and bone talismans hung in curtains across their chests, and most of the men had blankets draped across one shoulder and tied at the hip, leaving the upper paddling arm unencumbered. Their lower limbs were mostly naked, and many had small ornaments dangling from their penises, which swung against their thighs as they walked.

"I'd say I won," breathed Makal.

Anawa laughed. It wasn't the size of their organs that drew her attention but the men's regal bearing. Warriors of the sea: brave, strong, fearless. For the first time, pride in her daughter's union filled her heart.

11

So perfect was the feast, so lavish were the food and gifts that the Kahna-mut chief asked permission to borrow the whalers' word "*pa-chitla*," a superlative of abundance, to describe the occasion. The Kahnamut pronounced it "potlatch." The Chinook captives seethed when the whalers bestowed the word, for *pa-chitla* was one of their origin but lost to them now, as was their freedom.

For six days the spirits were feted in dance and song. Exhausted revelers lay sleeping where they collapsed. Now and then a participant nodded off into a spiritual trance, aided by bowls of berries fermented into a thick, black soup, and the smoke from kelp pipes making rounds. They ate, danced, and slept, then did it again until even the strongest were staggering, with bellies filled, bodies exhausted, and heads reeling.

The whalers sacrificed their first slave on the second day, dispensing with his life in one quick slash of blade across neck. The Kahnamut chief killed two of his own, proving his wealth was even greater than that of his visitors. The slaves' bodies were weighted with rocks and sunk offshore. As the boats returned to the cheers of both people, the chief announced his bride-gift to the whalers. Despite their studiously bland expressions, the chief sensed that the Nuu'chah'nulth were impressed. He was delighted the whalers had not brought a bride-gift of their own and he gravely accepted their pledge to return one day to reciprocate the gift. Obligation was mounting nicely.

A feast, in addition to a celebration, is also a time of forgiveness. The chief took down a shame pole topped with a single bulbous pair of frog eyes placed outside the longhouse of a man who had stolen fish from the drying racks of the chief's uncle. The chief angrily planted the pole of shame in front of the thief's lodge. There it would stay until he redeemed himself. An entire year passed and the pole remained, much to the distress of the extended family living in the longhouse. His wife, who refused to bed with him until the pole was removed, had recently gone to live in the lodge of her sister's husband.

On the third day of the potlatch, several commoners were honored by an invitation to join the chief and the whalers in the sweathouse. Awed, they stood on the steamy periphery while the more favored lay or squatted near the fire pit where it was hotter and free of fumes. On the fourth day, five boys were given adult names by their uncles in a ceremony before the whalers, casting their child names into the waters of the bay. Each of the fortunate boys also received a second name from one of the Nuu'chah'nulth to use for protection against the capricious waters of the Kahnamut Sea.

Uunutu flitted in and out of the feast like a nervous bird. It was the first time Anawa had seen him for days.

"He looks like a dying thing," she said to Makal.

"His eyes are black like the raccoon and he walks like he carries a deer on his shoulders," Makal noted.

"He fears I am angry and blame him," responded Anawa.

"And do you?" Makal asked softly.

"He was a fool," Anawa said, "but you are right, good has come of it." The thought of losing Gitsula still made her feel hollow inside, but she also felt the tremor of excitement growing. To be a healer!

On the seventh day as the sixth moon grew fat, the whalers prepared to leave. The bounty presented by the Kahnamut was greater than expected. They had come in peace and would leave that way. On the voyage home they intended to collect slaves from the Esquimalt, to replace those they'd sacrificed. Two small bands lived on a rocky shoreline at the southern tip of the big island just before the treacherous passage through Swift Waters. That was the joining of the Kahnamut Sea and the broad ocean. A shallow bay rimmed by red-skinned arbutus was fronted by a narrow spit of land and a lagoon. The geography protected the Esquimalt from the fierce westerly wind, which, 1,341 years later, a young man dubbed "the devil's breath." But the bay and rocks also effectively screened any approach from the east.

With luck the whalers would surprise the Esquimalt and take several boys and girls without killing. They weren't averse to killing. But stealing without killing required a higher order of skill.

The boats were prepared and blessed. The gifts stacked, loaded, and lashed down. Prayers were said and obeisance paid to the north-shore mountains.

"Guide us, guide us, follow us, follow us," the chant went up.

The Kahnamut chief waded out to each boat, his massive cape flowing behind, scattering feathers everywhere. The feather was a sign of peace but it was also a charm to ensure that no hostile tribes or malicious spirits attempted to stop them on their way home.

Uunutu crept up to his wife. When Anawa turned and smiled at him, his relief was almost comical. "Gitsula," he croaked, not having spoken for days.

"Come," she whispered. "Let us watch Gitsula and sing to the sea together for her."

✳

"Mmyah!" the women murmured approvingly.

"Ravens will fall out of the sky when you appear," giggled one.

"They will carry you off for themselves!" suggested another.

"You are far too beautiful to waste on those whalers," frowned a third as she carefully braided the thick ropes of Gitsula's hair. "Even a chief!"

At the end of each braid the woman tied a palm-sized, circular-shell medallion, positioning it so the iridescent interior faced out to catch the light. Then she fixed tiny shells along the length of the braids, finishing them off with three feathers tied tight against Gitsula's scalp.

In her hands Gitsula clasped a healing wand. Ah'we'tan had given it to her when the whalers arrived, and it had never left her side. The short, polelike handle was topped with the carving of a spirit helper—square legs with straight and slender arms crossed over its chest. The mouth was a round, raised button, the brow low and flat, and the head rose in a cone. The shamans used such wands to banish illness. Gitsula carried it to ward off strange ailments that might attack because she was of a different nation.

I am already ill, Gitsula thought clutching the wand. My spirit flies away.

She'd confessed her feelings to Anawa the previous night, when her mother brought a rough wool cape for her to wear on her journey, as well as deer-skin leggings. The cape, oily and thick, would shed rain, and the leggings, with the hair on the inside, would warm her during the long chilly hours of inactivity as the men paddled. Though Gitsula had been sequestered during the feast, she was weary with a lassitude that made every movement an effort. Even a smile taxed her. She longed to lie still, with her eyes shut and her head full of dreams. Lie in her own house on her own mat that she had used since childhood.

"Your feelings are natural," Anawa said hugging her. "You must ask your guardian spirit for strength and guidance. You must rejoice! Your father and I were wrong to be sad. We gave our sadness to you and now I take it away."

Anawa pulled a handful of salmon bones out of a small pouch. "Every spring we give the bones back to the river from the first catch so the fish will return year after year. These bones will bring you back to our land one day."

She took Gitsula's hand and scraped away at her fingernails with the edge of a fine, sharp shell. She cut a length of her daughter's hair and one of her own, placing everything in the pouch with the bones. Then she deposited a ball of spit on top.

"You too," she said, handing her daughter the shell. "Our bodies and spirits will mingle. When you have gone I will paddle until our bay is almost out of sight. I will give this to the waters, which will bring you back to me."

For the first time since Uunutu had lost Gitsula to the chief, Anawa sang, her melodious voice rich with the passion of her vision yet also soft with relief at her acceptance of Gitsula's fate.

"You must succumb!" Ah'we'tan had also urged Gitsula. "If you do not, you will be like the fox in a snare who has not met his death partner. It fights and tears at itself. The fox that has happily welcomed its death partner sits quiet and accepting."

The analogy of the dying fox did nothing to restore Gitsula's good cheer, but in her heart she knew the old one was right. The more she fought, the more she could tear herself up, so much so that her guardian spirit might leave her in disgust over her cowardice.

> Daughter of the land,
> People of the sea,
> Child of the salmon,
> Man of the whale.

Anawa sang while rocking back and forth. After a time, she opened her arms to her daughter sitting numbly opposite her, and hugged her. Then it came. Like the sudden, searing, last pain of childbirth. Like the final crash of a mighty wave upon the shore. Agony. Loneliness. Fear. Gitsula sobbed—hard, hurtful gulps. Anawa cradled her child and rubbed her belly as she had when she was little. As she rubbed the smooth, taut skin, her fingers unknowingly passed over the life growing within. The chief's child. Gitsula's baby. Anawa's grandchild.

Creamy dawn light sifted through the cracks in the seclusion house where Gitsula had been spending her days. Time intended for the strengthening of her spirit actually passed in a fog of desperation. While her mother sang and rubbed her, Gitsula finally resolved to present the face expected of her.

✳

The village women painted Gitsula's body and face, finished dressing her hair, and fussed over her garments. They wrapped her breasts in the softest cloth and hung around her neck a heavy necklace of quartered deer hooves. It started wide at the shoulders and tapered to a single hoof section just at her navel. Her skirt of split reeds hung long to the ground. On her head they placed the most important thing of all—a magnificent *teeka,* tall wooden hat.

From the *teeka'*s hard brim, four panels of woven cloth hung down her back, separated by a thick plait of the greenest grass and a soft rope of duck down. They represented the five basic colors of the Kahnamut world: *s'kayq*—black, *skwiy*—yellow, *sh'kwaym*—red, *s'iko*—white, and *sula*—green. Black from the boiling of hemlock bark in iron-rich mud, yellow from lichen boiled in water, and red from the pulverized twigs of red alder. They had no way of making green, a color owned by the spirit of spring and Sis'et, the elder moon, so they borrowed it. Similarly, white did not belong to the Kahnamut. They borrowed that from the down of a pale duck, which frequented the bay in winter. The women used urine as a mordant to seal the black and red in the dyed cloth while the green plait was soaked in an oily bath, then dried. Though it would fade over time, some green would always be evident, as it, like spring, was eternal.

"*Sie'm,*" they murmured approvingly to Gitsula. "*Sie'm.*" Lady, highborn one, woman of good fortune.

✳

The whalers' departure generated as much enthusiastic commotion as their arrival. After a spare predawn meal, energy returned, banishing the excesses of the potlatch. Gitsula walked to the shore, flanked by her entourage of women. Male relatives created a corridor. She placed her feet carefully, unaccustomed to the hat soaring above her head. With every step came a rustle, clatter, click, or thunk from the array of ornaments.

Anawa and Uunutu stood on the short, hard grass at the very edge of the beach. The family's simple dugout canoe was lined up alongside more than twenty others. Anawa and Uunutu would paddle out from the village to bid their visitors and their daughter a good journey. The chief's boat, which held sixteen, stood ready.

Gitsula glanced at her mother and father, forcing her chin up, bathing them with a shy smile.

"Oh!" breathed Anawa as Gitsula passed. Uunutu's heart felt as if it would explode.

Gitsula knelt on a small wooden raft, constructed for the occasion. Young boys pushed it out to the whalers' boats, while their mothers waded alongside, steadying it. She uttered no good-byes to either Anawa or Uunutu; there was no need.

Gitsula clung to Anawa's words. "My dreams tell me you will return. I saw the Raven with an egg in its mouth landing in the arbutus tree. The interpreter told me that you will come back in the form of your first son. I wait eagerly for that moment."

The high-pitched tones of the women and older girls met the morning sun and bobbed over the water. Each sang their personal song for Gitsula, waving long-feathered fans to push the words out to her. She would remember the words and music of each one, she promised herself, whispering her own song under her breath as the little raft bore her out. It was the song of her grandmother, which her mother had given to her.

The massive prow of the first Nuu'chah'nulth boat cast a cold shadow over Gitsula. She shivered, as a solemn-faced whaler reached over to steady her arm while two of the Chinook slaves laced their fingers for her to step on. Respectfully, none looked directly into her face. A bow seat had been prepared, so she could sit with her back to the wind. Once into the Kahnamut Sea and bearing toward the rocks of Swift Water at the big island's southern tip, the conditions would be difficult for one unaccustomed to open-water travel.

The whalers turned to face the north-shore mountains and began to chant their leaving song, finishing with a prayer to the gods who resided there to guard their passage home.

"Nuu'chah'nulth. Nuu'chah'nulth. Home! Home!"

The paddlers took their positions, each murmuring a good-luck chant that sounded to Gitsula like two grunts, a yelp, and two more grunts.

The first paddle struck water.

"We go!" roared the men in unison, bodies dipping as one, paddles sending the heavy boats across the bay.

A flotilla of dugouts and the village's two ceremonial war boats followed the whalers. Uunutu feverishly paddled their canoe to keep up, while Anawa flung lucky goose feathers on the water.

Gitsula's hand tightened on the medicine bundle of feathers given to her by Makal's two daughters. There were thirteen of them, one for each moon. The longest was a splendid tail-feather from Eagle-of-Snows, the white-headed bird of the mountains. The ends of the feathers dug into her palm. Gitsula looked down.

"Uuuh!" she gasped. Her shriek was lost in the breeze and the bellowing of the paddlers.

Eyes wide with fright, she stared at her hand. A pinprick of blood welled at the base of her thumb, but it was not that which prompted her terror. Several of the feathers were disintegrating, the down separating from the quill and clumping in her palm.

To the Kahnamut, everything in life had an opposite. That which symbolized the utmost good could also, when turned around, faced upward, or looked at in another light, be a harbinger of the utmost evil. Feathers represented peace and good luck. But stripped of their down, they were used to curse an antagonist. A handful of plucked quills attached to the door of a longhouse indicated that someone within stood accused of lying. When the matter was resolved, the quills would be replaced by full feathers.

The wind freshened. Unsettled, Gitsula wiped her hand on her reed skirt. Again and again, more rapidly, but the soft down stuck. The breeze caught one of the full feathers. Gitsula grabbed at it but it flew out of her reach, floating up, twisting and turning. The paddler directly in front of her bent low and pulled hard. On the recovery stroke he lifted his gaze, catching hers. Flat black eyes bore into hers. He smiled. It was the leer of a monster, his mouth wide and mocking, his teeth separated as if to swallow her. An unnaturally long tongue flicked hugely in and out. She glanced at the next man and the next, and the next and the next, they were all alike.

Gitsula moaned, teeth chattering. The wind sliced into her. She had never felt so cold. She caught sight of her parents paddling in the boat's wake. Both grinning and proud.

They do not know! I am doomed. I am doomed.

"Mother! Father!" she called out, pleading. The wind sucked her words away.

"Mother! Father!" They grinned and paddled and scattered feathers.

Time jumped on itself, speeding up the moment like a quickening song. Bellow, stroke, chant, and breathe. Gitsula's boat was reaching the point of no return. Then time abruptly deadened, every move slowed. Gitsula stood up. She shrugged off the heavy cape and dropped the medicine bundle, but the laces on the towering hat resisted her frantic fingers. The sounds of men and water and wind became a low, undistinguishable howl of noise. The lead paddler reached for her as slow as a glacier.

Then she was gone, up on the gunnels and over the side with a clean dive. Sound collapsed. Everything stopped. The dive lasted forever. This must be what the great eagle feels when it rides the wind, Gitsula thought as the world blurred. Her ears and mouth filled with brine. She heard the muffled scrape of paddles being pulled in as the flabbergasted men peered overboard trying to locate her. Had she fallen? Had she jumped? Had she been snatched away by an evil spirit?

It seemed like hours before she surfaced. Wind licked up the water. Wavelets broke at her face as Gitsula fought her way to her parents' canoe. Shouts from shore seemed to be urging her on. Her skirt dragged at her legs and her extravagant shell necklace made it difficult to catch her breath. Within minutes she was exhausted. Eyes blinded from the saltwater, she couldn't tell if she was getting closer, nor could she see if the whalers' boats were pursuing. She stopped and floated awkwardly for a moment.

The whalers were doing nothing. Shocked. Curious. Fearful. The black eyes found her through the haze. She flipped over, thrashing hard toward Anawa and Uunutu. In her mind, their warm, welcoming faces, their comforting arms drew her on, gave her strength.

A harsh bark from the whalers' chief. The men bent as one, digging hard at full cadence, pulling away as quickly as they could.

Anawa and Uunutu did not react, could not react. As Gitsula struggled toward them, their hearts seemed pulled out of their bodies.

Finally she was there. Gitsula grabbed the gunnel with cramped fingers, crying out with relief. She was home! She did not feel the first blow, but the second registered deep in her body. The paddle struck a third time, and the pain jumped up her arm. Her father stood over her, face contorted.

"Go back!" he shrilled. "You shame me!"

Crack!

"You shame your mother!"

Crack!

"You shame our people!"

Crack!

The blows of his paddle on her fingers grew harder, the last smashing two knuckles in her right hand. Gitsula clung tighter.

"Father!" she wailed. "Help me! I am doomed if I go. Please help me!"

"Doomed!" he shouted. "Doomed! You doom me."

Dimly, Gitsula heard Anawa crying and she thought she saw her mother's arms around her father's body, pulling him back. But blood clouded her vision. Still she fought to get back into the boat as heavy paddle-blows rained on her head and hands. Red spilled into the water, flowed into the boat. Still Gitsula refused to let go. She stared up into her father's face. She did not know it.

Uunutu held the heavy knife over his head. It was the one he had used since she was a baby, for taking off the heads of salmon before tossing the fish to her mother, who deftly gutted and filleted them for drying. The taste of the sweet, dried meat filled Gitsula's mouth. She watched the knife descend, heard her father's sobs, heard her mother's cries. Three fingers on the hand still clutching the boat fell away.

Gitsula felt no pain as she slipped under the water.

✻

Many different versions of Gitsula's story were told. Some say she sank beneath the sea forced down by her father's contempt and her mother's grief. In the depths, her spirit was taken by the dogfish, a type of small shark that preyed on salmon, biting chunks out of the living creature. Dogfish plagued the Kahnamut's fishing for several seasons after, and twice the Stahlo flooded spectacularly, drowning their summer camp, swallowing nets, weirs, traps, and racks. All because of Gitsula.

Others said her spirit merged with an eagle passing by when she dove from the canoe, that the body thrashing in the water was but a hollow shell.

The whalers told of a woman who was the most dangerous of creatures, a devious shape-changer, who almost infiltrated their powerful nation to learn the secrets of the whale hunt. It took another three centuries for them to return to Kahnamut's winter home on the broad bay that would someday form the welcome to Vancouver.

✻

Gitsula floated inertly for many hours in the bay, as a flowing tide carried her toward an island shaped like a bird's head. It was the almost-island opposite the bay where her people wintered. No tribes lived there. Deep in the heart of the island was a lake where the Raven slept. Disturbing it would bring the unwelcome attention of the powerful trickster bird upon the Kahnamut.

It had taken only minutes for the cold water to lower her heart rate and slow her breathing. Brisk northwesterly gusts chasing in from the mountainous north shore pushed her toward the sacred Sl'kheylish, Standing Man Rock. The narrow, towering cone of granite emerged from the water near the northern point of the almost-island, where Ak'aa, the first Raven, came to rest. Waves whipped into foam splashed across Gitsula's face. She choked and sputtered, coming to life, thrashing against the sea that heaved her toward the black, sharp rocks of the island. With each feeble stroke she took, the sea grew stronger and raised her higher before releasing her to crash ever closer to the killing shore.

Gitsula was past seeing, her eyes swollen almost shut from the salt. She heard the booming of the surf but thought it was the roaring of her heart. One, two, three more waves, and Sl'kheylish loomed. Death approached. Another wave—the knife edges of the rock beckoned. The water raised her, and a final mighty wave heaved her forward, squirting her through a gap between the rock and the cliff face of the island, and onto a small patch of sand and gravel.

All day, all night, and most of the next day Gitsula lay as if dead. Mice, crabs, and other little creatures of the tidal area investigated, congregating at her mutilated hands where the blood seeped. As the sun moved toward the second night, the Raven came. Large, blue-black, with a beak that opened wide to proclaim possession and protection of the thing on the triangle of sand and pebble. After dropping a small leather pouch on a nearby rock, it hopped back and forth along Gitsula's body, pecking at her clothes and pulling feathers from her hair. She groaned and twitched slightly from the poke of its beak behind her ear. The Raven hopped backward, eyeing her.

The Raven turned its head back and forth. It took up the small pouch. Powerful wings pulled the bird into the air. As it caught the breeze, the Raven opened its mouth and dropped the pouch onto Gitsula's chest—milky-green stones tumbled out. She pried her swollen eyes open to see the jade tears spilling across her breasts. Despite her pain, she pulled herself upright at the sight of them and feverishly gathered up the twelve sacred beads with her uninjured hand.

"Oh Father! Father!" she wept, cradling the seeds of her people.

"Caw! Caw! Caw!" shrieked the Raven, flying in ever-increasing circles overhead. If anyone had heard, they might have taken the sound for laughter.

PART III

Mindia
Eristavi

12

＊

"*Radidi Kve´qana!!*" whispered the shaggy-headed Georgian.

"What wondrous land!" he repeated in Spanish for the benefit of the scowling pilot standing next to him at the bow of the compact, three-masted caravel. Behind it two even smaller pinnaces rocked in the slight wake.

"It's not land we want," the old man growled, tucking his voluminous chin into the woolen scarf wound thrice around his neck. He'd stuffed the ends of the scarf into his high-necked jacket for warmth, giving him the appearance of a pouter pigeon.

"No matter what we find, the king could not help but be pleased with your discovery of these northern lands," the Georgian countered in a respectful tone.

"The king of Spain has more land than any five monarchs could control!" scoffed the old man. "He looks to take the legs out from under England, and what better way than lay claim over the northwest passage to the South Sea of the Indies?" He stared morosely out, toward the land becoming clearer to the naked eye with every league sailed. "I will give the king that power. If this bloody land ever ends."

Mindia Eristavi grinned broadly, the charm in his smile making up for a tooth missing in the upper row. Tall, with a mop of windswept hair the dun color and straw texture of a steppe pony, he always looked as if he was going somewhere, even when he was standing still. His lanky form was all elbows and knees, but when he did move there was no denying the natural grace. He didn't have the quickness of mind required for true wit, but Mindia's sweet humor would have made him a welcome *jeunesse dorée* in any café society, had his father sufficient wealth to allow him a life of fashionable ease.

"King Felipe is very generous with those who please him," Mindia pointed out. "Think of Oñate, Vizcaíno."

"Balboa! Cortés!" the old man barked back. "For every brave explorer amply rewarded for risking his life in this quest for new lands there are dozens derided or even punished for their efforts by the great kingdom of Spain. Even," he added, just to be sure the tall, gap-toothed boy beside him caught the point, "losing their heads for their trouble."

"Balboa was tricked by his enemies," protested Mindia. Despite his mere twenty-four years and a youth spent growing up as poor nobility in his native Georgia ("a bleak backwater of butchers and barbarians," according to the old man), he was an avid student of marine history. "He lost his head because he was not political," pronounced Mindia of Balboa, the first European to sight Pacifica, Ocean of Peace. "He would never have been accused of treason otherwise. In this world," he added, echoing the words of his father, "if you are not political you might as well be a peasant."

"No amount of politics would have saved his head," retorted the old man, pleased to offer a little instruction in sea lore to this boy who thought far too highly of what he knew. "He saw the Western Sea, but he lost his head to Pedro Arias Dávila. Dávila wanted the governorship of Darién, Panamá, and even, I am sure, all of Mesico. Balboa did things. Dávila just talked about them. Dávila was jealous and the only way to quell the sin of envy was to chop off poor Balboa's head. Politics! Pah!"

"No, no, no!" insisted Mindia, grasping the gunnels lightly to keep his feet as the ship slid down the side of a large swell.

He noted that the old man didn't even sway, let alone feel the need to grab anything to keep his balance. From the large pocket on the inside of his coat, Mindia pulled out a tattered monograph he had just finished reading, *A Briefe Historie and Dyscussion of Spanish Discoveries and Claimes Upon the New World*, written by an English scholar. "Balboa did not return to Spain after his monumental discovery in 1513," Mindia declared, his earnestness at odds with the comical gap in his teeth. "That was his mistake. Had he returned, he would have heard the court whispers that Dávila was not content with the governorship of Darién and had designs upon Panamá, California, Mesico, Nova Galicia, and Nova Spania. He wanted to become the most powerful man in the new world. Balboa was young, popular, famous, and absent. Dávila wanted to get rid of him and Balboa made it easy! It was politics! It's all here," he tapped the monograph authoritatively.

"Dávila was simply closer to the hairy ear of the king by virtue of fortunate birth," the old man derided. "Balboa was a bankrupt nobody until he saw Pacifica and became famous. Not politics, you foolish Cossack— family and money."

Mindia let the Cossack slur pass without comment. An army of beasts, if ever there was one, and he, a proud Georgian, had no desire to be lumped in with that lot. But he knew better than to debate nationality with the old man who had very firm ideas on the subject.

"Family and money—and politics. What's the difference?" Mindia countered mildly.

The old man merely grunted.

❋

Poor Vasco Núñez de Balboa. King Ferdinand chose to believe the poisonous words of the ambitious Dávila rather than the protestations of the young, stalwart explorer. Governor Dávila accused Balboa of selling maps to the English in 1518, a grave offense, and within months claimed to have the king's authority to behead him and the four who had accompanied Balboa on the fabled trip across the rugged interior of South America to the Pacific coast. Had the ax not descended on Balboa's unfortunate neck, Mindia Eristavi might well have been guided by a map drawn by the skilled hand of Balboa himself. Instead he charted treacherous new waters as the small fleet made its way along the increasingly chilly coastline of California for the greater glory of King Felipe and, hopefully, their own.

There were times when Mindia Eristavi could not help but hug himself inwardly with anticipation. With this old man and a fleet of three he would make history. The fabled Straits of Anian. The waterway between Pacifica and the South Sea, to be dominated forevermore by the invincible Spanish—once they found it, of course. The link between Asia and Europe. Mindia would bathe in pearls, gold, silver, and precious stones. His hand fairly twitched in his desire to seize his quill and ink bottle and begin drawing the map that would change the world.

The old man stepped forward in the gently heaving ship, unbuttoned his trousers, and rooted out his member. A yellow arc sailed overboard, not a drop flicking back to stain his clothes or boots. Impressive force and control for one of his age. Mindia chose his own moments carefully, having dappled his clothes more than once as the need to balance with his feet and legs, hold with his hand, and squeeze hard with his stomach muscles for maximum projection defeated him. The jowly, neckless Greek pilot beside him was a strange old goat for sure, but Mindia Eristavi, offspring of a minor Georgian diplomat and an even more minor English noblewoman, would follow him until the seas ran dry if it meant that he could pen the first map of the Straits of Anian through the continent of America.

The pilot, known as Juan de Fuca but born with the name Apostolos Valerianos, cared little about maps, except for their accuracy. The world was full of bad maps, fraudulent maps, and charts so ill-conceived they could not send ships to their grave any more surely than if they had been designed expressly for that purpose. But this map, which would be drawn by the excitable yet talented youngster, would be an exception. It promised fortune at last and status for his final days, which would allow him to purchase the company of any number of Kefalonian beauties, the women of his homeland. His calloused palms would hold their large, olive-hued breasts, and he would inhale the pungent aroma of flesh unadorned by the stink of perfume, which Spanish women insisted on dousing themselves with. Apostolos Valerianos hated Spanish women, their arrogance, and the ugly contrast between black hair and pale skin. Greek women were like the earth—warm and humble. At least that was how he remembered them.

"How long since you were last in Greece?" asked Mindia as if reading his mind.

"Uh?" grunted Apostolos, annoyed at being jarred from his pleasant mental meanderings.

"Greece," repeated Mindia. "Have you visited often?"

"Never."

"Not once?"

"Never. Forty years, maybe more. Forty years in Spain, the Indies, Philippinas, and now Nova Spania and Mesico. Forty years. Too damn long, serving those grasping Spanish idiots."

Mindia looked around nervously. When they'd set sail from Acapulco in Nova Galicia, the viceroy of Mesico assigned three emissaries, one to each ship. The pilot protested vehemently, saying there was little enough room for essential supplies without taking on three useless bodies. They were spies, plain and simple, who would watch their every move and report to the king himself once they sailed through the Straits and out into the South Sea. The viceroy had promised Apostolos he would receive rewards aplenty from the court once he delivered the map. But the old Greek didn't trust him. He was Spanish, after all.

Apostolos Valerianos was not a large man, neither tall nor well-fleshed, except in the short space between shoulders and jaw. His thin, straight calves bowed slightly outward at the knees, and his short, slender arms ended with hands more the size of a young girl's than a man's. These diminutive appendages had been a source of embarrassment to him all his life, so unlike his father's massive hands. Zepha Valerianos, a fig farmer, died when Apostolos was seventeen, nearly fifty years ago. Yet his son could still taste the oily sweetness of the brown wine the farmer made in wooden vats and drank in large quantities straight from the chipped lips of heavy, bisque-fired jugs that lined the wine shed.

Apostolos's father encouraged him to go to sea. "A mariner, my son!" he'd say between test sips, occasionally allowing the young boy a taste. "That is a life worth living. Better to break your back and see the world than break your back and see nothing but the same stone fences your whole life."

Apostolos still had the battered astrolabe his father presented to him when he boarded a boat at Argostoli for the mainland and his new life.

"That is why you speak so many languages," prompted Mindia, envious of the old man's life of endless exploration.

"Oh no. That is thanks to the Romans, Turks, Venetians, French, and the English, who have all *protected*," he drew the word out in a sneer, "us for a thousand years while our own country of Greece sits paralyzed. They drink our wine, eat our olives, and impregnate our women while we learn their languages."

"But the Spanish have never occupied your island, so why are you known as Juan de Fuca?" This was a matter of intense curiosity for Mindia, but he had never before dared to ask.

"We Kefalonians are nothing if not adaptable," shrugged the old man, his ears disappearing into his shoulders with the movement. "The Spaniards are more than happy to have foreigners as mariners, but when it comes to applying for license for one's own vessel—ahh, that is not so easy if you have an unpronounceable name."

For his first fifteen years at sea, Apostolos labored as a mariner on numerous Spanish vessels, gradually working his way from bilge pump to crow's nest and finally into the pilot's quarters, where he cared for maps, made navigational measurements, and took notes of any land forms spotted while the pilot slept. But it quickly became evident that no matter what quality of mariner he was he would never be admitted to the rank of pilot in any Spanish fleet, let alone aboard the ships plying the lucrative trade between Spain and the Indies. That is what he hungered for, the chance to participate as Spain bullied its way into the new world of black and brown savages, odd-shaped trees, fish, spices, and gold. Especially the gold! One day it would all belong to King Felipe, and Apostolos wanted his share.

Apostolos's plan took five years to unfold. He saved his meager wages, even selling his food allowance, worth one and a half reals for every day on land, as well as his weekly wine-and-rum allotment, to others on the ship. Finally, with a purse of thirty-five ducats, he purchased a Spanish birth card in the name of Juan de Fuca and still had enough left to bribe six pilots to stand for him in his application to Alonzo de Chiavez, the king's pilot major.

From there he, along with twelve others, endured two months of twice-daily questioning by Roderigo Zamorano, public reader of navigation. In fact, it was Zamorano's three minions who put forth the questions that rankled the Greek, since he suspected they did not have enough hours at sea among the three of them put together to compare with even the youngest of the applicants.

"If thy mast be broken by tempest what remedy wouldst thou use?" one of the pipsqueaks demanded.

"Should thy ship be set upon by pirates and leave thee destitute of chart, astrolabe, and other instruments, rendering thee helpless to take the height of the sun and position of stars, what course wouldst thou take in that extremity?" queried another.

"If thy ship should take a leak hazarding cargo and company aboard what remedy wouldst thou take to right the danger in the most expedient fashion?"

On and on it went, until finally the reader himself posed his own questions of specific locale. Apostolos requested to be examined concerning Nova Spania, Nombre de Dios, and Tierra Firma, regions of the New World that attracted the largest ships in the Spanish fleet and the most lucrative cargo. The king's claimed and unclaimed dominion was also relatively uncharted to the north of the Indies in the South Sea and even more so in Nova Galicia of Pacifica. The king offered handsome rewards for those who returned to Spain with proof of valuable discoveries. Then, of course, there were the Straits of Anian. Any man who found that fabled waterway linking the seas would certainly be granted title, lands, and wealth.

Apostolos spent many years in the Indies, and his acute memory allowed him to answer with near perfection the questions about the signs and marks of those lands. He devoted the last of his money to manufactured testimonials from fictitious relatives and friends, proving that he carried no Moorish or Negro blood. He shed his trousers before the committee to demonstrate that his manhood was not marked by the unholy knife of the Jew. He also swore on the Royal Book that he would never carry any chart, astrolabe, weapon, or instrument that had not been approved or signed and sealed by the pilot major and the king's reader who was also the royal cosmographer. He memorized the Aranzel, a table of rate and taxation that set both the value and the measurement of all known goods. How many *botijas* or *jarres* make a *tunne* of wine? How many *packes* of nails comprise a *quintal*, or hundredweight? And, most important, what precisely was the crown's tariff on each?

When the seal of the Contractation House melted the wax on his Letters Testimoniall, granting Juan de Fuca the right to serve as pilot in the realm he chose, Apostolos Valerianos felt his pockets begin to swell with riches. Alas, a series of painful misadventures over the years had left Apostolos rich with experience but light in the purse. This was his final chance to earn a retirement of ease in the Greece of his dreams. The alternative was the mariner's poorhouse in Madrid.

✳

Mindia had met the old man in a Venetian café eighteen months before this journey began. The week had been blisteringly hot—miserable, muggy heat that sucked air out of the day and energy out of the body. Mindia had a small room at the top of forty-two stairs. Ever the mapmaker, immediately on arrival he had paced off its dimensions (four strides northeast by three and a half strides southwest) and determined its orientation (the sun rose eleven degrees past the center of his single large window). The view was stupendous, as was the cold in winter and the heat in summer. Mindia's father, third assistant to the czar's emissary to Rome, had managed to procure an apprenticeship for him in Venice with Angelo di Montesantorini, a former student of the famous cartographer Judocus Hodius.

One day in July, six months into his apprenticeship, Mindia, unable to bear his tiny, stuffy room a moment longer, bundled up his charts and made his way down the stone stairs and into the cooler outdoor café across the street. Spreading his papers over two tables, he prepared to work. The café was almost full, but the proprietor turned a blind eye as he had designs on the tall, young Georgian for his beak-nosed daughter. Apostolos was not so understanding.

"Get out of the way!" he shouted at Mindia. "This is my table and I will eat my dinner here as I have every day for the past two weeks. Be gone or I will have your carcass in the gutter!"

"Calm yourself, old man. I will move. Give me a minute to organize my things."

"A minute, no more," growled the pilot, peering at the charts. He couldn't help himself. "I've never seen such inaccurate nonsense in my life," he scoffed. "Some scribe penned these who has never left solid ground. You waste your time."

"How would you know!" Mindia snapped back, not about to be bullied by this rude, ill-dressed cretin. "You look like the only exploring you've done is up and down your own member. If you can locate it, that is!"

Fortunately this struck the old man as amusing, and he allowed the boy to buy him a glass of wine, which Mindia could ill afford. From that cantankerous beginning, a relationship grew over the weeks as Apostolos waited impatiently for "a Turkish friend" to produce a promised 150 ducats as his share of a partnership in a venture to explore for the Straits of Anian. The money would be used as "court oil" to grease the way to an audience with the king, which would allow Apostolos, as Juan de Fuca, to plead his case for financing.

It entertained the king to have half a dozen of the greatest mariners on earth competing for the same cause, and to Apostolos's surprise, he was quickly granted the request for an audience at the pleasure of the Governor of Mesico. The king did not mention that his alacrity was prompted in large part by the English who were rapidly growing from irritant to plague in many of Spain's dominions. Francis Drake, that arrogant, immoral pagan, started it all in 1579 with his costly pirating forays up the coast of Pacifica in his hopefully named *Golden Hinde*. Others followed.

Despite the advice of the viceroy of Nova Galicia, backed by opinions held by the Governor of Mesico, Don Juan de Oñate, a former great explorer himself, that a northwest passage did not exist or, if it did, was so locked in ice it would be inaccessible, the king held the idea dear.

"I cannot imagine why the king has licensed this ancient, Juan de Fuca, to search for a route through land so abysmally cold and dangerous," an exasperated Oñate complained by letter to his emissary in Madrid. "Not even Vizcaíno could penetrate beyond 43°N. What in the saints' names does he expect of this decrepit pilot and a cartographer so young his voice still cracks? I beg you, dissuade the king as I have no ships to spare and rumors are that Cavendish is still about and determined to best Drake's shameful record of piracy."

Oñate kept Apostolos and his cartographer Mindia waiting in Aca-pulco for nearly a year while dispatches went back and forth.

"The king will not be dissuaded," his emissary responded apologetically. "Two more galleons have been taken by the English in Spanish waters near the Indies. He firmly believes control of the passage will guarantee our control over the South Sea."

Oñate shot back an angry reply. "Then I will give him a caravel and two pinnaces but not more. Further I will insist he takes a reckoning agent aboard each ship. If I am to be weakened by this folly then I will make damned sure that men I can trust will report directly back to me and ensure that credit for whatever he finds is shared by my command."

13

✴

"Look! Look there!"

Mindia waved his hands excitedly to the east. Apostolos secreted the shriveled lemon quarter in his pocket, which he'd been covertly sucking, and rubbed his eyes with cracked knuckles. Mindia caught the motion but didn't care. As far as he was concerned it was a pilot's privilege to feed himself better than the crew, nearly a quarter of whom were sickening from scurvy. If the old mariner believed chewing a lemon rind would protect him, then so be it. After all, if he fell ill, they were done for anyway. Mindia, so thin he was taking on the dimensions of a rope, had never felt more alive in his life.

"Do you see it?"

"If you stop yelling and jumping about I can look in peace," the old man said peevishly. Apostolos peered blearily through the fog that had clung to them for weeks. He was exhausted. The coast was an elusive dream, appearing then disappearing. Apostolos had lived this long by paying attention to the prickle of his skin when land was near. It had saved him on more than one occasion, even when the ship's captain vehemently disagreed. He had prevented enough wrecks that his "prickle" was no longer dismissed. He didn't trust anyone aboard but himself to steer clear of the increasingly vicious fog-enshrouded coastline, so he slept only an hour or two at a time. His eyes were caked and filmy. He could hardly see his hand, let alone something in the distance.

Suddenly it was there. A tall promontory capped with snow catching the midafternoon sun. It hung like a fingernail off the land, at least two hundred feet high, Apostolos estimated, perhaps far more. The cliff rose menacingly to its highest point and he could just make out a rocky bay below. Snow. They must be farther north than he thought.

"Bring me de Jode's map," he ordered Mindia.

Apostolos studied the coastline as drawn by Cornelius de Jode a year earlier.

"This is all wrong," Apostolos stabbed at the few inches of space between Capo Blanco and the meridian, the area first sighted by explorer Juan Rodríguez Cabrillo's courageous pilot Bartolomé Ferrelo. Ferrelo continued north past forty degrees after his master died in 1543, eventually providing the written information, which master cartographer de Jode later used to draw the map. Ferrelo marked the promontory as Capo Blanco and, not being able to continue farther, maintained that he believed it marked the entrance to the Straits of Anian.

"He missed at least five hundred miles of land and he has placed Capo Blanco at thirty degrees. That cannot be."

"We have certainly passed forty degrees," agreed Mindia.

"He shows we must sail at least nineteen degrees westerly to clear this land," Apostolos pointed to a massive peninsula de Jode had marked as Anian Regio, supposedly the southern boundary of the legendary El Streto de Anian. No one had ever seen it, but de Jode guessed at its location anyway. "But if he is wrong here," Apostolos tapped the point in the south marked *C. Blanco*, "then he may be wrong here." He tapped the entrance to the strait.

Even with an experienced pilot, captain, and legitimate map—there were plenty of the latter that could only be classed as mere figments—navigating relatively uncharted waters usually involved a litany of things going wrong, often terribly wrong. There were few who could observe latitudes and longitudes with perfection, and the best of the Spanish explorers were frequently off a degree or two. Juan Rodríguez Cabrillo was notorious for this. Apostolos knew it, counted on it. But the difference in his readings at Capo Blanco and those marked on de Jode's map were staggeringly large.

"The captain wishes me to tell you he gauges two days' supply of water at most," a mate announced politely. "Though several men are likely lost to scurvy, so he might stretch it to four."

"If de Jode is even partially right, we have weeks left before we reach the entrance to the straits. We will need provisions as well," the pilot muttered. "Tell the captain to prepare a landing party. We will anchor in the first suitable bay."

By rank the captain was in charge. But it was Apostolos who carried the letter from the king. This was his voyage. The captain was happy to let him take the responsibility. He would get five hundred ducats for the expedition alone, plus a hefty share of the reward once they sailed triumphantly through the continent into the South Seas of the Spanish Indies. The captain had already built a fort on the thousand acres of La Florida timber and farmland granted him by the governor. This would be his last voyage. He intended to spend his days supervising the importation of slaves from the Indies to work at his La Florida ranch. He would spend the court season in his sprawling home in Seville.

The three ships, tiny by the galleon standards of the Spanish fleet, had battled the powerful westerlies almost from the moment they'd cleared Acapulco thirty-one days before. But the night they marked Capo Blanco a warm front provided welcome relief from the bitter winds that had lashed them for so long. The winds shifted to the south and for the next two days allowed the ships to cover as much distance as they had in the previous week. Mindia stood for hours at the bow, eyes streaming with tears, mouth wide with delight as the land revealed itself to the east, unencumbered by the filthy fog that had obscured the coast for so long. His sketchbook was already three-quarters full, and he drew smaller and smaller notations of mountain, river, and valley. Everything he saw went onto those pages.

The third day after the winds changed, the night watchman of the caravel was startled half to death when the old pilot pounded along the deck toward him, shouting like a madman. It had turned cold again but the winds were light.

"Land to the north! We will ground! Wake the captain, give him these readings!" the pilot shoved a piece of paper in his hand. "Call all hands and signal the other ships. Quickly! Go! And send me two relays!" he bellowed at the frightened man's back.

The men were growing weak as they had yet to spot a good harbor along the rugged coast. But Apostolos's alarm made them forget their empty bellies and dry throats. The old man stared into the northeast, his grimy hands gripping the shrouds, nostrils wide for the scent of something different.

"Perhaps de Jode was partially right?" Mindia asked softly at his shoulder, suspecting they had at least five days yet before they'd reach the straits.

"Perhaps," was the only response.

They sailed this way for nearly an hour, Apostolos saying nothing, his fierce gaze not wavering a fraction. Then he knew.

"One degree three minutes west, then hard starboard on my mark," he called to the relay. The man ran to the captain and the second relay took his place. The ships bucked into the quickening winds toward the open ocean. Another hour passed.

"Mark! Hard starboard and hold!" The relay sprinted stern.

One good thing, Apostolos thought, this captain has no delusions of grandeur; he does what he is told.

"Straighten and maintain course!" he instructed the first relay a few minutes later. "Inform the captain I will join him shortly."

"Where are we?" puzzled Mindia, looking toward the pinking eastern sky.

"Welcome," the old Greek smiled for the first time in weeks, "to the Straits of Anian, passage to the South Sea!"

Night lifted quickly, the orange dawn peeling back to reveal a cerulean sky, calm waters, and the deep-green shoulders of land to the north and south.

"Note this," Apostolos instructed. "A pillar of conical shape, exceedingly high, guarding the mouth of the strait on the *nordeste,* northeast shore." He spoke it twice, in both Italian and Spanish to ensure Mindia got it right.

Mindia's fingers flew, sketching the land and Apostolos's comments. The pilot continued for several minutes, detailing land forms he wished marked. "Diverse islands," Mindia wrote in Spanish. "The entrance to the said Straits of Anian signaled by a spired rock, exceedingly high on the Hedland to the *noroeste.*" Noroeste he had heard from the cold, cracked lips of the old man. *Northwest.*

Landing parties were dispatched to a rocky cove to find water and game while the men in one of the pinnaces harpooned several small dolphins. By evening the water barrels were full and the meat rooms hung with slabs of fish and deer. The blood was carefully collected and the intestines cleaned to make sausages. No one mentioned the six scurvied bodies, sewn into sailcloth and heaved overboard with a minimum of ceremony.

The clear weather lasted barely three days, and for most of the next twenty, dark-bottomed clouds and heavy rain followed them. The air was near frigid and the rain more like wet snow. Even with full bellies, the men suffered terribly from the cold. Mindia shivered uncontrollably from dawn to dusk. Not even cupfuls of gristly soup warmed him. There wasn't a single sign of human life, and he concluded that it was simply too cold for habitation this far north.

Navigation using an astrolabe was virtually impossible with the overcast dimness of the days, but still Apostolos reckoned the straits were taking them east through the North American continent to the Spanish Indies, exactly as it should have done. It was, he had to admit, considerably farther than he'd expected.

"It is possible we will emerge far to the north of the Indies," he muttered, poring over his charts.

"Are you certain of the heading?" Mindia asked.

"Who are you to question my navigation?" snapped the old man.

"I am nothing but an apprentice cartographer, that is not in dispute, but I feel we head much farther north than east."

Apostolos grew angry at the suggestion. They *must* be sailing east. They *were* sailing east along the broad salty river that would connect Pacifica to the South Sea of the Indies. He was so out of sorts Mindia took care to leave him alone unless the pilot bade him to make specific drawings or notations. The cold was beginning to take a severe toll on the men, but Apostolos, gaunt-faced and white-lipped, didn't seem to feel it. He hardly slept at all and rarely seemed to eat.

On the twentieth day after passing the cone of rock that marked the entrance to the straits, Mindia reluctantly pulled his chilled body out of his bed and made his way to Apostolos's permanent post at the bow of the ship. His very blood seemed frozen. To his astonishment, the ancient pilot stood arms akimbo, swaying gently with the rocking of the ship, his gums bared in a mad grin.

"Oh ho!" he crowed. "Kefalonia awaits! I will drink the wine of my father again before I die."

Mindia rubbed the sleep out of his eyes with amazement. The landscape was transformed and the sea had taken on a different character. Floating near shore, like ducklings around their mother, were dozens of icebergs. Farther out to the center of the channel bobbed smaller floes. The strait itself had narrowed considerably and he could easily see up the jagged-faced fjords plunging inland on both sides. The air was so sharp his breath seemed to freeze the moment it was out of his mouth. But the magnificence of the vista chased the cold from his bones. Numerous islands dotted the strait shorelines, white-rimmed with ice. Higher ground shone snowy white.

"This," said Mindia, stating the obvious, "cannot be the South Sea."

"Clever of you to notice!" sang out the ebullient Greek.

"Could it be that we have emerged at Cartier's Baie St. Laurens?" Mindia wondered aloud, abandoning his previous suspicion that they had been trending north for at least the past two weeks. He had copies of maps bought or stolen from the French, Italians, and English. Maps of the great explorers and pilots: the Venetian-born John Cabot, the Portuguese Gaspar Côrte-Real, the Spaniard Juan Ponce de León, not to mention Verrazano, Gomes, and other men of the mariner nations all eagerly searching the Atlantic coast for Asia or a route to that continent. But it was his memory of Jacques Cartier's words more than half a century earlier that leaped to his mind as he surveyed their location.

It is composed of stones and horrible rugged rocks . . . this is the land God gave to Cain. There are icebergs in sight everywhere, hanging from cliff faces and rising in constant menace in our path. I believe some of them to be more than two fathoms in thickness. The territory to the north and south is mountainous but mostly in the distance and what rivers I can see look far too rough to attempt exploration.

"You speculated earlier of Nova Francia and Canada," said Apostolos. "I myself doubt it. I believe what you see before you is the North Sea itself and a route far to the north of what Cartier charted. Don't forget, he never found the passage to Asia. His Baie St. Laurens and Rivière du Canada ended in rapids, which he could not surmount. We see no rapids."

"Then what is this land?" Mindia gestured on both sides of the ships. "And whose?"

"I am sure it is beyond that claimed by France. If we sail farther north, we will find ourselves at the tip of Greenland," he said firmly. Contrary to Apostolos's conviction, the ice-laden land surrounding them was actually the northern reaches of the inside passage between what would be called Vancouver Island and British Columbia's mainland.

The men were horribly weak from scurvy and cold, some were mere skeletons. Apostolos was anxious to return to civilized Spanish territory lest he lose the entire crew. Watches and shifts of work had been cut in half and still many could not man their posts without falling asleep. The nails and fingers of most were black from bleeding beneath the skin and some of the men had lost more than half their teeth as their gums swelled and bled. Mutiny was always a possibility when conditions became this severe, even though only officers were armed and the armory was kept under lock and key.

Still, Apostolos insisted a boat be dispatched to the most hospitable spot they could locate, not an easy task. He gave the third mate command of the landing party and entrusted him with the Spanish flag, a single gold doubloon with the king's head upon its surface, a small jar of pickled olives, and a miniature flag of Kefalonia woven decades ago by one of his sisters.

Mindia was surprised. Never before had he detected even a dram of sentimentality in the old pilot. The landing boat nearly lost all hands when it collided with a submerged floe, but they slid off to the port side, narrowly evading disaster before making their way into a cove with a tiny pebble beach. The cliff was far too steep and icy to ascend, so they built a cairn of rocks and placed upon it the flag of the Spanish Empire. As the crew, mostly cashiered Portuguese sailors, cared little for the niceties of Spanish discovery, neither hymns nor other flowery words of claim were offered. When the flag was precariously wedged between two rocks, they hastily made their way back to the ship.

"We must try to improve our time back to Mesico," Apostolos ordered, now all business, to the captain of the caravel. "The winds now blow from the east," he noted incorrectly, "so they will be at our backs. Twenty days from this point of the straits' mouth at the north sea and back to the Pacific may be made in fifteen, or less."

They had barely enough food and water left to last the journey to the original entrance to the straits. Mindia had noted a broad bay one day shortly after entering the straits. It seemed to lead to a river but it was too far away to tell. He thought the bay was due east of them at the time, but if Apostolos was right it would in fact be located south. It might be a perfect spot to anchor for reprovisioning.

✳

The next week for Mindia passed in a whirl of sketching. He hardly saw Apostolos at all so busy was he dashing from one side of the ship to the other, drawing everything he saw. At night he took his notes and drawings and compared them, as best he could using the single candle he had left, with the copies of the maps he'd brought with him. As the days went on, doubt about their bearings lodged inside him and grew with every hour. Apostolos insisted they were now "carving the girth of the north continent from east to west," but the position of the sun, readily visible for the first time since Capo Blanco, was wrong.

"You know too little about the earth," scoffed the pilot. "We are near the North Pole and the earth narrows severely at that point. That is well known. It is also well known to those who have studied these things as I have, that the curve of the earth means the sun no longer rises and sets as it does closer to the meridian."

"But should it not have happened gradually as we sailed?" pressed Mindia. "As it is, the sun's position altered almost immediately upon entering the strait."

"And how would you know that?" Apostolos demanded tartly. "We did not see the sun at all or even the main shores once we passed the pinnacle of rock. Are you suddenly a pilot who is blessed with the navigation ability of a bird? Do what I brought you aboard to do. Map what we explore in accordance with the bearings I give you."

Stung, Mindia said no more on the subject.

The strait widened considerably as they neared the mouth and Apostolos guided the small fleet toward the bay and headland that Mindia had sketched before the fog and clouds had descended, obscuring their voyage. The land pushed out in a broad blunt prow, high cliffs at its front tapering, it appeared, to flatter land farther inland. On one side, south if Mindia was right, east if the old man was, there appeared to be a river's mouth with many fingers breaking around islands where it met the Straits of Anian. Around the other side of the promontory, north by Mindia's reckoning, west by that of the pilot, was a broad bay tapering to a narrow inlet and overlooked by extraordinary mountains, a long range of them running as far as the eye could see. It was still bitterly cold but they hadn't seen ice for some days. Nor yet had there been any indication of habitation.

Apostolos directed the ships to drop anchor just as the inlet narrowed between what appeared to be an island and the mountainous shore. In the morning he would send boats ashore to search for water, food, and fuel, and if they provisioned quickly he would explore and chart the inlet to its end. He would also sail up the big river as far as they could. As the day darkened, the pilot boarded the larger of the pinnaces to inspect stores and damage. He would remain there for the night.

In the absence of Apostolos and buoyed by their historic achievement in locating the passage between the seas, the men on the caravel ransacked their sea chests for thimblefuls of rum and the odd bottle of pine whiskey. Mindia shed his doubts to join them. What whiskey remained was foul stuff. You had to be well on the grog already in order to stomach it, which is why it had lasted so long on a voyage where normally the men would have drunk fermented urine given the chance. Mindia knew Apostolos had two jugs of port secreted in his cabin and Mindia himself had a single bottle of vodka, his favorite drink, which he had hoarded all the way from Venice. He'd intended to make it last for the return leg of their journey. But celebration was in the air, the passage had been discovered, their way home seemed clear, and they would all be rich, each according to his expectations and lot in life. By his second glass Mindia had convinced himself of his wealth to come and recognition as a world-famous cartographer. The man who mapped the Straits of Anian, the east-west link between the Pacific Ocean and the North Sea.

The men were able to scrounge a surprising amount of alcoholic drink, sufficient to put most of them to sleep in a matter of hours. As they were emaciated, wracked by scurvy and other ailments, a swig or two produced a drunken stupor in a gratifyingly brief amount of time. Even the captain was snoring by midnight. Mindia built up a roaring blaze in the deck brazier, then happily drifted off, serenaded by the music of two ill-tuned mandolins, humming as sweetly in his ear as if they were played by Europe's finest musicians.

14

*

Mindia woke in exactly the same position as he'd gone to sleep, buttocks buried deep in a coil of rope at the foot of the mainsail mast, bare feet hanging over the edge, and head cushioned by a bundle of oily rags he'd pulled out of a bucket the night before. His feet ached from the chill and he remembered that he'd built up a blaze in the pilot's deck brazier, then took off his boots and ragged stockings to warm his toes.

As he opened his eyes, Mindia's head spun but he'd felt worse many times; this would pass quickly. What he wouldn't give for a glass of his father's wonderful tea. Black, strong, and powerfully sweet. Unfortunately, tea, like so much else, had run out before they'd crossed forty degrees. He'd have to make do with a mug of boiled water laced with chicory powder. The natives of Mesico drank it liberally, and Apostolos had been persuaded to bring a barrel on board. Mindia was thankful, as the earthy-tasting stuff wasn't pleasant but plain water was even worse. God only knew what the water barrels held previously! Hopefully they would find fresh water today.

Mindia stretched comically, arms and legs straight up in the air, like a man stuck in an oversize bucket. Today he would accompany the shore tenders and sketch from every vantage point. Despite his throbbing head and paper-dry mouth, he was eager to get to work. Above him the sky was a rich blue, not the turquoise of Nova Spania or the azure of the Adriatic coast, but an intense, brooding blue tinged with purple. Craning his neck, he could just make out the snowy shoulders of a mountainous ridge. What a glorious country, far superior to the humid shores of Acapulco with its dirty-brown people and dirty-brown hills. Mindia groped for his stockings and boots and pulled himself out of his rope nest.

*

"Ha! Ha!" Mindia crowed, catching sight of the second mate propped upright against the rigging, sound asleep. "You certainly drank more than your share!" he called out to the man. "And you too, I'll warrant!" he hollered to one of the mandoliners asleep on his instrument, the neck of it visible on one side of his head, the round body protruding from the other. "That can't be very comfortable. Still, rum has a way of making a bed of nails seem like a mattress of feathers."

Mindia noticed a trail of blood seeping from the man's ear but thought little of it. It wasn't an uncommon sight as scurvy took firm hold on the body. In contrast to the revelry of the night before the boat was strangely quiet. No hands moved above decks and he couldn't smell the ever-present grease from the cook's quarters. If Apostolos was aboard he'd be furious. Mindia peered across the water at the larger pinnace pulling slightly at anchor. The light was so bright and his eyes so bleary he couldn't make out any movement there either. Perhaps the old Greek had unshipped some liquid stores for that crew as well.

He turned to step over the mandolin player's sleeping form. Something was odd about his head, the angle unnatural. Mere seconds passed, but to Mindia they were like hours. The head. The blood. The neck hanging to one side. And his eyes, they were open! Suddenly Mindia was on his knees, bile torrenting out of his mouth. The man's neck had been impaled from one side to the other by the mandolin. The wood had splintered as it had been driven into his flesh, and shards appeared out the other side in several places.

Mindia stumbled to his feet and made his way to wake up the second mate. There must have been a terrible brawl during the night. But just as he raised his hand to shake him, Mindia snatched it back, clutching it to his chest as if he'd been burned. The second mate was not propped against the rigging but also impaled, this time from belly to rectum with a harpoon, the tip of which was stuck into the deck. He hung there like a rag doll, the blood on his legs congealing in thick, black ropes. There was nothing left in Mindia's stomach but his innards heaved anyway with dry, hard coughs.

In the blur of minutes that followed Mindia found them all, twenty-two in total, ten lying in a row, their severed heads set neatly between their feet, the captain and cabin boys among them. Whoever had done it had tired of the sport or been interrupted; the rest of the crew were simply butchered and left to lie where they fell. Mindia noticed that every bit of decoration, including the many amulets the superstitious men wore to ward off evil, had been stripped from the bodies. Earrings pulled from lobes, fingers hacked off to get at rings, and even the cook's helper was missing his wooden foot.

Amidships he noticed a pile of things: items of clothing, tools, and cooking utensils. Mindia rushed forward to the bow, called hoarsely to the pinnace: "Help! Help!"

Belatedly it occurred to Mindia that calling attention to himself might not be the wisest move. For the life of him he couldn't figure out what had happened. Pirates seemed hardly likely! If it was a mutiny, where were the mutineers? In any event, a musket or pistol shot would certainly have woken him. Cautiously he walked over to the side of the ship where crew and ship's belongings were piled.

"Oooof!" He stopped so suddenly and drew in his breath so quickly, it was as if he'd had the wind knocked out of him.

"Dear Lord, save me," he whispered.

Four of them floated directly below. Immense canoelike boats with dragon heads on each prow, and twelve men holding paddles straight up in the air while two standing in the stern steadied the vessel in the light breeze. About fifty beings, so silent and motionless they could have been frozen. White bodies, black faces. While the creatures' legs and arms were bare, their chests and private parts were protected by what appeared to be bones sewn onto some kind of long vests. They stared curiously at Mindia and he stared back, equally curious, forgetting for a moment the atrocities they had obviously committed and the danger that so clearly faced him.

The man who must be the leader, so extravagantly was his body decorated, barked an order. Before he knew it, the men—if that was what they were—in one of the boats pulled close and a dozen scrambled up the side as quickly and easily as mounting a stairway.

"The end, oh Mother! Please forgive my sins, forgive the son who has not written to you, forgive my neglect, forgive my selfishness, forgive . . ." he rambled hysterically backing away from them, waiting for the terrible blow. But the creatures kept their distance as if he were diseased, circling him cautiously. They moved quickly to the bodies, snatching up the heads along with the various items that caught their fancy and tossed them overboard into the boats below. Then they were gone, down the ropes and back into the boats. Paddles smacked into the water and they pulled powerfully away, heading toward the island and a sharp pinnacle of rock.

As the savages paddled across the water and the air carried their laugh-

ter and songs to Mindia's ears, he realized what had happened. These creatures had attacked so swiftly and skillfully that no one on board had been
able to offer even token resistance. Then they'd loaded up their boats with
what booty they could carry and had just as brazenly returned for the rest.
That much was clear. But why had Mindia been spared? If they did not
notice him the first time, they'd certainly seen him now. Yet here he was,
indisputably alive. And what on earth was he to do now?

For a time Mindia stood dazed. He tried hailing the other boats but there
was still no discernible activity. Finally hunger and thirst goaded him to look
for food and the last of the ship's store of murky water. In the galley he found
biscuits and a half tin of chicory. With shaking hands he pulled a biscuit apart
and stuffed it, untasted, into his mouth. Then he heard the sound. It had been
teasing the edge of his consciousness for some minutes before he stopped to
listen. It was the ship's cat mewling for scraps, he was sure.

"Poor Boy!" he called out. "Come here fella, Poor Boy!" The sound
stopped. Mindia investigated the empty flour and sugar barrels stacked at
the far end of the galley. "Poor Boy! Come out, Poor Boy!"

The cook's helper had found the cat on shore in Acapulco, with a broken tail and enough fleas to make the entire city of St. Petersburg itch.
"Poor boy," he'd crooned to the skinny orange-and-white animal. "I take
care my poor boy." With that the ship had a new rat catcher, and the slightly
addled helper a friend. The cook threatened to make soup out of the
mangy animal just to tease his "crook boy" as he called his helper, but
everyone knew he never would.

The sound started up again. As Mindia moved toward it, he tripped
over firewood scattered about by the invaders and fell into the barrels. One
of the lids came rocketing off, and a man shot out waving a large ladle.

"Sons of bitches! Murdering thieves! Savages!" he screamed, brandishing the implement like a sword. "I'll get you bastards!" he foamed, spit cascading down his chin and his face still wet from tears of fright.

"Cook!" gasped Mindia. "You're alive! Dear heaven!" For a moment he
thought Cook was going to attack him with the ladle. "Don't hit me! I'm
the only one left."

"Have they gone them fockin' bastards? Where are they? Let me at'um!
Kilt ever'thin'. Kilt'um all. Not me," he babbled still waving the ladle. "I
fooled'um. Let me at 'um!"

"They're gone," soothed Mindia, "but so is everyone else. I thought the
whole ship was dead. How did you survive?"

"I fooled'um," growled Cook. "I were talking to mother," a sailor's phrase referring to urinating over the side, "when I heard a mighty crashing and me crook boy yelling 'n that was that."

"How did you get away?" pressed Mindia.

"Smart!" Cook tapped his temple. "I knows trouble when I hears it. It were right dark and no moon so I crep' up to rescue me crook boy but he were gone."

Mindia doubted this. Cook excelled at avoiding work that didn't involve pots, pans, and food, and he was positively allergic to any hint of danger, refusing to come on deck when the weather or the sea was even slightly robust. Mindia could no more imagine the man sneaking up to save his feeble-headed helper than he could picture him climbing to the crow's nest in a storm. Cook had obviously hidden in one of the barrels at the first hint of trouble and likely would be there still if Mindia hadn't stumbled across him.

"Wass the plan?" demanded Cook. "How we gettin' out here?"

"Welll," stammered Mindia.

He had no idea. He'd spent his entire life being directed—first by his mother, then by his governess, then by his father, next by his Venetian tutor, and, for the past eighteen months, by the old Greek. Mindia hadn't been asked to offer an opinion on any subject since his mother had inquired if he would be all right as she kissed her beloved son good-bye at the stairs of his tiny Venice apartment. His often lively conversations and debates with the old Greek never involved him taking charge in any way or creating a plan of action. He merely had the opportunity to exercise his mind while waiting on the pilot's pleasure.

"I suppose we should rouse the other boats," he reasoned. "They might not even be aware of what has happened. It's obvious we must get away as quickly as possible."

"Damn the other boats! I say we sail now. Haul anchor and away."

"But we must warn them!"

"An' what good that do?" Cook stuck his greasy nose inches in front of Mindia's face. "If they be dead, they be dead. An' we be target practice for the savages. If they alive they gonna bloodin' chase us when we go."

"We can't possibly sail the ship with two men!"

"Ya can't sail her with two dead men that be sure," retorted Cook with unassailable logic.

Lacking any other plan, they made their way carefully above deck, Cook lagging far behind in case a savage lay in wait. With an effort, Mindia forced himself to assess the situation. The invaders had not damaged any of the rigging or anything in the steerage cabin. They'd carted away as much as they could carry, but nothing essential to sailing the ship, at least short term. With only two of them they could probably manage with the supplies on hand for as long as ten days, especially if they caught some fish. But they could only sail on half canvas during the day, in calm weather, and when both were awake. They might have to anchor early on many days if they found a safe bay, which had been in very short supply on the inbound passage.

Mindia fervently wished for a different companion than Cook. Even his addled helper could do twice the work. He squinted into the sun at the two pinnaces at anchor. He still couldn't see any movement on the decks, no hint of life or even a signal flag run up the main mast. There seemed to be only two possibilities. The old man and the crew had seen the slaughter and feared attracting the attention of the savages. Or they were all dead.

In his heart Mindia believed they were dead, but Cook was right, either way they had to move this boat. He turned to the island and spotted what looked like a beachhead near the spire of rock. It was far smaller than the one they'd noted at the entrance to the straits. Mindia wondered what sort of omen the two pinnaces augured. They began to seem like grave markers to him.

"All right," he declared. "We'll go. I will take charge of the course and steering and you must man the rigging."

"By self!" Cook whined.

"Of course I'll help," Mindia soothed, "but we must work hard to clear the strait before they notice we're gone. Who knows what other savages are lurking along these shores. We can sail on one mast for the moment. The main thing is to get away as quickly as possible. You prepare the mainsail. I will chart our course."

Cook nodded sourly and shuffled off, furtively casting his eye about as if expecting one of the painted devils to leap out at him.

Despite their desperate situation Mindia felt a burst of optimism. He had issued an order and it had been accepted. Perhaps they could find their way out of this mess after all. The caravel was a nimble boat, relatively small for the task of exploration, but in this situation a boon. Two men could not hope to sail any of the larger boats in the Spanish fleet. Even so, it would be a couple of hours yet before they were under way with only the two of them to prepare the sheets. Normally it took four of the strongest crew to raise the big mainsail.

Within the hour Mindia had a good grasp of their course to the straits' mouth. Thankfully his notes were excellent. Managing the astrolabe was another matter. He had never used one and even the theory behind its use was a carefully guarded secret known only to the captain and the pilot. It was insurance. If the crew knew they couldn't make their own way home they were less likely to kill the captain and the pilot in the event of mutiny. Hopefully they could maintain sight of shore the whole way. As he worked at the pilot's desk Mindia heard a throaty noise. There in the ash bucket was Poor Boy. The cat stretched contentedly and began licking ash from its paws.

"Now," muttered Mindia, "is the time to be a cat."

Cook reappeared to say he'd unfurled the smaller sails as best he could and they were ready to be raised. Twilight was advancing and again no moon. He reckoned they could make Fuca's Spire, as the old Greek had dubbed it, guarding the entrance to the ocean within two days if they were lucky. Raising anchor was the tough part. Fortunately Apostolos had ordered only the two lightest set. The winds were calm and they had no need of the big anchor for the short time they had intended to stay. Now, of course, the caravel's crew would remain for all eternity.

The two of them could bring up both anchors and with tremendous effort get sufficient sail up to take them out of the strait. Once well under way they could raise more sail, but not too much. If they hit bad weather they'd be on the rocks before they could drop the sheets.

✳

"They leave us!" Cook ran shrieking back into the cabin. "They go! Bastards leaving us!"

"What are you saying?" Mindia demanded, his heart pounding painfully. "Who?"

They rushed to the bow. The two pinnaces, both under half sail and rapidly putting on more canvas, made toward open water. The light was dim but Mindia could make out the men feverishly raising more canvas and he could hear them bellowing encouragement at each other. He and Cook bellowed back, first in hope then in rage.

Mindia could not believe what he was seeing even as it was happening before his eyes. His throat was raw from screaming, and tears of exertion, fright, and despair coursed down his cheeks.

"Old man!" he whispered prayerfully as the boats beat it for the straits' mouth. "Old man, don't leave us."

Not once did anyone on board either pinnace acknowledge them as they ran for open sea. No semaphore signal. No light. No hail. Not even the warning flags they could easily have run up the mast, red-red-white, a code between Spanish ships meaning "danger, flee, every man for himself." Cook was fuming, stamping his feet and pounding the fore boom with his fists. Long after Mindia fell silent he stormed up and down the deck cursing the cowards and swearing vengeance upon their heads.

"I guess I would have done the same," uttered Mindia softly. "They must have seen the attack and assumed we were all dead. Or at least they didn't care to risk themselves to find out."

He didn't mention that he knew Apostolos had taken his eyeglass with him and could easily have made out the raiders as they chucked the severed heads into their boats and departed.

"But they got ears don't they?" protested Cook. "We been yelling like stink and they cud hear us easy cross water. They kep' silent gordamn bastards. They prepare to run like dogs but they done it quiet as can be. They know we be here."

"We'll just have to follow." Mindia straightened up. Though he was sickened by the knowledge that the old pilot had left them to die, he also felt better knowing that at least some of the crew of the two pinnaces were still alive. And he was sure Apostolos was among them. Their sudden departure had the mark of his professionalism about it. If they hoisted what sails they could and got under way they could keep the other boats in sight for a few hours. Surely once Apostolos realized they were following he would order their rescue.

"Come!" urged Mindia. "The longer we stand around crying the farther away they will get. To the anchors!"

Galvanized by his words, Cook rushed to the stern and began cranking mightily on the wheel to draw the anchor in. Mindia leaped to help him. Fortunately the gears and cogs were well greased and the rope ascended quickly through the chuck with one on each handle on either side of the wheel.

"We won't have much time after we hoist the second," puffed Mindia, unaccustomed to the exertion. "We'll raise the mainsail and then I'll have to steer. Can you manage the stays'le?"

"Ha! Manage!" barked out Cook, suddenly optimistic. "I'll her up 'fore you lay hands upon the wheel."

The anchor fluke was just visible.

"Here she comes!" shouted Mindia. "Harder now!" Suddenly his arms bore the full pressure of the anchor wheel. Cook had let go. Grunting, Mindia tried to hold steady but the anchor started slipping back slowly, then faster, until the handle was ripped right out of his hands.

"What's the matter with you man! That nearly tore my arms off! Why did you . . ."

Mindia looked up angrily and saw Cook's face, pale like the sheets themselves, staring out over the water. He followed the man's stricken look. More than a dozen craft were spread across the water. They had been clearly intending to cut off the two pinnaces, hence the ships' hasty departure. This is what the old man must have feared, Mindia realized, that the savages were only saving them for a second course.

Mindia examined the craft as they veered toward them. There was really nothing else to do. Resistance would be futile. Some of these boats were smaller and not as elaborately carved as those of the invaders who'd made off with the severed heads. The creatures inside looked like giant birds, their arms and legs festooned with all manner of feathers and their heads topped with extraordinary hats shaped like menacing beaks. Some were bare-chested though painted, and others wore the bone vests Mindia had seen before. The only indications that these things were human were their hands, with long, slender fingers, and their teeth, which were startlingly white, though not bared in a smile of welcome.

Did he faint or was he hit? Mindia couldn't figure it out. All he knew was that he was lying on his back in one of the log boats shooting through the water at what seemed an incredible speed. What vigor they have, he thought idly to himself. And then the blackness returned.

15

*

Like a child playing on a drawing-room rug, Mindia sat, legs sprawled apart, body leaning back. And, as though he were a child playing with adored possessions, a jumble of things lay on the ground between his legs. The astrolabe, two pipes, a speed tube, a watch, his quill pen, a silver inkwell, Apostolos's brass seal, and several fingers of red wax. There were spoons, twine, rigging needles, a magnifying glass, and a bisque-fired porcelain jar that contained various rocks the old pilot had collected in his travels: unworked chunks of Carrera marble, an alabaster egg, pink quartz, obsidian, pale pink and green jade disks with a dragon insignia, and his prize possession, a soft, black chunk of ebony so smooth and hard the brown-black wood felt like a large, light stone.

He heard groaning. Cook sat slumped in much the same position, blood dripping down his chin.

"Can you hear me, Cook?" whispered Mindia.

Cook groaned and opened one eye; the other was swollen shut. Most of his front teeth were knocked out or broken, and he gingerly ran his tongue over bloody stumps.

"They braked my fingers," he whined.

Cook, like Mindia, was tethered to the ground at his ankles and tied to a tree around his torso. Both hands were attached to stakes at his side. Several fingers were bent at terrible angles.

"Did you fight them?" Mindia asked sympathetically, wondering where the man's newfound courage came from.

"Started to. One ov'um whacked you with a big damn club. I thought he took your head off you went doon so fast. I hardly raised an arm 'fore a dozen jumped on me. Pissin' cowards!" Blood and spit popped and dribbled at his lips.

Mindia leaned his head back against the tree and instantly regretted it.

The movement turned the spot on the side of his head the club had hit into a throbbing locus of pain. But he was lucky. He appeared to have all his body parts. He hardly knew what to think. He assumed they meant to kill them. He prayed it would be quick and the savages not have sport with the two of them. But in his heart he feared that was the case. Why else would they keep him alive? He had heard lurid tales from the sailors and the old pilot himself of savages-and-explorer encounters gone wrong; of men staked by their intestines on ant hills, of others flayed alive or chased naked through the bush until they collapsed.

Terror now replaced the pain in his head. It lodged in his lower belly, leaving him breathless with the idea of torture. How would he bear it? The worst pain he'd ever experienced was a festered tooth, which had been pulled when he was fifteen. These were terrible people who would have no compunction about inflicting terrible things upon him.

A procession approached. Mindia recognized the first man, the one who appeared to be the leader of those who took away the heads. He craned to watch them as they neared. Cook didn't raise his chin from his chest. He looked as if he'd lost all hope. The group fanned out in front of them, chattering rapidly while pointing at and picking up the array of things on the ground. They ignored the two men. The leader walked back and forth, consulting with two of the women as if he were a Don on a shopping trip in an open-air bazaar, apparently weighing the merits of each object. One of the women was an ugly hag with empty breasts flopping on her chest only partially concealed by the coarse blanket worn around her shoulders. She gestured urgently at the pipes. These she wanted.

The leader shook his head and pointed at the jar full of rocks. When he squatted down Mindia could see brown flesh between the cracks in white body paint. The man hooked his finger in the jar, pulling out one rock after another. When he reached the pale-green jade disk he shouted excitedly. Several others clustered around. Mindia could smell a sweetness about them, sweat mixed with something else. The disk was thoroughly examined and commented upon. A very old man shuffled up, swathed from head to foot in cloth that looked like the bark of a tree. He wore a large piece of bone through his nose, and his eight fingers were pierced through the fleshy pad with quills. They looked like claws. He studied the green disk, tapped it on his teeth, and rubbed it over his chest. The leader pulled a heavy bone chain from his neck and gave it to the old man, who gently opened the pouch hanging from it and emptied the contents into his hand.

As he did, the leader barked an order and virtually everyone in the crowd cast down their eyes.

The old man and the tall leader carefully compared the dozen or so pale green beads with the jade disk, pointing to markings on the disk and then to the beads. Finally, the old man placed the beads back in their pouch and nodded definitively to the leader who smiled as if he had scored a victory. He walked away, cradling the jar in his arm. The ugly woman scowled in his wake.

"World's about thievin'," croaked Cook. "No different here than else."

With the leader gone, the rest approached the objects. There appeared to be a pecking order, as some stood back patiently waiting for others to take what they wanted. Here, as "else," the higher status dressed better and more flamboyantly. A young woman, surely no more than fifteen, stood in front of Mindia and selected two forks and a rigging needle. She scratched the fork against her arm and laughed. Two others of her age did the same and they giggled anew. Satisfied, she scratched herself all over, even running the tines over her breasts and nipples. Mindia's face flushed so hotly it made his head pound even harder. So crude, so shameless. Though he couldn't help noticing that they were rather nice breasts and nipples. A middle-aged woman knelt before him, grabbed a chunk of his beard, and began hacking it off. Mindia dared not move. By the time she finished she had a pouch well filled with wiry, auburn whiskers. She moved on to Cook's blacker beard, and he jerked his head back and forth, trying to get away from her. Grinning, she smacked the knife hard against his cheek, freezing him into stillness.

Then they were left alone for hours. Mindia was tied so firmly he couldn't stand or even kneel to relieve himself. In an agony of release he gave up and let his bladder go, his shame rising as the circle of darkened earth around him grew.

"Where do you suppose they live?" Mindia asked Cook, trying to distract himself. "I can't see shacks or any shelter."

"Holes in the ground," Cook grunted. "Like badgers or toads. Ugly bastards."

"I wonder if they make houses like the Indians I saw in Acapulco. You know, those mud huts? Or maybe they live in trees. There's an awful lot of those around."

"You be better off thinking 'bout how to get out of here," growled Cook. "I ain't spending my last days being played with by monkeys."

Surely the old pilot had simply withdrawn in order to regroup, Mindia told himself. Any minute he'd spot the masts of the two pinnaces in the broad bay. The men needed food and water before they'd have the energy to attack the murderers and rescue Cook and himself. Give it a day or two at most, then they'll be back. What good luck it was the caravel that had been taken. Though it was the larger boat, the other two were more heavily armed. There was one small cannon on each of the pinnaces, plus a goodly supply of muskets and a fireball catapult. If the bay was deep they could certainly come close enough to set the shoreline ablaze, which would give them an effective screen to dispatch rescue boats. The savages might have spears, perhaps even bows and arrows, but nothing to match Spanish muskets.

What a tale it would make for his mother! He'd draw it out deliciously, knowing the details would frighten her half to death. His father would be proud of his bravery. Mindia might gloss over the fact that he was unconscious for part of the ordeal. He was certainly conscious now. His fear began to abate; if they had intended to kill them they would have done so by now. And if torture was their goal, surely there would have been some hint of it from the group that looted the items from the ship. Come to think of it, what he remembered of the hideous sight of slaughter on board the ship was that every man appeared to have been cut down quickly. And when they returned to the ship they hadn't killed Mindia or Cook. Apparently there was a time for killing and a time when killing was over. That was a reassuring thought. Still, there was no explanation for why they hadn't killed Mindia along with the others.

"Get away!" Cook's strangled voice shot out. "Ugh! Filthy beasts! Monsters! Get away from me."

"What is it?"

"Look!" Cook gasped. "Look what that brute bitch got!"

A youngish woman had come up behind the two men. Strings of meat chunks hung over her shoulder. Mindia didn't understand Cook's disgust. Perhaps she had come to feed them. Water would be even better. As she bent over to study Mindia's face he saw what Cook had seen. Ears, dozens of them hanging from a hide rope like so many little fish. Mindia saw torn lobes and dried blood where the savages had ripped earrings from the crew's ears. Flies collected on the severed flesh.

Mindia turned his head away, feeling his stomach rebel once again. He was a well-educated young man and had read about the adventures of explorers both of his own country and others, but reading tales of savage behavior didn't compare to having examples of it dangled in front of one's face.

His stomach stilled, but spittle ran down his chin. The woman grinned broadly before setting down her dreadful cargo. She dug into a wooden bowl and her hand came away filled with a greenish paste, which she quickly smeared over Mindia's head. Pain shot down his neck. Her hand came away bloody. He must have been hit very hard.

The woman said something and pointed at the ears. For one horrible moment Mindia thought she was going to cut his off. Then he realized she was talking about the flies. She flicked at one then touched his head lightly. He guessed she was telling him the paste would keep the flies away. Mindia wondered whether he should smile or not. He settled for a quick nod of his head and a half-whispered thank you. She bent closer to hear him better, breathing softly near his ear.

"Thank you."

The woman fanned at her ear urging him to repeat the words.

"Thank you," he said again.

"Ta koo."

"Thank you."

"Thak roo."

"Thank you."

"Than kroo."

Despite his situation, a smile crossed his face. She was an attractive woman and eager to please. The woman smiled back and skipped away, her hips swaying provocatively. Then she turned abruptly to wave and, as she did, her calf-length skirt parted and Mindia's eyes widened. She was a man, unmistakably, sizably, protrudingly, a man.

❋

The days passed slowly. Mindia's eyes grew weary from squinting into the western sun, hoping for masts on the horizon. One day, the fourth, his heart leaped for joy. An enormous bird floated easily on the air currents. An albatross! It must mean the ships were nearby. But his heart fell quickly as the bird sailed closer and he saw it was black, far too large to be a crow or a blackbird. He had seen depictions of such a bird on the hats and capes of the people who came to give them food, water, and accompany them to relieve themselves in a mossy area of the forest.

Mindia hadn't seen the chief since that first day and wondered endlessly what they intended to do with them. Cook had become increasingly uncommunicative, swearing to himself in several languages, snarling at his captors when they fed him, and moaning in a fitful sleep. Mindia's arms and legs ached from the confinement and his buttocks were numb from the hard ground. Sleep was almost impossible, especially after some beasts from the forest, wild dogs or worse, wolves, emerged late one night and circled them, eyes glowing hungrily. The man-woman materialized from nowhere and, laughing, drove them off with a torch.

Early on the fifth morning, Mindia heard a large, noisy group of savages approach. They appeared to be arguing among themselves, for their voices were raised and excited—men and women alike with the high chime of children in the background. Once again they arrayed themselves in front of their captives, but this time the women quickly set about building a large fire and laying out a spread of food. As they talked, the men chewed on some dark-red meat skewered on sticks and roasted briefly in the fire. One basket held small blue eggs, and the children lined up as a young woman gently cracked the eggs and emptied the contents into their eager mouths. Mindia was starving. The rations had been meager. Even raw eggs would be an indescribable treat.

When everyone finished eating their fill, sharing nothing with Mindia or Cook, they turned their attention to their captives. Over the past days Mindia had picked up some words and expressions. *Mestiyew* seemed to mean both of them, while *Scha-us* seemed to refer to him alone and *Stesem* meant Cook. He knew words for "hair," "latrine," "face," "hands," "hungry," "thirsty," "man," "woman," "child," "bird." Cook appeared to know even more, for one day he lashed out at the two young men accompanying him as he relieved himself. Judging by the buffeting they administered to Cook's hide, his invective must have hit the mark.

"What did you say? How did you learn so many words?" Mindia had asked when he returned, deeply impressed. The man was full of surprises.

"I got ears, don't I? Least I do for the time being."

"But . . ."

"You spend enough time in ports of the world in the strange places I been, you pick up a few things. I kin name a woman's garden in thirteen diff'rent languages, four or five of 'em the tongue of uncivilized races."

"Garden?"

"You know. Hairy harbor. Pleasure palace. Forest of deelights."

They were the only eloquent words Mindia ever heard come from Cook's mouth.

✳

The group split into two, half crowding around Cook and the other half around Mindia. One woman touched his face, pulled at his beard, fondled the pale hair on his chest, and uttered some words to the chief. She appeared to tease a woman in the other group who shrugged and thumped Cook on the chest—much to his annoyance. Eventually it was settled. The children in Cook's throng happily untied his tethers while those surrounding Mindia flung themselves on his. He didn't know whether to be terrified or relieved. He stood, slowly stretching his stiff, aching limbs. The children fell back oohing and ahhing, impressed by his height. Cook's aversion to physical labor was not evident in his musculature. His chest and arms were lean and sharply defined. That was what the woman who'd thudded his chest seemed to be boasting of.

Ropes were attached to the captives' necks and each was led away from the pebble beach, into the forest and along a narrow trail. Cook never shut up. Every now and then a word he shouted was recognized, causing the savages to burst into laughter. Mindia kept his mouth shut.

Suddenly the oppressively tall, dark trees gave way to an open clearing around a small lagoon that appeared to drain in the direction of the same bay where they had been tied. Mindia estimated they were about two miles south of that place. There was a narrow sand beach and a low bank shore running in both directions, though to the north, where they had come from, the cliffs rose about fifteen feet high. The path must have skirted those cliffs. If Mindia had his bearings, the inlet where the three ships had anchored was also somewhat to the north.

He was about to pass on this information to Cook when he stopped dead at the sight before him. Buildings. Immense structures with soaring roofs and massive support timbers at the corners. Even more striking were towering carved poles depicting extraordinary figures along their length and colored in elemental shades of black, red, brown, and white. These were not the temporary structures of a nomadic people or the rough hovels he'd seen previously but dwellings of sophistication, with a good measure of architectural whimsy.

The poles, Mindia realized with a start, were entire trees, and the giant paintings on the front and sides of the building were strikingly bold and intricately done. With all his cartographic training and skill, Mindia couldn't approach the artistry. And the carving! Like anyone spending endless days on a sailing ship, he had tried his hand at whittling. He knew how hard it was to unlock even the simplest form from a piece of wood.

Mindia was intrigued by how things fit together, how one piece of land or water related to another. He was equally curious about buildings and once considered a career as an architect though his father had counseled against it.

"The world is looking away from the land, my son. Your future is on the water, where new lands are to be found, not in our old stagnant cities. Fame and fortune will come to those with courage and vision. Books are the expression of man's inner vision. Maps are the expression of man's outer vision." A sharp jerk on his neck interrupted Mindia's reminiscences, sending him stumbling along behind his captors.

As they passed close to one of the houses, Mindia reached out to touch the bulbous head of a creature carved into the pole set by the entrance. It had the eyes of a frog but the beak of a parrotlike bird. Before he knew it he was yanked backward, falling painfully on his tailbone. The man jerked the leash attached to Mindia's neck so hard it shut off his air, then, gesturing menacingly toward the pole, yanked it again for punctuation. Mindia got the message. Don't touch.

Apparently satisfied, the man gently tugged him toward the back of the house. Mindia was amazed. By counting his steps, he estimated the structure to be more than 150 feet on the long side. As he ogled the thick boards, he wondered how on earth they cut and planed them. For that matter, how did they fell these giant trees, larger even than the main mast of a Spanish galleon? He was tethered to a post set firmly in the ground while Cook was dragged off, protesting loudly, to one of the other houses.

Then they left him. Twilight came and he could hear the sounds of people moving around inside the house. A woman sang, more a chant really. Men laughed. Though he had seen many children, there were no sounds of babies crying or youngsters fighting with each other. When he was young, he and his brother had never got through a day without some kind of ruckus. Mindia was hungry, cold, and lonely. Tears filled his eyes as the night sky deepened.

The next morning Mindia, desperate to urinate, dying of thirst, and so empty-bellied he was ready to gnaw on the post, waited impatiently for someone to appear. Finally he raised himself up awkwardly. There was just enough slack to allow his hands to free himself from his trousers, which now smelled horribly. The stream burst forth. What incredible relief!

"*Ha, ho! Sqoqel! Titixem!*"

Mindia whipped around, hurriedly stuffing himself back in his tattered clothes. He believed the words meant something like "rank water." Seven women, old and young, contemplated him. Later he learned they were all wives of the village chief. The older ones had deeply lined faces with polished skin stretched tightly on prominent bones. The young ones carried themselves erectly, chins thrust out in the confident manner of those accustomed to privilege. Their eyes were small, dark, and almond-shaped, and their teeth were far whiter, straighter, and more numerous than those of most Europeans. Two carried wooden bowls. After a discussion they set the bowls on the ground and began cutting off his trousers while tugging at his waistcoat and shirt. They caressed his buttons, and one woman carefully chewed them off while his shirt was still on him. Mindia was embarrassed by her face pressed against his chest. Now completely naked except for his boots, he stood still as they coated him from head to toe with the thick, yellowish paint from the bowls. It dried quickly and began to itch. In the days to come he would be thankful, as the paste protected him from bugs and the sun. Finally they wrapped his loins with a piece of cloth.

Three men appeared next, accompanied by someone dressed head to ankles in feathers and entire bird wings. He carried a carved staff, which was also hung with feathers, and as the men untied Mindia and escorted him away, he pounded the staff rhythmically into the ground and danced a slow, hopping jig.

The chief or leader was sitting on a bench in front of his house as Mindia and, soon after, Cook were brought before him.

"Cook!" Mindia was never happier to see another person in his life.

"Treatin' you well, I see," said Cook, glancing at Mindia's caked body. His own torso was also covered with paint, but it was a deep red. And then Mindia got it. This was an ownership issue. Yellow denoted the house of the chief—he wore pale-yellow skins and his tall conical hat was also decorated with yellow feathers and amber-colored stones. The women all had something yellow on them, from blond discs that hung from lips or ears to flaxen or golden threads shot through the weaving of the capes they wore.

In contrast Cook's captors sported ornaments of a reddish hue. Judging by the stance of their bodies, there was a rivalry between the two groups.

"We're being basted up like pigs for the spit," snarled Cook, flinching from the prod of a stick.

"No, no, I don't think so," said Mindia. "I think they mean to keep us as slaves or servants."

"Can't do much work tied like a dog outside!"

"They seem to discuss and consider everything at length. I do not believe they make decisions quickly, at least not about ownership. I think they've been dickering about who gets us. Now the decision is final. That's why they've colored our bodies like this. I'm to belong to this house. It seems to be the biggest, so I assume it is the chief's."

"I don't belong to no one," Cook growled. "Least of all the likes of these."

From behind the throng a middle-aged man stepped forward. He was very small and stumpy-legged, with tiny eyes, but muscles padded his shoulders and thighs and he moved with the quick ease of the physically gifted. He was clad in red and possessed such an air of surety Mindia guessed he must be the leader of the house that now owned Cook. The red man, who Mindia was now certain was a rival of the yellow chief, began speaking. If he'd been a European, Mindia would have said from his tone that the man was boasting. The man pulled Cook toward him, one hand around the back of his neck as the other flashed to a belt at his waist. It happened so fast not even Cook could utter a protest. The knife, Cook's throat, and it was done. Blood cascaded forward, wetting Mindia from his knees to his feet.

Mindia strove with all his might to keep his composure in the face of Cook's hideous death. His own life might depend on it. The crowd was hushed but Mindia realized it wasn't from horror. The red chief and his people had the air of ones who have bettered an adversary. The yellows were downcast. The silence lengthened, and with it a feeling of expectation grew. Mindia tried hard not to look at Cook's crumpled form as he inched away from the spreading lake of blood.

The yellow chief stepped toward Mindia with the heavy movements of one about to perform a momentous act. Mindia steeled himself. At least this death would be quick!

The two men were almost the same height. He saw no malice in the man's face and calm, flat gaze, only curiosity. The man smiled and, instead of cleaving Mindia's neck, dropped to his hands and knees and began removing Mindia's boots, making him hop back and forth to keep his balance. With the boots off and Mindia's tattered socks pulled away, the chief stood up and bellowed triumphantly. Everyone crowded around to look at Mindia's feet. The three smallest toes on each foot were joined by webs of skin—a birth defect.

"*Utenok,*" his mother called him affectionately. "Duckling." His brother and boyhood friends had been less kind.

Tumult ensued. Women keened. Men groaned. In a flash of clarity Mindia realized that most of these people, both the reds and the yellows, had not known of his deformity. His cursed feet seemed to be a good thing, judging by their reaction, giving the yellow chief some sort of advantage over his red rival.

The deformity that had humiliated him as long as he could remember now saved his life. Mindia remembered waking up on deck bootless and sockless, his bare feet sticking up out of his rope-coil bed. The yellow chief had seen them then. In other circumstances Mindia might have laughed.

16

Mindia lost count of the months, let alone the weeks. At first he tried hard to keep the calendar in his mind, but eventually time as he knew it slipped into a series of daily events governed by the available light and the weather. In some ways he couldn't complain about his lot. Unlike the slaves taken from other tribes, more than two dozen in a village of roughly 170, Mindia shared the house of his owner and worked alongside other family members instead of being relegated to dirty tasks or collecting firewood. At first glance, finding firewood shouldn't have been a difficult chore in a land where trees were as plentiful as water in the ocean. But the village of the Kahnamut had been in the area since Gitsula washed up on shore 1,380 years earlier. Only after a big wind was firewood plentiful near the village.

✳

Though Mindia clearly held a favored position for a slave, Nik'ha'a, the chief, paid him very little direct attention, never speaking to him and issuing orders only through another family member. But the chief did spend considerable time studying his pale-skinned acquisition. Sometimes he just watched from a distance as Mindia performed simple functions, such as eating or attempting to clean his teeth with a sharpened stick. Other times he sat closely, even touching Mindia. The attention was not that of a man sizing up a friend, an enemy, or even an oddity brought from another place. It was the deliberation of a man trying to figure things out. Mindia had seen that look before in the face of his Venetian tutor, a fat, sloppy man with wet, red lips who looked like a scholarly monk studying the scriptures, when a map was placed before him. With little else to do, Mindia returned the favor, scrutinizing Nik'ha'a as carefully as he was being studied.

The chief was the tallest man in the village, and on the occasions when other tribes visited to trade or feast, Mindia noticed he was still the tallest.

Initially he wondered if the chief's physical stature alone had been sufficient to grant him the position he held. The chief was also darker-skinned than the rest, and when he was painted extravagantly, as he often was, the darkness of his skin stood out powerfully through the yellow and white paint he favored. The chief bathed frequently, which surprised Mindia, who equated cleanliness with civilization. When Nik'ha'a returned from the river, his paintless body was striking in its long, lean darkness, and Mindia could see another unusual feature about him—his hair. Unlike the Indians Mindia had seen in Acapulco—oh, that southern place seemed a visit in a nearly forgotten dream—all the savages here, the men at least, cut their hair to shoulder length or even shorter. The chief's hair was quite short but Mindia could see it was slightly kinky, not curly exactly but crimped somewhat. He guessed that was why one of the chief's wives so valued Mindia's beard hairs, which she trimmed regularly as if he were a sheep. Everyone, except the captive and the chief, had straight hair.

More than fifteen millennia had passed since Upper Paleolithic–era African blood had found its way to the Siberian Kamchatka Peninsula in the form of the great Nush-da travelers, the last of them Tooke and his grandson Manto. And ten millennia had been absorbed by the movement of people and animals in the northern reaches of the warming earth since Tooke, the last man of a destroyed civilization, had stumbled across deteriorating Beringia, the joining of northern Asia and Alaska. Had Tooke of the Nush-da escaped from his ravished homeland by venturing west into the territory of the nomadic Siberians, no trace of his heritage would likely have remained in the Northern Hemisphere. The people of the steppes were not forgiving of difference. In fact they feared it. Tooke would certainly have been killed. But the snow travelers of late–Ice Age Alaska lived by different gods and were ruled by different prohibitions. As a result, Tooke had been honored. The rich heritage of Tooke had become a trickle by Gitsula's time, but every few generations the old world of the African continent surfaced in a rounder eye, a longer face, a duskier skin, a denser musculature, coarse, wool-like hair, and sometimes great height.

As his grasp of the language improved and he started to understand their customs, Mindia realized that Nik'ha'a had achieved his position because he was astute. He did not so much accumulate wealth, though he had plenty of that, as he had the ability to create it for others. For that the villagers were grateful and beholden—but also afraid. One who could create and confer wealth could also take it away.

Nik'ha'a also guarded his stories closely, which gave rise to fears that the tales untold might be too powerful for ordinary ears. The stories the chief did tell emphasized his birth blessing by the Raven and his connection to the salmon-frog woman, Gitsula, who was the first to live on this almost-island. It was her legacy that kindled Nik'ha'a's interest in Mindia. Like Mindia, she was deformed, the offspring of a powerful salmon come to land and not able to shed its fish body entirely. The salmon had lost its way and had come ashore carrying its children in its mouth—two dozen small, pale-green eggs. The salmon, in female form, had few fingers, just finlike stumps at the ends of her normally shaped arms.

At the interior of the almost-island lay a small lake, thick with beaver, muskrat, ducks, and black frogs with yellow throats. In the spring and fall the frog songs could be heard for miles. The most powerful frog in that lake felt sorry for the salmon person. He loaned her his hands, which were long and dextrous, though webbed. In return she gave him the fins, which allowed him to swim far faster than any of the other frogs and eventually rule the lake itself.

But the gift became a curse. As his dominion increased over the swampy banks of the lake the other frogs were driven off to inhabit friendlier waters. He became lonely. Soon his plaintive *keeerrup! keeerrup!* was the only sound of his kind. Desperate for company, he sought out the salmon-frog woman to ask for his hands back. But she had become a great weaver, turning the *slowi* of cedar into soft blankets and skirts. She would not give back the hands. However, she did agree to marry the frog and give him a child to ease his loneliness.

When the child came, he bore no mark of either the salmon people or the frog, but they rejoiced nonetheless in his nut-brown skin and incredibly long, slender fingers. Nik'ha'a claimed descent from that child and at his naming feast boldly declared the black frog as his guardian spirit, claiming also possession of the green eggs, which he wore around his neck in a pouch made from the stomach of a bear. He was challenged by a family who had long carved their house totem with the wide mouth of the frog facing front and its arms and toes wrapped all the way around the pole. But Nik'ha'a spun his version of the story of his connection to the salmon woman and the frog so eloquently, so persuasively that no one doubted that it was true. The other family raged when it was decided he must indeed have the right of the frog. To their immense surprise, and that of the whole village, Nik'ha'a had no sooner been admitted to adulthood than he offered to share the frog.

"I will take care of my black-skinned, yellow-throated ancestor, but you must not abandon his brothers and sisters who are green like the forest," Nik'ha'a offered grandly.

In time, as water subtly demonstrates its power one drop at a time upon a rock, Nik'ha'a's generosity solidified his power in small and gradual ways. Upon that foundation was built his current position as chief.

And now this person had appeared in their midst, carried to them by the boat with white wings. That he was of the salmon Nik'ha'a had no doubt. Was he not marked as such? Were his feet not those of the fish or the frog? Why he was here was a different matter and it sorely puzzled the chief.

"I have wronged the salmon perhaps?" he speculated to the *sqomten*, medicine man.

"He was meant to live and walk upon our land," opined the *sqomten*, preferring not to answer directly until he understood the drift of the chief's concern. He was secretly as intrigued by the curly, light-haired one with the furry chest and whiskery chin as was the chief, but he dared not let on. His role was to interpret portents and seek answers where baser individuals could not. He'd learned it was best to seem detached from day-to-day matters while keeping his utterances as brief and mysterious as possible. In this manner he made himself seem wise and insightful.

The *sqomten* was also well aware that the frog-given family were among those who felt Mindia deserved the same fate as Cook. The frog-given family had never become comfortable with the chief's generosity, and the *sqomten* believed the more prominent members of the house were on the lookout for expressions of Nik'ha'a's weakness, which would allow them to regain their sole representations of the frog.

"Had it not been intended that he should feel our land beneath his feet," the *sqomten* continued, "he would have died beneath the wings of his boat."

"But why has he come?" pondered Nik'ha'a. "And what do I do with him?"

"You look at it crossways," corrected the *sqomten*, scratching himself with his divining stick, a rare, dead-straight piece of arbutus branch headed by dried horsetails bound to the end with gut. "You may not be required to do anything. His appearance may have nothing to do with you."

"But I am of the salmon woman and the frog!" the chief protested. "You saw his feet. He must be of the salmon. How can his appearance have nothing to do with me?"

The *sqomten* shrugged. "Perhaps he is your brother bearing the mark of the salmon, which you lack."

Nik'ha'a was shocked into silence. This was always the way with the *sqomten*, never producing a clear answer to a problem.

If the man they called Mindia was indeed his brother, he should immediately be given a place in the center of the longhouse—and also a chance to prove himself as belonging. No man wanted to be elevated without the pride of some deed to support him. That was fine for women—they were born more complete than men. But a man had to mark every important passage of age or situation by earning it, which was especially true of Nik'ha'a's family, because they were of the salmon that bravely fought their way from the ocean, up the mighty Stahlo, to mate, die, be reborn, and begin the journey again.

Nik'ha'a already had a brother, Siaq, a *stam'ya*—soft man—but all things considered, he wouldn't mind another.

✸

Most times Mindia felt like a ghost, tagging along behind one group or another, helping, learning, but rarely being spoken to by adults. After nearly a year with the tribe he knew the language well enough to converse, but no one seemed to care. He should be grateful, he kept telling himself, that his days weren't spent in the pouring rain gathering firewood or performing some other menial task. His owner family had long ago ceased to confine him, and he slept in one corner of the longhouse. He was also better fed than other slaves, especially at this time of year, late into winter, when the salmon stores for most houses, except the chief's, were long gone. While the rest were gnawing on the drier, more tasteless flesh of easily caught whitefish, the chief's family and Mindia enjoyed the oily richness of preserved salmon skin and fingerlike strips of dark-red meat, which had been dried and packed in eulachon oil.

But Mindia was lonely, overwhelmed by a yawning despair that ate away at his insides like an endless hunger. At times he felt so weak in his solitude he could barely move his arms and legs. One morning, when the malaise was too powerful to resist, he lay in his corner on a piece of rough hide, with a cedar-bark blanket wrapped around him, and didn't even lift his head as the family busied themselves stoking the fires, eating their first meal of the day, talking and laughing among themselves. It was early spring and the entire village was eager to prepare for the last hunt before they moved to the Stahlo for the first salmon run of the season.

It would be an exciting hunt, for they were to journey across the inlet to the mountainous lands of the Kiapilanoq, whose chief was widely regarded as one of the most powerful among the seven tribes and 127 *okwumuq*, villages, occupying the coastal areas running from Washington's Puget Sound to the northern tip of Vancouver Island, including the area which would eventually be the city of Vancouver and the broad deltas of the Fraser Valley. For several weeks they would hunt the elusive mountain goat and brown bear. The goats for wool, horns, and springy ribs, and the bear for its rich meat and hide.

The hunt was Siaq's time. For the past week Nik'ha'a's brother had slept apart from his wife—he had only one—and cleansed himself twice daily. In between he fasted and flailed his naked body with ropes of prickly blackberry canes, just as a girl at puberty would do to make herself alert and intelligent for her adult years. In the same manner, after every lashing he covered himself with a blanket to soak up the blood, which represented a girl's monthly flow. He bathed in the salt sea, crying out loud at the pain from the scratches on his body. Siaq also rubbed his body with cedar tips, as a girl would to encourage fertility and make herself attractive to men. During the week prior to the hunt Siaq had no contact with his brother or any other men of the tribe. Mindia dully pondered the reasons for this ritual. It bore no resemblance to anything else he had seen in these savages' various forms of worship. Early in the week he asked one of the older boys what it meant.

"It is for the hunt," the boy replied grudgingly. "You will see."

Since Mindia was not going to the hunt, he obviously would not see.

✳

"You come!" Mindia felt a prod in his back. The morning was well advanced but still he had not moved. "You come."

Mindia opened his eyes but couldn't make out the figure haloed before him as the morning light shot around his figure.

"We leave. You come. You travel with *stacem*. You will guard them and Siaq."

Mindia jumped up. It was the chief. Nik'ha'a hadn't spoken to him since he had been captured. Mindia's heart leaped happily as if a disapproving father had finally broken silence with an out-of-favor son.

Nik'ha'a was dressed plainly for such an important occasion, an undecorated cedar blanket draped over one shoulder, a short skirt of *slowi* covering his loins, his feet clad in simple moccasins. He wore little paint on his body.

"Where are we going?" Mindia ventured.

Nik'ha'a frowned and left the house. There was a piece of fat on the floor for Mindia to eat, and he noticed a wooden bowl with a milky substance in it for him to drink. He devoured both before dashing out of the house, shedding his malaise as if it had never been.

The boats were arrayed in the bay, thirteen in all. The chief occupied the largest with the males of his family, all except Siaq. One of the smaller boats held seven children, from about six to eleven years of age. The younger ones were crying, the older ones shushing them. Mindia recognized them as the *stacem*: children born to female slaves made pregnant by ranking members of the village.

On shore, a group of older girls, including two of the chief's daughters, danced on a wool-goat blanket just at the shoreline. Mindia recognized the intricate patterns. It was the *hausalktl*, or novice dance, graceful and slow, their movements paced by older women beating on cedar boards.

"Pretty girls," he heard a giggle at his shoulder. "You will dip yourself in one of them one day?"

Mindia turned, almost biting his tongue in surprise. It was Siaq, brother to the chief, the man-woman from his first day of capture. He was ludicrously dressed and painted as a woman. Even his voice was pitched higher, seductive. He grabbed Mindia's arm and pulled him toward the boat, his walk changing from the longer strides of a man to the shorter ones of a woman eager to attract the attention of a suitor.

"Where, where am I going?" Mindia stammered.

"With me of course. We ride the *stacem* boat. You are the protector."

"Why are the children in the boat and why are they crying?"

"Probably they have heard stories that some might be sacrificed. It is enough to make anyone cry," he added airily as if discussing a broken weir or a lost dog.

"Why are we going on that boat?" Mindia was instantly fearful. Perhaps that was his fate too.

"Because you are who you are and I am the soft man. To have the salmon man in the other boats would bring bad luck. Same for a woman."

"Why am I their protector then?"

"Why? Why? Why? You are like a child," Siaq teased. "You wear me out with your questions."

It was strange, after months of hardly being spoken to, suddenly to have the chief's brother chatting with him as if they were life-long friends.

"The *stacem* need a protector, or the orca, the black-and-white whale, might mistake them for food. With a protector on board, especially a salmon man, the orca will recognize that the children belong to humans and will not touch them."

Mindia desperately wanted to ask Siaq why he was dressed as a woman but he could not bring himself to pose the question. They were ankle-deep in the water with Siaq ushering him along. As they climbed into the boat, a plaited hide rope was tossed to one of the larger boats, which would tow them and the children. The knocking of sticks against logs on the shore beat a hypnotic rhythm and the girls swayed gently on the blanket. As they pulled out to the shouts of the oarsmen, the girls stepped off the blanket and the women flung themselves on it, hacking off bits of the rare wool to carry back to their houses. They would eat and drink frugally until the men returned, and carry their piece of the blanket as a talisman of their men's safe return.

The boat rounded Sqelc, the sacred standing-up rock where Gitsula once lay near death. Mindia could see the southern hills of Ialmuq, which one day would become Jericho Hill, some of the most valuable real estate in North America. Farther on, he spied the regal nose of Ilksn, Point Grey, where the University of British Columbia would spread out into the forests. On they pressed to Houltcison, Capilano Creek, home of a great chief.

17

*

"No one prepares herring spawn like Kiapilanoq women," pronounced Siaq, smacking his lips. Mindia knew the word for herring but spawn eluded him. "You will see," said Siaq when he asked. "Your belly will never be the same."

He leaned closer, the braids added to his hair brushing Mindia's shoulder and the boat rocking slightly with his movement. "I tell that to my wife and then she doesn't let me in for days," he laughed and sat back on his heels. "She is a good cook and is right to be mad for my praising the Kiapilanoq women. But when she lets me back in the house she prepares such meals! She never says anything but I know she is trying to prove to me that no Kiapilanoq woman can match her. I eat like a bear in spring."

*

Over the long winter months Mindia had slipped into a cautious acceptance of his fate. He had begun to decipher the ways of the Kahnamut, their curious sense of humor, and the elaborate structure of their society. In spite of himself he felt admiration for their skills, which created a standard of living in the forest to equal anything he had known in Georgia or Italy. The savages' massive lodges were comfortable, airy, and, for the most part, smoke-free, something he'd never known in Georgian winters, where fireplaces spewed as much smoke as an outdoor bonfire. Though many fires burned in each lodge, constant adjustments of the movable roof planks provided ventilation and draft. It was the woman's job to keep the planks over her family's area placed properly.

The Kahnamut had no written language but they had stories. As Mindia came to know them and heard certain stories told several times, he realized that their language was as different from his as a sentence from a painting. Everything said could be shaded and layered. Sometimes he thought that they didn't speak so much as evoke images shaped by the speaker as a potter molds clay.

✳

The Kahnamut had half a dozen ways of doing everything according to the tools at hand or the whim of the person doing the work. They took great delight in adding their own individual twists or signatures to that which had been done since time began. Even the simple task of drying the oily eulachon fish differed from one family to the next. Some threaded the six-inch-long bony fish on pliable cedar or hemlock boughs, then knotted the end of the bough to form a circle. Others impaled the fish through the gills with a thicker piece of hazel or hardtack. The women in the chief's family pulled the head of one eulachon through the mouth of another then hung the two joined fish over a branch to be dried and smoked. Each method had its proponents who would argue for hours about which produced the best quality, taste, and texture.

✳

Nearly a year after his capture Mindia felt he was beginning to understand these people. Except for Siaq. Mindia knew about male prostitutes and had often seen the she-boys of Venice parading their wares not far from the apartment he'd occupied until his fateful meeting with the old Greek. But the sudden transformation of a man he had heard boast of his sexual prowess and his ability as a warrior into this perverted, if rather convincing, figure was beyond his comprehension.

✳

"Get on with you!" shouted Siaq good-naturedly as Enoqua, son of Nik'ha'a and soon to be a man, stuck out his paddle from a passing boat and teased Siaq's added hair.

"Who does the lady choose!" the boy sang out.

"Not you, even if you were a man and not the son of my brother," retorted Siaq. "I would leave you cold and lonely to be eaten by the wolf."

"Then I would slay the wolf and wrap myself in his coat for warmth and not share the meat with the likes of you!" Enoqua shot back.

Siaq shook his head. "He will be a great hunter one day. Right now, he is fearless and foolish. But he has strength I have rarely seen in one so young. We will try to turn back the foolish in him with this hunt."

"Is that the purpose of the hunt?" asked Mindia.

"Of course. Enoqua will take the head of the Great Bear. We are here to help. The bear will provide Enoqua's dancing head until he is taken out of life, and the skin will give him a bed to lie with his first woman. That is," added Siaq, "if he does well."

"And if he doesn't do well?"

"Then my brother will be shamed and it is certain we will have poor catch when the salmon come back to seek their home."

Sometimes Mindia thought these people were just plain simple-minded for connecting the act of a boy with the amount of fish eventually caught in a net. But every now and then the firmness of the Kahnamuts' convictions made him wonder what they saw that he couldn't. Perhaps such convictions released a man from endless ruminations about his fate. Dear God, if he could only know what was in store for him, the sleepless nights, the loneliness, the pining for conversation over Venetian coffee and black Russian bread spread with fresh goat cheese might come to an end.

"There is another purpose to this hunt," Siaq confided.

"What is that?"

"The Kiapilanoq have been uneasy friends for many generations. We watch each other's fires across the water, on winter's nights, wondering about the next time we meet."

That was true. Mindia had seen it. During the cold, rainy nights Nik'ha'a ordered large fires built on the shores of their permanent village at Qoiqoi, around the point of the near island from Sqelc, the standing-up rock where Gitsula had met the Raven. There the villagers squatted in the heat of the flames, discussing their neighbors across the inlet who, in turn, noted the Kahnamuts' fires and built even larger ones of their own.

"And for the same time the Kiapilanoq have been long enemies of the Ukeltaws," Siaq continued.

"I have heard of them," Mindia offered. "Nik'ha'a's first wife was angry at her children and told them the Ukeltaws would come and suck their blood out. They cried and begged to be forgiven."

"They have not bothered us, because we are protected by the salmon-frog woman's eggs."

Siaq referred to lustrous, pale-green beads worn around the chief's neck on important occasions.

"How can little stones protect an entire village?" scoffed Mindia.

"They may appear as stones to you, but to everyone else they are the eggs of the salmon-frog woman. What is seen and believed is what is," Siaq said firmly.

"But how can they protect you?" persisted Mindia.

"There would be no point," Siaq replied. "If we were destroyed, the frog-with-hands would find the eggs and cause them to bring forth more of our people. But the Kiapilanoq have no such protection."

"So you believe your people are immortal?" asked Mindia, using a string of words that meant "never can be killed."

"No, no, you don't understand," chided Siaq. "We might die at the hands of the Ukeltaw, but our blood would take human form again, thanks to the salmon-frog woman's eggs. Nik'ha'a's grandfather was clever to make sure the Ukeltaw knew that so they would fear it forever."

"But if you have had no contact with them and their home is far away to the north, how did the information get to them?"

Siaq laughed again. This man might be of the salmon but he had a mind like roe box—the specially constructed cedar boxes made completely airtight, in which they stored salmon roe. The boxes were buried in sea water until the eggs had fermented into a delicious, gelatinous mass. Nothing could get in or out of these boxes. Mindia's mind was like that.

"You do not pass important information like this," Siaq leaned forward and touched his lips to Mindia's ear.

Mindia barely dared breathe, not wanting to insult Siaq by moving away.

"You do it like this."

Siaq lined up a row of six pebbles. He pointed at himself. "I am the chief's grandfather." Then he picked up the first pebble. "Stlatlumh." He uttered the name of people to the north who would be known as Lillooet. "Stlatlumh to Stó:lō." He touched the first pebble to the second. "Stó:lō to Tcilkotin." Pebble two tapped pebble three. And on he went down the line until he reached the sixth stone, which he picked up and touched to Mindia's ear. "And to Ukeltaw. Now they know."

"But how would he know the right information reaches the Ukeltaw?" puzzled Mindia. "After so many tribes passed it along, it might not be anything like what he wanted them to know."

Siaq sighed. The roe box of this one's head was very tight indeed. "It doesn't matter. The story grows and changes as it travels. The Ukeltaw warrior chief will know that. It will bother him, causing him to consider the story from all angles. He will wonder what the root of the story looks like if he has seen only the petal of the flower. He will consult his wise ones and they too will ponder it. Finally they will decide that it is best to leave alone what is not fully understood. And that is how we are protected," he finished triumphantly.

"In my home no one trusts gossip," Mindia used the phrase which meant "words passed along." "And we build fortresses to protect ourselves from invaders. We do not trust such a weak defense as stories that might not even be told properly."

"Truly, you have the wisdom of a mouse!" Siaq marveled. "Are all who live on the winged boats as simple as you?"

He continued on when no answer was forthcoming. "A long time ago the first salmon man explained how he came to walk on the land," Siaq pointed meaningfully to Mindia's webbed feet. "His words passed along saved *your* life. And," Siaq added referring to Cook, "stockades and winged boats did not protect the life of the skinny, angry man. How can you, of all people, doubt the power of these words?"

Mindia was so engrossed in the joy of having his first lengthy conversation in nearly a year he didn't notice how quickly they had crossed the inlet. The first Kahnamut boats were already beached and the men hauled baskets and weapons from them while the Kiapilanoq strung large deer-hide bags of supplies on poles.

Kiapilanoq women danced and chanted, entreating the men not to disappoint them in the hunt and imploring them to return home honored. Like the Kahnamut women across the inlet at Qoiqoi, when the men headed up river into the dark canyon, up through the dense forests and along the mountainous plateau where they hoped to find the Great Bear, the Kiapilanoq women would fast and drink sparingly until the men returned.

Mindia wandered around wondering what he was to do. At the river's edge he came across a small fenced enclosure where the children were penned. They were largely silent, wide-eyed, and pale. As he stared at them, pitying them in their terror, Siaq ran up.

"Come, come! We start now!" he shouted excitedly, his extravagant hair bobbing around his shoulders, the caked paint on his face cracking as he smiled.

"Bring the tall girl," he instructed, "and," he pointed to a small, shivering boy crouched in one corner, "that boy."

The girl stood rigidly, slowly shaking her head back and forth. "Not me!" her eyes pleaded.

They walked for hours. At first the going was easy along the broad, pebbled edge of the river, but as it began to turn north, cutting a canyon deep into the mountain, the way became difficult. Mindia had learned to navigate the forest but the land he'd lived on for the past eleven months was largely flat. This steep rocky terrain made him pant and slip as he tried to keep up. The two children had no such difficulty, nor did Siaq, who cavorted along the column of men like a grotesque village joker, pinching bottoms and slapping backs. Mindia could make out the voice of Enoqua calling out to the bear, warning he was coming.

That night they camped near a waterfall. Mindia, once again, was largely ignored. By the next night they were high up in the mountains. Siaq became even more frenzied in his entertainment of the men, teasing and cajoling them with an exhibition of the worst coquetry Mindia had ever seen. The third night the men set up a more permanent camp, building two large shelters using brush and the hide bundles they'd brought with them.

Siaq constructed his own small tent, searching for logs to make a rough foundation, then carefully securing a hide roof to the branches. Every man who passed was treated to his playful seductions.

"What are you doing?" Mindia demanded of Siaq, unable to stem his curiosity any longer. The words sounded hysterical even to his ears. "Why are you behaving like a . . . a . . ." he searched for a Kahnamut word that meant whore but the best he could come up with was "silly girl."

"I *am* a silly girl," Siaq responded matter-of-factly. "I am *stam'ya*, the soft one. I will take a man. Who I choose I don't know. If they are lucky I will take two or three."

Mindia was aghast. "You will sleep with a man!"

"All of them if I choose to. A man can easily be a woman," Siaq smiled. "All it takes is a little bear grease."

Mindia hadn't thought he could be any more shocked by Siaq than he already was, but the implications of his last statement made him want to vomit.

"You, you can't possibly sleep with *all* the men on the hunt!"

Siaq laughed. "I can choose all, or none, or only one. Even you!" He leaned toward Mindia, who recoiled so quickly he almost fell over. "You would like it. I know."

Thoroughly relishing Mindia's discomfort, Siaq danced around him, wagging his fingers, moving faster and faster until Mindia grew dizzy following him. Finally Siaq stopped and said in a more normal voice: "There is another purpose. The soft man fools the bear, who is not easily tricked. The bear knows women do not hunt, so if the bear sees a woman in camp it will not be nervous of us.

"But you have a wife!" sputtered Mindia.

"Of course I have a wife," Siaq explained patiently. "She is very lucky to have married the soft man. When the winter fish run out she still eats salmon from the chief's store."

"Isn't that because you are the chief's brother?"

"Oh no. We had another brother. He was poor and lazy. Nik'ha'a gave him food for a time, though he didn't earn it. One day he cast him out of the lodge, saying his name would be spoken no longer. Now we have no brother.

"My wife has a cape made of deer tails," Siaq continued. "And her own boat and many wool-goat blankets. Also, she has rights to a large clam bed. And, of course, she has me. She considers herself very fortunate."

Revolted though he was, Mindia couldn't contain his curiosity. "Do other people, um, practice this, uh, tradition?"

The garrulous Siaq was only too happy to expand on his proud role. He had nothing else to do as the hunters were busy scouting for scat and scratching trees or rocks the bears frequented.

"*Wamusp*," he said. "It is a borrowed word from the warm lands of the milk tree. Our stories say it is from those people that we learned. The *wamusp* are man-woman, both and neither. They do not help on the hunt or work in any way but they are teachers of children, and holy ones."

"Holy ones!" gasped Mindia. "In my faith such people would be cast out, or worse."

Siaq's expression made it clear he thought Mindia's land was full of people with ridiculous ideas.

"I have never met them but far, far across the big mountains," Siaq pointed to the east, "are the *winkte* of the Lakota. We do not trade with them, but we trade with the Stó:lō upriver and they trade with the Kootnai, and they trade with those who trade with the Lakota. In words passed along, I was given the story of the *winkte*. They are wise men who stay always as women. They are chosen for it as children."

Mindia's head spun. Siaq was enjoying his agitation hugely. These were serious matters, his role and the responsibility he had. But there was no censure against using his stories to make himself laugh inside by poking at the tall, ugly one.

A shout rose up nearby. Four men, two from each tribe, trotted into sight. They excitedly waved their arms and one rushed up to hug Siaq who returned the hug with a loving caress of the man's hair. Mindia shuddered.

"The bear track is found," Siaq declared. "It is unusual for it to happen so fast. We have very good luck. I told the Kiapilanoq it is you who brought the luck."

The men organized themselves into tracking and killing parties. They would find the bear before begging its forgiveness with the sacrifice of the first child. Enoqua would face the bear first, but he would not be expected to make the kill—only to behave as a warrior. After Enoqua's opportunity, they would bleed the bear by launching fifteen or twenty spears into its thick hide, taking care to avoid the head.

Enoqua was almost beside himself with anticipation. He jigged and hopped from one foot to the other, hoisting his spear high and shouting: "Success to me! Success to my house!" Once the bear was surrounded, he would have the honor of stepping forward to land the first blow.

Mindia heard a moan. The girl had been listening to Siaq's stories; now the reality of her situation returned along with her terror. In her keening Mindia could make out prayers for a quick death.

"You will go with Enoqua," Siaq announced to Mindia with a big grin on his face. "The chiefs think you have luck, that you will guide the boy's spear to the heart of the bear."

"Me?" Mindia said stupidly.

"You," Siaq agreed.

Nik'ha'a appeared. "Share your luck with my son," he said solemnly. It sounded like an order to Mindia.

They began the next morning in the pink-gray light of early dawn. The hunters had found the bear's track the previous day but it still took long slow hours to close in. The ground was extremely rocky as it rose from the canyon shelf. The bear was moving into higher ground and the men were anxious to drive it downward, closer to the canyon. Mindia was instructed to stay back with Enoqua and the other spear throwers, to be ready if the trackers turned the bear. Its winter lair was high up in the mountain but the food was lower down. The men were prepared for a long hunt. The breeze was brisk and from the south; they would have to be careful or the bear would catch the scent of man and either flee beyond their reach or turn and become the hunter himself.

The wind was unusually warm for so early in the spring. Mindia sat upon a rock and found himself enjoying the distinctive scents of fir and cedar surrounding him. It struck him that he now smelled things he never even knew had an aroma. Shouts floated into his drifting consciousness. His eyes snapped open. Enoqua was nowhere to be seen.

"Miaqutl! Miaqutl!"

Mindia knew the word. It meant the cinnamon bear, unusual so close to the sea. Miaqutl skins and heads were highly prized possessions of the Stlatlumh who lived farther north and deeper into the mountains. No one in the village had one. That Enoqua should have the chance to send the first spear into such a bear was an extraordinary stroke of fortune.

The boy came running at full speed toward Mindia. Almost screaming in his excitement he told Mindia his father had instructed them to stay near the canyon and wait for the bear to come to them. Enoqua would then sneak up and plunge the first spear. Mindia could hear a dreadful howling. The first of the sacrificial children, the boy, was cut in the stomach and staked to the ground. The bear was coming. The other would be sacrificed at the death of the bear.

The next moments were like a fast-moving thunderstorm, lightning flashes on top of thunder claps. Miaqutl came. Crashing through the brush it loped toward the sound of the crying child. Angry and hungry, the bear created an amazing amount of noise. Trackers moved softly through the woods. Once the bear was on the move and in the direction they wanted they drew back.

Suddenly it was in sight. Enormous, glossy, regal. Mindia crouched behind a boulder with Enoqua squatting beside him. Never before had he seen anything so magnificent, so terrifyingly powerful! Mindia and Enoqua crept forward. Once the first spear was set and the cry of success went up the other spear men would close in. Enoqua said nothing but Mindia could hear him breathing heavily.

For such an immense animal the bear moved with extraordinary speed. One minute it was nearly on top of the crying child and the next it whirled to face Mindia and Enoqua's hiding place. Rising on its hind legs, the bear sniffed the air, mouth open, eyes searching. Barely had Mindia time to admire the animal's height than it dropped to all fours and leaped toward them. Enoqua cannoned into him. Whimpering loudly, the boy dropped his spear, ran pell-mell for the canyon, and dove into a crevice just on the edge of the canyon wall. The bear pounded after him, roaring at the cowering boy who was just beyond the reach of its paws.

Where were the other men? Were they frightened too or did their culture demand that they wait for the boy to announce the success of his strike? Mindia snatched up a rock and flung it at the bear. A ridiculous missile. It missed. The bear turned at the clatter, small eyes boring into his. Mindia's heart swelled as if the bear's own rage filled him. He could smell the animal's sour breath and feel waves of dank heat coming from it. He hefted a second rock and threw it hard. It bounced off the bear's snout and the great beast bellowed in anger. It was now fully focused on Mindia. The spear! Where was the spear? Mindia's desperately groping fingers found it.

Miaqutl launched itself at Mindia, who braced his back against a boulder and drove the spear with all his might into the creature's eye. The bear dropped to all fours roaring, shaking his head back and forth, trying to rid itself of the irritant. Mindia knew that it was not a killing blow and the animal would turn on him in a moment. There was no escape and no sign of the other hunters.

Then it happened. One of the most surefooted creatures of the Pacific lands slipped. In its thrashings it turned too quickly and the force skittered its leg over the cliff edge. For the briefest moment the young Georgian mapmaker and the two-thousand-pound brown bear stared at each other in disbelief. Backward and down it went, bellowing until Mindia heard a heavy thud, then nothing.

✳

The celebration at Houltcison, the mouth of the Capilano River, was exuberant. So loud was the singing, cheering, and laughing that the women, children, and elderly at Qoiqoi could hear and knew their men had been successful. They immediately began to prepare for a feast of their own.

Enoqua had acquitted himself extraordinarily well. Mindia was given audience before the two chiefs and he described how the bear cornered them and how the boy had stood his ground, drawing the beast in, before attacking at the last instant. The bear had fallen to the river below but the men were able to clamber down and butcher it.

For bringing the boy such good luck the two chiefs granted Mindia his freedom. He was also given the *stacem* girl who had not been sacrificed after all. The bear was dead but the bait, the boy, still lived—at least for a few days. They decided that since the boy's death had not been needed to coax the life out of the bear, then the girl's was also not needed to help the bear spirit find a new form.

After several days of feasting, Mindia's head and belly grew heavy with a fine weariness. He danced, yelled at the moon, bathed in the saltwater at dawn, and covered himself with paint given to him by the Kiapilanoq. He felt strangely happy and sad at the same time. Once tears sprang to his eyes as he thought of his mother, and in a restless doze after dancing for hours his father's face appeared and smiled as if bidding him a good sleep, which he'd done every night when Mindia was a boy. His old world seemed as close as the images from a book just read.

The night before the Kahnamut left for their own village, Siaq came.

"When the sun rises I am man again. Tonight I choose to be yours."

Mindia demurred as politely as possible.

"Sometimes I choose for bravery. Sometimes for other reasons. Sometimes I do not choose. This time I choose only you."

"Why?" Mindia croaked.

"The boy is no coward but he would appear as one . . . if not for you."

"How did you know?" Mindia asked. Siaq could not have seen what happened on the cliff's edge.

"He was very troubled so he came to me. Things are said to the soft man that could not be said to anyone else."

"Why would he tell you? No one saw but me. A slave."

"What happens does not cease to exist because no man sees it."

"What did you tell him?"

"That the bear came to test *you*. It was proper for Enoqua to get out of the way. I told him his test would come one day. He would know it when it happened. And I believe what I told him." Then he added with a smile, "Almost every word.

"So now I choose you."

Mindia looked around. Some men were sleeping, others were eating. He could just make them out near the shoreline at the clam pits that smoked in the dim moonlight. Faintly in the distance he could hear singing.

Mindia opened his arms and stepped forward.

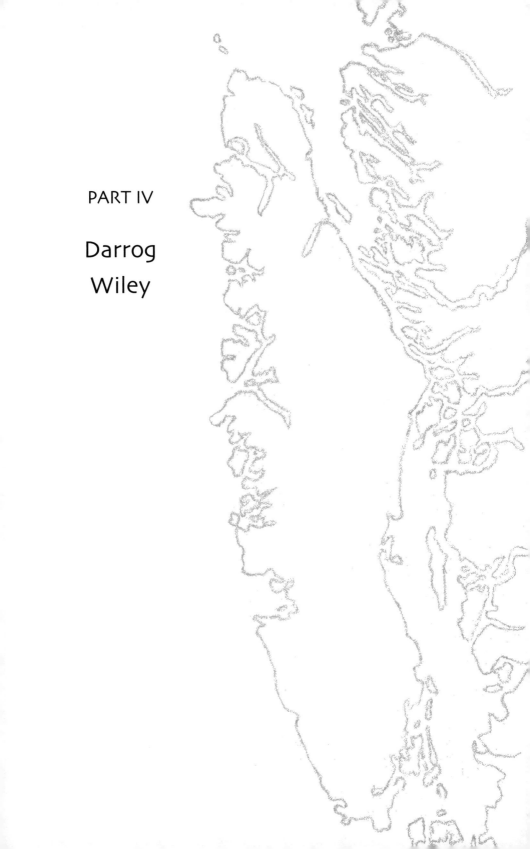

PART IV

Darrog
Wiley

18

✳

Henry Douglas sniffed, a grimace spreading across his long, droopy features. Glumly he poked a finger into the cloudy liquid and touched it to his tongue.

"Lost its pickle."

"I'd say," came the reply from a prow-chested, heavily whiskered man standing at his shoulder.

"What are we going to do?"

"Prevaricate." The fancy word seemed at odds with the rough outline of Darrog Wiley, Cameron clan, Glenlivet, Upper Banffshire.

Wiley had been a fur man since a cousin, Aeneas Cameron, recruited him for the service of the North West Company. Wiley turned eighteen on the Atlantic, twenty in a freight canoe on the St. Lawrence River, twenty-three on the diabolical Methy Portage connecting the far northern Churchill and Athabasca Rivers and counted his first quarter century sheltering beneath a lightweight *canot du nord* surrounded by Indian trade goods destined for the Sioux territory of the southern Red River. Wiley was a proud Nor'Wester, a voyageur who claimed dominion of the river and wilderness. He, and others like him, believed they were infinitely superior to the employees of the rival Hudson's Bay Company; men who sat protected in their forts and waited for furs to be brought to them.

At twenty-seven Wiley quit the North West Company and purchased his own canoe to work as a Freeman, selling beaver and buffalo skins to the highest bidder. There were many to choose from. In 1819 seven companies were pushing madly into the American and British northern and western territories. The real flurry that year was in Oregon, after the 1818 treaty required both countries to share their riches. In between trapping seasons, Wiley purchased slaves captured deep along the Snake River and sold them to Yankee skippers anchored in Astoria Bay at the mouth of the Columbia, who then traded them for sea-otter skins with tribes along the northwest Washington coast.

Wiley celebrated his thirtieth birthday inside the walls of John Jacob Astor's Fort Astoria, resting his head for the first and only time in his life on a down pillow with a silk casing. He'd won a night in the bed from the fort's second in command, a Boston man who taught Wiley the Cajun game of *poque*. Wiley also won the man's library, which consisted of a Bible and a dictionary, as well as the company of his two Flathead squaws, who had been captured to the north on the Spokane River. On the last night of his third decade Wiley slept with warm brown breasts pressed against his back and warm brown buttocks snugged into his crotch. He returned the slaves the next day but kept the Bible and dictionary. Reading was a legacy of his mother: "A single Cameron has more brains than a village of McDonalds! Get to tha' readin' young mon." As a result, Wiley knew a lot of unusual words. He liked to pull them out and show them off as if they were rare gems.

✳

"Prevaricate," Wiley repeated blandly to the frothing man beside him.

"How in bloody hell can you lie about four thousand salmon rotting in fifty-eight barrels because they've lost their pickle?"

"Who suggested we lie? I'm recommending some judicious equivocation, a slight obfuscation of the exact facts."

"Bloody lying in anyone else's book," muttered Henry Douglas. "Exactly what do you have in mind?"

"You'll recall we've still got sixteen good barrels."

"By sheer fool's luck," Douglas responded.

The previous winter, with the recently packed salmon barrels taking up every bit of spare area in the fort, Douglas had run out of room to store the pickling salt and musket powder from England as well as five hundred pounds of tallow, enough to last until the first boats arrived in the spring. The salt, powder, tallow, and sixteen leftover barrels went into the cellar. When the Hudson's Bay Company built Fort Langley on the banks of the broad Fraser River, fourteen miles upstream from the mouth, no one imagined that the big, sluggish river could turn so quickly into a swelling torrent. But then no one this side of Cherrapunji, India, where monsoon was a year-round event, had seen the like of these rains before either. The tallow and the sixteen barrels were the only things that survived the flood.

"We thought the barrels were ruint," marveled Wiley, "but the wet swelled the staves and they came through just fine. Not the best pickle but good enough for the Manchu's I'd reckon."

Henry Douglas sighed heavily. What a mess. He'd been at Fort Langley since it was built two years earlier, in 1827. Nine months ago, the chief factor Gilbert Thorpe was called to the carpet in London to explain their poor profitability. His return had been delayed twice, which left Douglas, his assistant, doing both their jobs while frantically scrambling to fulfill the company's ceaseless demand for profit. Though Douglas had all the chief factor's responsibilities as well as his own, he still collected only an assistant's pay. And the troubles were endless.

Since the North West Company and the Hudson's Bay amalgamated in 1821, Governor George Simpson, eager to drive other rivals under, had been sending ever more strident letters urging all the western and northern forts to be more businesslike and cut costs. Just how that was to be done was never specified. Simpson's generation was accustomed to profits of fifty percent or more on furs, and a hundred percent wasn't uncommon. But that was in the eastern Canadas and along the Red River. Life was different on the west coast, far different.

"We can't possibly send out a handful of barrels to Canton and Brazil and expect them to do anything but laugh at us when we ask for payment," protested Douglas.

"If I may take liberty with the Psalms," suggested Wiley, "the best way to get is to give. Cast your bread upon the waters. St. Joseph might not have had barrels of salmon in mind when he said that but I'm sure he'd approve."

"What in damnation are you talking about, man?" Douglas scrubbed a calloused hand over his face. He was only thirty-five years old but his body felt closer to fifty.

"I say we send half the barrels to Canton with the compliments of His Majesty's chartered Hudson's Bay Company and the other half to Brazil. We'll have McGoodan, the agent, on board and he can present them to the emperor and the governor at São Paulo. Northern sea fish have become *the* fashion in Europe, he'll tell them. That man's slicker than oil. If he doesn't return with a fistful of orders for next year no one could. That ought to keep the arseholes in London off your back and it's just the sort of plan that old prick Simpson will like."

"But what am I to do for barrels if we do get orders?" moaned Douglas. "We don't have a cooper. That's what caused the trouble in the first place.

The idiots who made this lot can't be trusted to saw a log in half let alone cut staves well enough to seal."

"We find our own cooper," Wiley said as if it was the simplest thing in the world. "A Highlander perhaps, though I'd even take a Glaswegian. Not one of the Upper Canadian pretenders or, gawd forbid, a Bostoner."

"Wellll," Douglas pondered. "If you can find me a cooper on this blessed earth who knows what he's about I might get my Molly to stitch you a decent pair of breeches and moccasins."

Darrog Wiley grinned broadly, his springy whiskers stuck straight out to the sides, giving him the appearance of a scruffy cat. Wiley's breeches were threadbare and his boots little better than slippers. He'd fashioned new soles out of wood but those too were disintegrating and they were uncomfortable and slippery. Nails were scarce and he had only a handful to pound through the wood to give him some grip on the slippery mud. The weather had been filthy for months. Nothing but rain, so cold it nearly froze on the skin, and a thick, depressing bank of cloud that hung like retribution off the shoulders of the north-shore mountains shrouding the Fraser River valley for miles. If Douglas's Molly (her real name was Sreeqin) stitched him a pair of moccasins to keep out the chill and damp, he'd be a happy man.

A native wife eased fort life considerably, but Wiley had never been in one place long enough to get one or need one. Nor'Westers were voyageurs, explorers, traveling men—unlike these fort-bound Hudson's Bay Company bureaucrats. They learned quickly to make their way in the wilds or they died. Simple as that. But forts were springing up on every river bend west of the Rocky Mountains as half a dozen companies vied with each other for control of the western trade. Native wives were a necessity for the "fort squatters," most of them still smelling of home and not having the vaguest idea of how to survive. No one could sew, weave, or fish like these Indian women, and if you picked right—a high-born lass—it automatically gave a man entry to a particular tribe and preferential treatment when it came to trading with them.

Shortly after enjoying the spoils of his *poque* win, Wiley met young Henry Douglas who was in the southern territories searching for a head trapper to be posted at the recently completed Fort Langley in the British Northwest. Douglas knew that Freemen, especially Nor'Westers, could be unpredictable and they were certainly an immoral lot. But no one could trap like them, and he quickly took a shine to the big Highlander. In a moment of weakness, while lubricated by the Bay man's unending cups of whiskey, Wiley promised to give it a try for six months. That was nearly two years ago.

At the bawdy urging of the other Langley trappers under his command, Wiley finally purchased a young girl from a tribe that called themselves the Kahnamut and lived at Khwaykhway, the thousand-acre almost-island that formed the western end of Burrard's Inlet. They were a rich tribe with extensive river rights along a section of the Fraser near the fort. Wiley never saw the girl before she arrived at the fort accompanied by several relatives. His vision of large warm breasts evaporated the moment he set eyes upon her. Thin and frightened, she cowered in the corner of his cabin whenever he came near. Her terror irritated him as he watched the other native wives confidently taking charge of the domestic lives of their Scottish husbands, cooking their meals, making their clothes, and warming their beds. Most of them went further, teaching their men how to wrap hooks for fishing, dress hides more efficiently, and fashion bones into a variety of handy tools, all essential when the supply ship was slow in coming. Douglas's Molly even ran her own trap line near the fort. In return the wives got extra provisions for their families, especially the desirable, dense, wool blankets the company brought in by the hundreds.

But this girl seemed to have few skills. Either that or she wasn't of a mind to use them for Darrog Wiley's benefit. Whenever he appeared in the cabin she shrank into the walls until he left. Despite his red hair, wild-looking pale-blue eyes, bulk, and irascible personality, Wiley was not given to temper. However, five minutes with this girl had him cursing, pulling at his beard, and feeling the urge to punch a tree. She was the worst deal he'd ever made in his life. No cooking. No sewing. He hadn't the stomach to exercise his mattress rights on such a pathetic creature.

Late one evening, lubricated by the last of his good whiskey, Wiley hesitantly broached the subject with Henry Douglas. Though younger, Douglas had spent a good part of his adult life among the natives of bush, prairie, and coast. Three years earlier he had been part of Jedediah Smith's extraordinary party that set out from the San Gabriel mission in California for the San Joaquin Valley far to the north and eventually east across the Sierras, "mountains of eternal snow."

Douglas returned with Smith on his death-defying trip back across the Sierras, dodging angry Mohaves and Mexican jail before landing up at the Hudson's Bay Company's post of Fort Vancouver on the Columbia River in the midst of Klikitat, Cowlitz, and Chinook territory. When it came to

Indians, both peaceable and warlike, Douglas was a voice to be listened to. Wiley had plenty of his own experiences with the red man but he'd been a voyageur for most of his life, rarely spending much time in one place. Here, holed up in the dank forests on the edge of the Fraser River, the white trappers and traders were in a different world.

"These savages are honest enough in their own way," Douglas explained. "But they're nothing like the primitives I've seen before. You always knew what an Apache would do. Kill you if they could, especially if you killed one of their own. Same with the Blackfoot and Paiute. But these ones!"

"What in hell's honesty got to do with it!" blustered Wiley.

"It's like this," Douglas said barely suppressing his amusement. "You paid for the girl with two ax heads, a skinning knife, six blankets, and a carot of tobacco."

"Yes," responded Wiley impatiently.

"A good enough price for a regular girl. But this is no regular squaw."

"What d'you mean?"

"She's pretty nearly a princess."

"A princess!" gasped Wiley. Her image popped into his head—scrawny, greasy-haired, and frightened. She was so slight he'd nicknamed her Scratch.

"Yes, indeed. Her uncle is head of at least two secret societies and her father, Sunak, isn't a chief, as far as I can gather, but he's held the biggest potlatch ever in this area, which puts him into direct competition with Big Noisy."

Big Noisy, a Stó:lō, was the dominant chief in the region defined by the river deltas in the south and the mountains in the north. He wasn't born into a royal family but he had earned his leading position by deft negotiation and sometimes threats of aggression with Musqueam nations farther downriver and with the Sqwamus in the area that would be Vancouver's mainland. Together their alliance had kept the stronger and more warlike Koskeymo Indians of Vancouver Island from absorbing all the best summer fishing grounds on the Fraser. Big Noisy married a well-born daughter of Sunak's Kahnamut, thus ensuring his tribe's easy access to excellent shellfish beds up the inlet and cooperation along the Fraser for salmon fishing rights.

Sunak, Scratch's father, promptly married a more royal daughter of the Musqueam—people of the grass. Back and forth the two men went, increasing their wealth and their alliances until Sunak staged a massive potlatch attended by nearly four thousand from seventeen different tribes speaking five languages. Seven of Sunak's own slaves were sacrificed. As well, the young men of Sunak's immediate family waded into the fast-moving river at their summer fishing grounds and tied themselves to rocks and snagged trees. They stayed there for three days and nights in the blood-chilling waters to honor the spirit of the woman who floated downriver on the branches of a giant tree in order to give birth to her children in the place where the salmon began their journey. The cheers, songs, jeers, and chants could be heard up and down the river and the glow from bonfires penetrated the blackest night.

When the men dragged themselves out of the river, Sunak impoverished himself by giving away, or ostentatiously destroying, every bit of wealth he possessed, including his store of precious coppers. He even bled himself to the point of death, proving that he was not too proud to give up his own life blood. Sunak's unheard-of display obligated every family in attendance to donate part of their own wealth in the effort to restore Sunak's. By doing so they hoped the great-man-to-be's honor would rub off on them. As a result, Sunak ended up even richer than before.

Big Noisy had been boiling ever since that bit of one-upmanship. Now Sunak had cemented his ties to the fort by selling a daughter to Wiley, which didn't improve the chief's humor.

"Scratch a princess?" Wiley repeated in amazement.

"Not full-fledged, mind. It's complicated, figuring their status. Very fluid. But princess is near enough.

"The other thing about Sunak are these green beads. He has them, Big Noisy doesn't."

"Green beads?"

"In their language they call them Tear Eggs. The story goes about some woman marooned at Khwaykhway, where Sunak lives. She cried for days and her tears became eggs and the eggs became children. It's a very important story for these people. I saw Sunak parade around with them at the potlatch. I think they're jade of some sort, but not from around here. All the jade here in New Caledonia is dark green and these beads are the palest ..."

"Good God!" shouted Wiley, interrupting Douglas. "What are you on about? Eggs and tears! I've got a woman who's useless to me."

"I'm just trying to give you the lay of the land," soothed Douglas. "Sunak's got these egg beads, Big Noisy claims they belong to the Stó:lō. Their little competition keeps things interesting and profitable. And you, my friend, bought a wife from one of the two most powerful men in all of New Caledonia."

"Yes, but I bought her fair and square. They sold me a lame horse. I should just give her back."

"Giving back is something you don't do with these people," chortled Douglas. "Here's where it stands. You bought Scratch, sure enough, but you paid only six three-stripe blankets. According to her status, she'd be worth at least that many four-stripe blankets and her father would probably make an argument for five-stripers."

The stripes on the blankets counted for pelts. Four-stripe blankets were equal to four beaver or deer skins, five stripes traded for five pelts, and so on.

"That was the price!" fumed Wiley.

"Yes and no. He asked for six blankets and you gave him six with three stripes. So he gave you the lame horse in his family. If you'd given him five-stripers you would have got the best daughter. Instead you got what you got!"

Wiley groaned. "No one never told me!"

"You never asked," shrugged Douglas. "Of course," he added, just to rub it in, "if you'd given him even one of your XYs he would have handed over his first wife, greased up and ready to go."

XY Company was one of the upstart fur trade enterprises eagerly trying to make a fortune from the western fur trade. Formed in 1795, its far from creative founders named it the New North West Company, though the well-established North West Company was still very much in existence. Often bales from both companies ended up on the same boat headed for London. Squabbles broke out over payment, which were invariably resolved to the older and more powerful company's advantage. By the second season all New North West Company's bales carried the broad black X or Y, and soon the name stuck.

XY Company got an edge on its rivals, the Hudson's Bay Company and the North West Company, by purchasing a hundred negro slaves to sew striking red or black blanket coats as Indian trade. Heavily fringed and occasionally decorated, they were highly sought after by Indians from Yerba Buena to the northern reaches of the Hudson's Bay Company's territory, and from St. Louis on the Missouri right across to the Pacific Ocean. Darrog Wiley had two XY coats; it was his fortune.

"Trade an XY for a woman? An Indian woman!" he sputtered. "No one would be foolish enough to do that."

"I gave ten muskets and ten five-stripe blankets for Molly," said Douglas mildly, citing an amount roughly equal to two XY blankets. "Ye don't hear me complaining."

Conversation paused for a moment as they quaffed deeply from their mugs. Wiley intended to save his coats to acquire sufficient bales to sell directly in Canton, then use the money to purchase a cattle ranch in Mexican California. Such private dealing was strictly forbidden by the Hudson's Bay Company, but with a little persuasion of the right sort he could convince the ship agent to take on his cargo without the Fort Langley factor, or his second in command, Henry Douglas, being any the wiser.

"I admire a man who stands by his principles," Douglas continued, smirking at Wiley's tattered trousers and his shredded boots. "But principles are principles, facts are facts. You pay this," he held out one empty hand palm up, "and you get that." He gestured at Wiley's attire. "And you're not saying but I'd guess you're not getting any of the other either." He punctuated his remarks by making an obscene gesture with his hands.

Wiley seethed. The idea of giving up an XY for a woman was infuriating. Even more aggravating was the fact that Douglas and the others plainly knew he was getting a bad deal and hadn't troubled to warn him about the three-stripe blankets. And worse, if it could get worse, was the knowledge that Sunak, the black-skinned son of a bitch, was laughing up his sleeve at Wiley. Sunak had used him to improve his position and gain advantage in his status war with Big Noisy. And the fact that a white man got tricked in the process added savor to the events. Wiley didn't care at all for the idea of being the butt of an Indian joke; such jokes hung around a long time, embellished with each telling.

Sunak was a clever bastard, no question. Quiet and very tall with a deep brow, wide fleshy lips, and skin so dark under his paint that it looked like mahogany. Not a trace of red or even brown about him. If Wiley didn't know better he'd take him for an escaped slave off one of the British ships that collected negroes from the Dark Continent along with ivory and wood and sold them for enormous profits. A few of the slaves were kept for labor as the ships traveled around the horn and made their way up the west coast to pick up furs for the China trade. Right now there were two at the fort, chained in the cellar with just enough slack to allow them to move around and kill rats. Every carcass they produced gave them an extra ration of food.

Sunak had been given a tour of the fort and he was fascinated by the negroes, immediately offering to trade for them. Henry Douglas hadn't refused outright but it wasn't politic to be handing over choice slaves to a man who wasn't a chief. Fueling the competition between Sunak and Big

Noisy encouraged both to produce more furs for potlatch items, which meant more trade and more profit for the fort. God knows the count had been meager enough these past two years. Helping one savage get clear-cut ascendancy might cut off trade altogether.

"I'll tell you what," said Douglas finally. "You find me a cooper, not a damn American, and I'll see what I can do about Scratch. If I can't exchange her then at least I might persuade Sunak to give up another daughter. That man would sell his mother if you met his price. And Molly *will* make you new clothes."

"I'll get you two coopers," Wiley vowed, though in truth it wouldn't be easy to find even one.

Tradesmen who didn't call themselves Americans were in short supply in the west. Ever since 1816, when Congress passed an act forbidding foreigners from trading on U.S. soil, every crofter, cattleman, hunter, and boatsman with something to sell became American overnight. Douglas didn't care for Americans, born there or not. Though he had been in the company of one of the greatest American explorers, Jedediah Smith, he considered most of them undisciplined and grasping. No king, no God, no controls.

"I must have one before spring run," said Douglas.

"What can I offer him?" queried Wiley, thinking it'd have to be plenty good to tempt one this far north.

"A pound a month and a half percent share," replied Douglas promptly. "And I'll guarantee a minimum on the share."

Wiley nodded. That might do the trick. A share in profits was almost unprecedented. Most in the Company drew straight wages only. It should be enough.

Wiley's idea was to travel overland to the Company's forts along the Columbia River and nose around for a cooper. There were plenty of French Canadians in the region, the roughest, hardest men he'd ever laid eyes on. Wiley was big and tough but there wasn't a single one among the Frenchies who he could outwrestle, outshoot, outpaddle, or outfight. To find such a one with coopering skills would be a triumph.

If he had no luck at Fort Nez Percés, so named by the Frenchies because the Indians all pierced their noses, he'd try Fort Vancouver, the largest in the Columbia River district. Nominally the Hudson's Bay Company forts cooperated with each other, but in reality it was every fort for itself, or, more accurately, every fort's profit for itself. Wiley would have to be careful; if they figured out what he was up to he'd get a good drubbing at the least. Should there be no joy in the larger forts there, he'd travel down to Fort French on the southern bank of the Columbia's mouth, where ships put in before they went upriver. A ship's carpenter would do in a pinch— would have to do.

"You'll be rid of me for a good few weeks," Wiley spoke into the gloom of his cabin that night. He thought he heard Scratch huddling in the corner. "Meek has its merits," he muttered, "but even the Lord Himself didn't have you in mind when he declared the virtues of humility."

Wiley had hit her once but it gave him about as much satisfaction as kicking a three-legged cur. He was hungry but his appetite fled when he entered his cabin. He lay down on the wooden bench-bed he'd made and softened with a bag of duck feathers and moss. His wife was there, breathing lightly, staring at him, he was sure. A chill gripped him. Did she hate him? Fear him? Wish to kill him? He had no idea. He forced himself to think about new breeches and the comfort a new wife would bring. Eventually, Darrog Wiley drifted off to sleep.

19

✳

"I'll not be hindered," growled Wiley.

"And I'll no be the one to hinder you!" retorted the long-limbed man standing defiantly in front of him, hands on hips, arms akimbo, and sharp beard thrust forward as if he intended to stick Wiley in the eye with it. "Quite the opposite."

"I'm bound to be back within the month and there's no ship to take us by sea or river, so overland is the only way."

"And what of it!"

"It's not a stroll through Edinburgh Park."

"And how do you think I got here?" Sharp Beard asked sarcastically. "Perhaps the good Lord plucked me from my cottage at home and delivered me here. I speak His word but I assure you I am not on those terms with Him."

Wiley chewed on his moustache. He'd found his cooper, but nothing was without its price. When he arrived at Fort Vancouver on the Columbia, the factor, Joseph La Prairie, told him his own cooper had been squashed by a tree fallen the wrong way and there wasn't another to be had in the six other Hudson's Bay Company forts along the Columbia and Snake Rivers. La Prairie had requested a replacement cooper a year earlier from London and he was still waiting for someone to arrive.

With a Chinook guide Wiley pushed south to the Williamette River, portaged across it to the Umpqua, and moved west along that river to the mouth. There was an abandoned fort there surrounded by a hodge-podge settlement of Montrealers and Métis left over from the North West days. They were Freemen trapping for beaver and otter.

Wiley intended to continue south toward Yerba Buena, hoping to find a cooper among the small settlement of Mexicans, missionaries, and Indians. But he had a great stroke of luck. A Hudson's Bay Company sloop was at anchor in Umpqua Bay with a broken mast and torn rigging. The shallow draft sloop had trade goods from Hawaii destined for the Columbia River forts. It would pick up furs and make the return trip to Canton. But not for weeks yet, not until the repairs were made.

And there on board was a cooper, the very cooper La Prairie was waiting for in Fort Vancouver. Drunk, smelly, and Irish, but a cooper. He'd signed on in the West Indies for a three-year stint supervising barrel-making for all the Columbia and Snake forts.

"This man on his own?" Wiley laughed.

"I know," agreed the sloop's captain. "He'd last no more than a month. He's been more pickled than the meat in his own barrels ever since we left the Indies. Useless."

"Let's save him a terrible fate," suggested Wiley. He pulled out a small sack of gold coins and played with it insouciantly.

"I'd hate to see a good man killed for want of care on our behalf," the captain opined, carefully not looking at the sack.

"That's very reasonable of you."

"I'm known for that."

"I'll take good care of him."

"I've no doubt you will. I'll be sure and tell his mother when I see her."

Wiley casually dropped the bag on a coil of rope where it was scooped up by the captain. Together they roused the protesting cooper from his slumber below decks. The captain told the cooper Wiley would escort him to Fort Vancouver, but, of course, they'd continue on up to New Caledonia and Fort Langley. The scrawny Irishman with enormous calloused hands wouldn't know the difference anyway.

The plan was unfolding wonderfully. Wiley could feel the thick, soft, deer-hide breeches, and his feet itched for the comfort of Indian moccasins. If he were lucky the soles would be made from tough walrus hide.

Then up pops this annoying preacher demanding to be taken along. Wiley refused outright. He was anxious to return to Fort Langley, there was precious little time left before the spring salmon run, and he wasn't about to be slowed down by some soft-palmed man of the Almighty. True, this preacher looked vigorous enough, but the wilds could turn the strongest man into a girl overnight.

"Ye'll not be denying me!" the preacher thundered.

"I'll deny you all I want!" Wiley thundered back, chest out. The nerve of the man. "I came for a cooper and a cooper I have. A preacher is as welcome in a trading fort as a farting pig in a lady's drawing room. Come to think of it, you can at least eat a farting pig."

"Hell will find you soon enough!" thundered back the preacher. "In the meantime I'll be pleased to pass on your comments to Sir George Simpson."

He flourished a letter in Wiley's face.

My dear Rev. MacDougall:

In contemplation of your family's extensive missionary experience with the Iroquois and Ojibwa of the New England states I consider you to be an admirable choice to establish a mission on the banks of the Frazer with an aim to civilize the natives all along the coast of New Caledonia. If we do not move forward then the Methodists, or worse, the Jesuits will surely insinuate themselves. With instruction in religion and morality we may encourage the Indians to adopt more British ideas of labour. Indolence is their worst vice and the Company has been required to import Montrealers and Métis to trap for beaver in order to keep the Americans from this area. It is, of course, far more expensive than our practice on the Snake and Columbia Rivers, where a single man of civilization leads a party of Indians.

Your instruction on matters of morality and the value of work will benefit both the Company and the savages.

In addition to your salary you are at liberty to take up to 5 beaver hides a month and as many otter as you wish and sell them through my acting agent, Henry Douglas, at Fort Langley. This alone should afford you an additional 25 pounds a year. Mr. Douglas will provide you with men to build a mission and he will ensure there is a good boat and reliable Indians at your disposal to reach their camps at the mouth of the Frazer and into Burrard Inlet where I have hopes of improving the coastal catch.

All HBC employees you encounter are directed to assist you in any way they can.

Regards, your servant before God,

Sir George Simpson

✳

Sunday. The day to trim whiskers and worship. It had become a practice in the fur trade community, in the absence of religious authority, for the chief factor or his assistant to read from the Bible. None of the trappers were church men but the word of God every week was as entertaining as anything else. Henry Douglas had done the honors for the past year, endeavoring to select rousing, adventurous passages to keep their attention, the Old Testament stories about David and Samson being favorites. The reading, followed by strong, whiskey-laced tea, hardtack, and beaver stew, had become a pleasurable few hours in a life filled with tedium and hard work.

Reverend Hamish MacDougall had different ideas about worship.

"Ye are fallen from grace!" he proclaimed to the ragged crew sitting and chatting in the anteroom of the main trading area.

Some lounged on bales of furs, others perched on caskets, and a few had already begun to enjoy the whiskey, which they'd later add to tea. Four native wives kneeled sedately on the floor at the feet of their men. Molly was industriously sewing blue trade beads on a beautifully woven hat.

"Be not deceived," quoted MacDougall, snatching a precious flask from one. "God is not mocked: for whatsoever a man soweth, that shall he also reap." He stared fiercely around the dim room. "And ye shall reap evil for filling your bodies with drink!"

Gwylim O'Connor, the cooper, turned his back to the reverend and surreptitiously poured a few drops of rum on the floor.

"'Tis the last of me rum, oh matey," he whispered. "Pray the Good Lord helps me reap more of what I'm sowing."

"Oh, 'tis a sad thing," the man beside him said dolefully, pulling off his hat in homage. "Specially 'cause this good man hasn't even had the chance to share his treasure with me and na it's gone."

"I'd humpbuck me own fayther afore sharing with a filthy Welshman like yerself," scoffed O'Connor.

"Forgive him Lord," the man responded. "He can't help being Irish."

"I prefer Song of Solomon," Douglas, standing by the door, commented acerbically to Wiley. "Thy navel is like a round goblet, which wanteth not liquor."

"Fornicators!" intoned the reverend, glaring around him, his eyes coming to rest accusingly on Molly. She giggled and the others joined in. They had no idea what he was saying but he was certainly excited about it.

"I'd not be speaking of navels to this laddie if I was you," advised Wiley.

"Fornication!" the reverend sung out, moving on to Philippians, "and all uncleanness, or covetousness, let it not once be named among you."

"If I recall, isn't that passage directed at saints?" queried Wiley.

"That it is and there'd be few enough of them among us," replied Douglas.

"This house of worship shall not be sullied by drink and sinful union," the reverend elaborated. "Leave thy lust and weakness at the door."

This particular house of worship smelled like a piggery, Wiley reflected. The miasma from the sow pen directly outside the only window wafted in on the morning breeze. Accenting it was the sour sweet aroma of ill-tanned hides. But Wiley had to hand it to the reverend. Even in such a place, with an audience of men who worshiped nothing and the handful of squaws who shared their beds (he didn't count the absent Scratch as one of them), the reverend's words of damnation found their mark. Most of the men shifted uncomfortably, eyes twitching, thinking of escape.

A pounding at the log chain over the gates of the trading post granted their wish. It was Big Noisy in a fury. He stormed up and down, shaking his head so hard his cheeks wobbled and clicked against his teeth. With him was a retinue from his tribe. All looked angry. When Henry Douglas appeared, Big Noisy began vigorously protesting the quality of the steel traps they'd traded for, claiming that the company had "magicked" them to convince the beaver to stay away while giving a blessing to the traps sold to his rival Sunak.

The tribes from the delta regions to the south, the north-shore mountains, the interior forests, and the villages of Khwaykhway on the almost-island at Burrard Inlet, would soon begin arriving at the river to establish their camps for the salmon run. The more powerful had the choicest spots while others were pushed to less desirable tributaries. Nothing had been seen of either Sunak or Big Noisy since the dying days of last season's fishing. But now they were back, jockeying for position, posturing, laying down conditions.

Big Noisy, short and blustering, created a fuss before they even began to catch fish to put Douglas on notice that he expected to receive preferential treatment. And he had Douglas over a barrel, so to speak. After two miserable fur seasons Douglas was placing his hopes on pickled salmon to boost revenues. But he was keenly aware that Big Noisy wouldn't hesitate to withdraw his trade if he wasn't pleased. Unlike the Cree, Flatheads, Iroquois, or even the murderous Sioux and Blackfoot, these West Coast Indians had no real need of white trade goods. Though the Hudson's Bay Company blankets were coveted, the women of the various tribes of Kahnamut, Musqueam, Sqwamus, and Stó:lō, whose permanent villages were within a few days' trek of the river, made equally warm, pliant, and sturdy blankets from the pounded inner fiber of cedar trees as well as from goat and dog wool. Big Noisy's wives were renowned for their woven hats decorated with dentalia shells, which he traded with people living far up Burrard Inlet at a place later called Indian Arm. There the more solitary Tsleil'waututh carved exquisite house and mortuary poles as well as glorious capes in desirable colors and unusual geometric designs closely resembling those of the Navajo. There was extensive trade inland also with the tribes of the mountainous interior, and once a year the Vancouver Island people of the island's ferocious west coast brought whale meat, walrus hides, and blubber to exchange for dentalia shells, blankets, tools, and eulachon oil.

In fact, the West Coast Indians had more and better of everything than any savages Douglas had ever come across in his years as a fur trader. It was a circumstance he tried to explain in his letters to London.

> *I feel they amuse themselves with us more than anything. They happily take our flour, sugar, tobacco, and molasses but they scorn trinkets and are hardly interested in tools, as theirs are more suitable for their work. On the next shipment it would be advantageous to us if you send us more tobacco, mirrors, and six-stripe blankets. It will not be necessary to include any more beads as I already have sacs of them here.*

But the damn beads arrived anyway, along with a letter tartly ordering that deer pelts not be substituted for beaver.

✳

"Molly tells me of a potlatch coming," Douglas said the day after Big Noisy created his ruckus at the gate. He scowled as he surveyed the twelve sacks of blue trade beads the men were unloading from the Hudson's Bay Company sloop.

"Another?" Wiley watched crates come off, fervently hoping to see the stamp of Glenlivet on one of them. The so-called whiskey left in stores was burning a hole in his stomach. He would give anything for a tumbler of good scotch.

"Aye, that's good for us."

"Dangerous damn things, those potlatches," said Wiley, hope diminishing as the last cargo was unloaded. "Someone always seems to get killed and it upsets the balance. I had Lillooet trapping last year and they're bloody good, but if they're bested at the potlatch they'll be sulking all winter."

"Forget your trapping, I'm talking about salmon. Big Noisy and Sunak are building their wealth like two men trying to outrun each other."

"Ahhh," Wiley got it. "So a little competition on the river for a big prize of . . . ?"

"This!" Douglas strode over to two large chests and flung one open.

"Bed warmers?"

"Bed warmers. One hundred and thirty of them. No more of this trade-bead nonsense. Fancy smoking pipes were my first choice, but these'll do. My cousin John is second to the head of the company's Indian Trade Department in London. I sent a letter on the last boat and I've been praying ever since. I'm betting all the tribes will fish around the clock for a chance at these—especially Big Noisy and Sunak."

"I wonder what on earth they'll use them for?" laughed Wiley.

"Use them? No. I'm betting these bed warmers will become like those coppers they're always hoarding or those jade stones of Sunak's. Valued possessions. If I tease 'em with these—I aim to give one each to Big Noisy and Sunak tomorrow, I'm hoping they'll fish like madmen to trade for the rest."

Wiley smiled at the vision of the potlatch feast with either Big Noisy or Sunak presiding over a mountain of bed warmers.

"Any grog in that lot?" O'Connor the cooper sidled up.

"Straight tea for you until I get my barrels," growled Douglas.

"A man can't work dry, you know," whined O'Connor.

"You've got three months and I need four hundred barrels. D'you think you can make that many?" he asked O'Connor hopefully.

"Dry or . . ." O'Connor licked his lips, "wet."

Douglas advanced on the Irishman, his fist clenched.

"All right, all right! Calm yourself. It all depends on how good your men are at rising staves," O'Connor shrugged. "I don't like the look of the wood much but it'll do."

"I'll send Wiley off to the pines under your instruction for staves," Douglas said. "And you take another group to cut hoops."

"We've got no time to dry the wood either, so you'll have to keep'um wet 'til they're shipped or we'll get no seal. What might you be thinking of filling them with?"

"Salmon, of course. We have a market in Lima and Woohoo." (The latter being Oahu on the Sandwich Islands.)

"And this junk fish fetches a good price?" O'Connor asked, amazed.

"Company business is none of your concern," Douglas snapped peevishly. "Just you worry about my barrels."

At £10 for a two-hundred-pound barrel, the pickled fish would never substitute for fur, but last year's business in pelts brought only £2,000 to Fort Langley, down a thousand. On the other hand there was a staggering abundance of fish. If the Indians, like Big Noisy and Sunak, could be persuaded to cooperate, it would be a simple matter to kipper several thousand barrels a season. And Douglas did need their cooperation. Their stone, basket, and tide traps were engineering marvels capable of diverting and snaring more than half the run of salmon in any given stream or river.

For every kind of water the Indians had a different kind of weir, net, or trap. One of the most ingenious was a wide hemlock lattice fashioned in an open V-shape and attached to posts secured by stones on the riverbed. They located the trap at falls in the river. As the leaping salmon missed their jump over the cascade, they fell back to be trapped by the lattice screen, making them easy to spear or scoop onto shore. There were grid traps for shallow, quick-flowing streams; log-dam traps for deeper water; and a terracelike double weir where the salmon leaped over the first barrier to become trapped against a higher second one.

✳

Early the first spring Douglas was in sole charge of the fort, they'd run terribly short of supplies. The Indians laughed long and hard at the sight of the trappers desperately trying to catch fish with a pole, line, and crude hook.

"Fish are a family," chided Sunak when Douglas bemoaned their lack of success. "They travel together. Why do you think you could catch them singly? Perhaps they will line up and wait for the hook?"

"It is the way Europeans fish."

"Then their lives do not depend on catching any," snorted Sunak.

✳

After several days of grumbling about the lack of white pine to make the staves, Gwylim O'Connor, still believing he was on the Columbia River, set to work on the ample, orange-tinged pine near the fort while Wiley assembled tools and men for a cutting party. Two days before they were to set out, Douglas appeared at his cabin, grinning broadly.

"Here you are!" he proclaimed, brandishing Molly's handiwork. "Henry Douglas is a man who keeps his promise."

"Aaaahhh!" breathed Wiley gratefully. "And in good time too, my boots and breeches are only fit for soup."

Douglas wrinkled his nose. "I see you anywhere near my soup pot, I'll take a stick to you!"

"Well, I know what I'll do with them then. I'll bury the sorry bastards."

Douglas laughed. "Well, do it far away from the fort or else the stench will keep the Indians away."

As usual, Scratch said not a word that night, but Wiley swore he could feel her scowling at him through the gloom. Her breathing was different. Quicker, stronger. He sighed inwardly. He could hardly wait until he got rid of her. Tomorrow he'd discuss that with Douglas. At least now he had decent breeches and walrus-soled moccasins.

The night was unusually warm for so early in the spring. Normally Wiley slept with his clothes on and a pile of Hudson's Bay Company blankets. But tonight he doffed his cherished doe-skin breeches and laid them carefully on the end of his rough bed. At the foot he placed his moccasins. He chortled contentedly to himself. He half thought about putting his new clothes in his trunk, then chastised himself for being so silly.

"Good night, Scratch. Your husband of sorts is now fit for any fine ball. Perhaps you'd be good enough to run away in the morning. I'm sure my finery would attract half a dozen more willing wives."

Silence greeted his remarks.

20

*

The dank, gray-white morning mist seeping through the board chinks brought the smell of food into Wiley's cabin. He sniffed hard, trying to figure out if it was Henry Douglas's soup pot or the clerk's stew pot that teased his stomach. Clerk, he decided. He felt around with his bare foot and touched the pliable hide of his new breeches. Not even the thought of a fortnight in the woods supervising the barrel-making crew—a bunch of disgruntled trappers and the fool Irishman—could dampen his spirits. Wiley made a resolution right then and there. Once the fishing season was over he'd bid Fort Langley good-bye. He heard a group of Métis were having great success on the Thompson River in the northern interior. The memories of life as a voyageur, once so tangible they felt like coins in his pocket, were fading into this fort-bound existence of tedium. One more season of counting, tabulating, and supervising, and he'd be gone.

Wiley rose quickly, eager to filch some food from the clerk. What a fine figure he must cut in his new breeches. As a boy he'd been quite handsome—more than one lass had consented to a little exploration during his teen years. Wiley smiled at the memory as he rooted around for his breeches. Some of the braiding must have come undone, because they felt odd in his hands. He peered closely at the hide, the pale light barely illuminating his hands. A gasp tore from him and he dropped his precious clothes as if they'd burst into flames. It could not be! He snatched up the breeches again. It was true! His fingers poked through gaping rents in the leather.

The long, angry bellow erupting from him brought the two dawn lookout men at a run.

"Bitch!" Wiley raged. "That good-for-nothing squaw bitch! I'll kill her, by God!"

"What's the matter?" panted one of the sentries. He'd been half asleep and Wiley's scream made him think Indians were attacking.

"Darrog's lass has done him dirt I'd wager," said the other, noting Wiley's purple face.

"Bitch! Dirty squaw bitch!" ranted Wiley, saliva spraying from his mouth and coating his tangled beard.

The two men edged closer. Hanging from Wiley's fist were the remains of his breeches, slashed to strips, every braid and bead cut off. Wiley stormed out of the cabin, the loose loincloth he wore Indian-style beneath his breeches unraveling as he went. The sentries followed, carefully suppressing their amusement. Wiley wasn't a man to cross when he was in a mood.

Squatting outside the cabin was Scratch—cooking. The sight momentarily stopped Wiley in his tracks. He had never seen her cook anything. Angled over the fire were three foot-long red alder poles split partway down. Chunks of salmon were wedged into the split, which was bound shut at the tip to hold them tight. Scratch was watching the fish intently, ready to turn it before cooking became burning. She looked up from the salmon, her eyes flicking over Wiley's face. He bore down on her, bellowing like a wounded pig. Scratch didn't move. Just as Wiley was ready to launch himself, the two sentries tackled him. Wiley, easily the strongest man in the fort, threw them off like he was shrugging off a cape.

"Let go, damn you!" he shouted. "I'll gut her like a fish!"

At that moment two reinforcements arrived and the four men barely managed to halt the big man's progress.

"Gut her all you want," grunted the senior man, a hardscrabble old trapper, "but I'd prefer . . . ooof! I prefer you leave it to the next watch."

✻

The following two weeks were among the most miserable Wiley had spent in the New World. He'd been holed up in ferocious storms in the mountains of Virginia, he'd dragged his canoe alone across a frozen northern Canadian river after his two companions were killed, and he'd been buried by an avalanche on the eastern flank of the Great Divide. He'd trapped for furs in some of the hottest, coldest, most inhospitable, bug-infested places that could possibly exist on earth. But never had Wiley been so miserable as he was leading a crew to cut and stack staves for the drunken Irishman's damned barrels.

Too large to wear anyone else's clothes, Wiley dug up his old breeches from the wet hole he'd buried them in and borrowed a pair of shabby boots from a man whose feet were smaller. His new moccasins were missing their walrus-hide soles.

Wood-cutting was not Darrog Wiley's idea of a fit occupation. It was for slaves, squaws, and those too simple for any other kind of work.

"Can't be just any old tree," O'Connor ruminated as they tramped through the damp dogwood brush about an hour out of Fort Langley. "It has to be straight-grained."

"We're making casks, for God's sakes, not furniture for the king," Wiley snapped.

"P'raps not, but your kippered salmon might make its way to The Majestic Buffoon, and if them barrels are as bad as your last lot he won't be none too impressed." O'Connor did not consider himself a subject of King George and refused to honor him in any way.

"Here's a good stand. Not too far from the fort either," Wiley said hopefully.

"Pah!" O'Connor dropped a glob of spit. "I wouldn't put this lot in me fireplace."

Wiley, the Irishman, and their crew of eight walked a good three hours more. In spite of his bleak mood Wiley felt the seductive magic of this land overcome him. Soft light, cool air, and the scent of ancient forest mixed with something else he could never quite identify. Humusy and sweet, it left a memory in the back of his throat. Above him the trees stretched to eternity. On days like this, when the mountain clouds crept into the valley and the trees poked out the top, a more fanciful man might easily imagine a host of heaven-sent souls perched on their branches, a fluffy, white lake spreading out below.

O'Connor stopped frequently to study trees, finally directing the men to bring down one magnificent fir that towered one hundred feet or more. It took them several hours.

"Nah!" spat O'Connor from a safe distance when it crashed to the ground splintering several smaller trees on the way down.

"What's wrong with this one?" asked an exasperated Wiley. His feet were beginning to ache.

"Knots."

"Where? How can you tell? It looks perfect to me."

"That's because you can only see what you see. I can see what I can't see."

"Well, I'm the leader of this gang and I say it's fine. We'll buck it up."

"Suit yerself," shrugged O'Connor plopping himself down and pulling out a tobacco tin. He gave Wiley the dimensions for proper stave-bolt lengths and smoked idly while the crew cut to his specifications. As the girth of the tree near the bottom was close to twenty feet, it took them most of the day just to get the raw bolt lengths.

"Split each four times," O'Connor called out when they'd finally worked their way up to the tree's lower branches. Once the bolts were split into quarters they would be returned to the fort for seasoning and dressing. The men had barely started on the splitting before one of them waved Wiley over.

"Look here at this mess."

Knots, not evident when they felled the tree and cut the rough bolts but clearly visible in the heart of the rounds. Wiley ordered a section split higher up the tree. More knots. O'Connor just smoked and smiled. It did nothing to improve Wiley's mood.

They were three days in the forests above the Fraser River when O'Connor found a stand that "might do." While the tree was being felled, Wiley turned to speak to the Irishman and found a group of Lillooet Indians standing at his shoulder, silently watching. He did his best to persuade them to help bring the wood back to the fort, promising them sugar, flour, and tobacco. The Indians spent several hours discussing the offer from all angles, drinking sweet tea, and happily tucking into the crew's provisions. When the food was gone they abruptly left. Wiley had the distinct feeling they intended to say no from the start but delayed just long enough to cage a free meal. His mood grew more glum and his feet more pained.

Finally, it was time to return home. They had two skids, which the men piled high with split bolts. It was brutal work, dragging the heavy load over uneven terrain, even with two horses. Rocks upended the skid and the horses struggled in narrow spaces where the trees were thick and the ground slick with moss. Every now and then, when they hit a particularly boggy patch, they had to stop and cut wood to create a corduroy road in order to get the skid through. Wiley would have done anything for a team of Suffolk Punch, the working horses his father raised in Scotland. These poor, rib-sprung beasts might be fine on the prairie or high desert of Oregon, but they were not fit for this kind of labor. The animals struggled so much Wiley ordered them harnessed together on the heaviest skid and rigged up a rough harness for six complaining men to pull the other one.

By the time the bone-weary wood-cutting party returned to the fort, nearly two weeks had passed. Their provisions were long gone, and they had been reduced to eating roots and drinking from muddy creeks swollen with runoff for the last three days. Wiley had left the ammunition in O'Connor's charge but he didn't notice when they stole the box of powder and balls. He'd been too busy enjoying an injun baccie smoke.

The men were delirious at the prospect of a good meal. A broad smile pasted itself on O'Connor's face as the fort came in sight.

Thinking of his booze, no doubt, Wiley thought sourly.

How the man managed to stay drunk on the meager rum and whiskey rations portioned out by Douglas was beyond him. He must have a stash somewhere.

As they drew up to the fort gates, a great tumult drowned out the ever-present calliope of the skids scraping over the rough ground. It sounded like a trading disagreement and a bad one. Wiley cursed. He'd told Douglas that trading should take place outside the fort, with the gate unchained, leaving them an escape route if things turned nasty. But Douglas believed they were safer with the gate secured and the Indians locked inside so no reinforcements could overwhelm them.

Wiley thumped and bellowed at the gate until finally he heard the rasp of the log chain pulled across and the gates swung open. There, in the common area where the Indians inspected their trade items, Douglas and the reverend stood toe to toe, snarling at each other like a pair of tomcats.

"I'll not be called a fornicator!" Douglas shouted, his face suffused and puffy. "And you'll not be calling my Molly a concubine." A sizable crowd stood around, fascinated by the spectacle. It dawned on Wiley that it must be Sunday and the reverend had gone too far with his sermon.

"I cannot tell you why the sky is blue, only that it is!" shot back the reverend.

"And I suppose your Dollymop of a wife is so pure Jesus Christ himself would not dare to touch her."

"Dollymop!" shrieked the reverend. "You dare liken my wife to a barmaid!"

"I cannot tell you why bear scat is brown only that it is!" Douglas said, mimicking the reverend's voice perfectly.

Wiley marveled at the very idea of the reverend having a wife. He almost choked at the thought of him sweatily groping at flesh under the covers. He shook off the appalling image and strode over to the two men. He'd better pull them apart or there'd be a donnybrook for sure. And he didn't like the much-larger reverend's chances once Douglas got his temper on, which turned the thin, intense man of average height into something very scary.

✳

It had happened only once in the two years he'd known Douglas, but once was plenty. A cow of a horse had kicked him twice as Douglas was attempting to nail in a loose shoe. Most would have dusted themselves off, sworn at the miserable creature, and vowed to keep a closer watch. Not Douglas. He proceeded to thrash the horse with both fists, actually bringing it to its knees with his blows. And now he looked to do the same thing with the reverend. Wiley ended the altercation by wrapping his massive arms around Douglas and frog-marching him away. When they reached the factor's quarters, Douglas thanked Wiley for doing the needful.

"That man's on the next boat if I have to pickle him in a barrel."

"What did he do now?"

"He wound up all the wives with talk of sin. Molly told me a few are thinking of leaving."

"They wouldn't do such a thing over that stick's pious ranting, would they?"

"He's talking about them rotting in the devil's cauldron! And staining their men with their sin! Molly understands well enough what he's talking about."

"If we had to have a preacher why did we get stuck with such a noodling fool?" groused Wiley.

"We'll have to make him understand," said Douglas in a worried tone, "that we can't manage without them. Indian politics are trickier here than in the king's own court."

Native wives were critical to the fort's relationship with the tribes. Molly gave Douglas easy entry to the Fraser River tribes. She smoothed the way during trade, established prices for goods, chastised and bullied other women to keep them in their place, and was an integral part of the hierarchy that kept the fort operating. It was Molly who convinced her own tribe, led by her uncle Whattlekainun, to catch fish for the fort.

It was also Molly who showed Douglas how to behave at a potlatch, what to bring, and how to accept gifts with the least amount of obligation. And it was Molly who explained that the white man's trade goods were more valuable as currency markers than as something desired for their own sake. If a chief destroyed 100 bags of flour, everyone knew the exact worth and dimension of his gesture. The act became something that could be bettered with 150 bags.

"Whattlekainun says the potlatch is war like the spirits wage," Molly told Douglas. "If you take blood and give blood in killing it takes a long time to bring the dead back in a form to fight again. But potlatching is war with what we can make, hunt, and find again. And do it much faster. The spirits do not destroy themselves to conquer their foes. They destroy what they can create again."

Wiley was sure it would take him a lifetime to understand the complexity of tribal rituals and societies on the Northwest Coast. For every if, there were twenty thens. But listening to Molly, he began to understand the potlatch.

"If my father holds a potlatch and burns thirty blankets or throws two hundred bundles of tobacco into the river, then others know the price of his importance. It is quite simple."

Molly and the other wives were vital ingredients in the subtle business of Indian trade. And now the Reverend Hamish MacDougall seemed determined to mortally insult every female who occupied a bed in the fort. In doing so he threatened to upset the delicate balance.

Wiley was so weary he was sure the hairs on his head were moaning for sleep. He left Douglas to take over the stacking of the stave-bolt lengths and stumbled to his cabin in one corner of the fort. He could easily have lodged inside the main building but he preferred his own "castle." His rough-plank bed, cushioned with its burlap bag of leaves, moss, and duck feathers, felt welcoming. There was no sign of Scratch. Without even taking off the boots that had blistered his feet, Wiley lay down and felt sleep rush up from his swollen toes.

Tired as he was he couldn't get comfortable; something dug painfully into the back of his head. Groaning, he sat up to move whatever it was and his palm brushed something soft. He pulled the lumpy bundle toward him. Bleary-eyed and fumbling, he unrolled material of some sort. Breeches! Wiley shot up and hurried over to the window. Honey-colored doeskin, finely tanned and sewn together with sinew and tiny stitches. Lightly fringed and heavily braided, the breeches sported a bucklelike closure made of carved antler. That's what dug into the back of his head. Wiley examined the beautifully fashioned thing. He could make out an eagle head with the moon in its beak, carved into the antler. He had heard of a legend belonging to Scratch's tribe about a brave warrior woman who swam across from

Englishman's Bay to Khwaykhway in order to save the tribe's children, whom she had turned into green beads and swallowed. Near death, she had washed up on the westerly beach and called for the children. The white-headed eagle, impressed with her feat, broke off a piece of the moon and dropped it at her feet. In the explosion of light the beads were changed back into children and the tribe, people who called themselves Kahnamut, the welcome ones, survived.

Studying the horn closing, Wiley knew the breeches could only have been made by Scratch. No other woman would dare usurp, even from a young woman so weak and perhaps even slow in the head, the design that belonged to her people. Still, he could hardly believe what he held in his hands.

Fatigue gone, Wiley limped out of the cabin. He could feel the blisters tear as he moved. He hadn't seen Scratch amid the confusion when he'd arrived back at the fort. Truthfully, he hadn't looked for her. He found her squatting over a cook ring, arranging a basket weave of sticks to produce a hot, quick-burning fire. Wiley called out. She didn't move. He was puzzled. Her back was to him, but why didn't she respond? She couldn't be angry at him, or he wouldn't be wearing these gorgeous new breeches.

"Thank you!" he ventured in English, feeling foolish, as if he were addressing a sister who had made him a too-personal birthday present.

"Thank you," he repeated, thinking she didn't understand the word. He tried to remember the equivalent in Halkomelem. "*Kleesaw,*" he tried. "*Kleewas!*" Again, but louder. No response.

He took a few steps toward her and tapped her back gently. Scratch started and fell to one side, her eyes round and shiny-black with shock. He had taken her by surprise. How could this be? No one had ever accused Darrog Wiley of being stealthy.

And then he knew.

"You can't hear, can you, lassie?" he asked her, watching her search his face.

It all made sense. Her fear, her refusal to speak, the long silent hours she crouched in his cabin. She was a deaf-mute! The other women adapted quickly to fort life and saw the advantages. But she could never adapt. There were no advantages for her among the white men, and she couldn't even communicate with the other women.

Darrog Wiley was not a man of strong principles. Pelts dictated his morals. Nor could he be accused of sentimentality or compassion. This was not a land where charitable thoughts got you anywhere. But as Wiley stared at the girl, her thick black hair cascading from beneath a simply woven, cone-shaped cedar hat, her lean face looking back at him watching him absorb what she could not tell him, he was overtaken with an unusual emotion.

Shame.

He smiled at his woman—in simple appreciation of her plight, as thanks for the breeches and, well, because it felt good.

Scratch smiled in return. Wiley felt his body warm, aches and pains falling away.

21

*

The reverend blocked the entrance to the anteroom of the trading area, arms crossed high on his chest, long legs spread, chin thrust forward ominously. His sandy-brown beard was still neatly trimmed to a point, and his clothes far cleaner than a man would normally expect in the grubby backwoods of the Hudson's Bay Company's northwest wilderness. It was Sunday and the men had already entered the room for the weekly Bible lesson, less eager than when Henry Douglas did the honors but still content to listen to hell and damnation, knowing a nip or three, some conversation, and some music would follow.

Five or six native wives trailed along, talking among themselves and bearing baskets of food. The women chattered happily, their excitement obvious. Indians were descending on the river from all over the valley, the north shore, and the coastal foothills. Most of the women would see their people for the first time since late the previous summer. All wore some item of European clothing, but since gowns were hard to come by on the Pacific frontier, the newer wives wore mostly native dress.

Molly looked beautiful in a vest and headdress that demonstrated her sewing skill, the position of her uncle Whattlekainun, and the wealth of her union with Douglas. The front of the vest and the entire headdress were covered with dentalia shells, almost tubelike in shape and creamy white, a fortune's worth. Each shell cost thirteen camas bulbs in trade. The bulbs, relatives of the lily, were eaten like potatoes. There were more than a hundred shells on her two garments. Camas didn't grow on Vancouver Island and the mainland tribes did not have the secret of harvesting dentalia. Similarly the island people did not have goats for wool while those across the strait did not hunt the whale. Bulbs for shells, wool for oil—that's what kept war at bay.

Molly's vest met a hooped crinoline, her favorite piece of clothing. She'd sewn baby mink tails to the hoops, which bobbed and swayed as she walked. Around her neck was a collar of small, polished vertebrae with an obsidian medallion hanging from it. And across her shoulders she carried a *slowi* shawl. Pieces of cedar had been so thoroughly pounded the fabric looked and felt as soft as good Irish wool. The last piece of her ensemble was a prized pair of ladies' high-buttoned boots of black kid leather. These she had braided onto a hide rope and tied around her waist. Though she would have caused stares and open laughter in London or Philadelphia, Molly looked every inch the frontier princess.

Hidden by the shawl was a wooden cradle shaped to the contours of Molly's back. In it a baby slept—four-month-old William. The proud father, Henry Douglas, had left a week earlier for the Columbia territory to sort out an imbroglio that unexpectedly threatened his plans to ship salmon to South America and Hawaii. Douglas learned that the Columbia district forts, which hadn't the slightest interest in salmon until now, had purchased a thousand barrels direct from the Spanish at Florida and 450 extra bushels of salt for pickling in an effort to get a jump on Fort Langley. That cunning dog Joseph La Prairie had quickly discovered what happened to his cooper and intended to make Douglas pay for it. With the right "encouragement" to the captain, La Prairie would overload the Hudson's Bay Company ship, expected in November, with cargo from his territory, leaving less room for fish and furs from Langley.

MacDougall seized the opportunity presented by Douglas's absence to arrange Sunday worship more to his liking.

"Concubines shall ne'er enter here!" he boomed, barring the door to Molly.

She stopped in her tracks. Douglas had urged her to ignore this strange man as best she could and encourage the other women to do the same. But Douglas was gone and this man was shouting at her like a mythic thunderbird. His endless talk of damnation and sin put a strange fear in her heart. She tried to sidle past. MacDougall stepped sideways, completely blocking the doorway.

"Did ye no hear me? Ye harlot! I'll no have unclean women at my worship. If ye sin ye must repent!"

Molly glanced at him and took another step toward the chamber. She could hear the other women behind her murmuring among themselves. She looked desperately past the reverend, hoping to catch the eye of the men within. They looked away uncomfortably. There would be no help from them. She looked around for Wiley but he was nowhere to be seen.

"Immoral! Unclean! Savages! Is it not bad enough to lie with a man who is not your husband? Yet ye must also defile this place of worship with your evil bodies and minds!"

Molly's English, after nearly four years with Henry Douglas, was very good and she well understood the gist of MacDougall's diatribe.

"We go in. It is our place," she said with summoned confidence to the other women and stepped forward again. The wives did not follow.

"Ye shall be damned and thy flesh rot from thy bones! Whore of Babylon. To hell ye all shall go!"

Hell. Hell. Hell. Hell.

The image bore into her. This one was so certain, so sure of himself. Molly had seen the power of the white men's god in their exploding sticks and the rocks that flew from tubes. She had accompanied Douglas on a navy ship that bombarded an abandoned Kwakwaka village farther up the coast. The ship thundered its cannon and turned the village into kindling, fire leaping to the height of the tallest totem. The village had become a place of bad luck after two chiefs died of the scab disease, which was increasingly common. All seven families remaining left to join with another related tribe. Douglas laid waste to the village, hoping the stories of his power would travel quickly along the coast. Molly was still frightened by the memory and the words.

"You'll go to hell if you cheat the crown!" proclaimed Douglas triumphantly after the first cannon exploded on the ground.

The Sky People's hell. Could this one send her there?

"The Lord sayeth women of filth in body and mind will be cursed to the cauldron of hell. You," the reverend shook his fist in Molly's face, "are damned!" Molly trembled. She did not want to turn her back on him for any reason.

The reverend poked her viciously with his iron fingers.

"Begone harlot!" he thundered. When Molly still didn't move the reverend swiftly backhanded her across the face with such force she stumbled to the ground, nearly falling on William.

"Ain't ye being a bit rough, Preacher?" O'Connor slurred out weakly from the anteroom.

"Silence, you drunken fool!" the reverend snarled.

An excruciating pain lanced through her jaw as Molly pulled herself to her feet and fled. The vision of the white man's hell overwhelmed her. Her concept of it was a terrible place of eternal torture where souls drifted. She would be stuck there between lives, and her family would be punished for her misdeeds. Weeping, she ran to the river and crouched low among the rushes.

"Where is everybody this fine morning?" queried Wiley cheerily a few minutes later. His new moccasins and breeches fit him perfectly and the scent of cedar resin from the needles Scratch rubbed him with after a cold river bath lingered pleasantly. His belly gurgled contentedly, filled with dried salmon, fresh rabbit, and bread roasted on a stick.

"You'd better be ready to share your stash, you Irish maggot," he called happily to O'Connor. "Or I'll have your insides out."

O'Connor held out his arms, palms up in empty-handed resignation. The other men looked crestfallen and something else—guilty. There were fewer of them than normal and no squaws. Only the reverend seemed happy, puffed up like a courting rooster.

"Where *is* everybody?" Wiley repeated. "The lassies?"

"I have righteously driven the heathen from this holy place," Mac-Dougall intoned. "We can now worship in sanctity as God intended."

Wiley shrugged. Something was wrong here but he was too happy to let this God-spewing fool spoil his excellent mood. Tea and a layabout would suit him quite fine, even if he had to listen to the man's pompous proclamations.

Two hours and a long, dry sermon later, Wiley came across O'Connor and a small group of men picking mud from their boots, sewing up jackets, repairing tools, and grumbling.

"No tay. No moosic. No room. No wimen," O'Connor growled. "Nuthin' but that prissy stick. I'll not survive your damned reverend that's for shore."

"*My* damned reverend?"

"You brought the shite here when ye tricked me. He's *your* damned reverend."

"O'Connor, you could survive the flood without an ark," laughed Wiley.

"Fik yew," muttered O'Connor.

"It'll blow over," assured Wiley, his fine mood too expansive to be easily dislodged.

"I'm na so sure," responded O'Connor. "Your reverend smacked Molly a good one."

"It'll blow over," Wiley said with considerably less assurance. A squaw wife was hardly a lady but MacDougall had no cause to hit the industrious Molly. Thank the Lord Douglas wasn't about.

"Blew ye fikkin' rev'rend, blew him right away," crooned O'Connor.

The other men picked up the melody and began adding lines, each one more obscene than the last. O'Connor added cheek music to their words. He plucked and slapped at his taut cheeks and lips, making an enormous range of sounds. Wiley was impressed by the display and he wondered if Scratch had ever heard music made thus. Heard. How stupid, she could not hear. He felt odd thinking of her so. An unaccustomed emotion filled him. Contentment, joy . . . something. How strange.

✳

Henry Douglas returned on the Hudson's Bay Company brig *Eagle* in record time from the mouth of the Columbia River to Fort Langley. His spirits were high. As he'd surmised, the salmon rumors were only partially true. The barrels hadn't arrived and there was no guarantee as to quality if made by the Spanish slaves at Florida. In any event, they'd ordered only a hundred, not a thousand. Furthermore, despite La Prairie's confidence, he had no firm arrangement with the Cowlitz, a notoriously fractious tribe, to catch fish.

Douglas had even managed to advance his own plans by persuading La Prairie to part with two hundred bushels of salt and a stationary jointer's plane O'Connor wanted for finishing the barrel staves to ensure a tight fit and proper bilge or belly to the shape. Douglas took with him forty bales of beaver pelts, and the Brazilian agent, who was visiting the company's Columbia region forts, bought them. Cash in hand, not on account.

Douglas also brought back tea, dried whale meat, Brazilian sugar, and beans, as well as ten yards of fine lace and an ivory handheld mirror. He could hardly wait to see Molly's face when he gave the treasures to her.

Wiley stood on the dock at Langley, watching the *Eagle* draw closer. He was worried. It had been nearly a week since MacDougall had "cleansed" Sunday worship. No one had seen Molly since and the men were unsettled.

The day after Molly disappeared, Scratch took Wiley to the small lean-to where Molly kept her fishing net, drying racks, and herring-spawn boxes. Molly gathered the kelp, thick with herring spawn, at the river's mouth and made the arduous paddle back to Fort Langley in a single day. After hanging the kelp to dry in the winds, she carefully scraped the ochre egg clumps into the boxes. During the winter, they added a pungent flavor to the bland diet. She had made a small pullout for her canoe near the lean-to. But the canoe was gone and there was no sign of Molly or the baby.

Douglas jumped off the boat and onto the dock without waiting for the gangway.

"I'll be chief factor yet, with these business dealings I've been cooking up," he crowed to Wiley. "A profit is assured next year if that damn O'Connor can make me enough barrels. The price of pickled salmon is up a pound a barrel, and the Columbia forts aren't going to be able to take up much of that.

"And I've got tea! No more of that filthy brew we've been drinking. Throw the bloody stuff in the river. And some whiskey . . ." Douglas's voice tailed off as he caught Wiley's furrowed expression. "What's the matter with you, man? You look like someone's razored your breeches again."

Normally that would have brought a rueful smile to Wiley's face. It had become a standing joke around the fort.

"It's Molly. She's gone."

"Gone? What do you mean, gone? Gone where?"

"That's the thing," said Wiley with difficulty, though he'd been considering the words for days. "No one knows. If the other women do, they're not saying."

"Gone?" Douglas repeated.

Molly never went anywhere without telling him. Not asking, mind you, just telling. She did leave three times a year: for the eulachon run on the tributary where her family had hereditary rights, the kelp harvest, and the late-fall spirit feast in her home village. But the eulachon run was finished and it was too early for kelp.

"And where's William?" Douglas asked quietly of his swarthy, dun-eyed son.

"Well." This was even harder. "It appears she's taken him with her."

Wiley tersely filled Douglas in on Molly's confrontation with McDougall. Douglas's expression darkened with every word. When Wiley mentioned the blow, the younger man clenched his fists.

"I wasn't there," Wiley said, meeting Douglas's eye.

"Has she gone back to her village?" Douglas asked, his voice icy.

"I sent Steg and Dwyer to check. Their wives are from the same village. I expect they'll find out quick enough if she's there. They took arms. If she ran away it won't be good for us," Wiley added.

"Molly, run away?" Douglas scoffed. "Don't be ridiculous."

Fur traders' native wives did occasionally run away if they were badly beaten or mistreated. And some pined so much for their old lives they preferred the censure of the tribe over another night spent in the bed of a hairy, smelly trapper. Occasionally trappers took their wives with them on the line and sold their favors to others in the bush. Those who didn't perish from malnutrition or disease returned as wraithlike creatures. But Douglas had taken a firm stance on the treatment of wives when he took over the fort. Two trappers had been killed by Scowlitz from Harrison Lake to the north because they'd allowed their women to be mauled by too many men. The trappers weren't that important, but that year no beaver pelts were brought to the fort by the people who claimed descent from the Mink and the Sturgeon.

Molly was the undisputed leader of the small group of the fort women. There were three Kwantlen, Molly's people; two Chilcotin; one from a Sqwamus tribe along the north shore of Burrard Inlet; and also Scratch, the daughter of Sunak of Khwaykhway. All spoke some dialect of the Halkomelem language common to many of the coastal people, and all deferred to Molly as they would to the first wife in a family. At the fort, Molly had wealth, status, and a kind husband. Running away was inconceivable.

A stony-faced Douglas ordered all men at the fort to search the woods, the riverbank, and the grassy flatlands on the deltas to the south. In an emotionless fury, Douglas left before dawn for Whattlekainun's encampment. Molly's tribe was constructing their weirs farther up the main river and building cylindrical basket traps, wide at one end, narrow at the other, for the swift tributaries. They placed the traps in water, the wide mouth facing downriver and anchored with stones, the narrow end tilted up on two crossed poles. People would be stationed on either side of the trap to beat the water and frighten the salmon back downriver. When they turned to run upstream again, they'd be forced into the mouth of the trap, which was quickly tilted up and the salmon captured.

Normally Douglas was fascinated by the annual ritual and the ingenuity of the various traps. This time he didn't even glance at the fish works as he went from one family group to another, asking about Molly. The second day Douglas returned, Whattlekainun himself stood on the high riverbank with men fanned out on both sides, blocking his approach.

"Go back," the regal old man ordered. Douglas was surprised. Whattlekainun had been the first to welcome Whan-ee-tum, the Sky People. And he was the first to allow the Sky People to take "a wife of our own ground," Molly, the daughter of his sister. He laid down trading terms and had been an ally in encouraging his people to use the more effective iron traps to capture beaver. It was also Whattlekainun who convinced several villages along the river and its tributaries to catch salmon for the fort. To have him turn against them would be a disaster, but all Douglas cared about at that moment was finding Molly and the child.

"You go back," Whattlekainun commanded again.

"I seek my wife," responded Douglas just as emphatically.

"Not here, go back."

"She has gone from me. She is mine. I will have her back."

"She is gone?" Whattlekainun's eyebrows rose almost to his hairline and the whitish paste coating his forehead and cheeks cracked in the furrows of his brow. "Or she is . . ." he used a word meaning "set adrift," implying carelessness by the owner.

Douglas could try to explain that Molly had been frightened, shamed, and driven off by the vicious tongue of the vile reverend. But he knew this would not impress Whattlekainun. The old man held him responsible for everything that went on in the fort. If MacDougall had driven Molly off, then Whattlekainun would expect Douglas to balance the wrong.

Douglas thought it safer to stay with the ownership issue. If Molly had sought refuge in her home village, he could make the charge that Whattlekainun had stolen her.

"I paid ten muskets, ten five-stripe blankets, ten carots of tobacco, fourteen knife blades, and many bushels of sugar. This you know," he asserted.

Douglas's raising the issue of ownership wasn't lost on Whattlekainun. By doing so he made Molly a shared problem. He found that subtlety was not a strength of the Sky People, but this one had his moments. A small smile broke the impassive mask of his face. He stared out at the White Mountain to the south then turned to contemplate T'lagunna to the north—two peaks the white men called Golden Ears. The best goat and deer hunting was in the foothills of those mountains. He was of a mind to kill this Whan-ee-tum and overrun their fortress. It would be easy enough to do despite their exploding sticks. He could claim all their stores and use it to shore up his own wealth in preparation for the potlatch to be held at Khwaykhway. Whattlekainun expected Sunak and Big Noisy to battle each other at the potlatch. With his additional wealth he would wait and see which of the two men appeared to be gaining the advantage and then throw his support in that direction.

But the Whan-ee-tum were endlessly interesting. Killing the chief would cut him off from their boats, tools, and building techniques, all of which intrigued Whattlekainun. Secretly he yearned to spend days inside the fort walls, watching how they did things. Even their method of cooking absorbed his interest, and now a new man had come to make round boxes. He studied one barrel and found the methods crude, but the tool used to shape the inside of the staves was like nothing he had ever seen before. Unfortunately, Whattlekainun could not give in to such a desire and still maintain his position. That was the reason he agreed to allow three women to marry the hairy beasts from the winged boats. They would learn much from their husbands and one day bring back what they had learned. In the meantime they gained strength from the trade alliance. Until now it had seemed a good arrangement.

The salmon were beginning to run, Whattlekainun reflected. He saw no advantage in killing Douglas at this time. Aside from anything else, such an attack might bring bad luck upon the season. Some of his people believed the white men were of the salmon. They must be handled carefully. Whattlekainun also worried about the disappearance of Molly. A portent? If so, of what? When he first heard she was missing, he studied the quills that his first wife dumped from a bag. They told him nothing. Then he had the bone reader examine the otter vertebrae. They indicated a long, cold wind and many frogs. That meant a wet spring. Roe and spawn would be difficult to dry. But did her disappearance augur more?

Whattlekainun made his decision. For the moment, he would ignore Douglas's insult and let him go. He saw a shadow pass swiftly across the top of the snowy peaks to the north. T'lagunna approved.

"Not here. Not among us. She could not come."

Did Whattlekainun mean "would not" or "could not"? Douglas wished he understood the language better. He took a chance.

"Why not?"

"Shame! A wife cannot return without payment, without permission. She would return only as a slave. She would not do that," Whattlekainun stated with certainty.

Douglas stared rudely into the older man's eyes. Whattlekainun allowed the chief Whan-ee-tum to search his face for truth. Douglas believed him. He nodded to Whattlekainun, turned quickly, and made his way back along the narrow cliff trail. Whattlekainun watched him go. As the disconsolate Douglas disappeared, Whattlekainun waved over two men from his own family and the shaman.

"Find her," he ordered.

"This is wrong luck," the shaman insisted. "Tomorrow we will bless the salmon and dance for its forgiveness."

"I want her found."

"You stand too closely to the Whan-ee-tum."

Whattlekainun angrily strode over to the shaman, drew a circle on the ground, and stepped into it.

"You must decide to stand close to me or live beyond the circle." He waved his staff in a broad sweep around his head. "I choose inside the circle. Which for you?"

There might be only so much room for good relations with the whites. Big Noisy and Sunak had staked their territory, as had Shashia, the most powerful Cowichan from Vancouver Island. The circle was becoming crowded. Whattlekainun wanted to be inside it.

"Find her," he repeated.

22

✳

They found her at Slikwhinna, the Big Horn bend in the Fraser River where it swooped southwestward toward the Pacific. Her body rested in the canoe as if she had just settled down to sleep. (Though it had rained hard the three previous days, her canoe was dry and the clothing covering her body only slightly damp.) Whattlekainun's men were afraid.

Molly could not have chosen to die in a more ominous place, which could only mean she had evil intent. Her years with the Sky People must have corrupted her spirit. The salmon were just beginning their journey upstream and no other being was more sensitive to death than the salmon. Yet here she was, dead on the banks of the great salmon river. Beneath her cedar-cloth cape they could see a bulge—the child.

Without touching Molly and doing their best not to look at her, the three Stó:lō towed the canoe to the beach at the fort, where they tied it to a tree and left quickly, paddling hard against the current, feeling the thud of their hearts. No one would be pleased with their news.

✳

Henry Douglas's arbutus walking stick would have fetched a handsome price at any fashionable market. Carved from tip to handle with an array of mythical beasts and spirits, its smooth orange-red skin polished to a sheen, it was a glorious example of artistry. Sunak had presented it to Douglas shortly after the fort's walls had been erected in two deluge-ridden months three years before. In return, Douglas had given the Indian chief an intricately etched and silvered Hudson's Bay Company presentation rifle.

Molly explained to Douglas that the creatures her people carved had many meanings, portents, and uses. House poles, for instance, held the stories of the family within the house. Massive figures were carved on the trunks of tall, straight, red-cedar poles. Few villages near the southern Fraser had them anymore, but they were common among tribes to the north, especially along the rugged, fjord-ridden coastline where life was much harsher. Molly's grandmother was Kwakwaka. Her people excelled in the carving of house poles and also enormous plaques that served as front pieces for their houses.

"This will be our house pole," she held the stick aloft. "It will guide us and protect us. When it is not in your hands you must keep it here." She laid it against the door frame of Douglas's quarters.

✳

Molly! A groan of deepest agony rose as Douglas brought the heavy arbutus stick down to meet the reverend's shoulder. The crunch of shattered bone brought a grim smile to his lips.

"Aaaaah!" howled the reverend, spinning round. "Oh God! You've broken my shoulder. God save me!"

"Don't speak to me of God," Douglas snarled. "You know nowt of God!"

"Help! Help! Save me!" screamed MacDougall. He backed up as Douglas advanced, coldly driving the stick into the reverend's abdomen. Undigested fish spewed over the ground. Weeping, the reverend held up his good hand to ward off a third blow.

"Please!" he begged. "Please, please have mercy!"

"I'll show you the same mercy you showed my Molly!"

Douglas brought the stick down again, catching the reverend's knuckles. "Unclean! Evil!" he snarled with the blow. "You disgusting offal!"

He swung the stick and missed, but the reverend pitched forward in fright, smashing his teeth on a rock. Blood filled his tidy beard, staining his collar and shirt front.

The fort was almost deserted; a hunting party had recently left while Wiley had the rest of the men outside the stockade, cutting hoops for O'Connor's barrels. Things had gotten so testy with the Stó:lō since Molly's death he'd ordered all hands to carry weapons. He did not need to know the half dozen dialects of Halkomelem, spoken by most of the people along the Fraser River and across the inlet to the northern shore mountains, to realize how angry and upset the tribes were. They had come to the salmon fishing grounds only to discover the specter of Molly's death threatening to haunt the season, perhaps even poison the fish.

Everyone was on edge. One of the other wives had left the fort without a word, and the fur trade had shrunk to a trickle. They had expected to take in five thousand otter and beaver pelts as the Indians converged on the river, bringing with them trade goods from winter hunting and trapping. Less than eight hundred lay in the fort's storeroom.

"You killed Molly!" hissed Douglas, standing over the whimpering reverend. "And I shall kill you."

He had a knife at his belt and a musket in his quarters, but Douglas had no intention of letting Hamish MacDougall die so quickly or neatly. He would not rest until the man's poisonous tongue hung lifeless from his head. He would deliver that tongue to Molly's people. They understood revenge better than anyone.

Thud. Thud. Thud. Sweat pouring down his face and body, Douglas grunted with the effort of each swing, and each impact on the pulpy form sent a shiver of satisfaction through him.

"What in the name of Mother Mary are you doing?" Wiley shouted, running up. Thud. Thud. Thud.

"Stop it! Henry!" In a killing frenzy, Douglas swung the stick with both hands, nearly taking Wiley's head off. Wiley ducked then charged, flinging himself at Douglas as the stick descended again. The two men fell to the ground.

"Dear heavens, look at him!" Wiley clambered to his feet. "There'll be hell to pay. How are we going to explain this to the church? I don't even want to think about the governor." There was no answer from Douglas.

Wiley could only imagine the letters MacDougall, if he lived, would send to Sir George Simpson, complaining of Douglas's brutality and the failure of the fort to adopt and foster Christian values. That's if he lived. If he died, Douglas would be called back in disgrace, probably jailed or even hanged. What a mess.

Douglas was already in bad odor with the company, as a number of sharply worded missives from London laid the blame for the decline in beaver pelts at his feet. Nor had any revenue been gained from the sale of salmon yet. If the natives attacked Fort Langley, or worse, should a war start among them over Molly's death and damage to the salmon run, problems could spread south, to the other Hudson's Bay Company forts on the Columbia.

As Wiley considered the unpleasant possibilities, the reverend mewled and coughed up blood. The man's too mean to die, Wiley thought with relief. As he wondered what to do, the rain came, the kind of downpour unrivaled anywhere in the world. There was more rain in other places, but nowhere else was there as much cold rain. Let it wash the reverend's soul clean, Wiley thought sourly, turning his attention to Douglas who sat in the mud, staring at his arbutus stick. Wiley dragged him to his feet and hauled him to his quarters before ordering two men to get the reverend off the ground and into a bed.

"If you are going to die, better do it quick," growled Wiley to the unconscious form. "I don't want to waste medicine on you."

Douglas barely moved for two days. Wiley desperately tried to coax him out of bed but Douglas wouldn't even respond.

"That's na going to work," announced O'Connor, who'd been entertained by Wiley's futile efforts to rouse the acting factor. "I tried 'im with a sip o' whiskey yesterday. If that don't raise him nuthin' will."

"How could this happen to a man like Douglas?"

"Ya hit a man in just the right place, you'll kill'im, no matter how big or tough he is," O'Connor shrugged. "Woman's death hit him in that place."

"It's a terrible thing."

"Very sad," O'Connor agreed. "Well, y'er in charge now. How 'bout doublin' the whiskey ration."

✳

Wiley elbowed O'Connor aside. "I'm a goddamn trapper," he muttered, walking toward his cabin. "But what have I done for more'n year. Wood-chopping! Fishing! Planting damned potatoes! Now I'm supposed to play factor and nursemaid."

Scratch greeted him at the door, eyes glued to his face in a way that made him feel as if she had crawled right inside of him. That look once gave him unpleasant shivers. Now tenderness, not chill, ran through him. She was a continual surprise, so slight yet able to carry enormous armloads of wood. That same strength was evident when her arms and legs wrapped around him late at night. Her skin was a fine brown hue, with the downy look of a child, though she must be in her late teens. She wore a cedar-cloth tunic, which hung straight from her shoulders, and over it a shawl-like cape that could be used for carrying things. Long strips of tanned hide were sewn to a belt around her waist. When she walked, they moved around her legs. Scratch wore little ornamentation except a carved horn amulet around her neck and two disks that hung from her ears—copper, the only sign that she was nobility. Her hair was wavy, coarse, and incredibly thick, quite unlike the straight, often lank hair of the other women.

"Daughter of the eagle," said Sunak when he'd sold her to Wiley. "She was born all black, with beak and claws to remind us of the white-headed eagle that helped the swimming woman bring back our people where they lay asleep in her green tears." Sunak touched the lustrous beads on his chest. "The eggs, the tears of the swimming woman, protect us still."

They had lived for months as antagonists and now awkwardly, slowly, they began to decode each other's gestures and preferences without the benefit of verbal language. Henry Douglas favored a hat with a sharp peak, so they referred to him by tenting the fingers of both hands above their heads. O'Connor was signified by the universal cupped hand and bent elbow of the tippler. They had no gesture for the reverend until Scratch saw him upbraiding a visiting Métis trapper who had two wives—bold, strapping women of the inland Kootenai people who could match the work of any man. Scratch caught Wiley's eye and, with a stern scowl, waved a scolding finger. Perfect, thought Wiley.

Wiley's first decision was what to do with Molly. The Indians refused to touch her body and even the company men were spooked. Wiley covered her with boughs, leaving a very reluctant trapper on guard to keep animals away. They could not wait any longer, they must bury her and her child.

"Men're no damned good at bodies 'n sich," opined O'Connor when Wiley fretted to him about what to do. "Specially wimmin's bodies."

"The other women won't go near Molly. They're all convinced she's got some evil spirit and they'll catch it too."

"Them Indians. Heads're cut half the time. Blootered fools. At least I enjoy meself when I'm seeing fairies."

"Well, I'd better see about burying her myself," said Wiley.

✳

Scratch found Wiley grimacing as he began removing the boughs from the boat, steeling himself for what he might find. She grabbed his arm and squeaked at him in the odd, high-pitched, breathy voice of those who have never heard or spoken. She pushed him away angrily.

Scratch went to one wife after another. They knew what she wanted but all refused her pantomimed entreaties to perform the duties of the *wutlzetca*, shaman of death. If it were a man who had died it would require a male *wutlzetca*. She must do it herself.

With Wiley watching and O'Connor lurking in the distance, Scratch pulled Molly out of the boat and detached the baby, whose dead lips were still clamped around her nipple. As she did this, Wiley's gorge rose up and he choked back the vomit. Even O'Connor winced.

Methodically, Scratch washed Molly from head to toe, oiled her hair, and painted her face a reddish brown. Then she rolled Molly over onto a blanket and positioned her on her side, with baby William against her chest and her knees drawn up to her bent head. Scratch pulled the down out of dried bullrushes hung in Molly's smokehouse and sprinkled it over them. She wrapped a large cedar blanket over the two corpses and bound them with braided hide rope. Above the pullout for Molly's boat she began to dig a grave, grunting with the effort to move the heavy clay. Wiley made as if to help but she sent him away. Four hours later, as the sun was finally making an appearance in the last moments of the day, Scratch was finished. The grave had been blessed with branches of fir, and she levered over a heavy stone to serve as a monument and keep the predators out.

Just as Wiley was wondering what next, Scratch marched off toward the main house. She had never before entered any of the buildings inside the stockade, let alone Douglas's quarters. She found him lying on his cot, one bent arm over his eyes and one leg half off the bed. She leaned over and shook him roughly. Wiley was amazed at her boldness. Douglas groaned and rolled over. Scratch shook him again, harder. The sight of her face propelled Douglas up, and for a dreadful moment Wiley thought he might have imagined it was Molly. Surprisingly, Douglas meekly followed Scratch. As they left his quarters, Douglas picked up his arbutus stick, which was lying on the floor. The reverend had done nothing but bleed and groan since the beating, so Wiley doubted there was any danger, but he intended to keep a sharp eye out in case Douglas tried to finish what he started.

Scratch took a long, sturdy pole from the smokehouse, threaded it through the rope binding Molly and the baby, then positioned Wiley at one end and Douglas at the other. The three of them walked solemnly toward the grave, their bundle swaying gently.

"How ye go is fur, fur more important than how ye come," uttered O'Connor solemnly as they passed.

The river grew inky with night. Molly and baby William were laid to rest. Douglas tried to put his carved arbutus stick in with them but Scratch firmly rebuffed him.

After Scratch had filled in the grave—she wouldn't let Wiley or Douglas help with this either—she picked up a small stone, cleaned off the dirt, and prompted Douglas to place it in his mouth. Throughout the whole ceremony, if it could be called that, Douglas said not a word. His face was set as if frozen, his eyes blank, his movements lethargic.

"What in the dear Lord's heaven am I to do with him?" Wiley worried to O'Connor the next day. "The chief factor won't be back from England for weeks yet and we've got to start bringing in the salmon. That's if we can get the Indians to fish for us."

"Lazy boogers. I coon't git a won to cut me rounds fer the barrel bottoms. I even give'em room, what little spot of it I've got left."

Wiley was sure O'Connor had plenty of "spots" of room—rum—as the man smelled of it most of the time. Giving over his favorite drink to cajole Indians to work for him would stick in his throat like the cook's morning biscuits.

"We've got big problems," Wiley ventured.

"Aye that *ye* do, right enough," O'Connor answered. "One hef dead in tha' head t'other hef dead in tha' body. Makes for an intrestin' situation."

"If MacDougall dies we'll have to bury him and send a report to London."

"An' if he don't die?"

"A navy frigate is due within the month to tow the *Selkirk*."

The four-gun ship, stove in from a chance meeting with a late-season floe a year ago, lay heeled over at the beach. Ice was rare in the river, so the ship's captain hadn't been watching for treachery beneath the surface.

"We could send him to Fort Vancouver. They're more able to patch him up than we are."

"An' when he wakes up what'll he say? He got hisself a wee hidin' from an angry leprechaun? Better for everyone if he dies," opined O'Connor as he stretched and sauntered away, happy to leave Wiley to his problems. "In tha' meantime," he shot back over his shoulder, "them savages are some twisted up. My hoop cutters got chased yesterday. Ever'one's as nervous as a virgin on her weddin' night. Not that I ever knew a virgin, mind. Mine have always been a wee bit experienced."

Wiley felt as trapped as an animal with Hudson's Bay Company iron clamped to its leg.

23

*

Wiley looked in on MacDougall. The reverend lay still, breathing shallowly, the smell of rot pervading the tiny room. Douglas was also sleeping and he smelled almost as bad, his sour breath from a long-empty stomach tainted the air twenty paces away. The cook was able to pour some broth down his throat a couple times a day, but that was all.

"Enjoy your snooze," Wiley grumped. "Left me in a fine pickle." The word brought a faint smile to his lips, rare of late. "Your damn pickle caused all this. If you hadn't needed a cooper, I'd never have brought that cursed reverend back."

Wiley walked slowly back to his cabin.

"Dey gone!" shouted Paul Dubois.

"Who's gone?"

"De women. Mine up and left while I was sleepin'." Dubois complained. "I checked. De rest gone too."

Wiley's eyes flew to his cabin. He took a breath. Scratch was there, tending the fire.

"Are you sure?"

Dubois snorted. "Travois gone, dog gone, cape and other clothe gone. Dat say gone to me."

Dubois, a former Nor'West trapper from Montreal, was one of the few men who spoke the local language well and seemed to prefer it over English or French. He called his wife by her real name, Seewali, whereas the rest of the men picked an English or French name, more often than not their mother's. Dubois also chose to live outside the stockade, in a cabin he built on the site of his wife's tribe's summer fishing grounds five miles downstream from the fort. Aside from Douglas himself, he was the best Indian man around.

"Molly death put da fear in dem bad," said Dubois. "It give me de chillies. And more bad. I heard dey diggin' pit house."

"Who?"

"Kahnamut, Stó:lō, Scowlitz."

Pit houses meant war. Bunkers to hide in. Wiley's heart beat a little faster and he wished he could rouse Douglas. He'd know what to do.

"Dey don't waste time building pit house in salmon season," Dubois added. "Not unless dey serious."

✳

Scratch gave Wiley a wooden cup with bitter Labrador tea brewed from narrow leaves she'd harvested and dried in an open basket hung from the ceiling. Wiley sat on the edge of his bed, sipping without tasting. When he looked up, Scratch was standing before him, holding a pile of fur-trimmed blankets in her outstretched arms. Wiley stared at her. What does she want? The late-spring evening was warm, he had no need of the blankets, and besides, these were the ones she was making for the potlatch at Khwaykhway. Scratch hurried to the corner of the cabin where she used to crouch for hours on end and returned with a small feast ladle. She dipped it in the tea and poured the liquid on the ground in a semicircle around Wiley's feet. Now he was really puzzled. Scratch fetched more objects, laying them at his feet. She urged Wiley to give her something. He held out his cup. She took it. Then he got it.

"You want me to hold a potlatch?"

Wiley squatted comically on the floor as he'd seen the Indians do, nearly tipping over with the effort to maintain his balance. He affected a stern, imperious look and pointed at the bare floor as if demanding that Scratch fill it with gifts.

"Is this what you mean?" he asked. "I put on a potlatch?" He pointed to himself.

Scratch grabbed his hand, pulled him out of the cabin, and waved her hands around her at the walls of the stockade.

"You want the fort to put on a potlatch." Wiley pantomimed eating and sleeping, then danced around from one foot to another, chanting, to Scratch's amusement. He wasn't fat, who could get fat in this place? But Wiley was big and graceless at anything but paddling.

"Food! Eat! Feast! Dance! Gifts!" he panted as he hopped around.

Scratch laughed and tapped his head. Her look said clearly: It took you long enough to figure out.

What a brilliant idea, Wiley exalted. It's never been done before! Who would have even thought of it? Scratch, that's who! He grabbed her arms and whirled her around until she was laughing so hard tears poured out of her eyes.

They plotted late into the night. Wiley lit every candle he had as they gestured to each other and drew on the ground, detailing the plan. The fort would hold a potlatch and do it quickly, in order to preempt the one to be held at Khwaykhway. That alone was unheard of. Potlatches took months, even years to prepare.

The potlatch, if it was done right, could accomplish many things in a single grand gesture. Whattlekainun, Sunak, and Big Noisy would be distracted from preparations for war. Wiley had no idea if the tribes were planning to attack each other or the fort, but if he were a gambling man he'd place his money on the fort as a target. And if he was wrong about war, the Sky People's potlatch might force Sunak to cancel his in case it suffered in comparison to that hosted by the fort. Douglas had been worrying that if Big Noisy or Whattlekainun were bested, those tribes might refuse to trade fish for a season. Even better, since potlatches were often used to wash away shame or guilt, the fort could seek cleansing for Molly's death.

No one would refuse the fort's invitation. The tribes would be dying of curiosity. Sky People holding a potlatch!

Lauwa, the red-fleshed sockeye salmon, didn't start running until early summer, about three weeks from now. As long as there was no war, once the first bones were returned to the river, all thought, all work would be devoted to the fishery. Wiley prayed there was enough time to pull everything together.

O'Connor worked with determination, once they'd settled on his compensation—two gills of rum, a double share, from the navy stores when the frigate arrived.

"Oooo an' I'll be away in tha' head decidin' about how best to honor Nelson's Blood," O'Connor smacked his lips. "Could be I'll start with a wee nor'west, seein' as that's where we are." A nor'west meant half water and half rum. "Then I'd be havin' to bow to the compass and let slid down me parched throat a north tot." Sailors drank by the compass, though O'Connor just drank, but he'd follow the tradition of the sea, naming each increasingly strong measure after the compass points.

That the plan involved more than a measure of trickery greatly appealed to the Irishman.

"I sucked the milk of guile at me mama's breast," said O'Connor as he

dove with uncharacteristic fervor into the work. First he built a raised platform, ten feet high, in front of the building used for trade and storage. On
top he constructed a thronelike chair out of logs.

Wiley ordered Dubois to gather every possible item of trade.

"Everything, you hear? Including the men's possessions, if they're
worth anything."

"My hide will not be worth nothin'," Dubois whined.

"It won't be worth nothing if we're not successful. Use your gun if the
men won't hand over their belongings."

The crippled ship at the Fort Langley wharf was a vital part of the plan.
A navy frigate was bringing supplies to make rough repairs before towing it
to the growing Spanish settlement at Monterey where the hull would be
made seaworthy. If the navy ship arrived ahead of schedule his plan would
be lost. "Good winds," he constantly whispered to himself, "blow foul and
keep that damn frigate away."

"Can you make her sound enough to ride the river for a few days?"
Wiley asked O'Connor.

"Aye," scoffed the Irishman with mock indignation. "I'm a cooper ain't I?"

Wiley didn't quite know how to get the potlatch message out, until
Paul Dubois had an idea. For three days he canoed along the Fraser and up
as many tributaries as he could. He took along the fort's junior clerk whose
only known talent was playing bagpipes. They stopped at each encampment and the lad, togged up in kilt, sporran, and tam-o'-shanter, squeezed
his bags mightily until the curious appeared, drawn by the terrible racket.
Dubois then invited them to the Sky People's potlatch at the fort, "one so
grand that the thunderbirds would speak of it for ever," he boasted.

For three weeks the work was frantic. Wiley was glad, as it kept the
men's minds off their missing wives and away from the prospect of attack.
None of them were soldiers.

Before dawn, at the end of the third week, just as the mountains
released their shadows, Wiley heard them coming. The sound was a wave
that never broke, a wind that rumbled as it gathered strength. He strained
his ears: no voices, only wood against water. He couldn't tell which way
they were coming from or how far away they were. He paced back and forth
by the gates as he'd done for most of the night. Scratch stood quietly, chin
raised, facing the river. She'd hardly moved for hours. Wiley pulled at his
jacket, yanked his collar, and rubbed his neck. The naval long coat was too
small, and the old tricorner hat, a souvenir he'd borrowed from the com-

modore quarters on the lame ship, made his head ache. His buttons shone even in the early dawn, and the leather-and-silver sword sheath squeaked and rattled as he walked.

Scratch ran to the gate and tugged at the log chain. In seconds, she had the heavy bolt released, then she was out and running to the beach.

If I were a religious man, Wiley thought as he followed her, I'd probably swear the ghostly host himself were leading a charge into the pits of hell. They came out of the dark and the early mists by the hundreds, the voice of their approach a muted symphony of thud, grunt, swish, and gurgle. The black water seemed to offer them up like sea birds on an incoming wave, but there was no wind and barely a ripple on the river.

Within hours, the mud bench on the river's shore was thick with canoes, some of them seventy feet long, with leering, leaping figureheads rising twenty feet into the air. The largest boat held a shaman, who disembarked to the pounding of paddles against the gunnels of their boats. When the chiefs alighted, each tribe attempted to outdo the other with chants and songs.

The noise, Wiley was sure, could be heard at the top of Golden Ears Mountain itself. It might even wake up Douglas. He looked around. Every trapper, trader, cook, and tradesman stood in silent wonder as the boats landed one after another. He spotted Whattlekainun, his massive canoe towing seven others, all brimming with gifts. Everywhere camps were being set up and tents pitched.

Sunak captured the best spot directly in front of the gates. To everybody's amazement, he began to erect a lodge with specially cut timbers and wall and roof planks ferried crossways on several canoes. The pièce de résistance was a seventy-foot-long totem pole strapped across three boats. With great hullabaloo they roped it up in front of the lodge. The other camps looked rather pallid in comparison.

"No amount of gold in the empire could match all this," he breathed to O'Connor, impressed in spite of himself.

"How did they do it in such short time?" the cooper asked.

"I can't imagine," said Wiley. "What about the ship?"

"She'll stay afloat a few hours yet," O'Connor gestured at the gunner boat bobbing at anchor. "I hope." O'Connor smiled when Wiley winced. In fact, Wiley thought he detected a list to starboard.

"Nahs the time," prodded O'Connor.

"I don't know what to say," Wiley said nervously, staring out at thousands of painted and elaborately costumed bodies. He'd never been to a ball, but he doubted whether even a celebration at Buckingham Palace itself could hope to compete with the finery arrayed on the banks of the Fraser, thousands of miles from civilization, in a wilderness ruled by trees.

"Has Douglas come to his senses?"

O'Connor pointed to the top of the platform and his giant chair.

"We hoisted him up like the Union Jack. He'll sit there 'til we bring him down. I filled his mouth with bandages just in case he does wake up."

Wiley twisted around and saw Douglas listlessly gazing out at the stupendous spectacle.

"Try a wee drop of medicine," O'Connor said offering a silver flask. "Works wonders."

Wiley drained it appreciatively, enjoyment rapidly turning to suspicion. This tastes like brandy, he thought, and the only brandy left in the fort belonged to the Reverend MacDougall.

"Decent stuff," O'Connor said, not troubling to hide a smirk. "Not whiskey of course. Still, it's decent."

Wiley took a deep breath, walked toward the platform. Scratch waylaid him and hefted a heavy cape over his shoulders. Every inch of the pounded cedar bark was covered with crisscrossed bones, tiny bird and otter bones, all painstakingly sewn. Around the bottom hung obsidian disks, and epaulets of eagle feathers stood out in a fringe. It must have weighed twenty-five pounds. She smiled at him and pushed him forward, his stomach unknotted for the first time in days.

As he climbed up on the platform Wiley glanced over at Douglas perched ridiculously in his chair like a child on a throne, his now cadaverous face sallow and blank.

"Great people of the river, the mountain, and the sea. I welcome you." Wiley's booming voice carried over the crowd, infused with power and clarity. His hand rippled down the bones on his chest; he felt taller, grander, greater than ever before. "I welcome you to the most important potlatch of all time. As I speak, the Grand White Father listens from his kingdom across three oceans, and sends his greetings. He has more children than trees in this land and all are honored by your presence."

He paused to allow Dubois to catch up with his translation.

"This potlatch will be spoken of for as long as people walk, fish swim, and birds fly. All others will be insignificant beside it."

He heard murmurs of doubt, mockery, even laughter. "It will be the greatest potlatch of all time because the greatest sin imaginable must be made right. A sin against the salmon, a plague upon your and my people, a pestilence upon our houses." He fervently hoped Dubois was translating this with the right balance of boasting and admission of shame.

"The most evil spirit of all entered the body of our shaman, transforming him, causing the spirits to abandon us." This brought another wave of comment. "We call upon our friends to help us drive away the wickedness, raze the taint of infamy, and . . . uh . . ." it had been a while since he'd read his dictionary, ". . . perfidy and evil!"

He caught Dubois eyeing him quizzically.

"This evil killed Molly, endangered the salmon spirit, and it is killing our chief!" Wiley flung his arm out and hundreds of eyes followed it to the chair. "Our chief bravely fought the evil! Now he can no longer speak or walk, his soul is frozen!

"Today we will vanquish this evil!"

Wiley clapped his hands sharply together over his head. The bagpiper strode out of the fort, warbling and gurgling a series of discordant notes. Six men followed, carrying a casket with the reverend's body. Conveniently, the day before, his pious but gangrenous self had departed for eternal plains. A tide of voices accompanied the casket as it made its way through their midst. Nine of the most powerful chiefs assembled stepped forward: Stó:lō, Kwakwaka, Sqwamus, Musqueam, Sechelt, Cowlitz, Lillooet, Kahnamut, Scowlitz. Each carried something in his hand—a staff, a spear, or a war hammer—which they rapped upon the sides of the casket.

"Our winged canoe will take the reverend shaman across waters to where the sea ends, and with him will go the evil. But first we feast!" The men set the casket down on the wharf. O'Connor sidled up.

"Trifle long-winded, once ye got going. I've got three men in the bilge pumping for all they're worth. Those canvas plugs wun't hold forever."

Wiley looked up at the sky. It was already midafternoon, and heavy black clouds were sliding down the north-shore mountains. Good. It would darken more quickly.

Again Wiley clapped his hands, and from out of the fort came venison arrayed on long boards and a dozen roasted pigs—they'd wiped out the entire piggery. Racks of smoked salmon followed—their entire remaining store—bins of hard candy, and every leaf of tobacco they could find. To this the various tribes added haunches of bear meat, raw whale blubber, clams, mussels, and slabs of sturgeon. Big Noisy brought an entire canoe filled with winkles—there must have been tens of thousands. They ate them raw, crunching the shells.

O'Connor had brewed several vats of yeasty spruce beer, supplementing it with every drop of alcohol he could find—except his own. He then "extended" it with water and "improved" it with several bottles of iodine, ink, and kerosene.

Dancing began, each tribe competing fervently. By twilight, twenty-nine marriages had been arranged, half a dozen shames expiated, and a sizable war canoe chopped to kindling to absolve its owner from a debt. The rotund clerk played a medley of Scottish fighting songs, the notes rising up above the cacophony of a dozen different dances and chants. Mindful of the leaking boat, Wiley readied himself to move to the next stage when O'Connor unexpectedly staggered onto the stage and burst into song. The Irishman proved to have a beautiful lilting voice, and he sang tragic lyrics involving lost loves, lost limbs, and lost wars. He crooned about the beauteous creature Spéirbhean and divine goddesses Grainneuaile, Roisin Dube, and Caitlin Ní Uallacháin. Wiley couldn't make out the heavily accented Gaelic but even so, the songs made him feel like weeping.

"Ah me laddie, these redskins have got nuthin' on the Irish for fairies and spirits," said O'Connor, wiping his eyes. "I'd say it's time to move on before our guests get carried away."

Wiley noted that a number of them had climbed up to inspect Douglas. Even more were taking a close-up look at the reverend. Wiley was amused to see one warrior poke him with his spear, presumably to see if he was really dead. He signaled the piper to sound his loudest, highest note.

"We have wronged the salmon god," Wiley said when he had their attention. "As an offering, we are returning his children to the river."

Fifty barrels were rolled out to the river's edge. With great ceremony, the men broke them open, tipped them into the river, throwing the barrels after them. Whattlekainun nodded approvingly. The whites had labored long and hard to make their silly barrels. They'd paid fairly for the salmon, which they were putting back. There was a balance here.

Wiley felt the rough throne beside him shaking.

"Are ye comin back to us then Henry?" he said with a chuckle. "I should have known your precious pickled salmon would wake you up."

More shaking as Douglas thumped his foot against the chair and fought against the bandages in his mouth.

"Hold your piddle. It's only last season's spoiled barrels."

The shaking subsided, only to intensify as the trappers, clerk, skinners, woodchoppers, and even the two cellar slaves fell to throwing a good portion of the fort's trading goods into the river—125 bags of flour, 500 bales of beaver furs, 22 traps, musket powder, 11 carots of tobacco, the precious tea—on it went.

When Douglas calmed down, Wiley would let him know that he'd reserved enough prime trading goods to see them through till the next supply boat. As a bonus he'd unloaded some of the untradeable goods that headquarters had stuck them with: thirty pairs of shoes, all left feet; a hundred yards of serge, whose color ran the minute water touched it; four heavily braided admiral's parade uniforms, which had inexplicably arrived on a cargo boat the previous year; fourteen pipes with cracked bowls; seven bales of white otter pelts shedding badly from an unknown disease; and twenty wrongly bored muskets. All ceremoniously went into the drink.

The men took fifty of Douglas's bed-warming pans and filled them with the last of their spermacin, highly-sought-after whale oil from Fort Wahoo on the Sandwich Islands. It was by far the best oil for burning. They presented each chief with a pan, then the next highest nobility, until all were gone. Wiley ostentatiously dumped his pan on the ground in front of the platform. Sunak immediately did the same, followed by everyone else. Fifty pans of oil formed a ring around the platform. O'Connor lit the oil with a torch and the ring exploded in quick flame. The resinous platform quickly caught fire.

Grease feasts were often the main events at a potlatch. The more oil burned and the better the quality of the oil, spermacin being the finest, the wealthier and more powerful the family. Great vats were lit inside the cedar lodges to burn throughout the activities. Composure was critical, as the heat seared the lungs and sometimes the beams and roof planks ignited. Then the host family strived to maintain maximum dignity even as they made their last-minute escape.

To this point, the Indians were approving but unimpressed with the display. Wiley wondered if he was losing ground. If he couldn't convince them that he had the power to drive the evil away, he had nothing left; the fort would starve.

Just as Douglas's chair began to burn, O'Connor yanked hard on a chain attached to one of the giant rungs and the assistant chief factor tilted over backward and somersaulted into a blanket held by four men. This finally brought an appreciative roar from the crowd.

O'Connor, swaying slightly, stood up. "Guess it's my turn," he slurred, pulling a hammer from his cooper's belt. With great flourish he secured the lid on the reverend's coffin with a handful of precious iron nails. Four stalwart woodchoppers heaved the box to their shoulders and carried it down to a dory on the shore. With O'Connor at the rudder, they rowed to the navy ship, and with much cursing succeeded in hoisting it onto the deck.

There was a lengthy silence, then several large splashes before O'Connor and the men made their way back to shore. Wiley could barely make out the outline from where he stood, but he knew there was a barrel, fastened to the stern of the boat. Curiosity and anticipation lay heavy on the crowd. Several minutes passed and nothing happened. The crowd grew restless. Wiley wondered what had happened to the two pumpers who were critical to the next moment. At last the boat began to move with the current. The pumpers had successfully raised the anchor and slipped overboard. Wiley prayed it wouldn't tip over as it was listing even more with the weight of water seeping through O'Connor's patches.

"The evil one is now on the water in one of our ships of battle. As penance we give both to the salmon."

Tensely he looked at O'Connor. "Now's the time to work your magic, my friend."

"Aye, now's a fine time for some magic," the cooper agreed but made no move. "'Tis your show."

Wiley snatched a torch from one of the fires and walked down to the beach. Scratch followed. Wiley drew a deep breath: he couldn't see the last man on the boat and had no idea if he was prepared or not. He raised the torch high, waved it a bit, and flung it far out over the water. Hiss, fizzle, out.

"Aaayahee!" the crowd sung out in disappointment.

A flicker appeared at the ship's bow, then came a bang and a tongue of flame shot up the main mast, which had been liberally soaked with whale oil. No one saw the man who'd lit the fuse scramble over the side.

Wiley's knees almost buckled with relief.

"Are you mad, burning a navy ship?" came a rasping voice. "And what have you done with the reverend? They'll put you in jail."

"Not me," Wiley said with a laugh. "I haven't done a thing. Far as the company's concerned, Henry Douglas is in charge of the fort. Darrog Wiley's just a simple trapper."

Douglas sputtered helplessly. The ship now burned so fiercely it lit up the river, and Wiley could swear he felt the heat.

"Oh the ship, the ship!" groaned Douglas. "The stores're all gone, the piggery's empty. We'll be eating rats."

"Yes, but we're alive, and with a little more luck we'll be back trading tomorrow," Wiley said, letting a little sharpness creep into his voice. "And as for your good friend the reverend, he conveniently died in his sleep as a result of the drubbing you gave him. I've written a nice note to the governor praising him to the sky and explaining how he'd set out alone to the mountains determined to convert as many Indians as he could lay his hands on. Signed your name to it. By the time he's missed no one will be the wiser."

"But the ship man, the damn ship!" demanded Douglas hoarsely.

"Ah, the ship," Wiley said, scratching his head. "Haven't quite figured that one out yet." Then he brightened. "But now you're up and about, it's your problem."

The ship burned for forty-five glorious minutes before it slipped under the water. For a second it seemed to be burning underwater, then it was gone. "They'll not soon forget that," Wiley said, his arm wrapped around Scratch.

Voices rose in awe and appreciation. No one had ever destroyed anything as valuable as a boat with wings. How many canoes would that be worth? How many coppers? Everywhere Wiley looked there was dancing. He heard singing and saw couples courting. There was one last thing to be dealt with.

Wiley strode over to Sunak. "A final matter," Wiley announced loudly in Halkomelem. "Something not finished. Between us only." Sunak narrowed his eyes.

The crowd grew quiet. Was this foolish white man going to ask for compensation?

Wiley could sense the nervousness of Dubois and the other fort men. Scratch tugged at his arm. What was he doing? her face asked. He'd kept this part of the plan to himself.

"A wrong must be made right!" Wiley thundered, praying he was getting the words right.

"What wrong?" Sunak asked.

"I have cheated you," Wiley continued to the astonishment of all. The fool! "Now I must give what is yours back to you."

"No one cheats me," Sunak replied belligerently. Any such suggestion made him look weak.

"You allowed me to take advantage of you." The crowd's low whistle of inhaled breath sounded like a flock of birds. This man treaded dangerous ground.

"No one took advantage of me," Sunak proclaimed.

"You let me take your daughter for too small a price. I have carried the shame of it with me."

Sunak bared his teeth. He could see Big Noisy and others enjoying his discomfort.

"Had I realized your daughter's true worth," Wiley continued, "I would never have paid so little. The price shames me."

The two men stared at each other.

"How do you make good?" hollered Big Noisy, happy to add to Sunak's embarrassment.

✳

Wiley whistled loudly. Two clerks brought out his foot locker as if they were transporting the crown jewels. Wiley delved into its depths and hauled out one of the XY blanket coats, which he draped over the first clerk's arms. This brought a hiss from the crowd; most had never seen these legendary items. Unveiling a second, even more elaborate coat with mother-of-pearl buttons, red-and-gold braid, and heavy embroidery on the collar, brought a louder reaction.

"My friends," Wiley said, hugely enjoying the moment. "These coats represent my wife's true worth rather than the poor assortment of damaged items Sunak so kindly accepted in the spirit of friendship. Of course, I could not now give him these coats, that would dishonor him further."

Wiley produced the razor Scratch used to shred his breeches. He beckoned to her, outlining a section of the blanket about two inches by six inches. Quickly understanding, she began to cut eagerly. Wiley presented the first piece of blanket to Sunak, who looked as if he'd swallowed a live frog. Together they distributed pieces to outstretched hands. Scratch's smile got broader and broader as she cut the coats. Women attached the strips of blanket to their skirts and hairpieces, men tucked them into their waist ropes or draped them from their hats.

Whattlekainun watched Sunak's helpless frustration. All he could do was pretend to be enjoying the joke. It was wonderfully done. Who would have thought a white capable of it—crafting such a perfect joke, one that would be spoken of and laughed about for years.

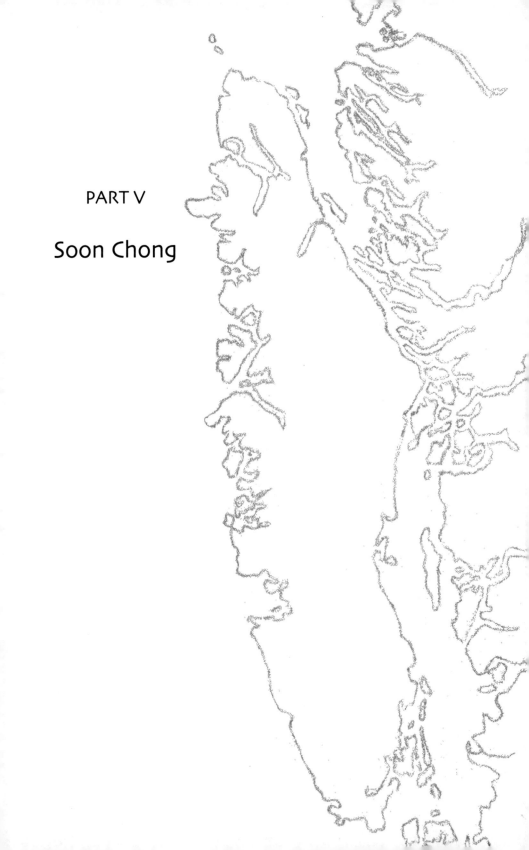

PART V

Soon Chong

24

✳

1844

Guangzhou, China

Soon Chong was born within sight of Huangpu Harbor on the northern bank of the Zhujiang (Pearl River) in the city of Guangzhou in the province of Guangdong. Surrounded by deltas of fertile, iron-rich red soil and bathed in a tropical climate, Guangzhou was known as Canton in the west. In the ancient legend of its founding, five heavenly beings riding goats and carrying rice stalks in their mouths discovered the region and populated it. The rice meant no one who lived in the area would ever go without food. In 1844 hunger was no stranger to the peasants of Guangzhou, but that, of course, was their own fault for not having the industry or aptitude to take advantage of what the gods had given them.

Strategically placed just upriver from the mouth of Zhujiang, Guangzhou, also called Yangcheng, the Goat City, had been a major port for nearly a thousand years. It was as a great-grandmother to the smaller, less sophisticated cities, which dabbled at sea trade but could not hope to approach the collective intelligence of this venerable port in the movement of goods and people. In 1757, more than a century after the Manchus of the north overthrew the Han dynasty, Guangzhou became honored as the only port in all of China permitted to trade with the west. Foreign goods entering China through the city were inspected by the Hongs, the emperor's bureaucrats, then transshipped throughout Guangdong, and on, into the rest of the country. All things exotic from around the world were handled by the people of Guangzhou first.

Soon Chong's family were landless workers, like millions of others living at the tumultuous heart of Guangzhou within sniffing distance of the vast docks. The Chongs were peddlers and had been since the city had opened its arms to the world. They lived in shanties near the docks. Most were "back men," selling what they could carry on their backs—rags, used clothing, occasionally new-made, and food meant to be eaten quickly. A few, like Soon's father, bettered themselves by securing work on the boats. It took two families several years to collect sufficient money to purchase a coveted place for Soon's father on one of the cargo gangs.

The family was the most important economic unit in China. Confucius decreed that peace, order, and good government flowed from the family. Moreover, social harmony and stability depended on fealty to the oldest male in the lineage. That was the theory. In reality such fealty was often the luxury of the well-to-do who could afford the time to pay obeisance and buy the medicine to keep the object of their respect alive into old age. Only one of Soon's grandparents still lived by the time he was born, his grandmother. She occupied a tiny corner of the family shanty and rarely moved, her consciousness long departed, snatched away by the chemicals she had worked with as a child in a nearby fabric factory.

There were 25 Chongs in Soon's direct family living in the two-room shanty, including two brothers and a sister, a married brother, his wife and two children, an assortment of unmarried aunts and uncles, and a cousin with twisted legs. The Chongs used the "hot mat" approach to make up for the shortage of beds. One room, completely covered with mats, was set aside for sleeping, which was accomplished in three shifts. When Soon got up, a brother took his place, and so on. In all, almost 175 interrelated Chongs, seven families, lived in seven adjacent shanties in a narrow gap known as Chong Alley.

At the opposite end of the city's hierarchy were the clans who owned land, ships, and buildings. They oversaw the government, controlled the flow of money, underwrote lawsuits, provided relief for the indigent, and built and repaired public buildings—particularly bridges. They alone could afford the costs of imperial exams for entry into the civil service.

The Chongs considered themselves fortunate. Most of their shanties had tin roofs with few holes; they supported themselves without selling a child into bondage or lopping a limb off a family member to provide an advantage in begging. They could even afford to have their homes inspected to ensure there was good feng shui. And each shanty door was guarded by an elaborately crafted portrait of a bearded and stern-looking Zhiang Tien Shi, the "catcher of ghosts." None of the Chongs owned land, or much of anything else for that matter. But if someone became sick they could afford basic medication or occasionally a visit from one of the herbalists who served the poorer inhabitants of the dock lands.

Soon had been helping to support his family since he was four and strong enough to wield the wooden paddle used to stir the *congee* as it cooked overnight. The thick, porridgelike rice dish, flavored with whatever was at hand, from vegetables to seafood, meat, or occasionally spices, was a staple on the docks. For the rest of his life, no matter where Soon was, it took little effort to evoke the earthy smell of steaming rice gruel.

"Upon my death my body should be wrapped in rice and mud like a century egg and buried for a hundred days," he joked to his sister. "When it is ripened it would be a grand *congee* flavoring for my grandchildren to use when the job of selling it is handed over to them."

"You're disgusting," his sister wrinkled her nose at him. "Is that all you can think of? Your *congee* pots!"

"The income buys your wedding dress!" Soon shot back.

"Hah!" she snorted haughtily. "And upon my wedding I will have a husband who tends his own fire *in one place* and does not have to roam about the streets like a beggar. Customers will come to him!"

✳

Soon carried his *congee* in two vats slung on a pole over his shoulders. The vats got fuller as he got older. By the age of ten, he'd developed calloused ridges at the peak of his shoulders and the nape of his neck. An hour before dawn Soon arose to ladle the simmering *congee* from the cook pots into the portable vats. His mother and sister were up even earlier, cooking it. On the street he spooned portions into paper containers folded into cone shapes, then flavored them to order with condiments he carried in pouches sewn into his tunic. Sprinkles of dried shrimp, berries, cured meat, fresh dog, and, when he could get hold of one, precious tidbits from a century egg, dramatically changed the taste and texture. He set a heated piece of iron into the vats to keep the *congee* warm.

When he was six, Soon went out selling *congee* with his brother Lim, then twelve. Two years later Lim joined his father working on the docks, and turned over the vats and carrying pole along with his purse containing a float for making change. Six precious words and Soon went from boy to man. "Little brother, it is your turn."

Each day, Soon proudly turned over his earnings, less the float, to his eldest brother, who then took a tithe to the Tong's dock boss. No business was transacted without the Tong, the underworld bureaucracy, taking a piece in return for keeping order and parceling out opportunities if a vendor died without an offspring or relative to take over. Yee As-wong, the dock boss, was rarely seen. However, his collectors could easily be spotted in their long jackets with a Mandarin crest stitched on the breast and the image of the imperial Foo Dog painted on the back.

People of Guangzhou rarely paid the first price for anything. The haggle was part of the purchase, as important as the flavor and consistency of the *congee*. In fact, it was often said that a successful haggle piqued the taste. And it was all given urgency by competition; dozens of peddlers hawked their wares and the customers were not rich—a better price beckoned around every corner.

Soon took pride in being the first on the street in the morning, never returning home until the last scrap of rice was sold. By the time he was eleven he'd cultivated customers who bought from him each day. Some he met at the doorsteps of their houses. But that didn't disrupt the haggle in the slightest.

"Hello and good morning, honorable sir!" Soon strode up to a narrow storefront hung with a dark-red banner advertising straw matting and nets. He bowed deeply to the man who was sweeping the cobblestones in front of the store.

"Good morning, most revered madam!" He bowed again to the man's stooped wife, on her hands and knees, scrubbing hard at invisible stains on the doorstep.

"Huh!" grunted the woman. "Come to steal our money again!"

"Oh no, dear-woman-deserving-of-much-respect," Soon bowed again. "I bring you the best and the cheapest *congee*."

"I have been buying from you for two years now," growled the man. "It is time you offered me a better price."

"For you I give best price, every day!"

"Today I will pay you your price less twenty-five percent, but tomorrow I will buy three times the amount for my wife's family who arrive for their annual visit."

"Ahhh, excellent idea, most honorable sir! Of course, for that price, which I have never given another, you would pay me the full sum now?"

"And how could I know you wouldn't run off with my money and not deliver the *congee*?"

Soon hung his head tragically. "Sir, great good sir! You know me!"

"Yes, and I also know my wife's family who would steal me blind if I didn't watch them every moment!" the man responded.

Though still a child, Soon nodded sympathetically. Denigrating one's relatives was a high art in Guangzhou.

"Perhaps an accommodation. I will give you fifteen percent under my best price if you give me three quarters the money for tomorrow's delivery."

"One quarter."

"Half and I won't charge for delivery."

"You never charge for delivery!"

Soon shrugged enigmatically. "Who knows what is contained in a price?"

The man broke into a broad laugh. "Are you telling me you have been including a delivery price while claiming you charge more to those who come to you on the docks?"

"Sir! I did not say that."

The man laughed again. The boy was good for a smile, which was far more than he had gotten out of his wife in the last ten years.

"All right. You give me fifteen percent under your best price today, and I will give you thirty percent toward the delivery tomorrow, but I want you to guarantee that price for a month."

Soon grinned. "Exactly what I was thinking myself, noble sir."

He sealed the deal with the deep bow and broad flourishes he'd copied after seeing what was accorded to a minor nobleman who once passed through the area.

Soon effortlessly calculated sums in his head, much faster than his customers. But he learned that feigning slowness often lowered a customer's guard.

Shortchanging a customer who politely paid the asking price with no haggle would be dishonorable to Soon's way of thinking. Shortchanging a customer who tried to cheat you was considered acceptable, even commendable. It wasn't that Soon ignored the moral teachings of Confucius, only that he modified them to fit his circumstances.

Soon would never keep any of the money made from selling *congee*. That belonged to the family. But what he made independently was his, not to be shared unless he chose. Occasionally a merchant or civil servant would give him a gratuity, a token in return for good service. That too was his. From his tips Soon bought a second purse to keep his own money. Infinitesimally, it grew.

Soon loved prowling through the dense city, home to five million souls. He loved the feel of the cobblestones under his bare feet, the smells—

not all of them pleasant, the lives that were lived out in full sight and hearing of anyone walking by. In the maze of narrow alleys he tried to decipher
the long, colorful banners hanging over his head. The banners, attached to
bamboo frames, advertised the various businesses located on the street. As
far as Soon knew, no one in his extended family could read. Most could
recognize their name chop for official documents but that was about it.
Over time Soon learned to match the characters with the business: money
exchangers, stores that sold bedding, herbs, and so on. The merchants
wouldn't let him into their premises but he could look from the outside.

Soon particularly liked the piers, where majestic brigantines, clippers,
and frigates, with their towering masts and elaborate rigging, loaded and
unloaded their wares. Hemming in the big ships were thousands of tiny Chinese junks, barges, and other floating craft made of wood, straw, bamboo, and
found material. On foggy mornings the shrieking of low-slung, oceangoing
teak junks as they jostled against each other was a siren call for him.

✳

When he turned twelve, Soon's father started giving him items for sale. "A
crate fell off the ship and broke open" was the usual explanation. Soon
doubted this; the variety of items—foodstuffs, bits of material, bottles—
suggested a more systematic pilferage.

Soon took care to offer these items only to his regulars, people he had
known for at least a year. That money belonged to the family. Recently, his
father had given him a pottery figurine about eight inches long, with a dark,
polished glaze. The face was round, the jaw jutting, and the forehead sloped
back from heavy brows over huge eyes lacking the Asian epicanthic fold. Soon
was fascinated by the combination of large breasts and male genitalia. Over it
was a tunic decorated with small, pale-green beads, each etched with an
inscription of some sort. Soon loved the piece from the moment he saw it.

Soon didn't know if the figurine had any value; he didn't think any of
his regulars would be interested. However, there was one man he could
approach.

25

*

The man appeared on the docks once a week without fail, stopping by the same vendors. Often he'd be waiting for Soon just as the boy arrived to set himself up on a lucrative corner to catch the first rush of early-morning trade. At dawn the *congee* was at its hottest, most flavorful, and thickest. The man always paid the asking price without demur. In turn Soon instinctively gave him his best price. To flavor the *congee* the man preferred *chow chow*, a sweet-hot mix of pickled ginger and orange peel in heavy syrup. The condiment was hard to come by and expensive, but Soon purchased a small supply and kept it hidden, especially from his sister who had a powerful taste for anything sweet.

Soon didn't know the man's name or occupation; he was obviously not from the docks, but his robes and shoes were fine, so the boy assumed he was a prosperous merchant. While eating, the man spoke of the weather, the river traffic, and occasionally the government. Soon knew the reigning emperor's name—Daogwang—and his other name, Huangdi, "Dread Lord," seventh imperial ruler of the Qing dynasty. But he had no idea who ruled the city, the province, or even the country. He simply assumed the richest controlled everything, just as they did on the dock, which had its own government—a ruling elite, police corps, corrupt officials. Soon didn't realize it, but the unelected and unacknowledged underground government of the dock lands exactly mirrored the Qing dynasty, from the imperial court at the emperor's Summer Palace in Beijing to his highest officials and on down to the lowliest local bureaucrat.

It was to this merchant that Soon hesitantly offered the figurine, minus the beaded tunic, which he couldn't bear to part with.

"Why have you shown this to me?" the merchant asked sharply.

Soon bowed low, hoping the flush on his cheeks wasn't obvious. "Forgive my forwardness. And forgive me for daring to waste the honorable sir's time. You are the only person I know who could appreciate its beauty." Soon bowed again, then said more quietly: "And its worth."

For a time the merchant examined the stone figurine, turning its rough but pleasing form over and over in his hand. He turned his scrutiny to Soon. "You are taking a great risk having such a thing in your possession, and an even greater risk showing it to me."

"I believe you to be an honest man," Soon replied simply.

"You have no idea who I am!" the merchant answered scornfully. "You don't even know my name."

"You will treat me fairly. That I know," Soon said, wondering if he had made a mistake. "I also know that my father expects me to sell this figurine."

The merchant didn't respond. Soon hurried on.

"To bring the statue back to my father would be disrespectful," said Soon, attempting to keep the pleading tone out of his voice.

The merchant studied Soon, who felt as if the man were boring holes in him.

"Tell me what you see when you look at this," the merchant asked, handing the figurine back to Soon.

"I am curious who made it." Emboldened by the merchant's question, Soon added, "The eyes are so different than any Chinese I have seen. The nose also. I once saw a man with a face like this. He was a black skin on one of the boats. I looked away, because the dark ones are bad luck, everyone knows that. But this," he pointed to the figure, "does not seem like bad luck at all."

The merchant grunted softly in reply. "Possibly."

Then he bowed to Soon; a brief dip of the head but a real bow nonetheless—not one of Soon's exaggerated flourishes as if to royalty or the bow one accorded to equals, but one of acknowledgment. No one of importance had ever bowed like this to Soon before.

"Come to my offices next week and we will discuss this further," the merchant said. "I will take it with me."

"I would be honored," Soon said, bowing in return. This time he copied the merchant.

As the merchant strolled unhurriedly away, the figurine out of sight beneath his robes, Soon suddenly remembered that he had turned thirteen the day before.

An hour earlier than the appointed time Soon presented himself at the address provided by the merchant. He was ushered into a large room where eight men worked standing up at long, narrow, highly polished tables. They were dressed identically, in long, dark tunics buttoned to midchest where the rough fabric scalloped out to one shoulder in the Manchu style. Their heads were freshly shaved, back to midcrown, and the older ones sported pencil-thin, greased moustache hanks hanging beneath their chins. Some fingered abacuses, while others made entries into long ledgers. One entire wall consisted of floor-to-ceiling shelves filled with the same ledgers. The only sound was the steady click-click of the abacuses. Soon found the sound pleasing.

Several of the men stared disdainfully, taking in Soon's grimy, bare feet, his frayed leggings, and ragged hat. No one offered him a seat, so Soon stood for nearly an hour, not daring to move, willing his breathing to be quiet. Finally a door opened and the merchant strode briskly in and beckoned the boy to follow. Soon could feel eight pairs of eyes between his shoulder blades.

To Soon's amazement, the merchant bade him sit in a high-backed chair covered in a soft, dark-red material. He had never sat in a real chair before, let alone one with a padded seat. The merchant lowered himself into a matching chair opposite and struck a small metal disk with a miniature hammer. A girl of Soon's age shuffled in, head bent, body inclined forward, eyes on her feet. She wore the pale robes of a virgin. Soon caught a hint of her delicious fragrance and longed to lean toward her and fill his lungs with the flowery smell. He flared his nostrils, inhaling as deeply as he could without making it obvious. The girl served the merchant first, pouring black, steaming tea into a delicate blue cup with red lettering. Then she held the tray out to Soon. He snatched at the cup and the burning liquid sloshed over his fingers. The sting brought tears to his eyes. As the girl backed away, he thought he heard the faintest cough of suppressed laughter.

"My daughter," the merchant said when she had gone. "Sat Yee. She's beautiful, is she not?"

Soon hadn't dared to look directly at the girl but nodded vigorously in agreement. He carefully mimicked the merchant's every move, and they sipped in tandem for a quarter of an hour while the older man spoke of the weather.

"You have presented me with a dilemma," he finally said. "I have been eating your *congee* for two years. You are a special young man of great potential."

Soon's face reddened with embarrassment. Praise was largely unknown to him, especially from a relative stranger. But he also became wary. He had heard stories of "special" young men from the docks recruited for uses he didn't care to think about.

"The figurine is ancient but it is not legal trade. As you know, foreign vessels are prohibited from going farther upriver, and they may not take any cargo that has not been approved. This was undoubtedly intended for one of those ships."

Soon, though he didn't know anything of the sort, nodded again.

"Foreigners buy treasures and sacred objects from China. They command great prices in faraway cities." The merchant sighed deeply. "Despite our recent defeat at the hands of the British over the opium trade, this trade in artifacts has been forbidden by the emperor and the British have promised to abide by it. You could not safely sell it. It would take years even for me to find the right buyer."

The merchant reached down and drew a brocade cloth bag out from under his chair. Inside was the figurine.

"I have read in books about a time when huge people with black skins lived in China. They were blessed by the dragon and became warriors that no one could defeat. It was only the great emperor, Dangzing, who drove them out of China and drowned them all in the sea. This piece undoubtedly comes from those times."

Soon breathed deeply. Dragons and black-skinned people who were not slaves. What a great story. He would swear Lim to secrecy and pass along the merchant's words.

"I have pondered the problem, and this very day visited a soothsayer for guidance.

"The soothsayer told me that the winds of change are blowing strongly. He said I could be borne away by this wind or I could sprout wings and fly along with it wherever it went."

Soon had no idea where the conversation was heading.

"You are like this figurine—crudely made and poorly finished but . . ."

Soon glanced uneasily at the door.

The merchant leaned forward.

"The Opium War has changed everything," he explained. "Guangzhou is no longer the only port open to the foreigners. With four other cities to compete with there are many more people going hungry. I have friends in government and they tell me there is great unrest. Rebels may rise against the emperor."

Soon stared. He knew the merchant was wealthy, but to actually have friends in positions to know such information put him on a different plane entirely—at least in the eyes of a boy who sold *congee* for a living.

"When flood waters begin to rise the wise do not build close to shore," the man said enigmatically.

Soon's head ached from the unaccustomed strength of the tea, the warm room, and the effort of deciphering the merchant's words.

"I would like you to begin working for me four days from now," the merchant was saying. Soon shot up in his chair.

"Work for you!" he blurted; surely he had heard the words wrong.

"You will start at first light. I don't tolerate tardiness."

"Work for you?" Soon repeated stupidly. He couldn't have been more surprised if the merchant's daughter had walked in and kissed him on the lips.

"I will pay the required indenture to your father, which should assist in procuring your beloved sister's dowry.

"You will have six months to prove your worth."

Soon, almost faint with the implications of what he'd heard, made up his mind before the merchant had finished speaking. He rose from his seat and bowed deeply, skinny arms clasped tightly across the front of his body. "I would be honored to accept your very generous offer. But sir, I have two questions?"

"The first?"

"What is your name?"

The man chuckled and bowed, "Sang Jia Yuan, at your service. I was firstborn in my family," he added, explaining the reason for his personal name Jia Yuan. "What is your second question?"

"What is my pay?"

"Ah so. Never accept first price. That is your motto. But I have taken first price from you all these months, now it is your turn. Learn the work first. Then the money will come. I will, however, feed you two meals a day and clothe you suitably."

✳

It turned out that Mr. Sang wasn't really a merchant at all, rather a bookkeeper. This was a disappointment to Soon. In his short experience, the only way to make money was in trade—goods for coins, coins for other goods, goods for goods, and sometimes goods for service.

Mr. Sang's clientele ranged from a jeweler to a small import-export house to a nearby brothel—the Palace of Extreme Unction—with an opium den–gambling room in the cellar. Occasionally Mr. Sang was asked to broker arrangements between his clients. He took a small fee for this service.

Shortly after the first Opium War ended, just a few months before, China had been forced to open the ports of Amoy, Foochow, Shanghai, and Ningpo to the rest of the world. It quickly became more difficult to get foreign goods in the city, as fewer ships now came to Guangzhou. Even worse, the ships' holds were crowded with opium chests and had less room for other, more mundane cargo. Still, Mr. Sang had a network of contacts with the Chinese boats that moved cargo from the foreign ships upriver or to other ports. He made additional money from his clients by finding the wealthier among them desired items, such as British whiskey.

Bookkeeping and brokering earned him a good income, but the core of Mr. Sang's growing success was the risky practice of lending money to those without sufficient stature, contacts, or cash flow to borrow from the established lending houses.

"I deal in capital," he told Soon six months after the boy began working for him. "Sometimes I see cash in one of my client's businesses and I arrange for it to be loaned to another in need, for a fee."

Soon learned that his employer had an interest in a dozen family-owned boats. He also owned a share in a boat-building yard. In all, he'd financed twenty or so enterprises, including seven peddlers.

"One business feeds the other, and they all feed my family" was another of Sang's favorite sayings.

For the first six months Soon accompanied the merchant on his rounds, setting off at dawn to collect interest and check on his investments. On the very first day they walked the exact route along the docks Soon had seen Sang take for years. As a weak sun was beginning to define the flocks of boats on the river, they arrived to find Yip Lee, Soon's brother, waiting for the morning rush. Grinning proudly, the young boy ladled huge quantities of *congee* for Soon and Mr. Sang.

"You must not do that, not even for family!" Soon chastised. "You have lost your profit before you have begun."

Soon spent the second half of each day learning to read and write and tally large numbers with an abacus. He loved the rhythmic clack of the ivory beads and the magic of calculating with the flick of a finger.

In the time Soon spent with Mr. Sang only once did someone fail to pay what was owed. It was a member of the flat-boat clan who plied the shallow tributaries of the delta for eels, crabs, and snails. He couldn't come up with his monthly interest because a flood on the Pearl River had spoiled fishing for six months. Sang took his youngest daughter in payment and promptly sold her to a brothel owner in one of the Three Counties surrounding the city.

"If you are careful who you advance money to," Sang told Soon, "you will rarely have to resort to extremes. Fortunately I have never had to threaten violence to collect a debt. But you must be ready in an instant if you feel that your money is at risk. Remember, your money is what protects your family."

"I look at a person's eyes," Soon said. "If they slide this way and that, I think he is dishonest."

"And if he is an honest man, how do his eyes behave?"

"They wash the face of the one he is talking to, then he looks away in respect."

"Yes," agreed Sang, "that works for the average man, but I have found, to my sorrow, that the biggest thieves and liars have the best grasp of etiquette."

"Then how can one judge?" asked Soon. " How do you decide who you will loan money to?"

Sang tapped his ears. "This is the secret. I listen to what people say and remember it. You never know when it will be useful. I make friends where I can. I do little favors. Ease people's burdens. And I listen and ask questions. Everyone is important. Everyone knows something that could help you. Even the boy selling *congee* on the docks," he said with emphasis. "Never be too proud to take information from a lowly source.

"You will have noticed that I visit Water Lily at the House of Extreme Unction each Friday afternoon. The child relieves me of the week's frustrations. Much to the appreciation of my wife. But she also provides excellent information—about our clients and business partners, hardly a one of whom doesn't visit either the girls or the gambling room, or take the pipe. If I owned such an establishment, I would be rich from the information alone.

"Yesterday Lily told me that Mr. Kim Ho of the import-export company had some erectness difficulty. And afterward he chased the dragon in the opium den for the first time. Today I looked over his company's books exceedingly carefully. I found nothing amiss. Doubtless it is a onetime thing with our friend Mr. Ho, but you never know."

Soon availed himself of the amenities of the House of Extreme Unction with an introduction supplied by Mr. Sang. The young lady went by the name of Scented Hibiscus. Soon prayed that his employer wouldn't hear of the sorry episode. He'd been so excited and nervous that he'd spread his seed all over himself and his clothes as he was pulling his tunic off. The second session was more satisfactory, with his seed being deposited where it belonged, but it was over in seconds.

There had been pleasure involved, but it had been considerably lessened by the fee, which, unlike a loan, would never be returned and paid no interest. All and all, Soon preferred to keep his capital in his purse and deal with his needs manually. He elected not to return for a third session.

✳

"She begged me to stay. She even promised me her younger sister. A virgin!"

"Did she take her clothes off?" Yip Lee panted out the question.

"Of course!"

"All off?"

"Of course."

"Did you . . . did you ever see a woman without her clothes before?"

"I am a man now," Soon said loftily. "Such things are common when you become a man."

"Do you see her every day?" Yip Lee thought that if a woman showed her breasts to him, let alone anything else, he would stay with her forever.

"Don't be stupid, little brother. She cries when I leave but I am busy. I have many obligations to Mr. Sang as his assistant."

Assistant. It had a good ring to it. Importance. Position. Purpose. Assistant. Though Mr. Sang never conferred the title on Soon and he was still referred to as "go boy" by the clerks, Mr. Sang's butler, Mr. Sang's wife, and even her maid, he considered himself an assistant. He'd tried out the title on some of Mr. Sang's lesser business associates, and they hadn't objected. Assistants, he reasoned, do not just carry and follow orders, they are involved in the business affairs of their employers.

Yip Lee was impressed both by his brother's great sexual escapades and by his title. The boy still wore pride in his work like a brand-new coat, but he dreamed of the day when he might follow Soon into the larger world of business beyond the docks. Yip Lee loved to serve his brother, always ladling out extra, as well as a double serving of Soon's favorite dried-shrimp topping. The inevitable scolding he received had become as comfortable as an old shirt.

"Cod balls! Cod balls!" A high, harsh cry joined the growing cacophony as the dock came to life.

"That one sleeps past dawn every day," Yip Lee derided. "No wonder that family doesn't even have their own home!"

"Where do they live?" asked Soon, listening to the cry gain strength.

"They feed the family of Chow Fat and in return take their mats at night."

The Chow Fats were "ghosters" who worked while the sun slept. Like Soon's father and uncle, the father and two sons were mules. They carried freight from the holds and set it next to the ship's gangway, where stackers moved it onto the dock in preparation for loading onto smaller boats or carriages for transportation elsewhere. Chow Fat had been born a poor peasant in Poon Yue County, north of the city. When his wife and daughter succumbed to cholera, he brought his young sons to Guangzhou to work. With no women to care for them, the arrangement with the peddler's family worked out nicely.

"Cod balls! Cod balls! Hiyee! Hiyee!"

"I have eaten his cod balls," sneered Yip Lee. "Old fat, no salt. Terrible."

"He will never be an assistant to an important man," declared Soon.

"If you are very lucky I will let you be my assistant one day," Yip Lee grinned at his brother.

"Tend to your business, boy," growled Soon, feinting with one hand then grabbing Yip Lee's chopsticks with the other. "Or I will take my *congee* vats away. The only other job you are fit for is washing the private parts of old men."

Yip Lee poked his finger through the front of his leggings and waggled it at Soon.

"The *congee* tastes better since I took over. All the customers say so," Yip Lee called cheerfully to his brother's retreating back. "But they haven't forgotten you," he hollered. "They often ask what happened to my dull-witted brother."

"Your dull-witted brother is now so rich he bought his own foot thongs," Soon shouted back, kicking up his feet as he skipped and ran happily toward Mr. Sang's house and offices.

Soon no longer waited silently at the back of the clerks' office while one of the sour-faced scribes went to inform Mr. Sang he had arrived. He strolled through the ledger room, glancing at books and ignoring the scowls of the men at the long, high bench. Now eighteen, Soon had taken over most of Mr. Sang's collection duties among the lower classes and twice had even closed two small loans himself—one to a matmaker and one to a breeder of Ho birds, fighting pheasants, whose daughter required dowry money.

This particular day Soon was in high spirits, with new sandals on his feet and a new accomplishment to report to his employer. For the past two years Mr. Sang had quietly paid for Soon to take English lessons. With the increasing British presence in China, Mr. Sang was among a handful of businessmen who suspected China would one day fall. When that day came about, those who could speak both the language of business and the language of the conquerors would be useful in the new regime. Even during the Opium Wars, when learning foreign languages was outlawed, Mr. Sang secretly studied the bewildering tongue. But in just two years Soon had easily outstripped his employer, language coming as naturally to him as numbers. Today Soon would tell Mr. Sang that he had finished reading his first book—*Physical Training Exercises for Young Men.* He laughed at the pictures and the peculiar physiques of the half-naked British men in the illustrations.

Mr. Sang was in the ledger room, speaking quietly to a boy a few years younger than Soon. Everything about him spoke of good breeding, from the tightly woven, heavy silk of his robes to the ivory clasp on his queue and the arrogant tilt of his head. He stared openly at Soon, not offering a bow or any acknowledgment. Soon hated him instantly.

"I'm glad you're here at last," Mr. Sang greeted Soon, who regretted the brief time he'd spent with Yip Lee.

"This is Wong Xu Hue, son of my second cousin."

Soon bowed respectfully. The boy barely tilted his head.

"Wong Xu Hue has arrived this day to begin his duties as my assistant."

Soon felt as if his heart had dropped to his feet. "Your assistant?" he managed.

"Yes," Mr. Sang replied, oblivious to Soon's dismay. "I have been waiting for him to finish his education at the Imperial Academy."

"And me?" Soon asked, reeling.

"You?"

"What, what will my duties be?" Soon stammered, aware of the collective smirks of the eavesdropping clerks.

"Your duties remain as they are until you set sail," replied Mr. Sang a little testily, "but Xu Hue will now speak with my voice."

Two words lodged in Soon's mind. "Set sail."

" . . . to the northwest coast of Mexico. It is called California," Mr. Sang was continuing, pronouncing the name awkwardly.

"The United States of America may one day soon own all of that continent. You will go there."

"Set sail," Soon repeated. He had lost his way in the conversation, so focused was he on those two words, "set sail." Mr. Sang had turned back to Wong Xu Hue and took up his explanation of the ledger-filing system.

Soon felt as if his body had suddenly frozen. He had never traveled more than an hour upriver, nor even to the far edges of the city. Virtually his entire life had been spent within a two-hour walk of Chong Alley. He was perfectly content doing what he was doing and had never even thought about going elsewhere. The idea of boarding one of those boats, which he had watched come and go since he was a baby, and sailing off to a land on the other side of the world made him dizzy with fear.

"What would I do there?" he uttered weakly, not caring that he broke into Mr. Sang's conversation.

Mr. Sang ignored Soon as he finished his explanation to his new assistant. Then he turned and spoke quietly, each word feeling like a little jab to Soon:

"I have spent a year researching this place. Gold was discovered last year, and I know that some of the British ships are loaded with iron for railroads. The United States of America is a primitive country but powerful. Mexico has lost its grip on the north. Some of the biggest landowners in the Three Counties are sending armies of men. If cities develop on that coast, one of them must belong to China. You will stay one year and return with your report on opportunities in the new land."

"I thought . . ." Soon no longer knew what he thought.

"What did you think?"

"I thought you wanted, you wanted me to . . ."

"To what?"

"Be your assistant," Soon responded, feeling foolish the second the words were out. He saw a broad smirk spread across Wong Xu Hue's face.

26

✳

March 1849

Approaching San Francisco Bay

Forty-three days, every single one of them worse than the one before.

Two hundred and seventeen countrymen. Three smuggled women. Five bodies—all tossed unceremoniously overboard. Respect for the dead was one thing; living with their corporeal form was another.

✳

Despite his earlier anxiety, Soon Chong's trip from Guangzhou to the deep harbor of Yerba Buena, which everyone still called it, began with thrilling anticipation. His passage aboard the Russian brig *Constantine* had been purchased by Mr. Sang. It was the ship's second visit to the small northern California port, the first time being January 16, 1847, just three days after the capitulation of Cahuenga, the final battle in the doomed Mexican war with the United States.

The first mate of the brig was in charge of the passengers: the Chinese, eleven British subjects, three Russians, and one German. Soon stood smiling at one end of the long, scrubbed deck with the throng of passengers waving boisterous good-byes to their families. His father, mother, brothers, two uncles, two aunts, and even his decrepit grandmother came to see him off. So too did his sister, her husband, their new baby, and several of his brother-in-law's family. Ticket prices allowed each passenger to bring along one trunk, usually made of wicker, or a large basket and two smaller ones. As the ship floated away from shore on the ebb tide, relatives flung tied cloth bags at their departing family members in an attempt to evade the rule. Most of the bags fell into the water, and for an hour after the ship headed south to the river's mouth, those left behind vied with the scavengers to get the sodden bundles before they sank into the oily water.

Soon leaned over the railing, watching his birth city recede. For a time he could make out the densely packed shores of the river—boats, shanties, warehouses, but they quickly melted into a blue smudge on the skyline. That had been his world. Now it was not. Soon turned to face the sun and the gray swells that stretched into his next lifetime.

Surrounded by his countrymen, he was certain no harm could come to him. True, they were mostly peasants, which he, most assuredly, was not. Though Soon Chong of Chong Alley did descend from rice carriers of Say-yup, the poor Four Counties of Guangzhou, he now considered himself elevated to those of Sam-yup, the commercial district of Three Counties, where Mr. Sang had his home and offices. By dress he could tell that only a handful of those aboard did not come from See-yup. Most wore the pale, rough leggings held up by a sash belt and an overshirt characteristic of peasants.

While he was contemplating his newly created origins, a sharp pain sent Soon down on one knee.

"Below! Below!"

He turned to face the sound. A bearded, scowling man, huge to Soon's eyes, waved a rod over the boy's head.

"Below! Below!" he shouted in dreadful Chinese.

As Soon raised his arm to protect his head, the man poked him hard in the ribs.

"Below! Below!"

Soon grabbed his belongings and dragged them after him as quickly as he could. He was not among the first group pushed roughly down the narrow stairs to the large hold, so the best positions against the walls were already taken.

"They let us smile good-bye, wait until we're out of sight, then shit upon us," one man snarled, shoving Soon's big, square basket off to one side to make more room for his own.

It took several days to establish a hierarchy. The more size, cunning, and meanness one possessed the more floor space one occupied. The status of the exalted Soon of Sam-yup was as nothing. Perhaps if the emperor himself was ensconced in the hold, he might be given a measure of lee-way—perhaps. Later Soon learned that each Chinese had paid as much for their stinking, stuffy, cramped quarters in the hold as the white passengers who traveled in comfort above decks.

Mercifully Soon didn't get seasick, though with the ghastly smell in the hold, he came close. The others weren't so lucky, and the waste buckets were always brim-full of vomit. Soon also mastered the art of sleeping propped upright, and managed four or five hours sleep each night. The Chinese were allowed on the after deck, out of sight of the other passengers, once in the morning and once in the evening, an hour at a time. By pumping briskly with a hand pump, they could wash up with freezing-cold seawater. No soap was provided. Fortunately, for those who could eat, there was plenty of rice cooked in large vats over oil braziers and dried fish served cold. Every few days a crewman would drop a box of the fish down into the hold and let the Chinese fight over it as pigs over scraps.

But now, forty-four days later, it was over. Sitting impatiently on his basket waiting for the call to disembark, Soon fingered the letter Mr. Sang had pressed into his hand before departure. It was a lengthy missive outlining Mr. Sang's own honorable antecedents, his existing family connections, and current business interests. He finished the letter with a request for a mutually profitable liaison in the New World, through his agent, Soon Chong.

"You will present this to the Chinese businesses you find in San Francisco," he'd instructed. "With it you should have no difficulty finding a responsible position. You are to keep your ears and eyes awake and return after a year to report on opportunities suitable for my business."

"As you wish," Soon bowed low. He was resigned to the voyage. After spending three months as assistant to Mr. Sang's new supercilious assistant, he was only too glad to leave.

"There is one more matter we must deal with," Mr. Sang said gravely. "I have finally disposed of the figurine you brought to me those many years ago."

"I had forgotten about that," Soon lied.

"It had been foremost in my mind," Mr. Sang assured. "But it has taken many hours of diligent inquiry to find a safe buyer." From out of the folds of his gown, he handed over a purse containing £50 sterling.

Soon goggled as he examined the money.

"You will use this money to finance your investigations on my behalf. If you present me with your written accounts I will reimburse your expenses on your return."

Soon was now taller than his employer, who suddenly seemed rather old. Mr. Sang bowed quickly to his apprentice and marched off without looking back.

Troubled about carrying so much money on his person, Soon consulted with his father.

"I may have something for you when I return from the shipyards tonight."

It occurred to Soon for the first time that there was much he didn't know about his father. In his entire life he'd hardly ever talked to him. In fact he knew more about Mr. Sang than he did about Wu Chong.

When Soon's father returned from work, he presented Soon with a smooth piece of porcelain about as long as a finger and cylindrical in shape.

"Here, let me show you." He twisted the cylinder in his gnarled hand; it was threaded in the middle so that the two halves fit smoothly together. "The money fits inside."

"Where do I keep it?" asked Soon with a sinking feeling.

"Here," his father said with a laugh, gesturing to his bottom. "Oil it and it will pop right in. No one is going to look there for your money!"

"It must have cost you a great deal."

"No matter. It is my parting gift. I am sure you will return a rich man and pay me back many times. It is said on the docks that Americans are so wealthy—everyone has a gun and a horse."

The two looked uncertainly at each other. Not since he was a baby had Soon's father touched him. He did not then either.

✳

Dragging his belongings out of the hold was not as difficult as dragging them in; Soon lost almost half to pilfering. Only by finally paying a guardian fee did he manage to hang on to the rest. The self-appointed guardians took charge within hours of leaving port, and they would set foot on American soil considerably wealthier than when they left China. They and those running the nonstop gambling games were the only ones to do so.

The mist was heavy, so the light didn't hurt Soon's eyes. His first impression was of hills rising sharply from the harbor. The second thing that caught his eye were the trees. Soon doubted there were as many in all of China, let alone a single one as large as these. Though the Mexicans and then the Americans had logged most of the first growth near the water, the steep hills were still heavily cloaked, and in the far distance he could see nothing but a wall of green and brown.

The sight filled him with dread. He was mesmerized until the first mate bellowed orders in his terrible Chinese to move along the long narrow gangway and off the ship.

"Gum San!" softly at first, then the volume rose. "Gum San! Gum San! Gold Mountain! Gold Mountain!" They pointed to the hills.

The voices of his countrymen stirred Soon. Many had been too ill or weak in the last few weeks of the voyage to say much at all. As they chanted the words strength flooded into his limbs. The ragged crowd shouldered their bundles and moved off, wobbly legged, down the gangway and onto the United States of America. For a moment the world whirled around him as Soon's legs struggled to balance on solid ground.

"Stop! It is an order! Stop!"

"Stop him!"

Three men ran by Soon. To his surprise, one of them was the brutish first mate. As he ran the man threw off his hat and tore at his navy jacket.

"Deserters!"

Six men pounded after the three. Pop! Pop! Soon had never heard a gun fired but they didn't make nearly as much noise as he expected. One man stumbled and fell, while the other dragged himself along for a short distance before he stopped, clutching his leg. The first mate, despite his size, ran like a gazelle. The guns flared again but didn't bring him down.

"I guess gold hunting is more appealing than another moment aboard that fetid cockroach heaven," observed the man who'd been Soon's left-side neighbor on the crossing.

Once accustomed to dry land, Soon looked around for the city before realizing that the paltry collection of small wooden buildings *was* the city. Oddly, many were unfinished, with doors gaping and roofs half completed. Despite the crowd at the pier there was an eerie quiet about the place too. Thousands of buildings would occupy the same space in Guangzhou. Pigs, chickens, and dogs ran loose. No one in China would be so careless about valuable animals. A little wire-haired terrier scooted by and Soon's mouth watered. Was food so plentiful here that people could afford to allow animals to roam free?

"Double wages, Johnny! Easy work!"

The words were first sung out in English by a white man wearing an enormous straw hat and carrying a gun as long as Soon's arm strapped low on his hip. A Chinese interpreter then shouted the offer in several Guangdong dialects. Groups of men from the ship clustered, and a rapid haggle began.

"Honorable sir," Soon bowed low to the interpreter. "I search for a merchant establishment. Kindly direct me to the business district of my countrymen."

The man laughed. "There's not much business around. Everyone's gone gold hunting. You'd best get yourself taken on by one of the white businesses. Everyone's hiring. They're desperate. Everyone's gone for gold. Even the chilis."

"Chilis?"

"Mexicans."

"What work is offered here?"

"Cook, laundry, cleaning, and, of course, digging."

"But I am a businessman."

The man glanced at Soon's filthy garments, his diaperlike leggings, his tattered *shen-i,* and snorted: "Businessman?"

When Soon left China, his *shen-i,* a one-piece garment of tunic and trousers sewn together, was clean and respectable. He had separated the tunic from the trousers because it had been so hot, and he'd knotted the trousers up around his knees to keep the bottoms out of the water and filth that covered the floor.

The man laughed again and walked off.

Soon had no intention of being taken on to wash someone's clothes. He touched the letter against his breast. His right-side neighbor from the ship, a congenial enough fellow, walked by, following another man, a cousin who had preceded him, arriving with the first boatload of Chinese in 1848, fifty-four of them aboard the brig *Eagle.* Soon followed them; he couldn't think of anything else to do.

The tiny Chinese community grouped around Portsmouth Square. The Chinese merchants primarily sold provisions: rice, mats, baskets, clothing, washboards, soap, and hardware—picks, shovels, and other mining equipment. Digger Johnnies with their own equipment commanded a higher wage in the goldfields. These businesses were owned by wealthy merchants from Guangzhou or Hong Kong, whose well-capitalized representatives had also arrived on the *Eagle.* Some of them landed with complete inventories and had set up shop in a tent within hours of walking off the ship. Soon recognized some of the commercial emblems of sizable Guangzhou trading houses.

Soon paid two pounds for the use of a wash-up cubicle and half a jug of clean water. He scrubbed hard, rebraided his queue, and changed into his best robe, his only other clothing. Then he called on the most prosperous-looking of the hastily thrown together commercial houses, where he was greeted cordially enough but given no hope of any job beyond the most menial.

Soon wasn't discouraged. After a century of life on the docks, the

Chongs were well accustomed to rejection. It had no meaning beyond what it was. Soon dutifully went from establishment to establishment, certain that Mr. Sang's letter would persuade a proprietor that good fortune had arrived in the form of this eager young man. In three hours he had approached every single establishment, from a one-person tent to a precarious two-story building with stairs running up the outside. No one was even slightly interested in reading Mr. Sang's letter, much less hiring him. The best chance was a grudging offer to work as a kitchen boy in return for food and lodging.

A stone's throw from Portsmouth Square, two white-owned businesses leaned toward each other—Horwold's Hardware and General Store and the Hotel Exotica. Soon loitered in front of both for fifteen minutes, pondering best approach. Mr. Sang's plan hadn't envisioned this eventuality. Should he use coolie English, or show them that he spoke quite well? Should he ask to see the owner or speak to whoever opened the door?

"Take a hike, chink!" growled a man on the porch of the hotel before Soon had even made up his mind. At the store, a twisted woman, her spine so bowed she could only stare at the floor, barked up at him: "We don't hire Johnnies here!"

The derogatory nickname perplexed Soon. Johnny was a perfectly good English name. The figure in *Physical Training Exercises for Young Men* was called John. Yet even on the Russian ship the crew had adopted the English insult. Soon assumed it was easier to call all Chinese John than wrestle with their real names. He had no idea the moniker was a corruption of the French *jaune*, for "yellow." Just as the French *sauvage*—"savage"—had become siwash, a common derogatory term for Indian, *jaune chinoise* had become Johnny Chinaman.

At the end of his first day Soon came to the conclusion that the city of San Francisco was little more than an illusion. Though thousands of people, including some thirty-one thousand Chinese, had passed through the former Mexican village in the last twelve months, the key phrase was "passed through." Most stayed a day or two, just long enough to find transportation to the mountains and as many pans, picks, and shovels as they could carry. The permanent population was less than two thousand and everything was geared to feeding and provisioning the miners and sending supplies by the wagon-trainload into the Sierra Nevadas, where prices could easily be multiplied by ten. The normal services, trade, and business of a city simply didn't exist.

Curiously, despite the exodus to the mountains, there seemed to be a dearth of beds for a good price. Soon had managed to hang on to his hoard of British pounds during the voyage. He was dismayed when the keeper of one rooming house demanded £3 for a single night—fifty times what it would have cost in Guangzhou. But he was warned that boats with hundreds more would be arriving daily, all of whom would need beds for a night or two.

"If you don't take it, someone else will," a Sam-yup hotelier, who ran the hovel that passed for a rooming house, snapped at him impatiently.

"Three pounds, one night. Water extra. You leave by seven A.M. or pay two pounds more. Now be quick!"

Three pounds bought one night on a bristly straw mat in a tiny room with ten others. Outside the door of the room a man was emptying his bowels in a bucket. Two more buckets of grayish water stood nearby.

"You want toilet, you pay more. Otherwise outside."

For another pound, Soon got a bowl of rice and some deep-fried fish, which the man's wife wrapped in newspaper before giving it to him. Everyone's making money around here, he thought glumly as he carefully chewed his food. At this rate, my fortune will last about three weeks.

After Soon finished the greasy bundle, he passed the time sitting outside on a bench—a piece of wood nailed across a stump—and read the oily paper to practice his English. For nearly two months he hadn't spoken a word of it and he didn't want to lose ground.

The article in the *California Star* was dated June 10, 1848, nine months earlier:

Every seaport as far south as San Diego, and every interior town, and nearly every rancho from the base of the mountains in which the gold has been found, to the Mission of San Luis, has become suddenly drained of human beings. Americans, Californians, Indians and Sandwich Islanders, men, women and children, indiscriminately.

Should there be that success which has repaid the efforts of those employed for the last month, during the present and next, as many are sanguine in their expectations, we confess to unhesitatingly believing that not only will we witness the depopulation of every town, the desertion of every rancho, and the desolation of the once promising crops of the country, but we will also see the population dwindling in the adjacent territories.

There is an area explored, within which a body of 50,000 men can labor without maliciously interfering with each other. Then, there need be no cause for contention and discord, where as yet, we are gratified to know, there is harmony and good feeling existing.

(Four days later the *California Star* folded when all the staff rushed off to a new gold strike at Sutter's Mill on the American River.)

"You can read that?" a boy, younger than Soon, said in the peasant Hakka dialect.

"Of course," Soon drew himself up.

"What does it say?"

Soon wasn't sure about "sanguine in their expectations" and a handful of other phrases, but he'd got the idea of it.

"It says everyone has gone to look for gold."

The boy snorted. "You've been staring at it for half an hour and that's all you got? I could have told you the same thing!"

"It also says there's room in the mountains for fifty thousand men to mine," Soon added stiffly, searching for some piece of information the boy couldn't know.

"Mmmph," the boy scoffed. "There's already that many, I'm told, and more going up daily, and still they're getting ten dollars a day for rough labor, easy."

He leaned toward Soon. "You know what a dollar is?"

"I most certainly do!" Soon walked away from the disrespectful nuisance. He wasn't too sure about the value of a dollar but he thought it took at least half a dozen of them to equal one British pound sterling.

That night Soon listened long into the early hours as the other bodies in the room tossed, turned, and groaned. From one corner came what sounded like stifled weeping. Though he was surrounded by people, he'd never felt so alone and lonely, or so confused. Nothing was as he'd expected. But as he lay there among his sleeping countrymen, resolve began to creep back into the eighteen-year-old.

"I did not come all this way to work in a laundry, or to be a house boy," Soon said to himself.

Most of the other Chinese staying in the rooming house were heading out the next day for the American River goldfields. Soon decided to follow. It couldn't be worse than staying here in this wet, cold, semi-deserted little town.

27

*

Soon joined a caravan of 137 people—Mexicans, Americans, British, Russians, Chinese—nine wagons and an assortment of spavined horses, cowhocked mules, and half-wild donkeys on the ninety-mile journey from San Francisco to Sutter's Mill on the American River in the foothills of the Sierra Nevada mountains. He'd strapped his basket to his back, hefted his carry pole over his shoulder, and within four hours was nearly in tears with agony. With each ensuing step, Gum San, the Gold Mountain, seemed to recede. Soon had grown soft in his years with Mr. Sang; no longer was he the *congee* peddler who could walk all day with a heavy load on his shoulder poles. His sisal slippers came apart by the end of the first day, forcing him to go barefoot. His feet, once thickly calloused from walking barefoot, blistered on the rocky terrain. He bound them as best he could with clothes from his basket. All the next day and the day after that people passed him, at least half of them wiry Hakka peasants who trod determinedly ahead as if they'd been trekking to the California mountains all their life.

Soon was delayed crossing at Sausalito, because none of the boats would take British pounds in payment.

"But this money is worth more than dollars!" protested Soon.

"We're Americans here, Johnny!" the boatman, a crofter from Dundee, proclaimed in his thick burr. "We use the queen's money for wipin' our arses. Greenbacks, gold, or go away."

Finally Soon found a man in uniform on a chestnut horse who agreed to take £10 in exchange for dollars, one for one. Soon stared at his $10 gloomily; it was like giving away money. A battered, handpainted sign advertised the cost of the boat trip as $5; $4, $3, and $2 were crossed out beside it. But when he set foot on the flat-bottom barge the crofter demanded seven.

"It'll be ten tomorrow, Johnny. Make up your mind!"

✳

At the end of the sixth day, Soon, among the last of the group that set out from San Francisco, reached the south fork of the American River. Just below what had begun as Captain John Sutter's gristmill to provide flour for the lumber camp higher up the river, a settlement of sorts grouped around a stockaded fort was taking root. Despite his agony, Soon marveled at the chaos and activity. Everything and everyone was in motion. There wasn't a clean individual anywhere, as recent rains had turned the shanty, tent, and "bush harbor" community into a muddy bog. Carts, axle-deep in mud, bullocks straining mightily, were carrying goods from launches, which could go no farther up the river. Dozens of sullen-looking men dressed in an odd combination of Mexican, American, and Indian clothing carried items from the launches, which couldn't fit into the carts.

"They look nothing like Chinese men," Soon said to himself, "and they aren't red at all, but a dirty brown."

Many were missing teeth, and they didn't appear nearly as impressive as the sturdy peasants of the Pearl River delta.

"You're soft," a voice declared in the Yue dialect, startling Soon from his reverie. He turned to find an owlish, overweight man sizing him up as one might judge a fish at market. The man cast his gaze over the other Chinese milling around and debating among themselves whether they should hire on or find their own spot on the river.

"Soft," the man said again, "but I think you'll do. I'll hire you. Bring your things." He turned on his heel and marched off.

"Wait a minute!" hollered Soon. "What are you talking about? Where are you going?"

"I need help on my claim. I'll feed you—one year only. Teach you how to mine. It's a good deal. Do you know how to use a pick? Do you know what a pick is? Do you own a pick?"

The man paused only long enough to see Soon shake his head. "You don't know the first thing about mining. You're no good to anyone else. I'll teach you, feed you. You won't have to spend any money. Best deal you'll find here."

"Why don't you hire them?" asked Soon, motioning at two strapping Hakka peasants walking briskly toward them.

"I doubt that you can work as much as they," the man acknowledged, "but I bet you can talk. Soft men talk. Hakka are only good to work. Too ignorant to talk. I value talk."

Once again Soon found himself carried along on someone else's tide. Mr. Sang's belief that he could find a position in a good business and then scout opportunities for his employer now seemed ridiculous. Nothing in this country seemed to matter but the gold. "The fat man's right," Soon muttered. "I know nothing about mining but what have I got to lose?" Shouldering his pole, he wearily followed the man who was already some distance ahead and moving quickly despite his girth.

"So, where do you come from?" the man asked when Soon caught up to him. But before he could respond the fat man launched into his own life story.

Tong Yuk Jee, Soon learned, had "in my once life" been a small-time labor supplier in Guangzhou. During the 1830s he'd done a good business with peasants, often second and third sons, who flooded into the city to work for a few months before returning to their farms or villages with cash and goods.

"You had to be plenty fast on your feet," Yuk Jee emphasized. "I took a percentage of each contract but I had to guarantee the men would serve out their time. If not, I had to pay money back. I hate to pay money back. If the men ran off to home villages before they finished, I chased them down. You bet!"

The first Opium War changed everything. Hundreds of farms were destroyed, peasants who labored on the land of the warlords who owned large sections along the river were displaced as British cannons shelled huge areas into oblivion. With the opening of four new ports there wasn't enough work in the city, and anyone requiring labor could easily find takers without paying extra to an agent like Tong Yuk Jee for his services.

"So here I am, a gold miner," Yuk Jee declared.

Yuk Jee's claim was far from the best, he explained, as Soon downheartedly surveyed the raggedy lean-to and the scrubby, stunted growth clinging to the rocky terrain. The mine itself looked like little more than chicken scratches in a bed of stones. Yuk's tools were battered beyond belief, the cooking pot dented and cracked, and even the cook fire, still smoldering from Yuk Jee's breakfast, looked forlorn. And as far as Soon could tell there wasn't another soul for miles around.

"Pretty terrible, eh?" Yuk Jee chuckled. "Took me a long time to find just the right spot."

"Terrible is not a sufficient word," said Soon, wondering if he could make it back to the fort.

"My first claim looked much better," Yuk Jee went on. "Good creek, nice big bar of sandy gravel, no big rocks. Perfect for mining. One day two white men with guns took it away. They were very polite. Said they'd blow my head off if I didn't leave. I left. You bet."

"Ah," Soon grunted in understanding.

"And that was before the whites were organized," Yuk Jee said with his ever-present chuckle. "Now I know better. I find the worst-looking place on earth. A place no white man would want."

Yuk Jee had staked his second claim in a dry ravine veering away from the American River's south fork, far from the main strike areas. It was also far off the wagon road. Water had to be hauled five hundred yards for washing the gravel and carefully conserved for rewashing. Hauling water was Soon's first mining job.

It was immediately clear that Soon's employer didn't really want someone to talk *to*, rather someone to talk *at*. "When I have two thousand dollars in gold I will be gone like a hummingbird," he said many times. "With two thousand dollars I can live my life like an emperor." The rest of Yuk Jee's conversation consisted of describing in elaborate and excruciating detail how he would spend sybaritic days in Guangzhou, at the Temple of Holy Bliss, where he was well and truly known.

Yuk Jee's time was to be focused on opium and a barely postpubescent girl called Delightful Eel. She was expensive because she was so young, with breasts still tiny buds on her chest. He held his little finger up to show how delicate and small they were.

"She will trill with ecstasy when I enter her," Yuk Jee said after a particularly vivid description of his techniques for bringing Delightful Eel to a fever pitch. "And she will beg for more when I am done. You bet."

Soon didn't point out that by the time Yuk Jee arrived back at the Temple of Holy Bliss, Delightful Eel would likely have a somewhat different shape.

Yuk Jee often paused in his work to give emphasis to a particular point, but if Soon stopped to listen, he would chastise him.

"You thief!" he scolded. "You steal from me! Every minute you rest is another minute I have to spend in this barbaric, cold country. Back to work! Immediately!"

When he wasn't discussing his plans for returning to China, Yuk Jee railed about the thieves and robbers who were as plentiful as maggots on the meat sold at the fort.

"If they think you're making money, the Red Bandannas will come one day and take it. Better that they think you don't know what you're doing. That you're too useless to have found gold. That is why I have no cradle or rocker here and use only Indian baskets and wooden pans." Only the poorest miners relied on such tools. He also hadn't sold any more of his gold than required to purchase food.

"Go to the assay office and sell your gold to those banker thieves from New York, and next thing you know the Red Bandannas pay you a visit. You bet," Yuk Jee said knowingly.

"Where is New York?" asked Soon.

"It is a big city full of Americans. What could be worse?" Yuk Jee paused to blow his nose vigorously.

"Round eyes, all of them! Stinking carcasses!" he added after studying the mucus carefully. "They think we Chinese are no better than the Indians. When I first come the whites sell me a barrel of flour for thirty-two dollars, and now they want fifty. Same flour! There is little rice but they will not sell me rice unless I buy flour too. Thieves! But," he shook his baggy eyes at Soon, "the Red Bandannas are the worst. We must always guard against them."

✳

Soon listened and worked and listened. True to his word, Yuk Jee taught him to be a miner, and fed him. The diet was simple. Rice when they could get it, unleavened biscuits, beans, and dried meat. Tea was a rare luxury, but coffee was plentiful. Soon's first taste of the oily, bitter brew left a vile aftertaste for hours. Soon had a voracious appetite all day long, but Yuk Jee ate little.

"You are the only fat Chinese around," Soon once pointed out. "And all you eat are beans and rice?"

"My stored-up needs for gratification are showing themselves in bodily form. It is not fat but stored-up *joss,* good fortune. When I return to my home city, I'll be as thin as your queue."

Nine months after his arrival in camp, Yuk Jee announced that he now had $2,000 in gold and he was leaving the very next day.

"I will not work a minute longer in my life. I will count the days back to Guangzhou."

"How can you stop now?" Soon asked. Though Yuk Jee had spoken of little else as the gold mounted, Soon had dismissed his words as empty talk. "We have just found larger grains!"

Yuk Jee smiled like a man after a satisfying meal. "I have what I need. Every day, every minute more I work is time away from my Delightful Eel."

Soon felt panic snatch away his breath. Tong Yuk Jee had become the most important person in his life—the only person in his life. The thought of losing him terrified Soon. Suddenly the fat, garrulous former labor boss was the best companion imaginable.

True to his word, Yuk Jee left for San Francisco at first light.

"This is yours now," he said before he left, gesturing to the shambles as if it were a manicured, thousand-year-old garden. "Take my advice. Work until you have what you need. No more. That is the route to happiness. Excess striving is the source of all unhappiness. I made a good choice in you. The time has passed quickly and pleasurably. I will see you in another life."

With the fat man gone, monotony and hard work made the days end-less. Yuk Jee's minute dissection of his yearnings had distracted Soon, but now there were only days of labor, the long nights, and endless stretches of silence. In Guangzhou there was always noise. Even in the young hours of morning no moment passed without contribution by humankind—feet padding by, consumptive coughs, the splash of urine in a ditch, the propo-sition of a woman, tears, arguments, laughter. But now, without Yuk Jee's gurgling snores and apnea broken by shuddering gasps, there was only silence. In time, Soon stopped listening to the emptiness, and his ears caught the rushing scamper of night creatures, the sounds of small lives being lost, the calls of greeting and warning. The wolves were the worst. He waited with shallow breath for the first howl. Lonely or threatening, he had no idea, but the keening made his stomach hurt. Then came the answering howl, the same but different. Yuk Jee told him he'd get used to it; he hadn't.

During the day, the clatter of rock against rock and his own grunts were Soon's only companions as he dug into the dry tributary of Gum San. His stock of gold was piling up. Six months after Yuk Jee left, Soon esti-mated that he had about $2,000 himself. Within a year he had doubled it. Gold consumed Soon. He abandoned all Yuk Jee's old routines and worked far into the night. He stopped only to sleep and, once a month, make the long trip into Mormon Diggings for groceries.

✳

When the Red Bandannas came, they didn't trouble with stealth, crashing out of the sunset late one day as Soon was squatting in the dirt, cooking a pot of rice flavored by a rare few hunks of fatty bacon. They were a terrify-ing legion with big horses, broad hats, and angry, mocking faces partially covered by red kerchiefs. It happened so suddenly Soon couldn't react, not even to shout.

Tax collectors, they called themselves.

"What have we here!" exclaimed the leader. "A yella! Hey boys, we caught ourselves a yella."

"Y'all workin' this sad old claim yerself?" demanded one. "Where's yer master, chink?"

"He gone. Back quick." Soon gasped out, feeling his pounding heart rise in his throat.

"He's lyin', Ralph! This here pigtail's got his own claim."

"Imagine that?" Ralph, the leader, said. "You all by yerself, boy? This here yer claim?"

"No, no! Boss man come. Back quick."

"Where you larn English, yella?"

"Boss man teach. Use book."

"Got some nerve!" barked another man with giant, fleshy ears and half a nose. "Got some nerve larnin' English. I've a mind to teach this yella prick a lesson! Lemme teach'im a lesson, Ralph."

Soon knew then that he was doomed. For the briefest second he thought about fighting. There was no gun in camp. Neither he nor Yuk Jee knew how to use one.

"It would only get you killed anyway if they come for you," Yuk Jee had advised him in a rare digression from his retirement plans. "Better to roll over and play dead."

The Red Bandannas found forgiveness in history, which portrayed them as relatively benign vigilantes. About seventy strong, the Bandannas did occasionally serve as a despotic adjunct to the law, hanging this or that person for claim jumping, whether they were guilty or not. But mostly they dispensed their own brand of justice to undesirables—nigras, injuns, chilis, and chinks. If an undesirable happened to have a pouch or two of gold, there would be no point in letting it lie around.

It was early in 1851 when eight men administered justice to the former *congee* peddler.

"Where's the gold, chink?" they demanded as boot heels and toes found their mark.

"Got no right to white man's gold, ya damn yella!"

"Dontcha know there's a new law says no chink can own a claim?" barked Ralph. "We gotta take yer gold. It's the law now, right, boys?"

Soon had no idea about any new law. Tong Yuk Jee had bought his claim like anyone else. But Soon had been so isolated he hadn't heard of the "America for Americans" slogan gathering converts all over the western states. While the Chinese were still allowed to operate businesses providing they paid the annual Oriental Tax, they could not own land, houses, or claims, making it bonanza time for good Americans who seized the property for themselves.

"These slanties are like girls!" crowed Half Nose. "Lookit'im. Curlin' up like gawdamn girlie girl."

"Where's the gold, chink?"

Soon had no trouble following one piece of Yuk Jee's advice.

"They'll expect you to make a lot of noise. They think we Chinese are cowards. Squeal like a pig, they say. Scream your heart out. I would. You bet!"

The second key to Yuk Jee's survival strategy was to have two stashes.

"Make the best hidden one your biggest," he told Soon. "Put eighty percent of your money into the big poke, because you want them to believe that's all you got. If they don't believe it's all you've got they'll keep going until they kill you. Better to live with almost nothing than die with a fortune."

Yuk Jee's words went through Soon's mind as his eyes filled with blood, his stomach heaved, and his bowels ran liquid. He prayed for unconsciousness but they seemed to know how far they could go before he passed out.

"He went down like nigra-lipped whore, but he's one tough little chink!" Ralph puffed, dragging his forearm across his brow.

Two of the men dragged Soon to his feet.

"Let's go git some gold, yella," said Half Nose. "Phew! I dunno what these ornamentals eat but it sure makes'em stink!"

"Look at the mess ya made of my boots," complained another. "I'll never get all the blood outta the stitchin'."

Soon scrambled crablike on all fours to the poke buried under a rock at the edge of his claim.

"Ain't that purty," breathed Ralph as he hefted ten small leather bags. "Dontcha feel better now?" he asked Soon who lay crumpled at his feet.

The men yowled and hollered, banging their pistols into the air, delighted with the unexpected size of the take. They'd expected a few hundred, no more. This section had been worked late in '49 by some of the original stakers and declared dry.

"Must be four thousand dollars here!" shouted Ralph.

"Pussytown, here we come!" bellowed Half Nose.

With one last desultory boot for good measure the Red Bandannas left the pulpy mass of Soon's body for the coyotes and vultures.

Soon lay there forever. At least it felt that way. The terrible pain was everything. Sometime on the second day, unusually warm for October in the mountains, a large bird landed on his back and began pecking at him. He managed somehow to muster up a shudder that shook the creature off. With the agony of movement the blackness returned, spinning him down into semiconsciousness.

By sundown of the second day Soon's thirst overwhelmed him. His throat screamed and his tongue lay swollen and cracked in his mouth. He crawled his way to the creek, minutely coiling and uncoiling himself like a caterpillar. Finally, he tumbled into the water, where he drank and retched, drank and retched. Blood mixed with the water and coiled around his body.

Once he'd kept a few sips down, lucidity started returning and with it pain so intense each breath felt like his last. The pain dominated him, strumming his body as if it were a stringed instrument. It seemed nothing less than a miracle when Soon realized he was actually hungry. Desperately trying to avoid dragging his tortured body over any rocks, Soon made his way back to his camp. It had been flattened as if by a typhoon. Half-cooked rice from his overturned pot lay scattered in the cold fire. He ate the rice grain by grain, not bothering to pick out the gritty charcoal. Never had the staple of his homeland tasted so good. His sheds were scrap, so he sheltered under a large rock with a slight overhang and slept for the first time in three days.

Each day he was able to do a little more. When the rice was gone, he mixed up a spongy paste of bug-filled flour, water, and sugar, and sucked it back. Miraculously he got better. After a week, he was moving gingerly about his claim. Though he still had plenty of blood in his stool and urine, thankfully nothing seemed to be broken.

While Soon was recovering he had plenty of time to think, something he'd done little of since his dismal landing in San Francisco. There was no point in lamenting his fate. Soon Chong of Chong Alley in Three Counties, apprentice to Mr. Sang, needed a plan. He had about $900 in his second poke, as well as about £20 in his anal cache, which he'd kept with the second poke. Also, carefully wrapped in leather, there was the letter from Mr. Sang and the silk tunic decorated with beads from the figurine. He'd stashed it all behind a stand of stinging nettles.

Two weeks after his visitors had stopped by, Soon gathered up his possessions, tied them on either end of a shoulder pole, and headed off.

28

*

A full day's limp took Soon to the Mormon Diggings at the Lower Mines. There he invested in a $5 bath, a $14 dinner of gristly stew and biscuits, and a $20 bed in a dank tent in the Chinese section. With his own bedroll, Soon would have paid $10 to flop in Mormon Sam Brannan's sheep shed, but several of the Red Bandanna's had relieved themselves on it. Soon fell onto the lumpy, horsehair mattress, exhausted and aching from the once-shaved crown of his head to his blackened toenails. He still had nearly $900 in gold scale in his buckskin poke and £20 tucked into his nether regions. Hiding the porcelain tube had been a painful feat, as the invaders hadn't spared that part of his anatomy with their hard-toed boots.

The man snoring beside Soon had enough whiskey in him to put a bull team under, but despite his advanced state of unconsciousness he never relaxed his grip on three leather sacks containing fourteen pounds avoirdupois of gold flake and scale, all fully washed and weighed. He'd chosen to sleep in the pigtails' tent because he didn't believe a Chinaman would dare rob a white man. It was his second haul, the Oregon man told Soon before passing out. The first, now resting safely in the Wells Fargo bank at Union Square in San Francisco, netted him sixteen thousand "sweet, green babies." He intended to take his fortune, a shipload of high-class injun trade goods, and his two wives—one a chili and the other a border squaw—back to Oregon and build himself a log palace.

Soon found himself envying the filthy stranger's plan.

Soon spent most of the next day trying to sell Tong Yuk Jee's claim. In 1850 there would have been dozens of takers at $5,000, but in 1851 even the newest miners wouldn't touch it after the state of California passed a law forbidding the Chinese from staking claims. The new law had been enacted to protect the "helpless celestials" from brutal claim jumpers. Soon dropped the price steadily all day, finally finding a taker, a drayman who hauled goods between Sutter's Fort, the Mill, and Mormon Sam Brannan's store at Lower Mines.

Fifty dollars. Soon tried to shrug it off. There was plenty of gold still there in Tong Yuk Jee's dry ravine, but what good was it if he couldn't defend it.

Soon waited all the following day for space on a cart leaving the hills for Sutter's Mill. Twice he was brusquely bumped by late-arriving white men. The first time the teamster refused to give him his money back. The second time Soon withheld his money until the cart was under way. Even so, two white men, laden with tools, flagged the cart down and roughly shoved him off. On Soon's third attempt he was left alone.

As the sun crept toward the ocean, two carts inched past them on the way to the Lower Mines. Both were brimming with his countrymen. They stared curiously at him. Soon stared impassively back.

"Why are you leaving?" their collective gaze seemed to say. "You must be a failure. Weak—not like us."

Soon laid his head down and tried to ignore the jolts that shot knives through his body. He was twenty-one years old.

Captain John Sutter's stockaded fort looked about the same as it had when Soon arrived over a year and a half before. But outside the fort, nothing was the same. The valley rolled off in all directions, pockmarked by every conceivable structure that could shelter an animal, goods for daily living, or a human being. Most were tents or rough shacks of branches and canvas but a few sported tin roofs and one or two solid walls. One man had upended a boat and was living under it with an Indian woman. He was selling week-old San Francisco newspapers for five times their original price while the woman repaired clothing.

Soon couldn't find a bed. The cart driver offered to let him sleep under the wagon, but Soon was loath to hand over another $10 to sleep on the ground. He dragged himself over to the Chinese area where the ground was free and curled up behind a small shed. He dreamed of climbing onto a mat still warm from his brother, waking to the comforting scent of *congee* cooking. Even in sleep his mouth watered.

"Wakee! Wakee! Havee glub! Good food!"

Soon cracked open one eye; the other was still swollen shut. A boy was squatting down, peering into his battered face. He spoke English with the harsh accent of the northern delta.

"You look bad. Very bad," he said, switching to Yue. "No gold, huh!

Here, your lucky day. Yesterday first time I have rice for a month. I made a big batch of *congee*."

"Your sales talk is poor," Soon croaked. "I hope your *congee* is better."

Grinning, the boy offered a steaming ladle of the pasty gruel to Soon. "Go ahead, you try. If you don't like you don't pay."

A sharp prick of memory and longing pierced Soon. What he would give to smell again the pungent, oily aroma of ships mixed with the thick odor of fish, food, and human waste. He took the chopsticks the boy handed over and helped himself to a mouthful. The main ingredient, after the rice, was chopped egg and a dash of something tangy the boy called chili paste.

"I'd offer you fish but there isn't any," the boy said apologetically. "No one fish here."

The chili made Soon's eyes water and his nose run but it was delicious and he said so.

"Rice is hard to get. All the Chinese want it. It goes fast. So I usually make American porridge out of oats," the boy said, clearly pleased by the compliment. "It's not nearly as good."

"Is this really the first *congee* you've made in a month or is it just your selling talk?" Soon asked. "What is the price for your best customer?"

"You are not my best customer," the boy replied indignantly. "I have many. All best."

Soon craned his neck. "I see no one but me."

✳

The boy laughed as they launched into a spirited haggle. Warmer and more pain-free than he'd been in days, Soon savored his helping of *congee,* which the boy had ladled onto a small plank with a rim nailed on to keep the liquid from spilling over the edge. Soon surveyed the boy. Fifteen, maybe sixteen years old, he guessed, and stick-thin. His head was perfectly shaved, Manchu style. A wide-brimmed hat hung at his back, secured around his neck with two frayed pieces of bright red ribbon, and a too-large jacket was tied across his chest. He carried his pot of *congee* on a pole over his shoulder with a rock tied at the other end for balance.

"You look like pig dung," the boy said after his own examination of Soon.

"You are very rude," Soon retorted, "for a boy of no importance."

"I live here more than a year now. Everyone is rude. I pick it up fast."

The boy offered Soon another helping after shoveling some into his own mouth straight from the pot.

"Don't you have any bowls?"

"Bowls cost big money. I made some out of thick pieces of bark but someone stole them for firewood."

"These are very clever," Soon said as he admired the wooden plates.

"Are you a miner or a businessman?" the boy demanded.

"How do you know I am either?"

"Everyone here either a miner or a businessman. Even Hakka say they are Sam Yup. Me, I'm a businessman too."

"Do Sam Yup control everything here?" Soon inquired.

"Own! Sam Yup own most things."

Soon couldn't suppress a sigh at the news.

"What you worry?" he boy asked cheerfully. "You big-time Sam Yup."

This was pure cheek. Though he'd spent years with Mr. Sang, no Chinese would ever mistake his accent for anything but what it was, lower-class See-yup.

"How do you stay in business?"

"Ladies in short supply. I let them have me, they leave me alone," the boy said flatly.

Soon gulped and quickly moved the conversation elsewhere. "What about the Tongs?"

"Not here yet. Whites still run most things. Chinese business too small. Laundry, lice pickers, barbers, sewing. But one day maybe. Then I leave."

"Why?"

The boy slapped his buttocks. "Let a Tong man inside me? Better to be dead!"

Tiny establishments in tents, under trees, and even in holes dug in the ground were the first signs of Chinese permanence outside of San Francisco. Even without the Tongs, if the Sam Yup controlled even the smallest business here as they did in Guangzhou and San Francisco, he would never be able to open anything in competition with them, no matter how crude their establishments, without paying an exorbitant agent fee, usually a hundred percent for several months.

Never before had Soon felt so strongly the impediment of his birth in Chong Alley. One's class was something that just was—like the length of one's arm or the shape of one's face. He had never questioned or regretted it before.

"I am a Hock Kah man," the boy was saying proudly. Soon guessed as much from the tidy shaved head and neat pigtail with the identifying knot at the end. Hock Kah were barbers, a notch above the Chongs of Chong Alley.

"Why then are you selling *congee?*"

"I apprenticed to my uncle. In 1849 big men from Captain Sutter came from America to Guangzhou and purchased his service for one year."

"Purchased his service for barbering?" Soon asked, surprised.

"No, no. For the road they build from the flour mill here to the lumber mill they were building on American River. We work for one year for $10 a month, then he pay us and we go back to China."

"And the Gold Rush happened," Soon guessed.

"When we got here we were second boat of Chinese and everything was crazy with talk of Gum San. All the Chinese wanted to look for gold but Mr. Sutter told us he'd have police put us in jail if we didn't stay with him for a year."

"Where is your uncle?" asked Soon, feeling that his absence was at the heart of this story.

"We were building a log road in bad section near the foothills. There are many streams there and it gets very muddy and slippery."

Corduroy roads consisted of a bed of logs laid across the trail and often secured with stakes or wire where it was steep or extra wet. They were the only way to ensure year-round passage in the foothills, which could be dead dry for most of the year and a slippery soup the rest. If a road sank into the marsh, the builders simply laid another course on top. If the terrain was particularly boggy they drove logs vertically into the mud, then laid the road on top.

Sutter could not afford to have the route impassable now that the miners were flooding into the territory. He was harvesting forty thousand bushels of wheat in his valley fields, worth a fortune sold to the miners as long as he could transport it to the Lower Mines and beyond.

"The work was terribly hard," the boy confessed. "I was tired all the time. I had never done anything like it." His job was to hold one end of the log steady with a big iron pry bar while a man at the other end fitted the log tightly against the previous one and then secured it with stakes. This particular day his uncle was wrestling with a badly trimmed log, hitched up on a branch protruding from its underside.

"And?" Soon prodded impatiently, for the boy had fallen silent.

"He told me to wedge the iron bar under the log to lift it so he could chop the branch off." Suddenly the porridge seller looked like the child he was; his face flushed, he fought tears. Soon looked away uncomfortably. Even in this raw, unprivate place where everything in a man was exposed, tears were unsettling.

"I was slow with the iron bar," the boy said quietly. "The log rolled over both of us. My uncle died."

The two said nothing for a moment.

"Captain Sutter fired me. He wouldn't give me my uncle's pay or the thirty dollars he owed me. Said he didn't need to, because we hadn't worked the whole year."

"Why fire you?"

"This," the boy tapped his ladle against his leg. Clunk. He pulled up the oversized leggings to show a wooden peg.

Soon gaped. The stump was still livid and sores oozed pus from under the crude strapping securing it.

"I am Fat Wan Lo," the boy said, changing the subject. "Share with me some good fortune. Yesterday a bag broke on one of the carts hauling coffee and I filled my pockets full before the driver took his whip to me." He laughed and showed off a welt on the side of his neck. "Not too expensive for enough coffee for a week!" he chirruped. "No charge," he added as an afterthought.

"I sell there later in the day, when it gets busy." Fat Wan Lo continued, pointing to a tiny lean-to, windowless but with a hole cut in one wall.

"Why don't you sell outside, where people can see you?" Soon asked curiously.

"While I serve one person, another steals from my pot. I cannot run fast enough to chase them away. And last week another porridge man threw dirt in my pot."

Soon peered through the hole. Inside, it was a little bigger than Soon had imagined. He could just make out a log for Wan Lo to sit on and a sleeping mat spread out in the corner. Outside the boy had positioned two more logs with a couple of planks across them to form a rough table.

The boy served out the coffee with a dash of sugar into two bean cans wrapped in burlap. Soon pronounced it the best he'd ever tasted. The only other coffee he'd ever drunk was Yuk Jee's, which he'd brewed by adding new coffee to the old grounds that didn't get thrown out until the pot was too full of sludge to add more water.

Fat Wan Lo beamed, gesturing for Soon to sit beside him on the log as he filled out the picture of a life not so different from Soon's own first fifteen years. As the boy talked, Soon examined the tiny shack. Though made with the roughest lumber and few nails, it was carefully constructed, with every plank meticulously cut, notched, and joined.

"After Sutter refused to give me my money, I stole a box of tools," he said, spotting Soon's inspection. "Shaping wood isn't so different from barbering."

A ruckus nearby jarred their conversation.

"What's that?" Soon asked.

"Someone lost money," Wan Lo replied with disdain. "Fan Tan."

Promising to return later, Soon followed the noise through a huddle of tents, past a stinking latrine, to a group of men gathered around a tree stump playing Fan Tan on a small board.

"Pick your corner. Find your spot. You in?" the dealer queried as Soon walked up.

"I'll watch."

"Don't play, don't win!" the dealer encouraged. "Seven only. I have one place left."

Soon demurred.

The middle-aged dealer wore a badly stained robe and spoke the Yue dialect with the clear intonations of the underclass. Even so, he handled the counting stick with style and flair. Perhaps not all is as set here as in Guangzhou, Soon thought. In China no See-yup would ever become a dealer, let alone own a board himself. Lotteries and games were strictly controlled by the men who could afford protection.

Fan meant turn (over a cup), and *tan* meant spread out (a pile of buttons); it was as simple a form of gambling as there was. Beads, jade, and ivory were used as buttons, and there was a rumor that diamonds were commonplace in the Summer Palace of the Qing court. Here in the foothills of the Sierras the man had a sack of animal teeth, which he had chipped and sanded as best he could into lumpy rounds. He'd managed to find some ink, so half the teeth were stained blue.

The dealer dipped his hand into a cloth bag and smacked his palm down on the board, quickly covering the tokens with a cracked leather cup.

"How many! How many!" he sang out. "Bet now. Take your corner."

Half a dozen men placed their bets on the square board, each side numbered one to four. A few risk takers chose to bet on a single number.

The others chose the corners, betting that either of the two adjacent numbers would be what was left when the dealer started counting down the tokens. With a flourish the dealer lifted the cup and separated the teeth out four at a time, until there were four or fewer left. Three was the winning number.

The losers groaned, while two winners—one on a corner, the other with a straight three—swept up their money. The dealer paid two to one for corner bets, three to one on the straight.

Soon could tell from the man's anxious eyes as the counting began that even a small run in the bettors' favor would put a strain on his purse.

In between games, Soon struck up a conversation with the forty-year-old Hing Li Ho from Hong Kong. "You are a long way from the tables in Hong Kong."

"Are you stupid!" the man scoffed. "I never touched a real Fan Tan board before I came here. Do you think the three families would let one such as me become a dealer?"

The man referred to the Wong, Zhu, and Ah Fong families, who had controlled lotteries and most gambling in Guangzhou and Hong Kong since the mid-1700s.

"I was clean-up boy," Li Ho said.

"But how did you get so good?"

"I watched, I practiced. In secret. Now I am here, I play. Here there is no one to stop me."

"What about the three families?"

"Not here yet. One day maybe, which is why my board is open every day until no one comes."

A line of impatient men was growing behind them.

"If you want to make lots of money, why don't you take more gamblers each game?"

"If seven men all win, I can take the loss. If twenty men all win, I am broke. Probably dead too."

※

Soon purchased four sweet buns sprinkled with sugar before making his way back to the shed. Wan Lo was delighted to see him again. He brewed more coffee and they ate together, squatting outside the boy's shack.

"You must stay here!" he insisted when Soon got up to leave. "Why sleep outside? Plenty of room on the floor."

"Plenty" was an exaggeration. Inches separated them, and Soon could feel the boy's breath on his face. Still, he was more comfortable on the dusty straw Wan Lo had laid down for his bed than he had been in a long time. As the boy snored gently into the night, Soon's mind clicked over the possibilities for his future, like beads on an abacus.

He had three choices. Return to China—he had more than enough for the passage. Hire on as labor—rates were now at $20 a month. Or he could do in this place what Mr. Sang sent him to do, if not in the way that Mr. Sang envisioned.

The first alternative was hard to contemplate, perhaps even folly. Two of the gamblers at the Fan Tan table had barely escaped from the uprisings spreading across China. They told of a madman, a Hakka named Hong Xiuquan, who was converting huge numbers from the impoverished hills of Guangxi to his vision of a new China with himself, second son of God and brother of the white Jesus Christ, at its head. He organized river pilots and lesser rice lords alike, and thousands were dead. The movement had spread to Guangzhou and one of the men said Hong intended to strike at the heart of the Qing dynasty itself.

The second option was certainly possible. Miners were bidding up the price of labor.

But in his heart Soon considered the final option the only real choice. He recalled some of Mr. Sang's advice:

"At the beginning of any enterprise there are two paths to success. One is to learn from the inside, and when you are ready to set out on your own you'll have knowledge of the competition's weakness, you'll have a place to strike. The second path is to make your own. Be the first and others will always be behind you. This path, of course, is one of greatest risk."

Soon considered the words carefully. In order to make a place for himself he had to be the first at something. But what? Until today he had no idea.

Soon knew nothing about gambling. What he did know was that the Hong Kong man had the only board in the mill but insufficient capital to run anything more than a limited game. Mr. Sang never did business with anyone he did not have the chance to fully study. But that could take years. Chinese years were northern California days. Soon's smile spread into the first grin of many months. A new business based on a one-legged boy; a wheezing, middle-aged Fan Tan dealer; and Soon Chong of Chong Alley. Mr. Sang would soil his robes.

✳

Delightful Eel Fan Tan House opened for business two weeks later. The ten-by-twelve log structure had a pleasing permanence thanks to Wan Lo's skill. Soon acted as the bank and assumed all financial risk, while Li Ho ran the games in return for twenty percent of the gross. Wan Lo was delighted with a small salary, particularly when he found out bending over wouldn't be part of his duties.

There was one more necessity. If Soon had learned anything in America it was that making money was pointless if you couldn't protect it. In China there was a long-established hierarchy of law and retribution for every class level. One group might prey upon another, but within each group justice was meted out effectively, as long as the proper duties and tithes were paid. In America it was up to the individual. And the most important individual in Sutter's Mill was Sheriff Riley Yates.

An enormous man, twice as tall as Soon, the sheriff appeared to flow out in all directions from his bulbous, open-pored nose to his thighs, which seemed ready to burst out of his deerskin chaps. He moved ponderously through Sutter's Mill, like a massive carp. All the other citizens of the town were like minnows, moving quickly out of his way. When Yates stared, his face draped with a long, thick moustache at the bottom and topped by a hat big enough to have a bath in, men shrank inside.

"Big man, big trouble," Li Ho cautioned. "Captain Sutter and Mormon Brannan brought him in to make law. He's the only white who dares to come into Chink Squat. Everyone's scared of him. Best to stay away."

Soon was also scared to death of Yates. But there was no one else. He watched the sheriff from a distance for days, waiting for an opportunity to catch him alone. Finally, late one evening, as Yates headed into his rough jailhouse, Soon stepped out in front of the man and bowed as if to royalty.

"Gleetings. Honable sheliff. Gleetings." Soon laid on his best coolie accent.

"Whaddya want Johnny!" Yates's voice sounded like a rock slide.

Soon felt like running but he plowed on. "Needie start business. Needie talk boss man. Muchee dolla."

Yates hitched up his pants and beneath the ankle-length duster Soon caught the thick gleam of two highly polished revolvers.

"Yeah. So what?"

"Business is weetle game. Chinaman game. Chinaman love gamble game. Muchee dolla. Easy money."

"What's that gotta do with me, Johnny?" Yates demanded, his voice dropping a notch and his half-lidded eyes narrowing.

"In China games own by few peopah. Same in San Fancisco. All otha kill if muscle in."

Yates's lip twitched.

"You boss man," Soon bowed low. "For evah fouh dolla I make boss man get one dolla. One dolla in fouh dolla. Easy money. For suah, two hunnand fifty dolla month. Minimum two hunnand fifty dolla."

"What you want for this two hundred fifty dolla?" the sheriff asked carefully.

"Weetle watch out. Keep white away. They lose money to Chinaman. Get mad. Bad business. New Chinamen come. Also keep away. No want."

"How do I know you won't cheat me?" The words were hostile but Soon assessed them as ritual negotiation.

"No cheat. Too flaid. Boss smart. Know if Johnny cheat," said Soon, ready to add the clincher. "I give you two hunnand fifty dolla now. Give you two hunnand fifty dolla fust day evah month. Nevah less. Maybe moh."

Apparently the answer was satisfactory, for Soon found himself staring at Yates's massive hand, palm upward.

Including the sheriff's $250 upfront, construction costs, food, and sundry other items, such as lanterns for the gambling club, which he'd paid dearly for at Walker's Warehouse, Soon had committed all but $300 of his capital—just enough, he calculated, to ride out a big winning streak.

When all was ready, Soon sent Wan Lo stumping through the shanties of Chink Squat, beating on a makeshift drum announcing that the Delightful Eel was open for business. One month later Wan Lo knocked down a side wall, doubling the space. Soon expanded again a year later, and by 1853 he'd added on a small opium den with just enough room for four people and four pottery opium "pillows" to cushion customers' heads when drug cloud dreams of home overtook them.

Yates's one dolla in fouh was now netting him an average of $750 a month, and he was worth every nickel. Whites who tried to crash the tables were quickly set straight. His favorite intimidation tactic was to sidle up to a man and bellow in his ear. Men peed themselves after this assault. If that didn't work, Yates's haunch-sized fist to the side of the head did the trick.

*

When a second, more substantial club offering lotteries, girls, and Fan Tan opened in a newly constructed building, Yates gleefully turned their fixtures into kindling.

"That sheriff is really a terrible fellow," Soon shook his head sadly, when he dropped by to commiserate.

"He leaves you alone," the competitor responded bitterly.

"Yes he does, doesn't he?" Soon said happily. "You made a serious mistake not looking into the situation more carefully. I fear that you wouldn't survive a second such mistake."

The man moaned in dismay.

"It's really a pity," Soon said. "There's certainly room for both of us in this business. If only . . ."

"If only what?" asked the woebegone owner.

"Well, I was just thinking that if I owned part of your business then it would automatically fall under the arrangement I have with Mr. Yates. But I'm sure that's not possible. I have no cash to invest."

The man begged Soon to accept forty percent of his business in return for his protection. Soon demurred politely, saying that he couldn't possibly undertake such a responsibility for less than sixty percent. The deal was struck. It was the shortest haggle in Soon's life.

Late one evening in the spring of 1853 Soon stepped into On New Hong, the pissing alley between the stables and the shanties, to relieve himself.

A whisper in his ear. "Chop off your head."

It was a favorite expression of the *poo tow choy*—the hatchet men, enforcers for the Tongs. They had arrived in Sutter's Mill. Soon didn't dare look around. "Our turn now," came the whisper. "Get out."

Mysteriously, two pigtailed newcomers were found a few miles below the fort, their own hatchets imbedded neatly in their chests.

29

*

1868

Sutter's Mill, California

"Got yer new cash crop, right here," Yates boomed as he unveiled three Chinese corpses heaped in his wagon.

The big man now owned a two-thousand-acre ranchero twenty miles from Sutter's Mill. Officially he was still sheriff of the dwindling sprawl around John Sutter's old fort, though his duties were much curtailed. By the mid-1850s virtually all the original Mormons were gone, having followed strikes in Utah and Colorado. With them went the population of the Sierra Nevadas. Nearly three-quarters of the newly landed Chinese were picked off at the docks by road builders and agents for the Central Pacific Railway. As the gold ran out in Gum San, the laundries, cook houses, and brothels gravitated toward the rapidly expanding Chinatown in San Francisco.

Wan Lo had built an ingenious portable gambling club that accommodated a dozen tightly packed players, the Fan Tan board, and a dealer. It folded up to the size of a dog cart, and with its two large wheels could be pulled by one man or a donkey. Within half an hour of arriving at a rail camp the club could be open for business. He and Li Ho had been following the gold strikes since 1856. They hid their money in caches as they went, and every six months Yates and Soon tracked the route laid out in the map Wan Lo sent back to Sutter's Mill. Soon traveled as Yates's houseboy. Aside from the occasional skirmish with road bandits, who were quickly persuaded of their mistake, Yates and Soon had been unmolested in their "banking" runs.

As the Civil War broke out moribund mines along hundreds of miles of the Sierras came to life again. Gold coin by the millions shipped out of Golden Gate for the voracious war appetite in the east. Wan Lo and Li Ho returned, and by 1862 Delightful Eel was once again relieving men of their labor wages.

Yates was as rich as any man in the Sacramento Valley and almost as rich as the biggest landowners in the city. But he saw no reason not to make a little extra if the opportunity presented itself.

Soon gazed at the three bodies, filled with what looked like bullet holes.

"Yessir, this here's the best idea since they put a bounty on injuns," he drawled.

"There is certainly an endless supply," agreed Soon.

At first he was horrified by the huge numbers of Chinese who died on American soil, most of them murdered or killed in the mines or on the rails. But by the fourth cartload his initial squeamishness disappeared. Until Yates came up with his disposal-service notion, most of the dead were unceremoniously buried, usually more or less where they fell. But as the numbers of Chinese began to swell so too did the fatalities and the concern over the remains by families in China. To lie for eternity in the ground of a foreign land was to curse the dead with an unsettled afterlife. Delegations representing a number of families began arriving from China in 1851 to dig up the departed and return to China with their bones.

"I've jes' added one and one together," Yates said to Soon one day. "An' figured out how to put two in our pockets."

"Bodies?" said Soon doubtfully.

"You don't gotta feed'em or nuthin'," replied Yates.

After that, when a Chinaman died anywhere in the vast region of the Sierra Nevada mines or within the Sacramento Valley, Yates did his best to find and claim the body. The first was Chinaman #1, short, missing finger. The most recent were Chinamen #231, scar on nose, and #232, skinny, big teeth. Well packed in salt, Soon stored the corpses in a shallow cellar underneath Walker's Warehouse, which he bought in 1855. If no one wrote to request the return of the departed, Wan Lo carted them out to the mission, where indigent Orientals were buried for a dollar, far away from the white graveyard. Grieving relatives who came up with $100, or the equivalent in silver or gold plus the freight costs, got their crated and desiccated dearly beloved back for a proper Chinese funeral. Sometimes as many as a dozen bodies lay waiting in the cellar as family back home desperately worked to come up with the required amount.

Yates clambered up on the wagon and rolled one of the bodies over. Despite the caved-in cheeks, hollowed eyes, and waxy skin, Soon could tell the corpse was of a very young man, possibly a boy. Chinaman #233. Soon thought briefly of his own first days in America and wondered what luck ran with him that he had avoided a similar fate. He pulled out a small note-book and began listing distinguishing features: acne scars, missing teeth, birthmarks, height. Occasionally they found identification on the dead, but it was rare. Fewer than half the corpses were matched to their correct fami-lies, but it didn't matter. By the time they reached China, the bodies were often so decomposed, despite the salt, no one could tell who they had been.

Soon left the current shipment of corpses outside and led the sheriff into the warehouse.

"I am pleased to serve you tea," Soon bowed to Yates.

"An' I'm pleased to make it drinkable," said Yates, pulling out a quart-sized flask from an inside pocket.

Soon was amused at the sight of Yates hunched over the low table in the little office Wan Lo had built at the back of the warehouse. Yates's sausage fingers curled awkwardly around the tiny porcelain cup. He sipped with his head angled back to avoid dipping his long moustache into the cup. They spoke of the weather, the recent earthquakes, and the continued enmity between the northern and southern states.

"Your system of government is too weak to prevent the country from tearing itself apart," observed Soon. "Too much leniency and no princes to enforce the orders of the president."

"Princes?" scoffed Yates. "Princes are definitely what America is *not* about. Fat lot of good princes have done your country. You Chinese are all coming to America because you can't make a living in your own country. And while your people starve, your wonderful princes seem ready to over-throw the emperor. Meanwhile the Brits wait in the wings."

Gradually, as they talked, it dawned on Soon that Yates's heavy drawl had all but disappeared.

Soon smiled. "Ah, yes, but rice lords and the land princes fight among themselves to see who will become the new inner circle for the emperor. The dynasty will continue. No one thinks of your president in the same way, so he doesn't last. Dynasties continue for a thousand years."

"What a dreadful thought," muttered Yates. "We haven't had a presi-dent yet that anyone could stand for more than a few years."

Soon had to know. "I do my humble best with your difficult language but I've noticed that you do not sound quite the same as the sheriff I am acquainted with."

Yates wiped drops of tea from his moustache.

"Ya done caught me," drawled Yates.

"Caught you?"

Yates tilted his chair back, scratched his crotch thoughtfully, and shone a mouthful of yellow teeth at Soon.

"It surprised me," he began with the broad vowels of a Massachusetts native, "to discover that appearances are as important on my country's frontier as they are at home in Boston."

"Boston?"

"A person does larn," Yates drew out the word, "a few things about putting on appearances after four years at Princeton."

Soon blinked in amazement. He'd heard of Princeton. It sounded like an exalted place, where wise scholars conversed about learned matters in hushed tones. As far away from the muddy, scrubby shack settlement of the Sierras as Chong Alley was from the Summer Palace.

"I came out here for the Gold Rush in '49, just like everyone else," Yates said, answering the unasked question. "Hated the mining. It was work and too damn much of it. I got made sheriff 'cause I was the biggest hoss around."

Yates laughed. "You lard your conversations with a few hosses, spit a lot, and you fit right in. I also learned to walk like I was born with a set of bull's balls, which was only enhanced when I bought the biggest damn hog leg I could find."

Yates patted his holster affectionately. "Dragoon Colt. I've hardly ever fired it. All I had to do was strut around like an angry cock and every now and then introduce people to my ten friends." He made fists of both hands.

"I thought you were a gunslinger. An outlaw."

"That's what I wanted everyone to think. Especially those Red Bandannas and the half dozen other gangs who followed them. Gold makes people crazy. I wanted them to think I was the craziest of them all."

A big exhale of air almost blew the candle out. "I never had so much fun in my life. I nailed my Princeton diploma right on the wall in the jail. No one ever bothered to read it. You're the only one who knows."

"I am honored," acknowledged Soon.

"I always thought I'd go back. My father owns a bank and couldn't spend all his money if he had five lifetimes."

"You came here to become rich, like your father."

"God, no. The rich just happened. It was the most amazing thing. This cheeky little pigtail made me a proposition. One dollah in foah dollah."

They looked at each other for a moment, as if for the first time. Yates sniggered. Soon smiled. Yates guffawed. Soon chuckled. Before they knew it, they were helpless captives of their own laughter. Deep, rich belly laughs. Yates pounded the table with his fist. Soon held his stomach with both hands; he hadn't laughed like this since he'd been a little boy in Guangzhou and his sister slipped and fell into the communal toilet hole. Finally they composed themselves.

"Unfortunately, the fun's over," Yates said abruptly.

"I beg your pardon?" Soon wiped his eyes.

"The fun is over," Yates repeated.

Soon's mirth fled at the serious look on Yates's face.

"We gotta problem," he intoned gravely.

"Problem?" Soon queried.

"Three bad boys from Pinkerton's rolled into Lower Mines a few days ago lookin' for a Chinaman—a very particular Chinaman," Yates revealed, lapsing into the more familiar drawl.

"Pinkerton's?"

"Private police, real hard cases. They knew your name, your *full* name, mind."

That alarmed Soon. Most whites called all Chinese Johnny, occasionally appending something like pigtail, celestial, washer, yellow, or the all-purpose chink to it, but rarely did they ever trouble to learn, let alone use, a man's full name.

"I have done nothing wrong," Soon said anxiously.

"It ain't about doin' the wrong ya know. It's about doin' the wrong ya don't know."

"What do you mean?"

"The South is near defeated, and when war's done, men come home. They want land. Trouble is, when our California boys were away making the Confederates bleed, debts didn't get paid, businesses went bust, and people like me kinda moved in and took up the surplus land.

"Now they're comin' home and suddenly the state found an old law on the books that no one bothered to enforce. Chinaman can't own land."

Soon's stomach churned. He hadn't forgotten the anti-Chinese lynchings of the fifties, the brutality of the America for Americans Committee, and the law that forced him to sell his claim for pennies on the dollar. But after California became the forty-ninth state, he'd quietly bought the warehouse and surrounding land.

"California gave up that law when it joined the Union! That was required."

"Sorta, sorta not. The Union said the law was unconstitutional, so the state fathers just ignored it. It's on the books all right, and they're gonna start enforcing it. I figure they're gonna confiscate land until Washington gets wind and tells'em to stop. The state'll sell what they take back to the soldier boys, an' everyone's happy."

"Except the Chinese," Soon squeezed out the words.

"Yup. 'Cept the Chinese."

"What about the Pinkerton men you saw?"

"There's a bounty. A bit hush-hush, but they got a list from Sacramento of all the Chinese registered as landowners. They find'em, bring'em in, and collect the bounty. There's already seven Johnnies in the Sacramento jail."

"Did they come to you to find me?"

"Well, they surely did. A big thug by the name of O'Shaughnessy offered me fifty bucks to help 'em collar this yeller fella by the name of Soon Chong. I jes' about laughed in his ugly mick face. I don't get outta my chair for fifty bucks. Hundred I'd have to think about."

"Thank you for your loyalty," Soon grunted.

"These boys could punch a steer to death without working up a sweat, but head work . . . well, I just played dumb and flattered them up a bit."

"They want to arrest me?"

"That's what they said."

"My business is gone," Soon concluded tonelessly.

"I'd say that's a good guess."

Soon's face felt as if it would crack in pieces. Yates felt sorry for the thin man who had revealed nothing about himself in the nearly fifteen years the sheriff had known him. The only glimpse Yates had ever gained into his life was the two times he saw him emerging late at night from Hoopi's Gal Palace at the edge of Sutter's Mill. That's where the dregs of Chinatown girls ended up once they were too used up for service in the slave dens on China Street in the heart of San Francisco's Chinatown. The kid—Yates still thought of Soon that way—had more smarts than any whites he'd ever met, including the Princeton lot. Too bad.

"I ain't gonna play sheriff no more," yawned Yates. "My ranch is doin' okay and one of them bride ships is comin' in from Australia next month. I got a lady all paid up on board."

Soon barely heard him. He could escape to San Francisco, he had money to pay protection and bribes, but if he showed himself too soon he'd be killed for his purse. And there were no guarantees he could buy into anything, no matter how much money he had. Money was only part of what made power. Organization was the other part. A one-legged man and a now-old Fan Tan dealer hardly constituted an organization. He shivered with fear and regret that he'd stayed too long in the foothills of the mountains when he might have been buying his way into a place in Chinatown. It might have taken him years, but now it was too late.

Yates watched Soon's struggle for composure. The scars drawing one eye slightly down darkened, and two of his fingers, permanently bent from the boots of the Red Bandannas, twitched against each other.

"I might have a notion to git you outta this fix," Yates said softly. "At leasty we can stop these boys from looking for you."

Soon looked up, his eyes widening with hope.

"What is your idea?"

"You ever go to the theater back in good ol' China?"

Theater? He'd been a street peddler. The closest he'd gotten to the theater was the occasional puppet show put on by street entertainers on the docks. Soon shook his head.

"Too bad. I did a little o' that actin' in Princeton," Yates said conversationally. "Wasn't a half bad Falstaff, if'n I do say so myself. My idea is we put on a little show for those Pinkerton boys."

✳

At five o'clock the next morning, spoon-thick fog coated everything with a vision-blocking, sound-muffling wrap as Wan Lo harnessed two horses to the corpse wagon. Soon still didn't like horses, but Wan Lo had become a capable horseman. He cursed and cajoled, using a mix of Chinese and bad Western slang. The animals snorted and pranced in the bracing, early-morning chill. When they first came to Gum San, few Chinese had anything to do with horses. Now it wasn't uncommon to see them driving wagons and even wrangling. But it still gave Soon a start to see an Oriental face topped by a cowboy hat.

Wan Lo tethered the horses a fair distance from the warehouse. Soon noticed patches of moss growing on the lee side, and places where the wooden foundation was sagging with rot. They pushed open the main receiving door, both starting slightly at the heavy groan of the hinges. Soon peered anxiously through the gloom inside. In the last few years they'd only used it to store bodies.

"Look out," Wan Lo cried, grabbing Soon's arm as something scuttled past him.

"It's only a rat," Soon scolded. "And I can't move with you hanging on to me!"

"Sorry," Wan Lo giggled nervously.

"I don't know why you're so jumpy," Soon said crossly, "you've been picking up bodies here for two years."

"This is different," retorted Wan Lo.

They made their way to the back of the warehouse. There it was. The set, as Yates called it. Two Chinese corpses sat in ladder-backed chairs, the only furniture in the place, both eerily lifelike, looking as if they were in the middle of a conversation. Soon tiptoed over. As Yates instructed, he carefully lit the lanterns, placing one in the window and two more on the floor near a pile of newspapers and several cans of kerosene. He opened one of the cans and poked a twisted length of cotton inside, letting the other end rest on the papers.

"I didn't think they'd mind we borrowed their bodies," Yates said the night before. "But we gotta move quick, 'cause they stink like pig innards, an' the coyotes and vultures will be after them."

Soon sent Wan Lo to stay with the wagon, then he crawled under the table with his legs sticking into the three-by-three-foot bolt hole cut into the wall. Facing into the office but hidden from sight, Soon awkwardly drew the nine-inch, four-and-a-half-pound Colt Yates provided.

"All ya do is squeeze the trigger gently an' make sure you aim at the wall," Yates instructed. "Empty the whole gun, throw it on the floor, 'n skedaddle. Oh yes, an' yell summin' in Chinese 'fore ya start blastin'."

Three hours later Soon was still waiting; in sweat time, it was an eternity. His back was cramped and his legs numb from lying on the hard floor.

"I'll get them there fast as I can," Yates had promised. "But they been drinkin' pretty good over at the Dead Dog, so it may take a while."

Soon nearly fainted when Yates's fist rattled the door.

"Open up, chink!" he boomed. "It's the sheriff!"

Caught by surprise after the long wait, Soon bellowed back the only phrase he could think of. "*Congee!* Get your hot *congee! Congee!*"

"We're comin' in, ya goddamn yella!"

When the door edged open, Soon emptied the gun into the wall, then scooted backward, pulling over the lantern as he went. He caught a glimpse of Yates as he backed out of the bolt hole. The big man had a happy smile on his face as he stormed into the dim warehouse, firing his gun. The Pinkerton's men were right behind him, but they didn't get far, as the flame caught and quickly roared into a blaze, igniting the paper, then enveloping the two corpses, which had been throughly doused with kerosene.

✳

Two hours later Soon and Wan Lo waited nervously in the wagon hidden behind a copse of trees. Li Ho would not come. He said he was too old. He'd rather run his Fan Tan game as long as he had breath in his body than run from the likes of Pinkerton men who'd likely catch them anyway. Riley Yates materialized out of the fog so suddenly that Wan Lo shrieked.

"Easy there," he soothed as one might a spooked horse. "Easy there. No cause for concern."

"Everything in order, Mr. Yates?" Soon asked formally.

"As orderly as one poor man can make this chaotic universe," Yates answered just as formally.

"And this evening's chaos?"

"Two chinks shot dead resisting arrest. Clumsy buggers knocked over a lantern. Burned themselves right up. Fortunately I was able to make a positive identification. A Mr. Soon Chong and his employee."

"The gentlemen from Pinkerton's are satisfied?"

"They were a bit wobbly from that pine-bark rotgut Charlie pretends is whiskey, but I think I convinced them they'd got their man. Though I can't say they're too comfortable right this moment."

"How so?"

"Welllll, they're cooling their heels in my jail."

"On what charges?"

"Offending me is the main one, but overbearing rudeness, stupidity, and poor table manners could easily be added."

"And how long might they be held on these very serious charges?"

"Couple or three days anyway, but I doubt they'll be able to travel inside a week. When I arrested them they made a serious mistake. Resistin'. Forced me to dust 'em off some."

"A week."

"Ain't long."

"It is a precious gift," Soon replied.

"Money buys all kinds of gifts these days. It was only 'cause of the money, you understand," Yates shrugged. "I don't cotton to chinks."

"Velly good suh," Soon bowed his head. "This chink no mind."

Two hours later, with the breath knocked out of him from an insanely fast ride down the road out of Sutter's Mill, Soon begged Wan Lo to slow down. The jade-beaded tunic he'd kept from the figurine was digging into him where he'd stashed it in an inside pocket. The gold in pouches around his waist was giving him bruises with each bone-jarring hole and bump. As he hauled in the lathered horses, Wan Lo asked Soon, "How far is this British land?"

"I don't know," Soon responded.

"Is it cold?"

"I don't know."

"Is it like San Francisco?"

"I don't know."

"There is gold?"

"Yes. Mr. Yates says the Yankee soldiers will be coming by the thousands. It will be like California fifteen years ago."

"I hope he is right," Wan Lo said, clicking his tongue at the horses to keep them moving.

"So do I."

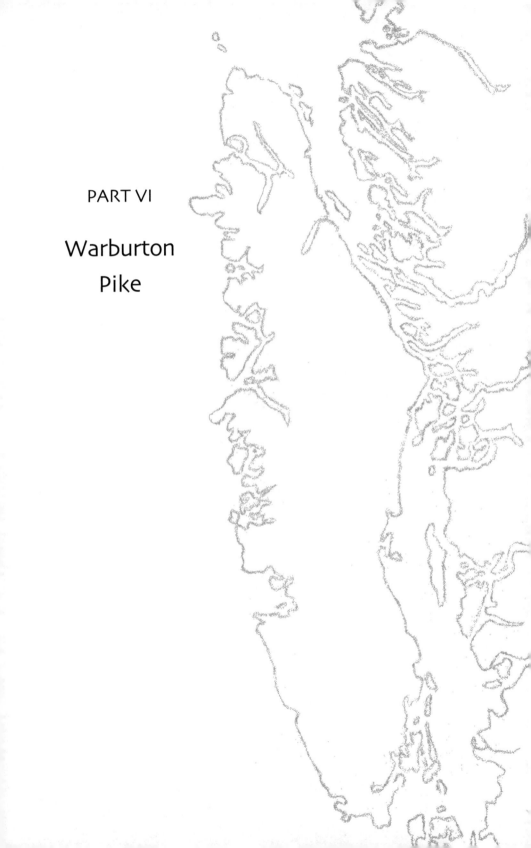

PART VI

Warburton
Pike

30

✳

1856

Aldershot, England

Warburton Pike loathed his father. "All he cares about is counting things, ordering people about, and making money," he complained to his mother.

"He knows no other way," his mother offered, unable to suppress a memory from early in their marriage when Kenderville Pike had insisted she fire her seamstress because the buttons on her bodice were out of alignment.

Everything in Kenderville Pike's life was ordered to perfection. Everything from the kitchen garden to the hay fields proceeded according to a logical plan. The shearing, milking, and harvest on the home farm were scheduled to the minute, and Pike had developed an ingenious punch-clock device to keep track of his employees. His textile mills, which he had cleverly converted from wool to canvas, were marvels of efficiency. He now supplied fully a third of all the canvas used by Her Majesty's Royal Navy. Recently he'd purchased a lumber mill in Liverpool and gained the contract for spars and decking timber for Her Majesty's China Fleet. The logs came from the northwestern British Territories.

"The territory called British Columbia is now safely out of the grasp of the Americans," Kenderville Pike instructed. "When you are old enough I will send you there. If the logs can be cheaply cut to size in the territory we can save thousands here on finishing."

"I don't want to go there," Warburton stated.

"What you want is of no consequence."

"I am *not* going anywhere called British anything!"

"You will do as I tell you."

"I will not!"

A sharp slap ended the conversation.

✳

As much as Warburton Pike loathed his father he adored his mother. Eva Warburg Pike, daughter of Rudolf Bismarck Warburg and cousin to the powerful von Schaumbergs, had four generations of Catalan nobility to thank for her black eyes and ebony hair, which Warburton spent hours brushing while she sang German lullabies and entranced him with stories of her childhood spent among her cousins on the von Schaumberg estate in Neu Gattersleben. She loved to read aloud, and her musical voice filled his imagination with heroic warriors and beautiful maidens suffering from hearts bursting with love.

"How did you come to marry Father?" Warburton once asked. Despite the constant drilling of the tutor and his father's proclamations on the importance of succession, preservation of family wealth, and forging important alliances through marriage, by the age of seven Warburton Pike believed fervently in hearts bursting with love. He was sure there must have been some of that between his exotic mother and his sandy-haired, upright father.

"It was an arranged union between our two families—as many marriages are."

"But did you love him? Did he carry you off and make brave sacrifices for you?"

Eva laughed with delight.

"Oh my little Warble!" she laughed, avoiding a direct answer. "My family in Germany benefited greatly from the association with your father even when I was still a girl. Your father is really very clever at business, you know."

"Yes, but did you love him like Guinevere loved Sir Lancelot?" he pressed, noting, even at seven, the lack of enthusiasm in her words.

Eva Pike hesitated. "We have come to respect each other deeply. Respect is as important as love."

Warburton pondered her words. He couldn't imagine the heroes or heroines of his mother's stories rising to a crescendo of excitement and longing over respect.

"Why does he always glare at me?" he demanded.

"He glares at everyone," Eva said, muffling a laugh with her hand. "He doesn't know any other way of looking."

Eva stroked Warburton's springy hair. It was like heather in full bloom. "Fathers have high expectations of their sons," she explained. "He simply can't imagine what is in your heart."

"But he's always glaring at me no matter what I do. His eyes go like the dead cod in the market. You know, the big ones, on ice?" Warburton pulled apart his upper and lower eyelids until his exposed eyeballs teared up.

"Don't do that, darling," his mother laughed, snatching at his hands. "That's very bad for your eyes. And don't compare your father to a cod!"

In truth, Kenderville Pike's eyes were a little bulgy, like those of a dead fish, and there was little warmth in them. Warburton caught his mother smiling. Warburton mimed fishlike mouth motions, which caused her to break out in giggles.

✳

As a young child, Warburton loved to tag along behind his father's gameskeeper or work alongside the stonemason while he repaired a cottage. When the perpetually exasperated tutor caught him, the inevitable scolding and caning from his father had the impact of rain on a rock. In later years, his diversions often ended up in swollen knuckles, a bloodied nose, or torn clothing. Warburton loved to taunt and tease, and though he was tall for his age, he was as quick with his fists and feet as with his tongue.

As he grew into his pre-adolescent years, Pike became the Questing Knight, foraying into forbidden regions of great danger—the Gypsy Forest being his favorite.

Every year in late spring, horse-drawn gypsy *vardos* rattled into the meadow that bordered the northern reaches of Kenderville Pike's estate. The land was common grazing, and it backed onto a thickly wooded preserve owned jointly by the three largest landowners for their hunting pleasure. To Warburton it was always the Gypsy Forest. Over the years, the gypsies had come to an uneasy understanding with the townspeople. They paid a fee for camping in the meadow and operating a small carnival, which consisted primarily of fortune telling and games of chance, with tinkering and jewelry repair among the other services offered. At the back of the camp, locals could find female companionship for a price. The carnival drew customers from dozens of surrounding villages, many of whom made purchases at the local shops, ate in the pub, and stabled their horses in the local livery. In return for attracting cash-paying visitors the gypsies were allowed to hunt and gather wood in the neighboring forest as long as they honored the boundaries of the three main estates, the largest being Mayhill owned by Kenderville Pike.

It was understood that the gypsies wouldn't visit the town in large numbers or indulge in thievery. Even so, local folk nailed down what was small enough to be moved and kept a wary eye on the rest.

To Warburton, the Romani men were men: arguing, brawling, drinking, coming and going as they pleased. Their ebullient gestures, mysterious language, and the colorful *diklos* worn around their necks, added to the illusion. The women's smoldering beauty, bold laughter, and blatantly curvaceous femininity never failed to unsettle his pubescent sleep. In the spring of his thirteenth year Warburton discovered Carla and Calaban, a brother and sister who operated the *churi*—knife-throwing—booth.

Carla was the lure. Calaban lazily outlined her wiggling, nervous body with knives to entice customers. A copper bought three opportunities to throw a knife into a target—a large round from an old apple tree, painted and suspended about twenty feet away. If one of the three knives landed true, the customer took a free turn, two out of three got the copper returned, and all three knives earned the thrower double his money.

Calaban accompanied the show with patter that carefully skirted the line between respectful gibes and outright insult. Carla collected the money, handed out the knives, praised the mark's skill and strength, and soothed away any annoyance.

Warburton noticed that people often won one free turn, less frequently threw two for three, and almost never got all three in the target. A few times a day, when the crowds were thinnest, someone would step forward and win several times in succession to the cheers of the onlookers, then melt away when the crowd swelled. The rare winners dressed like locals but Warburton never recognized them.

Before the gypsies broke camp that year, Warburton purchased a knife similar to the ones used by Calaban and Carla. The next winter he was Kat Vacuska: a Romany warlord romping through the woods, red scarf around his neck, uttering Romany-sounding threats. He practiced throwing the knife for hours at the wide variety of targets at hand until the kitchen gardener, gameskeeper, water man, thatcher, and cook all banished him. As he galloped through the woodlots and forest flinging the knife at trees, walls, buckets, and birds, Warburton imagined he was rescuing the beautiful Carla from an evil villain. Invariably the villain bore a striking resemblance to Kenderville Pike.

The following spring Warburton eagerly rushed to the meadow when word reached him of the gypsies' arrival. What good fortune that his father was in Scotland, inspecting a mill he was considering purchasing. Almost every day he escaped his tutor to walk among the noise and bustle and buy *bokoli.*

"*May kali I muri may gugli avela,*" whispered a woman of his mother's age as he passed close to her caravan. She seemed almost black-skinned in contrast to the bright-yellow scarves she wore and silver-and-gold jewelry on her arms and around her neck.

"I beg your pardon?" Warburton said.

"The darker the berry," she crooned, kissing at the air, "the sweeter the taste." She pulled up her shirt and circled her palm over her bare belly. Warburton was riveted by the rich brown flesh. A woman's stomach!

"*Ka xlia ma pe tute!*" bellowed a half-naked man emerging from the caravan. "I shit upon you!" Warburton scurried away as the first blow struck the yelping woman.

At the end of the first week Warburton noticed a small man with a neatly trimmed salt-and-pepper beard and a pronounced limp threading through the crowd as Calaban and Carla worked the audience.

"Old man doesn't look like he could pick up a knife, much less throw one," Calaban loudly commented, causing the passerby to stop in his tracks.

"I would not play at your sinful games, nor would I chance disease by lingering in your presence," the old man responded loftily, before moving on.

"Undoubtedly you are one of the old ones who condemn sin because you can no longer perform as a man with a woman," Calaban jeered, his thick accent making the barb seem even more insulting. "Though I bet the farm animals aren't safe around you."

"You are the devil's spawn!" huffed the old man, whose face had flushed an angry purple.

"Yes, I expect you're a pretty big man with the sheep," Calaban taunted.

Some of the women shielded their ears, and several men marched off in disgust, their families in tow. The old man limped toward Calaban, making as if to hit him with his cane.

"Please, sir!" Carla cried, flinging herself between them. "Have forgiveness! My brother is a reckless and rude young man. Accept my apologies." She punctuated her statement with a dramatic glare over her shoulder at Calaban, who looked sullenly on.

"He accused me of fornicating with animals," the man sputtered.

"Anyone can see you're a God-fearing man who would not indulge in such things," Carla said soothingly. "Please. A gift to you." She held out the knives. "Free." She whispered loudly, so the crowd could hear but not Calaban behind her: "Aim over the target. The knife drops quickly."

"It's known the Gyppo is slippery like the Jew," the old man said.

Calaban leaped forward, grabbed a knife from the box, and threw it over his shoulder, dead center of the target.

"Oooooh!" the crowd murmured.

"Take what the Gyppo girl offers!" came a voice from the back of the crowd. "Win all his money. That's the best way to take your revenge."

"I believe you're right, friend," the man said, addressing the unknown voice in the crowd. "God would want me to take His revenge on these heathens." He accepted the knives and weighed them in his hand.

The old man threw with insouciant ease, not seeming to aim and barely throwing hard enough to make it stick in. Each knife hitting the target was like a dagger to Calaban's heart. He sunk deeper and deeper into gloom as an increasingly distraught Carla handed over the money. Finally, a shame-faced Carla admitted they had to close. A growl rose up from the crowd.

"You Gyppos aren't going to get away with that!" a loud voice demanded. "I want my chance to win some of your cash!"

"Me too!" shouted another.

"Thieves!" a woman called out as the crowd's muttering took on an ominous tone.

Carla considered for a minute. "Calaban, they are right. Go and borrow some money so we can remain open."

After a brief argument in Romany, a furious Calaban slouched off. Eager customers stepped up for their chance. Warburton thrilled to the drama. It was better than any play.

Warburton had realized that the trick was in the knives. All the polishing and cleaning of blades was a cover for Carla's deft substitution of the proffered knives for identical ones of different weights, with different centers of gravity. Some were heavier at the grip and others in the middle, changing how the knife tracked as it flew toward the target. When he practiced all the previous winter, Warburton simulated the weighted knives by fastening fishing lead to the shaft with twine.

At the end of the day Warburton presented himself at the booth.

"Better show him which end to hold!" sneered Calaban.

"Leave him alone," Carla said, bathing him with a warm smile. "He's very handsome."

"I see a boy still on his mother's teats," Calaban scoffed.

"At least, *this* boy knows who his father is!" Warburton said hotly. The onlookers howled with delight at his sally.

The crowd cheered again when the first knife flew true, and groaned when the next two missed. On his second turn—Warburton had enough money for four even if he didn't win a single free turn—he landed two on target. On his third only one again—enough to keep him in the game. On his fourth set he got all three. An hour later he was still throwing, sometimes landing only one but most of the time two or more. The crowd had been with him the whole time, applauding every success, consoling every failure. With each toss Warburton strutted cockily and grinned broadly at the scowling Calaban.

A stranger offered Warburton a cup of water, which he took gladly. "Keep smiling and come with us," he whispered. The man seemed amiable, but his hand gripped Warburton's bicep painfully. When he didn't immediately move, Warburton felt a knife prick through his coat. Walking through the crowd he heard congratulatory laughter and felt pats on his back. The man linked arms with him until they were well clear of the booth, when a second man grabbed the back of his coat and hustled him through the door of the largest caravan.

Warburton had never seen the inside of one before, but the last thing he expected was a large desk similar to his father's sitting in the middle of the small space. At the rear were neat cubbyholes and shelves above a narrow bed. Behind the desk was a middle-aged man wearing a bright-red *diklo* with an ornate silver clasp, writing with a quill pen. It wasn't until he'd blotted the paper and looked up that Warburton recognized the old man with the limp.

The man looked Warburton over carefully. He felt as if the man's eyes were poking into every aspect of his life and personality.

"You obviously recognize me," he said matter-of-factly. "My name is Eli Frankham."

"You're the old man with the limp. You're a cheat!"

"Brave words, young man, but foolish. Tell me, how did you win?"

"I'm as good as any gypsy," retorted Warburton. "I throw every day."

"You are telling me you won with the knives Carla gave you? No substitutions?"

The idea had never occurred to Warburton. "Of course not."

"What am I to do with you?"

"You will release me right now. My father will have your hide for tanning if you don't."

"Not so quickly, I think. No one cheats the Romani."

"I didn't cheat," Warburton said defiantly.

"All the worse," the man said with a sigh. "Whatever happens, the Romani must never seem weak."

Calaban, watching in the doorway, interjected with a harsh burst of Romany.

"Boys disappear," the leader agreed, considering the pale face and hair of the boy in front of him. "You'd bring a good price in certain places." He gestured to Calaban, who leaped forward happily to grab his tormentor. He was a good six inches shorter than Warburton, but even with a fury of fists and elbows Warburton couldn't shake the gypsy off.

"A fat man will split you in two," leered Calaban, driving his thumb into Warburton's bottom.

"You wouldn't dare!" he shouted. His throat felt suddenly parched and his knees felt pudding-soft. "My father will have you in irons!"

"Who is your father?"

"Kenderville Pike."

The idea of selling the boy quickly dropped out of Eli Frankham's head. Too bad. Those of his age and complexion fetched the best price.

The Romani settled on the next best thing. Seeing the face of Sir Ramrod Spike, as the gypsies called the area's largest landowner, when Eli Frankham delivered his son through the front door of the manor house, would be worth as much as selling the boy.

Eight days later Warburton began a four-year sojourn at Balleydineen in northern Scotland. A good school. A famous school. A very strict school.

31

After his gypsy adventure, Eva couldn't stop her husband from banishing Warburton to Scotland, but she was able to persuade him to allow their son to spend the summers in Saxony with the family of her first cousin. It was like stepping out of a rain cloud and into the Mediterranean. The von Schaumberg boys, cousins, and assorted friends roved the vast estate like a wolf pack. They built rafts to sail to the New World and forts to defend themselves against the evil Prussians, and rode ponies at full tilt through forest and field, fleeing from Danish madmen. Alfred, second son of the old count, Frederick, immediately became Warburton's best friend.

The contrast between the German table and that at home couldn't have been greater. In England, supper was a somber affair, with servants whisking silently in and out like ghosts. The family ate quietly, as Kenderville Pike spoke of estate and business matters, corrected Warburton's table manners, and interrogated him about his day's lessons. His mother hardly spoke, and Warburton only when directly addressed.

In Germany, filling the stomach involved filling the mind and the heart. At night a hundred candles fired the red-velvet walls of the dining hall as a dozen voices loudly carried on disparate conversations open to all. No one was afraid to speak up as each opinion, no matter how foolish or ill informed, would be listened to attentively, discussed seriously, then disagreed with vociferously. Toasts were often offered, and the count had to be in a poor frame of mind indeed to fail to comment on the beauty of the women and the quality of the food. Once he surprised everyone by breaking into song after learning of the birth of a great-nephew. Another time he recited a poem, accompanied by flourishes with his soup spoon. And when a shy guest dropped her custard flan onto the floor, the count did the same to set her at ease.

Warburton lived for the summers, those sparkling days of adventure. The only darkness came in July of his second year.

✳

"What were you doing so deep in the forest?" inquired the count urgently. His face was pale from the sight of Alfred shaking with the pain of a badly broken leg.

"F-following the leader, sir. I was the l-leader," fourteen-year-old Warburton stammered, afraid he'd be sent home.

"Then what happened?" the count prompted.

"We were jumping fallen trees from the storm. At first, just at the edge of the cattle field, but there were better ones in the forest and I knew we should turn back but . . ."

"But?"

"It was so much fun. I just wanted to keep riding and jumping higher. I didn't hear Alfred calling to stop," Warburton's words tumbled over themselves. "The others stopped but Alfred kept following. He never gives up."

The count smiled faintly.

"Charger is smaller than my horse. He couldn't clear the last tree. He made a terrible sound when he fell."

The squeal of agony from Alfred's horse lodged in Warburton somewhere around his diaphragm.

"What happened to Charger?"

"I . . ." Warburton gulped back sobs. "I hit him, sir. Over one eye." He hadn't cried since he was ten but the tears could not be stopped.

"Did he die quickly?" the count asked gently.

"It was like blowing out a candle. One second he was there, the next he was gone."

Warburton sniffed loudly, remembering the shock through his arm as he brought the rock down with all his might.

"I should have stopped, sir," he whispered through his tears.

"Yes, you should have," the count said with a sigh. "But doing the wrong thing is sometimes the only way to learn how to do the right thing."

✳

During Warburton's third summer, the dastardly Prussians and wild-eyed Danes gave way to savage red Indians and brave Virginians.

"It's terribly exciting," the count said, handing a book to Warburton shortly after his arrival. *The Last of the Mohicans*, by James Fenimore Cooper.

"It's all the rage and I think you'll enjoy it. But no kidnaping of helpless women on my lands. Understand?"

The boys fought to portray Natty Bumpo, but Warburton coveted the role of Chingachgook, the Mohican. For long, hot weeks they freed Indian princesses and smote evil tribes. They drew their wooden pistols with lightning speed and died spectacularly. The dairy cows, buffalo in disguise, were chased and lassoed until the milk manager complained to the count. "They're drying up. Couldn't the young gentlemen at least bother the ones that need freshening?"

Before he returned to England, the count gave Warburton another book from his vast library in four languages.

"You really must read the explorations of this man! You won't believe the drawings," enthused the count. He flipped pages rapidly. "Just listen! 'The mountains are about 10,000 feet high, unequalled in any part of Switzerland for their peaks and beauty of form, capped and dazzling in their white mantle of snow.'"

Warburton agreed the soaring coastal peaks were exquisite in H. J. Warre's *Sketches in North America*.

"And here! Have you ever seen anything like this?" The count stabbed at a picture of a lone savage crouched by a beautifully shaped canoe with a dragonlike head at the prow and spears trailing fur and feathers leaning against it. Carved figures stood guard on either side with torn blankets draped over poles in the background.

"That's an Indian?" asked Warburton, taken by the vigil of a single man—he must be a warrior—in the midst of a towering forest.

"Yes, by a grave. I believe this is in British North America."

"My father insists I go there one day."

"What a lucky coincidence! You must keep this book."

✱

The summers of Warburton Pike's childhood ended on a muggy August afternoon of his seventeenth year. It had been a quieter time, with fewer boys, as several of the cousins and Alfred's older brother, Dieter, were at military schools where buffalo were scarce and Indian maidens even more so.

Shortly after Warburton's arrival, Dieter returned ill from Essen in Westphalia and was diagnosed with pleurisy. The family was relieved to learn he would live but permanent weakness in his lungs would prevent any form of stressful work. The strong, square-shouldered twenty-year-old seemed to shrink before Warburton's eyes. Dieter was to have served five years in the army before returning to Neu Gattersleben to begin taking over the affairs of the estate, which he would inherit. Now it fell to Alfred.

The change in Warburton's friend was remarkable; overnight he became serious and preoccupied. He began accompanying the count on his daily business. Warburton was invited along but he found the inspections of the orchards, the breeding sheds, and the abattoir stultifying. As politely as possible he began to beg off.

✳

"Life is all about change, you know," the count said one morning as Warburton waited glumly to see Alfred off for the day. "There's no getting away from it. I wake up in the morning and my back is stiff. It takes me fifteen minutes to fully straighten. That's a change I could do without, but kicking at it doesn't alter the fact."

"I don't want things to change," Warburton said petulantly. "I want things to stay the same."

The count stared over the rose garden and the ornate Italian reflecting pools as he puffed away at his *penitello,* one of the thin cigars that he kept inside his jacket.

"Some changes are more welcome than others," the count said softly. "Next week Alfred leaves for Essen to take Dieter's place. He's been avoiding telling you."

Warburton nodded silently. He'd feared as much. A sense of importance had grown in Alfred in a matter of weeks as he looked to his future more than the present. Warburton didn't like it one bit.

"This is our last summer."

"For now," the count agreed. "You, of course, will always be welcome, whether Alfred is here or not."

"I don't want to come back!" Warburton flushed the moment the outburst slipped out of his mouth. "I am sorry, sir. I couldn't bear to be here without Alfred." The boy was steeped in gloom. "It feels like everything is over," he added.

"Now you're speaking foolishness," the count said kindly. "I envy the life you have in front of you. You can choose your own path."

"Me? I live in England, in a dreary, old manor with boring people everywhere."

"Perhaps, but your life ahead is not circumscribed as mine was, as Alfred's now is."

"But you have all of this," protested Warburton, swinging his arm around at the most beautiful land he had ever seen in his life.

"Even so, it is not what I wished for."

Warburton was stunned. "What do you mean?"

"I yearned to be a scholar."

"Why didn't you?"

"I was the oldest son," the count said simply. "The weight of generations demanded I follow this path. The noble life is grand enough but it comes with hundreds of fingers holding on to you, holding you back. Any of my three younger brothers could have done just as well—I begged my father to pass on the succession. He would not. Nor can I. Alfred's place will be here. I am not unhappy with my life and I don't think Alfred will be either, but you have the rare opportunity to do whatever you want and be whatever you want."

"My father has everything planned for me until the day I die."

The count spoke urgently to Warburton, who could smell the fruity peat sweetness of the *penitello*. "That is a father's wish, which is a natural thing. But his plans for you do not carry the imprint of centuries. England is not as trussed up with tradition as we are. The new class emerging in England will lead the world, of that I am very sure. The merchants, the industrialists—the strivers and experimenters will strike out in new directions. You are of that class and I envy you for it."

Warburton contemplated the count's words. Nothing seemed stuffy or trussed up about life here.

"I'd still rather nothing changed," he repeated stubbornly.

The count puffed on his pipe for a few minutes. "Well, perhaps when we take Alfred to the train in Leipzig, I can show you how change can be welcome."

✳

The count promised the boys a splendid dinner in Leipzig before seeing Alfred off to Essen and putting Pike on the train to Calais. Leipzig was a grand city, a wise old duchess, still beautiful and imposing despite her years. There were many haughty hotels with silverware so heavy ladies complained of fatigue by the end of the soup course. But the count bypassed them, taking the boys to the Hochleiterstrasse, where they were shaved, even though neither sported much facial hair as yet. He bought them a new suit each, with several good pairs of boots for Alfred.

"If my experience is anything to go by, your main concern in the first months will be your feet," he told Alfred.

When their stomachs started growling with hunger, the count led them to a nearby gentlemen's club where he kept a membership and where the rooms were comfortable. They dined on fat oysters chilled in icy vodka, the taste enlivened by bitter greens sprinkled with dark-green olive oil. They sipped boar's-head soup and ate sausage stuffed with duck's liver. After finishing the light repast, the count announced he intended to retire for several hours to his rooms.

"We shall sup at eleven," he said. "I have informed the kitchen and will meet you back here."

Full of energy, the boys bounded up the stairs, chattering about how to occupy themselves until eleven.

✳

Breasts were things Warburton knew of in theory but had never actually seen. He'd kissed and groped a few farm girls, but that had been in the dark, and while it was vastly exciting he'd never laid eyes upon the desired objects.

Sitting on two large footstools inside their room were four breasts. Rather there were two women with four breasts so poorly veiled Pike could easily make out their rosy nipples. Shi and Sho, two girls imported from the Orient. They were mesmerizing, their breasts were mesmerizing. When they stood up and walked toward the boys, their breasts floated before them like a mirage.

Pike felt his penis abruptly harden.

The door behind them opened, and both boys whipped around, hands crossed in front of them, guilt flushing their skin.

"*Eh voici, les deux chers!*" a silken voice spoke from deep-red lips. More breasts. These thrust upward in great pillows toward the white neck of the speaker. They belonged to a woman in her thirties, still youthful despite her age, with creamy skin, a cat's green eyes, and dark red hair without a trace of gray.

"They have many skills," she said, gesturing at the two girls.

She touched each boy on the shoulder and both felt the ache in their groins intensify.

"*Prenez votre temps.*" She smiled and departed.

For the first time in his life Warburton Pike—the Questing Knight, Chingachgook, Kat Vacuska—hadn't the faintest idea of what to say or do. Words fled and his muscles froze into rocks as hot desire flooded through him. Fortunately Shi was well trained. With an economy of movement she led him to one of the bedrooms off the sitting room and undressed him carefully, her fingers gently teasing his skin.

Warburton inhaled deeply. The girl smelled of cinnamon, rose, and something musky. Her eyes hardly left his face. Her pupils were so large and dark he felt devoured by them. Shi reached for a pipe and lit it. The acrid, cloying smoke made him cough, but when he drew on the pipe his head grew light and dreamy. It was a wonderful feeling and he began to laugh.

"*This*," Shi said, uttering her first words and pointing to the pipe, "will make *this* last longer." She touched his erection, almost making him erupt on the spot.

The hours passed in a series of glorious explosions, some inside Shi's slender body, others in her hand or mouth. Pike's emotions bounced from embarrassment to lustful hunger. When it was over, Pike didn't know if the experience made him more of a man, but it certainly made him feel like doing more of the same.

✳

It took Pike only an hour after the boat left Calais to make up his mind. A year-old edition of *Harper's Weekly* in the first-class berth as he crossed the Channel reinforced that decision.

> The new colony of British Columbia bids fair to become a magnet for the enterprising, the freedom seeker and the adventurer. No boundaries hold a man, no conventions restrict him. The coastal natives are, for the most part, docile and their skill with wood and knife extraordinary to behold.
>
> At six o'clock in the morning in Fort Langley the massive bolts and bars are unlocked from the entrances to the stockade. The English, Scotch, Irish, half-breeds begin to make their appearance and the business of the day begins.
>
> Further along in Fort Yale is the main depot of the mining country. Gambling houses—of which there are five here—are in full blast, night and day, and the number of houses where liquor is sold is about nine out of every ten.

But for the man with a gun, a keen eye, a lion's courage and the desire to leave civilization behind, the attraction of British Columbia lies in its unexplored bays, mountains and watery deltas. For this kind of man the land is his for the taking.

"All right, father," he said aloud. "I *shall* go to British Columbia, but I shall do it as *I* please."

Just before departure he remembered to write to his mother, begging her forgiveness for his sudden decision. He asked that a bank draft "for the purposes of sustenance" be taken from the small account his grandfather set up for him and forwarded to New York. He hoped it could be accomplished without his father's knowledge. "I assume there is a Royal Bank of London in New York and you could send it there, dear Mother. Please don't worry, I promise to return within the year whereupon I shall follow my father's every wish."

Warburton was startled to find New York City every bit as dirty as London, though without the smoky gagging fog that often choked the older city. Most of the buildings were smaller and far newer, with a sharpness of design that matched the rapaciousness of the city and its people. There was a noisy, pushy eagerness about the inhabitants, which made the streets of London seemed muted. Hardly had he set foot off the ship when a tough in filthy plus fours grabbed at his purse. Warburton whirled and, without thinking, kicked the man's kneecap. The thief buckled, swearing angrily.

"Now you'll know better than to assault an English gentleman," he scolded gaily, walking off with his heart crowding against his tongue.

32

✳

1864

St. Louis, Missouri

The sign read:

COLORADO BOB: LIVERY AND OUTFITTER
TO BUFFALOE HUNTERS, MOUNTAINERS,
DROVERS AND RENDEEVOOS MEN.

Colorado himself greeted Warburton over the top of the store's Dutch doors. He was a little, wizened man with leathery skin and lengthy white whiskers drooping from the sides of his mouth and the tip of his chin. His goods were laid out on benches and hung on walls in the low-ceilinged barn that still had horse stalls in one corner. A young Mexican boy sullenly dusted with a mop of sheep's skin.

"Mr. Colorado, sir, I'm looking to be outfitted for the West and I'm told you're a fair man."

Pike had been told that by Colorado's spotter, who waited for likely looking young men off the trains from Chicago or Cincinnati. Those of English or German extraction were most valued. They all wanted the same thing—to become vaqueros, cattlemen, cowboys, and buffalo hunters. In the guise of a city employee offering directions and information, the spotter directed them to his employer.

"Colorado'll be fine," he said pulling the words out in a fine drawl. "What might you be called?"

"Pike, Warburton Pike."

"Warburton? What kind of name is that? Better stick to Pike," he advised.

Colorado Bob's real name was William Smith and he had never seen the Colorado River, much less anything else west of the junction of the Missouri and the Mississippi. Nor did he intend to. He was partial to Colorado because it sounded a little wild, an important attribute to a man outfitting would-be cowboys.

"You came to the right place, for certain. Colorado'll treat you right." He punctuated his statement with a flourish as he drew out a tin of flue-dried chewing tobacco from J. E. Liggett and Brother, the leading tobacconist in the city. Most bought the considerably cheaper fire-dried chew but Colorado favored the flashy red tin that spoke of a man with means. The gesture was lost on Pike, who knew pipe tobacco only.

"You'd be heading west, I take it. Texas? Arkansas? Mexico?"

"British Columbia."

"Where in the Good Lord's hell is that?"

"On the Pacific Ocean," said Pike eagerly.

"You mean San Francisco!"

"No, it is farther north."

"You'd be talking about Oregon then!"

Pike shook his head. "No, it's even farther north."

"Gor!" muttered Colorado. "Why would a man want to go there?"

"Because it is wild and unsettled."

"We've got lots of wild right here in America," responded Colorado. "But suit yourself. How d'you aim to get to this British whatyoucallit?"

A phrase from his shipboard reading, *The Bandits of the Osage: A Western Romance,* by Emerson Bennett popped into his mind.

"I'll be heading up the Cimarron Crossing Trail and then to the Oregon Trail," he said confidently.

"Well, then you'd be going north and south at the same time."

"I need to get to San Francisco," said Pike, irritated by Colorado's attitude. "There are ships to British Columbia, because of the Gold Rush. Everyone knows that," he emphasized the last three words.

"P'rhaps so. But I wouldn't be taking the Oregon Trail from what I know of the West. Little that it is," Colorado said stiffly.

Pike had no idea how to get to San Francisco, so he thought he'd better flatter the man.

"Everyone says you know all there is about the West. Can you tell me the best way to get to San Francisco?"

"Let's get you fitted first," said Colorado, mollified.

"Where should I start?" Pike asked, gawking at dozens of unfamiliar items.

"You'll be needing some artillery, a good kak, a hackmore or bozal, pair o' mule ears and gut hooks too, a John B., some *chaparreras,* and uh, lemme see, a shakedown and . . ."

"Wait," said Pike desperately. "What is all that?"

Colorado eyed him with exaggerated patience and allowed a put-upon sigh to escape. He loved this part.

"You got some larnin' to do." He emphasized the point by dead-centering another vile-looking wad into the spittoon. Colorado paused to reload tobacco before offering some to the boy, who shook his head vigorously.

"Artillery's your weapon, that's easy enough. And your kak's your saddle. Some call it a gelding smacker. It'll be like a wife to you if you treat it right. Many's the time I've spent three, four days straight in the kak during a drive, sleepin' in it, eatin' in it. One time during a blizzard I was scared I'd never get back on, so I pissed over the side. Har! Har! Har!"

Colorado laughed long and hard at the memory, wholly fictitious though it was. The only riding he had ever done was as a boy on the pony rides in Central Park in New York, that plus a good buck on the occasional soiled dove upstairs at the nearby saloon. Colorado was a salesman pure and simple: shoes, shirts, patent medicine, and now cowboy gear. Though he had not a whit of personal experience, he took care to absorb the lore.

St. Louis was a shipping point for the longhorns brought up from Texas or Arkansas and bound for eastern markets. Every year hundreds of drovers spent their long-drive money in St. Louis bars and brothels but some set enough aside to replace broken or worn-out gear. Colorado kept a couple of jars of pine whiskey for such men, which he doled out liberally to keep the stories coming. If Pike had happened into Colorado's store when a real cowboy was there, he would have been surprised to find a quietly deferential character in place of the garrulous salesman.

About a dozen saddles were laid out in one corner of the barn. To his delight, Pike found one he recognized, in pristine condition, under a piece of canvas. He picked it up happily. "This looks like a Phillips-Nash military close contact," he said, fondly stroking the long leg-flaps. "Where ever did you get it?"

Colorado's lip curled in contempt. "That's for girlsss," he hissed. "Nothing to jar their equipment." Colorado thumped the hornless pommel.

"Ride one of these hog-skinned kidney pads an' you won't last a day on the trail. Some easterner give this pimple up for a real saddle. He's a *man* now."

Pike dropped the saddle as if it were molten lava.

Eventually they settled on an elderly stock-saddle, at least forty-five pounds in weight, with a few tarnished silver conchos for decoration.

"Now let's get you a smoke wagon," Colorado announced. "Without one you'll be sent to heaven to hunt for a harp soon as ya cross the Missouri. All the injuns got cutters and most of them'll kill ya soon as look at ya. They got lead plum too, plenty of it, with the fur trade and all. I saw one man in the Utah Territory shot so goddam full of holes he wouldn't float in brine. Took the sawbones a day to mine the lead. Poor bastard died anyway."

It was a story he'd read in the *St. Louis Blower,* but Colorado told it as if he'd stood alongside the country surgeon while he fished for the bullets.

Pike didn't see anything even vaguely familiar in Colorado's gun room. The pistols were arranged on a table while the rifles and a few ancient muskets sat on wall racks.

"You'll need a pistol and a rifle," the owner advised. "If you can't afford both, get a rifle. Your choice is between the Hawken or the Sharps."

The .50-caliber Hawken rifle was made right there in St. Louis. Accurate at a range of 350 yards and equipped with a revolutionary percussion ignition system, it had been the workhorse of the plains since the 1820s.

"Mountain men love this un 'cause it hardly ever misfires. Mike Fink, Kit Carson, and Jim Bridger all owned these babies," he said as Pike hoisted the Hawken. His ears perked up at the mention of the fabled mountain men and scouts.

"Trouble is they're muzzle loaders. Hard as hell to reload when you're riding. These here are shorter than your Kentucky mountain rifles but still hard to handle, 'specially for a greenhorn. And they're tough to load lying down. And let me tell you, if you're in an injun fight, you want to keep as low as possible. Else you'll lose your scalp." With that Colorado made a slicing motion at his hairline and let out a blood-curdling war whoop. He spoke with such authority that Pike would have been amazed to learn that Colorado had rarely even seen an Indian and certainly not one bearing arms.

"Sharps is the one for you," Colorado stated emphatically.

"But it's four times as expensive," protested Pike, thinking of how much more he had yet to buy.

"The Hawken's fine if you want to save a few bucks, but if you want to live long enough to get to that Brit place, pick the Sharps."

The Sharps, a breech-loading, single-shot carbine was a remarkably flexible and reliable weapon. Short-barreled, it featured one of the first single-unit bullets, a linen-wrapped cartridge.

"You can get off four or five rounds a minute. Even the best muzzle-loader won't do better than three," Colorado added confidentially. "Might save your life one day."

※

Pike hefted the weapon and aimed several times, instantly comfortable with the feel and balance. He believed that weapons were very personal, and this one felt like a piece of him. Pike might not know a kak from a spur rowl, but he was well trained in the "manly arts," thanks to the school in Scotland. After three years topping all comers in target shooting, both pistol and rifle, he felt at home for the first time since walking through Colorado's doors.

"I'll take it," he said.

The response momentarily flattened Colorado, who was only midway through the sales spiel.

"Well, son, if you're sure, we'll put this aside."

"Excellent," responded Pike, warming into it. "What about a revolver?"

Pike knew from his careful reading of dime novels that the legendary frontier scout Kit Carson slept with two Colts at half-cock by his head and another under his blanket. In one encounter, Carson and a partner armed with Colts routed an attacking group of Kiowa and Comanche, reputedly killing or wounding more than a hundred. That was more than good enough for Pike.

"I'm looking for a Colt," he stated. "And I want the Navy model 1851."

Again Colorado was short-circuited, but he nodded approvingly.

"You sleep with five beans in the wheel of a King Colt an' you'll keep heaven and hell at bay for a while."

Of all his purchases Pike was most intrigued by his shakedown, or bedroll.

"Next to your saddle, my lad, and your hawg leg, this'll keep you alive," spouted Colorado, hauling one off a shelf. He got lucky with this bedroll, as its first owner brought it in for restitching, then got so drunk he drowned in the livery water trough before retrieving his property.

"It works like this," he instructed, keeping the bag's antecedents to himself. "You got your tarp here on the outside, an' if its raining out, you can get all covered up. Inside you got your *soogans* to keep your jewels cozy."

Colorado made the *soogans*, or liners, himself from wool he bought from the slaughter yards then combed into batting and stitched to strips of coats and pants that came off the corpses at the city morgue.

"You stick your war sack in the bottom." At Pike's blank look, he added, "Money. Roll 'er up like this. Lash 'er and you're done."

In an unusual fit of generosity, Colorado threw in a bright-red wipe, or neckerchief.

"Most useful thing you've got, next to your saddle," he said, forgetting he'd said precisely the same thing of the bedroll and weapons. "It'll protect your neck from sunburn or cold. They'll also double as ear muffs. Save your life during a dust storm. Wet it down and breathe through it during a prairie fire, or in summer set it in your hat to cool your brain pan. Serves as a towel, protects your hand from the branding iron. Then it's a pigging string to hogtie the cattle, a hobble for your horse, a tourniquet for wounds, a bandage, a sling for a broken arm . . ."

"Better make it two then, if they're so useful," Pike said to stem the flow. "I'll pay for one."

When it came to the boots, Colorado tsk-tsked for some time about the large size of Pike's feet before digging out a used pair. Pike commented on the beauty of the decorative embroidery.

"The fancy stitchin' ain't just decoration," Colorado said sharply. "Leather stretches. Stitchin' keeps it tight, 'specially at the ankles where it wrinkles and bags and at the tops so they won't break down and sag. The more stitchin' the more wear you'll get. Fancy stitchin's the sign of a good boot."

Pike's regalia was completed by *chaparreras*—chaps, a dark-brown John B. hat, and an oiled, yellow, cotton-duck slicker specially made to hook over the horn at the front of the saddle and over the cantle at the rear, keeping the rider more or less protected from the weather.

"If you don't hitch it just so," Colorado demonstrated, "your balls get wet an' get froze." Colorado paused and stared hard at Pike. "Tell ya the truth," he said in the manner imparting a hard-earned lesson. "Ya gotta be mighty careful not to get your equipment froze. A man can break it right in half trying to piss."

The purchases, including $30 for a brown-faced roan mare with the big, soft eyes of a cooperative mount, consumed Pike's entire budget plus $7.

Colorado took Pike's tweed suit to "square things up."

"You sure won't be needing it in Texas," he said with a barking laugh. He'd have no trouble unloading the high-quality suit to one of the bankers and merchants in St. Louis wanting to dress the part of a gentleman.

"But I'm going to San Francisco."

"Pr'haps so, but if you take the mountain route across through Utah you'll get yourself scalped sure as anything. If you want my advice . . ." He stopped meaningfully.

"Yes, yes, I do!"

"I'd join a drover outfit to Texas or Mexico, then hire on with one of the outfits shipping cattle to San Francisco. Gold's all gone there but it's quite the city now, I hear. Whores on every corner."

When Colorado informed Pike that the Bar S drover crew—which used to include the former owner of the bedroll—were a man short, Pike couldn't saddle up fast enough.

Dashing over to the hotel where Colorado said the crew was likely drying out after binging on drink and women, Pike passed the train station. For the first time in many days he thought about his parents. He wondered if his mother was crying and his father storming about in tight-lipped anger. He tied his horse to the hitching rail and hurried into the station.

"Can I post a letter here?"

"Certainly!" the apple-cheeked ticket agent beamed. "It will go day after tomorrow."

Pike quickly scribbled a few lines on paper he bought from the agent. He promised to write in more detail later and asked his parents to send letters to San Francisco, California.

At the hotel, the gang boss looked him over and grunted. "Dollar a day, bog rider and footer." His second in command added a throaty, "Yup," and they were off.

From St. Louis along the Missouri to Independence, where they joined the Cimarron Crossing Trail that would take them across the Santa Fe River and into the foothills of northern Texas, the gang rode hard on fresh horses, unencumbered by cattle. Pike spent the first week nursing his groin, getting used to riding with a long leg, and trying not to stick his horse with his sunset rowel spurs. Colorado recommended them over the flashier Texas-star rowels, with their longer, sharper points. The sunset had points set closely together, to inflict more of a poke than a sharp jab. As he held his heels away from his horse's side, Pike was grateful for the odd little man's advice.

33

✳

The drover's get-up was brilliantly designed for life off the ground but poorly suited for doing anything on two legs. Chaps, though saviors when riding through thickets of mesquite, were stiff and heavy, and they dragged as a man walked. Tall boot heels perfectly secured feet in the stirrups, and big rowels were excellent at persuading stubborn nags, but both made walking on the flat, much less uneven, terrain a challenge. The smooth soles were also slippery. Pike's first night on the trail, he fell twice en route to relieve himself. The second time he almost impaled himself on a wild-rose bush.

"You'll be pissing all over yerself at the rate yer flopping around," drawled the gang boss to general laughter.

Pike's accent earned him the nickname England, which distressed him, as it seemed so bland and unimaginative. Most of the hands had nicknames that were far more evocative. Brazos and Tex, Freckles and Stretch, Cat and Stinky. One of the drivers was called Windy on account of his ability to let loose thunderous farts at will. Pike yearned for something impressive, such as Kid or Pistol, but no one asked him what he wanted to be called, so he kept his mouth shut.

Thirteen days out of St. Louis the tired crew topped a mesa plateau to the east of the Bar S. Below spread the ranch, like a bunch of child's playing blocks strewn onto a barren piece of ground. Pike counted fourteen buildings, including the main bunkhouse and the breed shack for Mexicans and half-breeds who did the milking and pig work. The men stumbled into their bunks, swearing they'd sleep for a week. But Pike was so full of energy he couldn't lie down, let alone sleep. He roamed the spread for hours, thrilling to the openness, the bald hills stretching out to the horizon, and the smells of leather, manure, gun oil, and iron being heated in the blacksmith's forge.

"That mockey o' yours ain't good fer nuthin' but buzzard bait," Luke, the gangboss, informed him when Pike walked to the first horse pen, filled with milling animals. "Pick your remuda out o' this bunch."

"Mockey? Oh, do you mean my horse? I'm quite pleased with her," said Pike. The roan had been so solid on the ride to the ranch that Pike rarely rode his second-string horse, which Luke had picked up south of Independence.

"Mockey! Mare! Useless!"

"No, no, she's been an excellent mount."

"You git boggin' and she'll be bitin' the wind. Humpy'll help ya. You'll ride with him."

Humpy, or Buffalo Back, was part Comanche and part unknown. His name came from a prodigious swelling in the upper middle of his back, which had the effect of curling his torso into a bow. Even so, seated on his scruffy gray Indian pony, the half-breed seemed enormous in the buffalo cape he wore no matter what the weather.

In their first days together Humpy said only five words, all related to the horses they were cutting out in the paddock.

"Broncho," he said of a gorgeous buckskin—wild. "Crock head," he said of another—bad temperament. "Potros," for a too-green young bay. "Pinto." Approval. Pike selected the tri-color little gelding. Tiny, but calm-eyed and strong.

Words six and seven came when Pike saw a group of cowboys tearing up a nearby hill as if chasing a pot of gold.

"Humpy, what's on the other side of that hill they're riding up?"

"Nudder hill."

Other questions met with, "Ask crow," or "Ask gopher," depending on which animal was visible.

A few hours from the ranch on their first bogging run, the half-breed motioned Pike off the trail, finger across his lips. They waited silently for nearly ten minutes until three Indians materialized.

"Kiowa," Humpy said, spurring his horse forward to palaver.

Later that day Humpy did the same thing, but this time it was two hard-looking white men. Pike looked at the half-breed, who just shrugged, as if to say, "Don't know them and don't want to know them." Another day, when they were setting up camp, Humpy stopped in the middle of making a fire. He stood as straight as his back would allow, listening intently.

"Luke. Tex." Sure enough, the two men loped up three or four minutes later.

"How did you know?" Pike asked, thrilled at the mystical skill of his companion. "That was extraordinary. I didn't hear a thing. Can you teach me that?"

"Nope."

Breeds and Mexicans were usually assigned to the worst ranch chores, much of it done on foot. Bogging was filthy work, and most cowboys would rather have shot themselves than become bog riders. Despite his lowly status, Pike saw that the other men had a measure of respect for Humpy, and he soon learned why. One night a ferocious storm sent rare ball lightning exploding like cannon all over the ranch. Two hundred head of longhorns stampeded from a pen in a nearby canyon. Humpy was the man picked to do the dangerous job of heading—turning the lead cattle. Pike rode the safer outer flank. But even there the horrific sound of four hundred horns clacking against each other in the pitch black, coupled with the screams as animals went down and were trampled, kept his heart hammering like a gong for hours afterward.

When a new bunch of horses was brought to the ranch for breaking, the other cowboys hung back and smoked while Humpy quietly rode through the herd on his gray. Sometimes it took him hours, but no one moved until he slipped out of the paddock. From the mishmash of ranch-raised youngsters, Indian ponies, *mesteños* or mustangs, and army horses that had somehow "gotten away," Humpy picked out the ones best suited for cutting, line riding, roping, and night work. He was invariably right.

Still, Humpy was a breed, and bog riding was his job.

"Why do so many cattle get stuck in the mud?" Pike asked Humpy.

"Heel flies."

"Oh, I see, the flies bother them and they escape by wading into the mud?"

"Uh."

"But aren't the flies more common in spring?"

"Uh."

"It's not spring yet."

"Nope."

"Umm, so why are the cattle getting stuck in quicksand?"

"Sticky mud."

"Yes, yes, I figured out that part, but don't the cattle know enough not to go near the quicksand?"

"Nope."

Quicksand lay in wait at the bottom of shallow rivers and depressions, which held precious water for only a few months of the year. The quicksand of the western plains was unusually dangerous, because the grains of sand were flat and adhered to each other. You were safe as long as you kept moving, but cattle, not being the wisest of creatures, waded in to drink. As the tension pulled at their feet, they panicked. Pulling upward only increased the downward draw, and eventually they'd sink belly-deep.

At the first mired cow Humpy heaved himself off his horse and silently doffed his boots and pants, displaying an extremely shaggy posterior. He eyed the bleating animal a moment before crab-walking into the creek, carrying the loop end of a rope tied to Pike's saddle horn. When he was close enough, Humpy flipped the noose over the cow's head and signaled Pike to back up his horse to keep the rope taut.

Staying just clear of the frightened animal's horns, the half-breed began a strange dance, stomping slowly from foot to foot, forcing water into the sand to soften it as close as possible around the cow's legs. When the sand felt soupy underfoot, he used a bale hook to pull first one front leg, then the other, out of the sand, while Pike steadily increased the tension. It was dangerous work, as the cow flailed frantically and he had to free the hind legs quickly before the front ones sank again. When the beast finally pulled free of the muck, it angrily charged Pike, then raced away, bawling.

"Giddap!" Pike shouted, tearing after the animal. He'd forgotten to flip the rope off the cow's horns as it escaped. Returning to the ranch without his rope would be almost as bad as losing his horse.

"Got it! Oh my! That was exciting!" Pike rode triumphantly back to the creek, waving the lariat in his hand.

"Aren't you a sight!" Pike burst into laughter at Humpy's mud-dappled backside and waggling parts as he struggled out of the water.

"You next," Humpy said dead-pan. "Not funny then."

The night before they were to head back, they camped on a tributary of the Pecos. Pike swore he could hear the scrub talking to each other in a strange, scratching tongue. He dreamily wondered just what mesquite might say if it could talk in this barren land.

"You pass big water?"

At first Pike thought Humpy might be talking about relieving himself—"pullin' little man," the ranch hands called it.

"Do you mean the ocean?"

"Uh."

"I sailed from France to New York."

"Big boat?"

"Yes. It was a cargo ship with few passengers. I was worried we'd be stuck down with the bilge pumps," he paused. "Those are huge, noisy pumps that push out water that gets into the ship."

"Water in boat?"

"Well, no boat is completely waterproof, and when it is rough they all take on water, which has to be pumped out. Sometimes a captain will even pump in water, if a ship is riding high and the weight will improve the stability." He wasn't sure how much of what he said Humpy understood.

"You feared?"

"Frightened? Well, it was a big ship, so it wasn't like being on a little boat where you feel every swell and the water seems so close. But we had a big blow just a day off the coast of America. The waves were like mountains and we lost a mast. That got me saying my prayers."

Humpy fell silent.

"It's so damn big out here," Pike said at last, his words completely inadequate to describe the empty vastness. For long stretches at night, especially when clouds hid the stars, he felt as if every living thing but he and Humpy had been sucked off the face of the earth.

"Are you ever afraid out here?" he queried hesitantly.

Such a long time passed he thought Humpy had fallen asleep.

"Uh," came the affirmative reply.

✳

By the time Windy Charlie tried to bite his ear off, Pike had started to forget about his plans to go to British Columbia. Winter was coming and the days were filled with line riding and branding. Two men had been killed by Mescalero Apache raiders, their bodies beheaded, stripped, disemboweled, and draped over mesquite bushes, so the ranch was short of hands. Pike's work doubled. He loved the long days, the glorious fatigue as night fell, and every second Sunday, when Tattle Sue and Skit Mary rode out to the ranch from the fort at Pecos. They did six men each, drawing straws to see who got lucky. Pike won each time, happily refusing to sell his spot to the clamoring hands of the ones who'd lost.

Pike was idly stuffing a knotty chunk of cottonwood into the pot-bellied stove when Windy Charlie marched up and sunk his teeth into Pike's ear.

Pike leaped up, cupping his torn ear as the blood dripped into his sleeve.

"What the bloody hell are you doing!" he shrieked at the older man.

"You strung me a whizzer," growled Charlie.

"I did what?"

"Yer shakedown! It ain't yours, it's Hopi Craw's."

It was Hopi Craw, born Harold Crawford, who'd gone harp-hunting in the St. Louis water trough, which resulted in Colorado Bob's acquisition of his shakedown.

"Whaat?" Pike clutched at his ear.

"Betcha he hanked Hopi, too." Charlie's accusation caused a low rumbling among the other men in the bunkhouse. None of them had anything in particular against England, but from the beginning the youngest member of the Bar S gang had got under Charlie's skin like a cactus thorn. It was always Charlie who shouldered Pike away when the men clustered around the stove. The burly Tennessean liked to stick his foot out when Pike carried in the firewood. The first time Pike fell heavily, almost knocking his teeth in.

"Keep out of his way," Luke warned early on. "Windy was born with a chafed butt. Gets worse every day."

"You hank ol' Hopi?"

"What are you talking about?" said Pike irritably. He knew "hank" meant "kill," but he had no idea what this was about.

"Hopi supposed to be drowned but now I see you got Hopi's shakedown. I knowed it's his 'cause o' the patch on the bottom. I give it to him."

"I bought the bedroll from Colorado Bob!" protested Pike, starting to get his back up.

"Ya, an' I'm a porcupine fucker!"

"We're talking about a bedroll, not your mating habits," Pike snapped.

"Got you on that one, Windy!" hooted one of the hands.

"You boys gonna dance, take it outside," Luke said quietly from the corner.

At Luke's soft words Pike's anger flared, burning away caution and hesitation. He grabbed a stick and banged it against the stove.

"I'm calling you out, you mangy marsupial!" Pike shouted. He punctuated the challenge by pounding on the stove again. Anger and the power of youth combined to make him invincible.

"What in tarnation's a marsupial?" puzzled one of the men.

"Dunno, but it sounds bad," answered another.

"I'll be waiting outside," Pike marched out the door, giving it a kick as he went. "Unless you're too yellow to face me."

The cowboys, chattering eagerly, hastily laid down bets. Windy Charlie, at least sixty pounds heavier and snake-mean, took the odds.

"Ain't gonna last two minutes!" Windy taunted.

"Don't worry, I'll carry you at least that long," crowed Pike.

"No boy ain't gonna scritch me."

"When I'm finished with you, you'll be able to whistle in your own ear and lick your asshole with your tongue."

Each sally brought roars of encouragement from the men. "England's sure got some fast mouth," Tex commented to general agreement.

Pike grinned at the crowd, egging them on. As he did, Charlie charged low and hard, taking Pike's feet out from under him. Whump! He tasted dirt. Pike elicited a howl of laughter when he scrambled to his feet and put his dukes up in the best Marquis of Queensberry tradition. They wouldn't have laughed so loud if they'd met Pike's instructor at the Scottish school, a former infantry sergeant in the Royal Hussars, who seemed chipped from granite.

"Boxin's the sport of gentlemen, me lad," he often said. "But a gentleman should always know a little rough and tumble."

Charlie charged again. At the last instant Pike danced aside, hitting his opponent on the ear as he skidded past.

"That's for biting my ear!" Pike snarled.

The cowboys kyied and yipped, urging the combatants on. Nothing enlivened long, slow nights like a good fight. With plenty of room to maneuver, Pike backpedaled, landing jab after jab to the face, splitting Charlie's lip and bloodying his nose. He easily danced away from potentially punishing blows, leaving Charlie corkscrewing ineffectually in the air. After one of Charlie's misses, Pike pirouetted like a ballet dancer, then kicked his adversary in the ass to the roar of the hands.

Charlie stood panting, blood dripping. This wasn't going as expected.

"Let me know when you're ready to start fighting!" hollered Pike, feeling like a colt in spring. "I'm warmed up now."

At school, when one combatant was staggering and bleeding, the fight would be over. Here, on the hardback north Texas mesa, it had only begun. Pike just didn't know it. Charlie nursed his nose, looking thoroughly beaten. When Pike held out his hand to shake, Charlie made as if to take it. Instead he grabbed Pike's head, snapping it down into his rising knee.

Pike collapsed, stunned. "Oooo!" the crowd winced.

Through his tears Pike saw Humpy leaning massively against a fence post. Charlie could have finished the boy then and there, but he made a mistake. He drew his Colt.

"Hey!" Pike screamed. "I'm not armed!"

"Yah! An' I don' 'spect Hopi were neither when you drowned him."

"I didn't drown him, I tell you!" Pike yelped as a bullet smacked into the ground at his feet.

The roar of Humpy's Henry rifle pulled silence down on the eager watchers like water dousing a fire. Humpy waved the gun at Charlie's revolver and shook his head.

"Ain't yer business, breed!" spat Charlie, his voice tailing off into a squeak when the Henry roared again. Humpy walked over in his peculiar gait and held out his hand. Not looking at him, Charlie handed over the gun.

"I'd ruther hank'im by hand anyhow," he said unconvincingly.

"Gotta finish him," Humpy muttered as he helped Pike to his feet. "Hurtin's not enough."

Pike backpedaled furiously as Charlie closed in. When he got his breath back, Pike snapped off a five-punch combination into Charlie's face, this time putting his weight into the blows. Each one made a horrible, squishy, wet sound. Pain shot up his arms with every blow. Charlie's hands went up to his face, now a bloody wound. His eyes were swelling rapidly and his nose looked like it had been split in two with a knife. Pike turned to the unprotected body, focusing on the ribs, grunting with the effort he was putting into each blow. He'd heard ribs snapping on his last two punches.

"Had enough?" Pike gasped hopefully, hitting Charlie again in the same spot, then staggering backward.

Charlie made a strangled, snorting sound and charged again. Just as he reached Pike, he stopped dead with a surprised look on his face and crumpled to the ground. He was still breathing, but blood leaked from inside his ear, his face looked like a badly cut haunch, and he whimpered like a beaten dog. The cowboys bellowed their approval.

Pike was exhilarated. Even his hours with Shi couldn't compare. He could feel blood racing through his body. He heard Humpy's shout, "Finish 'im!"

✳

"I gotta let you go," said Luke.

"But Windy started the fight, and I never killed that man!" Pike said angrily.

"Don't matter. If you'd finished Charlie I coulda kep you, but it'll only cause trouble now. He'll be at you day and night. Charlie's my best cutter, I ain't letting him go. I got three men coming from Santa Fe. You'd best find another spread."

PART VII

Soon and
Pike

34

*

January 5, 1868

Head of Burrard Inlet,

Colony of British Columbia

The clammy damp licked Soon's arms and face. Cold, sticky. It wasn't rain or even a heavy mist, just thick, saturated air. He wiped his finger across his arm, and within seconds the moistness returned. Soon touched the shaved crown of his head. It too sported a sheen. His clothes smelled moldy, which, he supposed, was a small improvement over the rankness of his body, long overdue for a bath.

Soon raised his eyes and stared bleakly at the land mass rapidly approaching. What he felt in his heart was a cousin to what he felt on his skin—cold. The frigate ran quietly under sail, having cut its steam engines to save fuel as the wind now braced the sheets. He smiled grimly to himself. Imagine conserving fuel in this place where wood rampaged down to the shoreline like thousands of thirsty beasts surging forward to drink.

Soon tried not to think of Wan Lo. He missed him more than he thought was possible. It was only after Wan Lo died, the second day out of San Francisco, that Soon realized the boy—Wan Lo was long into manhood but Soon still thought of him as a boy—was as good a friend to him as he'd ever had. The illness had been strange and sudden. A ferocious fever consumed Wan Lo and delirium set in, broken only by moaning complaints of terrible pain in his head and neck. And then he was gone. The captain was furious and frightened. He confined all second-class passengers and aliens to their tiny quarters for five days. Only yesterday, after no one else showed any symptoms, had he allowed them above deck.

Soon stood freezing in the bow, hiding from Warburton Pike. Boisterous and heedless, Pike had no fear of catching any disease, and despite the captain's orders he'd come into the steerage and alien bunks to play cards night after night. He was also insufferably rude, looking directly and piercingly into one's eyes when speaking. Worse was his embarrassing intimacy.

The first day out of San Francisco he'd clapped Soon on his shoulder. It took all Soon's willpower not to shake off the offending hand.

And the questions, they never ended.

There was little to distinguish Soon, now thirty-five years old, from the 87,422 other Chinese who had flooded America over the past decade. At five feet three inches, he was of average height, though perhaps even more slender than his generally lean countrymen. His most striking feature was unusually sharp cheekbones framing deeply set brown eyes, so wide and hooded that they appeared as narrow slits in his face. A scar traversed his right cheek, and others were hidden under his clothing. His fingers were well shaped, but heavy scarring spoke of former hard usage. His crown was carefully shaved to the midpoint of his head, and his queue was unobtrusively tucked into a small, square, black cap. He wore a plain, dark *shen-i* robe, which came to his knees, and leather boots, a big improvement over sisal and cloth slippers or wooden shoes.

They were already seven days out of San Francisco, three more than the captain had anticipated, having been stalled and squalled upon and nearly wrecked first at Fuca's Spire and then in the narrow passage between the southern tip of Vancouver Island, the British colony, and the north shore of the new state of Washington.

> *We hauls she east and we hauls she west*
> *But hauls ye north and we be dead men I'll bet*
> *Oh heave mighty lad*
> *Oh heave and haul*
> *We'll fool the Spanish bastard by the morn'n yet*

The crew chanted those words over and over in the frightening day it took to get through "the Spanish bastard's" passage. None of them knew that the Spaniard was actually an old Greek pilot, or that his Straits of Anian was really a fish hook–shaped strait that curled around Vancouver Island's southern tip and opened out into the Strait of Georgia, which contained thousands of islands that chased each other all the way to Alaska. The barb of "the Spanish bastard's" hook was the entrance to what the captain called "the devil's own playground," where vicious waters seemed to ebb and flow at the same time, and winds tore in from all corners of the compass to crash against anyone fool enough to venture forward. Short of the Cape of Good Hope, there was no more treacherous stretch of ocean, in the captain's opinion. In a scant half century of navigation, more than fifty ships had already been lost, most with all hands.

The frigate, the *Lady Mary Green,* captained by Horatio Burke, was one of the better copies of the venerable *East Indiaman* but fitted with the modifications of a faster packet ship, which made her suitable for both the China trade and the West Indies run from the Atlantic coast to Liverpool. Though more full-bodied and not as speedy as the sleek American clippers, the *Lady Mary Green* made good way in open ocean yet was nimble enough to navigate the difficult coastline from the Oregon Territory through to the more northerly trading forts in New Caledonia, now British Columbia. She had a greater dead rise and a far finer run than the cumbersome cargo ships aboard which Burke spent his earlier career. And at 574 tons she was large enough to profitably transport bales of fur and barrels of salmon from the Hudson's Bay forts as well as the massive spar timbers destined for the shipbuilding yards in Liverpool and Bath.

"If those red Indians set out to design a way to keep us out, they couldn't do a better job than this bloody place! God only knows how they manage in those log boats of theirs," Soon had overheard the captain saying in the lull between two hard blows.

"In the open sea there's some honesty in the weather. Inside this passage it's all tricks."

"Are the Indians peaceable in British Columbia?" Pike asked, trying to divert the captain from the weather, which was his favorite topic.

"The ones closest to the coast are friendly but poor traders. They don't seem to have much of an interest in anything we have. The navy men have pushed most of the Musqueam and the Squamish out of the lands near the best bays, that'd be the English Bay and Burrard Inlet. If it bothers them they haven't done much about it. But inland and up the Fraser's River, it's a different story."

"The tribes are dangerous there?" Pike asked with relish.

"'Course things got a bit hotted up when gold was discovered in 1858. Nothing like fifty thousand miners stomping about to make things tense. No one knows how many lost their heads."

"Well, then my head is perfectly safe," declared Pike. "I have no interest in gold. None at all!"

"What kind of a man doesn't care about gold?" queried Captain Burke curiously.

"The kind of a man who's led the life I've led," Pike responded mildly. "Give me a bed under the stars any day rather than a desk in a counting house. A lady and a jug of whiskey would be nice too."

"I doubt I'd tire of the stuff," responded the captain. "I wouldn't mind trying."

Pike turned to enjoy the landscape. What an odd chap, Burke thought, taking in the Englishman. The rough outline of the lanky, young man who'd landed in New York nearly four years earlier was still present, but within the lines everything had changed. Any softness in frame and manner was long gone. In its place was a taller-than-average twenty-two-year-old body, which appeared to have been constructed by wrapping layers of muscle on top of one another, then pulling them tight around an iron core. What was inside the body had changed far more. From his battered hands to his eyes—glacier-gray—there were warning signs for those astute enough to notice.

But when Pike cracked his habitual wide smile, he was still the inquisitive boy who could get almost anyone to talk to him—and once you talked to him, you were usually a friend. Pike's dress was picturesque. A mix of English, California frontier, and drover, with a good dose of several Indian cultures mixed in. His hat—a black-felt Sam Yoke—replaced the one Colorado Bob had sold him. Wrapped around its brim was a rattlesnake skin complete with rattle. On his feet were *rancheros,* a combination of stiff-soled moccasin and low-heeled boot. His shirt was of pale-blue Egyptian cotton with a double-breasted front. He'd splurged on it in San Francisco just before boarding the ship to the British Northwest. The tightly woven fibers felt indescribably soft on his skin. His gray wool pants had been patched many times and were fraying at the cuffs. Over it all he wore a full-length, oiled canvas duster. No amount of rain could penetrate it, and the moth-eaten, rabbit liner was surprisingly warm.

Pike's hair, grown long, was tied at the back with a horsehair braid. Though he'd worn a beard and a moustache, his face was now meticulously shaven, both upper lip and chin, as it would be for the rest of his life. Around his neck Pike wore a bear claw hanging from rawhide, a parting gift from Humpy. Pike had planned to head directly to San Francisco after leaving the Bar S, but three years disappeared as he followed the cattle from Texas north to Montana and east to the cities of the Missouri and the Mississippi.

In spite of his appearance, the captain could tell that Pike had been born a gentleman. No amount of hardscrabble living could scour away the subtle signs of voice and posture that told of a life born into ease. Most of the Englishmen Burke ferried from California to the British Columbia gold-fields were destined for pain as they adjusted to life in the deep forests with little to eat but what they could shoot themselves. This one wasn't like that.

There were few other white passengers, as the Fraser River's bars had been mined out and the first cries of strikes in the interior had yet to make it to the United States or Europe. There was, however, the Chinaman and fourteen freed slaves, who'd been encouraged by Mifflin Gibbs, the colony's first black settler, to "seek the free life in Victoria on Vancouver Island." There were also ten Kanakas, or Hawaiians. Captain Burke treated them as cargo, keeping the Sandwich Islanders confined to the hold. He'd picked them up in San Francisco, where they'd been waiting a month for passage to the Northwest.

"Don't be fooled by those white-toothed grins of theirs," the captain warned Pike. "They have the heart of the Dark Continent in them. And they're too bloody good with boats to trust them moving about my ship without a musket at their back. Two Kanakas can do the work of ten on the water. Too bad they're a mutinous bunch," he'd insisted to Pike, when he mentioned that they looked harmless enough to him. "Cannibals too. They would eat you as soon as shake your hand. I'll be mighty glad to be rid of them. They're all going to work at the new mill in the colony."

At the mention of the mill Pike thought about his father. Wouldn't it be odd, he considered, to arrive in British Columbia only to find Kenderville Pike had got there ahead of him. He felt vaguely guilty about his mother. He had written half a dozen times since he left St. Louis, cheery letters with exaggerated descriptions of life in the West. Pike expected he made the days sound like one long shooting party in the deer forests of the Mayhill estate. One of her letters had arrived at the Bar S, but he hadn't received any more until he landed in San Francisco three years later. Nothing seemed to have changed in England. It was as if time stood still. His mother wrote of the gypsy caravans and an upset with a local landowner's daughter who had to leave suddenly and spend six months in France. There had been a small fire in the summer kitchen, an expansion of the rose beds, two lavish coming-out parties, and the appointment of Kenderville Pike to the Royal Industrial Society, which put him in line for a knighthood.

❋

"There's a fine inlet around this point," Captain Burke told Pike, tapping a name on his chart, Burrard Inlet. "According to the Admiralty, it's one of the best natural harbors in the empire. I'll leave the Kanakas there. I've got a boiler for the mill too, and some supplies."

"Is it a large mill?" queried Pike, pulling on his alderman pipe and staring at the chart in fascination.

"You won't hardly believe it until you lay eyes on it. It isn't so much the mill that's big, it's everything else around it. Timbers with girths so immense six men with their hands clasped couldn't circle the trunk. D'you ever read that smashing tale by that chap Swift?"

Pike smiled. *Gulliver's Travels* was a favorite. "'Philosophers are in the right when they tell us that nothing is great or little otherwise than by comparison,'" he quoted cheerily. "Lilliput is all one hears about but me, I'll take Brobdingnag any day. I rather like the idea of hiding between two sorrel leaves and 'discharging the Necessities of Nature.'"

"Personally I'd rather be in Lilliput, where Gulliver put out a house fire by urinating on it!" the captain countered with a laugh.

"I'd prefer to be small when all else was large," said Pike. "Think of what you could see with no one able to see you!"

"Well, you'll feel a right shrinking Gulliver if you venture too far from the mill."

"Are there rats with tails two yards long?" Pike asked eagerly, recalling Gulliver's battle with rodents larger than mastiffs.

"I couldn't say about that, but I've heard of bears as big as houses, stags taller than shires, and there's a river fish that looks like the devil's serpent. Twenty feet long, two thousand pounds, they say. It could pull a plow on dry land it's so strong."

There was nothing, next to hunting, that warmed Pike's heart so much as a rod, a creel, and a boat bobbing gently in the sunshine.

"Oh my! Where would a man find such fish?"

"What I've heard is they live in the deeps of this river." The captain pointed to the Fraser River and traced it from its double mouth west into the interior and then quickly north, far into Rupert's Land, as much of the north was still called.

"Fraser River." Pike bent his lanky frame to peer more closely at the map. "Fraser River. I say, will we be going anywhere near it?"

The captain, who'd tickled a few largemouth bass in his time, laughed. "This isn't the kind of fishing you've ever done in England. Not anywhere, for that matter. When I was running sugar and coffee from the West Indies after I got my first commission, I landed a king marlin off the shores of

Jamaica. You can't believe the fight in these things. They'd tear a man's arms out if you weren't braced. It took me four hours of hard work but I finally got the damn thing on board. Even without the tail and the nose, it was longer than me. Here," he stabbed at the throat of the river, "is a fish of a different sort."

"Oh," Pike said dreamily. "I wouldn't mind trying for such a creature."

"I was here fourteen months ago, taking furs from Fort Langley." The captain showed him the tiny dot on the map representing the Hudson's Bay fort near the lower reaches of the river. "A half-breed and two Indians were drowned when one of those sturgeons pulled their boat *straight down to the bottom of the river*. This wasn't a little dingy, mind. It was a big, log canoe, nearly thirty feet long!"

"I must have a try at one of those beasts," Pike repeated.

"Well, try all you want," Burke responded, "but I doubt we'll be going upriver. A letter was delivered to me at anchor in San Francisco from the *James Snow*, which left that place before Christmas. A freakish winter has iced in the lower part of the river, and the Hudson's Bay Company has been moving the furs overland to Burrard Inlet. The navy ships are wintering here and here," Burke added, pointing to spots farther up the inlet.

Pike sighed deeply and pondered the map. "It looks like a duck." He cocked his head and studied the little peninsula guarding the inlet. "It is. Don't you see? It has no name here. I'll call it Duck Island."

The captain looked closer. "You have odd-shaped ducks in Hampshire."

✳

Ducks! White man's talk is like ducks quacking, Soon thought darkly, as he walked gingerly along the deck of the rolling ship, trying to avoid being spotted by Pike. He didn't care for being onboard a boat any more than he liked traveling in a box behind a horse. The squalls had finally spit them out into a larger body of water pocked by varying-sized islands. Some rose steeply straight out of the water. Others lay flat with bays, beaches, and natural harbors. If this were China, there would be junks as far as the eye could see, and every stretch of even marginally hospitable waterfront would be teeming with houses, docks, businesses. And the waters would be boiling with fishing boats of every description. Why, even now, if we were sailing into Guangzhou, there would be water girls enticing us with clean water, floating vendors selling roasted meats and fresh eggs. Yes, and duck. What I wouldn't give for a bite of crispy-skinned, oily, roast duck.

Soon closed his eyes to summon up the cacophony that rose up from the Pearl River at all hours. Hawkers, shore scavengers, fishermen, and dive girls with extraordinary lung capacity, who scoured beneath the water for items to sell. They all had their own unique sounds, which blended together like the warbles of dozens of birds in a forest. Then there was the squeak of wood against wood, the curses of men and women when boats collided, the shriek of metal from the larger ships, and the ching and scrape of chain links wearing against each other.

Soon opened his eyes. The wind bit his face. "Eeee! Eeee! Ahhh!" Three gulls, snow-white with black markings, floated above his head. "Eeee! Ahhh!"—their broken call. He heard the slap of water against the hull and the gentle thunk and gurgle as the bow dropped into the troughs on the other side of each swell. Those were the only sounds. There was no one else on deck that he could see, as most crew were below, relashing the cargo that had shifted during the squall at the entrance to "the Spanish bastard's" strait. Soon cleared his throat just to make a noise to break the monotony.

"Have you ever seen anything like it!"

Soon started at the voice, sucking in his breath sharply and breaking into a cough as the damp chill poked at the back of his throat. The cough was joined by a hard wheeze as he struggled to get his breath, and in moments Soon was hacking uncontrollably.

"Good lord, man! Don't have a fit."

A heavy hand thumped Soon between the shoulder blades. Soon didn't know what was worse, the personal invasion by this overly familiar fool or near prostration at the man's feet in breathless agony. The closer they got to the northern territory the more his lungs seemed to rebel against the persistent chill. Finally Soon drew a shuddering gulp of air and fought against another cough. He stepped surreptitiously away from the tall, lean man with his face so long it appeared stretched.

"Don't mention it!" Pike said, having noticed the evasion. "You're perfectly welcome. Always pleased to help a fellow traveler."

He rubbed his hands together enthusiastically, and Soon took another step away, thinking for one awful minute that the man was going to touch him again. Pike laced his slender fingers together, arms raised to shoulder level, index fingers pointing outward, and spun in a circle.

"I say, have you ever seen anything like it!"

The ship was running smartly toward the head of the land Captain Burke would round on his approach to Burrard Inlet.

"Marvelous, isn't it? Sheer, bloody marvelous. Look at all that land. And the trees, my God, the trees!" Pike gripped the gunnel and thrust his long, narrow chin into the wind, eyes squeezed half shut and tearing with the cold.

Soon glanced at the man. *What does he see that I don't?*

California was nothing like this place. There were stands of trees in pockets around San Francisco. Coming out of the Sacramento Valley into the gold rivers of the Sierra Nevadas, there were extensive forests of lodgepole pine, cedar, and redwood, which the miners had to battle through. But they were nothing compared to this staggering vista of green. It wasn't the friendly verdant of tended fields and selectively logged woods. It was an oppressive assault.

They were nearly at the mainland. The boat tacked east around a broad nose of land that jutted out into the strait and headed toward what Pike called Duck Island, and Burrard Inlet. Soon's sense of foreboding grew. Fog claimed the view of mountains to the north and blanketed most of the land near the shore. He tried to shake off the chill hand on his heart and recapture the sense of anticipation he'd felt while trapped in the stinking hold of the tea clipper that had brought him to America. But he could not. He'd never felt so low, so despairing in his life. As he stood beside the awestruck Pike, Soon felt his spirit seeping into the gray mist.

35

✳

Warburton Pike scrambled up the main mast to get a better vantage. Dense fog still shrouded the approach, allowing only occasional glimpses of rampant greenery. Just as he reached the crow's nest, the gray blanket started to lift. Pike knew from examining the chart that a large bay—English Bay—would be exposed when they fully rounded the point. British Columbia. Newly named, newly trod by scores of eager gold miners, but still as wild to the eye as any place on earth.

Hanging on to the rigging with one arm, Pike ducked his head to his chest to shelter his pipe. He jabbed flint against rasp half a dozen times before the tinder caught. With one leg and one arm wrapped securely around the rigging, he puffed mightily until the tobacco glowed. What an odd place to light a pipe, he thought happily. Far below he heard angry voices; there would be hell to pay from the captain. But he wasn't troubled. There had rarely been a problem Pike couldn't laugh or fight his way out of.

For the moment Pike was where he wanted to be, doing what he wanted to do. Trouble didn't exist. He admired the scene as one might a painting, noting this or that detail, comparing and contrasting it to the many landscapes he'd seen before. Nothing came close. Not the mountains of Europe, the wilds of Scotland, or the hectic, crashing coast of northern California. Colossal trees crowded right to the water's edge. They grew so lushly and so closely together it appeared that one could simply saunter across their canopies. These trees didn't have the majestic dignity of the larger redwoods of California; rather, there was a thrilling, brooding menace about them. "Come, if you dare," they seemed to say.

Here and there Pike saw a blackened form shorn of green by a lightning strike, a skeleton casually stripped of flesh yet still standing as a warning and testament to the power of this land.

Tide was high, leaving little bank as the ship rounded the northern shore of the point. The steep rocky cliffs of the point were beginning to give way and in the distance Pike could just make out a sweep of sand in the southern curl of the bay. He spotted a flock of large, gray birds, perhaps four feet from beak to tail feathers, with long, spindly legs, standing in the shallows. They were hard to discern at first, because they moved so little, blending in with the blue-gray water. He saw one that appeared deformed, single-legged and headless. Pike snorted when he realized that it was resting, standing on one leg with its head tucked under a wing. He saw another strike so fast he couldn't be sure it had moved, except for an instant there was a flash of silver light from the fish flapping in its beak. Then it was gone.

His hunter's eye caught a movement at the top of one of the evergreen trees: a regal, white-capped bird with a dark body, sitting on a thick branch near the top. Eyes adjusting, he started to pick out more birds: one, two, then a dozen, perhaps hundreds in all, perched implacably in the trees along the bank. Usually birds congregating in such numbers make a terrific racket as they preen, squawk, and shift allegiances from one place to another. Even with the wind in his ears and the ruffle of the sheets around him, the noise of such a large number of birds would carry easily over the water. But Pike heard nothing. Each held silently to its spot as if it were guarding a throne—its attention riveted on the water. What were they looking at, what did they see?

As he considered the question, one hoisted itself aloft with an emphatic, double wing-snap. It caught the air and rode the currents in a languid, high circle overhead. It was some kind of eagle or large hawk, the predatory beak unmistakable. With a wingspan of at least eight feet, Pike guessed, it must weigh fifty pounds or more. As the bird soared into the disappearing fog with infinitesimal wing adjustments, Pike breathed deeply, his eyes glued to the magnificent ease of its flying.

To command the air so effortlessly must be a power like none other. He had a little book given to him years ago, *Wisdom of the East.* In it were sayings from holy texts. Two of his favorites came from the Bhagavad Gita—

Released from evil
His mind is constant
In contemplation.

The other seemed coined just for these birds—

I am sire of the world.

All things Eastern fascinated Pike. He thought about another book, which told of Hindu Yogis who had the ability to empty their minds like a bucket of water then project themselves into the souls of people and animals. Pike stared at the bird. "I am sire of the world," he whispered, concentrating hard as the bird banked and approached the ship. Sound dropped away. He felt only the wind passing. A tremor of joy seized him; devoid of complication it was serene and pure.

With an explosive clap of its wings and a hunching downward, the white-capped bird went into a steep dive so rapid Pike couldn't move his head quickly enough to follow the descent or see what happened when it hit the water. With powerful flaps the bird began its ascent again. It took Pike a few moments to identify the ropey gray matter clutched in its claws as one of the gray herons he'd been admiring moments before. In all his years of hunting Pike had never seen a more assured, efficient kill.

The ship cut across the wide part of the bay, heading toward the mountains and the chunk of land Pike noticed looked like a comical duck's head on the map. The sounds from below drifted up again.

"Let the bloody blighter fall!" Pike recognized the voice of the second mate calling out in his distinctive, sharp-edged voice from the deck.

"Aye, but it's not your head the shite fool'll fall on," came the grumbling answer.

The deck hands prepared to drop anchor once they passed the narrows between the duck head and the hilly northern shore and sailed into Burrard Inlet. Time enough to clamber down and face the music. An unusual formation, a rocky pillar, caught Pike's eye as they approached the gap. The shoreline, though low, was rugged, and trees again reached nearly to the water. Pike idly watched the dipping cormorants, diving underwater and not resurfacing for minutes at a time.

The first sign of human habitation appeared just past the narrows—a ramshackle collection of four buildings close to shore. Pike madly patted himself all over, searching for his eyeglass only to find it hanging from his neck by a lanyard. He squinted through the lens, hoping to see some people. Disappointed, he trained the glass on the buildings. The ship was close on shore and he had an excellent view of the untidy structures. But as his eye focused, Pike saw that the structures were carefully, even ingeniously, built. Each was placed to provide shelter to the next, and the longest of the group used the largest tree in the area as a corner post. The wallboards were immensely wide, with no perceptible gaps. More large boards appeared to be flung in helter-skelter fashion to make a roof, but Pike quickly realized that each overlapped the lower one, like giant shingles, to provide a rain seal and channel water downward and away.

He searched for the colorful murals or mammoth totem poles mentioned in the excerpts he had read years ago in *Harper's Weekly* but he could see none. In the foreground lay a dozen trees felled toward the water; some cut up into lengths, some lying complete. In the small, cleared area a log, peeled of bark and perhaps eighty feet in length, was raised off the ground through some contrivance not obvious to him. Amid the trees and other debris were a dozen canoes ranging in length from about ten feet to two slender pea-pods of sixty or seventy feet. Were these the oceangoing dugouts Captain James Cook described in his widely published journals? They looked so insubstantial, hardly sufficient to stand up to the Pacific waters.

When the frigate cleared the narrows, Pike saw the man. He'd been there all the time, sitting as still as a heron, in the shade on a platform cantilevered out over the water supported by poles, which were anchored to the base of the building nearest the shore. Pike could see little of the man's face or his clothing, but he saw enough to know he was a far cry from the boldly painted and naked primitives described by Cook or fellow explorer Captain George Vancouver. At that moment the man tilted his head toward the boat. His face looked almost black in the eyeglass, and Pike could make out prominent cheekbones and the slight droop of his shoulders indicating he was a long way from youth. The old Indian also had a pipe sticking out of his mouth.

From the angle of the man's head Pike thought he might be looking at him, so he waved his arm vigorously to no response. A shout was also met with no acknowledgment. There was nothing remarkable about the unmoving figure but Pike couldn't take his eyes off him. He didn't appear to be doing anything, just sitting. Pike screwed his glass deeper into his eye socket and refocused. Then the man looked at him—not just in passing but a hard, searching, knowing look. Pike felt a little dizzy.

I am sire of the world. This time he felt no joy or exhilaration, rather a deep, unfamiliar darkness. He sensed things fluttering at the far edge of his perception, but they wouldn't come clear. As Pike stared, the darkness intensified. He felt like an intruder but he couldn't put down the glass. For a moment he had the sensation of being grabbed at by hundreds of snatching hands and he found himself hugging the rigging as if a storm had struck. Sparks flew from his pipe as it tumbled toward the deck, leaving a smoky trail.

Pike drew a ragged breath. This is a strange place, he thought, gathering himself together, there's mystery here. Somewhat shakily he made his way back down the mast where he ignored Captain Burke's cockatoo's protests.

The bosun's mate, a Plymouth man, sidled over and surreptitiously offered a drink of rum from his hip flask.

"Are you daft, boyo?" he asked, not masking his delight in the little excitement Pike had provided. "That was about as stupid as getting married. Saw you romancing the mast up there. You black out?"

"I don't know," Pike answered, taking a long swig. "One minute I was there, the next I was somewhere else. I saw an old Indian and he looked at me."

"He's measuring you up to pick your pocket, I'm betting."

"No!" Pike said urgently. "It was as if he was trying to send me a message. Our eyes, they locked, and, uh . . ."

The bosun's mate snorted. "A little too much nipping in your cabin, me thinks."

Pike felt compelled to explain himself. "I felt a hand on me, like a dream, but I was awake."

The bosun didn't like talk of siren calls and visions.

"Thar sea'll do it to you every time," he said hastily, fending off further conversation. "Wobble legs, wobble brain. Being out on the ocean is one thing, but seeing land for the first time and bang! you're feeling like your sheets just unfurled in a hellish blow."

Pike didn't pursue it. Most of the crew thought he was crazy anyway. Never mind them. He caught sight of the Chinaman silently watching their interchange. Pike half thought about telling him of his experience. After all, he is from the East and they understand things that can't be measured, weighed, or calculated. As there wasn't the slightest hint of invitation in the Chinaman's gaze, Pike turned back to the scenery. The harbor, wide and almost completely sheltered on all four sides by land, was magnificent. There appeared to be no impediments in the water and a broad, deep channel. On the north and west side it was ringed with muscular hills—mountains they'd be called at home. Trees right up to the peaks painted the landscape several shades of green as far as he could see. Imagining the slopes teeming with bear, boar, deer, and wild cat, his fingers itched to close around the well-polished stock of his rifle.

It was rugged, raw, and beautiful but terrible also, with an undercurrent of threat. There are pleasures and dangers here that you can't conceive of, the wilderness seemed to say. Can you measure up? Pike liked the feeling, the sense of challenge he saw around him.

Pike heard the run of the chain as the anchors dropped in Burrard Inlet. His hand went to the bear claw. *I am sire of the world.*

36

Pike left on the first shore boat. Soon Chong and the Kanakas were left to the last. Captain Burke divided the crew into four. He sent one group off to load barrels with fresh water, the second to cut and buck up firewood, which they'd take on over the next few days. Another group would row over to the new Pioneer Mills on the north shore to assist in assembling lumber for loading, and the fourth would make their way south to join up with the False Creek trail leading from the lake that emptied into English Bay. That would take them to the naval reserve seven miles inland. The land had been set aside to collect spars. Frantic naval expansion during the Napoleonic campaigns had stripped Europe of spar-quality timber. Sweden had been the Royal Navy's primary supplier, but those stocks had dwindled to almost nothing. The captain also intended to spend a couple of days examining his preempted land lying halfway between English Bay and Burrard Inlet. There were signs of coal all along the coast and he hoped his parcel would turn into a rich mine. With access to Burrard Inlet on one side and English Bay on the other the coal would be cheap to mine and ship.

Europeans could preempt 160 acres of land anywhere in the colony as long as it wasn't occupied year-round by natives. However, since the tribes all moved to salmon grounds in the spring, none could prove year-round occupancy. The captain urged Pike to preempt, as there were several claims that had lapsed. But ownership of land held little interest for him.

"You're making a big mistake, my lad," insisted the man sitting beside Pike in the shore boat. John Morton was a Yorkshire man returning from Boston with brick molds and a potter's kiln in the hold. "My partners and I have pre-empted 550 acres and we'll soon be gentlemen thanks to fine clay bricks."

"You'd better hope all these forests burn down," Pike observed, gesturing at the seemingly endless trees. "Who in their right mind would buy *bricks* to build with when you have cedar, fir, and hemlock as far as the eye can see?"

"Bricks for ovens, bricks for foundations, bricks for forgers," the man enthused. "Bricks, my lad, build the world. And when this rude land becomes civilized it will do so on Yorkshire-made bricks!" Morton thrust his sandy beard to the sky as the words poured out of him.

"Morton here claims to be the first settler in the colony of British Columbia," the captain said as they were rowed ashore.

"Claim! Claim! I claim nothing of the sort. I *was* the first settler in this fearsome land. See over there?"

Pike looked to the shoreline and spotted a small cabin with two smaller outbuildings.

"That's mine. The kiln house will go there, just inland," Morton said excitedly. "I've found a good creek I can dredge to give me all the water I need. My partners arrive on the next ship and they'll build our loading dock. There's a Chinaman on board. If I can persuade him to work for me instead of going up Fraser's River to the gold bars, I can put up enough fuel to operate the kiln for two or three months. And if the captain here can produce for me some good coal out of his land next door, I can haul it half a mile to my factory."

Morton prattled on, but Pike paid little attention. When the boat scraped up on the pebbly shore, he leaped out, absentmindedly bidding the men good-bye. Pike had no idea where he was going as he picked his way along the waterfront. The air was full of the men's cries as they went about their business preparing for a hard week of work. Pike yearned to stretch his legs.

Without making a conscious decision, he set off toward the duck's-head island where he'd seen the old man smoking. The map showed an Indian village facing out toward the north shore and Burrard Inlet. A good foot-trail led the way initially, but it quickly deteriorated to little more than a game trail threading through the heavy bush thick with holly and tamarack. A moldering shack squatted in a clearing, likely a disappointed gold miner's. Pike didn't see anyone, and it looked long-abandoned.

The trail ended at an isthmus that kept the duck's head from being an island proper. A clearing ahead appeared hacked out of the thick growth. On all sides the forest was a dense thicket, creating a gloomy twilight as the sun failed to penetrate the trees' canopy. Just above the high-water mark Pike spotted a heavily bearded man lounging in front of a crude lean-to made of wooden poles propped against a huge deadfall.

"Dinna get many visitors out here!" the scruffy man hollered waving him over. "Come join me for a wee drap o' coffee."

"With pleasure!" Pike called back. "There can't be more than a few souls out here," he said when he drew nearer. "What good fortune that I should stumble across one of them."

"Fortune? There's not mooch of that as I can tell."

The man drained his cup, wiped it with his shirt end, poured it to the brim with black liquid, and presented it ceremoniously to his visitor. It took Pike some minutes to identify the unusual curved vessel as the cover of a ship's compass.

"Only one I've got," the man said. "I'm a wee doon on me luck." He pointed to a line strung between two trees, with three plump squirrels hanging from it.

"Squirrel stew morning, noon, and night," he said gloomily. "Thank God they're easy to snare. Care for a helping?"

"Perhaps later." Pike had eaten his share of rodent.

"Tobacco?" Pike offered his pouch, which was almost snatched out of his hand. "Don't have any papers but you can borrow my pipe."

The man burrowed into a trunk in the lean-to and pulled out a large book. Using a navigator's straight edge, he tore out a page from the illustrated version of John Bunyan's *Pilgrim's Progress*. Pike watched with amazement as the man carefully creased the paper, then poured a line of tobacco down one edge before rolling a cigarette as big around as a small cigar. Though he had to repeatedly relight it, he smoked with gusto.

"Canna tell you how lang it's been since I had a good smoke. Name's Colin Mcthrockle Glencannon," he said, proffering his hand. "T'would be a perfect day, indeed, if a man had a wee drap of God's nectar," he said wistfully.

"If you're speaking of whiskey, I can oblige," Pike said, producing his hip flask. He held out his finger as Glencannon reached out eagerly. "On one condition. Tell me the story of how you happen to be out here by yourself with no grog, precious little tobacco, hardly any food, and, from the looks of it, little else."

"I'd tell you me life story for what you've got in tha flask," Glencannon said earnestly. "Aye and tha stories of all me ancestors if it coomes to it."

Gleefully he wiped the compass glass with a rag and offered it up for Pike to fill. His hand shook slightly as he watched the dark-amber liquid rise in the glass. A few drops splashed over. Glencannon brought the glass to his lips and licked them off the edge before taking his first sip. "Oh mon! God lives in tha wild country." He took a deep lungful of air. "'Tis naa Scottish whiskey but it'll do." Glencannon consulted closely with the glass.

"Verra well. My story then. Being a Scot, it revolves around boats, tha sea, and," he held up the glass, "whiskey."

Glencannon moved over to settle himself in front of the fire. "With some tha downfall starts with a woman. With me t'was a boot," he said, gesturing toward his lean-to.

"Boat? What boat?"

"Yon boot," Glencannon pointed toward the lean-to.

Pike jumped up and peered inside. Sure enough he could discern the outlines of a boat. He judged it to be something over thirty feet, with a lapped clinker design to give it strength and stability in rough water. The craftsmanship appeared meticulous. There was a low-slung cabin in the center front with plenty of deck space for mounting cargo. A large oak tiller completed the aft. Pike noted that a system of pulleys allowed steerage from inside the cabin during bad weather. The boat itself was long enough and stable enough for careful exploration in open water. It was a perfect little craft, and Pike immediately lusted for it.

The image of perfection disappeared when he walked around the bow and saw a section of the prow stove in. Pike reached through the hole, feeling at least two broken beams and barnacles coating the boards. The boat must have been submerged for some time but was in surprisingly good shape. Pike lifted a tarp. His eyebrows shot up. A steam engine! Clearly adapted for marine work. Yellowish goo coated the working parts. Pike touched the stuff and quizzically held his fingers out to Glencannon who was making steady progress on the whiskey.

"Bear fat," he stated between gulps. "Bought it from tha primitives. Best I could do."

"You're a shipbuilder then?" Pike inquired.

"I'm a Scot," he emphasized. "I apprenticed in Glasgow to an engine builder for eight long years. There's no stationary steam engine I can't build or fix."

"You seem to be in quite a fix yourself," Pike joked.

"Dinna I tell you I ha' no money," he responded crossly. "If you loosen up your wrist I'll tell ye tha whole sad story."

Glencannon had been brought over from Scotland in 1862 to assemble and maintain the steam engine at Pioneer Mills then under construction.

"A fine modern mill it is, with no expense spared on the blades and engine," Glencannon said proudly as if he'd built and financed it himself.

At the time there were only a few hundred men in the lower mainland of the colony of British Columbia outside the traders at Fort Langley, the hands at the mill, and a scattering of settlers and businessmen in the newly crowned capital of New Westminster on the Fraser downriver from Fort Langley. The semipermanent population gave no hint of the fifty thousand men who had made their way up the Fraser to the gravel bars to pan for gold.

"Then I met the American," Glencannon said gloomily. "An American. I shoulda known."

The American was returning from the new strikes farther north and inland in the Kootenay goldfields. Unlike most, he decided to "retire" after a minor strike. He was closemouthed about exactly how much, but he claimed to have enough to start a small business.

"The idea was sound, I'll grant you that."

"What idea?"

"Well, he saw me workin' with tha steamer. Son of a bitch if he dinna convince me to adapt one to a small boat so he could run a freight and passenger service up tha Fraser. When I left Scotland they were playin' aroond with sich things. Tha boat made sense. There's two trails cross land now from tha inlet down to tha Fraser. But tha bloody mud stops horses half tha year. And tha big boats don't come near often enough."

Marine steam engines were still in their infancy, but a fast service and quick turnover would quickly offset the cost of bringing an engine up from San Francisco for Glencannon to adapt. The permanent population was still tiny, but a townsite was planned, New Westminster was developing, and predictions were that many of the gold seekers, not to mention Civil War soldiers drifting north, would eventually settle in the colony.

While the man was gone to California in search of an engine, Glencannon set about building the boat. He was to supply the boat and his labor on the engine in return for a hundred pounds and a case of whiskey. His partner would buy the engine. Profits were to be split fifty-fifty.

"A fine enough deal, I thought at the time."

"What happened?"

"I dinna reckon on a half-cocked idiot for a partner."

Six months later, when the boat was finished, Glencannon quit his job at Pioneer Mills to the fury of the mill boss. The captain and Glencannon set the maiden voyage for the next morning. The night was reserved for celebrations.

"Peter tha Whaler lives over at Brewer's Point," Glencannon gestured north, toward the narrows where Pike had seen the old native. "He 'n tha

Portuguese were going to bring their squaws and help us christen the *Pride of Charlotte*—the name of me darling muther."

"Settlers?" Pike asked, instantly interested. "I didn't think there were any yet. The captain told me most people were inland or up the river."

"Ship jumpers," corrected Glencannon. "If they tried to preempt land they'd be arrested, so they preempted themselves a couple of wives and went Indian. There's an old village round that point, overlooking tha narrows, what you come through on your approach. Some says it has magical powers. They call it Kahnamut or some such."

"What kind of magic?" To Pike this was far more compelling than the intricacies of engines.

"Used to be near two thousand Indians all around here, including on that island—though she isn't an island proper. Then tha smallpox came, like a hurricane in tha Indies. Wiped out three quarters of them. Only two villages weren't much touched, this one at tha point and one east along tha inlet, in New Brighton they're calling it."

"Yes, I heard the captain speak of it. Two of the men on board preempted land there and aim to farm pigs for the mill and the fort."

"That's it, true enough. The Indians call tha western village Kahnamut—it means 'welcome' or some sich. Peter tha Whaler told me tha two villages share tha same blood so that got tha big magic story going." Glencannon offered up his glass. "I could sure use a drap o' that fine dew before I tell you tha rest of tha sad tale of me boot."

Pike would much rather have talked about the magical villages but he doubted he'd get another word out of Glencannon before he'd exhausted his story of the boat.

"Just what happened to your boat?" he asked obligingly.

"'Tis simplicity herself. We got drunk as Irishmen. I passed out, to my everlasting shame. Bad whiskey no doot. The American—stupid bastard—in his cups, decides to take the boot out hisself and give tha Whaler and tha Portuguese a taste of her speed."

Glencannon paused, smacked his lips, and offered his glass suggestively to Pike, who had a swig from the flask while there was some left. Fortified, the Scot continued.

"Ah weel, you can guess tha rest. Bastard sailed around tha inlet then whooped it up through tha narrows and around to tha Siwash Rock, Standing Woman, 'cordin' to tha primitives." He blew a raspberry. "Devil Woman more, I'd say. Tha rock sunk my beauty and tha idiot partner drooned hisself."

"What about the money? Did you at least get paid for your troubles?"

"There's tha rub. Aye, there's tha rub. He'd only paid me twenty pund, with eighty to come. I owe forty for materials and no one will extend me a far-thin' in credit. I offered to trade my services at the naval reserve if they paid off my debts, but you'd think I was a bloody leper or something. The mill owner has been badmouthin' me all over tha place for quittin' on him. I even went to Mr. Muck Muck, Colonel Moody up in New Westminster. He's got fingers in everyone's beer around here and he's been layin' out a townsite just east of us. They're gonna call it Hastings. I told him I could rig up a stationary steam splitter to make tha clearin' more efficient. He says to me, 'I can import two hundred Chinamen for the price of a single steam engine.'"

Glencannon stared mournfully into his once again empty glass.

"I guess working at the mill is out of the question," Pike mulled. "What about the fort? Is there work there?"

"The fur trade's dropped off somethin' terrible." Glencannon shook his head ruefully. "Besides, I can't leave me beauty! The Indian'll steal anything he can carry. And some things you wouldn't think he could."

"I thought they were friendly."

"Got nothin' to do with bein' friendly," Glencannon said. "As far as I can figure, they dinna see it as stealin'. More like borrowin' to them. They dinna have tha same ideas about who owns what. Somethin's lyin' aboot with no one there, they'll take it if they want. When they dinna need it no more they'll up and leave it."

"These Indians have a marvelous culture," Pike enthused. "The captain had a book on board with lithographs of their costume and their art. I have never seen such hats and masks. The book also said their society is as com-plex as . . ."

"Other than that we get along fine," Glencannon cut in, not about to let his audience take over. "Traded my da's pocket watch for bear fat to pro-tect tha engine, some fish, and help pulling the boat out. Lumtinat's a squaw what lives in the village. She brings a fish now and then. Also tha Whaler's wife, they're from tha same village."

Glencannon frowned. "At least they don't expect anything back for it, which is more than I can say for those wharf rats on tha naval reserve and at tha mill."

"Why don't you sell the boat? Even stove in a bit, it should be worth something."

Glencannon shrugged. "The Indians offered one of their women for it. That was a month ago. I'd take the deal now. But they haven't been back."

A long silence hung between them as they pondered fate.

"What would it take to put your beauty back into shape?" Pike asked.

"A month and thirty pund, give or take. The push valves got damaged and tha piston's pitted from the salt bath," Glencannon said cautiously. He wondered if there was any more drink in the flask.

"Well, I have twenty-two pounds, some gold coins, and a few American dollars," Pike said. "If I set aside some for food, bullets, and tobacco. Hmmm."

"Sold!" Glencannon hollered at the top of his lungs, startling Pike. "Sold! Sold and double sold! As God is my witness." So great was his joy that he began capering around the clearing, holding up his compass glass as if it were a gold chalice.

"Wait a minute," Pike said. "What are you saying?"

"I'm sayin' that I'll sell her and fix her for whatever's left over from your computations."

"Surely she's worth more than," Pike did a quick sum in his head. "Twenty-nine pounds."

"Oh aye, she's my beauty and tha first steam boat to ply these waters, but I'll be well rid of her. She's brought no luck to me. Besides, sitting there all boosted up she ain't worth a farthin'."

"Well, all right," said Pike, making up his mind in a flash. "Here it is. I'll give you twenty-nine pounds but you'll still own twenty-five percent of her. That way we can both make a bit of money and I'll have use of the boat to explore. I want to go everywhere, and it seems that a boat is the thing in British Columbia."

"That's more'n fair. More'n fair. Now, I doon't mean to be critical, but you're a mite stingy with tha whiskey, partner."

✳

Glencannon began working at first light and didn't stop until he couldn't see the end of his nose. He labored over the engine and the broken beams while Pike scraped and oiled the boards and did innumerable little tasks Glencannon set for him. When there was nothing to do Pike wandered east, past where he'd landed, deep into the high lands overlooking Burrard Inlet to shoot game. He was a good and patient shot. Every night meat roasted in their fire. Halfway through their task, the *Lady Mary Green* departed fully loaded for Victoria, San Francisco, and Hong Kong. Pike barely noticed the ship leaving. Five weeks plus a day after he met Glencannon, Pike helped him roll the boat over logs on the beach and into the water. Glencannon had built her with a shallow draft; she'd bob heavily in a hard sea but she'd also be maneuverable along the Fraser's sand bars.

"To the *Marguerite Star!*" shouted Pike as the motor kicked in, faltered, then chugged throatily. Marguerite seemed a happier name to him than Charlotte.

"Aye, you've got that right, me lad. A star in the heavens she is."

Pike eagerly told Glencannon of his plan to explore farther up Burrard Inlet as they chugged toward Pioneer Mills.

"No offense, lad, but you're not goin' anywhere without me, though you've paid me fair and square. Besides, I've got us a little job takin' some passengers and freight over to Victoria. That'll be our first trip."

Pike was irritated at the mercantile turn of events but couldn't think of a good reason to veto it.

37

Pike barely managed the cargo trip to Victoria, impatient for the return and a chance to try his hand at a bear on the north-shore mountains or the giant fish in the Fraser River deeps. He cleaned his Sharps for hours as Glencannon happily piloted them through the islands of the Strait of Georgia to the growing community on the rocky southern tip of Vancouver Island. They were lucky with the weather, for the route took them close to the rocky cliffs of some of the larger islands. In a big blow, common in the straits, a boat such as theirs would be kindling in an instant. Victoria had become a proper town, rapidly developing around the Hudson's Bay fort into a center of commerce, with all the supply demands from miners, the expanding naval presence, the excitement over coal deposits, the export of salmon, and the fledgling timber trade. None of it interested Pike, and he couldn't share the excitement at Sir James Douglas's table about "development" and "growth" and "opportunities."

"There's no point in it," Pike declared to the smiles of the four women and the knowing head shakes of Douglas and the other men. "If we build everything up we'll just have to go somewhere else to find this glorious wilderness."

"If you had spent as much time as I have in the coastal frontier you would not be so eager to turn your back on the niceties of civilization," Douglas opined sternly. The recently knighted Douglas had, until a year earlier, been both chief factor of Fort Victoria and governor of the colony of Vancouver Island. He was stout and fleshy but solid, like a large rock. Pike noticed that the man never smiled and his every word was spoken with a sense of pronouncement.

"And don't forget women," shyly interjected Amelia, his half-Cree wife. "The colony needs women, but they are not inclined to come without the kindnesses of civilization."

"Perhaps so," replied Pike gaily. "But I confess that I would prefer a woman who spurns such kindnesses."

"Then you are fifty years too late," stated Douglas. "Those days of my youth, when rudeness of the wild was all we had, are now long gone."

After dinner Pike entertained the guests with randy songs he'd learned from the drovers, then Glencannon warbled his way through several ballads until tears of homesickness overcame him and several other well-liquored guests. It was pleasant enough, but Pike couldn't wait to get back to the mainland.

Three days later he and Glencannon, with four passengers, seven barrels of nails, two wagon wheels, four coils of rope, an assortment of tools, one petticoat, and three mules precariously tied amidships, were past the first sand bars at the river's mouth. The passengers were heading to the nearly depleted Cariboo goldfields, which Sir James had described as "the most inaccessible place on earth. Nothing but canyons, precipices, roots, and ruts." With each mile Pike's appreciation of the broad-chested Fraser grew. It was late spring, and snowy peaks framed both north and south horizons. Near the river itself, lowlands spread out in a watery haze. The *Marguerite Star* stopped briefly at Fort Langley, then continued past the first of the worked-out gold bars, tasting danger when the river grew narrow and angry at Hope. The dark little town was a fury of activity, filled with some of the more than one thousand men Sir James had assembled to blast and hack a navigable trail along the Fraser River into the Cariboo.

The passengers left the boat hoping to find quick transport on a mule train to the interior.

"Take care you don't meet any camels," called out the owner of the Hope Dry Goods & Etc.

"Camels? What on earth are you talking about?" Pike asked.

"A German fella brought 'em over a couple of years ago for transport," the man informed him. "Grand idea, except they'se feet are better on sand than rock. Most of them died but a few are about. One stampeded a mule train a month back. Scairt them foolish and the whole lot went over a cliff. All dead except a driver who jumped."

"What an extraordinary place," breathed Pike. "Camels in the north!"

He wandered the town until the light failed. On every corner someone was selling something, usually liquor. At one corner a man had set up offering temporary marriage licenses for $5. DON'T BE TIED DOWN FOR LIFE WITH A BUSH OR MOUNTAIN GIRL, the sign read. LICENSES GOOD FOR 6 MONTH ONNLY.

As they were departing Hope, much to Pike's disgust, Glencannon booked five passages back to Victoria for miners just off their claims and determined to spend their pokes on restaurant fare, hotel beds, and the fort's two brothels. He also extracted a fee for delivering mail to New Westminster and Fort Langley. Each time Pike wanted to explore an interesting river inlet or stop to hunt after spotting a fine elk rack, Glencannon kicked up such a fuss that Pike gave in.

"You've promised to deliver these paying passengers and their goods, not to mention Her Majesty's mail," Glencannon lectured sternly. "And deliver them ye will."

"I never promised anything of the sort!" Pike fumed.

"We've got a reputation to protect!"

"Reputation? What reputation?" Pike queried.

"The one we're building!"

✳

"I dinna believe it," Glencannon chortled as he handed Pike forty-one pounds plus thirteen American dollars, his share. "It's only September! At this rate we'll be rich men in a year. P'rhaps we'll even beat Johnny Morton tha brick maker to it!" He called out the last sentence to Morton, who was busy putting the finishing touches on a dry pan where he'd mix the binding ingredients for his bricks.

"Don't you go taking my name in vain, Mr. Glencannon, or I'll be charging you room and board."

"Shut your gob, Mr. Morton," Glencannon retorted. "I'll be paying ye for your hospitality—such as it is—with me next trip to Victoria."

"See that you hurry on with it. My Chinaman won't do a stroke. If you bring back another one like him, I'll be putting a hole in your precious boat." Morton gestured disgustedly at Soon Chong's little tent. When Morton saw him get off the boat, he had visions of a captive labor pool, but no amount of begging or threatening could get him to work for Morton beyond a few hours of laundry once a week in return for a few square feet of space where he erected a tent of sorts. Morton asked Glencannon to offer any pigtail they saw on the next Victoria trip two dollars just for coming to the inlet, and sixty cents a day, raising to seventy-five if any stayed out the month. He needed someone to carry firewood and finish the water slough. His partner would be returning within the month and Morton was eager to fire the first bricks.

Pike grunted, absentmindedly stuffing the cash into his pocket. They had flour, yeast, twine, and salt to deliver to Pioneer Mills. But Pike wanted to visit the chunk of land guarding the narrows, where he'd seen the Indian. Each time they'd passed the village it looked abandoned. On their last trip around Brewer's Point, Pike noted that several of the longer canoes were missing.

"Where did they go?" he asked Glencannon.

"Who?"

"The Indians. I saw at least one in that village."

"They come, they go. I dinna ken the why of it."

At odd moments during the past weeks Pike, lulled by the chug-chug of Glencannon's engine, found himself thinking about the Indian and the village, wondering how many lived there and what they did all day. At night, images filled his dreams. Eagles many times normal size, totem poles as he'd seen in the lithographs in the journals of Captain James Cook and George Vancouver. As night deepened, the carved figures came alive, writhing as if trying to free themselves from their wooden prisons. And always there was a woman, faceless and motionless, hovering in the background in his kaleidoscope of a dream. He didn't find the dreams frightening or even unsettling; they seemed more like an invitation, a promise. Pike told Glencannon about the woman as they prepared the boat for the run across the inlet.

"What do you suppose it means?" he idly asked Glencannon.

"It's simple as can be. It means you need a squaw." Glencannon punctuated his remark with an obscene gesture. "A man's loins can only go so long without attention. I've got me eye on one too. She's from a village on tha north shore near Pioneer Mills. Peter tha Whaler told me I could have her for a good price. One more trip'll do it. Tomorrow I'm going to make a down payment. I bought some fabric from Victoria and tobacco."

The next day Pike demanded that Glencannon take him to Brewer's Point, where he'd seen the old Indian. "I'll wait around until someone shows up."

"Ye dinna want to do that!" Glencannon said sharply. "Ye can't just go clumping in there like Sunday calling. They'd be verra cross if you arrived without permission. And they're not that tame."

"How would I get permission?"

"Presents, you fool! With presents anything is possible!"

"What sort of presents?" Pike asked.

"Drink's always good!" Glencannon said heartily.

"Maybe you could spare some of your fancy fabric."

"That's courting goods. Ye'll keep your blightin' hands off it."

"Well, I am going anyway. I am sick of being a boat for hire."

Glencannon clapped his hands to his head, moaning theatrically. "Just as I feared. Here I am, finally making a success of meself and I get saddled with a crazy mon who wants to throw it all away just to go watching savages." He dropped to his knees in front of Pike. "Why don't ye just shoot me in tha head and be done with it?"

Pike smiled at his friend's histrionics.

"Before I drop you off into the wilds to end your life, why not have a wee chat with tha Portuguese or Peter tha Whaler. He comes regular to Johnny Morton's. If you're determined to go nosing about, he'll tell you what to do."

"I'll do it. But if neither of them shows up, when you return from your courting you will take me to the Point with no more delaying," Pike said sternly.

✳

Soon Chong's spirits were considerably less exuberant. He got off the boat with the last load that included pigs, chickens, and four goats, all destined for the farm started up in the dark forest across the inlet from Pioneer Mills. Aside from washing Morton's clothes he spent most of his time in his tent, drinking the last of his tea. He thought about opening a store to supply the miners, especially the Chinese who were taking up the worked-out claims along the river. But most of the miners and Chinese laborers came through Victoria, where there were already two established Chinese stores, as well as a host of suppliers for pans, picks, shovels, dredges, and the clothes that miners needed. He considered some kind of trading post for the Indians in this part of the mainland colony, as the Langley fort was a considerable distance away. But so many had fallen to smallpox a year earlier; some of the whites onboard said almost two thirds were dead or diseased. Those that were left had little interest in trading. And besides there was nowhere for him to buy trade goods except Victoria, Langley, or New Westminster, and no means to transport what he purchased without dipping deeply into his cash.

Since he arrived it had rained constantly; he might as well be living at the bottom of a waterfall. The False Creek trail to New Westminster was so boggy even horses couldn't get through. Soon felt as stuck as if he was neck-deep in the mud. He considered going to Victoria, where a community of several hundred Chinese had settled, including a few women, but he suspected it would be much like San Francisco, where a few families controlled everything and he'd have to use up a great deal of money on bribes just to open a business. And what business?

While they'd been refurbishing the *Marguerite Star,* Pike, uninvited, had dropped in on Soon several times for tea. The first time Soon had been so gloomy he could hardly carry on a polite conversation.

"I have come all the way from China to be a fish," he complained. "Here fish don't have to be in the water to live, apparently."

"The rain will end."

"That I sincerely doubt."

"I thought patience was a virtue of the Oriental," Pike said innocently.

"Who has patience when they're drowning?"

The morning after their triumphant return to Morton's mucky clearing, Pike presented Soon with a huge, humpbacked salmon he'd caught two days earlier. He decorated it with pigtails braided from seaweed. He also brought a large umbrella purchased from the Fort Victoria store. The dour Chinese actually smiled when he saw the gifts.

Pike was itching to explore the Indian village but he promised Glencannon he'd wait for Peter the Whaler to appear while Glencannon took the boat to Pioneer Mills "to see ma lassie." The voluble Johnny Morton was too busy building his kiln for good conversation, but Soon, once thawed slightly with the salmon offering, offered a grudging listening post. With some polite probing Pike discovered the source of his scars, guessed he had money hidden somewhere, and sensed a deep disappointment in the slight man.

He is like a grazing deer, Soon considered while huddling in his blanket. A nibble here, a nibble there, and then gone. He endured Pike's familiarity and his questions, and listened as the man who seemed like a long, thin bag filled with bones talked on and on.

Glencannon returned in a jolly mood, with bloodshot eyes, breath like a buzzard, gas enough to power an engine, and a happy smile on his unshaven face. En route to the mill he'd skirted the Burrard Inlet's southern shore and on the beach by the navy's dock, at what would soon be the new townsite of Granville, he'd spotted two enterprising but exhausted men trying to roll whiskey barrels into a canoe. Despite the mill's rigid no-drink policy, the pair had walked twenty-two miles to New Westminster, bought the whiskey, then hitched themselves to the barrels like two dray animals, and dragged their precious cargo back along the Engineers North Road, which was little more than a seasonal track. Glencannon happily provided transportation across the inlet in return for two jugs of whiskey, one of which was nicely pickling his blood.

As Glencannon lurched off Morton's crude dock belching and calling greetings, Pike made a sudden decision. He hauled the protesting Scot— "Sleep mon, I need sleep!"—over to Soon's tent and parked him on a barrel under an overhang.

"Stay here till I call you," Pike ordered as he disappeared into the tent.

"A thousand apologies, my friend Soon, but I don't have time for pleasantries," he told the annoyed Chinaman.

"I have no more tea left," Soon said sternly, a little off balance from the sudden intrusion.

"Never mind the bloody tea! I am here about the moon, the sun, and the stars!" Pike jabbered.

"I beg your pardon?"

As Pike advanced on him, Soon stepped back in alarm, tripping on the sodden, frayed edge of the blanket he had draped around his shoulders in a futile attempt to keep warm. Pike swooped down to catch him and almost lifted Soon off his feet. A small bundle fell to the dirt floor. Pike bent down to pick up the beaded tunic, ignoring Soon's urgently outstretched hand.

"I say, what a charming little thing!"

Soon snatched it away. "It is mine."

Pike shrugged and rushed into the point of his visit.

"We have spoken of how there are currents in the universe that sometimes converge?" he said. Soon nodded, not bothering to remind Pike that it was only he who spoke of such things. "And a rational man who is properly trained in observation will be able to detect these events as they happen and influence their direction."

Soon nodded wearily.

"We are at such moment," Pike said with fervor. "We must seize it and make of it what will benefit us most. We must not let it pass and be squandered!"

Soon hoped the tirade would end before long. He had wrapped his pigtail around his neck for warmth and had just brewed some tea when Pike burst in. His belly ached for the heat of it. But he could hardly pour a cup after telling the man he didn't have any.

"Seize what?"

"The gypsies in England call certain men *Kat Vacuska,* those who take the moment in their hands. Here is the moment," Pike paused breathlessly and, without a sign of acknowledgment from Soon, plowed on. "I own three quarters of a steamboat, a marvel of modern man! It can make Victoria in eleven hours and New Westminster in thirteen."

"How wonderful for you," Soon said, well aware of the boat project, as Pike had spoken of little else while Glencannon was fixing it.

Pike leaned in so closely Soon could smell the venison on his breath. "I do not," Pike spoke each word slowly, "want the boat."

"What is that to do with me?"

"You will buy the boat, of course!" Pike shouted.

"I have no money."

Pike laughed. "Just as you have no tea?" He glanced pointedly to the teapot warming on the fire. Not even Soon could keep a twitch of chagrin off his face.

"I have another friend waiting outside. He is central to this important moment in our lives." Pike dashed outside before Soon could say a word.

Glencannon lay tilted at a dangerous angle against the tent wall, snoring in gentle repetitive puffs. Pike dragged him inside.

"Pikey me lad," Glencannon groaned. "Have mercy and let me poor body go with tha angels."

"Sit here!" Pike pointed at a crate that was Soon's only chair. "You can sleep later."

"Now would be better."

Pike turned to Soon. "Mr. Glencannon here can build and operate a boat as well as Her Majesty's best mariner. He owns twenty-five percent of the boat in question. He is my friend."

Pike turned to the heavy-lidded Glencannon. "Mr. Soon here is currently without occupation," he told the Scot. "But my suspicion is that he is a man of many talents. He is also my friend."

Each glared suspiciously at the other, like boxers in their corners.

"What has this slant-eye got to do with me boat?" Glencannon growled, his tongue thick.

"And what does this smelly goat have to do with me?" Soon retorted.

"Actually, Soon's eyes don't slant at all," Pike said mildly. "They're really quite straight."

To Soon he added. "He does look a bit like a goat, but he is an honest man and the smell is temporary."

Pike held his arms out, his pale eyes gleaming madly. "Mr. Glencannon. Mr. Chong. Meet your new partner."

Glencannon shot upright, now fully awake. Soon was so shocked he let his precious blanket drop into the puddles on the floor.

"Come now, Soon! Pour us some tea, before it tastes like boiled boot!"

Glencannon and Soon sat in stony silence staring at the floor, as Pike elaborated.

"The obvious thing is a passenger and cargo service between the mill and the mainland here, combined with regular trips to Victoria and New Westminster."

"No with a Chink partner!" Glencannon growled.

Pike ignored him. "You told me that the mill owner won't let workers drink anywhere on the north shore."

"What of it?" Glencannon demanded.

"Why not bring the lads over to Morton's dock on payday and sell them whiskey here, and isn't Gassy Jack talking about building a saloon once Captain Stamp builds his new mill on this shore? Then there's all the men hauling spar wood from the reserve to the inlet. A quick trip from the booming yards to Morton's or Gassy's could net a tidy sum."

Glencannon opened his mouth then closed it again with a snap.

Soon forgot the cold for a moment. He'd recently overheard Morton say that Stamp had English money to establish another sawmill on this side of the inlet. If that happened . . .

"Here's the deal," Pike said. "You two decide what is a fair price for Soon to buy me out."

"I have no money," Soon reminded him.

"I haven't forgotten," Pike replied merrily.

As he ducked out of the tent he called back, "Oh and you might consider building a barge to tow after the *Marguerite Star* for extra cargo, if she'll take the load."

"Don't be blaspheming me gel!" Glencannon shouted to Pike's back. "Take tha load! O' course she'll take tha load."

What seemed like hours later, Soon said quietly to Glencannon: "Just how profitable was this most recent excursion of yours?"

"I'll tell ye," Glencannon said with a heavy sigh, "if ye got something to drink other than yon babby's piddle."

✱

His share of the *Marguerite Star* had put the equivalent of seventy-five pounds in gold flakes in Pike's pocket. He would have just as happily pocketed twenty-five. He also would have sold his whole share, but when Glencannon and Soon began to squabble about who had final say, he agreed to hold on to a quarter of the enterprise "to settle any differences that might arise."

✳

Pike was astonished to find about fifty Indians standing near the shoreline when Peter the Whaler's dugout rounded the tip of land called Brewer's Point, the rocks of the narrows leading to Howe Sound in the north. An old man sat on a stump in front of the group, smoking a pipe.

"What are they doing?" he asked Peter the Whaler, a blockily built Londoner who paddled in silence all the way from Morton's cabin to the point. His wife, bronzed-faced and fat, sat just ahead of him in the boat.

"Waiting."

"Waiting for what?"

"You."

"I just met you this morning!" protested Pike. "How could they know I was coming?" Peter the Whaler shrugged. It had taken him only a few months to adopt the taciturn demeanor of his wife's people when dealing with outsiders. He was now so closemouthed even his shy wife seemed effusive in comparison.

"*He* knew you was come," Khapinaht, called Kappie by Peter, piped up softly in the English she'd learned from her husband. "It was told to him."

"Who?"

"*He.*"

"Who is *He*?"

"Chief," said Peter. "Khahtsalanough."

✳

After creating the reluctant partnership of Soon and Glencannon, Pike had scoured his meager possessions for gifts. He brought along one of two meerschaum pipes he'd bought in San Francisco, three neck scarves, a pair of bootlaces, and Glencannon's compass-cover drinking glass. He thought about his bear claw, but couldn't part with it. He also bought a barrel of beans and one of molasses from Morton. And while Glencannon was sleeping off his bender, he helped himself to the Scot's second bolt of "courting fabric." Pike smiled to himself when he appropriated Glencannon's remaining jug of whiskey, thinking of the commotion he'd kick up when he found out.

Peter the Whaler didn't ask why Pike wanted to go to the village, and now they were here no one asked why he'd come. The chief accepted the gifts noncommittally, while a short man in a bowler-style Western hat spoke to him. Pike stood to one side, feeling slightly foolish, wondering what to do next.

"What is this place called?" he whispered to Peter.

"Khwaykhway."

"Who's that?" he asked about an odd little man with a face that seemed fallen in on itself.

"Chupkheem, chief's brother."

"He lives here also?"

"He had a house and potlatch lodge at the head of False Creek but all his land was preempted two years ago," Peter said, using more words in one sentence than he had in the past five hours.

"He call up the eulachon," Kappie added. Certain elders had the magic to make valuable fish appear in the rivers.

"What is he saying?"

"They discuss your presents."

"And?"

"Chupkheem find them poor. Not many."

"Does the chief think the same thing?" Pike asked anxiously.

"Not say."

Khahtsalanough turned to Pike and spoke, his English halting but clear.

"Wise man always hold something back."

Pike grinned. This he understood.

He walked over to the beached dugout and with a flourish pulled out the jug of whiskey. He was of two minds about bringing alcohol. His last experience with it was terrifying. Indian whiskey, a vile potion, could include anything from kerosene to ink and snake guts. The concoction brewed up by the Bar S drovers to keep the Chickasaw friendly, sizzled down his throat before exploding like gunpowder in his stomach. One night after camping close to a Chickasaw settlement, he and Humpy drank until they were half mad. He had no recollection of the following two days, though he woke naked among a pile of Chickasaw bucks with blood on his hands and a sizable erection. Pike spent another three blurry-eyed days with a sour stomach and volcanic diarrhea, wondering about the erection. He hoped this whiskey, the real thing, would have a better result.

Khahtsalanough accepted the jug without a smile. He nodded curtly to Chupkheem.

"Eat."

The food made Pike's stomach forget the bland, limited diet of the past months. There was thick, grainy bread dipped in a gelatinous substance—oily and pungent. He ate salmon cheeks roasted on a stick, licked dried fish eggs from flat seaweed fronds, and sucked at small, raw bird's eggs. He chewed a root cooked to the point of sweetness and scooped soft fat out of a wooden bowl with his fingers. Pike ate, smoked, and sipped the whiskey from a porcelain chamber pot, identical to the chief's. Young girls serving him lingered to watch his expression as he tried each dish. With each lip smack, slurp, and belch, they giggled approvingly and urged more on him.

Then the talking began. Kappie sat next to him and translated in her soft, singsong voice, her broken English only adding to the fascination of the stories. Pike smiled at her gratefully. After a time, Khahtsalanough stood up portentously and began speaking in a somber voice.

"Old beginnings of people now gone," Kappie murmured. "Man and woman, come from far. Snow and ice. Walk many moons. He is of the Eagle. She is of the Moon. Bring seeds of people."

Khahtsalanough reverently held up something in his hand. Pike couldn't make out what it was.

Kappie pointed southwest, in the general direction of the mouth of the Fraser. "Story told for you."

The story wound on and on. Discussion followed many points. Sometimes the stones were called "tears" or "seeds of the people." Pike could barely follow it.

"Woman and Raven bring stone here. Escape the waters which bring them," Kappie struggled for the right word. "*Sl'kheylish*," she said, giving up and looking at Peter.

"Standing rock," Peter said. "On t'other side of the island."

Pike knew it. The odd conelike spire just off a rocky beach. He remembered seeing it as Captain Burke navigated toward the narrows on the approach to Burrard Inlet.

At a gesture from Khahtsalanough, Chupkheem walked around the seated group, holding out his papery hand, for all to see and touch the pale-green beads lying in his palm. Pike stared at them curiously. He'd seen something like them before, but before he could say anything Chupkheem walked on.

"More seeds of those people here," Kappie said, solemnly spreading her arms wide.

"Where?" asked Pike eagerly.

"No one know. Time is not come yet."

Khahtsalanough was just finishing the story.

"When sickness is gone from us, the people will come back and make us strong again."

"Where are those people now?"

"Gone," said Kappie. "They were Kahnamut. Gone now. This is their land. They come back and help us one day."

The evening was mild and the fire kept him warm. Pike lay back and watched the bruise of mountains on the horizon disappear into the black. As sleep cocooned him, he dreamed of big black birds, their mouths full of stones.

38

*

Late next morning, Pike was gently shaken awake by Khahtsalanough. "Come."

Pike slowly followed seven men along a moss-rimmed trail, compacted by many years and many feet. The trees astonished him, their magnitude far greater from the ground than the water. One behemoth towered at least two hundred feet into the air, with a girth of thirty feet or more. Each of the men preceding him paused and uttered a few words to the tree as they passed. After a fifteen-minute walk they stopped at the edge of a glen beside a small lake with a large beaver house at one end.

A shaft of sunlight beamed into the clearing, making it unbearably bright compared to the dark forest. When Pike's eyes adjusted, he saw a rounded, deerskin-covered structure—similar in shape to the beaver house. Beside it two ancient women tended an intense fire. As he watched, they used long sticks to maneuver a red-hot stone out of the fire and roll it along the ground until it dropped into a hole beside the shelter.

"Drink," Khahtsalanough ordered, ladling something out of a shallow wooden barrel. It tasted sweet, salty, and a little sour, all at the same time.

The men undressed, hanging their clothes on branches while the old women went about their business.

Though not modest by nature, Pike felt reluctant to bare himself in this strange setting. It didn't help when Chupkheem laughingly poked at his ribs and pointed at the sharp bones of his pelvis. Pike wasn't sure what he was saying but it didn't sound complimentary. The other men added jibes of their own and the two old women cackled.

Pike crawled into the structure, following the men through a flap in the end. He felt a little silly with his head down low and his buttocks stuck up in the air as he struggled through the opening made for people a foot shorter. Pike emerged into complete blackness. Already disoriented, he wilted in the blast of excruciatingly hot, moist air.

Hands guided him to a bench where he slumped, fighting for breath.

The lodge was larger inside than it appeared from the outside. Though narrow, it was excavated in terraces to provide headroom and, he later realized, to allow gradations of heat—higher being hotter. Cedar planks lay on the terraces, providing a sharp, resiny scent. Thankfully, the planks had been laboriously scraped smooth with stone, because cedar was notoriously prone to leaving jagged splinters that festered. Periodically the women rolled a hot stone into the hole outside, connected to a short tunnel leading into the lodge. The men threw ladles of water on it, producing belches of steam.

*

As his pores opened and sweat streamed down his body, Pike grew accustomed to breathing shallowly to protect his lungs. Someone handed him a pipe. He inhaled smoke, which was slightly bitter, with an aftertaste that numbed his mouth. Pike lay back on his plank and dozed lightly. He felt hotter than he'd ever been, but oddly there was no discomfort. It was as if the fire was part of him and he was part of the fire.

He dozed to the sound of a thousand hummingbirds beating their wings.

"You have come a long way to rid yourself of your father," a voice reverberated in his head.

Pike awoke to utter blackness. He didn't remember falling asleep. A dream floated just out of reach; something had made his father smile. He couldn't remember Kenderville Pike ever smiling.

The dark caressed him, the sound of other men breathing lulled him, and he slept once more. When Pike woke again, his body was light, as if it had been emptied of itself. He tried to sit up but a dizzy sickness overtook him and he slumped against the wall of the lodge. He was thirsty. He brought his hand to his mouth and licked—so thirsty—it tasted like blood. The dreams flew languidly in and out of his mind, like unsettled visitors.

Tears sprang to his eyes; Pike had no idea why. He wanted to wail like a frightened child. Images cascaded into his being. Brushing his mother's long, black hair. Throwing gypsy knives. Killing Alfred's horse with a rock. He saw Alfred and Shi dancing. His father was still smiling in a frozen leer. Alfred gave Shi a ring. As he did, an enormous black bird swooped down and plucked it from Alfred's hand. Pike lunged after the bird, calling out. It turned in a graceful arc and dove directly at him. Stop! He shielded his head with his arms. Awake again.

"Sun rises."

"What now?" Pike slurred.

"What now?" Khahtsalanough echoed.

"Yes," said Pike, his tongue heavy and his lips sticky. "What happens now?" He couldn't focus on anything except the rattle and bang of thoughts in his head. Thoughts with the substance of hard objects poking him and smacking him as they moved in and out of consciousness.

"We wait," the old chief replied.

"For what?"

"For, for . . ." the chief struggled for the English wording. "For shedding—like bark on the big red tree."

Light tickled Pike's consciousness from a great distance. Infinitesimally it neared. Weakly he opened his eyes. He was in the sweat lodge—alone, shivering. The flap at the end of the tent fluttered in the breeze, letting in blinding shafts of brilliant sunshine and cool air. Pike levered himself off the plank and crawled over to the fire pit. Cold ash and rocks. He crawled out of the lodge into the painful sunshine. How could he be so tired? Panting with exertion, he shakily got to his feet and tottered over to the lake where he drank his fill. Gradually the water brought his strength back. Lowering himself into the pond, he set out with a feeble dog paddle, which, after a few icy minutes, invigorated him wonderfully.

Emerging from the water, Pike found his clothes on the branch where he'd left them. He quickly got dressed and set out for the village. He looked up through the gaps in the trees to the sky above. The trees made him feel inconsequential. A mole must feel like this when it sits in its burrow and looks out, he thought.

He broke out of the forest into the opening on the shore where the village sat, a bunch of long, wooden boxes. No one paid the slightest attention to him. Several women were on the beach, digging a pit. Young girls were bringing smoldering wood, which they laid in the bottom of the pit. Nearby were several piles of what looked like seaweed. They must be cooking something, Pike thought, hunger buzzing in his ears so powerfully he felt faint.

The biggest lodge stood next to him. It was a magnificent structure at least a hundred feet long and as tall as a two-story house. Pike assumed it belonged to the chief. Was he supposed to leave? Stay and eat? His stomach hurt and his head felt light from the sentient dreams, which still pressed at the back of his eyes. Drawing a breath, Pike decided to enter the big house. Surely politeness demanded he say good-bye before leaving.

The entrance was surrounded, top and sides, by enormous painted boards covered with angular creatures squatting like griffons at guard. The colors were vibrant—rich scarlet, clear black, and splashes of white. Pike saw beaks and claws and felt himself drawn in as if the creatures were reaching out to him. There was also a house pole, rising thirty feet or more, standing like a sentinel. It was beautifully carved, with none of the geometric corners of the painting. Pike couldn't keep his hands off it. He stroked the round eyes of what seemed to be a frog and traced its fingers holding a ball. Halfway up, a bird in huge relief looked to be flying out of the pole itself with a small, egglike object in its mouth. Pike couldn't reach it but he felt the strong urge to grasp the bird's beak.

✳

"What are you doing?" Peter the Whaler asked quietly at his side.

"Oh, ah!" Pike shouted, heart slamming into his throat. "I, uh, was just going in to greet the chief. I'll be leaving, I suppose. I'd hoped to do some hunting but I don't imagine one just up and asks an Indian to go hunting, does one?"

"No."

At that moment Pike remembered his Sharps rifle. He'd left it in Peter's boat. He recalled what Glencannon said about how these Indians viewed property and theft.

"You think I should go in? Does one knock?"

"No," Peter chuckled.

"Thank you so much for your help," Pike said sarcastically, entering the dim recesses. This brought another chuckle from Peter.

The lodge was surprisingly light inside, as the setting sun pierced through the boards. In the middle a group of men squatted on piles of skins. He spotted Chupkheem near Khahtsalanough. Kappie, helped by two young girls, was braiding a woman's hair in the background. A boy with an older man beside him was hunched over a net, weaving a tool back and forth.

The chief smoked Pike's meerschaum pipe, talking between puffs and occasionally holding up an object. As Pike drew nearer, he saw the objects were the presents—three neck scarves, the bootlaces, Glencannon's compass-cover drinking glass and the courting fabric. Without looking up, Khahtsalanough spoke rapidly. At his shoulder Peter the Whaler whispered.

"Chief's still not happy with your presents."

The chief spoke again.

"He says you told him in the sweat lodge you had more."

Pike was baffled. "Why doesn't he speak to me in English? He did before."

Peter shrugged. Khahtsalanough spoke again, this time with great firmness.

"What is he saying?" Pike demanded. Kappie and the other woman laughed softly.

"You told him another gift in boat."

"What other gift?"

"The one in boat."

Not his gun! Pike was worried. Without his rifle he would feel more naked than without his clothes. Even a brief time in the American West had taught him that not even a horse compared in importance with his gun. He knew it was unlikely that he could buy such a valuable item in this desolate spot. The only guns available were old fur-trade rifles, which placed the shooter's face in more damage than his target.

"I can't give him my gun!" hissed Pike.

Peter the Whaler raised an eyebrow. "Can't?" Khahtsalanough and Chupkheem watched implacably.

"Don't want gun," Khahtsalanough suddenly spoke up. He gestured to his eye. Pike was puzzled. Khahtsalanough touched his eye again. Then it dawned on him. Pike recalled his eyeglass, also left in the bottom of Peter's boat.

Without another word, he dashed out of the longhouse. Sure enough, there it was, lying in the bottom of the boat along with his gun—untouched. The Pancratic eye tube—a small, handheld spyglass with changeable magnification, a marvel of modern science. When he returned, the woman whose hair was being braided had moved to stand beside Khahtsalanough.

"I have heard that Khahtsalanough is a man who carefully observes the world," said Pike, who had heard no such thing. "So I chose a very special present that allows the chief to better see the tops of mountains, the stars in the sky, the moon, and even his enemies as they come across the water."

Pike held it out to Khahtsalanough who ignored it. Chupkheem took the eye tube and placed it on his eye. A smile broadened his face. Khahtsalanough muttered something.

"He says that's more like it," Peter the Whaler translated. Pike now had a suspicion they were pulling his leg.

"You tell better stories than give gifts," the chief said in English.

"Oh," said Pike, not knowing what to say. What stories?

"Your father with fish eyes," illuminated Khahtsalanough. "Many days pass listening to your stories."

"Days," Pike said stupidly. "I've been here days?"

"Three."

Pike felt his world whirl. "How can that be?" he stammered. He could hardly believe that he had spent three days in the sweat lodge.

"You came a long way to find your father," the chief said.

The words sounded elusively familiar. Where had he heard them before? Find his father? He wasn't looking for his father. What nonsense. Still, he felt good and when he thought of his father there was no longer the mixture of anger and scorn burning in his gut.

The chief, reading the play of expression over Pike's face, grunted in satisfaction. Khahtsalanough motioned the woman forward.

"You speak of young girl in other world."

"I did?"

Chupkheem smiled lasciviously. "Chee?"

Shi. What had he said? Pike's face grew hot, remembering the young girl from Leipzig.

Khahtsalanough gestured to the woman. "This one not so young but yours."

Pike stared in amazement as she stepped out of shadows. "I am Itsu," she said in clear English, meeting his eyes calmly. "Itsu." She was the color of polished mahogany, smooth-browed, with hair past her waist braided simply but decorated with shells. She was taller than most of the women here and neither plump nor lean. Her cheeks were marked with smallpox scars and her eyes had lost the first freshness of youth. Her lips were wide though not full, and her nose was large and slightly flattened at the end. She was clean, and pleasant enough to look at, and there was no mistaking the intelligence in her steady, unabashed gaze.

"Mine?"

Khahtsalanough was already leaving the longhouse. Pike chased after him.

"Why are you . . . ?" he called out to the chief, forgetting etiquette.

The chief held up his hand for silence. He walked on toward the beach, and as he did, villagers fell in behind. When he reached the water's edge, Khahtsalanough spoke at length in his own tongue to nods and murmurs of agreement from his people. Chupkheem stood with his head bowed, listening intently. The chief flung his hands up and spoke loudly to the tree tops, then he turned to the water and spoke again. Finally he walked over to a group of children, reverently touching each of them in turn.

At a barked command from Khahtsalanough the villagers surged forward and began filling a boat on shore with bundles of fur.

Pike guessed that there were hundreds of them.

"Sea otter," said Peter at his shoulder again.

"Sea otter!" gasped Pike.

The animals had been trapped out on this coast decades earlier. Only in the far north were they still found in any kind of abundance. A fortune in the luxuriant pelts lay in the boat.

"Yours," Khahtsalanough said, waving his hand at the boat as if it were as inconsequential as stone.

"The boat and the furs are worth far more than my paltry offerings," Pike protested. He turned to Peter the Whaler.

"What was he saying to the village?"

"You have been chosen."

"Chosen?"

"You are one," explained Khahtsalanough in his halting English.

"The one what?" Pike asked, feeling like they were playing spin-blind, a childhood game where players were blindfolded, spun around, then released to find their way back to the touch post in the shortest time.

"The chief saw your spirit. You are the one."

"Just what have I been chosen for?"

"Find children," Khahtsalanough answered gravely, the deep lines in his face sagging downward as he spoke, his eyes dark with passion.

It took another hour for Pike to fully comprehend the story. At first he felt shocked, then sick, and finally angry. He had no brothers or sisters, but the chime of children on the von Schaumberg estate still rang in his ears.

Once word of gold on the Fraser River sand bars spread from Fort Langley to Fort Victoria, down the California coast, across the continent, and overseas, thousands of miners had found their way up the river. Aside from defending their claims and keeping their heads attached to their shoulders, the biggest challenge the miners faced was labor. Few trusted each other, and the work was too backbreaking for a man to do by himself day in and day out. Chinese labor, common in California, was rarer in the British colony, because up here the Chinese were free to stake their own claims and more belligerent about protecting them. The Northwest Indians, for the most part, were unwilling to do the white man's bidding.

But children . . .

The first boy child, a sturdy fellow of seven, had been stolen from a village on Burrard Inlet and quickly whisked overland on the rough trail to the Fraser. Normally, even the canniest trapper would have had difficulty stealing an Indian child, but disease weakened many tribes along the coast and up the river. Vaccination reduced the devastation of smallpox, but scrofula, phthisis, and influenza had all struck since 1860.

After the first child was taken, the trade in strong boys was brisk. By 1861 the miners no longer had to steal for themselves as the weakened tribes raided each other.

"Find children," the chief said again. "Bring them back."

"Why me?"

"White man steal. White man bring back."

"Where would I look?"

"Listen to spirit."

Pike found himself drawn in by the chief's ferocious certainty that he had been sent to bring back the village's children. He looked over Burrard Inlet to the darkening forests where he had planned to hunt bear, elk, and mountain sheep. He felt Itsu's eyes on him.

"How many children?"

"Seventeen, maybe more," Khahtsalanough replied. "Know three dead. You find others."

He inhabited a dream, Pike was sure of that. In a moment he would wake, sticky and thirsty in the sweat lodge. But for now . . .

"*Kat Vacuska!*" Pike declared. The villagers watched him curiously.

"I am sire of the world," Pike said softly, meeting Khahtsalanough's eyes.

39

*

Pike's brave words died in his throat when he saw Itsu gazing at him intently. He suddenly felt young, inexperienced, and awkward—more boy than man. It was time to go. But go where? Itsu stepped into the canoe, calling out two or three words. Several men scrambled forward, pushed the laden boat into the water, and held it there, waiting for Pike. As he walked toward the canoe, Chupkheem intercepted him.

"You need this," he held out the eyeglass.

"I gave it to the chief," protested Pike.

"Return it with his sister's son."

Pike strung the lanyard around his neck and looked across the sand-and-stone beach to the edge of the woods where Khahtsalanough stood. Even at a distance Pike felt the penetration of his eyes. How was he supposed to retrieve stolen children spread out in an uncivilized land with few towns, no police, and no law of any sort? It was a ridiculous task—like sending a man to the Orient and telling him to bring back a specific Chinaman with no known name, location, or occupation. As these thoughts pushed around his head, Pike realized that he was frightened. It wasn't the fear of physical danger, but a clammy, hollow anxiety. They expected something from him and he didn't know if he could deliver.

The canoe proved far harder to paddle than he'd imagined. The distance from Khwaykhway to Morton's cabin was only a mile or so by water, but as the boat nosed first one way then another with little forward progress, he wondered if he would ever make it. A slight wind picked up in the inlet, pushing them away from the shoreline. Pike dug in for all he was worth but it was only when Itsu crawled to the back of the boat and directed him to the front that the canoe finally began going in the right direction. Though far smaller, she propelled the craft with ease, leaning into the paddle and deftly steering with tiny adjustments of the blade.

"Good lord! You've got a small fortune there." Morton and Glencannon stared astonished, at the pile of silvery otter furs.

"An' what did you say you did to get 'em?" queried Glencannon.

Pike shrugged helplessly. "It's not what I did. It's what they want me to do."

"And that would be?" Morton asked, his heavy eyebrows arching to his hairline.

"Get me a drink first and I'll tell you all about it."

"Ar', you're in a wee bit of luck, me laddy," crowed Glencannon. "I've just towed that fine frigate into the inlet for Mr. Moody to fill up with spars and didn't they have a store of rum I took in part payment for the piloting. Go get Sour Soon and have him lift a glass of his piddly tea while you string us a yarn."

They all thought Pike was joking. Then they thought the Indians were having one over on him. But the fact of the furs remained, not to mention the woman watching at them from the corner.

"Couldn't you get a younger one?" Glencannon cradled his wooden mug. "She'll keep you warm, I suppose, but she's not first flower, I'll warrant."

Pike was starting to think Itsu wasn't a present at all—more like an overseer to make sure he did what the Indians wanted. That night Itsu refused the shelter of a tent Morton had erected beside his cabin. She insisted on sleeping in the canoe beside the furs. Without asking, she took Pike's gun and racked it ostentatiously before setting it beside her. Pike felt he should be hospitable, so he visited her before he succumbed to the rum. He heard her murmuring in her language as he approached.

She broke off at the sound of his footsteps.

"Prayer to papa," she explained without being asked.

"Papa your father?"

"Our papa in the above."

"Do you mean the Lord's Prayer?" asked Pike curiously. "In English it goes something like, 'Our Father who art in heaven.'"

Itsu nodded her head. "That it. Papa in the above."

"Where on earth did you learn that?"

"Mission man come from Fort Langley. Live at Sqwayus," she pointed south. Seeing Pike's blank look, she explained, "Sqwayus is where Xa:ls live. Xa:ls powerful magickers who change people to frog and other thing. Many lives ago my people were there. Mission man stay there and all think he will be turned to stone. But not, so we come to listen to story about white man magicker. Papa in the above."

"Are you not the same tribe as Chupkheem and Chief Khahtsalanough?"

"No, no. They are protector of me. Few of us left. We are Kahnamut Iqw. Lost Kahnamut. Some here, some there. With Khahtsalanough and Chupkheem we are sister people."

Magic, changing people into frogs, protectors—it was like a grand tale from childhood but real—at least in the minds of these people. And after his experience in the steamy lodge, Pike was starting to believe that these stories of the spirit and heart were every bit as real as the water around them.

"Why are you here?" blurted out Pike. "Are some of the stolen children yours?" He felt a little pang. It occurred to him that she might have a husband and family.

"No, no. One boy keeper of our people. When he taken our lives dead. No one want to live. But Khahtsalanough a great man. He ran the thoughts from us. He become keeper until boy found."

Itsu's voice was soft but clear; Pike could listen to her all night. He was surprised at how forthcoming she was, having heard many stories of the Indians' reticence or, when they spoke, how their words were like riddles. He was drawn to her quiet intensity and the dignified way she answered his questions. He quite forgot that he was squatting by an Indian canoe on an inlet of the great Pacific Ocean, surrounded by immense forests and mountains that no amount of brilliance in prose could possibly explain.

"You say the boy is a keeper. What does that mean?"

For the first time Itsu paused, struggling to explain something she knew would be difficult for a Xwelitem to understand. They called the whites Xwelitem, "hungry people," because they always needed food and weren't very good at getting it or storing it. Xwelitem were powerful in one way but weak in many others. They were impoverished, too, with only one god and few able to perform the transformations the Xa:ls could. Apparently whites could exist in only one form, and when they looked at a rock or a tree they saw only that.

"From when life began Kahnamut face many dangers. They forced from one land to other. They seek this place and find it. For them it is like your above land, but here on the earth. We different because we carry the beginning of us. They are the seeds. You see them?"

"Seeds. Do you mean like seeds to plant things?"

"Yes," she said. "Seed of our people. Chief Khahtsalanough hold them.

The seeds will borne our people again when the time is coming right. You see them—color like mountain water. Very shining and small."

"Yes, of course. I remember them! Pretty green stones. It was dark but they looked like jade."

Like all Anglicans, Pike had been raised to spurn the icons of the papists, cheap symbols that only served to reduce his Lord God and Jesus Christ to trinkets and trickery. But Itsu made it sound sensible—even practical. The essence of a disappearing people magically preserved in pale beads and handed down from generation to generation. They would burst forth when the time was right. To Pike, it was as credible a story as Adam and Eve.

"But why me? There have been many whites on these shores since the boys started disappearing. Didn't the first Gold Rush begin almost ten years ago? Have you not tried to find the keeper before? The Indian is far better in the wilderness than the white man. Surely you could find the children quicker than any of us could."

As he watched her consider an answer, Pike couldn't resist mentioning the thought that had been eating away at him since his ship sailed through the narrows into Burrard Inlet.

"You know, it seemed that everyone was waiting for me. The chief and Chupkheem at any rate. I find that unsettling." She looked at him inquiringly. "Unsettling? Strange, odd, eerie. Like a piece of my life was already being lived before I got there. They knew what was happening but I did not. It was as if . . . as if a piece of my life belonged to them."

"Lives not owned," Itsu said. "Not like stories."

"Then tell me!" he demanded. "How do you know you can trust me? Why do you want me to find the children?"

Itsu looked down at her laced fingers. "Why not?"

"And if I am a failure and we do not find the children, let alone this keeper, what then?"

"We wait for another to help us find them."

In the morning, Glencannon, Pike, and Itsu steamed over to the frigate with a dozen of the furs. The price staggered even Pike—twenty pounds for a single one. The tightly bound piles contained at least two hundred hides.

"You don't see such work this far south," the captain commented. "I've brought otter from Kamchatka and Alaska and these are as good as I've ever seen. Every one is perfectly scraped and dried. These Indians down here usually try to sell you mangy hides, hardly cleaned, let alone dried."

✳

It took the better part of two days to steam from the inlet, through the narrows separating the mainland from the north shore, around the broad snout that would one day be Point Grey and the University of British Columbia, up past the island in the mouth of the Fraser and on through the flooding waters to dock at New Westminster. They pushed past Hope and headed into a section of the river Pike hadn't seen before. Canyon walls rose steep and dark. Every now and then he saw the elaborate scaffolding of the river Indians cantilevered off the cliff face. Pike could scarcely believe how clever was the construction that allowed the flimsy-looking structure to securely support a man. He watched as one stood on a small platform and lowered a net to the water below. They skirted the rapids, so Pike had considerable time to study the man. He was grateful for having his eyeglass back. No sooner had the net touched the eddy waters than he began bringing it up again. It seemed like a slow way to catch fish, but Pike quickly changed his mind. In the time they passed out of sight of the fisherman, he snared half a dozen salmon, one as long as his arm.

At Yale, Glencannon let them off. A group of disconsolate miners hung about the dock, asking for return passage in return for work.

"Work?" mocked Glencannon. "The only work I'll be needing from the likes of you before you set foot on me beauty is the work of pulling money from your pockets."

Playing a hunch, Pike approached the scruffs. "Do any of you know the miner with the Indian boy working for him?" One man was about to speak when the other shushed him. "Like the Scot said, nothing's free in these parts."

"All right. If you tell me I'll pay your passage to New Westminster," said Pike. Glencannon groaned. "But if you send me on a wild-goose chase, we'll track you down. If I tossed a rock into the ocean my squaw could find it. And you won't like what happens."

The men looked over to where Itsu was standing.

"I'd like a bit of that," the third man stepped forward. "How 'bout a poke in return for what I know?"

"A poke would cost you as much as your miserable life is worth." Pike jutted his jaw. The man stepped back. Though skinny and young, this one had something in his eyes that said messing with him wouldn't be worthwhile.

"Fine! Fine! Don't get the wind up your tail. There's a shafter 'tween Little Canyon and Big Dip, just afore Soda Creek, where the old mule road passes. He's got a Siwash hauling rock."

"The man's called Bull Roberts, I'm told," another piped in.

While Pike talked, Soon supervised the loading of a small forge on an ox train destined for Soda Creek where it would be loaded on another river steamer to Quesnel and then to Williams Creek on the newly cut Cariboo Road. Strewn along the edges of the creek was what the shantytown fathers proclaimed was the largest settlement of white British and Americans west of Chicago. And it was, for a time. Not one settlement but three: Barkerville, Richfield, and Camerontown. Ten million pounds' worth of gold had been hauled up the area's mine shafts in the last eight years.

"Perhaps I will see you again," Soon said doubtfully.

"Of course you will," Pike replied jauntily. "I'm off for a bit of adventure and I'll return trailing children—like that fairy tale—the Pied Piper. Did you ever hear of it?"

Soon shook his head. The man was clearly mad. Glencannon was a lot to bear but what he wanted out of life was clear—whiskey and money. No puzzle could be more difficult to figure out than the young man who virtually gave away his business, went off into the woods for days, and then reappeared with a fortune in rare furs. He could live in leisure on the bounty from the furs, but he chose to follow an unattractive Indian woman into the darkest, thickest, most dangerous forests in the world. All in order to find children who were not his and probably didn't exist anyway.

Though the glory of the Cariboo riches was in decline, hotel rooms were still hard to come by. Pike was amazed at the whirl of activity along the single main street of Yale. Every second building was a saloon. Rousing songs spilled onto raised sidewalks balanced on stilts above the ever-present mud. Above Mucky's, a saloon, Pike took a room with two beds, a washbasin, and a passage on a rickety skywalk from the second floor to a brothel next door bearing the sign GIRLS: CLEAN AND FRESH. After paying for the room, he went in search of Itsu to buy her some dinner. There were seventeen establishments serving some variety of beans, rice, buffalo steaks, or fish fry. Two offered English puddings, while another advertised tripe and brains fried in grease. Pike searched for an hour and there was no sign of her, so he tried a meal of buffalo stew—he swore the meat came from a mule of considerable antiquity.

Next morning Itsu was waiting by the door of the hotel, urgency in her eyes.

"Bull Roberts's man. We go now," she stated.

Joining the ox train out of Yale to Soda Creek, they made painfully slow progress.

"Is it always like this?" Pike asked one of the drivers as they stopped for the tenth time to lever boulders out of the path.

"Oh yep, she drips rock all year," the driver gestured to the rock cliffs hanging hundreds of feet overhead. "At least we got a good wide road now and the stagecoaches can git through. You shoulda seen it when all we had was the mule road. This here's fit for a lady."

"You have a different kind of lady in this country," laughed Pike, forgetting Itsu jouncing on the board seat beside him. But her face showed no sign of offense.

The road had been blasted out of sheer rock by the Royal Engineers. In many places the cliff dropped in a straight line to the river below. Pike marveled at the engineering skill it took to forge such a route, and he wondered how anyone believed such a road was possible in the first place. But gold was gold, and he was sure men would build machines to fly to the moon if they thought gold could be found there. Pike stared down the canyon walls; it was mesmerizing. A large bird swooped close—an eagle of some sort, a bold bird, for it came at them two or three times. Itsu's eyes followed it intently. Pike saw something in her gaze. Certainty, fierce certainty.

"Good lord!" Pike shouted so loudly the driver started and one of the oxen bawled.

"There's something down there! A wagon!" Halfway down the canyon a two-cart train was impaled on a small stand of scrubby pine jutting out from a rocky lip on the wall. As Pike stared he could make out the bodies of several mules splayed out as if flattened by a giant hand.

"Oh, that's Noah's mule train. Happened last spring. He got chased by injuns coming back from Soda Creek with a load of gold from Barkerville. Stupid. There was a government stage coming back too, but he wouldn't wait. His sideman got cut in half and the injuns drove the mules over the cliff."

"And Noah?"

"There's bits of him all over, I dare say." The man thought this was hilarious and he laughed with booming appreciation for his grisly joke. "I heard it was the Lillooets what got him. Though up here there's half a dozen tribes that keep to themselves until they can't hold back anymore— and pffft! A little whoop-whoop against the white man."

"Did they attack to steal the gold?

"Hell no. That'd be too easy. You could jes give 'um the gold and be done with it. Nah, they're all in a prickle 'cause Davey Backus up at Quesnel took on a couple of injun boys to work for him, and when they stole from him he beat 'um bad. It was Davey's gold on the mule train."

Itsu gripped Pike's arm hard.

"Since we're going to the Cariboo I might just try my hand at a bit of digging," said Pike casually, getting her message. "D'you suppose I might hire some labor to help me?"

"You got a squaw," observed the driver. "Best labor going. You could try for a Chinaman in Barkerville, but they're hard to come by. Forget the young bucks. They'll do what they want then take all your food. I'd go for a kid if you can get 'um. But make sure you get 'um from down around the lowlands. The tribes around the Burrard Inlet are best. They'll never venture up here."

The man lapsed into silence as he started working on a big piece of jerky. With one cheek full of tobacco and the other stuffed with hard tack, it took all his concentration. Pike could hear Itsu breathing as the driver talked. He glanced at her face and caught the look that said, "See, it is true."

The adventure began to seem deadly serious. Pike thought about the horrific sound six mules and two carts would have made plunging a hundred feet to the rocks. Would they find even a single child, let alone Itsu's keeper, who would care for the jade stones now guarded by Chief Khahtsalanough?

Bull Roberts proved easy to find. Everyone knew him at the tiny wagon stop of Soda Creek where cargo switched from wagon to steamer. It was a hole punched in the forest with the debris of some godly fury scattered about. Deadfalls, rock, rotting stumps, and a thick coating of moss over everything. Roberts was a huge man with an enormous barrel chest and severely rounded shoulders. His beard hung in tatters on his chest and his faded blue eyes held the look of contempt for everyone and everything. His claim stretched for half a mile, a remnant of the Fraser River rush of '58, but yielding just enough for Roberts to keep hoping. His voice was scratchy, as if long unused. The boy was engaged digging a sluice to siphon off water from a shallow shaft. At the sight of him Itsu trembled so violently that Pike placed a hand on her shoulder to calm her. Pike made an offer, and to his surprise the man started dickering right away.

Roberts glanced at the boy and Pike was surprised to see a light of regret in his eyes. "Charlie here's just about used up anyway. I been fooling myself for long enough. This here claim's played out."

Fifty pounds, two tins of tobacco, and a bag of sugar secured the purchase.

The boy came willingly but didn't say a word. He couldn't be more than eleven, Pike judged. Itsu spoke briefly to him. The child looked cold but she didn't touch him or offer any clothes. Finally Pike wrapped his bedroll around him. That night they slept in the ox shed at Soda Creek. While the boy lay curled in a ball in the hay beside them, Itsu came to Pike for the first time. When he entered her body, power coursed through him. "I am sire of the world," he whispered triumphantly.

Itsu learned the boy was of the Musqueam people, from a village at the mouth of the Fraser. There were few people in the little community when they returned the boy; most were at their weirs on the lower sandbars. But it seemed like a throng of thousands with the keening, crying, and joyous shouts. The first smile crossed the weary child's face when an old woman came hobbling toward him as quickly as her bent legs would allow.

Pike felt like a savior. He was flushed from the easy success and half drunk with the sense of potency it gave him. That night Itsu came to him again, wrapping her brown legs around him as she pulled him down on her. "I am sire of the world," he whispered into her hair.

✱

Two hundred and seventy-three days later, Itsu left him. The baby was straining at her skin, turning vigorously, making comical bumps in her belly. She told Pike it was for the best. By then they had found seven children, most Musqueam but one from a Sqwamus tribe across from Burrard Inlet. Pike had purchased most of them, tussling only with one miner near Quesnel who took his money then drew his gun. But there were more to find, and so far no sign of the boy keeper.

"A boy," Itsu said when she returned just weeks later. Pike had stayed at Yale, losing at cards and learning how to play Fan Tan. He was surprised to see her so soon.

"Another woman," she said, touching her swollen breasts. A wet nurse. Pike loved her passionately at that moment . . . she'd left their child to continue their quest. A higher purpose—what glory. Pike ached to see his son, but the search for the children was even more compelling. He wondered if the police felt this way while on the hunt for a particularly dangerous criminal.

They pushed deep into the Cariboo, collecting information as they went. Word of their hunt got out, and a few miners, hard up for cash, sought them out, dragging pathetic children in their wake. Along the way, Pike's world changed with the force of lightning.

One minute he was crouched at the top of a narrow defile watching a boy place stones on a skid, and the next minute he was on his knees, vomiting violently. Itsu stroked his head as he retched. Together they retreated into the woods, so the man wouldn't see or hear them. The boy had been tethered around his neck and hobbled. He was naked, and the bloody sores on his backside obvious. Emaciated, he carried himself with the hopelessness of those praying for death. When he turned to move the stones, Pike, viewing him through his eyeglass, saw his face half-eaten away by some wasting disease. An image of the son he had yet to see flashed through his mind and grabbed his stomach in a sickening grip.

They found twelve more children, all belonging to the people of the lower Fraser or the villages near the inlet and the mountains. Only one came from Khahtsalanough's people.

"This one's fresh and he ain't going nowhere," the miner said defiantly, swinging his shotgun threateningly. "I bought him fair and square. He keeps me warm. Just like your squaw there. If you get my meaning."

Before Pike could reply, Itsu shot the man in the thigh, shattering the bone. "Now you can't mine. No need boy," she said with impeccable logic.

✳

Nineteen boys, but no keeper.

Late in the summer of 1869, a foul summer of hideous heat and mosquitoes big enough to bleed a man with one bite, Itsu told him she must go again.

"Child coming," she said, holding on to her huge belly.

"Have him here," Pike urged. He was sure it would be another boy. "There's a doctor in Barkerville and a hotel where I can purchase rooms for your lie-in."

"I do not need doctor," Itsu said. "I am not sick."

"You know what I mean! You will have care and our child shall be born so we can both look after him."

"I go."

Pike pleaded with her to stay. It seemed far more urgent than the last time. He talked often of the son who would be three years old as if the boy were living with him. He constructed for him a face, a body, and an impish look. Though he did not know it there were pieces of all the boys they had found in the imaginary picture he had of his son, now living somewhere with strangers.

Pike never saw Itsu again.

40

✳

Soon stared up at the slivers of gloomy sky, thinking about life. It was, he reflected, much like the poor excuse for streets in the British outpost—corduroy roads. Those wretched, bumpy trails constructed of logs that shook your guts like an internal storm and snatched apart wagons as if they were made of the thinnest kindling. The progress of life, at least his experience of it since he'd left China, was just like traveling such roads. You felt momentum gathering, but it came at the cost of prodigious bumping and jostling and then it was arrested, suddenly and painfully.

Soon wiggled his shoulders to ease the ache. His present situation was not good. He stood in a pit twelve feet deep and a foot wider than his shoulders. He was naked, standing barefoot in about three inches of mud. The sides of his prison were packed clay and seeping water. Overriding everything was an unmistakable outhouse odor.

✳

The heavy tread of boot on metal rattled the grate over his head. "Hello there! Johnny Pigtail!" a jovial British voice sang out. "Are you at home?"

"Ah yes, there you are," the voice boomed. "I say, how are you managing in your new quarters?" The voice stopped as if waiting for a reply. "Not too comfortable, I daresay. But we can't all live in fine houses, now can we?"

The feet moved away, stopped, then returned. "I say, old chap. I have something for you. Almost forgot. I've been saving it all afternoon."

Soon looked up hopefully, but the bulky figure standing on the grate above obscured everything. The warm stream of urine hit Soon's upraised face, stinging his eyes. He dropped to his knees, all he had room for. The rest of Captain Douglas Campbell's bladder emptied on his shoulders and the back of his bowed head.

"Those years with the Hong Kong police taught me everything I need to know about these chappies." Campbell appeared to be speaking to someone else.

"You mean there's actually someone down there?" A second voice filtered down.

"Yes, indeed. I call this my house of respect," the man explained. "I say, would you care to have a go at him yourself?"

"Er, no, thank you. I'm quite empty myself. What did he do to earn your attention?"

Stupid. Soon had been so stupid. Worse, arrogant. White men, especially fat, florid ones like Campbell, with bad skin and lips pursed from years of sucking on a bottle, seemed all the same to him. Greedy to start and untrustworthy to finish. Play on the former and you had a chance of avoiding the consequences of the latter. According to those beliefs, Soon had conducted his life safely and relatively profitably since he'd landed at Burrard Inlet years ago. If he'd stuck to what he knew for sure he would have been back in his shack near Gassy's. But stupidity had brought him here.

His grandfather, father, and brothers provided for the sprawling clan of Chong Alley by doing what they did, generation after generation, with little change. Occasionally some teardrop of the sun fell upon them, offering an unusual opportunity—a broken crate of goods that could be peddled, river salvage that scavengers would pay for if they knew its location, and once a beautiful, fateful piece of pottery. But they never went looking.

Soon Chong always went looking.

As a little boy, he'd spotted a piece of bright blue cloth caught by the breeze. It fluttered into a gap between two shacks, which was too low and narrow to accommodate even his small body. Flattening himself on the ground, he shoved his arm in as deep as it would go to grab the precious scrap. A starving cur sunk its teeth into his hand and would have chewed it off had his sister not heard his wail and pulled him away. That night, as his mother tended the wound, his father scolded.

"Why reach when you don't know what you are reaching into?"

"I wanted the pretty blue," Soon sobbed.

"Do not look for what you cannot see," came the stern response.

But Soon Chong always went looking.

He could have returned with Tong Yuk Jee to Guangzhou and lived like a prince with his California gold. But he went looking for more, and the mistakes that followed found him quickly. And here too. The freight service was a perfect business, which he and the Scot had mostly to themselves to begin with. Though the Gold Rush fell apart shortly after he arrived, the European appetite for timber and coal took its place. There were flutters about silver, the ever-growing export of fish, and the beginnings of a jade industry. Not the pale, sophisticated stone of the beads he still carried like a talisman, but hard, crude, dark green. Nonetheless, a market sprang up, bringing yet another wave of seekers to the Pacific coast. Canada had been a nation just eight years, and the township of Granville on Burrard Inlet a mere three years old, yet already there were promises of a railway across the country, which would bring more settlers west and take the riches of British Columbia east. Langley, around the old fort, had become its own municipality, as had Maple Ridge on the north shore of the Fraser. Several hundred farmers fanned out from both settlements, taking advantage of the nourishing alluvial land, renewed by the Fraser's regular flooding. Across the Burrard Inlet from Granville was the mill community of Moodyville. Promoters there promised it would become the most populated region of the new province. Married mill workers had established homes on dirt-and-stump-filled streets with grand names like the Rookeries, Maiden Lane, and Knob Hill.

Soon doubted the promoters. No community would grow where alcohol and brothels were forbidden. He estimated that on any given night in Moodyville or Hastings, to the east of Granville, fully half the citizens could be found drinking in Granville's four saloons or dropping their trousers for the sixteen girls who worked the area. Most of them were from the Indian villages at Khwaykhway and Musqueam near the mouth of the Fraser. They bent for a dollar, knelt for fifty cents.

Soon and Glencannon had a good business, but no enterprise operated in a bubble. The transportation of men, mail, and goods across Burrard Inlet, up the Fraser, and across the Strait of Georgia to Victoria soon attracted competitors.

Colin Glencannon, though a superior boat builder and operator, was useless at drumming up new business. He took what came his way. In earlier years, he never had to go looking. Now, to survive, they did. But any potential customers wouldn't deal with a Chinaman, especially after the vote was taken away from all aliens, anyone not white and European, when the province joined Canadian Confederation. Another mill opened along the inlet, a chain forger set up in False Creek, and a cannery, using mainly Oriental labor, was built at the mouth of the Fraser. The mail and provisioning contracts for each went to a competitor even before Soon became aware of their existence. Glencannon and Soon didn't lose the business they had, but they weren't attracting much more either.

While Glencannon drank up his profits, Soon invested his in a Chinese restaurant to the east of Gassy's on the edge of the new townsite of Granville. It had a laundry in the basement and a bathtub for rent sitting on a plank of wood in the muddy square of ground behind the shack. He stole all the wood from the salvage fires at the Hastings Mill. Late at night, when the watchman had fallen asleep, Soon pulled piece after piece from the blaze, saving the least burned.

Now Soon wanted more.

Captain Douglas Campbell appeared to be a pathway to that more. Glencannon mentioned the new head of the militia in passing one night, swearing to have his guts for guy ropes if he got half a chance. No Glencannon would pass a Campbell without attempting to cause mayhem to a representative of that clan, which had usurped the Glencannons some thousand years or so ago.

"You'll do no such thing!" retorted Soon upon hearing of Glencannon's plan. "How can you be so foolish? He is an important man and could be useful to us."

"No Campbell 'ud ever be important to a Glencannon!"

"We will see."

The man's appointment rekindled in Soon an old and previously successful idea. He called at the militia commander's office at the naval reserve—really just a single barracks block with fourteen men who spent most of their time playing cards. After the third attempt, he was admitted to Campbell's office, a small room just off the barrack's summer kitchen. Soon was surprised to see a rattan table holding a laquer tray with two tall sniffing cups and two squat drinking cups. Beside them sat a shiny enamel pot with a small spiral of aromatic steam rising from the spout. Soon had a cold, as he often did, but he could still detect the distinct aroma of Soi Sin tea. Even in China it was rare and had been a favorite of Mr. Sang, his long-ago mentor. Campbell sat down heavily, gesturing Soon to do the same. Soon found himself staring at the military man's head, which seemed far larger that it ought to be in proportion to his body. The imbalance was emphasized by Campbell's erect posture, which made his head appear to be bobbing like a glass float at sea.

Campbell served tea with a precise and practiced hand, first into the sniffing cups. They inhaled the aroma like two old friends, savoring it as the steam filled their noses. Then Campbell poured enough for two mouthfuls into the sipping cups. Soon murmured his pleasure as the rich, aged flavor caressed his tongue and warmed his throat.

Campbell leaned back in his chair, made a steeple with his fingers in his lap, and looked meaningfully at Soon.

"Thankee muchee tea," said Soon, using a less basic version of the coolie talk that had been so successful with Riley Yates. "This Johnny business. Know need velly good help. New peoples coming day and day. You help tell of new business me pay velly good. Many dollah."

Though he didn't move a muscle, the commander seemed to swell and his face grew alarmingly crimson.

"Let me get this straight," he said in a soft voice. "You wish me, a representative of the queen, to help procure new business for you, a Chinaman?"

"Yes, yes. I good businessman but no find new oppotunities. Kind of pahtner. You, me, my boat. You tell new business, me get wok, you get pay, all happy."

"Sooo, you are offering me a bribe to help you beat the other boatmen, British boatmen? Is that correct?"

This is not going well, thought Soon. His mind raced, but all he could think to do was nod in agreement. Campbell sat motionless, staring intently at Soon. The stare stretched on until there seemed nothing else in the world.

"I don't know who you think you are," he said finally. "But in this part of the world Chinamen don't make deals. You need to be taught some respect."

The words were still wet on his tongue as Campbell shot out of his chair like he'd been ejected from a cannon.

✳

"I grabbed the skinny little monkey and frogmarched him out the door! Imagine trying to proposition me!"

"He certainly doesn't look like much," the mystery man noted, peering into the grate.

"You should have seen the blighter's face when we dropped him down into the house of respect."

The hole was at the foot of Upper Town in the Granville township at the head of the False Creek Road, which ended at Burrard Inlet. Old coal shafts dotted the shoreline, one of them several hundred feet deep, but most were dry holes like this one, ranging from ten to fifty feet deep before the diggers gave up. The pockmarked shore was such a menace to wagons and horses that the newly elected members of the fledgling provincial legislature ordered grates made by the new foundry to cover them over until sufficient rocks could be brought in to fill them permanently.

Campbell's man, a Kanaka who looked like he could lift a horse, stripped Soon of his clothes and dropped him in the hole so quickly and efficiently he could have been unswaddling and putting to bed a newborn. Perhaps Campbell doesn't want to damage a prospective business partner, Soon thought hopefully, as the Kanaka handled him quite gently. That was before Soon was showered with the pungent, yellow stream.

He'd been down here nearly a day, Soon estimated. Several times men had walked overhead; Soon thought it wise not to draw their attention to him.

"What are you going to do with him?"

Pike! Warburton Pike. Soon finally recognized the distinctive voice of his strange acquaintance and former partner. Some fateful wind kept throwing them together. Here he was, witnessing this British pig urinating on him. Soon's humiliation kept him from addressing Pike. Besides, the two men were chatting together like friends.

"You see, Chinamen aren't made the same as us," Campbell earnestly explained, as if giving a primer on the care and feeding of Orientals. "They can live on a few grains of rice and a thimble of water for weeks. Very difficult to hurt or even kill. That's what makes them so valuable to the empire."

"I've heard that," Pike replied dryly.

"It would be interesting to see how long he lasts, don't you think?"

"Sort of a scientific experiment," Pike observed.

"Just so."

Soon's heart began interfering with his breathing.

"What did he want from you? It takes a bit of brass to pay a visit to the militia commander. Why would a Chinaman bother? How on earth would he get up the nerve?"

"They may be able to live on less rations than a cat, but when it comes to money they can sniff it out quicker 'n a cat will find a bird with a broken wing. He's a boatman and he's on about information or something. I doubt it would amount to much. But if I'm to be in this dreary little corner for a few years yet I'd better be teaching these celestials respect. Ten years with the Hong Kong constabulary taught me a thing or two about them."

"A boatman, you say," Pike said, considering. "The only Chinese boat-man I know of is a chap named Soon Chong, very reliable for a Chinese. He's been quite successful, I hear." Pike lit a match and stooped close to the grate. Soon saw Pike's grinning face, as big as the harvest moon, appear above the grate. One eye opened and closed in an exaggerated wink. It was the most wonderful thing Soon had ever seen.

"It's very dark down there," Pike ventured. "And of course all these monkeys do look alike. But I do think this is the very fellow."

"Are you certain?"

"Can't say as I am, but if it is Soon Chong, it could mean money in your pocket. And if it's not, what's the harm? You can always throw him back."

"You've got a point. I'll have my Kanaka fish him out. You won't want to be near him, he'll stink."

After roughly rubbing himself down with a piece of sheeting offered by the Kanaka, Soon pulled on his tunic and leggings. The Kanaka watched him silently, then showed him into the same room in the barracks. Pike, struggling to contain his amusement, was there as well. Soon walked stiffly forward. The tea service still sat on the rattan table but this time Campbell didn't offer him any.

"Now then, where were we?" Campbell said jovially. "Mr. Pike here vouches for you. So I'm willing to listen. But none of that cheeky Johnny coolie talk. I spotted it as phony the minute you started speaking."

"Yes, sir," agreed Soon deferentially, "with your kind permission."

"Capital! Let's get down to it then."

"I am told that all permits for new businesses are to pass through your hands?"

Soon made it all sound far more organized than it really was. With roughly a thousand natives and barely eight hundred whites living on both sides of Burrard Inlet, the community of Granville, which everyone called Gastown, after Gassy Jack Deighton's lively hotel, was still a jumble of thir-teen nationalities. There were exactly three Granville-area businesses acknowledged as such by the provincial administration in Victoria, and eleven more, like Glencannon and Soon, who simply set up and took what came their way. There were no permits, taxes, or fees—just timber, water, and fish.

"Yes, the governor has been kind enough to show such confidence in me," Campbell agreed.

Pike knew Campbell's main task was actually to make sure no one made off with the naval reserve's timber, as loggers had already stripped the best wood nearest the inlet. The single government building was inhabited by Jonathan "Indian" Miller, nominally the area's constable. Miller had been logging Khwaykhway when he was appointed. His tiny cottage beside the saloon boasted the only flower garden in the township, which garnered him teasing most nights at Gassy Jack's Bar. He built a small jail where he kept injured animals and the occasional Indian dog. He was also supposed to collect customs duties and taxes. But when informed of American or Russian ships in the harbor, he merely waved and promised the messenger he would attend to matters shortly, which he rarely did.

But now that British Columbia had become the fourth province of Canada, amenities and people were bound to follow. And Soon Chong desperately wanted a part of it. He had no intention of chugging back and forth across the inlet, over the stomach-churning Strait of Georgia and up the Fraser River for the rest of his life.

"Your experience and personal force have made a considerable impression on me," Soon said carefully, wondering what might have been in store if Pike hadn't come along. "I need guidance on how to conduct my business. I am Chinese, and many matters in the English world confuse me. I humbly ask for your assistance. I will pay well for information and introductions."

✳

"I have not seen you for many years," Soon said to Pike outside the barracks an hour later.

Pike drew hard on his pipe.

"I built a cabin up Indian Arm. There are the most marvelous clam beds there. And the hunting!"

"That is good," Soon replied, wondering why on earth a man who could choose to live anywhere would isolate himself in the forest.

"Itsu and I had two boys, you know," he said. "The oldest would be eight now."

Pike's face darkened quickly, the pain in his eyes was naked. Soon looked away while he composed himself.

Suddenly Pike thumped him on the back.

"I almost forgot!" he said brightly as if the subject of the children had never been raised. "You dropped this when Campbell relieved you of your clothes."

He handed over the figurine's tunic, now fairly shredded but with the pale-green beads still attached with silk thread. Once again, Soon wanted to snatch it back. The jade stones seemed so private to him. He willed himself to reach his hand out slowly.

"Thank you," he said.

"I swear I've seen beads like these somewhere before. You didn't buy them around here, did you?"

"No."

"Hmmm. Well, I do know I've seen them."

"Thank you," Soon said, stuffing the beads inside his shirt.

"Don't mention it." Pike turned and waved gaily. "Time to make that scoundrel Gassy Jack uncork the scotch he saves for himself."

Pike's feet thumped against the board sidewalk as he walked away, leaving Soon staring after him. Sometimes I wish I had his approach to life, Soon reflected, stretching his neck and shoulders stiff from his cold confinement.

41

*

1893

City of Vancouver,

British Columbia

Soon filled his lungs with the rich sea air laced with the ever-present scent of wood-slash piles. Since 1886, when the city of Vancouver came into being, the fires had been burning nonstop. Not even the terrible blaze of that year, which destroyed every building but four in the original Granville townsite, had stopped the slash burning as the timber was pushed back mile upon mile to accommodate the growing population. From ninety-six buildings at the beginning of 1885 the city had grown to occupy nearly thirteen hundred. The Canadian Pacific Railway had proven to be the canniest land speculator in the Western world. Variously it had announced the terminus of the transcontinental line to be in New Westminster, Port Moody, and the southern shore of English Bay, where young Gitsula's winter village once stood. The line to that point had been used once, just long enough for the CPR, the province, and early landowners to make a fortune selling to those who wanted to be near the terminus. No sooner was most of the land sold than the CPR changed its mind and, with the province's blessing, relocated the end of the road to the heart of the small Granville settlement.

To add a little spice to the transaction, two CPR directors, Donald Smith and Richard Angus, also happened to own the land where the CPR finally came to a halt. In return for selling this land to the railroad they were rewarded with almost six thousand acres just south of the city's 1886 boundary and nearly five hundred acres in what would become Vancouver's downtown core.

Soon sniffed again, inhaling that uniquely Vancouver smell of damp, salt, cedar, and smoke. The land dance in Vancouver was just like the cup of chance on a Fan Tan table. The eager and greedy could always be counted on to keep flinging money in the hope the number they chose would be what was left of the token when the dealer counted down. Soon could still recall the Pearl River stench of bodies and rotting food that permeated the dock lands. The hunger for fortune was no different 6,700 miles across the Pacific, but in Vancouver, if one speculative sally didn't work, another would be right around the corner. In Guangzhou an opportunity came rarely, and even more rarely did one come twice in a lifetime.

Saltwater City, the 2,764 Chinese inhabitants called it. Home. Soon allowed the word to lodge in his mind. He still hated the endless cold rains of winter when the air was so moist fish could swim in it. Soon chuckled. An old joke. But hardly a week went by that wasn't relieved by a few hours of glorious, clear sunshine, which chased away the fog and rain. When that happened, the spirits of the small city of 18,000 rose on wings.

Soon squinted north to the Lions, two hunching bulks of rock that crowned the North Shore skyline. The whites called them the Lions, but Soon thought of them as dragons. As long as he could see them his luck would hold.

"What are you going to do with your share?" Soon finally asked of the man leaning idly against a hitching rail and smoking.

"Why do you keep pestering me about that?" Pike responded a little peevishly. "I told you to hang on to it."

Soon snorted. "I can't just hang on to $250,000."

"Why not?" Pike asked innocently.

"Money has to be working. If it is not working it disappears," Soon stated as if it were a self-evident, universal truth.

"You sound like my dear, departed father. All he cared about was putting money to work, as if paper and coin were oxen."

"Still, you must decide," Soon said, unimpressed by the imagery.

"Well, put it to work then. I'm sure you've got a yoke or two on hand."

Glencannon's boat grew into G & S Freight with seven small, highly maneuverable steamships and a dozen barges. Glencannon's eldest son, Hamish, only twenty but with more of a mercantile bent than his father, signed up over a third of the new industries in the booming city. They even snagged the government mail contract. Unfortunately, Glencannon was already six years in the grave. To his surprise, Soon found he missed the garrulous Scot; all those zeroes would have kept him grinning and drinking into the next century.

But it was Pike, by the sheerest accident, who pushed the whole enterprise beyond anything Soon had dreamed of. He never stopped searching for his sons and he had paid staggering amounts of money for clues about Itsu's whereabouts. Soon would see him three or four times a year when he was alternately wildly optimistic or suicidally hopeless. On one occasion, in 1888, he had spent three months in the deep forests beyond Yale on the Fraser River. Discouraged, half starved, and utterly dejected, he stepped in front of a CPR train. To everyone's amazement the train was able to stop in time. On board was President William Van Horne, the legendary American who had driven the railway across the country, some said by force of his own will alone.

"Are you mad! Completely mad! How dare you stop a Canadian Pacific Railway train," he bellowed out of his thick, gray beard.

Not a word about Pike's near death, only a tirade about interfering with the schedule of the CPR. This struck Pike as hugely funny.

Over dinner the heavyset, bombastic railway president and the emaciated adventurer talked, drank, and ate well into the early hours of the morning. When Van Horne mentioned that he planned to buy a shipyard to build a fleet of four fast steamers for the mail run between Vancouver, Victoria, Seattle, and San Francisco, Pike mentioned in return that he owned a small part in G & S Freight.

Ideas and opportunities came to Pike like that, as butterflies on a strong wind. The previous summer Pike had taken the commander of the British Pacific naval fleet fishing for giant sturgeon in the Fraser. When the man became violently ill from eating fish liver, Pike dragged him all the way back along the rutted Victoria Road to the Gladstone Inn east of the city. While settling his stomach with French brandy, the commander bemoaned the long wait in the busy Vancouver harbor for fresh water and provisions to be delivered to his ships. Pike told Soon, who promptly sent Hamish Glencannon to the still-recovering commander with the guarantee of cheap water delivered quickly.

Then, on a hunting expedition with Vancouver's first and wealthiest industrialist, David Oppenheimer, Pike learned that the City of Vancouver was having trouble getting enough gravel to seat the roads, which were swarming out from the city. His chief engineer was planning to bring it overland from the interior at a tremendous cost.

"Wouldn't it be cheaper to bring it by sea?" Pike asked.

"From where? There's no gravel beds to be found along the coast. Too many bloody boulders and the grade's poor to boot. Too much granite, not enough lime."

"What about the scree gravel near the limestone shelves on the north end of Vancouver Island?"

"What limestone shelves?"

And so it went. Ideas and opportunities plucked out of the air. All Soon had to do was listen and reap.

A young boy of ten brought steaming bowls of *congee.*

"You are velly slow," scolded Pike. "Chop! Chop! I velly velly hungly. Wait too long."

The boy giggled and ducked out of reach as Pike lunged for him. Joe, the youngest of Soon's four boys and two girls. By 1880 Soon had brought a wife, his brothers, and even his sister to the city. The Chongs were now the largest Chinese family in Vancouver. The sight of Joe, whom Pike adored, ate at him like a hot coal in his guts. He envied the family with a ferocity that startled, even frightened, Soon.

"I would like to give you your money," Soon was saying.

"I don't want it or need it."

"Nonetheless, the sale of G & S Freight provides an excellent opportunity to settle our accounts."

"Keep it for now," Pike waved his hand. "There is always time."

Soon sighed. Pike was as stubborn as a mule. Once he'd made up his mind, Soon had never been able to change it, not even a little. The problem was simple. His partner had never taken a penny of profit from their business since he'd sold all but a quarter share of the steamboat twenty-eight years earlier.

In the ensuing years, Pike's share had so intermingled with Soon's growing empire that it pained him to think about how much it might be worth. To complicate matters, the infernal man actually trusted Soon to do what was right. As well, Pike had no way of knowing the $250,000 from the sale of the freight line represented only the tip of Soon's operations.

Pike, of course, knew of the three laundries, four restaurants, and two gaming clubs and opium dens owned by Soon. What Pike wasn't aware of was the processing factory in the heart of Vancouver's growing Chinatown turning out a staggering profit. Though banned now in the United States, opium was legal everywhere in the empire. Soon bought opium base in Guangdong, processed it into powder, then sent it via coolie train to Port Townsend in Washington State, where it was hidden in flour sacks and sent by rail to San Francisco, Los Angeles, and the hungry eastern cities. Initially there were more than a dozen independent factories competing against each other, cutting into profits. Using his police contacts to good advantage, Soon consolidated the business. He now owned the largest factory in Chinatown.

Then there was the counterfeiting. That had been the inspiration of Wan Lo, Soon's oldest son, when a crate of whiskey Soon bought for his clubs arrived with no labels.

"How could such a thing happen?" Soon worried that something else was in the bottles besides whiskey. Wan Lo gave some to one of the bums on the city wharf to no ill effect. But customers expected to see labels.

"You fuss too much," chided Wan Lo. "It is a simple matter to fix."

Now Soon paid half a penny for six empties, so every houseboy in Vancouver brought sacks of them to Chinatown. In a puddle-filled basement of a warehouse, also purchased with Pike's money and not far from where Soon had been entombed in a pit by Douglas Campbell, an assembly line of workers, directed by a calligrapher brought in from Hong Kong, replaced the old labels with duplicates of expensive British, Scottish, and Irish brands. The bottles were then filled with a concoction Soon had learned about from a man who'd been a gold-camp laborer. One quarter real whiskey, one quarter spring water, one quarter waste water from Wah Chong's laundry, and the rest a mix of powerful medicinal alcohol that could blind a man if drunk straight.

After forging whiskey labels it seemed natural to keep his artists busy by looking for other things to duplicate, postage stamps for example. The stamps were meticulously steamed off the envelopes, then the cancellation mark washed off. It took many tries before his workers got it right. At first glance, the bogus postage stamps seemed a small-margin business. But there were twenty thousand Chinese spread over the province, and most of them sent money home to China at least once a month. The stamps were sold locally, through the Chinese hardware stores operated by his brother-in-law. It was a reliable business, generating guaranteed profits, and now that white stores had started buying the discounted stamps, Soon was considering exporting them to other cities.

Head-tax documents were a higher-margin business. Real documents cost $50. Soon also sold his for $50, the difference being that he was willing to take the money out in labor. Soon thought the head tax repugnant but, if someone was going to collect it, it might as well be him. About half of all the Chinese who ended up in British Columbia had phony head-tax documents provided by Soon's artists.

From the beginning Soon bought land. He purchased the first parcel at Vancouver's inaugural land auction, close to the final terminus site of the CPR. That proximity play was sheer, blind luck. Soon ended up with seven of those forty lots, ranging in price from $350 to $1,450. He had seven different front men bid on them, and supplied the documents and money for them to take possession of the deeds, which were promptly made over to Samuel Pilar, Esq.

It was easy for Soon to mask his dealings, because the registry office was in chaos, and in any event officials couldn't tell one Chinese from another. The original owners of one piece of property, for instance, were listed as Chang Foon Hung, Chin Fong Hong, and Sou Hong Ho. These names were crossed out on the ledger and replaced by Chin Foon Hong, Chin Hung, and So Kon Ho. After several more increasingly vehement crossing-outs, the final entry read simply "owned by three Chinamen." Occasionally the owners were listed only as Chinaman Number 1 or Chinaman Number 2.

The first births in the Chinese community also caused problems. The four boys of the Chow family all ended up with different surnames because their father used a different interpreter for each birth registration. John had the best interpreter, so he ended up with Chow. Ed became Ed Joe, Bill became Bill Chew, and Tom became Tom Shoe.

Soon smiled indulgently as Pike whirled the screaming Joe over his head at arm's length. How does he do it? How does he remain so much the boy? Soon often wondered. Without question, Soon was doing very well. No one had the slightest inkling that he was by far the richest man in Vancouver, even though recently he had started quietly loaning money to a number of white merchants and industrialists, all at arm's length, of course. But his position in the Chinese community was well known among the Chinese. It was only natural that his power should eventually attract certain elements.

In early 1880 a splendidly attired and well-mannered Chinese gentleman, Chaing Yun Hak from Hong Kong, paid Soon a visit. It had been arranged by intermediaries. Chaing had been born into the Green Tong, China's dominant organized crime organization and deeply rooted on the docks. The Green Tong, later called the Green Triad, would one day boast Chiang Kai-shek as its most illustrious member.

"I have been expecting you," Soon said.

"Me?" Chaing asked surprised.

"One like you," Soon explained. "One who is not a thug."

"Just so," Chaing inclined his head. "My father wishes me to pay all respects to the honorable Mr. Soon. He is very admiring of what you have accomplished here."

"I am certain that you are too important and too busy to come all this way to pass on your father's compliments," Soon said carefully, "pleasant as they are to hear."

"We would like to help you."

"I do not require any help."

"You will. I can guarantee it."

It was a deal with an expected enemy, a deal Soon realized he would have to make some day. He had no powerful connections in China, no one to persuade the Tong to leave him alone. The deal was quite simple and more advantageous than Soon had hoped for. The Tong would control emigration from Shanghai and Hong Kong. In return for continuing to supply the head-tax documents, Soon would pay an annual fee. He also agreed to purchase all his opium base directly from the Tong as well as whiskey, most of which was stolen from British ships. In return, the Tong would protect Soon from "undesirable elements" and "open other doors to good fortune."

Before Chaing left, he produced a small metal stamp. On it was the sign of the Foo Dog. Soon remembered it decorating the tunics of the dock boss's enforcers. Chaing took a miniature brass brazier from his valise and asked Soon for a glowing coal. He set the stamp on the brazier until it glowed hot.

At the time, Soon was fifty-eight years old. Though his face was remarkably unlined, his body felt pain, he was sure, far more easily than it should even for an old man. He watched the stamp and knew what was coming. His breath grew short and he desperately tried to think of ways to avoid the branding that would mark him as a member the Tong society. But he could not. When the skin on his forearm smoked sickeningly, his knees buckled and vomit flooded his throat. It was over in less than ten seconds, but the pain stayed with him for days.

As it turned out, a more painful intrusion was yet to come. Pei-ying, Chaing's eighteen-year old daughter, "the delightful glue of our arrangement," Chaing told him happily. Alas, Pei-ying was shrill and unattractive, though reasonably willing in bed. Over the next ten years she provided eight children for Soon. One died at birth and the last, a disfigured girl, was quickly drowned.

"What would I do with that much money anyway?" Pike said with a laugh.

"You could always buy more guns to shoot Germans."

Pike smirked. "You heard about that, did you?"

"It isn't every day that a British gentleman is arrested for firing on guests of the queen who are hunting legally."

"That's just it! They weren't hunting legally, they were on Indian land. They took twenty-seven grizzlies and were aiming for more."

That had been Pike's latest escapade when he returned for the eighth time to the ancient lands of the mysterious Tsleil'waututh who lived on the cloud-shrouded shores of Indian Arm, the extension of Burrard Inlet. Pike believed that was where Itsu had gone. The hunters were camped on the edge of the reserve, and Pike had heard them blasting away like cannons shelling an enemy stronghold. He returned the fire. When the hunters decamped—hastily—to Vancouver with tales of bloodthirsty attacks, which made all the newspapers, Pike could not resist correcting the story. He was arrested for a day but released when he claimed to have been acting in self-defense.

Pike grunted as Joe landed a solid fist in his stomach.

"Stop it!" scolded Soon in Cantonese. "If a policeman comes you'll be arrested for hitting a white man."

"You can't hurt Wobble Pike," proclaimed the child in English. "He is un, un, unvincestable."

Soon shooed the boy away.

"What's troubling you?" Pike asked, forgetting the bothersome issue of the money. Soon, always serious, had a hard line of worry creasing his forehead.

"A man with children, two wives, and a modest home has no troubles."

"Two wives!"

"Yes, of course." Soon tucked his hands into the arms of his robes. Poor circulation in his hands, thanks to the boots of the Red Bandannas those many years ago, made his fingers numb and cold all the time.

"Where is the second?"

"In Guangzhou."

Pike was nonplussed. He had known Soon for twenty-eight years and had never heard a word about another wife.

"How did you marry her?"

"She was a letter bride. My brother arranged it."

"You married a woman just by sending a letter?"

Soon said nothing.

"Will you bring her here?"

"No, never. Her family manages my business affairs in China. It is really just a business arrangement."

"But you always told me you wouldn't return to China."

"Just so. But a man who does not understand the rabbit will one day get stuck. Two holes from the den are preferable to one."

Soon appeared to make up his mind about something.

"Come, I will show you what occupies my mind."

Pike ambled beside Soon on the walk east along Carrall Street and into Shanghai Alley. There Chinatown spilled out in shanties and unpainted clapboard buildings. One brick building, with the recessed balconies and wrought iron typical of southern China, was constructed in a large square, with an open courtyard at its center. Away from the eyes of the street, gardens were grown, children played, and private meetings were held. Soon's wife, Pei-ying, whom he discouraged from walking in the street, took her daily air in the courtyard.

"The less the whites see of us the better," Soon instructed firmly.

Soon led him through a labyrinth of tiny rooms extending far back from the street, up to the second level, into the six-foot-high cheater floor where Pike had to bend over to avoid hitting his head, up through the next two stories, and finally out to a tiny balcony overlooking the courtyard. Pike lost count of the rooms, let alone the narrow beds he spotted through half-opened curtains.

What appeared to be three different buildings from the outside was actually one, with a single inner-perimeter wall. From above Pike could see the courtyard had four alleyways leading into it. An individual unfamiliar with the setup was faced with a myriad of wooden doors, iron gates, and passageways, making it impossible to even enter the compound without a guide.

Pike noticed that several rooms and corridors had doors to the outside. Soon caught him looking at one with a puzzled expression. He walked over and opened the door, stepping around two women who didn't look up from their fine handwork on tailored shirts. The door opened to a shaft between two walls and a narrow ladder that led to the ground floor. One room on the second floor featured joined closets with a concealed push door, which allowed secret passage from room to room without entering the main corridor. In the attic a heavily barred window could be swung outward allowing easy access to an escape route over the roof.

At each revelation Pike clapped his hands in appreciation of its cleverness and peppered Soon with questions.

"Where does that lead to?" he asked like a delighted schoolboy allowed to play in a maze.

Soon walked back to the main room of the floor they were on. He pointed out the window.

"See that?"

Pike noted a large grate below.

"It took ten men three months to tunnel to the old G & S warehouse. There is a false floor, and we can get a hundred people in there hidden in less than thirty minutes." Pike wondered just what else might be secreted in the subterranean depths.

By the time they reached the balcony over the courtyard, Pike had run out of superlatives. He fell silent, wondering about the fear that drove his friend to such elaborate measures.

"This is my problem." Soon handed Pike a City of Vancouver Declaration.

"A cubic-air bylaw?" Pike said, reading the document. "What nonsense is this?"

"Every occupant must have at least 384 cubic feet of space as well as an opening window," Soon said.

Pike hadn't seen a single window, opening or otherwise, in any of the rooms, some of which held as many as twelve narrow bunks.

"That means eight feet by eight feet and six feet high for every single person. More than half the Chinese population will be out on the street if it is enforced."

"And I bet there's a bylaw forbidding sleeping on the street," hazarded Pike.

Soon nodded. "Already several houses here have been searched, as well as two warehouses near the city wharf. The police have taken thirty-seven people, including children, to jail because they couldn't pay the fine. The fine is not just per family, it is per person."

Pike watched Joe hit a tin can in the courtyard with a bamboo paddle. Ting. Ting. Ting. He struck it rhythmically, his pigtail bouncing up and down his back as he ran.

"Sometimes, in order to solve a problem, you need to turn it on its head," Pike said with a happy grin. "I think I see a way you can fix this up."

The next night the Chinese Consolidated Benevolent Association passed a resolution calling for all Chinese who were charged under the Cubic Air Bylaw to choose a one-day jail term instead of paying a fine, even if they could afford it. Any who refused would find their names posted on a shunning board. But those who dutifully spent their time in jail would be paid $15 by the Benevolent Association once they were released.

Overnight the jails filled with Chinese. For a time the three-member police force stubbornly kept arresting violators, and within a week had used up an entire year's food budget as the law required them to feed the prisoners, even Chinese, three meals a day. Pike charged off to New Westminster, where he knew he'd find Israel Fink, a Jewish lawyer with an unusual shock of orangey hair and a temper to match. Fink got by on bits of business other lawyers didn't want. "Putting it up the back end of the Vancouver snoots and anti-Semites" would give him no end of pleasure.

With Fink's help, the Benevolent Association filed suit against the police for violating the Cubic Air Bylaw by housing more than one Chinese per 384 cubic feet, almost exactly the size of a jail cell. That was the end of the Cubic Air Bylaw in Vancouver.

42

*

1895

Chinatown, Vancouver

"Clean the ashes, you lazy monkey!" Pei-ying harangued her thirteen-year-old houseboy in Chinese. "The stove is filthy and will not light properly. I tell you every day. I tell you to do it better! Why do you wait for me to tell you again?"

Pei-ying addressed Nellie Chu over the games table. "I pay his passage," she shook her domino tile for emphasis. "I pay his father in China and I promise to bring two brothers here. I feed him rice every day," she raised her voice slightly, "and he eats enough for two people! All I ask in return is five years of easy work."

"You are too generous," murmured Nellie.

"Every day he wakes me from my sleep with the noise he makes raking ashes. So I tell him to clean the stove after I am awake. But he forgets! Every day he forgets!"

Nellie Chu shook her head in sympathy. "Houseboys are all lazy." She drew her lips together so they almost touched her nose. "I have had three since I came to Vancouver and they are all trouble. Sometimes I think it is better to do the work myself."

She placed a tile neatly blocking a series of moves by Pei-ying, who scowled, suspecting Nellie adjusted the positioning of the tiles while she was distracted by the houseboy. "Truly, they are not good for much."

"Unless you are a white woman." Pei-ying dropped her voice.

Nellie's hooded eyes rounded, her eyelashes disappearing beneath the heavy creases. "What do you mean?"

Coquettishness sat poorly on Pei-ying's features; the knowing smile unfolded more like a snarl. She shrugged elaborately as if the words had been accidental. "It is nothing."

"Pei-ying! You tell." The foibles of white women were a favored topic for gossip. And they had plenty of grist, because nearly every white woman in Vancouver had Chinese servant boys.

The houseboy strained to listen.

"The Golden Rule women," giggled Pei-ying, referring to a recently formed group of society ladies with a mission to encourage citizens of the young city to honor the Golden Rule in all areas of work, law, and government.

"Do unto others as you would have them do unto you," chanted Nellie, mimicking the words of Fong Dickman, a young Chinese man recently converted to the Methodist faith, who preached at the end of Shanghai Alley every night accompanied by another young man playing a small, portable organ.

"Golden Rule women listen very carefully to those words and apply them to their houseboys—*in their bathtubs!*"

"Washee backee litter boy!" sang out Nellie in English.

"Not only backs," hissed Pei-ying, glaring at the houseboy who looked in their direction. "But fronts and," she stuck her head out, her words barely audible, "*their flower places too!*"

Nellie let out a delicious gasp of shock.

"Get about your work!" Pei-ying shrieked at the houseboy. "How dare you listen to your betters?"

Pei-ying's voice easily penetrated the reinforced wall separating the women from the receiving room of Soon's opium company. Though less than 150 square feet, it was opulently furnished and hung with beautifully lettered, bright-red banners like those he recalled from the streets of his childhood. The room held three carved chairs for customers, each with the symbol of the lion embossed on the seats. At one end a tall, tin-plated chest with dozens of small drawers held opium powder and expensive vials of tincture that was much more difficult to make and lethal to take in large doses. There were no windows, but the glow from four gas lanterns was sufficient to read by. Soon was reviewing his accounts.

Since the railroad had arrived in Vancouver nearly a decade earlier, opium had become ever more popular and he was considering building another factory to process it. There were two other opium manufacturers in Chinatown, but one of them mainly supplied the white population, something Soon avoided. The other sold poorly processed euphoric to the clearing gangs employed to dynamite trees for the rapidly expanding city. It was dreadful stuff that robbed the men of their senses far more quickly than the unpredictable dynamite robbed them of fingers and sometimes eyes.

Soon ran figures through his head. The problem was supply. He didn't want to build another factory only to let it sit idle if he couldn't bring enough raw opium to Vancouver. He felt sure the answer lay in India, where opium production was increasing. But he had no connections in India.

The knock and slap against the hidden outer door jarred Soon out of his contemplation. It was unusual to be disturbed this early in the day. The rap followed by a palm smacked against the door signaled a family member. Before Soon could call out permission to enter, Joe burst into the room. The boy was sobbing wildly, his words lost in small screams and groans.

"Pappee!" he keened. "Wobble dead! Torn up so very bad."

"Calm yourself. Are you hurt?"

"Not me! Wobble. Dead! Oh Pappee he is dead!"

Soon jumped up. "Quick, show me."

"I can't," Joe hiccuped. "It is too bad. Too terrible!"

"You must. Stop crying now and show me!"

Joe ran out of the room with Soon trotting close behind.

Between the city wharf and the Hastings sawmill, city council allowed the Chinatown merchants to construct a pier of their own. Shabby but functional, it jutted into Burrard Inlet in a long U. The whites laughed at the strange shape but swallowed their derision when they saw how many small fishing boats could tie up on the inside while still leaving the outer edge free for the bigger boats. On the garbage-strewn beach Soon spotted a distinctive Indian canoe. Four Indian men, dressed in an odd assortment of bowler hats, berets, ties, and native leggings, were standing in front of the canoe, shielding whatever was in it from the curious stares of the people on shore.

Soon peered into the boat. Mangled fingers, swollen lips, pieces of broken teeth on the ground flashed at him. He felt the blood, smelled his own vomit, heard the crunches as the Red Bandannas' boots crushed his bones so long ago. Drawing his hands to his stomach, Soon tried hard to not cry out at the sight of Warburton Pike.

"He said to come to you, only you," one of the Indians uttered in Chinook, the pidgin language used by virtually every nationality working the waterfront and waterways.

"He is dead?"

"Almost. Breath still comes."

Bubbles of blood and mucus on Pike's mouth and nose expanded and contracted infinitesimally. Soon turned to his son. "He needs medicine quickly. Find Wo Ping and bring him to the smoking den. Tell him there is much blood. If you cannot find him, go to Miss Agnes at the school. Tell her we need a doctor. Quick! Run!"

✳

It took Puller Leach nearly six hours to piece Pike's body back together. He was Soon's last resort; Wo Ping was visiting family in Victoria, and not even the school teacher, Miss Agnes, could persuade two of the city's three doctors to venture into Chinatown. The third couldn't be found. Leach was a dentist who supplemented his income stitching up horses torn by falls or wire, and cows with prolapsed uteruses after delivery. His shirt was dark with sweat when he finished.

"Jesus and Joseph, Mr. Chong! I haven't shoved so much back in a body since Henry Mutrie's dog got gored."

"What happened to the dog?" Soon asked dully. He was as exhausted as if he had done the doctoring himself.

"Oh he died damn quick. Good thing I got paid first," he added pointedly. Soon reached into his sleeve and retrieved some notes from a purse he kept tied to his forearm.

"You will come back if I need you?"

The dentist looked down at Pike who was breathing shallowly.

"I doubt that'll be necessary. Pike's a tough one but he's done it this time. I tol' and tol' him to quit messing with those Indians. They're all ratted up these days about the Kanakas blasting fish with dynamite. Bad voodoo or something. White is white when the red men are pissing up the pole. One scalp's as good as another, I guess." He leaned over his patient. "Funny. They left his hair alone."

✳

When Pike woke up five days later, the first thing he noticed was the sweet smell of rot in the air—the skin on his leg, curled back on itself where the stitching didn't take, was now festering. He also smelled cloves from Wo Ping's various ministrations. It reminded him of Christmas, he thought, before a suffocating gloom overcame him.

Soon entered the dim little room just off the smoking den and lit a lantern. Pike was breathing more deeply. He saw the tracks of tears down Pike's face. He cried every day and, Soon was sure, not from his wounds.

Pike ate nothing and drank little. He seemed to be caving in on himself like a piece of fruit drying in the hot sun.

Soon took no intoxicants except his beloved tea. He'd never sampled the opium that was making him rich, nor even the whiskey he cut many times. Pike adored his cigars and cigarettes almost as much as he did French brandy and blood-red wine, which puckered the tongue it was so dry and heavy with tannin. But as far as Soon was aware he had never chased the dragon. The man was so wretched, maybe heaven smoke would bring him out of his misery.

The sun was just glazing the water of the inlet as Soon picked his way over the bodies of men who still lay where they had chased the dragon the night before. Opium ghosts. They would rise shortly and stumble out into the streets for sweet pancakes, rice, and *congee* from street sellers before heading to the sawmills, laundries, smelters, and canneries where they worked. Vegetable farmers would appear shortly, baskets strung from poles across their shoulders, to supply peddlers who sold on the streets and door to door.

Soon went into his receiving room to get a pipe. He carefully scraped all the soot from the bowl onto a piece of paper. In the kitchen he found mashed potatoes from the night before. Dry and hard, they were the perfect consistency. He mixed some with the pipe cleanings and rolled them into thumbnail-sized pills. When he returned to Pike, his friend's eyes were open, tears rolling down from the corners into his ears. Soon spread Pike's lips with his finger and forced the opium into his mouth. Then he squeezed a cloth dipped into cold tea onto Pike's lips until finally he licked the liquid and swallowed the potato. Satisfied, Soon carefully trimmed the wick on an opium lamp, lit it, and began heating the grayish substance until it bubbled. He spooned some out and placed it on the pipe, which he held to Pike's lips. Pike pushed at the pipe with his tongue but Soon held it there until Pike drew on the stem, shallowly at first then steadily.

✳

"You would like Itsu, Mother," Pike said softly, the movement of his lips cracking the blood on his cheek.

"Tell me about her," Soon replied.

"She is not fat, not thin, just right. Like the fairy tale," he laughed. "You remember?"

"I do," Soon said.

"She is like a princess. You know she wasn't red at all!" Pike giggled. "Not a bit. She wasn't brown either. Very dark, almost black. I never told her this because she might be angry but she looked a little like a Negro person."

"Where is she now?" Soon prompted, happy at the first sign of life in Pike. But he quickly regretted his words, as Pike's face contorted with pain.

"Lost. So lost," Pike wailed. "Why did she get lost, Mother?"

"I do not know," Soon said softly.

"It's her people. Silly people, they got themselves lost too."

"Who are her people?" asked Soon. He remembered what Pike had told him years ago about an ancient tribe who once were spread out over Kitsilano, downtown Vancouver, English Bay, and into Stanley Park. That had been the whole reason for Pike's mad chase throughout the interior of the province looking for stolen children, in particular looking for one child. Itsu seemed to think he was some kind of messiah. It was ridiculous; Soon said so at the time. Itsu's people were decimated as were most of the Indians around Vancouver. No messiah would bring them back. But that didn't stop Pike looking, as if he was some kind of knight common in English fables.

"The Kahnamut!" shouted Pike. "Itsu was Kahnamut. They owned Stanley Park. Now the child is gone, green stones gone too, Itsu gone. My sons gone."

Soon had heard many stories about Itsu's people from Pike during his periodic forays into Vancouver. He knew she'd left to bear Pike's children, two boys, among a related tribe. He also knew that Pike had never seen his children, nor had he laid eyes on Itsu in a quarter of a century. Soon didn't understand Pike's anguish. Half-breed children were worthless and a hindrance, unless you were a farmer and needed the labor.

Soon had not seen Pike since his old partner had neatly solved the cubic-air problem. He had taken up photographing and spent months with a strange young Austrian by the name of Franz Boas, cataloging moldering Indian villages all along the coast.

"Tell me about the stones," Soon urged, concerned that Pike had fallen silent for so long.

"The old chief had them," Pike responded slowly, his tongue thickening as the smoke found his brain. "Safekeeping. Itsu said he would bury them like treasure until we found the keeper. But we never found him, Mother! I couldn't find him, and the stones are gone forever."

"Where did he bury the stones?" Soon asked.

"In Stanley Park," muttered Pike, angry now.

Pike had been furious again when Stanley Park was created in 1888. A year earlier he had put together a consortium to purchase the island from the Canadian government and lease it back to the city. When that failed, he tried to get permission to sink coal shafts, as many still believed the island sat on a rich carbon vein. That made good sense to Soon at the time. Now Soon wondered if Pike's scheme had really been about finding the mythical stones. For a few minutes Soon considered retrieving the tunic and showing it to Pike. It was a rare fanciful moment for Soon. What did a handful of old jade beads mean anyway? Even if his were similar to these ones spoken of by Pike. What did it matter?

Soon offered the pipe again and Pike sucked greedily on it.

"We found lost children!" Pike said loudly, driving the thought of the stones from Soon's mind. "Lots of them! Stolen. Poor things. All trussed up like mules and hauling skids. They buggered them too!" he shouted, half sitting up. "I only saw Itsu cry once. We found a boy hauling gravel to a sluice. Miner had him tied up so all he could do was walk to the sluice and back, pulling a cart. He was sick. Poor thing. A little boy. All bleeding from his backside, with the flies all over."

Pike fell silent.

"What did you do?"

"Killed him, of course."

"The boy?"

"No, the miner. But," Pike sighed again, "the boy died anyway. We took him back to his people and they were mad. The men were going to war but Itsu talked them out of it. You would like her, Mother."

"Does killing this man trouble you?" Soon asked.

"I had a rattler crawl in my shakedown once in Texas," Pike answered. "I killed him because he scared me. I felt bad. He was just looking for a warm place, that's all. I have the skin still. Where's my hat?" Pike flailed around.

"Here it is," Soon took his own cap off and handed it to Pike.

"See? Here's the skin and the rattle. Still fine after all these years," Pike traced his finger around the cap. "I felt sorry for killing the snake. I liked killing the miner."

Soon refilled the pipe.

"I had to kill a horse once. Didn't like it. I liked killing the miner."

"We found nineteen children," Pike spoke again. "Four died. Eyes like diseased dogs. Crazy look."

Pike's voice grew fainter and his words more jumbled as the sweet smoke took hold.

"She took the children. Stole them all. Ran away."

Soon was confused. "Itsu stole children?"

"Yes, I tell you!" Pike shouted. "My children. I have two sons! My sons."

Soon was sure that Itsu was dead. The sons also. Indians, Soon believed, would not survive on this coast much longer and few lived past the age of forty. Itsu would be nearly sixty, he estimated, if she was still alive. The Indians couldn't adapt, not like the Chinese. They were becoming a nuisance in the city, drunken bundles sleeping in doorways in Chinatown. Bad for business.

As it sometimes does, the opium fog lifted and Pike sat fully upright, his voice now clear and his words lucid.

"I wish you would talk to her, Mother."

"What would I tell her?"

"'My children will live in the Indian world,' that's what she said. She went up Indian Arm and far beyond the reserves into Lillooet Territory. Tell her to come back."

"You went looking for them and you were attacked?" Soon prompted.

"Canoe. Lost. Busted. No food. So tired."

"The Indians attacked you?"

"Wolves. Pretty wolves. Big teeth. I ran and ran. They caught me and I fought them. Got away too! Then I fall down and down and down. Do you know?" Pike said, his voice again oddly clear. "I thought I was in heaven. But I'm home now, Mother. I'll find the boys another day."

Pike held out his hand for the pipe, filling his lungs with the wondrous smoke.

Soon watched the man he thought of as invincible lying there weak and broken. He felt unaccustomed tears prick his eyes. He thought Pike the oddest person he'd ever met, infuriating, outrageous, and rude—but never weak, never defeated.

"I will sleep now, Mother. The bird is coming to sing to me."

Pike closed his eyes, smiling happily as a large black bird swooped into view.

✳

"Where will you go now?" asked Soon a week later. Pike had regained a measure of his zest, and though he still limped badly from the terrible bite on his leg, he was getting more active and vigorous by the day.

"I may go to Germany for a bit," said Pike, stretching and scratching at his gray hair and newly shaved face. "I have family there I haven't seen since I crossed the ocean. Alfred is ill now, and I would love to see him once again. My mother and father are gone, and he is the closest family I have now."

No mention of Itsu or his sons. Good.

"Family is important," agreed Soon, though privately he considered them his major source of aggravation, particularly his wife.

Pike looked up and down Hastings Street and over to Burrard Inlet. "Who would have thought that the little mud hole we landed in all those years ago would become a thriving city?"

"I thought so."

"You would," Pike chuckled. "I somehow believed it would remain always as it was."

"I wouldn't have stayed if it had," answered Soon.

"And I kept wanting to leave because it kept growing. All the marvelous things it was are no longer."

"Will you be back?"

"I expect so, but who knows?"

With Pike, no truer words were ever spoken. He turned to the only man he could really call his friend. "You are older than me, but I expect you will live to see the century mark, long after I am dead and gone."

"Not with the demands my wife and children place on me," retorted Soon.

"I would ask a favor of you," Pike said gravely.

Soon stiffened. Pike wanted his quarter-share of the business. Damn his soul! Soon had dreaded this day for almost thirty years. Sometimes he calculated what the quarter-share was really worth, then debated with himself how much or, more correctly, how little he could get away with giving Pike.

"Itsu and the boys are lost to me. I see that now. And I'm starting to see it is for the best. Itsu understood right away. No Indian, no matter how strong, can flourish in our two cultures right now. Hopefully in time." Pike cleared his throat.

"I find myself with a rather large fortune." Soon relaxed. "While under your care, I came to a decision about what to do with it." He handed over a folded sheet of paper, densely covered with longhand. "This is my will."

"I do not wish such a responsibility," Soon demurred.

"Perhaps you should read it first."

Soon took the paper as if it would burn his fingers. It was headed "Last Will and Testament," naming Soon Chong as executor. He read it through carefully twice, then he shook his head. This was much worse than having to hand over money.

"Now I'm absolutely sure I do not want the responsibility."

"I am asking a favor in light of our long friendship," Pike said, staring him in the eye. "As you can see, there's plenty of money. And if you run short, use the quarter-share you're always trying to get me to take."

"But this is foolishness," Soon sputtered in a rare loss of equanimity. "The Indians are doomed. This will not save them!" Soon shook the paper. "Then what will happen to all this money?"

"Nonetheless, you must promise!" Pike said fiercely. "You must swear this to me. And you must promise to find a way to make what I wish happen long after we are both gone."

Soon had so many things to think of. Opium from India. A processing plant. His wife's demand to bring over more family members. The tiresome Italian gangsters who needed slapping down again. He did not want the complication of Pike's obsessions. He sighed deeply, the pouches underneath his eyes sagging into his cheeks as he exhaled. At least he no longer had to worry about the quarter-share.

"I will do as you wish."

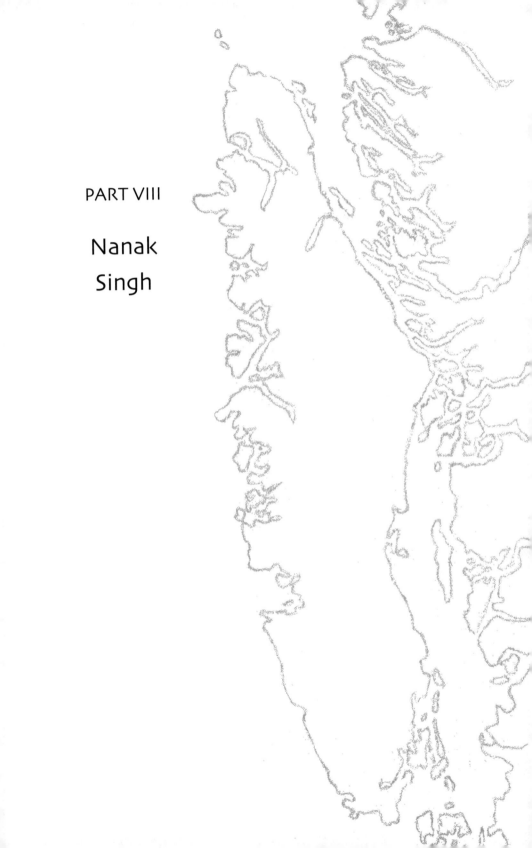

PART VIII

Nanak
Singh

43

*

1897

Port Moody, British Columbia

As the transcontinental Canadian Pacific Railway train pulled by Engine 22 smoked into the station—Port Moody, population 376—Nanak Singh made a fateful decision.

Now twenty-three, Nanak had left the Punjab and his family seven years before. There was little trace of the quivering sixteen-year-old boy who had bowed to his father and promised to carry on the proud Khalsa warrior tradition within one of the Sikh *misls*, or divisions, of the British India Army. Two of his great-great-grandfathers had fought beside the squat, ugly, charismatic Ranjit Singh to create the short-lived Sikh kingdom a century before. Young Nanak adored his father's tales of those exploits, especially the spicy bits about Ranjit Singh's love of drink, women, and fast horses. The anecdotes were always appended with some form of "great men often have great weaknesses but . . ."—the parental brow would frown at this point—"such weaknesses serve as a warning, not an example."

Nanak's grandfather had helped demolish the British forces in February of 1849 at Chillianwala only to lay down arms a month later at Gujarat when the British prevailed with the help of treacherous Sikh anarchists. Out of that bitter defeat came a type of honor as the British absorbed the best of the Sikh fighters into their own army. The British, not forgetting for a moment the humiliation at Chillianwala, spread the Sikh soldiers widely, isolating their various divisions from one another. Nanak's grandfather became such a supporter of the crown that he added English places to the names of his three children. Nanak's father became Qurban Surrey Singh, his uncle Gopal Bath Singh, and his aunt Nanki Thames Kaur.

Nanak's father took the tradition a step further by adding English descriptions of character to his children's names. Nanak's older brother was Pritam Happy Singh, while Nanak became Nanak Simple Singh. Simple was chosen because Nanak's father thought it mean "solitary" or "single" which was appropriate, because he rarely cried as a baby and was content to be left alone gazing for hours at trees or flowers. Nanak dropped that part of his name exactly a week after he joined the British army.

Seven years. It should be long enough to please any father and any God. Though the white man's God seemed a malleable deity; pleasing Him seemed to be more a matter of pleasing oneself.

"Enough of that," Nanak admonished himself. "Don't let your distaste for the British army lead you to tarnish their God."

Seven years. He'd done his duty. Duty was central to a good Sikh. Duty to family, to clan, to country, and, of course, to God. Nanak, named after the first Sikh guru, was well steeped in his obligations. Now this one was satisfied, he hoped to become a poet or perhaps a writer of history. The fledgling Khalsa College of Amritsar had already expanded once since the British had established it in 1893 and Nanak could think of nothing better than a life of contemplation spent inside its walls pondering the great truths of the Granth Sahib, the Sikh bible, or adding a chapter to the short but exciting history of the Sikh Punjab.

But at this moment, more than anything, Nanak yearned to be alone.

Though the Sikhs were a close-knit society, many living in large extended families, Nanak Simple Singh preferred to be alone. For seven years he had marched with, fought with, lain with, eaten with, and defecated with thousands of other men. They were sons of *shadra*—peasants—as well as professional soldiers, farmers, clerks, and tradespeople. The vast social differences among them never bothered Nanak. He just hated their all-consuming presence. Their sweaty bodies, their constant gossip, endless questions, complaints, and low humor. The idea of being alone had grown into an obsession as strong as his countrymen's desire for home and a warm cup of buttermilk with a bowl of *sarson ka saag,* a flavorful mash of mustard leaves.

And the business with the damned language made things worse, much worse. There were many times now that he cursed his grandfather's worship of all thing British. Along with the added names, English songs, stories, and poems were a tradition in his family. As a result, Nanak had a good working knowledge of English, a fact quickly discovered by the commander of the regiment who immediately appointed Nanak translator.

"We want no misunderstandings, you see?" the man commented gravely. "Misunderstandings get people killed. You speak English far better than my officers speak Punjabi or Urdu, so I want you on hand at all times, as required."

"As required" meant hours spent trotting back and forth between soldiers and officers, Sikh and English, like a *dajoika*, delivery boy. It forced Nanak into constant conversation, explanation, and contact. The English officers often asked him to settle disputes among the men or get to the bottom of complaints that were sensed but not voiced, or to run errands because he was available. Nanak found that an intermediary is resented equally by all sides.

If the Sikhs didn't care for an order, they found it convenient and a good deal safer to abuse Nanak, the messenger. And if the Sikhs displeased the English, they acted as if Nanak was somehow responsible. Nanak's extra duties came with no elevation in rank, pay, or even improved rations. He was the most junior officer in the division, ranking barely above the enlisted men. But Nanak was often told he was "invaluable." Nanak thought the English word perfectly summed up how he felt: beyond value, but without value.

✳

Just as Nanak's division was preparing to stand down for a two-month leave, after which he intended to file for his honorable release, new orders arrived. Two hundred elite Punjabi Lancers were to proceed forthwith to London, England, as color, entertainment, and novelty for Queen Victoria's Diamond Jubilee celebrations. The month aboard a troop ship from Shanghai to London was excruciating. Officially, Her Majesty's troops were equal within their rank and Nanak found that to be true—in death. In reality, even the lowliest white British soldiers lived in the above-water deck, while the "equal" Indians were jammed like sardines in the bowels.

The troop ship had a rounded bottom to allow it to carry more cargo, human and otherwise, and it was also cheaper to construct than the V-hulled military ships. The rounded hull, despite stabilizers, rolled alarmingly even in a calm sea, turning strong men into shivering, retching babies. Nanak suffered horribly from every pitch, the slightest of which turned his stomach upside down. There was no relief anywhere. He couldn't even hold down the cold soup and black, treacly potions the doctor's assistant pressed on him.

"Can't have any more of you dying," the man said briskly. Nanak didn't know a person could die of seasickness. "Though from the looks of you, it might come as a relief."

Ah, thought Nanak, once again the peculiar English sense of humor.

He felt like telling this jester that if he wanted to fix his *garmy* stomach he could get him some *lassi,* a yogurt drink that cooled the body and soothed the digestion. But the man wouldn't believe such humble food could cure illness; in any case, there wasn't any yogurt to be had.

Nanak tried walking on deck but the motion, coupled with seeing the horizon bobbing about, made the sickness worse, and the sea breeze chilled his weakened body to its core. At least in the tiny bunk there was a semblance of warmth; unfortunately, along with warmth came fetid odors— urine, excrement, sweat, vomit. All food turned against him—even his beloved *masal* of onions, garlic, ginger, and tomatoes fried in *ghee.*

In London, after what everyone agreed was a splendid display of marching, dancing, and sword work by the Sikh lancers to honor the Queen, orders were cut to take the Sikhs back to the Punjab.

"We will be sailing by the very same way in return?" he asked the captain's adjutant anxiously. The man everyone called Jolly Roger laughed.

"If we do, we might as well take that blighty belly of yours and bury it right here. No, son, we'll be crossing the Atlantic and then taking the train across Canada. It's bloody cold, I'm told. But less time for you on the sea in one go. We'll be shipping out of the port city of Vancouver to Hong Kong and Shanghai. Then home for you."

✳

After chugging through thousands of miles of rock, forest, prairie, and mountains, Nanak was just days from the last leg of his seven-year service. It was Monday, September 10, 1897. On Wednesday the Sikhs were to board the *Empress of China,* a mail steamer. He estimated that he would be back in his village for his father's birthday in early November. His fingers caressed a small book, a rare miniature version of the Granth Sahib.

"I cannot take it!" Nanak said, both honored and fearful, when his father pressed it on him.

"I expect it back in its proper place when you return to take up the next part of your life," his father insisted solemnly.

Nanak did not consider himself a particularly religious man, but he loved the texture and sound of verse on his tongue. Words had a sensuous quality as they moved from brain to mouth and out. He found the hymns of the Granth Sahib very comforting, even in battle. The bible was a cherished possession and he could not wait to set it back on the small ivory stand his grandfather had carved for it.

The train shrieked to a jerky stop.

"Make sure everyone stays put," an officer called to Nanak. "Hop to it, I don't want to be rounding you fellows up!"

Nanak had been daydreaming.

"Disembarking not permitted?"

"Not permitted. That's what I said, now spread the word!"

Nanak hurried after him. "Sir, please," he saluted. "I am begging for a short walk."

The officer considered. "I can't have you lot running all over the place."

"Sir, yes, I am understanding," Nanak said unctuously. "I'll be back before you are knowing."

The officer liked Nanak well enough for a wog. He did what he was told and rarely complained. He nodded curtly. "Find out from the conductor how long the stopover is, and don't let the others see you go."

Nanak continued on to the toilet facilities in the next car. He loved the Canadian privacy rooms. When he emerged, freshly washed, he headed to the exit door, the platform, and freedom.

"Be back in an hour 'n a half, coon!" hollered the porter at Nanak's back. "Or you'll be left behind. Then all you'll be is someone's tame monkey." The man roared with laughter. "You'd look plenty good in a cage."

Nanak had no idea what a coon was, but he assumed, judging by the man's tone, that it wasn't a pleasantry. The porter was the only aspect of the train trip that Nanak had not enjoyed. The man was furious at being assigned to a car full of "darkies" and "ferners," and didn't trouble to hide it.

It would be decades yet before Nanak came across the term "redneck," but when he did he immediately thought of the porter, whose neck and every square inch of exposed body skin was flushed. Nanak didn't know if the redness was a permanent affliction or one that came upon him when he saw Sikhs.

"It will be as you are saying, great one, oh respected guardian of other men's leavings," Nanak replied in an obsequious tone.

"Your fancy talk won't help you if you're late."

"You are saying in one hour and a half the train is leaving?"

"Your ears plugged with that head bandage? An hour 'n a half."

Nanak jumped down to the wooden step-box on the platform, his *kirpan* sword banging on the train car. An hour and a half. An eternity!

The porter smiled nastily as Nanak walked away. The stopover was for a bare twenty minutes as the train was late and they were taking on only mail.

At the very least the cheeky bastard would have to run his ass off to get back on the train, and with any luck they'd leave him behind. Fact was he'd like to leave the lot of them behind. They smelled bad and they were so, so very polite. But underneath the politeness lay the trace of a sneer. Why on earth the Queen should want a bunch of monkeys with rags on their heads prancing around for her Diamond Jubilee was completely beyond him.

His thoughts stoked the anger burning in the pit of his stomach. It was an accustomed anger, a righteous anger. Born in the shadow of the Cheviot Hills just north of Newcastle, Martin Effelwick's father, a third-generation miner, had been drawn to British Columbia by its rich deposits of high-grade coal. There were tremendous opportunities for a man who understood the black devil. He rose to supervise three mines on Vancouver Island before landing a job in Vancouver in 1887, just a year after the city was named, as coal-shipping manager for the CPR. In Newcastle he would have likely served his entire career "down shaft," perhaps, if he was lucky, one day becoming the shift manager. Here the Effelwicks lived in a beautiful stone-and-clapboard house on the slopes of Fairview overlooking the young city.

In 1895 his father had actually been invited to a ball at the Hotel Vancouver owned by the railway, as most things seemed to be in this city. The president himself, Sir William Van Horne, was to be in attendance. Martin's mother spent weeks preparing herself. She had three dresses made, discarding them one after the other. A four-in-hand picked up his parents, looking for all the world like members of the royal family. Young Martin admired them as they set off down Oak Street for the new bridge across False Creek and then to the intersection of Granville and Robson.

It was the Orientals who'd sunk the up-and-coming Effelwicks. Martin's face suffused as he watched the lanky Indian walk quickly toward the station, almost bouncing as he went. The CPR brought in gangs of the beasts to labor on six-month contracts, replacing them with more men when they returned to China. The slanty-eyed bastards worked for half the price, twice as long as white men, and only ate a handful of rice a day. They did everything from dock work to digging. And, like these gibbering monkeys, they were so, so polite. His father vehemently opposed their increasing numbers and fought to have more experienced coalmen brought from Wales, Scotland, and northern England. He took the battle all the way to the president of the CPR, writing a letter to Sir William explaining his objection to the "yellow blight," which was being carried by the CPR ships themselves from China.

But it turned out that Sir William, expatriate American and a collector of

Ming dynasty pottery and porcelain, had a powerful appreciation for the diligence and culture of the Chinese. With the West Coast building boom of the late 1880s and early 1890s, combined with the desperate shortage of labor in the coal mines, Van Horne considered the Chinese a necessity. Astonishingly he even believed they should be allowed to settle in Canada after a mere six months of work. In one of his last acts as president of the railway, William Van Horne arranged to have Gilbert J. Effelwick fired.

Occasionally Martin pondered how a career, twenty years in the making, could be unmade in a matter of months. His father suddenly found work scarce. They moved from Fairview south to Hicksville, then again to scruffy Ramtown on the northern side of the Creek, facing a sewer runoff. Within eighteen months Martin had been yanked out of his school and set to work as a glorified servant on the CPR's cross-country run. It was only a favor begged by his father in a sober moment that got him the job.

Martin Effelwick patted the little badge sewn to the vest under his porter's uniform—Asian Expulsion League, a small group of like-minded men who would soon set things to rights. He smiled thinly, then chuckled aloud as the raghead disappeared behind the station house. There goes one cheeky monkey about to get his comeuppance. For a moment the fires within were banked.

The small station with an adjacent bunkhouse was the only building on the west side of the tracks with a tiny town starting to grow on the east side. After a pleasant fifteen-minute walk Nanak found a private grassy spot beneath a tree. He sat cross-legged, holding the bible unopened in his lap. He shut his eyes and savored the warm sun on his shoulders. Nanak welcomed the sense of well-being that grew up from his toes like a glow. It had been so long since he'd felt this way he didn't recognize it at first. After five minutes of dreamy reflection he opened his eyes to the most splendid sight of his life. A mountain unlike anything he had ever seen.

Growing up in the northern Punjab, close to some of the highest peaks in the world, he regarded mountains as obstacles and all too plentiful ones at that. Marching through the high passes of Kashmir and patrolling India's northeastern boundary made Nanak appreciate the low, green valleys of cultivated farmland in the southern Punjab. But here, in the midst of a broad valley, not unlike that which swept out richly from the banks of the Punjabi Sutlej River, was a mountain. A mountain that appeared by its very isolation to be far higher than those of his homeland. In fact, it was far smaller, but its majestic white crown, long, sharp ridge, and sloping shoulders of deepest green made it a queen of the landscape.

Nanak sat absorbing its beauty, inhaling the freshness of the air, a peaty smell. His eyes closed and he began to hum softly, the words of a guru forming in his mind.

As a team of oxen are we driven
by the ploughman, our teacher
by the furrows made are thus writ
our actions—on the earth, our paper.

Nanak jumped to his feet, the depth of his peaceful reverie disorienting him for a moment. He thought a black cloud had come and taken over the day. He couldn't see the train and the station was dark in the distance, and the shadows long.

He must be dreaming. Running to the tracks, he tried to calm his heart, which beat painfully in his throat, making his head throb at the same time. Not a soul was about. It was no dream—the train was gone. He ran around the station, frantically calling: "Oh sir! Hello! Someone to help?"

Only one train traveled across this vast country each day. He would get no assistance until the next day, perhaps not until late afternoon. The knowledge gave him hope. If he waited, he could simply board the train tomorrow for Vancouver and join the regiment at the militia barracks near the docks. Nanak caught the ghostly glow of Mount Baker. Suddenly the queen of the Fraser Valley did not seem so benevolent anymore. She appeared to be glowering at a stupid, insignificant Sikh marooned on a train platform.

✳

Nanak woke again to the sound of a door slamming. Stiffly he rose, trying to work the ache out of his muscles. Sleep had not been refreshing. It had rained hard during the night and the wind had driven it into the only shelter Nanak could find, a shack next to the station, without doors or windows. He was damp through to the skin. The uninhabited bunkhouse was locked and shuttered; Nanak could have walked into the village but he didn't dare leave the station in case somebody in authority came back. He made his way into the ticket office, where a man in an immaculate uniform sat transcribing the Morse code from the overnight traffic. Though he must have heard footsteps, the man continued with his business. Nanak cleared his throat. After a long moment the ticket agent looked up.

"Yes?" he said in the flat voice favored by minor functionaries the world over. If the man was surprised to see a turbaned Sikh standing in front of him he gave no sign. "What can I do for you?"

"Mr. Agent, sir," Nanak said. "I am being in a serious pickle, indeed. I have been falling asleep this past night and now I am missing my train. Kind sir, be good enough to discharge me upon the next one." Behind the agent Nanak saw a kettle burbling on a woodstove and the makings for tea on the counter: a tin of Darjeeling, sugar, even a small pitcher of milk. Never had he craved anything as much as he now did a cup of hot tea.

"There's only one thing I detest worse than a liar," the agent said, ostentatiously reaching over and locking the door into his cubicle, "and that's a deserter. You may have thought you'd slithered away unseen, but the porter," he shuffled through the cables, "ah yes, Martin Effelwick, an alert lad, spotted you sneaking off with your pack and rifle."

Nanak was dumbfounded. The telegraph started clicking away. "Here's another transmission from the authorities in Vancouver. Apparently your sort is running like rabbits. Disgraceful. We go to the trouble of civilizing you and then you run away like the unfaithful animals you are."

"I am not running away!" pleaded Nanak. "I am falling asleep!"

"You can explain all that to the authorities!" the man said. "Though I doubt they'll listen to a deserter."

The word was terrifying to Nanak. He had observed several times as one of the regiment, usually a cowardly Hindu or Muslim, decided to leave his army boots behind. In seven years five deserters had been shot, two more jailed, and at least one other unfortunate hung. Nobody was interested in explanations, particularly from a Sikh. And one thing he knew for sure: once the army decided you were something, whatever that something might be, it was virtually impossible to change their minds.

At first Nanak was too confused and frightened by his predicament to be angry, but fury overtook him at the cruel fate that put him at the mercy of this sanctimonious clerk. For an instant his anger was so great that had the man not been protected by a sturdy iron wicket, Nanak would have reached in and throttled him. Instead he grabbed the wicket and gave it a mighty shake. Just as quickly as the rage kindled it was quenched, and he became aware that the man was talking excitedly as his fingers clacked away at the telegraph keys.

"Deserter here now, stop," he said as his fingers flew. "Attempting to break in, stop. Armed and threatening, stop. Fear for my life, stop. Come at once, stop." He looked up with a smile at Nanak. "That should just about seal your fate and that of those other wogs."

Nanak recognized a large boulder rolling downhill when he saw it. If this man and the porter were able to lie so easily—the why of it mystified Nanak—what hope had he that the authorities would believe he had simply fallen asleep? While it was unlikely that he'd be shot—they weren't in the middle of a war, after all—desertion was still a very grave crime. At the least he faced a long spell in one of Her Majesty's military prisons and he'd rather be shot than spend a night at the mercy of British jailers. At the moment he was fresh out of optimism toward any English-speaking person.

"For your edification, kind sir," Nanak said, making his decision, "we wogs were civilized when those of your country were still eating tadpoles out of puddles."

"Mind your tongue or I'll take a stick to you."

"You are welcome to attempt such," Nanak replied, eyeing the pudgy body and paper-white hands. The clerk didn't make the slightest move. "Very well then, I am bidding you a good day."

"Stay right there! You are under arrest!"

Nanak turned and walked out of the waiting room.

"Where are you going, you coward!" shrieked the agent. He left off stabbing at the telegraph keys for a moment and rushed to the wicket. "I order you to stay right here!"

"I am doubting they will ever find me," Nanak shot back imprudently.

"Aha! So you admit it. You are a deserter! God save this country from the likes of you."

"You call upon your God and I am calling to mine. We will be seeing who is answering first."

44

*

Nanak awoke for the third time since he'd left the train to find a ghostly apparition leaning over him, staring intently.

"Are you an Indian?" the apparition demanded. "One of the deserters?"

Nanak groaned. He'd been walking and running for two days, hardly pausing. Last night he'd become so hungry he nerved himself up to approach an isolated farmhouse to ask for food. He'd hardly gotten within hailing distance when the farmer emptied both barrels of a shotgun at him. Nanak had been shot at in battle many times, but the unexpected pellets whizzing by like furious bees terrified him. He ran until he collapsed.

He sat up, almost bumping noses with the woman who continued to examine him as if he were some strange beast. After the Diamond Jubilee he was accustomed to gawkers. The entire time they were in England people gaped at the Sikhs wherever they went. Not unlike the circus, Nanak thought. The regiment toured the London Zoo shortly before they were shipped out to Canada, and Nanak knew exactly how the lions felt pacing back and forth as visitors lined up to peer at them. But this whey-faced creature's stare contained more than curiosity.

"Are you one of the hindoos? You don't look as dangerous as they say."

"I am not being dangerous in the slightest," Nanak said. "And I am most definitely not Hindu, I am Sikh."

"Sick? I'm not surprised, sleeping in the open like this. But I suppose as you've run away you didn't have much choice."

"I am begging your pardon but I am not running away. Being most unfortunate and falling asleep, the train was departing without my person. And," he added, "I am not unwell. I am Sikh. That is my faith. I am from the Punjab."

"That's not what everyone's saying. We're a bit out of the way here but word does get out. Sikh, huh? How interesting. My dear brother will have apoplexy."

How she talked! A straight run of words with no intonation, just like a box had been upended and the contents dumped out. She had a narrow, angular face with prominent cheekbones, a pointed chin, and the reddest hair he had ever seen. But it was her eyes which were most remarkable, the palest green that only served to make her complexion seem all the whiter. Her skin looked a bit like the dough used to make *naan*.

"Could you be kind to tell me where I am being now?"

"British Columbia," she said, puzzled.

"I am knowing of that, but more precisely in what place?"

"Well," she replied cheerfully, "Fort Langley is that way," she pointed south and east, "that used to be a Hudson's Bay Company fur trading fort, but they closed it down last year. No one cares much about furs anymore. New Westminster is that way," she gestured vaguely west. "It used to be the capital of British Columbia, but the railway rules everything here and the mucky mucks decided Vancouver should be the terminus for the railway and made Victoria, over on the island, the capital."

As she paused for breath, Nanak asked diffidently: "Could I make my way to Vancouver tonight?"

"Good lord, no! Not unless you have wings underneath your clothes."

She spotted the *kirpan* poking out of his long, white muslin tunic. "That is a very long sword," she said, touching the leather scabbard.

Shocked at her forwardness, Nanak scrambled to his feet. "Not a sword, it is a *kirpan*. All Sikh are required to wear. It is part of our faith."

"No wonder everyone thinks the deserters are dangerous, if you are carrying weapons like that."

"Who is everyone being?" Nanak was getting the impression that the entire population of British Columbia was massing for a giant manhunt of which he was the target.

"Well, in truth, just my brother and Sam Morris. He has the closest milking farm to us. Too bad I didn't find you sooner. Sam's gone to Vancouver to pick up some coolie labor from the *Empress of China*. She docked a few days ago and I expect she'll be leaving soon if she's not gone already."

Nanak's spirits dropped like an anchor. He imagined his regiment standing on deck, backs to the Canadian colony, faces toward the Orient, hearts eagerly anticipating their return to the Punjab.

"Would you like my lunch? A cheese sandwich and an apple—our own apples and Sam's cheese. You must be hungry."

"A thousand times thank you." Nanak was ravenous. Though he didn't

care for the tasteless aridity of the leavened bread, he devoured the sandwich in a few bites. Amused, the woman watched him eat. He was a strange
fellow, to be sure. It was hard to make out his face beneath the whiskers that
seemed braided, folded back on themselves and tucked into his turban. It
made his face look puffy and dirty but she supposed he could not help that
as he had obviously slept in the rough for two cold nights.

Nanak wanted to ask more questions but he didn't know how to phrase
them. Except for the Women's Temperance League in London, which had held
a tea for the regiment and a dance where the Sikhs were allowed to attend and
watch but not participate, Nanak had hardly seen a woman in seven years, let
alone talked to one. In Hong Kong a number of the men visited prostitutes, but
Nanak couldn't bring himself to consider the idea of having sex with a woman
not his wife. Besides, he'd sent every shilling he was paid home to his family.

"I love this place," she said, saving him. "Near the inlet most of the trees
have been cut down for farms, but this little forest remains and I come here
often. If you climb that hill you can really see Mt. Baker well. I usually come
to read." She leaned in to him. He smelled a flowery freshness. "Especially
books my brother would not approve of." The book she brandished, *The
History of Tom Jones: A Foundling,* meant nothing to Nanak.

"He doesn't believe a woman should be reading such things. Rough
books, he calls them. Sometimes I think he isn't even happy that I learned to
read, though he's happy enough that I am available to write letters for his
flock. So," she changed the subject abruptly and growing serious, "what are we
going to do with you? I fear that they'll beat you or jail you if you are caught."

Nanak expected as much.

"Come, I'll take you home," she said abruptly, offering her hand. "I
can't wait to see Matthew's face when he sees you on his doorstep. Don't
worry, he's all bark and very little bite. A bit of a hypocrite but he has a
good heart. We'll see how he manages with a dark fox like you among his
Christian charity rabbits.

"By the way, I'm Katherine. Kate, most call me. What do I call you?"

"I am Nanak Sim . . . Nanak Singh." Nanak almost included his second
name but he had no desire to appear foolish before this woman.

✳

"What of the Good Samaritan?" submitted Kate, who could out-Bible her minister brother with her eyes closed. "Was he not of dark complexion? *This* man
could be a descendant of *that* good man, yet you would turn your back?"

"I don't recall that the Samaritan was a deserter," Matthew Darrington replied, striving for and not quite achieving a reasoned tone of voice. Trust Kate to twist an argument.

"Now you're being ridiculous, Matthew," she said bluntly. "He gave me his explanation and I accept it, completely. If he was a deserter he would have killed me, and here I am, entirely whole! He has a marvelous sword and he could have slit my throat just like that! And if he's a deserter, where's his baggage? This man doesn't even have a coat!"

She snapped her fingers, making her brother blink.

He hated it when Kate became so . . . so physical. She spoke of gruesome events and body parts as if one were speaking of vegetables in the field. And now she had brought *this* home. Matthew strode to the window and peeked out. The hindoo was standing there almost at attention.

"Even if we believe him, no one else will!" sputtered her brother. "And we will be tarred by his crime."

"His *supposed* crime," corrected Kate.

"Yes, well, I expect the best thing is to notify the authorities in Burnaby who will hand him over to the Vancouver militia."

"There are no authorities in Burnaby," Kate reminded him. "They let the policeman go last year." In 1896 a herd of swine running loose on the dirt streets of the small Fraser River settlement outside Vancouver had caused the carriage of a reeve to bolt, giving him a fright that required a full day in bed. A week later a policeman was hired to take care of the animal problem and control rowdy youth. He lasted less than a year before the village coffers ran dry. In lieu of back pay the man was allowed to keep his hand and leg irons, and uniform.

"It's our Christian duty to help him," Kate stated.

Matthew knew he'd have no peace unless they helped this Indian. Kate was like that with his parishioners, bullying them to do this and that, fix this and that, arrange something else. Anyone would think she was the minister and not he. But he had far too much work to worry about a single man and, despite what Kate said, a likely criminal.

"All right," conceded Matthew. "I shall allow him to stay a single night. Then we shall arrange transportation into Vancouver for him. What happens from there will be his own business."

Kate smiled broadly and hugged her brother; the concession of one day could easily be wedged into a week. "I knew you would see it my way." Gracious she was not. Before he could say another word, she swept open the door and bade the man enter. Despite his rather dirty clothing and greasy head garment, Matthew was surprised, in spite of himself, at the impressive figure the Indian cut. He wasn't terribly tall, or broad, but even with his peculiar hat he had a powerful dignity.

Nanak offered his hand in the Western way. Matthew hesitated but he could feel Kate glaring at him, so he quickly touched the long brown fingers then snatched his hand back, burying it in his jacket pocket. Nanak was surprised at the difference between the two. Where Kate was tall, angular, and lithe, her brother was short, round, and pudgy. His eyes were small and nervous, like a village money-lender's; an odd face for a man of religion charged with caring for people's souls.

The next few hours dragged into eternity. Nanak sat stiffly in a chair while Kate busied herself in the kitchen. That morning she had begun making candles, and the wicks were ready for dipping a second and third time. Their house was so small that her brother's parish office consisted of a desk set to one side of the fireplace. The heat from the blaze made Nanak feel faint. He desperately wished to say his prayers but he didn't want to offend by leaving the room or praying in front of the brother. Though Matthew was a man of God, Nanak knew from experience that religions often mixed poorly. A jaguar and a tiger may both be cats, but cage them together and they would kill each other.

After a bland but filling dinner of potatoes and boiled mutton with onions, Kate demanded to know more about Sikhs. Matthew grew increasingly uncomfortable with each question.

"It is a simple faith," demurred Nanak.

"Oh come, come!" urged Kate. "We have not had a visitor for ages who could talk about anything but dry wells or dry cows or their children's boils. We have fed you. Now you cannot deny us conversation."

"What are you wishing to know?"

"Everything! What exactly is a Sikh? Where have you come from and why do you wear that contrivance on your head? They called it a turban in the paper. It seems very impractical. Do you sleep in it?"

Nanak glanced again at Matthew, who was resignedly studying the gristle on his plate. What harm could it do?

"Sikh is very young religion. Only four hundred years old," Nanak said, striving to make the complex understandable in a few words. "It began with my naming sake, Nanak, who was very first guru."

"Your first guru was a man, not a god?" Kate quizzed.

"That is correct," Nanak agreed.

"That is unusual, is it not?" interjected Katherine. "As far as I know, no other religion is based on the word of man. In all other religions the word has been passed down directly from God. In the case of Christianity the teachings were passed down by God through His divine but earthly son, Jesus."

"Guru Nanak was unusual in very many ways," responded Nanak. "When young he was preferring reading of religious matters to his family business. It is written that they were very upset."

"Families can be difficult," agreed Kate, glancing at her brother.

"In those times holiest of Hindus and Muslims walked the countryside, speaking about the word of their faith. Guru Nanak was pestering at them and poking the holes in their teachings. The holy men were not taking kindly to this. I am from Punjab, which is far north in India. My people have been believing a long time that persecution of us is great. Guru Nanak was pushing forward this point and he was blaming the Muslim and Hindu faiths.

"His family were all unknowing what to do with him," Nanak continued, warming to his story. "He gave away his monies, everything. But then he took a wife and all life went to normal."

Kate laughed. "I keep telling my brother that. Get yourself a wife if you want to live a normal life in this country. But he has a sister," she shrugged, "who looks after him, so I can't budge him."

"Kate!" Matthew interjected sharply as if she were revealing the most intimate family secrets.

"Then is coming another great change. Nanak leaves his village and family and became like a holy beggar. His life is prayer and meditations."

"I have never understood the good of that in any religion!" snorted Kate. "It seems just an excuse to do nothing."

"Kate!"

"Don't 'Kate!' me. You have often said yourself that the holy orders of the Catholics and Jesuits could do more good in the world if they spent less time praying and more among the people."

"That is not how I put it," Matthew's nose and cheeks burned pink.

"It is close enough. How did this guru go from there to creating an entire religion?"

"Nanak believed his purpose was bringing of Hindus and Muslims together. He was teaching that love of each one other is leading forward to loving of God."

"Love. I like that. We are so afraid to say that in our stiff Anglican faith."

Matthew didn't respond to her provocations. It just made things worse.

"Nanak was believing in bringing up women and low castes," Nanak said shyly, guessing that Matthew disliked his sister's manly, forward nature.

"Then I shall become a Sikh," declared Kate. "We are far more suited to caring for the souls and bodies of people than men are."

"He was called a gentling man but his teachings left, ah," Nanak searched for the word.

"Wounds?" Kate supplied.

"Yes, his teachings left wounds. Wounds of spirit heal most poorly. I believe he was not meaning hurt but his beliefs were strong," Nanak said. "He thought people were coming before ritual."

"Oh Matthew, will you listen to this! How often have we discussed this very issue."

Matthew's head inclined slightly in grudging acknowledgment.

"Perhaps I have a story you will like?"

"I tell the children of the parish so many stories, *I* would love to hear one for a change." Kate's eyes sparkled and her face grew warm with enthusiasm. It makes her look healthier, less pale, Nanak thought.

"Hindus have many holy beliefs about the great river Ganges. They are throwing water into the river for honoring of departed ancestors. When Nanak is visiting Ganges he takes water and throws it in other direction. The holy men were most unhappy. 'I am watering my field,' he told them. 'If you can send water to the dead in heavens, can I not send it to my village in the Punjab where it is being needed?'"

"I like your Nanak, he has a sense of humor."

"Yes, but he was pricking the strong faiths and many hated him for that. Nanak always made for peace, no mattering how much his teachings were disliked. He also taught us the body is holy and deserving in respect. So we do not smoke or drink alcohol spirits."

Matthew guiltily let his hand slip away from the glass of claret. Kate smiled and finished hers.

"We work hard to honor God and obey nature."

"How is it, if Sikhs believe in peace, you and your comrades are in the army?" Kate asked.

"This is a most interesting question. Nine gurus, one after each, were teaching peace, and many, many were following their words. But guru number nine, Tegh Bahadur, was being ordered by Mughal emperor to return to the Muslim faith or to die. Our guru refuse but it was being believed he had a secret to stop the sword from cutting his neck. The emperor is wanting this secret. On the day of execution, Guru Tegh was writing the secret and ties it on his neck so no one can see. He is killed and the paper is found."

"What did it say?" brother and sister demanded almost in unison.

"'I give my head but not my secret.'"

"What did that mean?" Kate asked.

"No one knows," Nanak admitted with a wry smile.

"And his death began a war?"

"Not quite fast. His son called Gobind became tenth guru when he was only ten years old. He was sickened by what happened to his father. He was training also in arts of war. He said, 'When all other means are failing, it is righteous to draw the sword.'

"I will be making you tedious," apologized Nanak.

"No! No! This is fascinating," insisted Kate.

"The very most cherished thing for warrior is such words of Guru Gobind." He paused for a moment, struggling to get the English correct. "'Sikhs are as sparrows, teach them to hunt the eagle and each man will have courage to fight an army.' That is what he said."

For once Kate was silent. The powerful words flowed through her like an invigorating tonic, filling places that so often felt empty.

"Are all Sikhs warriors?" she finally asked.

"Oh goodness gracious, no! Most Sikhs are thinking of themselves as farmers. The Jat Sikhs.

"I am missing what is very most important. It is not fighting but joining. Guru Gobind named all men Singh, for 'lion,' and all women Kaur, for 'princess.' It was to be making us equal. In days when it was forbidden most strictly to touch one of lower caste, or talk or drink from the same vessel, he made followers do all of that. There was great consternation. His first warriors were five, all from differing castes. Khalsa, he called them, 'pure.' They were the Punj Piyaras, Five Beloved."

"Oooh," breathed Kate. "What a lovely description. So much more romantic than our church, which seems to frown on every bit of beauty and romance."

45

✻

"According to *both* the *World* and the *Daily News-Advertiser,* there were most definitely Sikh deserters," Matthew said triumphantly. "Your friend is clearly identified as the ringleader."

"Show me!" demanded Kate. She wore plain clothing: her dress had a snug, light-blue bodice and simple sleeves. She wore a shawl over her shoulders, and a navy skirt buttoned up the front with the most modest petticoat underneath. Billowing petticoats and lace would not do for the reverend's sister. Still, Nanak could hear the rustle of her skirts as the sensible grosgrain cloth rubbed against itself when she rushed to look at the day-old papers, which had arrived that morning. The long article on the "Hindus" was accompanied by a drawing of what looked like a sinister monkey wearing a turban and brandishing a sword.

"Oh dear. More than a dozen, it says here, but they expect to catch most of them, as they have no money or food except what they stole from the train. Look here, the *Empress of China* left this morning at dawn."

The drawing of the ship steaming away west, to the China Sea, hit Nanak like a fist in his stomach. He still could not believe that after seven long years in the British army his life was going to end like this, stranded in an isolated colony and likely hanged or shot. Hearing that others had deserted struck him as equally wrong. Why would they? They were going home. The men talked of nothing else from Liverpool to Halifax, then from that rough Nova Scotia port all the way across this extraordinarily vast country. Perhaps the report was merely exaggeration, an excitation of the spirit at the idea of exotic, dangerous men from the East running around loose. Whatever the reality, he had to find out for himself.

"Supposing there *are* being deserters," Nanak said. "Where are they going?"

"I don't know," puzzled Kate. "Vancouver is a pretty big place. The population isn't so large, twenty thousand or so, but it's very spread out. There's bits of the city popping up all the way from New Westminster right through to south Vancouver. Why, there is even a little fishing village now at the mouth of the Fraser, called Steveston and it's full of Japanese! I went there once with my brother and it was just like setting foot in Japan itself. And the fish! You can smell the canneries there for miles around. Then you have the Kanakas, those are Hawaiians, near Fort Langley, and there's a settlement of them close to Stanley Park. And, of course, the Chinese—they're everywhere these days."

"Those would be *legal* people," Matthew reminded her. "I think what he wants to know is where a criminal would go." His last words fell like little hatchet chops.

"Where would not-legal people be going?" Nanak pressed. "Where could they be hiding if such a thing is happening?"

Kate had no experience with such matters. Her life was the countryside around the once-booming town of Port Moody. Now sunk into depression after the railway located its terminus farther west in Vancouver. Kate spent little time there, choosing instead to help the farmers and their families. A bit of midwifery, filling in when one of the two teachers in the area fell sick, and occasionally counseling young women who had fallen. The rest—the deaths, the births, the sermons, which didn't change from one year to the next—she left to her brother.

It wasn't a life Kate would have chosen; her heart beat stronger at the thought of silk skirts and music that wasn't just mournful hymns. But at least here she was free, in a manner of speaking. She rode her own horse astride, drove her own cart, and spoke her mind. There had been two suitors in the six years since she and Matthew had moved into the farmhouse after their parents had died of influenza. Neither could coax more than a polite smile out of her. Kate reserved her passions for her books; she particularly liked books of dangerous matters, of obsessions she would never entertain, and of sins she could only imagine. But the printed page was as close to the world's dark underside as she'd ever been. She almost lost her brother's words in her musing.

"There's a hobo squat in the woods near the swamp, south of the Chinese piggeries," Matthew was saying. "Maybe forty or so lost souls at any one time. Drunk Indians, Chinese without papers, and white drifters, mostly American. All the riffraff ends up there eventually. I'll take you there."

"Bravo!" Kate clapped her hands. "Now we're seeing your charitable side."

Charity had nothing to do with it. Matthew wanted this strange, dark man out of his house. He had been waiting two years for the spring of 1898, just eight months from now, for the archbishop to visit Vancouver to bless Christ Church Cathedral, which had been finished in 1895. Several times Matthew had made the long journey to Vancouver from Port Moody to watch the spires go up, the slate roof tiles laid, and the mahogany altar set in place. The archbishop would deliver his blessing and select someone to give the first sermon. Matthew longed to be that someone.

Matthew's flock on the farmland and dark forests in the region between Port Moody on Burrard Inlet and the Fraser River fifteen miles to the south were more interested in earthly matters: clothing for the extra unexpected child, comfort for the death of a husband or wife, assistance in a dispute with a neighbor, and support when some slip of judgment brought them before the magistrate who traveled to Port Moody once every two weeks. Matthew yearned for the experience of an audience who actually cared about the interpretation of holy decrees and the true meaning of the scriptures. He worked tirelessly for the opportunity to raise himself in the church. He had chosen this placement over a smaller, less complicated parish in the developing working-class area in the south of Vancouver, feeling that one was never anointed for serving easy time. And now the archbishop was coming. And this chirruping man of India, this deserter, could ruin it all.

"First you must disguise yourself," Matthew said, fighting down his distress. "That, uh, contrivance on your head must go. It's a certain giveaway."

It had never occurred to Nanak that he would ever be without his turban, the nearly seven yards of cotton worn since *dastar bandhi,* the turban-tying ceremony performed when he was six years old.

"It is not allowed," Nanak stated firmly.

"For heaven's sake, why not?" Kate scoffed as she might at a child holding tight to a silly idea. "You might as well carry a placard saying FUGITIVE FROM JUSTICE." She paused for a moment. "And, after all, it's only a hat."

"It is not only a hat," Nanak said firmly. "It is being part of my faith."

"It doesn't matter what *you* think of it," Kate emphasized. "It is what *other* people think of it. To them it marks you as the man in the drawing. The deserter." She showed Nanak the exaggerated sketch in the newspaper.

"No Sikh can be in the public without this." Nanak touched the steel-blue turban, the color of warriors. Normally he was fastidious about keeping it clean, but his two days on the run had left it badly stained and he felt awkward about asking his hosts for washing water.

For once brother and sister agreed. The look that passed between them was clear.

"It is being part of our belief," Nanak stumbled on, straining to make them understand. "It is same for hairs and beard, we never cut. And all body must be kept clean."

"You mean you've never cut your hair and it's all under there?" Matthew asked.

"Yes."

"Do you sleep in the turban?" Kate jumped in.

"No, it is coming off for slumber."

"Well, then, pretend you are sleeping," she suggested. "I am sure your God will forgive you."

Kate found it difficult to sympathize with the idea that a piece of cloth might hold more significance to a faith than life itself. Yet, as she watched Nanak wrestle with his decision, a powerful wave of emotion caught in her chest.

"Come brother, help me load the bales of clothing for your trip," she said, feeling that the man deserved a little privacy. She tugged at her brother's sleeve. He was reluctant to leave. "He's not going to steal anything!" she hissed softly.

As they left, Nanak drew his razor-sharp *kirpan*. God would know what was in his heart.

When they returned, Kate was astonished at the transformation. Nanak's face, made puffy and round by the beard, suddenly looked lean and chiseled, if scraped a little raw. He had a finely shaped head and a jawline that spoke of determination. His eyes were still flat and black, and hid their depths, but the menace was gone from his face. Odd, she thought, how difficult she found it to judge the man when he wore the turban.

"Now what will we call you?" she said quietly. "You certainly won't pass for a Chinaman."

"I suppose we could say he is a Nobilly," offered Matthew. He too was taken aback at the transformation of the deserter. If Matthew were able to open a pathway deeper inside himself, he might have admitted that the "hat" inexplicably made him uncomfortable, regardless of what the stranger had or hadn't done.

"Yes! Perfect!" agreed Kate.

"What is Nobilly? Please."

"Italians," explained Kate. "A few came here before the big Gold Rush of '58 with Father Nobili. They settled the interior of the province, where it is very dry. I suppose, much like Italy. After the Rush, others came and now there is a small settlement of craftsmen in Vancouver. Everyone's just taken to calling them Nobilly's. They're Catholic."

Nanak found the dozens of branches and offshoots of Christianity decidedly odd.

Roughly shaved and cropped, wearing a set of clothes culled from the parish poor-box, Nanak Singh could certainly pass for a swarthy Italian. He carefully wrapped his turban, *kirpan,* and Granth Sahib in some burlap sacking. In time he would need them again.

Though soul-sick at the loss of his hair and turban, when he looked into the mirror, Nanak had to admit that his mother wouldn't be able to recognize him.

"I could be your brother," Nanak remarked to Matthew, a trace of his characteristic humor returning.

"You'll not say things like that!" Matthew retorted.

"Don't dismiss him so quickly!" laughed Kate. "Mother always teased you about having a touch of the olive in you. All these years of wandering the countryside in an open wagon has served to make you very brown indeed."

Matthew marched stiffly to the horses. The sooner they were off, the sooner he could be rid of the unwelcome visitor. While Nanak was cutting his hair, he and Kate loaded three bales of poor-box clothing onto the wagon, together with vegetables and fruit donated to the church by parishioners who had no money for collection. It was his practice to take a load of charity to the cathedral twice a year, feeling that such generosity from his poor parish reflected well on him.

They rattled out to meet the newly graveled road connecting Port Moody with Vancouver.

"Logs have a better time of it than people," grumbled Matthew, a familiar complaint. "A nice float down the river to the mills, but people are jounced half to death traveling the same distance."

"There's not nearly the profit in people as in logs," Kate replied, as she invariably did.

But now the graveling was done, matched by the surfacing of the Dewdney Road that reached deeper into the Fraser Valley. If it didn't rain, the road would hold up and a straight run to Vancouver would take only six hours.

"This is as far as I go," Kate said, stepping down from the wagon. "God speed."

Nanak's last sight of Kate was a statue, hand raised in a manly salute, skirts mushrooming around her in the breeze.

"The hobo squat isn't a safe place for a woman; come to that, most men either," the reverend said as Nanak stared back at his sister for longer than Matthew thought seemly.

Katherine Louise Darrington held her hand up until the wagon was out of sight. Her back felt cold and hollow despite the autumn sunshine. Her cheeks itched. She wiggled her mouth to relieve the chafe, and the salt from a tear surprised her. Both cheeks were wet.

"What on earth are you on about, you silly spinster?" she chided herself. "Be thankful Matthew has agreed to take him to the city. He couldn't stay here. No, he couldn't." She didn't fool herself for a second.

The trip of six hours became ten, as Matthew stopped at several little settlements along the shores of the inlet visiting many impoverished families whose men had been earning good wages in the sawmills until 1891, when everything went flat.

"Vancouver has taken a pause," observed one editorial, "in its pell-mell race to become the number one city on the Pacific Coast." It was an over-statement neither Seattle nor San Francisco would agree to, but boosterism was virtually a job description for the local papers, which cared little about fact or proportion. Some of the people living along the inlet had been without steady income for years. A few pigs, some chickens, and the charity of neighbors kept them alive. News of the Klondike gold strike in the far north was just beginning to trickle into the city, and within months most of the men would be gone, eager for their fortune and equally eager to leave their dull-eyed children and nagging wives behind.

It was immediately clear to Nanak that Reverend Matthew Darrington was a popular man. Dutiful inquiries about Kate made him think she was more respected than liked. Matthew introduced Nanak as Giuseppe, a recently arrived Italian who would be working as a stonemason at the new CPR pier, which was just under way. The lie was told easily. Nanak watched the faces of the people carefully and saw no trace of suspicion.

"My best advice is to smile when spoken to and no matter what they ask turn the question to the weather; it's been raining a lot lately. That will get you by. I doubt anyone along the road has ever met an Italian, so they won't know better," Mathew told him.

They skirted the city. Nanak had seen few buildings, though he smelled the effluent of the sawmills as they passed. The sun was just a blurry orange memory when the tired horses drew to a stop after a bumpy thirty-minute pull south of the main road. Nanak looked around dubiously. Aside from a smoldering fire, a few scraps of canvas tarpaulin, and garbage strewn, there was no hint that anyone called this clearing home.

"They fade back into the woods when they hear someone coming," Matthew explained as he lit a lantern and placed it on the wagon seat. "They'll come out again when they feel safe." Sure enough, within fifteen minutes a dozen individuals sifted out of the twilight to surround the wagon. Matthew began handing out food and clothing. Nanak marveled: the purse-lipped, nervous man he'd so briefly known was replaced by one comfortable and at ease.

"Anything unusual happen lately?" he asked a sullen Chinaman, receiving a hostile look in response. Matthew cheerfully continued, asking variations of the question until he hit upon a more talkative individual. Grizzled like an old wire-haired dog and gaunt to the point of emaciation, the man looked far too old to be living outdoors.

"I bet yer talking about the Injoos," he said slyly. "A few more of those fine carrots might help me remember. A chunk of your missus's cheese too." Matthew dug into the donations, which he'd kept aside for Christ Church. "Not red men like that billcan over there," he said, gesturing to a small, crooked Musqueam from one of the villages in the delta lands to the south of the Fraser River. "Indian Indians, from Injer," he pranced as he spoke the words in a mocked-up British accent. "Scairt they are! They're hiding up on the hill," he pointed to a dark rise not far off. "I tried to talk to them but didn't have much luck. I thought they might have some backie smoke or somethin'. They just jabbered and waved their swords. I left right quick."

Information poured out of the little man almost too fast for Nanak to follow. Unlike most others, he appeared to be here by choice. A chain forger by trade, he'd found laboring over a hot forge in the chain works at False Creek not to his taste. Long ago he discovered that the abundant woods and many creeks surrounding Vancouver supplied easy game, roots, berries, and fish. He proudly showed them a little lean-to he'd built back in the bush, which looked remarkably weathertight and comfortable.

"Sometimes I walk into town and trade a few furs for some flour and backie smoke. A bottle too, if I get enough cash, though if the Dry Ladies have anything to do with it you're gonna need a blessing from God to buy a single honest shot."

About the only thing the old man apparently missed was conversation. "Half o' them here don't speak English and them that do don't have anything interesting to say."

The little old man stared hard at Nanak. "You're one of them, ain'tcha. You just don't have those bandages on your head."

"I, uh . . ." Nanak was startled to be pegged so easily. "I am Giuseppe—Italian."

"Sure you are, an' I'm a leprechaun," the old man danced about. "I'll take you up there if you want. Went up to have a chatter with them when they first arrived," he said, repeating himself. "They're very shy. A bit rude, I thought."

"Go with the old man," Matthew suggested. "I'll finish up here."

Nanak was horror-stricken at the thought. Would Matthew leave as soon as he was gone? Matthew Darrington wasn't his choice for a companion, but he and Kate were the only allies he had in this strange country.

"I'm not going anywhere just yet," Matthew said, reading the concern on his face.

"Thank you," Nanak said humbly.

"I'll not wait forever though, so be off with you," Matthew responded gruffly. "I'd like a bed before dawn breaks, and the horses need a rest."

Nanak heard Matthew's soft words following him: "Happy are those who reject the advice of evil men, who do not follow the example of sinners."

✳

As they walked toward the dark slope, Nanak was dimly aware that the old man was continuing his barrage of conversation. He wondered what was waiting for him. They quickly came to a smaller clearing where a dispirited group slumped around a tiny fire. Nanak saw at once that they were indeed Sikhs, but they showed little resemblance to the crack military troops they had been a few days earlier. No guards were posted, no food was in sight, and no shelter was in existence or under construction. The men had their packs, weapons, and field gear, but they lay haphazardly about. Nanak recognized the five as foot soldiers from his troop.

"Sturdy and strong. Better than pack animals," his British division commander often commented.

When Nanak and the old man entered the clearing, the group jumped to their feet and stood in a fighting stance, *kirpans* drawn or rifles cocked, so quickly the old man dropped to his knees and covered his head with his arms.

"Careful there, careful there, we're friends," he mumbled, face to the ground. "I'm leaving, so's you take it out on this feller." He scurried back on his knees, then stood up slowly. "You natter up there. I've got better things to do than get shot or stuck." He hurried away.

At least they still show some semblance of their training, Nanak thought. I'd better say something before they shoot me by mistake.

"Attention!" Nanak barked in Punjabi, in his best junior-officer parade voice. The effect was like a cannonball in their midst.

"I am ashamed of you mangy dogs," Nanak boomed. "A few days without officers and you're snuffling about like animals."

"Who is this speaking to us in the language of the Punjab but garbed as a white man?" demanded the largest member of the troop, Rajinder Basant Singh, a farmer from Lahore who stood six and a half feet tall and was broad to match. He was fearless on the battlefield and carried the weight of two men during the regiment's miserable crossing of the Safed Koh Range between Peshawar and Kabul to defend India's northwestern border against the Afghan raiders.

"I am Nanak Singh of Her Majesty's First Sikh Lancers."

The five men went wild, gathering around Nanak, thumping him on the back, grabbing his arm. The questions came quickly, as they do from desperate men. "Is it really you, Nanak? Where is your turban? What have you done with your hair and beard? We've been looking all over for you. What are we going to do? Where will we go?"

Nanak observed that Bohun, the youngest member of the troop—no more than twenty he judged—was bright-eyed with unshed tears. Rajiid, another man he didn't know well, had an ashen complexion. "All in good time," Nanak responded, cheered by the hearty welcome. "First I must return to the clearing to speak with the minister who has helped me. Perhaps he has more food and clothing he will be willing to give us. When I return we will worship, then we will talk."

But the question scratching at his mind burst out. "Before I go, I must know. Why did you desert?"

"You gave us the idea," one of the men responded. "We were surprised when we learned you had deserted. But we figured you had a plan. We wanted our chance to get rich too."

"I don't understand," Nanak stammered. "What are you talking about?"

"We will not be well off like you when we leave the army," Rajinder explained. "You have your family's five acres waiting for you and oxen. Your father has a good job and you have an education. You can even read! But us. Nothing. We have no land. None of us. We figured that if the richest and smartest man in the troop thought it was a good idea to stay here, then that would suit us too."

These idiots deserted because they assumed I had, thought Nanak. What irony.

The five stood, looking expectantly at Nanak, waiting for him to tell them what to do. The joy that welled up at the reunion with his countrymen evaporated. The only thing worse than being marooned in a strange country was to be marooned with five men dependent on him.

For a moment, Nanak Simple Singh considered asking Matthew to take him back to the farm; to take another fork in the road. Instead, he began giving orders as if that had been his intention all along.

46

✳

"You lost a man?" Nanak asked incredulously. "How is that possible?"

"We got separated after we left the train," Rajinder explained defensively. "The monster trees hid the sun. We chose this hill as a landmark, but Santa must have gotten confused and wandered off to some other hill."

"And why haven't you gone looking for him?" Nanak demanded.

"We thought he'd find us," Rajinder replied lamely.

"What if he's injured?" Nanak demanded. The idea hadn't occurred to Rajinder or the others. And why would it? They were used to following orders, not thinking for themselves.

Nanak immediately sent Rajinder and Bohun out looking for the missing man, ordering them to stay away from any sign of people. Here, on the far eastern outskirts of the city, it was mostly isolated, poor farms, logging shacks, and a scattering of Indians shoved ever farther east by the expanding city. If they were careful, they could search without raising alarm. Nanak also moved their campsite to a more sheltered spot a hundred yards farther up the hill, where a concave depression gave protection from the north wind. There was also a good view of the hobo squat and the cart track heading to it. With a fresh sense of direction, the remaining men set to work, stringing a large field tarpaulin and gathering firewood.

"We retraced our steps as best we could," a dejected Rajinder reported late in the evening. "No sign."

"Warm yourself by the fire," Nanak clasped the big man around the shoulders. "Have something to eat. We'll all go out in the morning."

The next morning Rajindar, posted as a lookout, spotted the skinny Musqueam Indian with yards of steel-blue cotton wrapped around his neck and trailing down his back—Santa's turban. He quickly fetched Nanak.

"Po' man give me. Mine," the Indian said belligerently.

"No poor man is having something so fine as this," challenged Nanak. "Where are you getting it?"

"I say po' man. Go away. Stink man." The Musqueam spit copiously in the direction of Nanak's feet.

The squatters gathered around excitedly. The Indian carried a small hatchet, which they'd seen him use on a previous visit to the squat when he carved up another hobo with astonishing dexterity. On the other hand, the new man had a wicked-looking sword.

"I am not going away until you are telling me where it is coming from."

The Musqueam began flailing his ax; Nanak dodged with each swing. It went on like that for several minutes until Rajinder lumbered over, deflected a blow with his massive forearm, and snatched the weapon away. While the Musqueam was still trying to figure out what happened, Rajinder grabbed him by the scruff of his neck, lifted him off the ground with one hand, and shook him like a terrier would a rat.

"I am offering a very good bargain," Nanak said, hefting the Indian's hatchet. "I will trade you this fine ax for the cloth and what you know."

"Mine there! Give it!"

Rajinder roared, shaking the man so hard that if he'd had any teeth they would have been rattling in his head.

The Indian rapidly told them where he'd "found" the turban. Nanak guessed that he was telling the truth but thought it best to hold on to him, just in case.

✳

They discovered Santa Teli Singh that afternoon sleeping in the sheep shed of a rough little farm four miles from the hobo squat with only his thin army uniform and bedroll to keep him warm.

He was so soiled by sheep urine and excrement that the men couldn't get within ten feet of him.

"Maybe your relationship with the sheep was more than just for warmth," taunted a much-relieved Rajinder. "Maybe we should call you Santa Shit Head . . ."

The other men chimed in with suggestions, finally dubbing him Santa Pee Pee. Even Nanak had to laugh. Santa was a banty rooster of a man. Though short and scrawny, he was combative and always game for any kind of one-upmanship. And best of all, he took no permanent offense.

Santa eyed the shorn Nanak.

"My father would cut off his member if he saw his son as I see you."

"I heard your father cut off his member when you were born," interjected Rajinder, picking at his teeth with a small knife he'd found in the sheep shed. "Your face frightened him so much he swore never to have another."

"My face is not the most important part of my body," replied Santa gravely. "No woman need look beyond this." He grasped his crotch with both hands.

"That's because no woman has ever had the misfortune of getting close to that pig's tail you call a member." Rajinder eyed him speculatively. "And even if she got close I doubt if she could ever find it."

They trudged back to the clearing, only to find their campsite above the squat had been raided and the little food Matthew had left with them gone along with all their firewood. Below the hill, two dozen men sat around several sizable fires. Not one of them had looked up as the Sikhs passed by.

"We need to find a better place," Nanak observed. "And we'd better start posting a permanent guard."

"What about food?" bleated Bohun.

"We'll steal it," Rajinder declared. "This land is so vast they won't miss a thing."

"We can't afford to take the chance of drawing further attention to ourselves. I have told you, the authorities are well aware of our absence."

"Absence! That's good," remarked Santa. "I do not think they hang people for absence."

That night it snowed, a great white clasping blanket more than a foot thick.

Nanak's little group huddled together, shivering so hard they seemed to vibrate as one. In the morning Santa leaned over and woke Nanak. He looked so comical with ice hanging from his beard and a crown of white on his head that, despite his misery, Nanak couldn't help but chuckle.

"Save your merriment. I have bad news."

"I haven't had any good news for so long it could only be bad," Nanak muttered.

"Rajiid is dead."

Nanak leaped to his feet. Curled against Santa's back during the night, Rajiid had stiffened into a turtlelike shell.

"I would have told you earlier, but even dead he was keeping me warm. But now he's stiff and smelly. He let go in his pants. His charm has gone for me."

"How did he die?" Bohun asked. By now the rest were awake. "Is it catching?"

"Don't be an idiot," Santa responded. "He was weak, always coughing, slept all the time. He just wore out."

"There's an old well over there," Prem Singh gestured toward the city. "I found it when we were looking for firewood. We could throw him down there. No one would know."

Nanak shuddered. He barely knew Rajiid, a mournful-looking soldier who said and did as little as possible. He was quite surprised when he discovered him among the deserters, as he didn't think the man had the gumption for anything so risky. But despite what he thought of him, every Sikh deserved a proper funeral, which meant a cleansing cremation in a funeral pyre. There was no eldest son to light the blaze, nor even a close relative, so one of this pathetic band would have to do. "Rajiid must be seen off properly," he declared. "We will go deeper into the woods."

"But everything is wet," Bohun whined.

"Why not burn him here," suggested Santa.

Nanak drew a deep breath and pointed down the hill at the huddles of sleeping men. "There are people here who, for a hunk of bread, would be happy to declare to the English police that we killed a man by burning him to death. Deserting is one thing, they may forget about us in time. But if it is found what we have done to a body, people will be afraid, and then they will really hunt us down."

"We cannot hide anyway," moaned Bohun. "We are too different. We must give ourselves up—explain it was all a mistake. Then they will let us bury Rajiid and go home."

"Go home, baby sister?" Rajinder snorted, pushing the boy backward with the flat of his hand. "Were you always so stupid, or did the British drill all your brains out of you? No one is taking us home. Nanak is right. We must honor Rajiid. He was a pot of water that never boiled, but it is our duty. And not here."

Rajinder settled the matter by wrapping the stiff, smelly bundle in a blanket, flinging it over his shoulder, then marching off into the deep woods without a backward look. Within an hour they found a small clearing surrounded by towering trees. The wet snow changed to a drizzle, which soaked them thoroughly while they scavenged for wood. It took most of the morning to build a decent-sized pyre. It should have been at least eight feet high and twelve feet across, but this damp land of trees gave up its firewood grudgingly.

Nanak produced a matchbox, and everyone cheered when Santa pulled out a small can of kerosene. No one spoke as the match flared. Out. The wind was playing with them. They crowded around to shelter the flame and nearly set Bohun's clothes on fire, as wet as they were. Two, three, four matches, and not a single one caught.

"God's tooth!" swore Rajinder. "Give me that!" There was only one match left. Rajinder rained curses on everyone and everything he could think of. He selected a piece of wood sticky with resin, slivered it carefully into a pile with his *kirpan*, then they poured the kerosene on it. Calmly he looked around, winked at Nanak, then struck the match to the kindling, which ignited with a great *whoosh*.

Half an hour later, the pyre burning merrily, the men were finally warm. Even the looming trees didn't seem so threatening. They sang hymns to honor the passing of their comrade.

> *He who made the night and day,*
> *The days of the week and the seasons,*
> *He who made the breezes blow, the waters run,*
> *The fires and the lower regions.*
> *Made the earth—the temple of law.*
> *He who made creatures of diverse kind*
> *With a multitude of names,*
> *Made this law—*
> *By thought and deed be judged forsooth*
> *For God is true and dispenses Truth.*

"Howdy, folks!" a voice boomed out of the darkness.

"Eee!" shrieked Bohun, almost falling to his knees.

"Shut up!" Rajinder hissed, drawing his *kirpan*.

Two large white men strolled into the clearing, cradling heavy-caliber deer rifles. Though they were many years apart in age, they were virtually identical, one a slighter shorter version of the other. By the light of the fire each face was narrow, like an ax, with a prominent nose and close-set eyes framed by a single, unbroken eyebrow. Their clothes were a mixture of native-sewn skins, burlap, blankets, and a few items purchased from the Hudson's Bay Company store near the heart of Vancouver.

"Saw yer fire," started the older man.

"Lordy!" interrupted the younger one, "smelled it afore we saw it. I been drooling like an old hound ever since."

"We're after deer," the older man continued. "Got turned around in the bushes and saw yer fire. Too damn cold for hunting. Weather around here's as changeable as a woman's mind. All right if we warm up?"

With their backs to the fire, the pair made an eerie scene; damp steamed from their overcoats, which looked like old blankets with head holes hacked out.

"Mighty big fire ya got here," observed the younger. "Funny place to have one. No houses hereabouts. Hey!"

The Sikhs stood as if paralyzed.

"Don't pester'em, Arvil," chastened the older man. "For'ners are shy. For'ners, right?" Receiving no answer, he continued: "If ya don't mind I'll give ya a bit o' advice. Them hats of yourn are poor. Too much rain here for that deesign. You'll be carrying a hunnert pound on yer head afore ya knowt. Ya really need something that shoots the water off." He held out a leather hat with an extra-wide brim at the back, to send the rain away from the neck.

"See, an here's my secret. Beaver!" He showed the men a round of beaver pelt pushed into the crown. "I never get cold with this! Nor with this," he pulled out a pint bottle, which he upended into his mouth.

"That'll kill the demons," he said with a barking cough followed by a mighty shudder. He offered the bottle around, but the Sikhs all shook their heads.

If the hunters were bothered by the lack of response to their conversation, they gave no sign. Nanak was so startled by their sudden appearance that he forgot all his English. The others smiled foolishly, trying to convey their friendliness. They were all uncomfortably aware of the loaded rifles.

"Heard your singing. Nice havin' a singsong on such a mis'rable day."

Hearing no answer, the man consulted his bottle again before essaying another conversational gambit. "Say," he said, sniffing ostentatiously, "what are you fellas cooking? I'm so hungry I could eat an ox."

"Amore!" shouted Nanak. His tongue loosened and he threw out the only Italian word he knew. "Amore. We Italian."

"Oh, sure, well that 'splains it. They drink wine, Arvil," he added to his son.

"Sure wouldn't mind sharing a bita that meat ya cookin'," Avril said, wiping a string of drool off his face.

Nanak grinned happily at him. "Amore! Amore!"

"No speekie English, eh?" the older man said loudly in a manner that suggested all was explained. "We'd better not help ourselves, Arvil, it ain't polite."

Finally they picked up their guns and made to depart. "Well folks, thanks for your hospitality. Mighty fine fire. So long."

The Sikhs stood in silence until they were out of earshot.

"What did they want?" whispered Bohun in a querulous voice.

"They wanted to eat Rajiid," Nanak said with a straight face. "Said he smelled like he was done."

"What did you tell them?"

"You heard me. I told them *amore*, the only word I know in Italian."

"*Amore?* What is *amore?*"

"It means," Nanak said stiffly, trying to quell an enormous bubble of laughter. "It means something like I love you.'"

They roared and screamed with laughter, shouting until their sides ached and tears wet their cheeks.

"*Amore! Amore!*" they chanted.

47

＊

1899

Hastings Mill, Burrard Inlet

"Just what kind of deal are you talking about?" The whiskered man pulled at the stained shirt, doing a poor job of containing his belly.

"A very good one," Nanak replied.

"It'd better be good 'cause I hire locals and Kanakas—big and strong and dumb. They do what they're told."

Matthew arranged the meeting with Elwood Casey, manager of the Hastings Mill on Burrard Inlet, telling him the Italians were good workers. During the two years since Kate found Nanak, Matthew, though stiff and disapproving as ever, had proven himself a friend. Once the fuss about the deserters died down, he persuaded a dairy farmer in the tiny community of Eburne, a couple of miles from the mouth of the Fraser, to hire the Sikhs when he tripled his herd. Since then they'd been working for food. But now they needed proper wages in order to purchase passage back to India or, as they'd discussed many times, settle in Vancouver and one day bring over families and brides. All of the Sikhs had farming roots and were impressed with the quality and quantity of the farmland, much of which hadn't been cleared.

"We are smaller," conceded Nanak. "But we are working most quickly and are very good at following the orders."

The man shot him a quick look. Was this Itie poking at him?

"I saw Italians before, you don't look nothing like them."

"We are coming from Corsica. Different language, much different."

The mill boss was sorely tempted. Orders for railway ties were flooding in to the Hastings Mill, and he didn't have the men to fill them. As a result he'd lost two orders to the Moodyville Mill across Burrard Inlet, and it infuriated him. Hastings Mill, with the city wharf on one side and the foundry and lime kiln on the other, had once been the largest in the colony, but that was long before Vancouver had officially become a city in 1886. Now Moodyville had taken those honors away.

With the gold craze in the Klondike no one wanted to work the mill. Even the chinks were heading north, and the Indians preferred working in the canneries if you could get them to work at all. And just recently the discovery of copper and silver in the Boundary Bay area, southwest of Vancouver near the American border, had siphoned off more workers. When Casey had arrived from Minnesota to take over management of the mill in 1889, there were ten mining companies registered in the city. Now there were nearly two thousand on the books. It seemed everyone was unemployed in 1895, and now no one was.

"And the discount?"

"We are taking fifty percent of white wages. But you are promising to hire us each and every one. And we must have shelter."

The mill boss considered. This one certainly wasn't an impressive specimen, but if they didn't work out he'd just get rid of them. Half price was very attractive.

"I don't allow no drinkin' and no wimmin on the property. If you've got to get your pipe pulled, then do it on their turf. I don't want no fights over wimmin."

"No drink. No women. No pipes," agreed Nanak. "You have shelter?"

"Oh yeah, I got shelter. A farmhouse. You'll see it t'other side of the skid road. Jess don't come whining to me about leaks and such. Got it?"

"Got it. The pay is coming how and how much exactly?"

"You ain't done one lick o' work and yor comin' on about pay?" the man huffed for a bit. "Seventy-five cents a day, that's half," he lied. It was closer to a third. "I pay Thursday, ev'ry Thursday 'cept this one for your boys. It's already Sunday and I couldn't do the payroll in time. You'll get yours next time."

✳

"We have it!" Nanak declared triumphantly. "And a farmhouse too!"

"Let's go!" shouted a delighted Rajinder. He was sick of sleeping in the damp barn.

"No, first you must cut your hair and beard. We're supposed to be Italians."

Dismay wrote itself across the faces of the men. They hadn't needed to make that sacrifice hidden away on the isolated farm. Only Nanak came in contact with outsiders.

"What about our turbans?" Santa asked, anxiety heavy in his voice.

"We put them away," stated Nanak firmly. "One day we'll need them again."

Almost as one the men fingered their turbans and the coarse coil of beard hair around their jaws. Cut it. No knife had ever touched their heads.

Rajinder's mother was Hindu and his father a Gude district farmer whose own mother had also been Hindu. Of all the men, he held least closely to the Sikh traditions. He squatted down in front of Nanak. "I was born without a turban and I can die without one. And a beard is just a beard. Off with it!"

Not a word was said as the *kirpan* scritched-scritched against Rajinder's long, oily hair. First one hank fell to the ground, then another. The men stared disbelievingly at the growing pile. When Nanak was finished, Rajinder stood up.

"Who next?" he challenged.

✳

"What will you do with your first pay Santa Pee Pee?" Rajinder asked.

"I will buy butter! I will buy a hundred pounds of butter and bathe in it, I will make *ghee* and drink it, I will smear it all over my body. Then I will buy wheat flour and make *naan, naan* so large and greasy and stuffed with charred onions that it will take me a week to eat it." Santa sighed happily in anticipation.

"And what will you buy?" Santa asked the big man walking beside him.
"More guns."
"Guns?"
"Guns," the big man replied.
"What for? We are Italian mill workers. What do you need a gun for?"
"I conclude that everyone in this country needs a gun."
"Ha! You'd probably shoot off your little monster if you ever got your hands on one."
"Half my little monster is worth all of yours at full attention."
"Oh, be careful, my friend," urged Santa seriously. "I am slight of four limbs but massive of the fifth. One sight of it, and you will fall down dead in a faint of envy."

✳

Listening to them, Nanak didn't disagree with Rajinder. He wouldn't soon forget the lies of the train porter and station agent that got him in so much trouble, or the theft of their unguarded food at the hobo squat. At some point they might have to defend themselves. All the men were trained with rifles, but they had only two, and few bullets. We should have at least one weapon for every man, he thought.

Nanak was crestfallen when they actually saw where they were to live. The farmhouse was in dreadful shape. Barely half the roof was still intact, and the heavy West Coast rains had rotted much of the floor. The smell of decay was powerful, and piles of garbage were strewn everywhere. Markings on the walls indicated that some of the denizens of the hobo village had lived there before moving on to a more habitable site.

"You're too fussy," Rajinder said, brushing aside Nanak's sour mood. "You would find paradise and complain that it was too warm or the grass too green or the water not blue enough."

"It's a dung heap!"

"Needs a little tidying up," Rajinder countered. "Otherwise it's fine. The foundation is sound and the field beside the house looks like it can be made to grow food."

The men surprised Nanak by setting about cleaning up without complaint. Their canvas field tarp was stretched over the hole in the roof. When the garbage inside the house was hauled out they made a find: an aged pot-bellied stove buried under the debris, which Rajinder cleaned and coaxed back to life. The world started to seem a better place with a warm fire and tea brewing on the stove.

✳

"This is much better than living in a barn," said Kate a week later. "I'd say this is a big improvement. You've done a good job."

"Many thanks to you," Nanak said awkwardly. He searched desperately for something else to say. "How is your herd being?"

Kate frowned, "My herd? We don't keep any animals."

"No, no, I am thinking about your peoples, who you are helping. Do you not call them your herd?"

Kate threw back her head and laughed. "Oh my, that is very funny."

The other men glanced over, curious at her peals of laughter. Nanak glared at them furiously.

"Flock. We call them a flock in religious circles, though only the Lord knows why. And I suppose I am the mother hen caring for my little chicks."

Nanak had the urge to ask her why she didn't have a husband.

"What are you smiling at?"

"I am thinking . . ." he caught himself, horrified at what he'd almost asked, what he'd been thinking ". . . of, of food. Yes, the food you are bringing. That is very kind of you."

Kate held his eyes for a moment.

"It's nothing," her voice sounded flat to her own ears. Stop it, you silly old spinster! What did you expect?

Matthew and Kate had brought along two sacks of flour, a flagon of oil, some tea, a small box of salt, and a half barrel of pickled beef. The men unloaded everything happily. "I have several more boxes to deliver in Hastings," he said. "There's a family come down terrible with ague. Poor woman has six children, and her husband lost his leg cutting shingles. Let's be off, Kate!"

Kate glanced back once as the wagon rattled toward the main road leading to the old colony townsite of Hastings to the east of the city. Nanak, whose attention had been taken by Santa, missed her quick look. Kate drew a long breath.

"Are you tired, Kate? You look weary; we can put in for the night at Johnson's Livery and deliver the boxes in the morning."

"No, brother. Not at all, do stop fussing at me."

✳

"No butter," Santa said sadly. "Oh well, this wretched oil will have to do. Hurry up, Bohun, make my *naan*!"

"How shall we cook it? We have no grill," asked Bohun.

"Perhaps one day, young Bohun, you will tell us what we can do instead of what we can't," chided Rajinder.

Naan was usually cooked over a hot fire on a flat iron griddle, but here they didn't even have a frying pan.

"The buckets! We can use them," Nanak said, picking up one of the old ash buckets lying in the yard. "We'll turn them over and cook on the bottoms. It'll be perfect."

"Bohun! If Guru Gobind were here he would proclaim you the bucket boy," said Rajinder. "Since he's not here, *I* proclaim you bucket boy. Turn the bread often and don't let it burn, or Santa Pee Pee will be so distressed he will be unable to work tomorrow and the English will throw us into the sea."

The bread was barely cooked in the middle, charred at the ends, and garnished with the bits of ash that Bohun hadn't been able to scrape out. But it was unleavened, oily, and the best thing any of them could ever remember eating.

Bohun began to sing softly, *Satnaam, Wah Guru*—"the true name, the wondrous Guru." His voice was high and melodious. Delight filled the room. The morose boy had never shown a hint of such talent before.

"I was to be trained as a *raagi*," he explained. "My father was also a hymn singer. But he died and my uncle said the British army was the best way to help the family. I thought it meant I would sing for the Sikh troops, but they sent me to be trained on the cannons with the Muslim gunners. That is how I ended up in London."

Bohun's gunnery division had brought ten of the famed Sikh cannons made in the time of Maharaja Ranjit Singh to Queen Victoria's Diamond Jubilee. Each cannon had a slightly different "throat," and as they boomed out in the main courtyard of Buckingham Palace, a deafening symphony could be heard by the throngs standing miles-deep around the palace. That night the Queen went to bed with a nostrum for her headache.

"Sing on," encouraged Nanak. "Sing of *raj me jog* and tell us how to be of the world but not worldly."

"I do not have my harmonium."

"Never mind, sing on."

Bohun raised his chin and closed his eyes.

The lotus in the water is not wet
Nor the waterfowl in the stream
If man would live, but by the world untouched,
Meditate and repeat the name of the Lord Supreme.

The men smiled and nodded their heads to the melody. Nanak noticed Rajinder sitting rigidly, seemingly far away. Never had he seen such a look of melancholy.

Nanak read aloud from the Granth Sahib, as one by one the men nodded off to sleep.

"What of your home, Rajinder?" Nanak asked the big man, the only one still awake. It bothered him that the strength in their group was so mournful.

"I will tell you on one condition. I have a paper, which I have carried for five years, since I joined the army. I cannot read and I would like you to read it to me."

"Gladly."

"I am Jat Sikh, a farmer, that much you know."

Nanak nodded.

"My village is Gude in the Lahore district. I had always wanted to be a Khalsa warrior, but I have three sisters. I have a brother too, but he was born with shriveled legs and cannot work. I always asked my father when I was young how I could become a Khalsa warrior, and he would always say to me, 'The desire is in your heart but let your head guide you to your duty.' The farm was my duty."

"I too had desires," Nanak murmured sympathetically. "But they were to study and teach, not to march and kill for the British."

"It is too bad we could not have traded places," Rajinder sighed deeply. "I married at seventeen and my wife . . ." he clasped his hands to his chest. The loving gesture pained Nanak. Rajinder cleared his throat. "When the British raised taxes, my father was forced to sell half our land to pay them. There wasn't enough left to support me and my new family, so I joined up." Another heavy sigh. "By then, of course, I didn't want to leave my wife and children."

Nanak was silent for several minutes but he could not contain himself.

"Why then did you desert? You have a wife, your wages, and . . ."

"And two sons."

"And two sons! You had little time left in the army but you ran away."

"I did not run away!" Rajinder scowled. "I thought about my home and how my father was right. The land was in my heart. All those years in Amritsar and then in the army. It took me that long to feel the land in my heart."

"But you could have purchased more land."

Rajinder shook his head. "It is difficult in my district now, and all my wages went to marry off my sisters and support my wife. There was little left."

"I still don't understand why you left the train."

"Land," Rajinder responded simply. "Didn't you see it from the train? Everywhere you look there is land, good farmland, especially along the big river. It is flat and looks rich, much like the valley of the five rivers in the Punjab." He tapped his knuckles against his *kirpan*. "I will own some of that land one day. And then I will bring my family over."

Nanak once again fell silent. Rajinder's story made his own bumbling misadventure an embarrassment.

"I left the train because you did. You showed me the way. I wouldn't have had the courage otherwise."

"Why did you think I'd deserted?"

"At first I didn't believe it," Rajinder admitted. "No one from the train saw anything, you were just gone. Everyone was very upset. Then the officers read a statement from the porter who said he saw you running away through the woods. Then another from the ticket agent, who said you threatened to cut his throat."

Nanak seethed at the lies, even though they were two years old.

"The train stopped just before we were to enter Vancouver. There was a large animal dead on the tracks. It was then I decided to go. I grabbed my pack, slipped off the back of the train, and ran to the woods as fast as I could. When I looked back I saw the rest of them following me." He flicked his fingers at the slumbering lumps on the floor.

"I am not a leader like you are. This bunch couldn't wipe their bottoms without being told how. But I knew we'd find you. Just as I knew you had a plan."

"There is no plan," Nanak said carefully, trying to decide what to tell this man who had risked so much on a false assumption. "I did not desert," he said softly. "I fell asleep and the train left without me."

Rajinder stared at him disbelievingly.

"You fell asleep?" he asked, the words rumbling out from deep within his chest.

Nanak simply nodded.

"You did not mean to stay here?"

"Not at all. I have served for seven years, my term was finished. It was a beautiful day. I sneaked away just for a short time to say my prayers, and I fell asleep."

"Asleep! We are here because you fell asleep! And there is no plan? Never was a plan?"

Rajinder narrowed his eyes and hunched his massive shoulders. For a moment Nanak thought he was about to be ripped to pieces. Then the laugh came, rippled up Rajinder's bulky frame and shook his body. Barely a sound escaped his lips but his shoulders twitched as if pulled by a puppet master. When he recovered, Rajinder shook his head, wiped his eyes, and said, "Now you owe me a reading." He handed over a battered wad of paper, many times folded and furry at the edges with handling.

My honored husband,

Your face and body are with me every night as I say my prayers. Your smile is on the lips of your sons. I touch them when they sleep . . .

Nanak looked up, embarrassed, but Rajinder had his eyes closed and a happy smile on his face.

"*. . . my finger to their lips as mine to yours. The flower of my body . . .*"

Nanak couldn't continue. His face burned and he stumbled over the last words.

"What is wrong? Go on, go on."

"You speak well, not like a peasant, but you can't read?"

"If I could read would I have you read my wife's dearest thoughts aloud? My wife is from an educated family, though poor. Her father believed all should read. My father saw no need for it."

"I am embarrassed to be intruding upon you and your wife in these most intimate moments," Nanak admitted.

"If I am not embarrassed, why should you be?" Rajinder responded with his down-to-earth logic. "Now get on with it."

"I can't help it," Nanak said.

"Put away your embarrassment, it's spoiling my enjoyment. Start again at the part about her flower."

48

✳

1903

Coal Harbour

Nanak stood nervously on the Coal Harbour dock; to his left, the sixteen-year-old, thousand-acre Stanley Park where the ancient village of Khwaykhway once stood. Away to his right was the smoke of furious industry. Vancouver was booming. The economic pause of the mid-90s had evaporated in a swell of land speculation, railway building, international trade, and, of course, gold. The Kootenay rush to the interior of British Columbia was the fourth major gold strike in the West since the middle of the last century, and each one brought a new wave of men—innocent, grasping, hopeful. There had also been significant finds of silver, copper, and zinc, which meant the building of smelters and more rail lines to carry the ore to port.

Nanak cared nothing for gold or any other metal. The ship he waited for contained something more precious: his countrymen, at least twelve of whom were on board. More than five endless years had passed since he and the others had been marooned in Vancouver, and they eagerly awaited the first boatload of legal Sikhs. They hadn't expected them to arrive for some months yet. Then, a few days ago, on one of her periodic visits to the mill, Kate showed him a newspaper article headlined "Noble Exotics From The Spice Continent." They were to arrive the following Monday. After much puffing and blowing, Elwood Casey gave Nanak the day off—"no pay"—to meet the boat. "But none of the others, mind."

New arrivals were also eagerly anticipated by the city. As the prosperity of the area grew, labor of all sorts was, once again, desperately needed. This group came from the river valleys in the Punjab and were reputed to be splendid farmers, something that was in short supply as so many men had turned to mining or timber. The writer applauded the newcomers for being "cleaner than other Orientals" and, having served with the British army, they were familiar with the culture of His Majesty's citizens.

Nanak hoped that an older man was among the passengers, perhaps someone with religious training, who would lift his burden of leadership. He also prayed that this boat would be a first step in normalizing his men's lives as Sikhs in their new country. Everyone was heartily sick of pretending they were Italians and all longed for a larger community. The next step would be to bring women and families to British Columbia. He knew there were already many Chinese wives and some from Japan.

The ship stood offshore while the immigration officer processed the crew and passengers—checking their detainment papers from Albert's Head in Victoria where they'd been deloused and disinfected for smallpox with foul-smelling powders. A Vancouver doctor examined each again, because a woman of "ill repute" en route from San Francisco had recently passed through the Albert's Head checkpoint with full-blown venereal disease. Before she succumbed, she'd passed it on to the ship's purser, a subeditor of the *Vancouver World,* and a traveling salesman.

A stately man of middle years with a stiffly erect posture appeared, wearing a gleaming-white turban and a flowing, spotless muslin robe. Following him was a bedraggled group of thirteen tired, bleary-eyed, and dirty men. The first man had a way of casting his eyes around as if seeing things not discernible to others. He spoke with the cultured tones of the educated, asking a government customs agent in English where accommodation could be found. Nanak pushed through the crowd and addressed him in Punjabi.

"Who are you?" the man demanded, surprised to be spoken to in his own tongue by a foreigner.

"I am Nanak Simple Singh of the village Sur Singh. I welcome you to this new land."

"Where is your turban?" the man demanded. "What has been done to your hair?"

"I beg your forgiveness for my appearance," Nanak said, quite taken aback at the man's harsh tone and lack of pleasantries. "It would be best if we discussed the matter later, among our own."

"A Sikh without a turban is not a Sikh at all," the man declared.

Nanak did his best to ignore the man's rebuke. "I would be grateful to know your name, sir."

"Giani Bhupinder Gill Singh," he said stiffly.

This man thinks well of himself, Nanak thought. "Giani" was a Sikh title, that meant "learned teacher." It was rarely used when one person introduced himself to another, unless pomposity was his leading character trait.

"I cannot believe what I see before me!"

"There are many things to understand and know about this new country, Sardar Bhupinder Gill Singh," Nanak said respectfully but pointedly using Sardar, meaning Mr., instead of the more elevated title.

"The others are as you?" the man demanded.

"All six of us," Nanak admitted. "You see when we arrived . . ."

"I'll hear your excuses later," Bhupinder cut him off sharply, his face creased with displeasure. "I will now go to the *gurdwara*." In the Punjab, a *gurdwara* served as a place of worship as well as shelter for visitors and the needy.

"We have not one as yet. There have been some difficulties with our presence here, but now that you have arrived I believe . . ."

"No *gurdwara*! With no gateway to the Guru, he is lost to you."

"We have found ways of keeping His spirit pure in our hearts," responded Nanak, starting to get his back up. What did this man know about the conditions here? And who was he to judge them?

"What prattle!" Bhupinder scoffed. "You stand before me with no turban. Hair and beard shorn. Clearly you have abandoned the Wah Guru."

"We have not abandoned the path," Nanak bristled. "It has been necessary to chart a new one through the forest. This is not the Punjab."

"What have you arranged to accommodate us?" Bhupinder asked in the pinched and weary tone of one expecting the worst.

Nanak fought down his irritation for the sake of the men who had spent every spare moment enlarging the farmhouse since Nanak learned of the Sikhs arriving. Their joy could not be contained. Every morning they said *japji,* the morning prayer, with such enthusiasm it sounded more like the songs to celebrate victory in battle than the reverent uttering of *mool mantra,* the most fundamental expression of the Sikh faith. They smiled, joked, and laughed, and the twelve-hour days flew by. Soon there would be people from home.

"Our farmhouse is less than two hours' walk," said Nanak.

"We must walk!" Bhupinder harrumped.

"Only for a short while."

"Wagons should have been provided."

"We did not have sufficient money for wagons," Nanak said flatly.

They did have money, but the men agreed that none of it would be touched until they had enough to purchase their own farmland.

"I think you will find the accommodations at our place of work gracious though poor," Nanak said, trying to be encouraging.

✳

The farm was their pride. The summer after they moved in the men planted a garden and tended their rows jealously, comparing their harvest and boasting about the size of their carrots or the sweetness of their peas. Santa purchased two brace of chickens, quickly adding several pigs and three cows. Bohun shyly traded vegetables to a nearby farmer for more chickens and presented them to a delighted Santa. Rajinder and Santa planted strawberries and raspberries, and a native Indian family from the north shore appeared one day with blackberry roots, which Nanak exchanged for broken mill tools they'd scavenged and repaired.

When Elwood Casey saw the improvements made by the Sikhs on the land and buildings, he began charging rent, which he doubled the next year. "'Course you can always move out," he told Nanak.

"That's capitalism at work," Kate stated bluntly after Nanak complained of the man's avarice. "Like it or not, that's the way things are. It's all about ownership. Those who own call the shots."

"It is not so different back in the Punjab," Nanak reflected. "But things move much more quickly here."

"Then why not give Mr. Casey a taste of his own medicine?"

"A taste . . . medicine. These English sayings are still puzzling to me."

"Mr. Casey doesn't own the mill," she told him. "He just acts like he does. I doubt that Mr. Casey has even told the owners he's renting the land to you."

"So as far as the owners are knowing, the land is unused?" Nanak said, starting to catch on.

"I wouldn't be surprised."

The next day Nanak proposed that Casey tell the owners he had a buyer for the two acres.

"Get out with you! I'm not running around for you like some kind of nigger helper."

"I am understanding. Of course," Nanak said deferentially. "I was only contemplating that you are doing the owners a favor."

"How do you figure that?"

"It must be quite a nuisance, collecting rent every month. I am thinking the owners would be preferring a larger sum to rid themselves of land not needed. It could be a falling wind you bring to them. And, of course, there is the fee for the finding."

Casey scowled. Falling wind? The groveling idiot must mean windfall.

"It's worth . . ." Casey was about to say "worthless." The land was of no value to the mill as it was too far back from the beach to build on, and the fact that it happened to be well situated for a few bushels of carrots meant nothing. But as the words entered his head he grasped what the slippery foreigner was up to. He was subtly threatening to approach the owners directly about the rent that was not, in fact, entered on the books. The conversation quickly took a very different turn.

✳

Casey negotiated a deal for $2,000, to be paid in equal installments over seven years at three percent interest, slightly over the going rate. Nanak later learned it was the same amount the owners had paid for the entire hundred and twenty acres the mill stood on five years earlier. No matter, it was theirs. He considered the $200 he turned over to Casey as finder's fee a bargain.

✳

Bhupinder swept past Nanak and stepped on a chest the Sikhs had unloaded from the ship.

"This man who greeted us is not of our faith though he pretends to be." He nodded disparagingly toward Nanak. "He would have us cut our hair and abandon the path of our belief. We will make our own way or else we shall be lost as he is."

Beside himself, Nanak called out to the exhausted, dispirited group who followed Bhupinder off the boat.

"I'm sorry that I have disappointed your enlightened leader," he said sarcastically, purposely using Punjabi phraseology that implied the man's head was in the clouds, not fully connected to earth. "We have done the best we can and with your help we shall build a community here."

Nanak saw the men shifting uncomfortably from foot to foot. They were peasants and soldiers, and they too were astonished at his appearance. Desperately he recited,

He who made the night and day,
The days of the week and the season,
He who made the breezes blow, the waters run,
The fires and the lower regions.
Made the earth—the temple of law.

He who made creatures of diverse kind
With a multitude of names,
Made this law—
By thought and deed be judged forsooth
For God is true and dispenses Truth.
There the elect His court adorn,
And God Himself their actions honors:
There are sorted deeds that were done and bore fruit
From those that to action could never ripen.
This O Nanak, shall hereafter happen.

"What do you mean, they left?" Rajinder's face was dark with disbelief and anger. The rest of the men stood around with crestfallen expressions.

"Left. Gone. Not coming," Nanak said with exasperation. "Right on the dock, Bhupinder spoke to a sawmill agent from Washington who convinced them they'd be happier there. When I protested, the agent said it was only fair to come up and take our 'hindoos,' what with British Columbia importing cheap Oriental labor then shipping cut-rate rail ties and boards to be sold in their market."

Rajinder didn't care about business, he fixated on the idea that thirteen Sikhs from the Punjab had set foot in Vancouver but refused even to visit their countrymen.

"Do you mean to tell me that these Sikhs, including a man of good family, simply went off with two Americans to work in their mills because we cut our hair?"

Nanak was too depressed to do anything but nod his head.

That night the men were as full of suppressed anger as they had earlier been brimming with happiness and anticipation. Even evening prayer didn't lift their black mood. It was a grim group that walked over to the mill the next morning at six A.M. to start their twelve-hour shift.

Though no one challenged the fiction that the Sikhs were Italians, few believed their homeland was anywhere near Italy. One hundred and twenty-seven men worked at the mill, fifty-two of them Chinese or Japanese, who kept to themselves. They were just numerous enough to avoid much trouble with the whites; the six "Italians" were not.

From the first day, feet appeared from nowhere, spilling Sikhs with timber on their shoulders, and showers of sawdust greeted those who carelessly walked under the storage bins. Once Bohun nearly fell through the trap in the sawing floor, when a pile of slabs ready for resawing into pickets and lathe strips inexplicably tumbled toward him.

Just before lunch on the bleak day after the ship arrived, Rajinder was almost crushed when an improperly fixed log rolled off the carriage. He glared at the two doggers responsible for securing logs. They hopped and clucked around like barnyard chickens, daring him to retaliate. It took Nanak and the rest to hold the big man back.

"We must put a stop to this nonsense," Nanak, who had always previously urged restraint, told the Sikhs during their half-hour lunch break. "But not with our largest, rather our smallest."

Santa Pee Pee was by far the smallest. He was also the fastest, and had been the most lethal hand-to-hand fighter in the entire Sikh regiment. "His little hands are like stones," Rajinder had once observed. "Too bad his head is made from the same material."

"Size is important to these men," Nanak emphasized. "If our smallest beats their toughest, their balls will shrivel around their ears." He outlined his plan. Santa and the others smiled for the first time since Nanak had returned alone from Vancouver.

Just before shutdown, Santa sauntered over to Samuel Hardy, informal leader of the whites, and the head saw-man. He was as tall as Rajinder, with the same craggy physique. The top of Santa's head barely came to the man's shoulder.

"Whaddya want, woggie?"

"A gift for your mother," said Santa, whose English was getting quite good. He spit copiously on Hardy's right foot, then on his chest, before the big man could react. Santa quickly circled away, just out of reach, waiting until the entire yard was assembled, eagerly anticipating the show.

Then he attacked, ducking under the man's windmilling punches. Five strikes, two to the head, two to the body, and one to the kneecap. Hardy toppled face-forward, stone-cold unconscious. It was disappointingly brief. Santa strolled up to the prostrate body, casually rolled him over with his foot, and stood on Hardy's chest facing the crowd, looking like a miniature lion asserting his ascendancy.

Stunned at first by the devastating demolition of their champion, the whites surged toward the defiant Sikh only to be stopped by the snick of *kirpans* sliding out of leather scabbards.

"The blades you see have many times killed for the British army," Santa said happily. "We were taught a hundred ways to kill. We can be popping out eyes with a single finger or making your balls into ornaments. We will not be gentle as I was with this pig here. Who knows what we will do. Are we not animals?

"Now is a very good time to be going away."

With a high-pitched scream Santa advanced, swinging his *kirpan* so rapidly it seemed a solid object to the eye. The crowd dispersed.

49

*

1906

Coal Harbour

This time Nanak was prepared with a wagon and a team of horses. Dwight McKenna, new manager of Hastings Mill, was easier to deal with than Elwood Casey, whose list of ailments had grown with the size of his belly. Six months earlier Casey had succumbed to gout, which the local doctor attempted to cure with a series of pukes and purges. In the course of endless vomiting, he suffered a hernia, which the enthusiastic healer attempted to fix surgically when a truss didn't work. The ether made Casey violently ill, and gas pains ensued for days, made worse by the peritonitis, which set in after the doctor stuffed the bowel back into the abdominal cavity with a finger recently used to free another man's blocked colon and insufficiently washed afterward. Casey's beleaguered gut wasn't helped by a bout of urine retention, which led to a bladder infection when the doctor catheterized the poor man who was in such agony that the idea of death made him positively joyous. He wasn't long denied.

By trading two days of free labor, Nanak got use of a wagon to meet the CPR steamer, the *Empress of China,* due in from Shanghai and Hong Kong, loaded with rice, silk, cotton, 14 Japanese, 175 Chinese, and 60 men of the Punjab. The irony was not lost on Nanak that the ship was the very one they had all missed nine years before.

"I'll not be promising to hire a one of them," Dwight McKenna warned Nanak when he agreed to provide the wagon. "Vancouver's bubble has burst and I'm betting we're on the slide for some time yet."

"Very good, sir. I am asking only for the use of the cleared field beside the skid road to house them most temporarily. We are collecting fabric for one year now and are making very good tents."

"How enterprising of you," McKenna said. "But tents or no tents, they stay one month and one month only."

Nanak couldn't keep his hands from his head. He caressed the folds of cloth tucking in bits of stray hair. Nine years, four months, twenty-two days. His head welcomed the turban as a mother does a lost child. It felt like an embrace around his head. Nanak had gone into the woods alone to wrap and secure it before dawn that morning. His fingers had not forgotten the soothing routine.

Nanak watched the steamship round the point of Stanley Park. In less than an hour his countrymen would be on shore. It wasn't cold but he found himself shivering as he waited.

He was nervous, far more nervous than he had been three years earlier standing in the same spot.

Vancouver had changed dramatically since Nanak found Rajinder, Santa, and the others near the hobo squat. The railway no longer controlled civic affairs, and the power of the social elite was giving way to a new class of entrepreneurs. The first bridge had been recently built across the Fraser River at New Westminster, and fishing was so valuable to the economy that government-built hatcheries placed over 100 million salmon fry in the Fraser every year. Though the giant Moodyville Mill closed in 1901, many more opened along the river. It was the perfect time for immigrants to find their way in the new world. Or would have been, if the economy hadn't stumbled. As it turned out, it would be a small stumble but sufficient to stir the glowering crowd standing fifty feet away. The Asiatic Exclusion League.

GOLLIWOGS, CELESTIALS, NIPS NOT WANTED HERE
WHITE CANADA FOR WHITE MEN
HINDOOS HEAVE HO

Nanak felt a ripple of irritation at their presence, which he hoped wouldn't interfere with his plan to turn the small band of Nobilly's into legal inhabitants of Vancouver. Ironically, the scheme had been created by Jupta Singh, Nanak's father, who as far as he knew had never previously entertained a single dishonest thought.

It had taken Nanak almost three years to work up the courage to write to his parents, though he regularly wrote letters home for the other men. Still officially a deserter, he was sure their disappointment in him for betraying the Khalsa spirit would never be set aside. It was Kate, on one of her periodic mill visits, tending to sick or injured men, who finally persuaded him to write.

"It will never arrive," opined Nanak bleakly.

"The CPR mail ships are the fastest in the world! Of course it will arrive."

"They cannot read."

"But you told me the priest in the *gurdwara* provided that service."

"They will never be believing me."

Kate sighed, with lips drawn into a tight circle of disapproval.

"Nanak Singh, are all Sikhs as pessimistic and easily discouraged as you?"

One December morning, five months later, to Nanak's amazement, a return letter arrived with the boiler coal. He crept off down to the rocky beach, away from the log pond and the area where hundred-foot trees, too large to go up the jack ladder into the mill, were split into smaller pieces by gunpowder charges. He told no one. It was dereliction of duty, leaving his post at the gang saw sorting the cants and odd sections of timber into uniform boards, but Nanak couldn't resist.

On the first page, there were only four words. At first Nanak thought it was a dismissal. His eyes cleared and he focused. "O Nanak, be saved."

The words of the first guru, his namesake. Prayer is the purifier to cleanse the spirit, rinse the soul of impurities, taught Guru Nanak. Nanak recalled the rest of the passage:

As hands or feet besmirched with slime,
Water washes white;
As garments dark with grime,
Rinsed with soap are made light;
So when sin soils the soul
Prayer alone shall make it whole.
Words do not the saint or sinner make,
Action alone is written in the book of fate,
What we sow that alone we take;
Oh Nanak, be saved or forever transmigrate.

Oh Nanak, be saved. Nanak cried his first night in the British India Army. He cried again when a man he called a friend died fighting the Afghan insurgents in '95. On December 3, 1906, Nanak Simple Singh cried for the third time in his adult life. A flood of despair and guilt poured out of him like a poison, searing his skin and soaking his shirt. With the tears came howls of release from a pain that had tightened around his heart for so long. When it was over he lay back exhausted and fell into a deep, peaceful sleep.

✳

The plan was simple yet ingenious. After begging his son's forgiveness for violating the example of honesty every father owes his son, Jupta Singh outlined his idea. Nanak's father had been saving every rupee he could. By late 1906 he had 2,000 rupees, sufficient for a healthy bribe. He entrusted the money to a friend who carried it all the way to Calcutta, exchanged it for pounds sterling, and bribed the first mate of the *Empress of China*. The mate surreptitiously added six people to the ship's manifest.

The boat was tied and the gangway lowered. Nanak's heart was near exploding. Men flowed off the ship, catching themselves and laughing as their sea legs wobbled. Carrying everything from leather suitcases to baskets and military duffels, they swarmed over the newly replanked dock. The music of languages and dialects met the crisp midday air. There they were. Ten, then twenty, then suddenly dozens of men in turbans of all colors, with *kirpans* at their sides. Most had a discernible military bearing and many wore military medals or campaign ribbons on their civilian clothes. They caused quite a stir among the onlookers.

The next hours were a blur. There was no Bhupinder Singh, no supercilious dismissal of Nanak. Nanak organized six of the men to pass through the immigration line twice, with different identification papers also paid for by his father.

"They will never notice," he assured them. "We all look the same to them."

The men were so fatigued from the journey that Nanak feared they would collapse. They set off along Water Street toward the mill, the weakest in the wagon, the rest walking. Nanak's hand slipped inside his shirt where he'd tucked the paper: NANAK SING, BRITISH SUBJECT written at the top with the red stamp of His Majesty's Immigration Service at the bottom.

✳

The problem, of course, was work.

"I can't possibly hire on more. I told you that," said McKenna, irritated that Nanak was even asking. "I gave you the land for a month and now you're asking for more work!"

"No, not more work. Same work, more people."

"What are you getting at, man?"

"There are six of us working here now. This is correct?" McKenna nodded suspiciously. He liked Nanak well enough and couldn't fault his labor or that of the other "Italians." McKenna knew full well that Nanak was no more Italian than he was a Negro. But he couldn't care less, as long as they continued to work like dogs for low wages and didn't make trouble.

"Which six it is being, is of no matter."

"You sneaky bastard, I see what you're up to. You can forget about it!"

"Please, reconsider!" Nanak held up hands in entreaty. "I give my holy word that six men are working all the day until no more light, and all the days of the week."

McKenna thought it through. He'd get more work for the same price. In his two years supervising the mill not a single one of the hindoos had been injured or sick. They worked harder than the whites or the Chinese, and never got drunk. Pretty Kate, on her last visit, had brought him news that the Women's League was bringing a complaint to the city council about the Hastings Mill workers, among others, frequenting the "vipers of Dupont Street" and encouraging prostitution. Secretly McKenna wondered what these hindoos did without women, as he'd never seen one of them set out west toward Chinatown on "dame patrol."

An idea stirred in McKenna's head. Rumor was that the British Columbia government was loaning money to Vancouver to allow the city to march ahead with several school building projects in the east-end workingclass neighborhood of Grandview and in middle-class Mount Pleasant. Zephraim Miles, owner of the mill, would love to have sufficient boards on hand to bid for those projects as well as for the street blocking, for which the council had already set aside money. Most of the roads were dirt or gravel in the city, but increasingly they were being upgraded with wooden-block paving or the new tar-macadam. All it took was a swell with a prominent name like Odlum, Marpole, or von Schaumberg getting one of their fancy automobiles stuck to suddenly put a street on the list for upgrading. If McKenna stockpiled paving blocks and boards without spending an additional penny for the work he'd certainly earn a feather from Miles.

"I'll give it a try for one month."

"Four."

"One."

"Perhaps two?"

"Done, but you'll have to house them yourself and don't start bleating like sheep to me about problems."

"Sheeps? Oh no sir, we are not like sheeps."

More like oxen, McKenna thought, watching him go.

When the first group of new workers was acclimatized, Nanak began substituting them into the mill work crew, always ensuring that one of his original group was on hand to supervise. The rest he put to work extending the farmhouse and planting more crops. Bohun had created a mini-*gurdwara* for the Granth Sahib his father had sent from the Punjab. One of the men, usually Bohun, opened it every morning and wrapped it for "rest" every evening. Bohun had made a switch of horse hair to substitute for the yak-hair fly whisk continuously flicked over the head of the bible reader in *gurdwaras* at home. But the holy resting place had to go. Six men could sleep in bunks in the pantry, actually twelve if they slept in shifts.

"Life here is always compromise," Nanak commented to Rajinder as a crew tackled the building projects.

"That is true of life everywhere," said the big man.

"If that was so for my former life, I do not remember it," replied Nanak, touching his blue turban.

Rajinder caught the gesture. He intended to keep his hair short. Turbans were impractical for work in the dirty mill, and they soaked up Vancouver's incessant rain like sponges. In his heart Rajinder wasn't a believer in the way that Nanak, Bohun, or even Santa Pee Pee were.

"That is your problem, Nanak Singh, you think too much and make yourself unhappy. Look at me, I think of nothing and I smile all day."

"Is that why I must remind you of your duties each day?" Santa interjected as he passed.

"You work like a buffalo with three legs!" Rajinder shot back.

"Ha! I am *fauj*, as an army compared to you."

"An army of Muslims perhaps, and all of them smoking *bhang*."

✳

Rotating nearly seventy men in jobs meant for six couldn't work for long. Squabbles erupted when one man took over a shift from another. Nanak, as usual, was thrown into the role of mediator. Rajinder wanted to let them fight it out, but Nanak had promised no trouble.

"Why not approach other mills?" asked Kate on one of her visits. She came more often, Nanak noticed, and usually had tea with McKenna in the small parlor he had built beside his office. They shouted politely to each other over the noise of the saws.

"Moodyville has closed but there is a new shingle mill at False Creek, and at the river near Eburne a second sawmill has just opened."

"But hiring is not going well, some are even being sent away as we are speaking."

"I bet Dwight has been spinning you those tales to keep you here, working like horses."

Nanak noted her casual use of the mill manager's first name.

"Even if I am placing these men elsewhere I cannot be rushing from one mill to another."

"Who says you need to?"

"They are as children and I am standing in the middle always. They speak hardly one word of English and they worry about families at home. I read prayers every day and I am collecting the money together. We must grow our own food and who will be supervising that?"

"Nanak Singh! Listen to yourself. You're like a mother hen who doesn't want to let any of her brood go. Are you too proud of yourself to let them be men?"

Nanak was stung. Pride was not a virtue. In his heart he knew Kate was right. He'd hated his role as interminable go-between in the army but had become resigned to it here. And now, with the influx of Sikhs, he was taking on the same role as if he'd been anointed to the task.

*

The next day Nanak traveled south on the new interurban train back to the little community of Eburne on the Fraser River where they'd first worked on the dairy farm. The conductor forced him to ride in the last car, with "the nigras." Nanak didn't care; he was too busy planning what he would say to the mill managers when he arrived.

As Kate had told him, there were two sawmills, a cannery, and a shingle mill in the village a few miles west along the river from the bridge to New Westminister, which had been constructed with much fanfare and hyperbole in 1905. Ignoring the stares of the men in the yard, he knocked boldly on the manager's door. After introducing himself, Nanak plunged in. He had learned a great deal about directness in his years among the Canadians.

"I will provide to you with a crew of twenty Sikhs, including my own self, who will work for you absolutely free of charge for a week. At that time you are choosing to hire us or not. Whichever way, I am giving to you the week as a gift."

The manager examined the proposition from all angles and couldn't see any way that he could be tricked or otherwise taken advantage of.

"Supposing I wanted to hire you and your men. What then?" the manager asked craftily.

"You must be hiring at least twenty men and they must be working together," Nanak explained.

"I can't pay you what the white labor gets."

"Seventy-five percent will do. And since we are doing two times as much work, it will be the greatest bargain for you. Also, we will take those shacks by the water for our housing."

This all seemed fine to the manager; he had been planning to knock down the smoke shacks ever since they'd run off the last of the Indians who'd used them for the spring and summer salmon run.

Three days later Nanak and Rajinder appeared with a hand-picked crew—only the largest, strongest, and hardest workers. "We must work as if our lives depended on it," Nanak warned them. In the yard, the whites used pushcarts to move the cut logs around, while the Sikhs ostentatiously hoisted the timbers on their shoulders and double-timed to and fro. It was teamwork as much as brawn. By the end of the day one Sikh crew of ten had stacked an entire barge with rough planks, which would be towed down the river, around the big green snout of Point Grey, soon to be its own municipality, and loaded onto a CPR ship bound for England. Normally the job took a gang of twelve two days. The next day Nanak slipped in ten fresh replacements who were camped in the woods at the foot of Granville Street, then substituted in the rested ten the next day.

"I'm glad you came by, Mr. Singh," the mill manager said on the last day. "I have decided to hire seven of your workers starting Monday. However, I can only pay sixty percent of the standard wage, not seventy-five as you demanded."

"That is most satisfactory but with one exception," Nanak stated. "You must hire all twenty to get that price."

Nanak waited while the man mulled it over. "The arrangements are, most naturally, private between you and I," Nanak added, sweetening the offer. "How you manage the books is most definitely your own business."

The manager's eyes lit up like torches. Cost the darkies out as if they were white and pocket the difference.

"All right, I'll take fifteen of your people." The manager quickly estimated that paying fifteen men sixty percent wages but costing them at a hundred percent gave him a nice bonus of about five dollars a day. He would have his longed-for Packard a full year earlier than anticipated.

"I am most grateful," Nanak bowed low so the man could not see the smile of triumph on his face.

Nanak traveled to seven mills. He barely rested or ate, but each success fueled his spirit like a feast. Within three months he had every single Sikh placed within Vancouver's lower mainland. There was still so much to do— arrange for collection of their wages, write letters, purchase food for the communal kitchens each pod of Sikhs quickly built wherever they were placed. Since none of the new arrivals spoke English he sent Santa, Rajinder, and Bohun to head teams in three of the larger mills. He would deal with the ones closer to the inlet himself, on his day of rest.

50

✳

1907

Vancouver

This is the voice of the west & speaks to the world,
We'll hold by right & maintain by might
Till the fore is backward driven.
We welcome as brothers all white men still,
But the shifty yellow race,
Whose word is vain, who oppress the weak,
must find another place.

Then let us stand unite all
And show our father's might,
That won the home we call our own,
For white man's land we fight
To Oriental grasp and greed
We'll surrender, no never.
Our watch word be God save the King.
White Canada forever.

(THEME SONG OF THE ASIATIC EXCLUSION LEAGUE)

After 1906 Sikh immigrants arrived in droves. Every boat from Hong Kong or
Shanghai to Vancouver carried men from the Punjab, mostly ex-soldiers, many
farmers. Word of excellent farmland, good jobs, and a climate not unlike the
valleys of the Punjab brought them to the west coast of America and Canada.
Some arrived via Australia, where they tried to land but were turned back. By
1908 there were at least 2,500 Sikhs officially in the province, and at least as
many who'd slipped over the border from the United States. They worked on
rail gangs and farms, in mines and mills, from the north shore of Vancouver to
the Fernie mines in the foothills of the Rocky Mountains.

At first they were welcomed as a solution to a desperate labor shortage, as Vancouver's economy roared once again. But as their numbers increased, so did the opposition. Still, the discrimination was nothing compared to what the Chinese and Japanese faced; they were far more numerous and visible on the streets and in the factories and homes owned by whites. Unlike their Far East neighbors, few Sikhs owned land or operated businesses. They also had a powerful connection to the empire from their service in the British army. And when the Sikhs were pushed, they pushed back. Until 1907 the various anti-Asian groups had concentrated on the far more numerous "chinks" and "japs."

To Kate's outrage, several prominent women from the Women's League joined the anti-Asian organization, helping swell the numbers to more than a thousand.

"I can't believe how they justify their actions!" sputtered Kate to Nanak as she was leaving Hastings Mill one day after tea with Dwight McKenna. She came every Monday and every Friday. McKenna, in spats, suspenders, and a fine woolen suit, drove his gleaming, black sixteen-horsepower Franklin Touring Car from the mill to the west end of the city for an "At Home" in the mansion where Kate rented rooms. Nanak saw the car advertised in the paper for $1,850 and marveled at having that much money to waste.

"I am sure it is the jobs," responded Nanak. "But I am stuck, because I cannot ask for men to leave their work and I cannot ask the owners to pay us white wages. I also am thinking it is the turbans. It is like a pink flag to a bull ox."

"Red," muttered Kate. "It is a red flag. No, I think you are wrong. It's your underwear."

"Underwears?"

"Yes, your people work in those bloomers with bare legs, and many don't wear shirts, so the Women's League has issued a proclamation that their dress is indecent and corrupting to our youth."

Whatever the cause, a very nasty undercurrent swirls about our feet, Nanak thought. Perhaps the *gurdwara* would give the growing community a focus. The more we stay out of the way of the whites the better off we will be, and with their own church Sikhs would have a place to pray and work out their squabbles, which were increasing among the lonely men crowded together with no women. An unusual man by the name of Bhai Arjan Singh from the village of Malak in the district of Ludhiana had arrived a year earlier and, with Nanak's support, promptly took charge of collecting funds for a *gurdwara.* He quickly gathered a sufficient sum to purchase land, and every Sunday gangs of men cleared the property.

Just as tensions appeared to be calming, the problem in Marysville erupted. Across the border, in the state of Washington, twenty Sikhs were building a rail bed. The American branch of the Asiatic Exclusion League gave the workers one month to quit their jobs and leave the country, or face the consequences.

The foreman of the work gang was Bhai Vir Singh, a Khalsa warrior and one of the very few Sikhs who rose to become a British army officer. Most of the men working on the rail crew had served under him in India. When Bhai landed in Vancouver in 1906, he'd stopped over at the farm, as most of the early immigrants did. Though he and his men were contracted to work in Washington he wanted to meet the "deserters." For three days and nights Bhai, Rajinder, and Santa talked nonstop. They spoke of weapons, rehashed battles, and recited favorite passages from the warrior Guru Gobind Singh. Rajinder and Santa had been stockpiling weapons for years. Occasionally they tried to coax money out of Nanak, who took a tithe from each man's wages for general expenses and for building the *gurdwara.*

"We should use some of that money to purchase weapons," insisted Rajinder.

"What good are guns without a *gurdwara* to look after our spiritual well-being? Remember, weapons and violence are a last resort," retorted Nanak.

"What good is a *gurdwara* without a means to defend ourselves?" Rajinder responded firmly.

"You can pray all you want," chimed in Santa, "but without a head, pffft!"

Nanak wouldn't budge, so Rajinder began collecting his own tithe. Nanak suspected this tithe wasn't entirely voluntary.

✳

After Bhai's arrival, Rajinder and Santa pored over the arsenal: twenty-one rifles, two pistols, several dozen knives, and ten *salotars*—long wooden spears with a double-headed blade secured to the end. Rajinder had even picked up an ancient nor'wester, the trade gun of the fur industry. The flintlock was handsome with its snake-decorated sideplate polished to a radiant gleam.

"How on earth would you fire such a thing? It does not take bullets?" pondered Bhai, admiring the remarkably light old gun.

"I wouldn't have to fire it, just wave it around," Rajinder said. "It looks dangerous enough to loosen anyone's bowels."

When Bhai sent word of the expulsion order, Rajinder and Santa were like men reborn. They and five others made the trip to Marysville, where they were greeted as heroes. Nanak included himself—"to keep you idiots out of trouble."

"Whites are dangerous because they are undisciplined," said Rajinder.

"They're not military men," agreed Bhai Singh. "They'll anger easily and frighten easily. We can use that against them."

"Large groups of men are unpredictable," Rajinder emphasized. "Like wild animals, there's no certainty in what they will do."

"Let me show you what I've got planned," Bhai Singh said, unrolling a hand-drawn map of the area.

"Now you're talking!" Rajinder said happily, hunching his massive form over the map.

"Here and here," Bhai said, pointing with his finger, "is where they'll come from. And here we'll command the high ground."

Rajinder whistled his appreciation. "But what about . . ."

Despite himself, Nanak was drawn into their excitement, the cleverness of the plan, and the confidence Rajinder and Bhai had of success. Though it had been years since he'd fired a rifle, he had once been an excellent shot.

"I will station you here," Rajinder spoke to Nanak and tapped the map. "You'll be far away from the crowd but ready if we need you. Just don't shoot yourself in the nuts by mistake."

In the area where the Sikhs worked they set up barricades to narrow their exposure. The barricades were in the shape of a funnel, allowing no more than six or seven whites to engage them at one time. Bhai Singh built a low-slung platform out of railway ties set on top of a railcar, allowing three riflemen to lie in a protected, prone position and fire into the mob, should they overwhelm the barricades. It would be a deadly kill-zone if it came to that. Rajinder, Bhai, and Santa pronounced themselves happy with the arrangements. Long before dawn on the expulsion day they were ready. The men who still had British army uniforms wore them complete with their medals and campaign patches.

By the time the sun was up, an enormous crowd had gathered in Marysville's main square. On a platform built for the purpose, officials of the Asiatic Exclusion League recounted their successes in purifying America and bellowed out their plans for the hindoos who'd been warned "fair and square." They carried a hodgepodge of shotguns, pistols, rifles, sticks, and clubs. Speeches were made and flasks were passed from hand to hand. When the crowd was sufficiently incensed, the leaders urged them to march forward for righteousness.

Whatever they expected, it wasn't thirty turbaned Sikhs in British army uniforms with wicked-looking lances, repeating rifles, and bandoliers heavy with bullets. Nanak, from the vantage of the platform atop the rail-car, felt great pride in his countrymen. Though outnumbered a hundred to one, the men stood calmly, confidence clear in their faces.

Rajinder was magnificent, brandishing the old trade gun in one hand and his *kirpan* in the other. Nanak noted that the crowd bulged markedly away from where Rajinder stood. The few whites with military experience, noticing the way the area had been laid out, quietly moved to the back of the crowd.

A florid-faced man stepped forward, his hand on the butt of a pistol strapped to his hip.

"This country is filling up with garbage and riffraff from all over the world," he declared to deafening cheers. "We aim to clean up the garbage."

"Hear, hear!" rose into the morning air. "Get rid of the wogs."

"You lot have been warned! Now go back to the jungle where you came from." The man preened with triumph as the crowd noise surged even higher.

Nanak realized with a start that the white man was Martin Effelwick, a little heavier and more red-faced than before but definitely the same man. "I wouldn't mind finding you alone in the jungle," Nanak muttered.

"Goodness gracious, what a terrible waste of your time," Bhai Singh said mildly when the crowd quieted. "We are not going anywhere. The work is not finished."

"You've been ordered out!" Effelwick barked to more cheers. "You tell those darkies."

"But the work is not finished," Bhai spoke as if reasoning with a child. "How can we go?"

Effelwick seemed stumped. "I thought you were religious men," he sneered, taking another tack.

"We *are* religious men," Bhai Singh said equably. "Men of peace. We are here to work only."

"Then why are you armed?" Effelwick shot back.

"These?" Bhai looked at the revolver in one hand and the knife in the other as if seeing them for the first time. "These are for the purposes of self-defense. You need have no fear of the weapons. My men are all former soldiers of the British army. They have fought in many battles, killed many men. Their rifles will not go off by accident." Bhai had been speaking softly but bore down on the final sentence. "The rifles will not go off by accident," he repeated.

"We're not afraid of you monkeys," harrumphed Effelwick.

Bhai lifted his hand. The Sikhs began singing.

"What are you doing?" Effelwick scoffed, trying to mask the worry in his face. In the background the crowd was urging, "Attack! Run them off! Do it now!"

"We are making peace with our god," Bhai intoned solemnly. "We are now ready to die." As an afterthought, he added: "Do you need time to make peace with yours?"

Thirty rifles racked at a second hand-signal from Bhai, sending an uneasy shiver rippling through the crowd. Those in the front of the mob edged backward. At that moment, a stone hit Bhai on the forehead, knocking him flat. Rajinder roared and charged. The Sikhs surged forward, chanting and methodically swinging their *salotars* at leg height. The nearest five whites went down, then the next five. Within seconds, all the Sikhs could see were the backsides of the rapidly departing crowd.

"Chase and harry," ordered Bhai, struggling to his feet, blood streaming from his wound. "But do not kill."

Salotars raised, the thirty Sikhs chased thousands through the small town. Nanak slipped down from the platform and ran after Martin Effelwick, who showed a surprising turn of speed for such a portly man. As he tired, Nanak closed the distance, pricking his ample bottom with the *kirpan*, which spurred a fresh burst of speed. Nanak whacked him with the flat of the blade until the former porter fell exhausted and frightened to his knees.

"Don't kill me!" he whimpered.

"I feared I would never see you again," Nanak said, swinging the *kirpan* inches from Effelwick's head. "What a happy surprise."

"Murderers, deserters," Effelwick shouted in a show of bravery. "You're all the same."

Effelwick's bulging eyes were transfixed on the *kirpan* raised high up in the air. For a moment sun danced off the blade, then it descended. He passed out just as the point buried itself in the ground, a finger's width from his throat.

Nanak chuckled as a urine stain grew on the man's crotch. "You're too pitiful to kill," he said to the man who'd caused him so much trouble.

✳

Two years later, Nanak stared out over Burrard Inlet into mist so heavy nothing could be seen beyond a few feet of the shoreline. He was thirty-five years old, and after twelve years in Canada, he was tired, very tired. After the Battle of Marysville, as Rajinder happily called it, Nanak found himself increasingly pressured by the various communities of Sikhs clustered around mills, farms, and mines in and around Vancouver, about writing letters, sending money home to the Punjab, mediating the growing number of disputes—both among the Sikhs and with their white employers. Disagreements were a common occurrence, and the Sikhs were acquiring a reputation as quarrelsome and dangerous. For two years Nanak had been trying to bring wives and families from the Punjab. To date, not a single Sikh woman had set foot in Vancouver, though two boatloads of Japanese women had landed and Chinese women had been in Vancouver for more than twenty years. Three times he'd met with the interior minister of the federal government to plead their case.

It was ironic, Nanak mused. We built a *gurdwara* in Vancouver and have a priest, to whom we pay $36 a month. We have a place for men to worship, yet they argue about the bylaws among themselves, complain about the money required to support the temple, and all the while the whites are growing ever more determined to get rid of us. We must be strong together, yet we are splitting apart. Only with families can we build a community. We need our women.

"So does everyone."

Nanak jumped to his feet.

"I beg your pardon?"

"You said you need women," Kate said.

"I was not aware I was speaking aloud."

"You were having quite a lively conversation," she laughed. "An argument, really. If anyone else happened by, they'd likely lock you up as a madman."

Nanak smiled. The inlet shore was dank and isolated, and the air choked with the acrid smoke from the mill's boilers. It was not the kind of place people chose for a stroll. Kate must have sought him out. Her pale face was a beacon in the dark afternoon. Corkscrews of curly red hair escaped from her hat. She was carrying a black leather bag. She must have just finished her clinic at the mill. Nanak wondered if she'd had tea yet with Dwight McKenna.

"What troubles you so much?"

Nanak pulled out a clipping from the *New Advertiser,* reporting on the passage of a law declaring that all people of East Indian origin were required to have $200 on their person in order to land anywhere in the Dominion of Canada.

"This is the third insult," Nanak said quietly. Kate watched him, realizing with a shock that she had known him for more than ten years. She had become accustomed to the turban neatly wrapped around his head. It seemed fitting. But her feelings were not shared by most, she knew. How odd that a piece of cloth could be the focus of so much hatred.

"I don't suppose your people would be willing to take off their turbans and cut their hair, as you did when you came?"

Nanak laughed bitterly. "I do not think it matters. Look at this." He had a small pile of newspapers at his side, which he had been reading and rereading like a wounded man picking at a scab. It was the text of a speech made at a meeting in the Oddfellows' Hall in Vancouver two nights earlier.

The Hindus never did one solitary thing for humanity in the past 2,000 years and will not probably in the next 2,000. These Orientals are continually harping about what they did in the Indian Mutiny. But if you look at British history you will quickly see that if they had not come to the assistance of the British they themselves would have been in peril of annihilation by the Mohammedans who stood 24 to 1 against them.

I tell you that the Hindus will not assimilate and thank god for it. They wish to bring their women here but without the morality of whites they will breed unconscionably and develop a race of antagonists who will strip us of the very means of putting food on our table. If we do not allow the women but permit the men then they will eventually take over our daughters and sisters with their dark ways.

"It's bad enough that they hate us," Nanak said, trying to lighten the mood. "But must they call us Hindus?"

"Two prominent men of the clergy support this," murmured Kate. "And look at all the businessmen's wives." As she spoke the names, it was all she could do not to spit, especially as she knew that one of them, St. John Stevens, owner of Fraser Mills, was the biggest employer of Sikhs in the province.

"The Sikhs made them rich," she continued angrily, and now, when there is a surplus of white labor with the new immigrants from eastern Europe, they are quite happy to drift with the tide of popular feeling, even though it is wrong."

"We have one supporter," observed Nanak bleakly. "A Mr. Konrad von Schaumberg, who is owning several mining companies in the interior of the province." He rummaged in his pile of papers and gave a clipping to Kate.

"I would rather hire whites if I can get them" went the comment from the wealthy owner of Cariboo Consolidated Company in the *Province* newspaper. "But these Hindus are all old soldiers. I see no harm in giving employment to these old men who have helped to fight for the British Empire than to entire aliens."

"Such voices are as a straw to a breaking dam," said Nanak when Kate finished reading.

He leaned his head against the mossy tree trunk behind him. First there was the law forbidding any "Orientals" to land in Vancouver if they did not sail direct from their homeland. However, there was no direct ship from India. Then came a second order-in-council, demanding that all "Hindus" be deported to a British colony, such as the British Honduras. And now the $200 head tax, which was not being applied to the Japanese or Chinese, though the latter were being beaten so regularly in Vancouver's East End by gangs of roving white thugs they were called yellow punching-bags. "And we mean yellow in every sense of the word," proclaimed one leader of a clean-out crew. "At least the japs have a bit of gumption to them."

Nanak closed his eyes.

Her hand startled him. He stared at it where it lay across his slender, ropey forearm, pure white upon brown. She had never touched him before. Everything inside him moved, blood flowed painfully in torrents, his skin shrank then expanded, his eyes seemed to swell, his heart and stomach met each other. His other hand hung by his side and he gazed in fascination as it began to move of its own accord across his body and through the air to clasp Kate's soft fingers. Neither spoke as they watched their fingers explore, tip against knuckle, curling around, stroking, his calloused palm against her incredibly smooth freckled skin.

Twelve years. Eternity. Longing, secret and forbidden, so much a part of him that now, allowing it to escape, made him ache as if every tooth was being pulled from his head. Their eyes could not meet. As two shy dancers, they bent so cheeks would touch. Kate felt his whiskers and turned her lips to rub against them, every prick and scratch sending a shock through her so powerful she could not hold back the moan. Nanak allowed the edge of his lips to lay against hers. For many minutes they were still as death, breathing in the scent of each other.

It *was* like death—this pain, this release. Nanak's hands encircled her waist, barely touching. Kate inhaled deeply, trying to swell herself into his grasp. She wore only a shift beneath her blouse and skirt, the corset's whalebone stays being too restrictive in her work. Nanak could feel her ribs. He pressed his thumbs gently into the hollow where they joined. Her head dropped back and he saw the patch of skin beneath her chin that was not covered by her high collar. His lips found it.

It was the sudden cracking of ice after holding up a great weight. They dissolved arms into arms, lips silently devouring each other.

And then it ended. Nanak and Kate shot apart panting, their eyes locked and a message of fear and hopelessness traveling between them. Kate spoke first.

"Oh, Nanak!" she gasped. "I . . ." she couldn't continue.

He tried to lessen her agony. "Perhaps we Sikhs are deserving of our reputation of immorality after all."

She took him wrong. "No, no! Please don't say that. I wanted . . . I have wanted . . ."

"I know," Nanak said softly. "And I too, far more even than my heart or head ever knew."

"There are places!" Kate blurted. "Places in the colonies where society is not so, so damned bigoted." Nanak smiled. He had never heard her swear before. "I am told the Canary Islands are full of men who have taken native wives, and the Sandwich Islands also." She stopped at his expression.

"And how many places are you knowing of where a man from a Dark Continent is taking a white woman for a wife?" he asked softly.

They sat for a lifetime, staring out over Burrard Inlet as the day warmed and the mist lifted to reveal the soft ridges of the north shore mountains.

"It is said that there are Indians, red Indians, living in those mountains who have never seen a white person and refuse to have anything to do with us," Kate finally spoke.

"For some peoples the making of terms with conquerors is a difficult thing."

"It is also said that they hide an extraordinary treasure of rare jade, gems, and gold that came here thousands of years ago with Oriental sailors. An old Indian on the reserve in Deep Cove told me that the men across the waters will come back to reclaim their prize one day."

"I do not think the treasure is in danger from any of us."

Kate turned her head and looked at him. How she loved his sense of humor, though it surfaced so rarely. When he was happy, his thick black lashes tangled at the corners of his eyes. She thought of her own skimpy, pale lashes and wondered what a child of theirs would inherit. She slammed the door shut on her thoughts.

"Mr. McKenna has asked me to marry him," she said with a harsh edge to her voice.

Nanak searched her face, finding no guile. He was instantly ashamed for even thinking Kate was capable of saying something to provoke him at such a moment. There was only the fact of the words uttered.

"And will you be marrying him?"

"I don't know," she sighed. "I've been trying not to think about it. Until today I didn't admit to myself why." Another sigh. "I'd better say yes then. After all, I'm getting to be rather an old maid."

Kate's words hung heavily between them.

*

Kate never again sought out Nanak at the mill after she became Mrs. Dwight McKenna. For his part, he never came forward to greet her, even though enough years had gone by for their acquaintance to pass without remark.

One day, eight months after her marriage, she was waiting for him as he emerged from the sawdust room beneath the main saw. Nanak approached her slowly, his eyes carefully aimed away from hers.

"Hello, Kate."

"Hello, Nanak."

"It is a pleasure to see you looking so well."

Kate's hand strayed to the swell of her belly. A few more months. Dwight chastised her for continuing to see to the needs of the workers in her condition. She cleared her throat.

"Mr. McKenna told me that the owner of this mill has another on the Fraser near the village of Mission. He is moving it closer to New Westminster to be nearer the ships. The old mill is out of date, with ancient equipment, and no one will buy it for that purpose, even though business is in a better state than last year."

Nanak listened intently.

"Mr. McKenna, uh, suggested that if the Sikhs were to own more of their own businesses, pay taxes, and hire their own kind, the province might look more kindly upon your presence and allow you to bring wives and families."

Ownership wasn't a new idea to Nanak. He had tried to purchase small farm plots in the south near the river and in the north near the inlet to allow the Sikhs to grow their own food. Each time he approached an owner, the price of the land mysteriously doubled. But a mill! Their own mill!

"Mr. Miles would be open to an offer on his property?"

"I feel sure, at least Mr. McKenna does. He has nothing against Sikhs, as you have made him very wealthy with your productivity."

"I shall thank Mr. McKenna."

Kate turned to leave but the rough ground caught her heel. Nanak reached out a hand to support her. She drew back. Regret flooded her face and Nanak wished he had words to console her.

"Well, then," her normally strong voice was barely audible. "I will bid you good-bye—Nanak Simple Singh."

She made her way up the path, concentrating hard on not stumbling. She felt the warmth of his face at her back.

"Kate." How like treacle was his voice. She turned, pushing her hair from her face so she could see him better.

"I am betrothed," he said simply. "My parents arranged it last year."

She did not trust herself to answer.

"Her name is Bibi Kaur, of the village Bhikhiwind."

Kate faced him squarely and summoned a smile.

"I am glad, Nanak. Truly glad."

Watching her departing back, Nanak murmured to himself in his own language, "I know that you are, my Kate, sweet Kate."

51

*

1916

Mission

When the rest of the men arrived, Rajinder hoisted the canvas bundle onto his still massive shoulder and headed off across the fields, toward the woods beyond. He seemed to know exactly where he was going. The five, the original deserters, spoke not a word as they tramped along. It took them almost two hours to cross the extensively cultivated fields of the Fraser River's alluvial valley and enter the woods. Rajinder pushed on through slender new growth until they reached larger, older trees. Finally, he gently laid the bundle down in a small clearing.

"A man ought to weigh more," Rajinder said as he started to pick up branches.

"He hardly ate last year," Bohun commented. He'd grown sturdier in body and personality in the almost twenty years since they'd arrived in British Columbia but, thankfully, his voice hadn't coarsened. He still sang hymns at the *gurdwara*.

"The white woman ruined him," Santa said bitterly. He hardly seemed to have aged and carried himself, as always, like a banty rooster.

"From the beginning they itched for each other, sure enough," Rajinder agreed. "You could see it. For years it went on. Making each other more and more uncomfortable. Many times I told him to take her and be done with it."

"A Sikh and a white woman!" one of the others said in disgust.

"I agree," Rajinder said wearily. "Their women hold no interest for me. They look like ghosts. How could they have any substance in bed? But those two, they were on fire for each other."

Rajinder motioned for Bohun to help him with a particularly large branch, which they dragged over to the pile.

"All those years," sighed Rajinder, "wasted. If his mind didn't know that he wanted her, his body certainly did. His balls were as blue as your turban."

Everyone laughed, but it was the laugh of men making an effort.

"When the white woman married the mill manager," Santa stated, "I thought that would be the end of it."

"It was in a way, and in a way it wasn't," Rajinder admitted. "After that he let his mother select a bride for him. She'd been pestering him for years. And he threw himself into work, more than ever. That was when he devised the scheme to smuggle my wife and his Bibi here. He called it a test run."

Every Sikh in British Columbia knew the story; it was as much the property of the community as it was of Rajinder and Nanak. Late in 1910, the two women set out, each with a brother for protection, along with Rajinder's twin boys, then sixteen. Their papers were correct, except the women were identified as men. Everything went smoothly until they arrived in Hong Kong, where Bibi Kaur developed a cough. It was nothing. But the doctor placed her in quarantine, threatening to jail her when he discovered she wasn't a man.

"Nanak never lost hope, even when she did not arrive," Santa said admiringly.

"He carried on," Rajinder agreed. "That's the way of him. The rest of us would shout and pull our hair. Not him, he cried inside. But the wedding nearly broke him."

The wedding was intended for Nanak and Bibi Kaur, but when the boat landed without her, Nanak suggested that Rajinder remarry his wife.

"You shouldn't have agreed," Santa said accusingly.

"What could I do?" Rajinder protested. " I just wanted to take my wife away and get to know her again, if you understand my meaning." The other men nodded knowingly, all of them remembering the acute envy they'd felt when the woman arrived. "But Nanak was adamant. He told me it was my duty, that the community needed something to celebrate. I could never say no to him when he was like that."

"You still shouldn't have agreed! If there had been no wedding, the white woman would not have come!"

"You're telling me what I already know!" Rajinder shot back at Santa. "Nanak and the priest wanted to invite whites to the wedding to show them we are not monsters and our families pose no threat."

"But no whites came except that woman!" Santa pressed. "She stabbed a dagger into Nanak with every minute of her presence. It was a stupid idea."

"It was not my doing!" Rajinder protested.

"The wedding was truly wonderful," interjected Bohun, trying to diffuse the situation. "Everyone was so happy. It was just like being home."

"Yes, it was," Rajinder agreed, his anger evaporating as quickly as it had flared. "Nanak was right. It was grand. Two thousand of us, all in one place, singing and dancing. That was quite a sight. And my dear wife and sons loved it. After waiting by herself for fifteen years, she deserved it."

A dreamy expression overtook Rajinder as he remembered holding one end of a scarf with his beautiful wife holding the other end. Ten men stood in as her brothers and male relatives to escort her as they made four trips around the Granth Sahib. When the priest pronounced them joined, Rajinder felt the years of separation melt away. He spotted Nanak at the front of the crowd and saw the lie in his smile.

"Nanak talked about going to the Punjab to marry Bibi but she wouldn't hear of it. She'd been learning English and was determined to come to Vancouver."

"That was when he heard about the *Komagata Maru.*"

"The whites were never happy with us being here, especially when there was more than a few hundred," Rajinder pointed out. "A boat with so many Sikhs was a mistake."

"It might have been all right if we could have stopped the Natal Act," piped up Bohun.

"That was a black day," spoke up Santa. "How could we have stopped it? We never knew of it until it was passed."

The Natal Act, a federal law, forbade immigrants from India to land in Vancouver unless they came directly from their country of birth. Since there was no direct service from Calcutta to Vancouver, the act effectively ended immigration from the Punjab. For a while it seemed as if all was lost, until in 1914 a group of prominent Sikhs in the Punjab chartered the *Komagata Maru* with their own money and set sail from Calcutta bound for Vancouver, with 376 Punjabi aboard.

"Bibi was on board. Nanak was so hopeful," sighed Rajinder.

"It was a grand sight when the ship anchored and all our people lined up on deck with thousands more on shore," Santa reminisced, breaking twigs as he talked.

"It was grand enough, until the bastards wouldn't let anyone get off," Rajinder retorted.

For three months, the ship sat embargoed in the harbor. Everything was attempted: negotiation, lawsuits, bribery, and even violence. Nanak was in the thick of it, aching more with each day, knowing Bibi was aboard and helpless to bring her the few hundred yards to Canadian soil. And what he kept to himself was that he'd smuggled six other women onto the manifest. His guilt grew the longer they were marooned. What agony of thirst, hunger, and filth were the poor women suffering? And all because of him. Finally, on the verge of starvation, the passengers took over the ship and threatened to ram it ashore.

"Let's get on with this, you all know how this shitty story ends as well as I do," Rajinder said grouchily. "We need more wood!"

On July 23, 1914, a Royal Canadian gunboat, the *Rainbow,* forced the *Komagata Maru* out of the harbor and into the sea at cannon point.

"On the way home poor Bibi Kaur died of dysentery," Bohun stated solemnly, unable to let it go.

"And Nanak died with her," Santa added.

"He wasn't about to fall on his *kirpan,* that would be too easy," Rajinder said. "He set about working himself to death and only ate enough to sustain a canary."

"He waited until he figured out how to get our women here," one of the others piped up.

"Yes, and when he got all your betrothed here and you all properly married . . ." Rajinder's voice caught, anger and sadness stopping his words.

This time Nanak bypassed the Canadian authorities entirely, routing the women through Hong Kong to Brazil and on to Mexico. From there he chartered a boat to take them close to Port Townsend, Washington. They landed at night, just out of view of the harbor. An armed escort led by Rajinder and Santa slipped them through the unpatrolled Cascade Mountains that touched the Canadian border.

When the pyre was large enough, a good ten feet tall, Rajinder drew himself up, as if to speak. "I can't say the words, Santa. Will you do it?"

"We have much to thank the Guru for," Santa began solemnly. "We own a saw mill. We own farms, of such a size our parents would be amazed. We are surrounded by ten thousand of our countrymen, and though we are not completely welcome here, it is our home. We thank the Guru."

"We thank the Guru," the others repeated.

"And we have our women and children! For that we must also thank the Guru and Nanak's grand plan to settle in this new world."

Bohun began to sing. Rajinder could not contain himself anymore.

"Plan?" he interjected. "What plan?" Tears coursed down his cheeks but he didn't trouble to wipe them away. "There was no plan."

The others stared at him.

"What do you mean, no plan?" puzzled Bohun. "He had a great vision. I know it. It was what kept us alive."

"And he told you this?" scoffed Rajinder. "He told you of this grand plan to leave the train and re-create the Punjab in Canada?"

"Not in so many words, but . . ."

"Nanak fell asleep, you fool! He took a walk and fell asleep. The train left him behind." The last words were spoken softly, as if a tremendous weight lay on Rajinder's chest.

The pyre was forgotten.

"Then it was all a mistake?" said Santa disbelievingly. "We left the train to follow him thinking he deserted, but he had just fallen asleep?"

Rajinder nodded wearily.

"He must have thought we were such idiots," Bohun whispered.

"Yes," Rajinder agreed. "But mostly he was embarrassed."

"Embarrassed?" several said at once.

"Yes, he was embarrassed that we thought so much of him we would risk our lives to follow."

There was a long silence as the men considered how their fates had all been determined.

"Oh Nanak," Rajinder chanted, stepping forward to light Nanak's funeral pyre. This time there was no difficulty and the flames reached for the sky.

As a team of oxen are we driven
By the ploughman, our teacher
By the furrows made are thus writ
Our actions—on the earth our paper
The sweat of labor is as beads
Falling by the ploughman as seeds sown.
We reap according to our measure
Some for ourselves to keep, some to others give
Oh Nanak, this is the way to truly give.

✳

Hours later, Rajinder Singh stood vigil by himself over the few smoldering branches. "Well Nanak, my friend, you've finally got your chance to be alone."

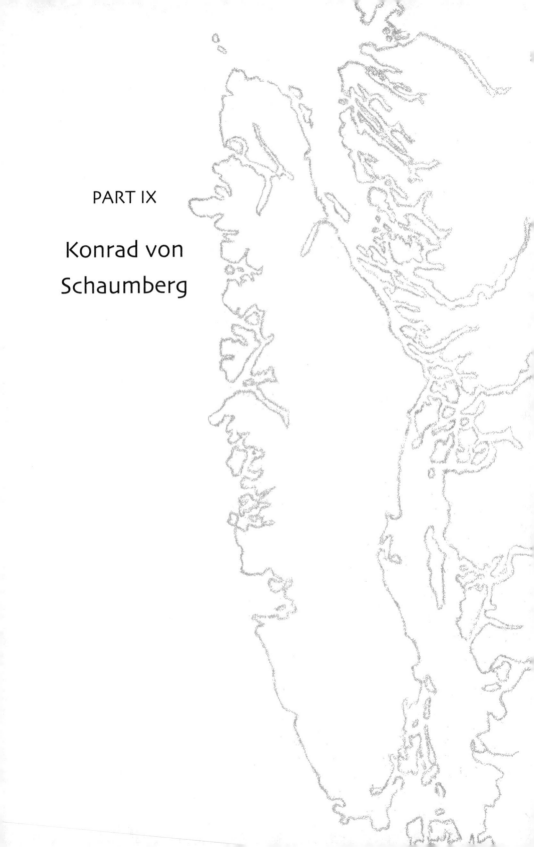

PART IX

Konrad von
Schaumberg

52

✳

Konrad Erich von Schaumberg stood on the wooden pier, gazing unappreciatively over Burrard Inlet at the icing of late snow coating the shoulders of a mountain range that stretched as far as he could see. The early morning sun played with the ice crystals, making it seem as if the horizon was blanketed in diamonds. He turned his back on the white peaks, the narrow gray-blue stretch of water, and the steamship bobbing against its pilings to survey the waterfront bustle of Vancouver's inner harbor. Disappointment painted his face.

The twenty-four-year-old third son of Baroness Amelia Verstag and Count Alfred Gustav von Schaumberg—former ambassador to the czar of Russia—expected something more. Actually, he expected something less. Less activity, fewer people, fewer buildings. He'd come halfway around the world for cowboys and gold. His pockets were empty of the latter and the streets empty of the former.

Konrad fingered the few coins in his pocket and sighed. The scenery was pretty enough, but he'd grown up in the most beautiful part of Germany, surrounded by miles of tended fields and managed forests. There even the mountain ranges and passes seemed engineered. The fifteen-thousand-acre family estate in Neu Gattersleben boasted some of the best land in Lower Saxony. Three rivers carved through the estate, which included two castles, one of them dating back to 600 A.D.; five villages; seven churches; two flour mills; two quarries; a textile factory outfitted with all the best equipment of the new century; and four sawmills. Seven hundred and fifty men worked the lands, raising hay, grain, and livestock. The count's precious orchards included twenty-two varieties of apples, seventeen of peaches, and a dozen types of pears. The count also proudly boasted the largest herd of angora goats in all of Europe. The carefully carded, silken wool from their coats warmed royal backs from England to Russia.

The thought of the great estate, its precisely laid out fields and fences, its cultivated orchards, tidy barns, and efficiently run mills, brought on a giant, jaw-cracking yawn. Konrad had come all the way around the world for adventure. This busy, scruffy little town hemmed in by dense unkempt forests, mountains, and a wide, still river the ship's captain called the Fraser, might have been an exciting western outpost forty years ago, but now it seemed nothing more than a pretentious settlement hovering on the Pacific Ocean.

And not a cowboy in sight.

"Lawndee! Lawndee! Washee lawndee! Mistah need washee lawndee!" The boy rushed from passenger to passenger, urging them to give him clothes soiled from the long voyage for washing, pressing, and delivery to their hotel the next day.

"Wheah stay, mistah! Flee delivalee."

"*Nein!*" Konrad waved him off.

"No mistah! My familee washee all impotent people clothe in Vancouvah. Bess people, bess clothe, bess lawndee."

"*Aufgang!* Get out of my way, you dirty child."

The boy shrugged, moving on to the next passenger.

Konrad pulled an envelope out of his pocket and studied the name on it, written in his mother's exotic script. WARBURTON PIKE. His second cousin on his mother's side.

He's a charming man. He visited us some years ago and renewed acquaintance with your father. Everybody loved him. I have never seen your father laugh so much as when Warburton was here. And the girls thought he was rather special too. He has wonderful manners.

His mother is, of course, long dead but I remember her from when I was a child. She married a nichtsgeboren *from England. Everyone felt sorry for the match and couldn't imagine her living out her life as a merchant's wife. But for all that he did well, and came to own a great deal of property, coal. He also bought himself a peerage, which meant she could hold her head a little higher at court.*

But I ramble. Warburton was rather wild in his youth and nearly broke his parents' hearts when he ran away to the New World. Sadly, both died before he returned. But he has redeemed himself with great success in a place called Vancouver. It is quite wild, I understand, with buffalo in the streets and red Indians everywhere.

The count will write to you about business issues, and in the meantime I will do my best to encourage him to increase your allowance. I am enclosing a letter of introduction to Mr. Pike. I am sure he'll arrange for you to meet the right people.

I am certain he is a very successful man in that place and will help you establish a position. He is much older than you, sixty-one by my calculation, so you will have the benefit of his wisdom and experience.

Do try and find something to make you happy, my darling Konrad. It needn't be anything terribly important, but if you do well your father will bring you back and I am sure I can persuade him to settle some lands on you.

With much love and tears at your continued absence, I remain your mother.

✳

Konrad doubted if a letter from his father discussing "business issues" would arrive anytime soon, nor would there be any more money, let alone the offer of lands. The count had sent him to the army when he was eighteen and already an established wastrel. "Military training will give you ambition, my boy," the count instructed, ignoring his son's protests. "Everything is too easy for you around here."

The artillery corps most emphatically did not transform Konrad, though he developed an even finer shooting eye. He spent three years at a post in northern Poland, receiving 150 marks a month from his commission as well as a 500-mark allowance from his father. Konrad had the knack of losing both easily and happily, often in a single night of drinking and gambling. When the money was gone, he simply borrowed as much as he could get. Konrad was a popular companion and there were always officers happy to lend him what he needed.

In 1902, deeply in debt, Konrad was cashiered out of the corps over a silly unpleasantness with the wife of the post commander. Rigid with anger and barely hidden embarrassment, the commander demanded Konrad make good on his debts, and sent a rather fiercely worded letter to the count along the same lines. When Konrad arrived home, delighted to be released, the count refused to see him. Two days later a servant delivered to his bedroom a terse note from his father telling him never to come begging for money again and an envelope containing a steamer ticket to El Salvador, where his sister and brother-in-law owned several coffee plantations.

"Money doesn't grow on trees, you know!" Joachim bellowed at him fourteen months after Konrad arrived. "You have to earn it!"

Earn it. Fed up with his dissolute ways, Joachim offered him a choice—work or leave. His sister was no help at all and refused to intervene. As it happened, Konrad had been recently playing faro with one of Joachim's coffee-plantation foremen and the man told him he was saving money for another six months, then heading to Alaska, where gold flowed out of the rivers in such quantity that prospectors were making their fortunes inside a week.

Konrad chose to leave. His plan was simple—rest up with this Pike person for a few months, and do a bit of hunting and perhaps fishing while he planned his venture. Undoubtedly Pike could be encouraged to set him up for a sojourn to the goldfields. Konrad was an expert in charm, particularly when it came to women and the elderly. He made a little bet with himself that he would have the required sum committed within the month.

Passengers were disembarking and making their way through the various barkers offering rooms, carriages, and laundry service. The first-class passengers all seemed to have acquaintances and destinations. But a number of those in steerage stopped, grateful to have suggestions for what they hoped were cheap rooms and good food. Konrad, for the first time in his life, traveled steerage after losing his first-class ticket to a sharpie with a deck of cards—marked, he was sure. He scratched hard at his hair and chest. Aside from a goodly supply of eager gamblers, steerage also contained more than its fair share of nits.

Konrad glanced at the envelope again. He'd better get on with it and find the old man. Hoisting his treasured rifle, a valise, and a fine duffel made from El Salvador alligator, Konrad set off along the dock. Vancouver was such a small place this Warburton Pike was undoubtedly well known. He waved the Chinese boy over.

"Washee lawndee?" the grinning child said happily.

"*Nein*. But I will give you an American penny if you tell me where I could find a gentleman of this city by the name of Warburton Pike." As he spoke to the boy, Konrad seemed to inflate. Generations of privilege had bred into him a smoothly overbearing manner when addressing his lessers, which he could not have turned off even if he'd been aware of it.

The boy held out his hand. Dropping the penny into the child's palm Konrad impatiently prompted, "Well?"

"No undastand English, solly!"

"Pike, you idiot. Warburton Pike. He is a leading citizen in this city."

"Pike? No Pike. Solly."

The boy scuttled off.

"Give my penny back!" Konrad called out irritably. But the boy melted into the throng.

Following the crowd, Konrad searched for someone who looked as if he was a citizen of Vancouver. As the crowd began to thin out, he spotted a scruffy man slouching against a two-horse surrey.

"I'd be grateful if you could tell me where I could find a man by the name of Warburton Pike."

A plume of yellow juice erupted from the man's face.

"This ain't no information service, sport! Fifty cents to a hotel of your choice, another fifty and I'll git ya a clean girl."

"I'd be happy to pay for the information."

"Information's a buck, and none o' that Yank money neither."

A dollar would seriously cut into Konrad's tiny reserves; he counted on this man Pike to bail him out. He kept walking. Shortly a commotion on a dock caught his attention. A group of whooping street urchins were conducting a game, pitching pennies against the side of a shed wall. At the center of the action was an old man, throwing his pennies as gleefully as any of the boys. The pitch that got closest to the wall was the winner and took all the other pennies. Between turns the man leaned against a bollard, puffing on a pipe. Smoke wreathed his lanky gray hair, which was braided Indian-fashion and decorated with several feathers. The man was dressed in buckskins, much like those Konrad had seen in western novels, though these were not nearly so well fitting. Bits of fringe were missing, and oily stains darkened the jacket front.

At first Konrad thought the man was a real, live Indian. His feet were bare and filthy and his skin was dark enough. Konrad had never actually seen a red Indian, but he considered himself somewhat of an expert, having read vast numbers of western novels during the long, hot afternoons in El Salvador after mornings spent shooting game. But how many Indians smoked a meerschaum pipe?

Konrad approached.

"*Guten Tag, mein Herr,*" he began courteously. "Good day to you, sir." The man turned worn, hazel eyes in his direction. At first Konrad thought he detected the tiniest hint of amusement in the man's face, but he must have been mistaken, for on closer examination there was no hint of anything on the creased and leathery visage.

"I require directions to the place of a prominent Vancouver citizen by the name of Mr. Warburton Pike. Could you give me assistance?" Konrad spoke with the crisp enunciation of one addressing a subaltern.

The question brought a titter from the boys who stopped their game to listen. The faded eyes took in the Tyrolean felt hat, wool hunting jacket, neatly knotted silk cravat, whipcord breeches, and exquisitely tooled water-bison boots. They came to rest on the lovingly polished rifle at the lean young man's side.

"Something that size'd knock a buffalo down a mile away, I'd guess."

"Yes, indeed," Konrad gushed, forgetting his mission. "I haven't met a man yet who could match me with this." He patted the rifle proudly. "Where would I find a buffalo?"

"I ain't seen a buffalo since I got my first woody and that'd be more 'n fifty-two years ago."

"Woody?"

The man stuck an erect finger at his crotch.

"Do you know Warburton Pike?" Konrad said loudly, ignoring the man's crude behavior.

"Made his acquaintance," the man admitted.

"Well," Konrad said after waiting fruitlessly for some elaboration, "then I would be grateful if you could tell me where I might find him."

"Haven't seen him for a while."

This earned another laugh from the group, which seemed to have gotten larger.

"*Ach Scheisse!*" Konrad muttered under his breath. "Can you suggest to me where I might look?"

"What do you want him for?" the man asked.

"That's none of your business!" Konrad responded sharply.

"If I don't know what you want, how can I decide whether to tell you where he is?" the old man said reasonably. "Pike isn't the sort to appreciate having a tin horn sent after him for no good reason."

Konrad snatched up his belongings and marched off. If all Canadians were as stupid and uncooperative as this . . . A further burst of mocking laughter from the urchins burned his ears for several blocks.

✳

Warburton Pike tapped out his pipe, tucked it in his belt, stretched might-ily, and slowly followed the young man. He watched as Konrad stopped at the first hotel, a modest establishment with rates published outside. Kon-rad wearily dragged his bags up the stairs. As he opened the door, the old man grabbed the handle.

"Look," he said in a friendly manner reaching for Konrad's bag. "We got off wrong back there. I'm Pike."

"The hell you are!" Konrad snatched away his bag. "I've had quite enough of you!"

"It's true! Warburton Pike reporting for duty. Show me your letter."

"How do you know I have a letter?"

"Your sort always has a letter. Anyone who lands in Vancouver dressed like you and looking like a game of cards would wear him out has gotta have a letter."

"Manager!" yelled Konrad to the white-shirted, middle-aged man busily shuffling papers and trying not to make his eavesdropping too obvi-ous. "This man is bothering me."

The fat fellow rolled out from behind the scarred desk and looked appraisingly at the older man.

"Can't have you bothering the Kaiser here," he said briskly. "Best be on your way before I have to, uh, duff you up a bit."

Pike obligingly sauntered out the door, the manager's hand at his back. Once out of Konrad's sight, the manager clapped him on the shoulder.

"Never thought I'd be able to say I threw Warburton Pike out of here!" he laughed.

"Duff me up?" Pike sniggered. "That was a nice touch."

"It seemed like the right thing to do. Is the young fool really related to you?"

"'Fraid so," Pike said with a laugh. "His father wrote to me, making out his son to be worse than a Frenchman. Imagine that! Called him a loafer and a dozen things I don't quite remember. But I do recall him asking me to do nothing for him."

"But you couldn't resist checking him out," the manager said know-ingly.

"Well," Pike said unabashed. "I've known a few Frenchmen. Rather liked them. I thought I'd buy him a drink and see what he was made of for myself. But apparently I'm not what he expected."

53

"A decent hotel would provide clean water for the guests," Konrad von Schaumberg complained imperiously. The long sea voyage from El Salvador had not been kind to his breeches. He scrubbed away at a series of stains. The water he dipped the cloth in was cold and obviously used.

"I quite agree," the manager stated. "A *decent* hotel would do such things."

"Then where is the clean water?"

"Still in the ground, I'd expect."

Konrad couldn't decide whether the man thought he was being funny or was merely a dummkopf. The latter word seemed to be peppering his thoughts ever more often since he'd landed at Pier Number 3 in Vancouver. After choking down what passed for dinner at the hotel last night, mostly a potatolike vegetable called a rootbegger, he'd made further inquiries about Warburton Pike. Everybody seemed to know of him but nobody seemed clear about where he could be found.

"And do you think you could get the water out of the ground so I could have a bath?"

The manager chuckled in appreciation at the joke. "My best advice is to find your way to Chong's steam baths. They look after you good there, and the water's clean, hot as well. Johnny Chong's got a laundry too, and them chinee girls do a nice shave. One, two, three, you're done!"

"And how much will this cost?" asked Konrad.

"A buck and a half should cover it.

"Will you be having breakfast?" the man continued. "If not, I'm closing up and going fishing. Elseways we've got oat porridge and last night's soup."

Konrad grimaced: rootbegger soup, gruel, and watered-down milk. He had precisely $14.92. Enough for almost a week in the hotel but no extras, including a proper breakfast. He sighed in frustration.

"I still don't see why I can't have a bath here in clean, hot water."

"That'd be because there isn't any."

Konrad felt like biting the man. "I can see that," he said, not liking the shrillness creeping into his tone. "Why not?"

"I've been waiting on the smithy to fix the water pump but the salmon's running . . ."

"You knew that there was no water when I checked in last night and you didn't tell me," Konrad accused.

Unbidden, the manager walked into Konrad's room and peered into the washbowl.

"This is water," he said, stirring the water with a chubby finger. "It's pretty clean. No one has used it before you."

"No, thank you," Konrad said through clenched teeth. "I will take your suggestion. And where will I find these steam baths?"

"Can I hail the gentleman a cab?" the manager beamed, happy his guest was leaving and giving him an extra hour of fishing.

"*Nein*, I will walk. Directions, if you please."

The manager sent him toward the main pier and along Water Street. "Take a hard right at Gassy Jack's place, can't miss it. Just beyond you'll see the cobbler and next to him the laundry. Steam bath's in the back."

As he waddled out the door, the manager asked, "You be staying on, matey?"

"In all chance, I will stay with Herr Pike after today."

The manager nodded enthusiastically. "Of course! Just needed to know so's I can pass your water on to someone else in case the pump isn't fixed."

Konrad distinctly heard a quiet "Happy hunting, Kaiser" as the man left. He thought to take the man to task for his impudence but decided to let it pass.

✳

The weather had, once more, dealt Vancouver an unbeatable hand. Dry and crisp with the promise of warmth later on; salt and cedar perfuming the air. The winds blew softly from the west, clearing away the eye-stinging smoke of the coal-fired mill boilers along the inlet and up into Indian Arm. Konrad had traveled widely to all the required places from Berlin to Moscow and from the delightful wilds of Morocco to the plantations of Latin America (he didn't count his enforced stint in Poland as traveling). Still, he had to admit as he walked down the narrow steps of McNeil's Guest Hotel, that the setting of this little town managed an impact on the senses that considerably exceeded its size and importance.

The street leading to the water was steep, giving an excellent view of Burrard Inlet, the curving shoulder of Stanley Park and a panorama of mountains to the north. As far as he could tell, the entire north shore of Burrard Inlet was relatively uninhabited, though he could see a few smoke spires drifting up from the rocky beach and plumes erupting from a mill almost directly across from Vancouver. "Indians?" he wondered, studying the beach fires. The thought of squaws quickly followed.

As he walked, a smile played across his lips. Konrad had happy memories of the natives in El Salvador. Giving folk, especially the women. Absolutely no morals at all. He had the acquaintance of one woman who, after a brief, grunting, fully clothed coupling against the side of a well, promptly offered him her daughter who couldn't have been more than thirteen. Konrad turned her down, not because he had scruples about children but because he preferred a bit of flesh on his women and the daughter was stick-skinny. A gentleman could do a lot worse than spend his life on a coffee plantation in El Salvador despite six months of stinking hot weather and another two of impenetrable rain.

Heedless of his nearly empty pockets, Konrad found himself humming as he sauntered along. He eyed the heavy green blanket of trees across the inlet and a boat chugging toward the pier, listing hard to port as it towed an enormous boom of logs. He hadn't expected a town so developed when he landed in Vancouver, but perhaps the place had potential. Over the last fifty years the forests in Germany had been razed to power the industries of Leipzig, Frankfurt, and Berlin. What large tracts of timber remained were owned by the Kaiser himself or nobles such as his father and kept for big game–hunting and other sport. Wood was becoming increasingly scarce.

Just before Konrad left for El Salvador, the count had met with two of Kaiser Wilhelm's top naval commanders. His mother told him that they'd brought the news that the Kaiser had authorized them to commission the building of thirty-five additional warships. But finding good timber would be difficult, they'd stressed, hoping the count would use his contacts in the West Indies and Latin America to facilitate the supply. They also hinted that the count might deed the timber rights of four thousand acres to the kaiser until supplies improved. The count was annoyed at the suggestion, especially since he'd already given over a portion of his coalfields in Herzegovina to fuel the Kaiser's obsession with building up his precious navy.

Perhaps I will write to him and tell him about the forests here stretching as far as you can see, Konrad ruminated. Almost the instant the idea popped into his head he shooed it out again. The thought of actually working with his father, even if at a tremendous distance, wasn't appealing. No one ever worked *with* his father. You worked *for* him or you didn't work at all.

Several wrong turns later Konrad thought he must be nearly in sight of his destination. "I could have sworn he said hard right at Gassy Jack's," he muttered, having passed the saloon a good ten minutes earlier. Two women walked toward him, carrying parasols and holding their skirts up to cross a muddy culvert.

"I beg your pardon," Konrad stepped out of their path, swept off his hat, and bowed.

"You see, Edith!" the taller woman said triumphantly. "I told you we'd find a man with good manners in this place."

Edith smiled shyly and returned Konrad's bow with a slight dip of her head. He hoped his boots and breeches didn't look too grubby. Fortunately his jacket and hat were presentable.

"I am Konrad von Schaumberg and I require directions," he said, "but perhaps you are new to Vancouver just as I am?"

"New and not so new," the taller woman said promptly. "Edith here's just come from San Francisco but I've been here for two years. Two looong years," she drew the word out. "Hetty Henley-Galen's my name.

"I've been telling Edith there's not much sophistication in Vancouver, not like Chicago—that's my home, you know—and the folks here are a bit, well, *rough,* but we do our best to find good people among the population, though," she sighed heavily, "you couldn't fill a steamer trunk with them. But *you* at any rate know how to greet a woman properly," she smiled coquettishly.

Konrad shuddered. The woman was bold and obvious and all too talkative. Whatever "good people" she knew in Chicago wouldn't get an invitation to his mother's annual servant ball.

"So where are you going that you need directions?" the woman chattered on, oblivious to his disdain. "I can probably help out. I take my walk every day, rain or shine. It even snowed for three weeks straight and I had my China boy shovel me a path."

Edith had said nothing during her friend's monologue. She gazed at the wooden walkway beneath her feet as if it held an important secret.

Konrad jumped in. "Actually you could help me, yes. I search for Water Street and I also search for Herr Warburton Pike."

"There it is, right there," Hetty swung her arm toward the water. "They call it Water Street because it runs right along the water! I wouldn't walk there if I were you. Indians, drunks, and chinkies. Too many bars and gambling, oh my dear, gambling like you've never seen before. Of course I don't know myself, but I keep an ear to the ground. I've told my husband, Mr. Henley-Galen, that Vancouver will never hold its head up as long as such places exist. Did you say Warburton Pike?"

Konrad nodded and was about to explain he was a relative of the important man.

"I was afraid so," she turned to her companion, and affected a confidential tone. "The man's a scandal! An absolute scandal. One time he even brought an Indian woman into the Vancouver Club."

Konrad kept his connections to himself for the moment.

"My husband, Mr. Henley-Galen—he's a lawyer *and* a businessman— doesn't like me to say it but I can't help it. He's a strange one. 'Hetty,' my husband says, 'a man such as Warburton Pike has earned his eccentricities and don't you go spreading such opinions around.' But I can't help it, the man's odd."

Hetty Henley-Galen paused for a great sucking breath and Konrad leaped in desperately. "And what business is your husband in?"

"Canneries! Canneries!" she yelped. "That's the business to be in these days. My husband, Mr. Henley-Galen, always says, 'Hetty, there isn't a better place to be a fisherman than on the west coast of Canada.' Of course," she added with a deprecating laugh, "my husband doesn't actually catch fish! He likes to call himself a fisherman though. Mr. Henley-Galen doesn't like to be thought of as too rich. He always says, 'Hetty, this isn't the old country where titles and such matter. Nooo, this is a country of workers. It's work that matters here, so we shall be workers.'"

Konrad couldn't decide who was more obnoxious, Hetty, with her bellowing pomposity, or the pious Mr. Henley-Galen.

"And what business might you be in?" Hetty was asking.

"Ah, I am in . . ." Konrad glanced up at the forested north shore mountains, "timber, ja, I am in timber."

"Oooh," Hetty replied appreciatively. "Then you are an export man as well. I am sure you and Mr. Henley-Galen have much in common." She turned to Edith, "He's forever talking about currency and shipping and such, isn't he, Edith?"

Konrad looked carefully at Edith. She was a short woman, almost plump, with white-blond hair, blue eyes, and a calm expression that his mother would say came from thinking good thoughts. He hoped to hear her speak, but to his disappointment she only nodded her head shyly. It was as if her friend's verbosity drew all the words out of the air.

"Well, I must be off, ladies. Truly it was a pleasure." He decided not to mention Chong's Steam Bath House as his destination. "Do you walk this way every day?" he asked Edith hopefully. It seemed, for a moment, that she would answer him.

"Oh my, yes! And elsewhere too," the indomitable Hetty coursed on. "But there are some places a lady must be careful of. There's madmen about!"

Konrad couldn't imagine anyone daring to take on Hetty except, perhaps, a madman.

"Madmen?" he couldn't resist.

"Oh my, yes. Up the Fraser River. There are white men living in the woods who *never* have any contact with civilization."

"You've seen such madmen?"

"Oh Lord, no!" Hetty fluttered her handkerchief in front of her face. "My husband, Mr. Henley-Galen, would have a fit at the thought! He won't even allow me to take the steamer up the river to watch the Indians do their salmon dances in the spring," she giggled. "Doesn't feel it's right for ladies to see half-clothed men." The handkerchief again. "He's right, of course, isn't he, Edith?"

Perhaps the girl is a mute, considered Konrad. The thought warmed his heart. A poor thing, beautiful but wordless, an appealing fantasy.

He tipped his broad alpaca hat, styled rakishly in the popular Tyrolean fashion.

"A pleasure to make your acquaintance," he said with a little bow.

"He certainly has nice manners," said Hetty watching him go. "Of course, he is German. My husband always says . . ."

Edith didn't reply. With Hetty it was better not to. But she continued to watch the back of the dark-brown wool jacket as its erect and broad-shouldered owner, still clutching his funny hat, walked quickly out of sight.

✳

Dodging a group of boys chasing a wheel down the road and jumping out of the way as a streetcar clanged up behind him, Konrad made his way down the street. He hadn't noticed much when he'd disembarked the day before, beyond the lack of cowboys, but this morning Konrad was struck by the activity everywhere. Not only were there men hurrying from one place to another but the streets near the docks were crowded with carriage traffic, Chinamen pulling little carts, four-horse drays delivering cut lumber to the ships, and the noise was extraordinary. There must be a foundry nearby, for he could hear the distinct sound of hammer against metal.

Looking out over the harbor Konrad could hardly see the water for boats. It wasn't an ordered movement of traffic, rather a lurching, jostling, higgledy-piggledy to and fro with horns tooting impatiently for slower boats to move out of the way. Tied against the three enormous piers were steamships and the odd triple-masted schooner. He counted twenty-three ships before giving up. Aside from the majesty of the mountains in the distance he still couldn't call it a pretty town, but Konrad had to admit it was certainly busy enough, and busy meant prosperity, and prosperity meant, if not goldfields, then men with money. In Konrad's experience, men with money were always eagerly looking for ways to lose it. Though he'd had a bad run of luck surrendering his first-class ticket in a game of cards, Konrad was sure the experience wouldn't be repeated.

Across the street Konrad spotted what he was looking for. The sign was in need of repair. CHONGS STE M BAT H SE. At the bottom, in small faded letters, were the words, LAUNDREY I BACK. He marched across the street to the group of men sitting in front and smoking. Damn! One of them was that odious old fellow who'd tried to pass himself off as Pike yesterday; still barefoot.

"Howdy!" he greeted Konrad in a poor imitation of a western drawl. "Didya find that Park chap you were searching for yesterday?"

"Pike," snapped Konrad, "Mr. Warburton Pike."

"Right-ho! Pike. Any of you boys know where that scoundrel Pike is about?"

Konrad turned to the others who looked of a better class, their handlebar moustaches neatly trimmed and waxed, patent-leather shoes shined, and though their clothes were of an ordinary cut and ordinary cloth, Konrad doubted better fabric would be available in this outpost.

"Saw him a minute ago," one of the men said, picking his words carefully. "Do you want us to give him a message? I'm sure he'll get it."

"Yes," Konrad worked to keep the exasperation out of his voice. This Pike was harder to catch up with than a mountain goat. "Please inform him that Konrad von Schaumberg is looking for him."

"Got it!"

"Well then," Konrad said. "I have been directed here for a bath and a shave. Would you say this is a good establishment?"

Another of the gentlemen, a round-faced fellow with ballooning, vein-shot cheeks, looked up at the sign as if seeing it for the first time.

"Fancy that! And all these years I thought Johnny Chong was a tailor. I went in there to get a suit made last summer and I guess they've just been washing the cloth over and over again. No wonder I'm nearly in rags."

The buckskin-clad man guffawed. "You're in rags because you're too cheap for anything else. I heard you tried to sell one of your shirts that was missing a sleeve for twenty-five cents."

"I marked it down, didn't I?" the man said with a wounded expression.

Taking pity on the newcomer, the other neatly dressed gentleman jumped in, "Don't pay any attention to Hec Brundage." He stabbed his cigar in the direction of the plump-faced man. "It's been slow here since '95, and Hec don't have anything better to do than pester people with his bad jokes. You go on inside and Johnny Chong'll look after you fine."

Though the front of Chong's Steam Bath House was narrow, just fifteen feet across, it extended far back in a warren of alcoves, rooms, and at least three stories. Konrad was led into the tiled baths by a young boy who stood—head bowed, arms outstretched—waiting for Konrad's clothes, which would be brushed and pressed for fifteen cents. Despite the thinness of his wallet, Konrad splurged on a new collar.

Konrad lowered himself into the hot plunge; he'd follow it with a long sit in the steam rooms. The boy who took his clothes giggled as Konrad had to squat slightly in the water to get his more than six feet of height wet up to the neck. A small wood fire burned in one corner, and the boy threw on some cedar boughs that crackled and gave off a delightful aroma.

From what his mother said, this Pike was rich, perhaps not on the scale of the count but certainly rich enough, and he must also have an appetite for risk. Why else would he have holed up in this grubby little place for so long? Konrad intended to offer Warburton Pike twenty percent of all the gold he collected. Naturally Konrad would subtract his costs first but it was a good deal. He'd be doing all the difficult work, taking a chance on being mauled by bears or set upon by Eskimos or Indians or whatever savages inhabited the goldfields.

Konrad was nothing if not charming and persuasive, he knew that well enough. In addition he was athletic, handsome, and from impeccable stock. Anyone would be delighted at the opportunity of doing business with him. Before Konrad was through with him, Warburton Pike would be begging to be allowed to invest in his plans.

Six massive steamer trunks were waiting for him in San Francisco. He planned to return inside a year. Next winter the magnificent Caruso would sing in the city. Though he'd lost his first-class passage, the first day out of El Salvador, as the boat pushed along the Mexican coast and up into American territory Konrad had managed to win a pair of tickets to Caruso's performance from one of the British. He had tucked the tickets inside his dress boots, locked the trunks, and sent the Grand Hotel's bellboy off to secure them for his return.

Konrad calculated that nine months gave him just sufficient time to catch a boat from Vancouver to Skagway, Alaska, and journey overland to make his fortune. He had an article in his bags from the *Neu Welt* magazine, detailing the route. He'd left a few free weeks in his schedule to bag a caribou, huge deer apparently sporting "racks so big it takes two men to lift them." With his fortune Konrad intended to purchase a large tract of property. He hadn't settled on exactly where, perhaps here in the mountains of British Columbia. He would build a marvelous summer home modeled on Schloss Gossweinstein, the magnificent home of Baron von Sohlhein, and invite friends from Prussia, Bavaria, Paris, and London to shoot and enjoy the Wild West. It was, he congratulated himself, an excellent plan.

Of utmost urgency now was finding Pike. He had $12.75 left, enough for a few more days at that wretched hotel but certainly not enough to get to Alaska. The four men were still sitting out front. Konrad addressed himself to the one with manners.

"Sir, I would like to make an appointment with Herr Pike. Can you direct me to his main place of business?"

The man looked at the old ruffian as if expecting him to have the answer.

"Hmmm, well," he ventured when nothing was forthcoming. "It's hard to say where he might be. He could be anywhere. Why don't you tell me what you're about?"

Everyone seemed interested in his private business, but Konrad had little choice.

"He is going to be my partner in an enterprise in the north. I must find him and make arrangements."

"The north, eh?" Hec Brundage nodded knowingly. "Lot o' young fellas going up north. After the gold, I expect. That what's on your mind?"

"Well, yes, that is my reason also. I will stake a claim and work it on behalf of Herr Pike and myself."

A phlegmy rumble emanated from the buckskins.

"No question, Pike's gotten pretty decrepit." Brundage's words were greeted by another rumble from the buckskins. "Say! Did you know that we had a bit of a gold rush here?" Hec asked innocently. "'Course it was some years ago."

Konrad perked up. "Is there still gold in these regions?"

"Some says yes, some says no," Brundage said craftily.

"I expect I can inquire at the mining office? There is a registrar?"

"Er, yes, but, you see, he's gone fishing. Big run now on the Fraser and just about everyone who's got a stick and a string's out there."

Konrad's face fell. No matter where he turned in this cursed town he faced an obstacle.

"How on earth does anyone conduct business here?" he asked.

"It ain't the same as you're used to, I expect," Hec commiserated. Then he clapped his hands together. "I say we give this young man a hand. We shouldn't stand in the way of a hardworking son of Germany."

Another gurgle from the buckskins. The man's chin was sunk on his chest and the disgusting sound was the only hint he was still alive.

"If you can't run down Pike, come and see me. I'll help you all I can. Even if you find him, why not come to dinner tomorrow night and bring the old gent along!" He took a small brass case out of his pocket and extracted a business card, "H. Brundage, Import–Export," with the address neatly lettered in gold along the bottom.

Konrad almost forgot himself in his relief. "I can't thank you enough, sir! It has been difficult my first day here to find my way about and get things under way, so I certainly appreciate the assistance."

"No trouble at all, son, happy to help. Lots of opportunity here, gold or no gold, that's for sure!"

"'Gold or no gold'?" Pike snorted. He raised his chin off his chest, scrubbed at his face, and stared after Konrad walking vigorously back toward his hotel. "'Gold or no gold'?"

"Well, what did you want me to say? I was just trying to make the poor fool feel better."

"Poor! His father could buy British Columbia with enough left over to purchase a couple of small countries. And he really does know the Kaiser."

"You're related to all that wealth and still you sit with a bunch of paupers like us?"

"Guess I'm not particular about who I sit with," Pike retorted. "But I think his father's right. Young Konrad is uncooked steak. And he badly needs seasoning."

54

✳

Konrad left the bathhouse full of anticipation. He felt as if he had been adrift for months on an unknown sea, bobbing here and there, directionless, helpless. Here, on the busy shores of this small, hastily built town filled with a lot of bad-mannered people, Konrad had felt lost for the first time in his life. Or at least he would have felt lost if he had spent a moment considering the unfamiliar emotion. The last day and a half had somehow seemed longer than his entire three years with the artillery in the Polish hellhole. Now, if not Warburton Pike, he had made the acquaintance of Hec Brundage, who seemed an amiable sort and might be persuaded to help him along his way.

Konrad hurried back to his room to make out a list of provisions to present for Mr. Brundage's advice. He knew exactly what he needed, having carefully consulted *Sourdough Sam—Tales of a Boston Lad in the Canadian Wilderness.*

Certain his fortunes were on the upswing, Konrad splurged on a cab. The horse plodded up Granville Street and then west along Davie, where an enclave of large, recently built houses looked south to the beaches of English Bay and cliffs of the Spanish Banks. There was a little madness in the architecture, as if each builder had been directed to include every fanciful style of the Victorian period in a single house. Though the calmer design of the new Edwardian era had begun to soothe the senses in London, New York, Boston, and even Toronto, here in Vancouver the style of the late queen's era was very much alive. After paying off the cabby and gaily adding a fifteen-cent tip, Konrad was now well under $10. He bounded up the stairs, pausing to smooth his hair under his hat. He tugged his cravat and rapped confidently on the heavy door.

He was met at the door by a dark-skinned liveried butler of undetermined heritage, who took his hat and coat before ushering him into the study. "The count is here," he announced in rolling accent. Count. Konrad's spirits were too high to bother correcting him.

Hec Brundage, jacketless and shirtsleeves rolled, beckoned him over. He was leaning over a small table in front of a huge fire, studying something intently. Konrad noted with a little thrill that it was a map encompassing British Columbia and the lower reaches of Alaska and the Yukon Territory. They shook hands warmly, like two old friends.

"Any luck finding Pike then?" Brundage asked.

"I'm starting to believe the man doesn't exist!" Konrad said somewhat plaintively.

"That's his place just up the hill," Brundage said, pointing through the study's bow window to a massive, double-turreted house. "I haven't seen him for some days. Pike's a friend, an old friend, but I wouldn't be talking out of turn if I told you he was a bit unreliable."

"I've heard he is also a little, er, eccentric?" Konrad wasn't sure how far he should go in his assessment of someone Brundage called a friend.

"Eccentric!" Brundage brayed. "My boy, you have no idea!" He bent to examine the map again.

"I was just trying to decide what I'd do if I was in your shoes," Brundage said, gesturing toward the map. "That is if I was a young man again. I know you're set on going to Alaska and you strike me as a determined sort, not easily dissuaded. But there are other places."

"Nein," Konrad protested quickly. "I mean, I would be most interested in having the benefit of your opinion and experience."

"All right then, for what it's worth. As you know, the big rush was on in the Yukon Klondike in '98." Konrad, who knew no such thing, nodded vigorously. "Never been up there myself but I hear there isn't enough gold left there to support a Chinaman. Alaska's the big thing now. Of course, everybody and their grandmother is loading up for the Alaska fields. We've had thirty-five thousand go through here since the start of the year. They've bought up every shovel, pick, and pan I can bring in, and the fares have tripled going up the coast. Sometimes it sickens me how people take advantage." Brundage stroked his ruddy cheek thoughtfully.

"But you know, there's one thing I've learned in business. Sometimes it pays to go with the crowd, sometimes it doesn't. Knowin' what I do now I'd be half inclined to give the Fraser a try."

"The Fraser?"

"Yup, that'd be the big old river about two hours' ride south of here. It's one of the biggest in the world. Practically makes Vancouver an island. There's fine fishing near the mouth. But farther up, you wouldn't know it was the same piece of water. Vicious and mean. That river's killed more men than I'd care to count. "

As Brundage studied the map again, Konrad took in his surroundings. He stood upon a thick silk rug—a dozen shades of white, cream, and gray, like every mood of a cloudy day. The escritoire was a fine example of Queen Anne–era craftsmanship. Overhead, a twenty-four-light crystal chandelier shot prisms onto the walls, which were washed silk of a pale moss-green. A group of brocade-clad chairs faced a large, almost pure-white marble fireplace topped by an extraordinary terra-cotta mantle with gargoyles posted on the corners, feeding out ropes of grape vines, which twisted down and around the mantle supports. The room spoke of success and good judgment. Konrad felt completely at home.

"My nose," Brundage said, tapping his sizable appendage, "tells me that there's still gold up the Fraser. Plenty of it. The easy boys chased out of there to the Cariboo and Kootenays long before it was played out and then the call took 'em to the Klondike. But you're young and I sure enough understand you wanting to chase the crowd to Alaska. Now! Let's go get our dinner while *I'm* still young enough to enjoy it."

✳

Alsace Riesling and thinly sliced cold salmon topped with onions and thick cream. Claret with sorrel-and-mushroom soup. Burgundy and venison with small boiled potatoes and roasted carrots. Steamed pudding with tart berries and whipped cream accompanied by a tawny reisling. Port and mild, white, nutty cheese. Konrad sipped his brandy, trying hard not to groan. His stomach had shrunk after his sea voyage. Though not an educated man, Brundage was good company. He'd set foot in Vancouver a week before the fire of 1887, which wiped out all but four of the buildings in the day-old city. Brundage seemed to know everybody and everything. He had wonderful stories to tell of the Kanakas, legendary Hawaiian strongmen who worked in the Moodyville and Hastings mills. Stories of the 120-foot tree felled and transported all the way to London in one piece. Stories of bears rampaging through the streets and a wild battle with Indians who came across the inlet from the north shore mountains. What a time it must have been. Konrad had come two decades too late.

With the cheese, served by the Kanaka butler, came slices of a pale, crispy, heavily salted meat. It was oily and delicious.

"Mmmmm! What is this marvelous taste?"

"Jumbo dick."

"Jumbo dick?"

"Aye, sir. Jumbo is an elephant. There's a good story there about how the railway brought the poor brute over from Africa and then proceeded to run it down with its own locomotive but I'll tell that another day. This here's what we call jumbo dick, elephant penis or, more politely, geoduck."

"It doesn't taste like any kind of duck I've ever eaten."

"That's because it's a clam. A huge thing. It's got a foot on it this long," Brundage drew his hands three feet apart. Looks disgusting uncooked, but once in the pot you can't beat it."

A young Oriental slid into the room and cleared the plates.

"If you ever settle around here, you'll have to get yourself a chinee," emphasized the older man. "I've got three: a yard boy, the cook, and a houseboy for the missus. Costs me less than a dollar a day for the set."

"Where is the missus?" Konrad asked, a little surprised she hadn't been mentioned before.

"Attending a 'Keep Vancouver White' meeting," Brundage replied without a trace of irony. "She's convinced there won't be a white face left on this coast if we don't put a stop to all the newcomers. Myself, I don't care. But the missus is in with the League of Responsible Women and they're trying to block a petition to allow the India Indians, the japs, and the Chinese to bring their wives in." He stretched, allowing a series of wet belches to escape. "She's probably right. Women make us think of things other than work. Ain't that right?"

Konrad laughed. "At this point I'd be happy to investigate that opinion. There weren't many women you could safely touch on board my ship." The next hour passed quickly as they traded reminiscences of fair flesh—of both the light and the dark-skinned variety.

"Perhaps the Fraser *would* be a better place to try my hand?" Konrad said finally, taking a long puff on a rummy cigar. "It certainly isn't as far away as Alaska."

"P'rhaps so, but you got yourself a few problems. First among them being there isn't any land left worth working that isn't staked. The second being that most of the claims that aren't being worked as we speak are being held by plungers."

"Plungers?"

"Yup. You spend enough time in this *land of opportunity,* and you'll find plungers of all sorts. Generally they buy up something they expect is going to be in short supply, hold it back awhile, waiting for the price to rise, then sell it for jacked-up prices. Sinful practice but there you go."

"So these plungers are holding claims along the Fraser and waiting until . . ."

"Yup, until prices go scooting up as they always do when gold's involved. You'll never get your hands on any of those claims unless the kaiser himself bankrolled you."

"But I thought you said most people believed the gold is all mined out on the Fraser."

"I did say that. Belief's the key word. As long as there's easy takings elsewhere, most are gonna hold to that belief. But the smart folk know that it's just the easy stuff that's gone. They're waiting until the mines play out up north and the gold diggers head on back for a second try."

"I guess I'll have to go back to my original plan," Konrad shrugged. The Fraser sounded too tame anyway. He'd rather follow the footsteps of Sour-dough Sam.

Brundage took a long, speculative look at his guest. "You seem like a fine fellow, and I'd like to help you out. Vancouver needs more people like yourself. I'll tell you what. If you're really interested in something on the Fraser I can nose around tomorrow and see what I can find."

"I thought you said there weren't any claims available."

"No, son," Hec Brundage shook his head at the slender, impatient young man. "What I told you was there isn't any land worth anything that hasn't been staked. I did not say that none o' those claims aren't available."

The sentences filled with negatives confused Konrad.

"You're saying there might be some claims available?" he asked hopefully.

Brundage beamed as if a slow pupil had come up with the right answer to a complex bit of arithmetic.

"There might just be. There might just be. Help yourself to another glass of brandy and tell me more about hunting in Morocco."

✳

"You've found something?" Konrad asked late the next afternoon when he met Brundage at his office, a red-brick building a short distance from Christ Church Cathedral, rather a grand name for such a minor-looking parish church, Konrad thought. He'd spent the day in high anticipation while fighting his way out from under a severe hangover.

"I got lucky," Brundage chortled, looking none the worse for wear. "Have a look." He spread a map out on the table.

Konrad had a hard time not rubbing his hands together. He always was lucky. He knew that about himself. Even when things were at their bleakest—such as the day he'd been stripped of his rank and discharged from the artillery—something else came along. And now, standing in his new friend's office, he sensed that his recent bad luck had changed.

"This here's a good-sized claim up at Texas Bar. Perfect spot. Easy panning and there's a sluice all set up. There's even a cabin."

"This is not a fresh claim?" asked a disappointed Konrad.

"She ain't a virgin, I won't tell you that. But like I said there's not much along the Fraser that hasn't been touched. But this spot was only worked a month or two before the fool who staked it got himself shot."

"Indians?"

"Nah, shot himself. Nearly blew his head off cleaning his gun. So there you have it. Texas Bar can be all yours."

Konrad's spirits climbed again. Now all he had to do was find Warburton Pike and wheedle a loan out of the old man.

"I'll take it!"

"A wise choice, my friend, a wise choice."

55

*

"I laid out cold hard cash to the widow on your say-so," a suddenly far less agreeable Hec Brundage barked the next afternoon. "Now you tell me you don't have any money! What did you expect me to do? *Give* it to you?"

Konrad, who'd been thinking precisely along these lines, quickly demurred. "Most certainly not. Never. I had hoped perhaps for a loan."

"Claims are a cash business," Brundage said, eyes slitted, "and I've found it doesn't pay to loan money to friends. No sir. They don't stay friends for long that way."

The von Schaumbergs were not in the habit of begging, but Konrad, fired with his mission, pleaded with Brundage to give him a day to find Warburton Pike. Again he trudged the streets of Vancouver, stopping anyone who was well dressed to ask if they had seen him or knew of his business address. It was astounding that the man was rich and well known yet no one could say exactly where his offices were located. Konrad even walked an entire hour to the house Brundage had pointed out in the West End only to find the place was empty, save for a Chinese gardener who didn't speak English.

The hours raced by and Konrad was exhausted from ascending and descending the steep streets leading from the waterfront. His final stop was the Pacific Club, where Brundage said Pike often ate midday. He staggered into the foyer and quickly dusted himself off, hoping the odor from his exertions wasn't too obvious.

"Mr. Pike is in attendance," the doorman said stiffly. He glanced discreetly at Konrad's tooled boots, the diamond-and-ruby ring on his middle finger, and the large ornate watch he pulled out in frustration and flipped open. "Would you like me to see if he can be disturbed?"

Konrad brightened. At last. "Yes indeed, that would be most helpful. Thank you."

"A sherry in the reading room while you wait, sir?"

"A sherry would be most pleasant. This town has many hills, and even a horse would be tired from all the miles I have walked today searching for Herr Pike."

✳

"Well, if it isn't the Kaiser." An irritating drawl pierced Konrad's thoughts. It was the seedy old bandit. At least the scruff was wearing shoes—a heavily worn pair of boots. And the dirty buckskin jacket was gone, replaced by a barely presentable dinner coat. How on earth did a man such as this gain admittance to a private club?

"What can I do for you?"

"You can leave me alone," Konrad said brusquely; he'd wasted far too much time on this ass already. "I am waiting for Herr Pike. And I don't wish to be disturbed."

"Have it your way, Kaiser," the man smiled. "Have it your way."

✳

Time passed, the sherry was gone, and there was no sign of Pike. "Did you have a word with Pike?" boomed Hec Brundage, sweeping into the room, the bonhomie back in place. Konrad started to his feet.

"*Nein,*" he sighed. "He has not come in to speak to me yet."

"That's not like him," Brundage said. "Pike has his faults but he's not the sort to cut someone who wants to see him."

"But he won't see me," Konrad said disconsolately.

"A man sees what he wants to see," Brundage said, tucking his thumbs into his waistcoat and strolling over to the fireplace to gaze at the painting above the mantle. "Take this painting. Woman did this, a friend of Pike's. Pike loves the paintings but they give me the shivers. I never could understand why he insisted the club mount it here."

Konrad hadn't noticed the work before, more a large sketch really. He wasn't much interested in art but he wanted to be polite. He was quickly running out of hope, not to mention energy and money. And this man was his last chance. Short, sharp black strokes created ghostly trees that ran into each other with no beginning and no end. In the foreground wooden shacks rimmed a bay with the water drawn to look like smooth, flat rocks frozen in a gentle midswell. A small figure sat alone in one corner, head covered in a bowl-like hat.

"Emily Carr. Strange tub of a creature. Rude too. But Pike thinks she's wonderful; buys as many as she'll let him. Otherwise she can't give them away. He tried to get a bunch of us to buy her work, but tell me, why would I hang something in my house that gives me the creeps?"

Konrad looked closer. There was certainly an aura of otherworldliness about the picture. It wasn't pretty, as you would expect a woman's art to be, but it held the eye. Looking at it, he suddenly felt indescribably lonely, but since he didn't recognize the emotion, he took it to be hunger.

"My point is that there's no predicting Pike. He lives by his own rules. He decided to help this woman," he pointed to the picture. "I don't know why. For some strange reason he doesn't want to help you. I don't know why either. But that still leaves us with some business to settle."

"Well, I suppose our deal is off then," Konrad said heavily, admitting defeat. "I have no other resources, no other prospects."

Brundage pulled out his watch. "Let me think on this. Meet me at my office at eight o'clock tonight." He turned quickly on his heel and left before Konrad could say a word.

❋

Konrad recalled a small steakhouse on one of the precipitous streets leading to the harbor. HARRY'S 99—FULL MEAL 99 cents. BEER PICHER 99 cents. That would do nicely. Turning left out of the club, he walked for ten minutes into the gloom. The sun had disappeared behind the mountains on the northwest shore, and all that could be seen across Burrard Inlet was a darkening blanket and a faint haze of gray from a mill that was still busy at work. Konrad thought briefly of the picture in the club and for a moment felt what the artist must have felt when she sketched those trees, so entwined they seemed as one.

"No need to go farther," a breathy voice issued from a doorway. "The best of Dupont Street is right here."

Konrad peered toward the pleasant sound and found himself looking into the frothy cleavage of a well-endowed young woman. He must have turned the wrong way out of the club.

"I was looking for steak. Harry's," he smiled at her.

"I got a rump you could chew on, mister," she purred, keeping her lips tight together so her lack of teeth didn't show. This one was well dressed. She'd like to reel him in.

"I bet you do," Konrad grinned. "But a man must eat to keep up his strength." He rested his leg on the doorstep inches from where she was standing. Cherry-red nails slid over and patted his knee, then again a little higher. Konrad had excellent legs, he knew that. Long, lean, and hard from hunting and riding. His breeches and trousers were carefully cut to show off the muscular swell of his thighs. His stomach growled, but the growing warmth in his loins kept him in the doorway. Not since the lovely darkie who worked in his sister's laundry had Konrad enjoyed a woman. That was nearly two months ago. A record for him.

"You're plenty strong as it is," the girl crooned with an appreciative squeeze. "A man like you shouldn't be alone on a night like this." It was her standard line, uninventive but she hadn't put two thoughts together in so long she never considered coming up with a better one. Besides, at the lower end of Dupont Street, ladies like her didn't attract too many men who unbuttoned their pants for conversation. She squeezed again.

"Company won't cost you much."

The mention of money blew a cold wind on Konrad's rapidly heating loins.

"How much is not too much?"

"A dollar. Mouth work's extra."

He looked at her mouth, which she neglected to keep shut. The yellow cast from the lantern hung up in the doorway to mark her territory highlighted the toothless stretches of gum. The moment was lost, and Konrad's stomach overrode his groin.

"*Fraulein,*" he murmured apologetically, "you would help pass the night most pleasantly but I am short of money and also hungry."

"One dollar? Night's early and I ain't busy!" she urged.

"*Ach, nein.* I must go." Nothing would persuade him to stay now. His sweaty encounter with the none-too-clean laundry darkie whose breath reeked of cloves and garlic seemed different somehow, more appropriate in the wilting steam of the tropics. A grab and grope with this already well-faded rose suddenly felt repulsive in the soft air of Vancouver's twilight.

As he moved away, the woman lunged forward, snatched his hand, and stuffed it into her bodice.

"I ain't never done one like you, so pretty," she wheedled.

Konrad yanked his hand back so violently he pulled the woman right out of the doorway and sent her stumbling into the street. Three men passing roared with delight. One stopped and pumped his hips.

"Doin' the Dupont Dance!" he crowed.

The woman whirled around, hissing like a cornered cat.

"Fockin' bastard!" she snarled, swinging wildly at Konrad's head.

Konrad bolted back in the direction he'd come from, moving quickly until he could no longer hear the shrieks that followed him. It was a beautiful night, and couples strolling along Granville stared curiously at the well-dressed foreigner hot-footing it away from the brothel district. Granville, lined with shops and services, seemed like a welcoming metropolis.

"Harry's 99, sir! Do you know where it is?" Konrad breathlessly asked the first gentleman he came upon.

"Ayyye, aye! That I do. One block that way." The man pointed up the hill south along Granville. "Turn left on Georgia and you'll see it right there. You'll get a fein cut from Harry, my lad."

Seated on a worn bench seat with a thick candle dripping wax on a dented tabletop and a frothy "picher" of beer in front of him, Konrad felt somewhat better. Nothing was as expected about this place. It appeared as if Vancouver was like any other young city in the new world, hastily built by strivers and decorated around the edges with a civilized veneer. But everywhere there were surprises and an ominous sense that another power was in charge beyond man and his works.

Konrad had yet to see the Fraser River except for the briefest glance at dawn the day he'd arrived, and he'd only viewed the mountains from the safety of Vancouver's muddy streets and wooden sidewalks. But he had a looming sense of one's destiny being in someone or something else's control. It kept a person off balance. Konrad didn't like the feeling.

With forty minutes left before his meeting with Hec Brundage, Konrad reluctantly pulled himself out of the booth and paid Harry's missus—$1.98. He'd given up counting but guessed he had less than $6 left.

A fat golden moon hung in the sky, overwhelming the glow of the city's new electric streetlights.

Gold, thought Konrad, staring appreciatively at the orb. A good omen.

✳

Hec Brundage was slobbering over a cigar the size of a stovepipe. Ashes dropped to the creamy carpet beneath his feet.

"There you are! Come. Come."

He led Konrad past the exquisite Queen Anne desk, through a set of heavily leaded doors, and along a narrow corridor lined with wainscoting of a dark, unusual wood and covered in the same pale moss-green silk. Six drawings mounted in plain cedar frames caught his eye.

"I thought you did not like this artist?" he asked, noting the forceful signature "M. Emily Carr."

"Yess, well. When you meet Pikey you'll find out what a persuasive fellow he is. Every time I walk down this hall I am reminded of an old nursery rhyme that warns children not to venture too deeply into the woods. I take it seriously."

Open-mouthed creatures leered from a hard, gray-black backdrop of trees. The pictures looked disheveled, with tall, carved poles canting in all directions. Konrad tried to imagine what his mother would say if he gave her one of these drawings.

"This poor child must have gone mad!" she'd exclaim before consigning the canvas to the nearest fireplace.

"Here we are. What do you think of this lot?"

Brundage opened a door at the end of the hallway leading to a small room that could have been an old pantry. Arrayed on the stone floor were boots, several hats, two shovels, a pickax, an assortment of hand tools including an adze, a small ax, and a saw, three stacked objects that looked like large pie pans, two buckets, a lantern, a battered canteen, and a pile of blankets. Brundage handed him an envelope, which contained a train ticket to a place called New Westminster and a letter of introduction to Stuart Halley, Esquire.

"This'll get you to the Fraser," he tapped the ticket. "This'll get you passage upriver," he waved the letter.

"How is this possible!" Konrad exclaimed happily.

"You gave me the idea this morning."

"I did?"

"When you asked for a loan."

"You said you didn't loan money to friends."

"Yes, quite right," Brundage said almost gaily. "But I've struck on a way to loan you some money without abandoning my principles of many years. Collateral."

"Collateral?" Konrad knew the word but had no idea how it applied to him in his circumstances.

"That, 'n that, 'n that, 'n those."

Brundage pointed to Konrad's gold watch, his ruby-and-diamond ring, his beloved rifle, and his water-bison boots.

"Where did you get my rifle?"

"Had it brought over from your room. I know the proprietor. Man can't fish to save his life but he's convinced the problem's with the boat, so every few years he buys a new one from me. I told him we'd made a deal."

Konrad gasped. The gall of the man to simply march in and seize his belongings when not even a handshake had passed between them.

"Oh yes, you'll be wanting this." Brundage handed over the claim.

Anger pushed up from the pit of Konrad's stomach.

"My watch belonged to the uncle of our Kaiser! See?" He flipped it open to show the royal seal. "A thousand dollars could not buy this anywhere in the civilized world."

Indignation built.

"And this ring was given to my mother's father by Czar Alexander. You want me to exchange these things for, for this stuff?"

Brundage considered. "Yes, you're right. All this stuff's probably not worth more'n a hundred bucks on a good day. Claim maybe another three hundred. Why don't you hand over four hundred and we'll call it a square deal."

Brundage had him. Even if Konrad resorted to begging his father for money it would be many months before it arrived—if it arrived. He could certainly wait until the elusive Pike appeared, but his initial optimism that the old man would finance him on the strength of a letter was fading. And what use was a ruby ring to a gold prospector anyway?

"All right. Here is the agreement," Konrad began, forgetting for a moment Brundage held all the cards. "I will do as you ask but I ask in return that you keep my things for three months. In that time I intend to make my fortune and I will buy them back from you."

"We'd better settle on a price then. Say two thousand dollars?"

"Two thousand dollars!"

"You just told me all your things are worth so much, and I've gotta keep 'em here for three months, out of pocket for my expenses, waiting for you to return. You could get killed or something, and I've gotta spend time selling them. Seems reasonable to me."

Konrad wished he had kept his mouth shut about the value of his property. Still, what did it matter? Three months was plenty of time to make his fortune, and he was eager to be rid of Vancouver.

"Yes, I will agree. Except for one thing. I must have a gun. Mine is most valuable, but if you will find me a good one in replacement, then we have a deal."

Brundage reached behind the door and pulled out an aged Winchester two-shot.

"This should do you just fine. Brought down many a duck in its day. It was given to me by my own dear father." Konrad was not naturally a cynical man, but after a day of being tossed here and there by people like Brundage, who always seemed to leave out some vital piece of information in a conversation, he had serious doubts that the rifle had ever been any-where near Brundage's "own dear father."

Konrad sighted down the barrel, snapped open the breech, and turned the rifle over in his hands carefully. Even a neglected gun like this gave him pleasure to handle. He could bring this one back to life.

"It will do." He stuck out his hand to seal the bargain.

56

*

Konrad mounted the platform of the Canadian Pacific Railway passenger car with his duffel and supervised the car boy loading his chest—his *Koffer*. The compartment was only second class, but the seats were well-kept dark-red leather, the rugs new, the wood trim inside the car polished, and the service as good as on any first-class European train.

Settling down Konrad pulled out a pamphlet given to him by Hec Brundage, *Important Facts for Gold Prospectors*, published by Dominion Mines and Resources. Sluices, scree, nuggets, pans, slurry, sediment. He read avidly. In the middle of the booklet was a grainy photograph of a man holding up a fist-sized nugget recovered from a tributary of the Fraser River. A little thrill rippled through him.

Once clear of the railway warehouses on the waterfront, the train slowly chugged past the piers lined up on the shore like soldiers, past the outskirts of Chinatown with its higgledy-piggledy houses and past the Hastings Saw Mill belching smoke. Around the mill was a small shanty-town, the remnants of a large squatter community where the so-called *rancherie* held sway—nervy Indians, Kloochmen, miners' wives—usually abandoned—and the most disreputable whites. Their reputation for immorality and every vice known to man meant that only missionaries dared venture into the area. The train pressed on through the working-class neighborhood of Strathcona and a newly opened area called Grand-view. The homes were small and few were painted, but compared to the squalor of Chinatown and the degradation of the dwellings that housed the *rancherie*, they were relatively tidy despite lacking water, sewer, or electricity, all of which were enjoyed by those who lived downtown, in Vancouver's upper-class West End and the growing middle-class districts of Mount Pleasant and Fairview.

The small houses on east Vancouver's fringe quickly gave way to another rabble of shanties with moss-laden roofs, holes dug in the ground for the inhabitants to perform their private duties in plain view, laundry hanging from trees, and tiny glassless windows covered with bits of salvaged cloth. As the train turned south toward New Westminster, sudden movement caught Konrad's eye. Hundreds of gray, long-legged birds rose like dust out of a carpet from the shallow waters of False Creek flats. False Creek itself lay farther west, but its overflow waters turned several hundred acres of land, the flats, into a heron's paradise. Just as the herons disappeared from view, Konrad caught sight of a small band of men, women, and children wading slowly through the ankle-deep water, bent low and occasionally snatching something out of the water. Indians! He craned his neck hard to get a better view, but the train was gathering speed.

*

After little more than an hour the train pulled into the bustling waterfront station at New Westminster. As Konrad alighted he was struck by how much the town resembled a large factory, with the smell of fish, salt, and wet wood pervading everything. High on a hill overlooking the Fraser Konrad spotted a group of boldly colored houses with high, white balustrades shining in the morning light. On the waterfront, log booms stretched as far as he could see, boats weaved in and out, jockeying for position. It took him a moment to identify an eerie screech symphony that underlaid the general racket of motor and horse. Logs. The booms rose and fell with the slight swell of the river causing the captive logs to rub and howl against each other.

When Manto and Inish had floated downriver to the Fraser's mouth, the land that was destined to become the city of Vancouver was like an uneven hand, lying palm-up, fingers protruding into the Strait of Georgia between the mainland and Vancouver Island. New Westminster sat in the middle of the wrist. A long bulbous thumb was the mountain range of Vancouver's north shore. The index finger lay separated from the middle finger by Burrard Inlet to the north and, to the south, False Creek, which once had been a true river plunging deep into the interior to meet its parent, the Fraser. The middle finger commanded the long peninsula, which became Vancouver's central residential core ending in the steep cliffs, sandy beaches, and wide green nose of the University of British Columbia's endowment lands. The third finger comprised the islands lying in the final fork of the Fraser, the settlement of Richmond, and the little finger, the forests and deltas that made up Vancouver's most southerly lands.

Outside the station Konrad was delighted to see a freight carriage waiting for cargo from the train. HALLEY'S FORWARDING, the black-and-gold lettering read. Brundage assured him that there would be at least one carriage
meeting every train. Konrad supervised the unloading of his *Koffer*. Now
stripped of his obviously European clothes, he blended more easily with
the rough working people.

"I have passage to Chilliwack aboard one of Mr. Halley's boats," he
informed a man lounging in the driver's seat and smoking while he waited
for the cargo to be unloaded.

"Find yerself a place then. We'll be brim-full within the hour an' this's
the last train we're meeting today."

Konrad occupied his time with the old Winchester. Rust had invaded
the barrel, trigger, and cock, and he diligently worked away with an oiled
cloth to bring the metal back to its former glory. The sight was bent, but an
experienced shot could compensate.

*

"Y'all read it to me," commanded the beefy person of Stu "Sawbush" Halley
when Konrad presented his letter of introduction.

Dear Mr. Halley,

*Here is a young man from Germany who aims to search for gold up
river. I have set him up with a claim at Texas Bar and outfitted his
person for that purpose. If you go beyond Chilliwack kindly provide
him passage as far as Crikshead unless the River is high enough to
land him at the Bar. I would consider it a personal favor.*

Regards, Hector Brundage Esq.

"What year would it be?" Halley puzzled.

"1904," returned Konrad.

"Ain't you a mite late?"

"Late?"

"Yeah, late. Been nearly fifty years since the Rush."

"Yes, well, Mr. Brundage explained that to me well enough," said Konrad, eager to appear informed. "Most of the prospectors abandoned perfectly

good claims for easier money in the north. Mr. Brundage believes there's plenty of gold waiting to be gathered up."

"Could be, I s'pose."

"And now with such good times for timber, people such as yourselves are occupied with that instead of prospecting."

"Five bucks to the Bar."

Konrad fully expected the passage to be gratis, based on the letter from Brundage. In Germany and, indeed, most of Europe a letter from a prominent person to someone else of any station in life would have automatically meant a favor was being called into play. But the only favor Sawbush Halley intended to perform he did at that moment, reaching out a black-toed boot and kicking away a dog that had begun to raise its leg against Konrad's leather duffel.

"Five bucks and be quick about it. I gotta git this stuff loaded."

Konrad pulled out what was left of his cash. No matter. Gold was tender in any part of the world. He also had his gun and four boxes of bullets. He could easily feed himself until the first gold appeared.

Halley pocketed the money in a blink.

"Think we'll get ya to the Bar all right. River's up. We's loaded heavy and we'll draw big but the Bar ain't usually a problem till midsummer. Git yer stuff for'd, starberd the bridge."

Konrad waited for half an hour for someone to move his *Koffer* onto the boat. It easily weighed 150 pounds. Three men worked steadily, hauling cargo off the carriage and stowing it. They stopped for a smoke. Konrad stared at them and they stared back, but no one made a move toward the large chest. The crew were casting off lines when Konrad laboriously maneuvered the chest up the plank and over the side, where it fell with a clatter of pans and shovels. No sooner had he righted himself than Halley barked at the man below decks to pick up his pace shoveling coal into the boiler.

The big brown river, more than two thousand feet across, ambled west to the Pacific. Even heavily loaded, the boat had no difficulty bucking the current. The high land of New Westminster disappeared speedily and the shorn banks grew back their treed fringe. Konrad leaned over the edge, watching in fascination as small dextrous boats wove in and out of booms anchored to shore. There were hundreds of logs in each boom.

"Chew?"

Halley's drawl woke Konrad from his reverie. With a start he realized an hour had passed. The mountains to the north seemed closer now, darker, higher. But the land to the south was low, gentle, and startlingly green.

"Dairy mostly out here."

Halley shoved something brown at him. It looked like an oily, flattened cigar.

"Injun candy. I swear to the Almighty, they put sumtang in it that makes a man crazy fer more."

Konrad sniffed the stiff finger of meat.

"It's fish, dried salmon. I bet you ain't never tasted an'thang like it before."

Konrad took a bite. Sweet, salty, and pungent.

"When we get closer to Hope, you'll see 'em settin' up their dryin' racks. 'Bout the only thang them injuns do that's worth a damn. Making this injun candy. Back in '96 I got stranded way upriver in the canyons in a storm that'd rip apart a navy fleet. Boat pounded to kindling. Lost a man an' three of us took a week to git back to New West. All we had to eat was this here candy. Never been without it since."

"*Mein Gott!*" shouted Konrad.

Halley stepped back in alarm.

"Jeeesus man, whassamatter with you!"

Halley followed Konrad's astonished eyes.

"Oh yes, the Queen. She does that to ya."

Konrad von Schaumberg had hunted on the slopes of the Matterhorn. He had ascended partway up the rocky slopes of the Eiger with four Swiss guides who packed along wine, cheese, and a whole pig to a late-summer picnic for Konrad and his party of ten. And many times he had skied down the snow fields of Mont Blanc to the winter villa of the Mumm family. But never had the sight of anything struck him so forcefully as what lay before him now.

The Queen. Mount Baker rising unexpectedly on the southern horizon out of land that was retreating in fields and deltas to the sea, leaving behind the sharp, young peaks of the coastal range on the other side of the river. She was all alone, regal and white, as if she had just been dropped there as an afterthought.

"She's jes about the on'y thang you can count on along this here river," opined Halley, adding, in a rare poetic moment, "She fills you up better'n a hot meal."

Konrad gaped at the slightly lopsided tower of white, seemingly close enough to touch. In reality, as the crow flies Mount Baker was nearly seventy miles away, across the American border, in the state of Washington. It wasn't even very big as mountains go, just less than eleven thousand feet, a mere pup compared to the peaks of Konrad's homeland. Nor was it a difficult mountain. Its north face was readily accessible to any of average mountaineering skill. A ridge route went up to a false summit, then dipped into a snowy valley before a second ridge ran up to the top. It had been walked by men, women, and even children. But no one could take away its startlingly solitary position, like a queen without a court.

Three hours later the boat ducked out of the river's center, swung around an island, and chugged toward a pier and a pile of buildings flung along the bank. Smoke rose from a cluster of shacks on the islands, and a group of Indian children were pulling nets out of the water—the boys nearly naked, the girls thigh-deep in the water, with Western-style skirts swirling around them.

The town of Mission was a fury of activity. One passenger train was leaving toward Vancouver while a long, dirty freight pulled in behind. Waiting to be loaded at the railside were rows of milk cans. It was strange to see, after hours of flat fields, this buzzing town erupt in the middle of nowhere.

"I could have taken the train this far?" asked Konrad as Halley came forward to supervise docking.

"Yup, but it wouldn't git ya where'n yer going. I'm landing you south side of the river at the Bar an' way above Hope. Yer damn lucky. Most times I jes go as far as Agassiz. CPR'll take ya upriver all right to Hope, but how's ya gonna get that great bloody box of yourn across the river? It's tricky at that point. And ya gotta know where to go or you're lost."

✳

Konrad heard a warble and turned his attention to the main wharf. A group of boys in white trousers, red jerseys, and pillbox hats parked smartly to one side of their heads were singing enthusiastically.

He hath sent me,
I shall go,
for my soul invincible.

The Indian boys, charges of the Oblates of Mary Immaculate, turned their brown faces to the peaking sun and galloped through the hymn. An ancient priest sat in a chair beside the choir, his head nodding rhythmically to the song, one hand propped on a cane, the other waving in the air. Next to him an unusually tall young girl stood stiffly. As the knitted blanket slid from the priest's lap, she tugged it back in place. The old man laid his knotted hand across her smooth brown one in appreciation.

For the second time in a few hours Konrad's heart leaped painfully in his chest. The Indian girl was indescribably beautiful, with full lips, breasts, and hips. Her face had none of the exaggerated flatness featured in the photographs and drawings he'd seen in his readings about Indians. Konrad guessed her age at no more than fourteen, but her poise and presence were of a much older person. She paid no attention to the activity on the wharf.

"They bin practicing for three weeks fer some bishop or other. You'd never think the injun could look so pretty would ya?" Halley leered. "They don't last though."

When the old priest was looking the other way, one of Halley's crew ostentatiously rubbed his crotch as he passed her. If she noticed she gave no indication.

"Red meat!" the man smacked his lips. "Bet that one's never had the pole," he said to Konrad.

"You should not speak in such ways!" Konrad snapped.

"Well, don't that beat all," Halley roared with laughter. "Our Mr. Kraut got himself a sausage goin' for some of the local color!

"Maybe you need a little reeleef," he drew the word out, "before you go make your fortune on the Bar."

Konrad blushed uncomfortably at the attention his outburst attracted. He didn't know why he'd spoken up for the girl. She was no different from the darkie he'd so happily used on his brother-in-law's estate. He glanced at her once the crew had resumed their unloading. She stared straight ahead as if intently listening to the boys singing, but he could have sworn her lips moved—just a fraction, but they moved.

Konrad didn't want the girl; well, he did, but for some strange reason—the two bore no resemblance to each other—she made him think of Edith, the silent blonde he'd met perambulating with her awful friend in the streets of Vancouver. Konrad watched the girl, as they chugged up the river, until she was a speck.

Around the lower part of the hook that formed the southern course of the Fraser, small settlements clustered on or near both banks: Fort Langley—the original fur-trading post on the south bank, Mission and Hatzic on the north, then Chilliwack on the south, and Agassiz—the last village before the river turned sharply north, its personality changing as it went.

The boat passed dozens of islands, where birds lifted into the sky like gray sheets floating in a strong wind. They moved a little more nimbly now, with the two heavy stoves for the Oblates and several tons of boom chains offloaded. By late afternoon they were rounding the blunt nose of land lying between the river and Agassiz.

Pop! Pop! Pop! Rifle shots.

Halley jumped out of the bridge, binoculars in one hand, rifle in the other. Konrad's sight was excellent and he could easily make out five figures running hard to the water's edge where two Indian dugouts bobbed in the reeds.

"Thievin' bastards," the shouts floated across the water, even above the sound of the boat's raspy engine.

Pop! Pop! Pop! The pursuers were firing enough lead to fell a herd of deer. But not a single shot went home. Konrad grinned at their ineptitude. The Indians were in their boats and paddling madly downstream as the white men came panting up to the shore, swearing and shouting in their frustration.

"Stop 'em!" they shouted, waving encouragement at Halley.

"What the hell!" whooped Halley. "Let's have a little fun."

"Goin' scalpin'!" hollered the crew.

Halley turned the boat expertly and chugged full-throttle after the canoes. They had a good head start, but their speed was no match for an experienced river captain heading downriver with a full head of steam at his disposal. They were able to avoid being rammed by darting in and out of shallows and cutting close to shore when the bigger boat was forced to go wide. But the bank grew steeper at this rounded point on the Fraser and they had no protection from either shallows or islands. The crew were jumping up and down with glee as the boat drew within twenty yards.

"Get the net!" yelled Halley. "We'll catch the red sumbitches like fish!"

One of the crew pulled a heavy net out of the storage hold and dragged it forward.

"Pull 'er close!"

The crew grabbed sections of the net, ready to fling it overboard. Just as they pulled alongside one of the canoes, an Indian stood up suddenly in the center of the boat, balanced carefully and . . .

"Look out!" screeched Halley when he saw the harpoon in the man's hands. The Indian's face was painted completely red, a hideous mask made all the worse by his bared teeth.

"Yahhh!!" His body jerked forward and his hand snapped the release. It flew straight and found its mark.

"Ughh," a heavily bearded crewman dropped to his knees, blood surging out of his inner thigh. A prodigious throw, thought Konrad.

"Uh, uh, uh," the downed man stuttered in surprise, looking stupidly at the harpoon imbedded in his leg.

"Take the wheel!" Halley roughly shoved one of the men.

Konrad peered cautiously over the edge of the boat. The two canoes were pulling rapidly away but the harpoonist was looking back and laughing. They were heading into the Cheam Slough, where Halley couldn't follow. They were almost out of sight when Red Face stood up again and faced the idling riverboat. He flipped up his loin cloth and waggled his manhood in triumphant derision.

Konrad sprinted to the back of the boat, jumping over the puddling blood from the weeping crewman's leg. Halley was tying a rope tourniquet.

"Shuddap, ya fat pig! If ya didn't eat so much ya coulda gotten outta the way."

No one paid any attention to Konrad as he burrowed among his things, pulled the old rifle free of its oiled cloth, and slammed two bullets into the breech. Ignoring the bent sight, he squinted along the barrel, compensating slightly for what he expected would be a bias to the right. He could just make out the figures through the reedy banks of the slough. Konrad sucked in his breath, paused, then squeezed softly.

"Fuck me!" squeaked the wheelman, half fainting as the first bullet whined past him. He hit the deck, ignoring the boat now drifting close to shore.

The old gun had quite a kick, but Konrad was well planted and it took only a second to bring the barrel back in line with his second target. Breathe. Hold. Pause. Squeeze. Crack!

"Pull 'er port!" bellowed Halley. Konrad's second bullet flew. The wheelman didn't move. Halley abandoned the injured man and yanked the wheel around.

Everything was suddenly quiet. Halley steered the boat back into the channel.

"You coulda kilt me!" the outraged wheelman thumped Konrad in his chest.

"No, I could not. I was not aiming for you."

"Aimin'! Aimin'! Any bullet comes that near my head and I don't care about no aimin'!"

Halley pointed toward the slough. One of the canoes was drifting back toward the river turning sideways in the slow current.

"Get the hook out," Halley instructed. "And you, quick shot, cover 'em."

Two men lay in the boat. The third must have jumped overboard and escaped into the bushes. Red Face's hand was shattered. The second bullet had creased a crimson ribbon across the side of the other man's head. He lay unmoving but breathing.

The crew yipped and danced. They pulled the canoe against the boat with a long grappling hook. Red Face glared ferociously, cradling his arm.

"We'll take 'em back to Agassiz and the farmers'll have a fine time with them tonight. What'd they take, anyway?" Halley asked.

Konrad peered into the canoe. "Looks like apples."

"Mighty expensive apples, if you ask me," Halley said happily, turning the boat again.

After dropping the two men at the Agassiz flats, much to the delight of the fruit farmers, Halley turned to Konrad.

"You mean to do that?"

"You ask if I meant to hit them?"

"Hit 'em like that, yeah."

"Of course."

"Why dincha just kill 'em?"

"They were not my apples."

57

The lower part of the Fraser, a south and west sweeping hook, was a tease, a façade concealing its true character. As the steamer neared Hope, the river began to divulge its secrets. Narrower, darker, swifter. Water plunged and pulled at them, forcing Halley to pay closer attention to his navigation.

They tied up at Hope for the night, the last town of any size before the river unleashed what Halley called "a witch's cauldron."

"We go through that to get to my Bar?"

"Nah. 'Bout two miles north o' the Bar the river gets plum angry till ya hit Yale. You're just below it but you still gotta watch the river. She looks sweet but in the right weather those rapids reach way farther south."

"What is beyond Yale?"

"Ahh, now yer talkin' river like no one seen afore. I hearda men who fell in an' their arms, legs, and head were ripped right off their body!"

Konrad was eager to see such a fury of water, but for now he'd settle for Texas Bar. There would be plenty of time to explore with gold in his pocket.

"The best man that ever drove this river was Captain Billy Moore. A German, jes like yerself."

"With a name like Billy Moore?"

"He was Wilhelm somesuch, but no one could pronounce it, so he changed it. Had this boat he built hisself, the *Henrietta*. She dint draw more'n five inches. He could sail her on heavy dew. Once he did the trip from New Westminster to Yale, fully loaded, mind, in twenty-two and one half hours—takes me twenty-eight with a light load. Christ, that man had bear balls. Got hisself over sandbars along this river where a bird'd get stuck. Ol' Billy probably took more gold downriver than half a dozen other pilots put together."

Konrad's ears perked up at the word "gold."

"When was that?"

"Oh, back in '58, '59. People were loco, to hear it told. Lotsa them diggers ended up right here in Hope—still hoping, I guess."

"Fifty years ago?"

Halley laughed at the German's distress.

"Ya figure they done took it all? Mebee. But p'rhaps the man who sold ya the claim is right. Gold diggers are as fickle a bunch as ya'll ever find. They git theyselves a stake, some nice flakes comin' out, then someone hits the big one and off they go. Chasin'. Chasin'."

Men did still pan and operate small dredges along the river. Most were hermits, some with obvious mental disorders, and all had made peace of sorts with the Indians, the land, and the river. Halley knew for a fact that there was still gold. The Indians knew how to get it. Halley had a secret compartment deep in the hold of his boat. No one but he had ever seen it. Well, one man had. A woodcutter sold him some fuel a couple of years ago at the mouth of the Silverhope Creek, just south of Hope, in return for passage to New Westminster. That night Halley found the man burrowing around in the hold, looking for things he could pocket. Damn if he didn't somehow stumble on the cache. Halley broke a perfectly good blade in the man's back.

But the Indians had gold—dust, flakes, and the occasional nugget. Enough to pay for a load of blankets, tools, or whiskey. Halley made sure he had all three on every run—the thinnest blankets, cut whiskey, and tools no white man would use, but most of the Indians were long past any kind of serious resistance to the white man. Halley never knew when a canoe would come gliding up alongside. Now he almost had enough to get himself a fine house on one of Vancouver's hills with a long white porch, windows as tall as a man, and a grand view over False Creek. Halley never asked the Indians where they got the gold. He figured they had a mountain of the stuff stolen from miners in years gone by. But no need to tell the German that.

Hope was a hopeless sort of town, hemmed in by hills, dingy and glowering in the day's last light. From the main wharf the buildings all seemed to loom and the people on the streets looked furtive. Konrad shuddered and wrapped himself against the chill in one of Halley's meager blankets. Tomorrow the Bar. He had a flask of brandy, which he'd use to toast his first fistful of gold.

＊

"This is it?"

"No, that is it."

Halley pointed to a crook in the river where the tops of several sand-bars just broke the surface of the water. Texas Bar. The cliffs rose steeply almost from the shoreline. All Konrad could see were black rocks, trees, and sharp banks. The pleasant fantasy of strolling out and shooting game for dinner evaporated. No man could possibly walk through such a tangle, let alone see clearly enough to shoot anything.

Halley was in a hurry to leave. He had a load to pick up in Hope on the way back and eight passengers. He ordered the crew to ship the German's chest over the side, lowering it to the water with ropes.

"You cannot dock at the shore?" Konrad asked plaintively, suddenly realizing he had to wade to the bank.

"I ain't drawing no five inches. Be quick now. I want to be into Hope before dark."

As the boat nimbly whipped around and steamed downriver, Konrad, waist-deep in water, hauled his duffel and trunk to the shore, desperately try-ing to keep his rifle dry. He pulled everything onto the first of a dozen little sandbars. The boat was almost out of sight, moving swiftly with the current.

"Come back!" The words were out before Konrad realized it. Just a whisper.

"Come back!" This time he screamed. Then again and again, until his throat flamed with the effort. "Come back!"

Konrad suddenly felt very foolish, like a weepy girl. This land took the man out of a person, if you let it. He was thankful the boat was out of earshot. He'd survived three years in the Prussian army's most desolate post; he could certainly survive on Texas Bar. Halley said he'd come back in a month with supplies if Konrad posted bond for the passage and the goods. He didn't have anything left of value except his grandmother's engagement ring, which he wore for good luck around his neck. Women thought it incredibly romantic (he told them it had belonged to his betrothed who'd died of consumption just before their wedding day). They played with the ring like a third nipple on his chest. But Konrad doubted if such an opportunity would arise in the near future, so off came the twenty-four-karat band plainly set with three large pink diamonds.

True to Hec Brundage's word, Texas Bar clearly showed signs of former habitation—a long sluice box, several broken shovels, and a rocker used to sift gravel by separating out the heavier gold. There was even a cabin—actu-ally a lean-to with rather too much lean and most of its bark roof missing. Slimy moss covered every bit of wood, most of which disintegrated under the slightest pressure from his fingers. The smell of rot pervaded the air.

When Konrad gave the sluice box—a long series of wooden troughs on a stiltlike foundation—a shake to test how solid it was, the bottom half of the structure collapsed into the water. There were bits of garbage, a broken plate, and a tin bowl oddly wedged in the crotch of a tree. Konrad also found a sprung trap—a heavy-jawed leg hold with a few chunks of dried flesh still attached to the teeth.

"Well, at least whoever was here caught something," Konrad said loudly. His voice was swallowed up as if he'd spoken into a pillow.

It took him three full days to bring some order to the little encampment. Though he was aching to lift his first shovel of gravel, he forced himself to make his surroundings as habitable as possible. The weather was beautiful and each night he slept in the open with just a blanket, listening to the trees and the river talk.

Finally, Konrad had a roof of sorts over the lean-to, and a bed made with long strands of hanging moss pulled off the trees. He dug a latrine a good distance from the shore, set up a fire pit, laid out his tools, oiled the rifle, and read his pamphlet several more times. He was ready. Gold!

The next morning broke slowly, with thick mist hovering inches above the water. Konrad attacked the gravel on the shoreline, enthusiastically scooping loads of water and rock into his pan. After two hours his shoulders and knees screamed from the agony of squatting and shaking the heavy pan back and forth then flipping it forward awkwardly to send gravel over the lip. After lunching on his store of beef jerky and black tea, Konrad decided to try his shovel and the sluice. It was hard work, heaving gravel into the box then carefully washing pieces back into the river with buckets of water but definitely easier than the panning. It took seven shovels of dirt to yield the first show, a few little flakes nestled among black sand at the bottom of the box. Konrad leapt into the air, shouting and waving his arms. He hugged himself and danced in a circle, scaring birds out of the trees.

"I'm a king! The gold king!" he crowed. He scooped dirt out of the box, carefully spreading it in one of his pans to dry, so he could pick out the gold shards. Never had he known such joy, such a feeling of self-worth. Nothing, not even bringing down a massive bull elephant in Rhodesia when he was seventeen, compared to this. He grabbed himself and wished at that moment for a woman. A cheap one that he could take quickly and roughly.

"In time, girls," Konrad bellowed, "you will see me in good time!"

✳

Rifle and rod clutched in one hand, bleeding fingers of the other hand grabbing rock and bush for balance, Konrad inched precariously along a crumbling shelf. Thirty feet below lay the water. Above him more rock and gnarled trees clinging somehow to a steep granite face. It had rained solidly for a week and a half; the river was high and running hard. Ninety-one days had passed since Halley dropped him like a sack of goods in the water off Texas Bar. There'd been no sign of the man since and no sign of gold after that first show.

He had been taken, plain and simple. First by Brundage selling him a worked-out claim, and then by Halley who now owned his grandmother's diamond ring. Sometime in the second month Konrad grew so angry thinking about his possessions in the hands of thieves that he smashed the shovel against a tree again and again until the blade flew off and the handle shattered. Konrad didn't know how but he'd make them all pay eventually.

✳

The rains started partway into the second month. After the second day the Bar disappeared, as the water claimed the new sluice box Konrad had built. The next night he woke up to the river lapping at his ears, and feces from the flooded latrine bobbing around him.

By day eight of the sheeting rain Konrad had eaten his way through the last of his jerky. He'd caught fish when the weather was fine and shot several birds, including a heron that provided a few bites of incredibly tough meat, but the rain made the footing so treacherous hunting was impossible and the fish seemed to have gone to other waters. The fire went out that night and Konrad used up the last of his matches desperately trying to rekindle it. All he had left was a tin of bitter tea. He made a brew with the cold, muddy river water and sipped it slowly out of his tin mug.

Konrad remembered the river running due north after Hope. If he stuck to the precarious shoreline he figured he could make it to the town in a couple of days. There was no point in staying a moment longer on Texas Bar. Thankfully, as Konrad climbed, the shelf widened and the cliffs moved back from the bank, allowing him to walk more easily. The rain relented, giving way to a heavy mist; still he could see little but the faint shadow of mountains. Even the river itself was obscured.

He almost stepped in the little creek before he saw it. Though it too was flowing rapidly he thought he might have a chance of catching a fish. There was just enough gravelly bank to stand on. Konrad turned over rocks looking for worms. He cast, let the line drift past him, then cast again. In another life, he thought grimly flinging the line out, this would be pleasurable. The hook stuck on something and Konrad's temper flared. He yanked hard and the line snapped back to him. For a moment he thought he had a fish but it was a long piece of rough, brown, woolen cloth. Peering into the mist he saw a tiny rocky island in the middle of the creek. He was wet anyway; on the chance of finding abandoned clothes he'd cross the creek and risk a soaking.

Konrad smelled something rank and cloying, the odor rising above the mildewy wet of the forest. Climbing to the top of the rock he grasped something that came away in his hand—a boot. He climbed higher. Staked out, like Gulliver in the land of the Lilliputians, was a body. With horror he realized the stakes were driven through the man's flesh, not just his clothing. Konrad's empty stomach recoiled and he spewed yellow bile on the body's leg. Tears streaming, Konrad slid down the rock, but the thought of finding something salvageable drove him back up. Trying not to look at the stakes piercing the armpits and hands, he rummaged through the lower pockets of the body's jacket. He debated taking the jacket off, but no matter how cold he was he couldn't bear the thought.

"Arrrrrsssh!"

Konrad tumbled backward. Panting with fright, he felt sudden warmth as his bladder released.

"Heppp!" the body slurred.

Though not a religious man, Konrad would have much preferred the Devil to snatch him up at that moment and carry him off to the cauldron of Hell than crawl toward the hideous sound.

"Heppp!" the thing gurgled.

Konrad gathered his courage and willed his stomach to be calm.

"*Mein Gott*, Halley!"

The river pilot's face was a mass of crusted sores. One eye stared straight up, the lid sliced to prevent him closing it. The other socket was simply a black hole.

"Halley!" gasped Konrad again. He'd never seen such horror. How could the man still be alive?

"Ku muh! Ku muh!" Halley gurgled urgently a bubble of blood and spit oozing from his cracked lips.

The life was obviously draining out of him. Who could have done such a thing? And why?

"Ku muh!" Halley babbled again.

Kill me, Konrad suddenly realized. "Kill you! *Allmächtiger Gott,* I cannot do such a thing!" he said. "I will try to free you."

Torturously, Halley shook his head and opened his mouth. Reluctantly Konrad crept nearer.

"Eeeeha." Halley's tongue was severed so deeply it looked as if it had been torn out. Halley frantically rolled his eyeball downward. Konrad bent his head and murmured a prayer. What murderous animals? He hadn't noticed the thick mass of blood and maggots at Halley's crotch. His stomach rebelled again and he heaved hard and painfully, nothing coming up but sour bile. The animals had cut off his penis, leaving the bloody mass open to the elements.

Adrenaline shot through him. Forgetting his rifle, Konrad grabbed a heavy rock, swung it high, and bashed it down on Halley's wretched head. Again and again, until nothing but bone shards and pulp remained. Sobbing and moaning, he half fell from the rock, stumbled across the creek, and dropped to his knees on the gravel bench. He wanted only to curl up, cry himself to sleep, and awaken in the morning to his mother's warm hand on his forehead and the peaceful view from his large bow window in the east wing of the *Schloss* with a fire burning in the black marble fireplace. He would see green rolling fields, stone fences, and the faint puffs of smoke in the far distance from his father's mills. Safe. Away from the constant wet, the black terror of the forest with thieves and murderers everywhere he turned.

Konrad had no idea how long he lay there. Five minutes, an hour, a day? He was chilled, frightened, and hopeless. Cramped in every joint, he forced himself to stand. What he saw sat him right back on his buttocks. Four Indians stood motionless less than ten feet away. Unlike the two he'd shot, these ones did not have red faces, only a few lines of white and black around their ears and foreheads. They wore conical hats like upside-down baskets and each carried a rifle. Three wore Western shirts, while the other sported a white man's belt around his naked torso.

Aren't they cold? Konrad wondered idly. All feeling was gone. Even the prospect of pain didn't bother him. He waited dully for the attack. But the men just stared.

"*Haben sie sich an mir gerächt!*" he croaked. Take your revenge on me. "*Schnell! Bitte!*" Quickly, please!

✳

Feet swollen, blistered, and bleeding from the rocks, every muscle screaming with fatigue and pain, Konrad walked on. He had long passed the point where Hope should have appeared. He was trapped in the mountains' black embrace skidding aimlessly from cliff side to creek bed. The sun had not shown itself since he'd left Texas Bar and the clouds were so low they seemed to rest on his shoulders. He had no idea which direction he was going, and every time he tried to follow a tributary, which should logically have led to the river, he was thwarted by the damp grasping jungle or precipitous rock that was impossible to scale.

The Indians left him alone. Konrad had no idea why. Perhaps he was too pathetic to be bothered with. Halley told him there were a few rene-gades along the river yet, Indians who refused to be tamed by government or mission. Still, there hadn't been a white man killed by an Indian in a long time. "Leastwise no one's lived to tell of it," Halley had added with a laugh.

"Wouldn't he be pleased to know he was the first?" Konrad said to the forest.

Konrad had seven bullets remaining. If only he could reach some level ground, he could lie in wait for a bird or rabbit. He had no matches, but he'd eat the warm meat raw and savor it.

When the forest and mountain suddenly released him, Konrad could hardly believe it. He gaped stupidly at a series of broad, cultivated fields. The transition was startling. Cliffs and trees one minute, fields the next. Cultivation meant people. White people. Konrad knew enough now to realize the coastal Indians were fishermen and hunters, not farmers.

He began to run, weeping, laughing, whooping.

"*Oh, liebe Mutter*," he yelled. "Your Konrad is saved."

✳

The woman who answered the door had a puff of flour on her cheek and her hair had partially escaped from a graying chignon at the back of her neck.

"May I help you?" she greeted him as if filthy strangers with wild, hungry eyes turned up at her door every day.

"Where I am?" Konrad stuttered.

"Right at the moment you're standing on my porch."

Konrad beamed at her wit. He hadn't done that in a long time.

"No, I mean where exactly is this place? You see, ma'am," he said unnecessarily, "I am lost."

"Do tell! From the looks of you I'd say you've been lost quite some time." Her voice had a soft Irish lilt. "This is the O'Connor farm. I am Mary, and this place is called Rosedale. And that would be in the province of British Columbia."

58

*

Dear Mother,

I feel terribly guilty for not writing in such a long time. You would hardly recognize me these days. I have been among ferocious Indians and in country so wild you would think I could not survive an afternoon. But I did. I bought a gold claim from a dishonest fellow (there are many such in this country) and nearly got myself killed looking for gold that did not exist. Please do not worry, for I have gone from there and am among civilized people once again.

I would prefer it if you did not inform Father of my failure in gold, as I have some good news to impart. I have spent the winter stacking hay cakes for farmer Bryant O'Connor who took me in for the winter after my ordeal on the river looking for gold. I have also helped him tend his dairy herd (do not laugh, Mother!) and can now milk a Bessy, he calls them all by that name, almost as well as he can, who has spent his life with cows.

I am, however, heartily sick of the strange bread his wife (who is a kind woman) makes. Gray in color, it leaves a film on your teeth for hours after eating. She calls it soda bread and tells me the Irish have existed on it for centuries. I would like to express my opinion that this poor excuse for Bröt may well be the reason the Irish have never been able to rise above their British landlords.

I would also be happy never to see a potato again. Eight months—and potatoes for every meal. We are surrounded by cows, yet a good repast of meat is a very rare thing. Though a tributary of the Fraser, the East Yale River, is an hour's ride away, they seem to have a suspicion of anything which comes from the water, and fish graces the table less often than beef.

I find to my surprise (and yours too, I am sure) that I don't mind the work. The salmon fish run will begin any day. The Fraser River here is like the Elbe or the Rhine, and all the world on this northwest coast has some business with it. I have got myself a situation on a boat (perhaps you should tell Father I am a partner in a fishing venture) and I expect to do very well in a single season. Every day in Vancouver boats line up in the harbor waiting to load salmon fish for the Orient, Europe, and America's East. The competition for fish is so strong that I have heard agents from these boats arrive on the banks of the Fraser and bid for the cargo before it is even caught.

But Konrad, I hear you say, you have no experience with fish. Ah, but you forget it was your little Konrad, still in Kneibundhose, *who won the fishing derby at Mittenwald so many years ago.*

Wish me viel Glück.

I will write to you again very soon, I promise,

Your loving son always, Konrad.

"If you think of a fambly with everyone lookin' different, actin' different but somehow also bein' the same, then you kin jes about understand the salmon."

Konrad fed trolling lines while Solly—Sorry to most—checked the spoons, metal disks that danced and jigged as the boat moved along, hoping to distract the single-minded salmon for a moment from their mission to return to their home waters in the nooks and crannies of the Fraser. They surged upstream deep into the Shuswap, lying on the western flank of the Fraser, into the high land of the Chilcotin, which rises to meet the coastal mountains, and even as far north as Stuart Lake, seven hundred miles from the Fraser's mouth, within hailing distance of the Alaska panhandle.

"We'll be after the spring salmon with these lines. They's the only ones that'll bite out at sea this time o' year. Later we'll troll again for the bluebacks, the coho. Some go after 'em as early as May but I don't bother till we stop haulin' up the Alaska reds. Bluebacks'll be back late on in summer an' it's a good run most years."

"How will you catch the reds?"

"They's called sockeye by some," Solly continued, ignoring his questions, "but wait'll you cut one open and you'll see why they's called reds. Flesh the color of fresh blood. Quite a sight."

Konrad flashed back to his so-long-ago meal of sockeye salmon with the scoundrel Hec Brundage. He dreamed of wrapping his hands around the man's fat neck. When he thought of Brundage and the elusive Pike, he inevitably found the image of Edith crowding into his mind. What an arrogant cockatoo he must have seemed to her.

Sorry, who could have been forty or eighty, checked the gurdy, a winch at the back of the boat to haul in the trolling lines. Konrad worked the winch as Sorry took off the fish and quickly checked the spoons as the lines came in. The salmon runs had been so good the last few years that many fishermen didn't bother with the spring, or tyee, waiting until the sockeye run started a month or so later. The oily sockeye were much smaller, ten pounds at most, compared to the spring, which could top forty-five pounds. But the canneries paid double for the red flesh, which retained its flavor wonderfully after processing.

✶

"Then you got the little humpbacks," Sorry continued. "Kinda like the runt of the family. When they get to spawnin' the male grows this big hump, ugly thing. Canneries take 'em, but you don' get sockeye prices."

Sorry stood up, stretched his back with numerous cracks and snaps, packed his cheek with tobacco, and gazed across the delta at the Fraser's mouth, where they were tied up, making last-minute repairs and double checking nets while they waited for the call that the first run had been spotted.

"I grew up haulin' crabs in the Carolinas. Every day crabs, crabs, and more crabs. Decent livin' as far as it went, but the diff'rence between there and here is like the diff'rence between breakin' rocks fer a livin' and minin' fer gold. Basic work's the same, but the payoff ain't."

Konrad winced at the mention of gold, praying this boating venture would not turn out the same.

"Fin'ly ya got the keta. Some calls it chum, though God knows why, 'cause it ain't nobody's friend. Injuns won't touch it. We'll take it if it comes, but it's a sloppy fish, ain't got the muscle nor oil like the others. Sometimes I kin sell a load up to Chinktown in Vancouver. They'll eat anything."

When the run started, it was like nothing Konrad had ever experienced. Though Sorry told him the number of boats doubled when the sockeye began running in early summer, Konrad was not prepared for the staggering flotilla that invaded the river. Within days nearly a thousand boats of every description, many barely seaworthy, competed for the fish.

There were actually two mouths of the Fraser. The river began to fork at New Westminster, breaking around the large island of Richmond. The northern fork, which formed the southern boundary of Vancouver, broke again around Sea Island. Sorry was anchored at Sea Island with half a dozen other boats.

"Most others start way down on the south fork o' the Fraser, which is a whole lot closer to the Strait, which is a whole lot closer to the Pacific," Sorry explained. "But me," he added smugly, "I'm smarter. Them peckers coon't find fish if one jump in their boat. They on'y catch 'em 'cause they run right into the schools. Can't help but catch 'em. I don't fight it out with them idiots. The spring don't stick together, same with the sockeye. I swing wide an' north an' got whole damn schools to myself."

Those were as many words as Sorry spoke at once over the next weeks, as many words as he had time for. Dawn ran into day, into dusk, and into night with no cessation of work. They only stopped when the blackness or the fog closed in so tightly that getting from bow to stern was a dangerous balancing act.

The spring gave way to the sockeye, which would never take hook or bait in their single-minded quest for their spawning grounds. With the sockeye, Sorry and Konrad gill-netted until the hold was full of the valuable blue-skinned, red-fleshed creatures. Then Sorry put in to Sea Island where two "jappy boys" unloaded and packed the fish in ice for the trip across the Oak Street bridge, down the muddy Granville Street, to the cannery at the Vancouver docks.

Sometimes Sorry rejected offers from the Japanese, British, and American agents who came up from Washington and San Francisco, and took his load to the docks himself where a lively barter among buyers usually netted an extra penny a pound. Everybody hated the agents.

By mid-August Konrad's world was saturated with the smell, taste, and feel of fish. There wasn't the thrill of stalking game, but each time they reeled in the gill-net jam-packed with protesting fish, he totted up what the haul would add to his share. As a "puller," Konrad got $4 a day plus twenty percent of every pound they took in over Sorry's minimum.

"If we have a bad season, you git your piece, but if it's a good'un, you share," Sorry explained.

Sorry could afford to be generous: he owned his boat. Still, Konrad, son of the eighth wealthiest man in all of Germany, was grateful.

They made seven trips to the cannery in New Westminster and ten more directly to the Vancouver docks. They hauled sixty-six tons of fish, one of the biggest catches Sorry could remember, "discountin' oh two o' course, which were like a tidal wave."

"Back in the Carolinas I'd be lookin' to hire out for the winter, fixin' nets or crab pots or sumfin'," Sorry said. "But Vancouver lets a man get his strength back over the winter."

"Does that mean we're finished?" Konrad asked incredulously.

As the rhythm of the days and months wove a constant pattern of work and sleep, his body overcame the agony of the first weeks and grew strong. His hands, at first horribly cracked from the salt and torn by lines, became calloused and impervious. He had come to believe his days would go on forever just like this.

"Yup, done."

Sorry used his profits to buy farmland along the lower Fraser. "I figger this town'll be one big city sometime and then my grandkids can live right, without having to work like their ol' salty grampa."

It was the first Konrad had heard of a family, and he was astonished to learn that Sorry had a half-Musqueam wife, who farmed the first plot of land Sorry bought on the slopes of south Vancouver. He also had nine children, with the oldest three marrying white.

"Tell ya the truth, you looked soft and lazy to me, but the O'Connors sweared by ya. I'd be glad to have ya back next year," Sorry said awkwardly, extending a rough paw to shake Konrad's hand. "If'n yer intrested I'll be tied up, same place on Sea Island, 'round late March."

"You will not be able to keep me away," Konrad said enthusiastically as he swung his gun; his few possessions; and his bag of money, $750; on his shoulder and waved good-bye. He'd never felt so good in his life.

A year earlier, if Konrad had come into this much ready money, he would have immediately spent it on a fine suit of clothes, an elegant pair of boots, a box of the best cigars, and a few nights in a first-class hotel with a couple of fancy girls. He briefly considered hot-footing it into Vancouver and taking a suite at the Hotel Vancouver, the elegant Canadian Pacific Railway hotel frequented by moneyed visitors from all over the world. Instead he decided to hang on to the money for now. He'd earned it with his own sweat and he enjoyed knowing his pockets were full.

The inn Sorry recommended on south Granville Street was surrounded by the modest homes of working-class people, many of whom made a living in the mills and factories along the river. The inn's porch was well swept, the steps clean, and the flower beds free of weeds. It would do nicely. He opened the door and was greeted by the smell of apples cooking.

No fish for dinner tonight, he vowed. No fish for a week! No fish for a month!

"You hardly look like the man I met on the streets of Vancouver," a soft voice said at his shoulder.

Konrad had been scratching his name in the registration book. He whirled around.

"Edith!"

Her eyes laughed at his surprise, embarrassment, and unsuccessful effort to hide his delight.

"Edith," he repeated.

"You remember my name," she teased.

"How could I forget? You have been in my thoughts," he said boldly, then regretted it. "I'm sorry, I didn't mean to be so, um, forward."

"What are you doing here?" Edith asked, trying to quell her own thrill at knowing he had been thinking of her. She was curious at his disheveled state, a far cry from the dapper blade she'd met a year earlier. He smelled fishy and his hands were calloused. Dirty, smelly, unshaven, and ragged, but more appealing than that silly peacock of a year ago.

"I'm afraid I would bore you with the details," Konrad smiled.

"I am not easily bored," Edith replied. "After all, I survived many months living with Hetty."

The laugh welled up from Konrad's boots; rich, warm, and happy.

"I thought you were a deaf mute!" He reminded her she had not spoken a word at their first meeting.

"Why, I believe that wouldn't have been a bad thing around dear Hetty."

They fell silent, the air between them carrying messages.

"Could I persuade you to have dinner with me?" Konrad asked shyly. He looked down at his stained trousers. "No, no, not tonight!! I have been dirty for so long I have forgotten what it is like to have clean clothes. Tomorrow, perhaps? I will find some suitable clothes then. Will you still be here? I am sorry to be so unpresentable. I would not shame you by forcing myself on you as I am. Perhaps . . ." he babbled on, desperate to keep her there yet aware of his filth and now, to his horror, the odor rising from him.

Edith shook her head. "I am here for one night. I am visiting a sick friend and then I must return to my school. I will still have dinner with you tonight. I teach among farmers, so dirty clothes are not new to me." Eyes twinkling, she added: "The fish is very good here."

Edith spoke her sentences as if reading lines from a poorly written play. It was the only way she could keep the joy out of her voice and manner. She supposed she should have demurred, at least for a gracious period, but since leaving the city to teach in the tiny farming community of Ladner, twenty miles south of Vancouver, she seemed to have left her ladylike manners behind in Hetty's parlor. The community had none of the pretentiousness of booming Vancouver and the people were simple folk, mainly from Holland and Scotland. What came out of the ground dictated the pattern of their plain lives. They were strict with their children, and dedicated churchgoers, but nothing was done to excess, be it prayers or the ornamentation of their houses.

"I would be happy to have dinner with you," she repeated as Konrad looked at her blankly. "Say eight o'clock?"

Konrad tore off to his room, barely remembering to say good-bye. "Yes, eight, perfect, eight, thank you, at eight."

Fish. He could hardly wait.

59

✳

1907

Vancouver

"Credit? For how long and to what limit?"

"Forever!" boomed Konrad. "No limit."

"Don't be ridiculous," the editor of the *Vancouver Province* snorted. "You have been in business . . . let's see," he consulted some papers on his desk, "four days. Four whole days. And now you ask for credit. Matters of finance don't work that way."

"Hah! You talk like the sour old bankers in Germany. This is the new world," retorted Konrad. "We must develop new ways."

"Bad debts are bad debts, here or in Germany. They're not something my publisher considers desirable, no matter how they've been accumulated."

As Konrad leaned across the man's mahogany desk, the sleeves of his full-length alpaca coat slung across his shoulders fell forward, sending papers skittering to the floor.

"There will be no bad debts!" he thumped his doeskin gloves on the desk. "You give me one month for my ads and I will pay you two times your rate. After that no more timid talk about limits."

It had been a good fall, no, a great fall, the editor mused. Propelled by an avalanche of real estate ads, lineage and revenue had doubled over the previous spring. Virtually all were paid in advance. Unknown to the publisher, he gave credit to a select few advertisers who paid him a little bonus for the privilege. The bonuses had financed the purchase of two building lots on Fairview, a quickly developing rise of land south of False Creek, with spectacular views of downtown and the snow-capped north-shore mountains. It wasn't the West End, perhaps, with its porticoed mansions, or the new and exclusive Shaughnessy Heights in South Vancouver, but a good neighborhood nonetheless.

Unlike many other new developments in the frantic boom that had swept up the entire city, these lots came already serviced with water, electricity, and even the promise of sidewalks.

The editor stared at the tall, excited German with the thick, groomed moustache and pale eyes. Was he really a count, as he claimed? Or was he one of the tricksters and confidence men swarming in the New World like flies on manure? He wouldn't know an aristocrat from an argonaut, but this count, or whatever he was, certainly couldn't be described as ordinary. What did he have to lose? If the man didn't pay, he'd just write it off with no one being the wiser. He wouldn't even record the debt until the man anted up; that way, if he defaulted, the publisher would have to compare lineage with the advertising ledger and he was unlikely to do that.

"All right," he said with a world-weary sigh. "Show me your ad."

SCHAUMBERG FINANCE AND GENERAL INVESTMENT CO.

Best investment advize in the city. I can astounding oportunnities provide. No delay. Vancouver in 20th century is to be a great city.

DO NOT LEFT BEHIND GET

Attend to the office of Count Konrad von Schaumberg and assuring your future.

Hours of office 8 in morning to 10 in night.

The editor began methodically striking out the numerous spelling and grammatical mistakes.

"*Nein!*" Konrad ordered. "Don't change a letter."

"I can't run that!"

"Why not?"

"It is full of mistakes. People will laugh."

"Let them laugh," roared Konrad in his excellent English. "I believe people vill be interested in dis dummkopf German who doesn't know English but sees opportunities," he said putting on a heavy German accent. "If twenty people do not 'attend,'" he drew out the word, "my office the day after this ad is printed, I will pay you in gold coins triple your price the day after and never bother you again."

The editor shrugged. Damn German fool.

By noon on the morning the paper came out with Konrad's full-page ad, eleven people had dropped by his office, half to correct "the Kraut's" spelling, the rest curious about just what opportunities he had in mind. Konrad turned on the charm. By five o'clock the number had risen to twenty-five; about a third he judged to be serious prospects. By evening he had two $100 deposits for land in the new, all-white area of Kerrisdale, which, he promised, would soon be serviced by city tram and was miles away from the pestilence of Chinatown. A suggestion had recently been debated in city council to allow only Chinese carrying service passports to cross into the western sections of Vancouver after it was discovered that one real estate speculator had been selling huge amounts of land along the eastern side of Granville Street to Chinatown merchants.

"Your women and children will absolutely be safe here," Konrad beamed, stabbing his finger at a Vancouver map.

Early the next morning Konrad was waiting for the registry office to open so he could find out who owned the Kerrisdale land. He certainly didn't! Most of the property was still in the hands of the Canadian Pacific Railway. Softened by a $10 bill, the clerk admitted that a large chunk of it had just changed hands but the conveyancing had not yet taken. Another ten elicited the information that a Samuel C. Pillar would eventually be the registered owner of ten prime lots along the major thoroughfare. A final ten, and the clerk "managed" to find the address.

521 W. Cordova St.

Off Konrad hurried, his coattails flapping behind him. Cordova ran one street up from the water. He found the address in a three-story brick building, almost black with the soot from the harbor industries.

Pillar Forwarding Ltd. It was closed and dark, with no notice of operating hours. Konrad quivered with nerves. He waited impatiently, smoking one cigarette after another, until a portly man arrived and opened the door. The office was tiny, with a single chair in the waiting area. The man carefully examined the freshly printed calling card.

"You would be inquiring about land?"

"How did you know?" Konrad was surprised.

"It is a small city. Please proceed to this address." He held out a scrap of paper with "724 Princess St." written on it. "This is Mr. Pillar's normal place of business. He is expecting you."

Annoyed at having to make a second stop, Konrad left without a word, and with a burst of speed was able to hop a tram as it clanged by, heading east. The address was on the fringes of Chinatown. A strange place for a landowner, such as this Mr. Pillar, to set up. And what had the fat man said? "He's expecting you." How could that be? Never mind. He must make a deal quickly or he would have to return the $200 he had in deposit funds.

Konrad was counting on Mr. Pillar being eager to turn a quick profit on a portion of his new holdings, which would allow him to hang on to the rest and sell gradually as the prices rose. And rise they would. Konrad was completely certain of that. Land fever burned in every corner of Vancouver. Most nights at Scotty's Ale House he listened to frenzied conversation about this property or that. From mouth to ear to greased palm, real estate tips were exchanged quicker than information about a blisteringly fast breeze time at the racetrack. Even the most dubious characters had a lead on a bit of land they intended to resell before the ink was dry. Rumors flew that speculators from Seattle, San Francisco, London, New York, and Toronto were flooding into the city, buying options on land with cash and paying heavily for tips about who might be selling or buying.

724 Princess Street. A small office among a rabbit warren of them, all occupied by Chinamen doing goodness knows what. Konrad presented his card to a young Oriental girl, asking for Samuel Pillar.

"This way, preese. This way."

She waved him toward a curtain. Konrad folded his six-foot-two frame under the low doorway. In the darkness sat a man so ancient he looked more like a dried apple than a human being. He was dwarfed by a large red chair with carved lions sprouting from the arms. He puffed on a thin cigar.

"I am here to see Mr. Samuel C. Pillar," Konrad announced. He worried that some game was being played.

"Soon Chong," the withered thing in the chair inclined his head.

"Where is Mr. Pillar?"

"Soon Chong," the old man repeated. "The English alphabet is a useful thing. Letters can stand for one thing or another. S is as good for Soon as it is for Samuel. And C might be Chong, or any other name, for someone who might be considered a pillar of the community. I believe you English have a phrase, sleight of hand? 'Samuel C. Pillar' is a sleight of alphabet."

He chuckled happily to himself, a gurgling, hiccuping laugh. "My friend Warburton Pike calls Mr. C. Pillar a 'cut out.' I rather like the term."

"You know Warburton Pike?" Konrad asked as if he were addressing a rattlesnake at close quarters.

"Forty-two years," Soon answered. "You wouldn't be here if he hadn't spoken for you."

Hairs prickled on Konrad's neck. Pike, again. He didn't feel grateful, rather spooked by the man who kept popping up in his life. But this time he at least knew what Warburton Pike looked like, thanks to a chance meeting a year ago.

After two summers on Sorry's fish boat, he'd taken a night watchman job at the Brunswick Cannery, which provided a small overnight room. He couldn't bear to be away from Edith for the whole salmon season. During the day he shot game and sold it to Vancouver's better restaurants and private clubs. He got thirty-five cents for mallards and forty-five cents for a brace of pigeon and teal.

One night, while he was drinking schnapps on the steps outside the kitchen with the Bavarian chef of the Vancouver Club, he heard a familiar voice.

"I'm certainly honored to receive this award but I want to know why the president of the club sent me a note reminding me to wear shoes?" the voice said to a roar of laughter.

Konrad crept into the foyer and peeked into the dining room. It was the old ragamuffin who had tried to pass himself off as Warburton Pike, Konrad realized.

"It's not what you've got on your feet we're worried about," one man called out. "It's what you might have on your arm." The heckler was referring to a celebrated incident in which Pike, against all taboos, had brought an Indian woman into the club.

"What's that old fool doing here?" Konrad demanded of the chef.

"That's Warburton Pike," the chef said in a manner of one surprised at common knowledge not known. "He was just made a fellow of the National Geographic Society of England in honor of his second book. Something about mountains, I believe."

Konrad felt a burning flush of embarrassment. Warburton Pike. He was both angry and chagrined. But somehow he had the feeling he'd brought the whole thing on to himself. He left the club that night hoping never to lay eyes on Warburton Pike or hear his name again. And now here he was.

Soon had no intention of retaining the land. He'd purchased it through a white contact and would sell it again in the same way. He hadn't expected such a quick turnover when Pike showed up, long gray hair flying around his head, urging him to see this German.

Konrad had heard dealings with the Chinese were painfully slow and required a great deal of patience. To his surprise, Soon Chong had the deeds on the chair beside him and was ready to deal. He had paid $500 for each of ten lots. After a bit of haggling Soon reluctantly agreed to let two of them go for $1,000 each, but only if the cash was in hand within forty-eight hours. Konrad slapped down the remaining $170 from the deposits, supplementing it with $50 from his rent money. Before he opened up for business as a land financier he'd saved up $1,437. "Fish money," he called it, but after renting an office and buying new clothes and a book about investment terms, there was little left. He fidgeted while Chong instructed his assistant to write out a receipt. Only as he was leaving did he notice the word "non-refundable" across the bottom. With a curt good-bye, Konrad rushed out, the sweat of elation running down his sides and backbone. The girl giggled as he gave himself a resounding thwack on the head on the low door frame.

It took every ounce of noble charm Konrad possessed to persuade his two prospective buyers to come up with $1,500 each—$250 more than they'd agreed to pay the previous day—without any sign of the deed. Konrad told them that similar lots in the area of Kitsilano, which lay closer to English Bay, were selling for $2,250 and virtually all were spoken for.

"So you see, you're already in line for nice profit, thanks to me," he soothed. "That is what happens when you trust the right man with your hard-earned money."

❋

Even in late December the Sunday crowds filled the beach and stone walkways of English Bay. The water was flat and hard, a contrast to the soft bruise of hills guarding the entrance to Howe Sound and the wilderness beyond. The air felt like April. Vancouver was like that. She threw a reprieve at regular intervals during the eighty-seven inches of cold rain that fell between December and April. Winter turned to spring and even summer on occasion, and the city became giddy with it, flinging off coats and boots, casting aside woolen hats, and wearing in December clothes that would not normally be warm enough for May.

Heavy clouds waited on the west side of Vancouver Island, an area of furious geography and hideous weather. One day soon they would heave themselves over the mountainous rib that bisected the island, sail across the Strait of Georgia, and bring their load of near-freezing rain to the city. The reprieve would be over. But Vancouverites, young and old, lived these sunny days with a reckless passion. Even the nursing nuns tittered among themselves about the babies that would arrive in greater than normal numbers in forty weeks' time.

The chief of police canceled holidays and personally hauled constables out of bed when the spring-in-winter light crept west from the dark caverns of Yale and Hope, flooded the Fraser Valley with warmth, and teased the city out of lethargy. The unnatural weather brought out the worst in men. The shantytown around the Hastings Mill would cough up its citizens, normally too beaten down by rain and work to cause problems. Even men of business lost their heads too easily in these days and the drinking started hours earlier than normal. There would be arguments about debts and fights over deals. Men became manly in the shock of the warm sun, turquoise sky, and gentle salt breeze rising from the harbor. And nothing, the chief of police knew, was worse than men being manly, especially if they'd been saving it up.

The girls on Pender Street didn't mind. They emerged from such days with more bruises than normal, breasts and buttocks tender from desperately grasping hands, privates swollen from the urgency of men who normally lasted minutes but during these winter reprieves found themselves with hard, long stamina. The girls on Pender Street didn't mind; their purses were full.

Edith fingered the letter she had just read to Konrad. With her other hand she rolled a diamond ring in her palm. The stone was the largest she had ever seen. It would look ridiculous on her small hand. But Konrad, being Konrad, would only have thought about the biggest, the best for her. Almost every Sunday since they'd remet eleven months before, they'd come to the teahouse overlooking the beach at English Bay in Stanley Park. They watched the Negro Joe Fortes, self-appointed lifeguard and swimming instructor, as he patrolled the shoreline, shepherding children back to their families if they strayed too close to the water. In fine weather they walked to the roller skating arena on Denman Street nearby and shakily rolled around the boards, clinging to each other. Today, they just sat, enjoying the sun. Edith played with the ring. She had both been hoping for it and dreading it for months. Because now she would have to say what could not be avoided.

"If I go against them I shall be without family."

"You don't need them. I am the only family you need."

Edith wanted him. She wanted him so badly her nights were constantly interrupted by thoughts of him. When she was lying in her bed in the large, comfortable room she rented in a Ladner farmhouse, a short buggy ride to the two-room school where she taught, the tangy scent of his body seemed to invade the room. She would fling herself facedown into her pillow, grab the edge of her bed with both hands to prevent them from straying to her skin. Her breasts were small but her hips and thighs round. "I wonder how Konrad would like me," she mused to herself more than once on those nights. She'd allow her hand to massage the ache in her soft belly then let it stray to the mound of hair below . . . "Oh, damn you, Konrad!"

"'The match would be unsuitable,'" Edith read. "To my family 'unsuitable' is a strong word. They want to say 'forbidden' but they will never bring themselves to utter it. They will not be able to imagine me going against them."

"'Forbidden!' 'Unsuitable!' To marry the son of a count. I could have any woman in Europe! In Germany mothers would call such a match *die Eintrittskarte*—admission ticket. My family is connected to the best houses from Moscow to London. And look at me now. I have a fishing fleet. I own three houses and a merchant building downtown. I have investments in coal and iron and interests in lumber. And all of this less than two years after selling ducks to restaurants. 'Unsuitable!'" He shouted the words, startling two couples sitting close. Edith laughed.

"How can this be funny? What is wrong with your parents? 'Unsuitable!' Ridiculous."

"You are funny, my Konrad. If you could hear yourself. You sound like a street hawker touting his wares," she looked at him sidelong. "Any woman in Europe?"

Konrad had the grace to be moderately abashed. "You know what I mean."

Edith shielded her eyes against the late-afternoon glare bouncing off English Bay. The day was beginning to cool but it had lost none of its glory.

"There is another problem, which is really the same problem."

Konrad was surprised. "Whatever can that be?"

Edith had thought about how to say it. How to express the simple word with such complex significance. A word that tore nations apart and incited men to commit such dreadful acts that it became easy to believe the Devil walked the earth. She had thought for hours, days, months, saying the word in many ways in many different sentences until it no longer had any meaning to her.

"I am a Jew."

In later years Konrad would like to have looked back at that moment with pride. He could not. An invisible fist met his diaphragm and his hand sprang open, as if of its own accord, dropping hers to the table.

"It is," she said sorrowfully, "the magic of birth. You were born to a Prussian count and I to devout Jews."

Konrad's father had recently been instrumental in altering banking laws in Germany to suit the Kaiser's desire to "clarify" the realm's finances. It was a delicate matter, as Kaiser Wilhelm's court was deeply in debt to Jewish moneylenders and the new law improved the kaiser's balance sheet considerably at the expense of the lenders. It was an article of faith among the count's contemporaries that Jews used unscrupulous means to inveigle the better races into debt. The count had long warned the Kaiser about the dangers of indebtedness to a people whose only concern was profit and whose only allegiance was to their own race.

"They will hamstring you without a moment's hesitation," argued the count.

"*Eine Jüdin?*" Konrad whispered, staring in disbelief at her white-blond hair, warm-ivory skin, and brown eyes. "*Eine Jüdin?*"

"Russian originally," Edith said matter-of-factly, as if she were teaching a class in genealogy. She felt so much better now the truth was out. "My family built boats for Catherine the Great. We are, in our own way, nobility too. My great-grandfather's designs are still in use today, though I doubt whether your kaiser would be willing to admit his fastest warships owe their speed to a Russian Jew."

She caught him studying her Nordic features and blond hair. "We don't all look like trolls and toads, you know. This hair has saved many lives in our family. My grandfather was nicknamed Bela, which means 'white.' Though he carried the Jewish brand when he fled to France with his family, he was able to convince soldiers on the toll road that he was a poor craftsman who owed money to Jews and when he was unable to pay they sent collectors who beat him and branded him and his children with the Star of David. Because the children had the same hair and features, they got through as well. But my grandmother looked as you," she said the word pointedly, "expect all Jews to look. She traveled separately so as not to endanger the children."

Edith looked down at the large diamond.

"My grandmother did not get through. They had arranged to meet in

Paris. She carried all the money, because my grandfather thought she might have to pay many bribes along the way. He waited for years, always believing she would come. It is a sad story."

Konrad gazed sightlessly at the children playing in the last of the day's sun. A Jewess. A Jewess. A Jewess. The word struck him again and again. How could she have deceived me, he thought angrily. I have courted her for nearly two years. Deceit. He recalled a drunken evening with his father, brothers, and a large group of friends after a successful hunt. His father was teasing a neighboring farmer about his Jewish mistress, a woman of such remarkable beauty and lushness that it was said she could have seduced Pontius Pilate himself.

"She'll cast her Jew spell over you," the count had warned. "You can't trust them. Jews are like a disease. You'll catch it, I promise you, if you keep plunging your rod into that temptress's body." And that is exactly what happened. The poor man died of venereal disease, having passed it on to his wife, who later killed herself over the shame of it.

"No matter how much you need a woman," his father said on the day of the man's funeral, "never, ever be tempted by a Jew. Colored women and mixed breeds are the best. They always know their place. They'll be grateful for what you give them. Jews are grateful for nothing."

Deceit.

Konrad's face was as readable as the morning newspaper. She had her answer.

"And this is a sad story too," Edith said softly as she rose.

Minutes passed. Perhaps hours. Konrad had no idea. He looked at the space where she had sat. The ring lay there, sparkling, catching the final rays of light.

60

*

1912

It was only eight A.M. when Konrad arrived at his Granville Street offices, yet a small crowd of men was already gathered, including a tram conductor who had simply stopped his car in the middle of the street to await Konrad's arrival.

"What say, Count?" bellowed one as Konrad's Packard Tourer roared up to the front of the building.

"Boys, boys," grinned Konrad, "a man hasn't had his breakfast, or even his first cigar, and already you're on the hunt."

"Word's around that you're up to something?" asked one, not quite begging.

"I am up to nothing," mocked Konrad, as he pulled out a cigar and rolled it in his fingers. "*Nichts*, zero."

"Word is you're after a big piece of property," one of them persisted. "Just a hint is all we're asking."

A clamor ran through the crowd: "Just a hint, Count! Just a hint!"

Konrad smiled to himself. He was indeed after a property, he was always after a property. If chasers like this lot knew where it was, they could make some money on the pickings, selling either information or options on nearby but less desirable property. But this one was no ordinary deal. He would keep it to himself for now.

"Boys," he said, taking a slow, deep pull on his cigar, "come back in a couple of days and I might have something for you." A whoop went up, and the crowd dispersed like delighted school kids at dismissal bell. One or two would wait behind, he knew, hanging out in alleyways or bars until he left his office. He'd likely have at least one tail determined to unearth his secret.

As Konrad watched the men make their way down the street, he puffed away, reflecting happily on his good fortune. In 1907, the year he'd started his real estate business, only forty-two properties changed hands in the city of 63,000 people. By 1912 the city had mushroomed to 127,000 people, jammed into every rooming house, basement, and hotel. And all of the new arrivals seemed to be looking to buy land. It was only June and already more than seven hundred transactions had taken place. Three more clerks had been added to the city's land office, but deeds and documents still lay piled up in every corner of the registry.

Often a property changed hands three or four times before the clerk managed to record the first sale. Options on property—the right to buy a piece of land at a certain price by a certain date—were in almost as much demand as the property itself. It wasn't so much a speculative frenzy that gripped the city but a rapacious hunger far exceeding, so the old timers said, the gold fever of the last century. It wasn't only Vancouver that was booming—throughout most of the civilized world the euphoria of prosperity promised that the new century would result in wealth for all classes and endless peace.

Konrad currently owned fourteen sizable properties, each one a levered purchase. Their combined value as of eight A.M. on June 12, 1912 (by noon the valuations would all change) was over $5 million. But Konrad had committed only $87,000 cash to secure the land. While his carrying costs were $1,100 a day, he estimated the land was increasing in value by $4,000 in the same period, so the bankers were happy to lend him more.

At first the land was enough, but Konrad lusted after more. He didn't want to be lumped in with rapacious land speculators. Almost overnight Konrad von Schaumberg remade himself. Early in 1911, he built an elegant, fourteen-story terra-cotta building in downtown Vancouver—every single stone was imported. It was a marvel of design and architecture with an all-steel frame—the first in the city and one of the first in all of North America. Konrad vowed to follow it up with a fifty-story edifice, skyscrapers they were being dubbed. Everyone thought he was mad to attempt such a tall building, which, no doubt, would fall down, but no one said that to his face.

With success came courage. Since he'd written to his mother in 1907, a formal letter had arrived every year near his birthday in October from Count Alfred von Schaumberg, one page—never more. On a glorious summer day in 1911 the annual letter arrived early.

"My dear son," his father wrote. Konrad's heart twisted. It must be bad news. "I am encouraged to write this letter after a visit from my cousin and dear friend, Warburton Pike." For five pages his father went on about Pike, reminiscing about their adventures, hinting at stories he dared not commit to paper. Tears welled up in Konrad's eyes. For once he was happy to hear Pike's name. The waiter serving him breakfast was concerned and asked if he was ill.

"Not ill," declared Konrad, wiping away the tears. "Just foolish." He left that afternoon on the transcontinental train to Toronto, then on to New York, and a fast steamer to Europe.

By late 1912 he counted seventeen companies among his empire, ranging from a whaling fleet based on the west coast of Vancouver Island to a wild-cat oil-drilling outfit exploring in Alberta and Texas and a moribund coal mine in Issaquah, Washington. J. P. Morgan had just purchased mineral rights to the Mesabi iron range, which sprawled over Minnesota, a belt of high-grade ore that ran as deep as five hundred feet into the earth. No sooner had Morgan signed his name to the deal than he committed to purchase all the coal Konrad could produce in Washington.

Much of his initial financing came from Germany. Baron Lustveig von Meistermann, a friend of his father, was an important investor. The garrulous noble was delighted with the bustling young city and the extraordinary beauty of its surroundings. Von Meistermann came for a month on Konrad's recommendation to search out investment opportunities on behalf of Reichschancellor Theobald von Bethmann Hollweg, Field Marshall August von Mackensen, and his own cousin Emma Mumm, the canny inheritor of a champagne dynasty. He also intended to kill a few animals.

Trophy-hunting in the Wild West had become fashionable of late, with articles in *Harper's Magazine,* the popular British publication *Abroad,* and *Das Großwild* extolling the thrill of bringing down elk, bear, big-horned sheep, and full-racked bull deer in the Canadian wilderness. "Safaris have become far too tame," the publisher of *Das Großwild* wrote. "Combing the weld for lions and other big game has become a tedious checker game with bunches of colored boys trapping the prey and the hunter left only to shoot the beast. Canada's west has to be the very best place to find what all true hunters seek: challenging terrain and animals dangerous and difficult enough to provide the thrill so often lacking in our civilized lives."

Throughout 1911, 1912, and most of 1913, hardly a train pulled in from the east or a boat from around the Horn without a group of Germans equipped as if for an assault on Everest. Konrad made a very good thing of quietly purchasing large parcels of land for his countrymen who were enamored with the city, the wilds, and the potential. In the interior and the north of British Columbia staking for coal, silver, and copper properties was almost as furious as residential and industrial land speculation in Vancouver. Von Meistermann had easily financed his entire trip with a five-hundred-acre parcel near Revelstoke in the Selkirk Mountains, deep within the province. He bought it his first week and sold it his second.

The night before von Meistermann left, the two men dined at the Vancouver Club. After a meal of wild mushrooms in heavy cream, roast venison, salmon grilled with tangy Indian berries, custard, and June straw-berries, followed by German cheeses that Konrad insisted the club import, the men retired to the smoking room to digest. The waiter brought in a heavy silver tray laden with lead-crystal glasses full of ten-year-old port so rich von Meistermann declared it "blood of the gods." The waiter bowed low in appreciation of the guest's good taste. As he did so, his eyes fell upon Konrad, who smiled broadly as the man's eyes opened wide.

"I see you have graduated from the kitchen!" Konrad said.

The waiter was surprised at Konrad's knowledge of his first job accept-ing and storing food as it was delivered to the club.

"Oh yes, dammit! I know you," Konrad continued with taunting delight. "I'm the man who used to sell eggs and butter at the back door." He turned to the grinning men gathered around. "And mallards for thirty-five cents and pigeon and teal at forty-five cents a brace."

He turned back to the waiter. "That was me! Now stop your gawking and get on with your serving." He tossed a yellow hunk of Jarlsberg back on the tray. "Take this away, it is far too young."

Flushed, the waiter scurried away with the laughter of the members and guests at his back.

"You see, my good Baron, that is what this city is all about," pronounced Konrad. "Opportunity. Here a man can catch fish and shoot game for a living one minute and own a steamship fleet and coal mines the next. In Europe that couldn't happen. One is always blocked by birth. Even in the United States they are starting to become more concerned about the who than the what and the how." He drove his thumb into his chest. "I am your what and how."

Long after midnight Konrad found Chinjun at her accustomed place on Pender Street. The night was slow, and she was mending petticoats when Konrad burst in—unlike most men, no amount of food or drink quelled his desires.

Chinjun was an unusual combination, a Chinese father and a Squamish mother from the ragged tribe across Burrard Inlet. It was a rape like many oth-ers on the dark Vancouver streets along the water—a man stupid with rice wine and angry over gambling losses and a woman who had the bad luck to be searching the streets for garbage near a Fan Tan game house.

Both cultures rejected the child, but Pender Street did not. Her birth name was Ilik but Konrad called her Chinjun, his Chinese injun. Barely five feet tall, she was almost exactly Edith's height, but there the resemblance ended. Dark-haired, with sleek, deep-mahogany skin, broad cheekbones, and an angular body, Ilik claimed to be eighteen to sidestep periodic child-prostitution sweeps along the Pender strip. She was just fourteen. Konrad had known her for a year.

Ilik never knew what mood might be driving Konrad. He could be a rutting bull, hurtful with his massive size inside her small body, heedless of her pain and the blood that often came afterward. Or he could woo her with gentleness, warm kisses down her belly, his wet tongue softly caressing her pubis then finding its way to the hard knob of flesh that shocked her with its sensitivity. Ilik never knew which Konrad would come through her door.

But one thing was always the same. In the moment of his release, a name, uttered as a sob. "Edie! Edie!" She never asked.

That night, after his meal at the club, Konrad was a jovial gentleman. He brought Ilik flowers and a beautiful hat pin with a polished jade stone at the end.

"Tomorrow," he crowed to her, "is the day."

With Ilik cradling his head against her thin breasts, he detailed his scheme as if she were a business partner. Ilik only half listened as his voice rose and fell with the tale of riches and revenge. Money meant nothing, she would never have any, and if she did she wouldn't know what to do with it.

His words finally wound down. "Tell me a story," he said softly after a long pause. Ilik smiled in the dark. It was a little joke between them. A bedtime story. She began her tale as she began most of them.

"The lost tribe of the Kahnamut once owned all of the land in Vancouver and as far as you can drive in any direction in a day. My mother came from a most royal line of those people."

"Tell me about the treasure in Stanley Park," Konrad murmured. He didn't believe the thousand-acre park held any ancient secrets. Shafts for coal had been sunk all over the near island, most of its trees had been logged, and squatters of all sorts had lived there for more than half a century. But he loved to hear about dreams.

"It is such a great treasure," breathed Ilik. "Once it's found, the world will change."

"How did it get there?"

"If you be quiet I will tell you."

*

Hec Brundage, drawn in like so many others to the fury of land speculation, had taken an option on ten acres of land near False Creek. There were plans afoot to dredge the silting creek, more a small lake than a creek, and provide another docking point for cargo ships with ready access to the new Canadian National Railway station and its track along the south shore of the Fraser River, a competitor to the CPR, which ran to the north.

"Brundage sent me on a wild-goose chase," Konrad often said to himself, "and one day I shall goose him in return." Now that chance had come.

So confident was Brundage of his ability to raise money to close the deal that he trumpeted his success-to-be all over town and had even begun discussions with two different cargo lines for exclusive rights to the first docks he intended to build. His financiers had impeccable credentials: real estate broker C. D. Rand and banker Donald von Cramer, both founding members of the new Vancouver Stock Exchange.

The opening of the Vancouver Stock Exchange in 1907 had sounded the financial death knell to the provincial capital of Victoria, a pretty, stuffy little town at the south end of Vancouver Island, with lingering pretensions of being the major city for trade and finance on the West Coast. As Victoria sagged from prominence, Vancouver loudly and brashly took over.

But the Exchange struggled, stung by the stories of bucket-shop promoters selling nonexistent claims and hastily printed shares to take advantage of "exciting new strikes" in the interior, then disappearing to St. Louis, San Francisco, or Toronto with pockets bulging. The words "stockbroker" and "highway robber" had become synonymous. Even the local bankers, despite the respectable von Cramer's involvement, wanted nothing to do with the fledgling Exchange.

In early 1912, over large chipped glasses of warmed Cognac in Gassy's, Rand bellyached to von Schaumberg about the Exchange's slow start.

"If these slippery devils selling worthless bits of paper, *unlisted stocks*," he snarled over the words, "were forced to put their own money behind those companies, you'd see an exhibition of welshing and quitting that would awe both men and gods."

Konrad nodded equably, puffing on his cigar and interjecting periodically during the rant, one he'd heard before. "The Exchange's reputation isn't the best," he agreed.

"We are none of us salesmen, not one among the ten founders, and these silver-tongued devils charm money out of people's hands while we try to gladden their hearts with sound business arguments. And which approach do you think is more successful? Huh! An easy answer. We need a man of your promotional abilities."

They sipped in silence for a few minutes. "I don't suppose I could persuade you to take a seat, could I?"

"Perhaps," said Konrad after an appropriate pause, "as a personal favor." Rand hung on Konrad's words as he relit his cigar. "But I would need a favor from you and Mr. von Cramer in return."

It took Konrad two months to arrange the most critical element of his plan, a meeting with eighty-one-year-old Soon Chong, who still occupied the rabbit warren on the edge of Chinatown.

"We are well aware of Mr. Brundage and his wife," the wizened little man said. "It would do wonders for the racial climate if they were, uh, diminished somewhat. I'm sure easing relations between our two cultures is your primary concern and not, for example, something like revenge?"

"You have assessed my motives perfectly," Konrad agreed.

"Perhaps if Mr. Brundage's missus could not afford so many Chinese houseboys, she wouldn't have time to get up to so much mischief, such as her support of the act to deport all Chinese women and children," Soon said with a rare and quite awful laugh. "Let's see what we can come up with."

✳

Hec Brundage raged. Donald von Cramer sat impassively in the carved ebony chair imported from Africa to accent his new position as president of the recently formed Vancouver Trust Company.

"My hands are tied," he said calmly to the purple-faced fury stomping up and down the Persian rug–covered floor of his presidential suite. "The rules are very clear." It was rather nice, putting the boot to Brundage, who was, in his opinion, a vulgarian of the worst sort, with a shrill wife determined to social-climb her way onto the List of Four Hundred, the ladies and gentlemen in the city's elite social register.

"I have contracts in hand!" bellowed Brundage. "Within seven days I will have down payments of $250,000 against property on the waterfront section. These are legitimate contracts from two of the largest dock builders in North America. Where is your risk!"

"The risk is, Mr. Brundage, you have signed your hotel over as security on a loan from us, which will be *your* down payment on the land which you intend to sell at a vast profit, in fact have already sold a good section of it at a profit, even though you do not yet own the land."

Von Cramer sat in solemn disapproval, as if completely unaware that such flipping of land had become the norm in Vancouver.

"But I don't have the money in hand yet!" sputtered Brundage. "I have promises, of course. Profits are built on risk. *I* am taking all the risk, yet you seem determined to cut me off."

Von Cramer held up his hand to ward off Brundage's argument.

"Your deal is to close at four P.M. today, yet this morning I discover that there is a lien against your hotel. I call that our risk."

"It is of no consequence!" Brundage hissed. "It dates back to my first days in Vancouver, when I purchased the hotel with a small amount of help. I have long since paid off the loan. I simply neglected to have the lien removed."

"The lien holder is rumored to be a Chinaman," von Cramer stated.

"Ridiculous," Brundage faltered. "The loan was arranged through my good friend Warburton Pike and the lender was Samuel C. Pillar."

Von Cramer frowned.

"Have you ever met Mr. Pillar?"

"Well, no. But there was no need. Pike's known him for years. There was no need," he repeated weakly. A cold feeling grew inside him.

"Samuel C. Pillar is an alias. I do not know whether he's one of us or an Oriental, but he has an office in Chinatown. He is rumored to be a very powerful man in certain circles."

The cold turned into a burn of fear in Brundage's belly. Samuel Pillar. Why hadn't he insisted on meeting the man face-to-face?

Von Cramer wasn't about to budge. "No, Mr. Brundage," he said, shaking his head. "The lien must be removed."

It was one P.M. Pike was not about, as usual. The old man had taken to spending months at a time in a rough cabin on the shores of Indian Arm. Brundage jumped into his car and raced to Chinatown.

Samuel Pillar was nowhere to be found. Not only that, but no one seemed to know who he was, where he lived, or the address of his business. Brundage ran up and down Pender Street, dodging stinking barrels overflowing with revolting things that looked like entrails. He stopped at every business and asked the same question. The answer was always the same: "Solly."

Brundage tore back to his house and rummaged furiously through his papers. Sweat soaked his linen shirt, his collar was sprung, and damp panic made the inside of his thighs stick to his woolen trousers. Three P.M. All he needed was receipt of the final payment. It was nearly eighteen years ago, but he was sure he had it. He knocked over a Pairpont lamp, puffy balloons of glass in fanciful candy colors. It shattered on the Aubusson carpet. "Fuck!" he screamed, kicking aside the shards. Three twenty-five. There! The receipt, he had it.

The car coughed twice, then fired. Brundage flew up Granville Street, crossed Georgia, and headed south to the bridge across False Creek. He turned left sharply at Broadway Street, smiling grimly. He could see the lands at the head of False Creek through the heavy smoke of the industries just below the bridge. "Mine," he muttered. "Mine."

At city hall he took three steps at a time and raced into the land registry office. It would go smoothly now. He knew people here. Three forty-seven.

"I am sorry, sir. We must have a release of lien form signed and notarized. I'm sure you understand. This signature could be anyone's." He added, pushing the receipt back across the counter.

Brundage was sure his body would explode on the spot. The man behaved as if he had never seen Brundage before in his life.

"You know me!" Brundage shouted. "My word is good! Here is proof the money was repaid. Now remove the damn lien! Do it!"

Three fifty-two.

"I'm sorry, sir. I suggest you take this form and have Mr. Pillar sign it."

"I can't find the bloody man!" Brundage shouted. "I'll have your job if you deny me this!"

Brundage vaulted across the counter and grabbed the man's lapels, shaking him like a terrier with a rat. He was a big man, and the little clerk's head snapped back and forth. It took three people to haul Brundage off.

Four oh-two.

As Brundage was being dragged to the door, he saw the time. Tears poured down his face. "I am ruined! I am ruined!" he sobbed hysterically.

His escorts shoved him out the door in disgust. The wobbly-kneed clerk dusted himself off and patted his pocket. "If I had known he would get violent I would have demanded far more from Mr. von Schaumberg," he muttered.

✳

Brundage was forced to sell his house and adjacent hotel. C. D. Rand kindly offered to cut his agent fee to almost nothing. Normally the hotel and the double lot it sat on would have been worth $52,000 in that frenzied market. With only a day to raise the promised option money Brundage had no choice but to let it go for $30,000. The purchaser, Fraser Valley Timber and Boom Coy. Ltd., gave its address as Texas Bar.

61

*

August 23, 1914

"He's in jail?" Edith dropped her knitting in her lap and her hand flew to her mouth.

"Not jail exactly," corrected Hetty Henley-Galen. "Detained. He has been detained. Mr. Henley-Galen says it amounts to the same thing as jail."

Hettie said the word with a happy emphasis. She never liked the tall, arrogant man. She thought him trouble from the start and couldn't imagine what Edith saw in him. It certainly wasn't money—he was good at making it, that's for sure, but Edith never seemed to care much about wealth. More's the pity. Hetty spent years trying to kindle her interest in eligible bachelors, among them a banker, a partner in a meat-packing plant, and the owner of two dry-goods stores. Edith was unfailingly polite, but not the least bit encouraging. Hetty had only one success in her campaign to improve Edith. She bullied her younger friend into putting her name forward to teach at a new private school on Vancouver's West Side, in the heart of the exclusive Shaughnessy Heights mansions, then badgered her husband to ensure Edith got the job.

"Ladner is all well enough, but you can't spend your life marooned with farmers, Chinamen, and jappy fishermen. And those Indians from India, with the silly hats, are moving into the area. Mr. Henley-Galen told me the fields are full of them and the mills too. You're not getting younger, my dear. Your life will be over before you know it."

Edith adored the little two-room school with its odd mix of students—Japanese, Chinese, Germans, Irish, Italians, and even two Indians. The Musqueam boys didn't last long, however, when wind of their attendance reached the ears of the Board of Education. The last she heard they had been sent to the Mission school on the Fraser River, "to be with their own kind."

Rumors of impending war shook the school. Several of her German students stopped coming after one of the older boys had his nose and several fingers broken by a group of students of Scottish descent.

During his last visit the district supervisor warned her the school would close, because a new school with an indoor washroom and electric lights was under construction closer to the village. All her students would go there, she was told. Edith knew better. Most of her children—she thought of them that way—lived within walking distance of this school. Their parents wouldn't think education was worth an hour's buggy ride every morning and afternoon. But there were already three teachers in Ladner, all with more seniority than Edith, so she reluctantly took the new position.

The Crofton School for Girls was lovely. The brick-faced building blended into the acres of arbutus, oak, and tall firs as if it had been there for a century. As she walked through the imported-mahogany double doors inscribed with the date of construction and the school's name, Edith couldn't deny the sense of peace that settled upon her. Everything was quiet and controlled. The girls came from excellent Vancouver families. The very best, of course, sent their daughters to finishing schools in Switzerland or France. Poised and well-mannered as little adults, the girls giggled and chattered in the corridors and dormitories but in class they were attentive and respectful. On her first day Edith looked out over her French grammar students: thirteen neat heads, immaculate pinafores, bent over leather-bound books. No aroma of pig, no pungent smell of fish, no salty odor of bodies long needing a wash. She would not be riding a horse bareback to school anymore, nor would she play hockey with the children at lunch, and there would be no more slabs of perfectly filleted fish or baskets of carrots and cabbage arriving on her doorstep.

"He's been spying on us for years and shipping all that coal to feed the kaiser's steel-making," Hetty informed Edith. "What do you expect? He's German!"

"But it's only rumor, surely!" protested Edith.

"That accent of his is all the proof I need," sniffed Hetty. "Besides, how else could a man make so much money so fast? Why, we met him by the docks ten years ago and I'm sure he didn't have a dollar in his pocket. Then suddenly he's entertaining the likes of John D. Rockefeller and the Astors!"

By late 1913 Konrad required $15 million annually to finance his numerous schemes. It was men such as Rockefeller and his European contacts who happily provided it. The price of everything had been rising by the month as the collective industrial might of the Western nations fed the largest consumer binge in history. But the tide of money changes with rapid ferocity.

Konrad's annual visit to New York in October 1913 netted him a few promises but nothing more. All his former sources of capital wanted to do was talk about the German war machine. For the first time Konrad was forced to commit nearly a million dollars of his own funds in order to meet his payroll. Three months later he sold fifteen hundred acres of land in Vancouver. Quickly as land fever had soared in the previous years, it dropped twice as fast. Even his Shaughnessy lots went for thirty-five percent less than he'd paid for them. By March 1914, Konrad was stretched so thin, he sailed for Europe to search for operating capital. It is a strange thing in the world of business that companies and the men who run them are far more eager to invest in something that exists only as an idea than they are to lay down money to keep an actual enterprise operating.

"Dreams," Konrad said in an address to Vancouver's Empire Club that same month. "Give men dreams and they will come to you. Reality they are far less interested in."

The reality of 1914 was war. World markets suddenly shrank back in on themselves. Konrad was certain the ridiculous threat would pass. Germany could not afford to go to war with Britain. It was a different world now than fifty years ago. Investment linked the advanced nations. Kaiser Wilhelm was not the best businessman, being too inclined to ring up debt he could not service, but he assured Konrad that he wanted to expand his interests in North America, particularly the resource-rich West Coast of Canada.

When Britain declared war against Germany at 8:32 A.M. Greenwich Mean Time on August 4, 1914, Konrad was two days out of Copenhagen, bound for New York, then Seattle, and finally Vancouver. He had raised not a single mark from his former investors and worse, several, including the Kaiser himself, reneged on previous financing commitments.

On the long boat voyage to New York and then again on the continental train, Konrad read and reread a letter that had found its way to him in Europe. He winced at the words across the top of the page.

Dominion Rating & Mercantile Agency

OUR SYSTEM GETS THE MONEY ANY OLD PLACE. NO COLLECTION NO CHARGE. WE FURNISH LISTS OF DEADBEATS AND LOCATE NON-PAYING DEBTORS WHO HAVE ABSCONDED.

Direct inquiries to: 244 W. Cordova Street, Vancouver, British Columbia.

What followed were a few terse, ungrammatical demands for payment of money borrowed to open the Issaquah mine and purchase a coal freighter. It wasn't the only such letter he had in hand.

Deadbeat. Konrad cringed. He was a builder! A developer. He wasn't like so many in Vancouver these days who created nothing but paper in their speculative schemes. Oh yes, he'd had his hand in a few of those, but everything he devoted his considerable energy to was *intended* to be a real enterprise. No puffs and bubbles for him. He built buildings, opened mines, set ships a-sail, and consorted with aristocracy and business leaders from twenty-two different countries.

Deadbeat. Konrad didn't feel a shred of guilt for all the money he owed. Business was like that. Men took risks with their money and suffered the consequences. He vowed to return to Vancouver where he'd reorganize and emerge stronger than ever. Perhaps he could arrange a loan in Seattle. The steel manufacturers would certainly capitalize on the demand from both sides for ships, tanks, and planes. Now that he really thought things through, Konrad came around to the opinion that war in Europe would be his savior.

By the time Konrad reached Seattle he was so sick of the chatter, first onboard the ship and then on the train, about assured victory within the month, that he retired to his compartment and took his meals there.

"Konrad von Schaumberg?" The constable who'd been waiting at the terminal stumbled over the name but had no trouble handing over a heavy bundle of documents.

It took two days to process Konrad's detention requested by the Canadian government at the behest of the British Foreign Ministry. He sat bleakly in a guarded room in a smelly hotel overlooking the fishing piers until a letter from the Custodian of Enemy Alien's Property informed him that he would be jailed if he crossed the border into Canada and that his "property all and in its entirety was sequestered in the name of the Queen."

"What about my cars and my wines and my houses!" Konrad raged to a representative of the British Columbia Military District in Vancouver who'd hand-delivered the letter to Seattle. The man merely shrugged and stared at him coldly. Just one more kraut trying to take over the world. Well, they stopped this one, he thought to himself with satisfaction.

Konrad's ability to funnel German funds to Vancouver had given him cachet and power only a year ago, but now it was evidence of dark conspiracy. Stories with nameless sources appeared, proclaiming him to be an illegitimate son of Kaiser Wilhelm and a spy to boot. One report had authorities finding huge stocks of guns and explosives in one of his houses while another suggested his canneries were intended as refueling depots for the Kaiser's navy once it invaded the West.

Konrad's developments, which were once trumpeted as making Vancouver the great city of the twentieth century, were now sinister plots to rape the natural resources of the West Coast to benefit the Kaiser's war effort.

"It has come to the exclusive attention of this reporter," one columnist began, "that there is now definitive proof that the fraud we once hailed as 'the count' is, in fact, a mere limb of the horrific octopus that is Kaiser Wilhelm's military machine.

'The Count' dances to the tune of the Kaiser, plain and simple. A telegram from one known German agent to another was fortunately intercepted by the British and now exposes a plot to starve His Majesty's air force of vitally needed aeroplanes. You will be as shocked as I was at the audacity of this turncoat who used Vancouver and its good citizens for his own black purposes.

Here is the evidence as plainly outlined in the telegram from one secret ministry of the German war monster to another:

Von Schaumberg will present a plan with reference to the purchase of the Wright aeroplane factory in Dayton, Ohio. If he is successful, we would be in a position to prevent the export of flying machines from the United States and keep the British flying forces where they belong, on the ground.

Konrad simmered when he read the column. He knew nothing of Dayton, Ohio, let alone an aeroplane factory. The next day grim-faced American police officers escorted Konrad to the Seattle jail, from where he was quickly whisked away to Utah and a camp for undesirable aliens. The joint arrangement between the American and British governments housed nearly 350 men, many of them scientists, former businessmen, and inventors of German descent.

✳

On February 3, 1921, Vancouver slowly dug itself out of the snowstorm of the century. Sleighs were seldom used in the city, as snow rarely stayed more than a few days, just long enough to remind West Coasters that they shouldn't be too smug about the mild winters while the rest of the country and the North and East of the United States were regularly paralyzed by Arctic conditions. On the hills of Mount Pleasant overlooking False Creek and all through downtown children zipped down the streets on anything that would slide. There was no danger from cars, as none could negotiate the slippery conditions, and for a day or so the children, with their schools all closed, owned every rise and fall in the roads despite the best efforts of the police to banish them.

The train from Los Angeles and Seattle was three days late. Twice it was halted, and early on the third day it seemed as if it would not be able to cross the Fraser en route to Vancouver because of fears the bridge would collapse from the combined weight of the snow and the train. But the head conductor knew his business. He uncoupled all the freight cars, had them shunted off to a siding, then cajoled the grumbling passengers into walking across the bridge on foot before the engine crossed. All the toilets were blocked up and food had run short, as the snow had stopped the suppliers from reaching the Bellingham station before they'd set off for Vancouver.

Konrad uncoiled himself from the cramped seat in the third-class car, carpetbag in his hand. Seven years it had been since he'd last set foot in Vancouver, seventeen since a foolish twenty-four-year-old got off the passenger ship at Coal Harbour. As he looked across Burrard Inlet to the north shore mountains, he realized he had come to love the city, though he never acknowledged the feeling the whole time he lived here. Fittingly, Vancouver was unusually shrouded in snow, which made it look as foreign to him as Constantinople. The station was almost as busy as he'd remembered, but it was a different feeling. Quieter. Less energetic, and there were far more women. It seemed there were three to every man.

Seven years. He walked slowly down the platform and gazed again at the mountains and the smoke rising from the north shore factories. There were more of them than when he'd left, no doubt as a result of the war. He took in the broad flank of Grouse Mountain, which he had begun negotiations to purchase in 1913, with plans to build a funicular railway and a skiing facility at the top. It all seemed a lifetime ago. He couldn't help but smile when his eye rested on the Lions. The twin peaks guarding the city. While imprisoned in the Utah camp with little to look at but dirty, bald hills, he'd thought of them often.

The letter from the Department of Confiscated Property explained bluntly that though treason charges against him had been dropped and he was free to travel in Canada, there would be no repatriation of his land, buildings, or bank account holdings.

"I'm sure they've drunk the damn wine," he muttered to himself, reading the letter. "I'll show them. I'll build it up again," he vowed, but the words sounded hollow. In truth, Konrad von Schaumberg had no idea what he wanted to do. His entire fortune consisted of a hundred dollars the Red Cross had given him when he left Utah.

In the camp he occasionally allowed Edith to penetrate his thoughts, not so much with yearning—he'd lost the knack for that—but in wonderment that he could have been so stupid. After years of carnage and loss, the origins of one's blood seemed laughably inconsequential. He'd treated her abominably and she was long gone; rightly so.

"Father," he murmured, "if you could see your son now landing for the second time in this city, the first time young and broke and this time old and broke." The count had died of pneumonia in 1915, and he'd received a letter from his youngest brother in 1919 saying his mother had succumbed to scarlet fever. He had no idea what was left of his family's holdings after capitulation, as he hadn't heard a word from his brothers. His sister sent a brief letter in early 1920 to the alien imprisonment camp saying Joachim had sold his coffee plantations at a tremendous loss and they were leaving to join a small group of investors on the Yucatán Peninsula in Mexico, where hotels were being erected on what she said was reputed to be the best beach outside the Riviera. She promised to send more information later but that was nearly fourteen months ago.

"At least I won't be tempted by gold schemes," Konrad said to himself with a chuckle as he pulled open the doors to the station. Several other passengers glanced curiously at the laughing man. They were relieved to have finally arrived, but after a three-day delay no one felt the slightest bit like celebrating.

With a little burst of his old energy Konrad marched across the concourse, the sound of his worn boots against the polished pink granite floor bringing a few memories back.

"Forget the memories!" he said sharply, drawing a few more stares. "Forget the past. Start again. You'll find something."

The first necessity was a room. He doubted too much had changed south of Georgia Street, and there would likely be many vacancies in the cheaper hostels. He'd read an article on the train about how difficult times were for rooming houses that had once served traveling salesmen, as so many of that generation were dead. Konrad felt oddly detached when he read it. He had missed the entire event. Event. Some devil had waved its hand and wiped a generation off the face of the earth while he, Konrad von Schaumberg, was harvesting rocks for railway beds.

Konrad neared the massive brass doors leading out to Cordova Street. He breathed deeply, pulled his gaunt body to its full height, and pushed them open. Konrad's eyes immediately teared up at the bright light bouncing off the snow. He peered across the street, trying to decide which way to go. The seedier areas were to the east; he would head in that direction. He took a step and noticed a small figure standing with a suitcase. Life has changed so much, he thought. When I left Vancouver you rarely saw a woman alone. He looked at her, wondering if she was one of those who'd lost a husband to the war. Then he gasped, coughing as he drew in the chilly air.

"No, no, it can't be," he moaned. Eyes still blurry, he rushed across the street, slipping in the slush and almost falling again. He slid to a stop. No words would come. He panted as if having run several miles at full tilt. The snow bank absorbed the impact as he dropped to the ground in front of her.

"I am still a Jew," Edith whispered.

"I, I am . . . Oh Edie, Edie, Edie." It was the first time in years that her name had crossed his lips. He tasted her on his tongue, savored the syllables. "I am sorry. So, so sorry."

"There is nothing to forgive," she said, her voice still soft.

Konrad had not dared look at her and still did not. He scrambled to his feet and swept her small, plump body into his arms.

"Edie!" he sobbed, tears rolling down his cheeks, wetting her hair, filling his mouth.

Konrad had no idea how the next few hours passed. Somehow they made their way to White's Hostel for Gentlemen, where Konrad flung two $10 bills at the astonished clerk to look the other way as he and Edith careened up the stairs like drunken fools, words tumbling and crashing over each other like children playing in the surf. Sentences began and never finished, smiles dissolved into tears, and lips found lips, ending thoughts in mid-expression. His hands raced over her, feeling her body beneath her clothes as if he couldn't yet believe she was real, as if she would evaporate any moment. She felt his desire, pain, and shame, and knew, even without probing, that Konrad, this thin, tired, middle-aged man, was her Konrad. The same Konrad, only better.

When a peaceful silence finally descended for a few moments, Edith gave him the ancient leather suitcase with tarnished buckles and cracked straps. A long canvas-wrapped object was strapped to the side.

"What is it?" Konrad said, wiping his eyes that seemed like a fountain. "When I saw you with the suitcase I thought you were going away on a trip. I never dreamed you were waiting for me."

"After you were sent to Utah, a very strange fellow came by my school and gave me this. He told me it was yours and you would come to collect it one day."

"What man and how did he know I would ever come back?" Konrad was perplexed. He hadn't communicated with anyone in Vancouver.

Edith played with her fingers before answering. It was a habit he remembered fondly.

"He seemed quite certain you'd be back," she said. "Quite certain. It gave me hope! Though I never thought you'd ever want to see me again."

A groan rose from his belly like dying sounds of a large animal.

"There is no fool like I, no one who deserves more to be shot at dawn, to be run off a cliff, to suffer a lifetime of torture!"

Edith smiled. The years had taken some of his hair, added lines to his face, and a gray, papery quality to his skin after so long in confinement, but the spirit was still there. "When he gave me this suitcase I felt I had a piece of you, and somehow I couldn't let go. It was a curse really. Think of all the marriage proposals I turned down," she teased. "Hetty quite gave up on me."

"Who was the man?" Konrad asked.

"His name was Pike, Warburton Pike. Odd old fellow. He must have been over seventy, but I quite liked him. He said he was sorry about what had happened to you and he thought you might be interested in a few mementoes, that was the word he used, when you came back.

"I told him again that I doubted you would ever be back and he said," Edith paused for a moment with a funny look, "he said if you were too stupid not to come back to me, then he'd badly misjudged you."

"That old scoundrel," Konrad said.

"How did he know we had once been together?" she asked.

"All the scholars in all the world would never be able to explain Warburton Pike. What is inside the case?"

"I've never looked." She hung her head and the years of sadness crept into her face. Konrad wished he had a knife and could stab himself without her seeing. "I couldn't look, though I thought of it often. After a time it just became like an old friend. There but not really there."

Suddenly Konrad thought of her appearance at the station. "How did you come to meet the train?"

"It was quite strange, really. An Indian came to my door. Frightened the daylights out of me before he handed me a piece of paper, then disappeared without saying a word. The note said, 'Go to the CPR Station and meet the Seattle train. Take the suitcase.' It was signed 'Warburton Pike.'

"I didn't even think about it," she continued. "I just went to the station the next day, and the next, and the next, because, of course, your train was delayed."

"You stood in the snow waiting for me?"

"I didn't think I was waiting for you. I really didn't. It was almost as if my will was not my own. It never occurred to me you might arrive. I had heard so many things, the last of which was you had returned to Germany to fight for your family lands. That was after I heard you'd been in Vancouver all the time. Before that I heard you'd been shot to death escaping and after that I heard you'd been seen cutting quite a figure in New York. I believed all of that and none of that."

Konrad stared at her in wonder. She pointed at the case. "Open it. I've been curious for years."

He pried open the top, which creaked in protest. On the top lay a pair of tooled water-bison boots with double-stitched soles, the leather dull with dirt. He lifted one up and something fell out. A heavy diamond-and-ruby ring. He lifted the second boot and an object slid from toe to heel. He tipped the boot up. His watch. Edith smiled as he wound it and held it to his ear. Tock, tock, tock. The canvas, he now knew, held his prized rifle.

"Good lord," Konrad whispered. "How on earth did he manage to get these from old Brundage?"

"There's something more," Edith said, pointing to a wrapped package in the bottom of the case.

Konrad pulled the paper free, a smile spreading across his face. It was the gloomy, frightening painting Brundage had hanging outside his office. By Emily Carr. But somehow the picture seemed far less ominous than when he'd first seen it. It had a dreamy quality.

"Oh Konrad, it is beautiful," breathed Edith. "Hetty's ladies find her far too masculine but I love her boldness."

"It is beautiful," agreed Konrad.

There was one more surprise. Edith picked up an envelope that was jammed into one corner. Her name was on it. Inside was a certificate of ownership under the Homesteaders' Law of 1919—deeded to Edith West-cott—a hundred acres on the west side of the Fraser River, and another hundred acres on the east side known as Texas Bar. The signature of the former owner was at the bottom: "Warburton Pike."

Konrad began to laugh. Chuckles, bellows, aching guffaws of sheer joy. He had seven years of laughing to make up. No, fourteen years, from the day Edith laid his ring on the bench at English Bay. He laughed until his ribs hurt and his stomach muscles throbbed with the effort.

"What will you do with it?" Konrad said when he could finally speak.

Edith stared at the document, her hand caressing its surface. And then she knew.

"We will live there."

"Live there?"

"Yes, live there," she repeated firmly. "Since you have been gone, a con-siderable community has grown up along the river. Most of the towns have electric lights, and a good road connects Hope to Vancouver. And there is the railway on both sides of the river, and there are farms, and . . ."

"Of course!" bellowed Konrad, startling her. "We will live there, you and I. We will have a cow, and pan for gold, and swim in the river with no clothes on! We will live there—you, me, my boots, the ring, the watch, and this magnificent picture."

"And don't forget the children," Edith teased.

"Yes, yes! How could I forget," Konrad's lips brushed her neck. "Let us waste no time."

Konrad took his grandfather's ring and put it on Edith's finger.

PART X

Walter
Dolby

62

✳

1968

Vancouver

Walter Dolby lurched eastward along the wide sidewalk of Georgia Street, downtown Vancouver's main east-west artery, eyes darting from the newly laid paving stones beneath his feet to the buildings beside him. Every now and then he hopped slightly to avoid stepping on a crack, which inevitably put him in conflict with people walking toward him.

"Watch it, buddy!" laughed one man, sidestepping a collision.

"Drunken asshole!" muttered another, less charitable soul.

"Forkin' veeehickles!" snarled Dolby, ignoring the people but shaking his fist as the cars streaming into the heart of the city sent cascades of water onto the sidewalk.

"You'd think the goddamn city cud figger out a way to get rid of the goddamn puddles. Two forkin' weeks of rain and now it's sunny I'm still getting soaked."

"Pardon me?" an elderly woman said, thinking he was talking to her.

"Shaddap."

Dolby could have avoided the rooster tails of water shooting off the cars by walking closer to buildings but that would have left no margin for reaction should a cat cross his path.

Dolby remembered his last cat disaster with burning acuity. A moldering orange tom swaggered out of an alley next to the Marine Building near the waterfront at 11:32 A.M. on July 7, 1964. Dolby didn't see the cat because he'd veered toward the building to dodge a group of street musicians working pedestrians for handouts. As he did, he tripped over the squealing cat and fell face first, smashing his nose.

At 12:07, after unsuccessfully trying to hail a cab, Dolby, nose streaming blood, flagged down a police officer, who deposited him at the emergency ward of St. Paul's Hospital a mile south on Burrard Street. And there he passed out. At 1:00 P.M., while Dolby was still unconscious, the option he had in his pocket to purchase twenty-five thousand shares of Silver City Mines at seventy cents a share expired. The stock was selling for $1.18 a share, which meant a tidy profit of $12,000 if the option was still good. "Twelve forkin' big ones flying out the window" was how Walter Dolby put it. All because of a goddamn cat.

As he bobbed and wove up the street, Walter Dolby cut anything but an impressive figure. Though his suits were top-of-the-line worsted wool from Bachelor's on Park and Fifty-third in Manhattan, and his coats the best cashmere, specially cut for his "challenging build" by Marvin at Hind's Furnishings on Saville Row, he invariably looked like he was outfitted by army surplus.

Dolby never for a moment imagined himself as anything but what he was—five-feet-two-and-a-quarter-inches tall, jowly and balding, with a prominent beaked nose that finished in a small hook. He was also irredeemably fat and unathletic. Unappealing as a baby, even to his mother, Dolby grew up a target for bully boy gangs as he hawked newspapers in New York's Washington Square. All the running he did never helped with his physique. Nor did it improve after a summer in his teen years spent as a pack horse for a Mesabi iron-range geologist. Later, as an assistant to an eternally optimistic rock banger in the early 1930s, he crisscrossed the rugged Canadian Shield in northern Ontario, swatting blackflies and prospecting for gold, silver, and lead.

Through it all Walter Dolby was fat and jowly, and he certainly hadn't gotten any taller. But with Walter Dolby everything was deceiving. He could still walk all day in the bush if he had to, and he had a handshake to make Charles Atlas wince.

The distance from Dolby's suite in the Sylvia Hotel overlooking English Bay and the ocean beyond to his habitual weekend morning haunt, the Dockside Café, was about three miles. He walked it easily in thirty-five minutes, allowing for several stops along the way. An impressive pace, considering his short-legged gait and detours.

In later years, his route through the West End to downtown would pass through one of the largest gay communities in North America, past architecturally avant-garde condominiums (many of which leaked in the winter rains), and through a dense corridor of high-rise apartments. But on this day in 1968, Dolby trod past majestic houses, interspersed with small businesses, Nat Bailey's White Spot drive-in among them. As Dolby marched along, he banged on the window of the restaurant to be rewarded by Nat's languid salute. Nat, a dedicated loser in the penny-stock market, could always be counted on to put a few thousand into a new promotion. On Dolby strode, toward Christ Church Cathedral, where he vigorously crossed himself (the wrong way) to ward off possible evils and on the grounds that it couldn't possibly hurt. By then Burrard Inlet, set off by the dark-green shoulders of the north shore mountains, was easily visible.

"How's they hanging, Wally?" croaked a tall, wizened man who'd sidled up Burrard Street to Georgia to hit him up before Dolby cut down to the water at Hornby by the Canadian Pacific Railway hotel. Dutch Eldrich, a fellow stock promoter. Once fastidiously dapper, Dutch's expensive check suit was frayed at the cuffs and stained along the sagging pockets. On one cheek were bits of fiber from a gas-station paper towel he'd used to clean himself up. He looked two decades older than Dolby's fifty-nine years, though they were about the same age.

"Forkin' loose and forkin' comfortable," Dolby responded. "Loose and comfortable. The way they forkin' outta be." Profanity was Dolby's first language. Crudeness never went with cleverness, he reasoned, and the less clever one appeared in his game the better.

Eldrich laughed delightedly, an early-morning cackle of nicotine phlegm. He kept at it long after the humor of the remark melted away, pushing out the guffaws like offerings to the stumpy figure before him.

"Need a loan, Dutch?" Dolby asked roughly, a tone of voice which passed for friendliness in his limited range of expression.

"An advance," Eldrich corrected eagerly. "I've got a line on a property in the Sierras. I just need to get cleaned up and put her into play."

"Moose pasture," grunted Dolby, the expected answer.

"I got assays!" Eldrich protested indignantly, also as required. "Hundert percent legit."

Dolby chuckled. "Moose pasture" was street argot for worthless land that, with artful promotion, could be transformed into a potential mine site.

"Hunnert percent, huh? Can't get much better 'n that." Dolby dug around in his pocket, separating the roll of twenties from the tens and fives by touch. He didn't bother with ones and twos, leaving them on shop counters if given in change.

"Better make it a hunnert," Dolby said, peeling off four bills, then another. "If you're workin' a promotion, you'll need flash money once you're cleaned up."

The man almost squeezed himself in joy. "You're the tops, Wally! The absolute tops!"

Dolby watched the man hurry away. Largesse was another of his super-stitions. He believed that handing out cash preserved his own luck.

A block farther, half a dozen men loitered in front of the Georgia Hotel, also waiting for Walter Dolby. One was another down-at-the-heels promoter working as a street-board boy for a brokerage firm, chalking up stock prices on a sidewalk blackboard to entice pedestrians. Two were bums who'd been regulars of the corner for years. One of them had a toffee-sounding English accent and called him "Guv." Dolby peeled off a twenty just to hear the "Thank you, Guv. You're a toff."

Two others, long-haired, half-asleep young men, were newcomers.

"Got some green for the love machine?" they chorused as he approached.

"Take a hike, ya lazy hippies!" Dolby snorted.

"Just groovin' here, man, waiting for the sugar bear," protested one with crinkly locks past his shoulder. If anything, they were dirtier than the bums. "We heard you were cool on helping your fellow man."

In 1968 flower power was emerging like a shy bud in Vancouver. The Canadian West Coast quickly emulated San Francisco by enticing society girls, good-family girls, girls from homes with double garages, to swallow bits of brown paper, suck on ganga pipes, and toke until their nose hairs burned. Fourth Avenue across the Burrard Street bridge and Gastown on the waterfront were becoming Vancouver's calmer, more polite Haight-Ashbury districts. If one looked hard amid the hippies, one might find teenaged Margaret Sinclair spreading her wings. She would go on to marry the charismatic Canadian prime minister Pierre Elliott Trudeau, then shock the country by cavorting with the Rolling Stones in New York's Club 21.

Dolby worked on the edge of the law every day of his life, but he was conservative to the core. He loathed the very idea of hippies—their ridicu-lous language and everything they stood for, which, as far as he could determine, was dirt, free sex, and indolence. He liked sex plenty, but he was intensely suspicious of "porkin'" any woman he wasn't married to, or any doll who didn't ask for cash on the barrel before he unzipped his fly. Both being pretty much the same thing to his way of thinking.

Thank Christ on the cross, his own two children hadn't been infected by this hippie disease, he thought, glaring distastefully at the shaggy young men.

"Whattya say, man, be cool, huh? Lay on a little bread."

"Fruits!" spat Dolby.

"Ahh, spare a little bread," wheedled the crinkle-haired one.

"I ain't given a forkin' penny to bums," Dolby said, lightening his tone. "But I'll spot you money for a haircut."

"Far out!" they chorused.

"Forkin' a-OK then," Dolby said, turning on his heel.

"Where ya going, man?" crinkle-hair asked plaintively. "I thought you were giving us some bread."

"I'm gonna pay for a forkin' haircut," Dolby responded equably. "Like I tol' you, so I'm going to the forkin' barbers! Where else d'ja gonna get a forkin' haircut?"

The young men slunk off, to the jeers and catcalls of the onlookers.

Dolby picked his way among sidewalk cracks, keeping a sharp eye out for ladders and cats. Half a block from the first commercial wharf, George Gates, newsletter publisher, editor, writer, and delivery boy of *The Street Squabble*, a daily guide to insider doings on the Vancouver Stock Exchange and the unlisted "pink sheet" market south of the border, fell into step with him. Gates was another Saturday-morning habitué of the Dockside Café. He had skin the color and texture of an iguana, with the personality to match. Rarely did Gates go anywhere without a shroud of cigar smoke wreathing his head.

"Heard about Macklin?" Gates managed to ask out of the corner of his mouth despite the presence of the cigar. His voice was soft and raspy, as if his vocal cords had been cured in whiskey. Morty Macklin was Dolby's main stock-promoting rival.

"Had a heart attack whilst getting a blow job at his desk?" queried Dolby hopefully.

Walter Dolby had nothing against a good blow job, but there was a time and place—i.e., bought from a woman who arrived at his hotel in a taxi. She'd parade a bit, do the job, pocket the money, kiss him on the top of his head, then leave him to a good night's sleep. But Macklin had them for breakfast on his office desk. Sometimes with other people watching! He even kept a hooker on company payroll full-time, but she sure wasn't there to keep the typewriter keys loose.

Dolby had nothing against a hooker being a secretary if she could type and didn't bring her other work into the office. In fact, his own was a former Granville Street slouch; regular typists didn't stick, because of his working hours and vile language.

Dolby spat copiously on the street, barely missing Gates's shoe.

"Macklin's a walkin' talkin' boner."

"Maybe so, but that boner up and flew out of town," Gates bubbled over his cigar butt. "I was just over to his hotel and he's cleared out—lock, stock, and pecker."

"His office?" Dolby asked, interested now.

"Same thing: lock, stock, barrel, and hooker."

"Pricks like him make it hard for the rest of us to make an honest forkin' living!" Dolby bellowed, startling a man washing windows. "Forkin' markets gonna be flat as an old whore's tits for weeks. Shit! That means I gotta get back on the forkin' phones and calm my investors, or everyone'll be jumpin' out the winda. Shit! And I just got Molly goin' good."

"What's it to you?" Gates asked, already knowing the answer but seeing no way to stem the tirade.

"What was his stock trading at on Friday? Eleven forkin' dollars! What'll it be trading at Monday morning? Eleven forkin' cents! An' the whole goddamn exchange'll follow him into the toilet. Always let 'em down gentle. Itsa rule!" Dolby said as if reciting a lofty moral principle.

"Yeah, yeah. You and your rules," Gates said with a barking laugh.

Dolby did have principles of a sort, though when he enunciated them they sounded like anything but. He usually had six or seven shell, or moribund, companies in his stable, but only one company actually under promotion. He'd bought his current play, now called Molly Mines, in the late 1950s to stockpile for a future promotion. For $15,000 he got forty claims and an assay report that showed not a trace of gold but sizable amounts of quartz molybdenite, or molybdenum, a mineral no one had ever heard of and no more valuable than salt.

Years later the unexpected happened. Molybdenum became useful as an alloy in the steel industry. Its base price rose from nothing in the early 1950s to $1.67 a pound in the early 1960s. Dolby heard molybdenum mentioned on the radio several times one day in 1965 and remembered the old assay reports. Dolby never picked up the trick of reading, but part of his secretary's job was to read the business page of the *Western Miner* newspaper and assay reports, in that order.

Molybdenum. Dolby tried out the word a few times but the combination of consonants overpowered his tongue so he gave it up, thereafter steadfastly referring to the mineral as molly.

Dolby renamed the worthless claims Molly Mines Inc. in 1965. Then he commissioned the *Vancouver Sun* newspaper's lead business writer to produce a "tout sheet" boosting molybdenum and mentioning that Molly Mines was exploring a site that already had "strong indications of the presence of the mineral." Dolby distributed a hundred tout sheets to news-papers, newsletters, television and radio stations, and to selected investors.

"It's one forkin' thing to tell somebody somethin's great," Dolby often explained. "And don't get me wrong, that's ninety-five percent of the forkin' sale. But you hafta have something to hand them. Something that looks real. That forkin' seals it."

As further sealant Dolby also slipped the writer a thousand shares of Molly Mines. Three weeks later a sizable feature article fronting the business pages proclaimed molybdenum the "Gold of the Sixties." Toward the end of the article it was mentioned that Molly Mines, a Vancouver Stock Exchange–listed company, was exploring for molybdenum in the vicinity of Williams Lake in British Columbia's interior.

Meanwhile Dolby was busy creating a market out of thin air. This he did by wash-trading—buying and selling shares to himself. Dolby called it "Hungarian magic." Using twenty-six different accounts in eight different firms, all in different names, he eased the stock up from two cents a share to nine cents over a week, where he kept it hovering for ten days until several days of legitimate trading by speculators pushed it to thirteen cents. Dolby then floated it to just over twenty cents, where it stayed for another week until the "Gold of the Sixties" newspaper article catapulted it over fifty cents, all on legitimate buying. As it went up, Dolby unloaded a portion of his own shares. With a little legerdemain Dolby turned a company he'd put together for less than $200,000 into one with a market capitalization of more than $1 million, and he was just getting started.

Over the next eighteen months, Dolby slowly worked Molly into the $3.50 range, where it traded until the previous week when it moved, seem-ingly of its own volition, into the worrisome $4.50 zone. He was able to ease it back down to $3.50 by selling fifty thousand shares.

"If someone buys at three dollars and they lose—that hurts, but not too much," Dolby intoned to Gates. "They don't like it but they'll come back for more. When they buy it at eleven and it crashes, that stings. That stings real bad."

Right now Dolby faced the unusual problem of keeping the share price down. Molly Mines was taking on a life of its own, threatening to push the stock back up over $4 a share. Dolby could live with a four-dollar stock, though he preferred the $3 comfort zone. In over twenty-five years of pro-moting nearly a hundred companies, he'd never allowed a stock to go over $5, not even once.

Macklin doing a bunk would depress the entire market and do exactly what Dolby wanted, but he was certain Molly Mines would slide too far and too fast, panicking investors.

"Dink forkin' weed!" He stomped his foot. "I outta go down to that desert hideout of Macklin's and yank his forkin' balls off!"

"Since when did you get teary-eyed about people losing money?" scoffed Gates.

"Ten forkin' years ago we had two hundred and twenty-seven companies listed on the exchange. Now look! Four forkin' hundred."

Actually there were four hundred and thirty-one, and Gates knew every one, but he wasn't about to correct Dolby when he was in one of his moods.

"They got choice sticking out their ass. Too many choices. Gotta stay competitive. If I let 'em lose too much they'll be lining someone else's pocket. And that," Dolby snorted, sucked, and filled his mouth with mucus, "forkin' chafes my butt." He deposited the mouthful on the sidewalk.

"Meanwhile that prickarolla is down in Arizona with a broad on both ends and one in the middle."

The normally phlegmatic Gates laughed hard enough to cough the cigar out of his mouth. "What do I know? I'm a simple newsletter publisher. Fighting to publish the truth. You guys make the big money."

"Stop, you'll make me cry," Dolby said without a trace of sympathy. "Maybe I should organize a charity drive for ya," he said, peeling off several bills from his roll with a great flourish, then pressing them into Gates's hand.

"Is that all?" Gates said, fingering the bills. "I spend more than that on cigars."

"If ya ain't the richest guy on the exchange I don't know who forkin' is," Dolby shot back. He considered the "simple newsletter publisher" one of the savviest people around, if only because he kept his own counsel.

"You wrong me," Gates demurred, his reptilian features collapsing in on themselves. "I've barely got two dimes to rub together."

"Probably the first two forkin' dimes ya ever made," Dolby said, eyeing Gates's clean but elderly suit. "And I wouldn't be surprised if ya took 'em out of a blind beggar's cup."

Gates's cigar hit the sidewalk again, punctuating a cascade of laughter. "You kill me, Wally! You really kill me." Dolby enjoyed the sight of his friend breaking up so much he almost missed seeing Gates slip the twenties into his pocket.

63

*

Dolby stumbled awkwardly to avoid stepping on a crack. Gates alertly grabbed his arm and they bumped together, almost hugging to recover their balance. At that moment Nathan Wingate, owner of Western Securities and the unquestioned power on the Vancouver Stock Exchange board of directors, hove into view. Behind Wingate bounced Will Barnaby, his young second-in-command.

"Gentlemen! Gentlemen!" Wingate boomed in his deep, hard voice. "What you do behind closed doors, disgusting as it may be, is your own business. But keep it off the street. If you don't stop groping each other, I'm calling the cops."

Wingate didn't miss a stride as he continued on past, but Barnaby giggled so hard Dolby thought he'd piss his pants.

"Happy to provide some cheap entertainment, Nate," Dolby hollered to their retreating backs. "Thinks his shit don't stink," he added to Gates.

"Doesn't Barnaby look like a rabbit?" observed Gates.

Dolby stood with his hand in a theatrically pensive gesture on the side of his drooping cheek. "Not a rabbit," he said slowly, "more like a forkin' weasel, I think. Specially in the face. Kinda snakin' along, isn't he?" he added as Barnaby's unfashionable, pencil-trousered legs churned after the long-striding Wingate.

Wingate was one of those rare men who always seemed bigger and more powerful than they actually were. While Dolby seemed shorter than his five feet and two and a quarter inches Wingate seemed taller than his five feet nine. And while they were similarly overweight, Dolby seemed obese, while Wingate's girth generated an aura of power and force. Dolby appeared bundled in his expensive clothing like a hastily wrapped and awkwardly shaped present. Wingate's hand-stitched suits and perfectly starched shirts hung from his body beautifully, enhancing his image.

"Forkin' prick thinks he owns the world these days and he don't give a hippo turd for anyone else," Dolby muttered darkly. "Guys like me do all the forkin' dirty work and he makes the money."

Gates sighed. Since Wingate had become the undisputed leader of the largest venture capital market in the world, he'd heard Dolby's rant so many times he could recite it by heart.

"If it wasn't for guys like me there wouldn't be a forkin exchange," continued Dolby.

"You're not bellyaching about all the work you do. You're just frosted Wingate has his hand in your pocket."

"Fork yooo."

"Look, it's not so bad that Wingate's brought in all these new rules and regs," argued Gates. "We've got too many companies and too much money invested in the VSE for all the trading and public offerings to be controlled by promoters, like it used to be."

"Hey, doncha lump me in with vultures like Macklin."

"Walter, I'm not comparing you to those assholes, but nowadays we got ten times more promoters running off half-cocked. It's a good thing they've got to run their IPOs through a brokerage house and make their own trades that way too."

"They treat us like we outta be forkin' grateful if they place an IPO, and if they don't it's our forkin' fault 'cause the promotion's lousy, the property's worthless, or some other forkin' thing. And who takes the fall if things go wrong?"

"Wingate brought in the new regs forcing promoters to use brokers, but everyone else voted for them," Gates reminded him.

"Yah! Buncha butt-forkin' sheep!"

Before the rules changed, a promoter like Dolby could apply directly to list a company on the exchange, make an initial public offering of shares, promote the market, and supervise all shares bought and sold. Gates smiled remembering Dolby standing on the sidewalk in the 1950s, selling share certificates right out of his pocket. He'd approach people he didn't know, most of whom thought investing meant buying bonds. But more than half the time Dolby made the sale. Those were the days. Promoters had teams of salesmen going door to door, selling stock certificates printed so colorfully and elaborately they were works of art.

The new rules meant only firms with a seat on the exchange could sell shares to the public, and all initial public offerings had to be funneled through a member firm that undertook to sell the offered shares. Most promoters made their money by selling claims or land they owned to an already listed company, or by selling the below-market-cost founder's shares promoters took when a company was formed. Dolby did all that but he missed the days when he could look someone in the eye, take their money, and hand over the shares—a paper dream.

"Bloodsuckers! It ain't the cut they take and ya goddamn well know it. If them leeches just sucked away at their sales commissions I'd be such a happy man I wouldn't need a hooker to get me off. But when I brought Molly into play an' made a 250,000 share offering, guess whose hairy hole showed up demanding founder's shares? He ain't got no right to founder's shares when I'm the forkin' founder."

Western Securities had become so big that thirty percent of all new share offerings went through his firm. As an additional cost of underwriting the stock, Wingate forced the promoters to kick back a chunk of their own founders' shares. A promoter who gave his firm problems, like releasing positive information without telling Wingate first, could suddenly find himself in a sliding market as Wingate dumped his shares. It pushed promoters like Dolby farther away from the control of their own company.

"What's your beef? So Wingate and the rest of the firms are taking a bite, but you're getting a bigger bite because they can sell way more shares than you ever could. Besides, now promoters are cozy with the brokers, they're going to protect all those illegal accounts of yours if the superintendent of brokers should come calling."

"I gotta better chance o' bein' laid by Brigitte Bardot than that happenin'. The superintendent of brokers and Wingate are so tight you can't see where one begins and the other forkin' ends. No forkin' way Wingate's gonna protect me if the SoB wants information."

"Wingate's never going to blow you off. Some days your trades still account for a quarter of the VSE's volume."

"Yeah, well, I didn't do my bend-over-and-bang-me act for Wingate when Halo Hills Mine din't turn up diddly on the copper assays. So whachoo think Wingate did?"

Gates knew but he let Dolby tell it.

"He forkin' spilled to his pal judges and government bozos, so they dumped before I had time to get my investors out. He was supposed to wait, for fork's sake."

Brokers used to be simply middlemen, holders of accounts for the investing public. In effect, now two kinds of promoters worked the junior market and their goals were not necessarily the same.

"Well, what are you going to do about it?" Gates asked.

"Nothin'," Dolby answered glumly. "Nothin' I can do. But that don't forkin' make it right."

What particularly galled Dolby was Wingate's relationship with Gerald Day, the superintendent of brokers—SoB—responsible for legal matters relating to the VSE. Regulation and enforcement was a collegial affair between the two men.

"He's a friend of mining and loves British Columbia and would do any-thing to help make this province prosperous," Wingate once gushed to the *Northwest Mining* newspaper. "Say a prospector comes into his office and needs a couple of hundred bucks, I'm betting Day will give it to him, because he knows that if this fellow gets out in the field with that two hundred, and two hundred more he gets from someone else, and hits something that's great, it'll do something for B.C., and," he dropped his voice modestly, "maybe I'll get something out of it." His last comment drew a big laugh from the reporter.

The two men were so tight Wingate could get verbal commitment for an underwriting, the issue of new shares, and the company listed on the board before even a scrap of paperwork was completed. The process took everyone else months.

"Pretty forkin' soon there ain't gonna be but one promoter around—Macklin!" complained Dolby, "and one broker—Wingate! An' if ya complain about anything, Wingate slaps another noxious rule on the table for a vote. An' ya can double up your bet the rule ain't gonna benefit people like me."

Dolby's rant conveniently wore down just as they reached the Dockside Café. It was one of Dolby's favorite spots, made more so by the fact that the now ramshackle three-story building cantilevered out over one of the main fishing piers that had once been Konrad von Schaumberg's property. There was a picture of von Schaumberg in a prominent place in the exchange's board room. Dolby never let on to anyone, but if he ever had a chance to be born again to a little more height and a little less girth, no, check that, a lot more height and a lot less girth, he'd like to be modeled after the elegant German.

✳

Waiting in front of the restaurant for Walter Dolby was a man almost as elegant as the fabled von Schaumberg. Cloaked in a buttery-soft, full-length leather trench coat over a monogrammed, heavy silk shirt with long,

up-to-the-moment collar points, and wide-bottomed pants with cuffs was
Dr. Warren Finlayson. On one wrist he wore a heavy gold chain and on the
other a watch costing more than the average car. Dolby forgave the man the
"faggot" jewelry and his obvious manicure—it just seemed right on him.
Though had Dolby known that the immaculate, wavy, blond hair and long
sideburns were permed and dyed, he might not have forgiven that.

Finlayson, physician to Vancouver's rich and famous, was a doctor by
profession and a gambler by avocation. An inveterate penny-stock plunger,
Finlayson bought any story going, winning just often enough to keep his
wallet open.

"Heya, Doc! Slummin'?"

"No, no, not at all," Finlayson responded smoothly. "A pleasure to see
you both this fine morning."

Dolby peered at the doctor's face. "You're lookin' a little peaky."

"I have, uh, a small problem," the doctor said sheepishly.

"Oh, don't forkin' tell me!" Dolby groaned and made as if to pull out his
almost nonexistent hair. "Don't tell me ya hung on to Macklin's stock." One
look at the doctor shuffling his feet like a schoolboy gave him his answer.
"Whadda I tell ya? Whadda I forkin' tell ya? I tol' ya on Thursday to sell that
shit. It got too goddamn high. I didn't know Macklin was gonna skip but a
stock rises that high is just waitin' to fall. How much?" he demanded.

"Thirty thousand," Finlayson said sorrowfully.

Gates let out a long, low whistle.

"How forkin' much?" Dolby repeated sternly.

"Well, actually, fifty thousand and, um, I uh, borrowed the money."

"Ya stupid bastard! Whadda I hafta do, break your forkin' arm before
ya listen to me?"

The doctor would have been disappointed if he didn't get this kind of
rough talk from Dolby.

Dolby had appointed himself the doctor's protector two years earlier,
when his teenaged daughter, Tiffany, while paying a surprising and
unwanted visit in the summer, came down with some sort of woman's
plumbing problem. Dolby was too squeamish to inquire about the details.
Terrified that Tiffany would ask him to take her to the hospital, Dolby
called Finlayson, who arrived at his hotel suite twenty minutes later.

"She'll be right as rain," Finlayson assured Dolby in his silken voice.
"I'm going to run her over to my office and I'll have her back tonight. Just a
few routine tests. Nothing to worry about."

Dolby fled from the hotel suite as quickly as he could, in case either Finlayson or Tiffany asked for his help or decided to get specific. When he returned just before midnight, he sucked in a deep breath before peeking into her room. Tiffany, wavy hair scattered over the pillow, was sleeping peacefully. Dolby was grateful. He'd never been to a doctor himself but he knew they normally didn't make house visits twenty minutes after a telephone call and sure didn't drive patients to their office for tests, especially a fancy-pants like Finlayson.

"What can I do for ya, Doc?" Dolby asked sorrowfully.

"I need to recoup . . ." He drew Dolby to one side. "I've got to replace the money in my wife's trust. She has a meeting with her advisor next month and they'll sniff it out."

"But Doc!" Dolby groaned again. "Dincha think of that when ya bought the forkin' stock?"

"Macklin promised a quick turnaround. Buy at eight-fifty, hold for no more than two days, and then sell."

Dolby sighed heavily. "Two days gave the forker enough time to fly south with your fifty large."

"If you can just give me a heads up on Molly Mines, I can recoup on that."

Dolby let out a long sigh. "How much d'ya already own?"

"Five thousand shares I bought at a dollar. Another five thousand at two dollars. It's selling for around four."

"I know how forkin' much's selling for!" Dolby said with exasperation. "It's my forkin' company! It ain't goin' nowhere for a while, till Macklin's turds fly off the fan."

"So you think it will go down?" The man was so pathetic Dolby felt like kicking him.

"Tell ya what I'm gonna do," Dolby said. "Though with your track record you'd be better to sell everything now. If ya did, you'd put twenty thousand profit in your pocket. That's not too forkin' shabby on a fifteen thousand investment—over six or seven months. A hundred and thirty-three forkin' percent."

Dolby might not have been able to read but he could absorb a page of numbers at a glance and do complicated calculations faster than anyone could wield a calculator.

"But I need more!" the doctor responded, looking less the society physician with every word.

"OK. OK. Don't bust your suspenders and pay close attention. Molly's gonna drop to two-fifty before lunchtime Monday," Dolby said. "What with Macklin gone and all. It'll start down from the bell, so put in your short order first thing for half the shares you own. When she hits two seventy-five, buy the forker back, ya got me? 'Cause I'm going to be buying hard soon as it hits two-fifty. Don't forkin' wait for another quarter in the price. Got it?"

Finlayson bobbed his head happily, relief stretched over his tanned cheeks.

"And the rest of your stock. When it hits three seventy-five again, ya gotta unload her. Got it?"

"Got it. But Walter, don't you think I should hang on to a few shares? Those assay results sound excellent. The newspapers are saying the site could become the largest producer of molybdenum in the world. Then we'd be looking at a takeover by a major . . ."

Dolby gripped the doctor roughly by the padded shoulders of his coat. It was an incongruous sight: the rumpled, stubby stock promoter manhandling the immaculate six-footer.

"Now you forkin' listen to what I'm forkin' telling you," Dolby said, shaking the man heavily to emphasize each word. "There ain't no mine there. Never will be. It's just like pro wrestling, 'cept I make the rules. When I tell you to forkin' get out you get out. Now repeat it after me. Dump at three seventy-five."

"Dump at three seventy-five," the doctor repeated.

"Dump at three seventy-five," Dolby stressed.

"Dump at three seventy-five," the doctor chanted back.

"Ain't no forkin' molly in Molly," Dolby hissed.

"Absolutely not," agreed Finlayson, thanked Dolby, and hurried off.

✳

"He's not going to sell," Gates predicted.

"Nah, he ain't," Dolby agreed sadly. "He never does. He'll short Monday morning, wet his forkin' drawers with the money he makes by lunchtime, buy her back, then hang on till she slides."

"What is that anyway, a new technique of stock promoting?" Gates asked caustically. "Tell the guy the stock is fake?"

"Maybe I stumbled onto somethin' here." Dolby laughed. "The more I told him there weren't gonna be any goddamn mine, the more he got a hard-on for the forkin' stock."

64

✳

"Pass the wine please, dear," Rita Dolby asked her husband, who cursed softly under his breath. Rita was a CC-and-7 girl until she started attending the Sotheby's auctions in New York to pick up a few "items of conversation" for the house. Now meals were accompanied by a crystal decanter filled with red or white swill. Dolby hated the sickly aftertaste, the dry puckering it caused at the back of his throat, and the coating wine left on his tongue. It seemed that the more expensive the bottle the more objectionable it was.

"Yeah, sure," he responded, leaning across the table to slop the scarlet liquid into her heavy Waterford glass. If you could belt the stuff, it might go down better, but it had to be sipped as if he were an old broad taking tea. Dolby stared mournfully at the decanter. Once it had been kept brim-full with bourbon.

To his left, across the trestle-legged quarter-cut oak table, his twenty-year-old daughter Tiffany smirked. "How do you like the claret, Daddy?" she teased. "Don't you think it has a lovely bouquet?"

"Terrific, just terrific," Dolby responded. "Great fork' . . . friggin' bookay. Just great."

Rita'd picked it up at an auction in New York. Bought a whole god-damn case of the stuff. Dolby could have a truckload of his favorite Southern Comfort for the same price.

"It's thirty years old and gets better every year," Rita crooned. "We decline with age but good wine only gets better. Isn't that wonderful?"

Dolby would much rather suck on a thirty-year-old dame than dip his tongue into this stuff. If he drank slowly, maybe he could make the glass last all dinner. Afterward he'd scour out the taste by cracking a fifth when everyone was in bed.

"No more, thanks," he held his hand out. "Gotta keep the gout at bay. 'Sgreat though."

Tiffany cruelly poured his glass to the rim anyway.

"I'm glad you like it, dear," Rita said. "We described your tastes to the man at the auction. He said this vintage would be perfect for you. We should really have cellared it. Still, it is very nice. I'll put down the other bottles until next year."

He'd be delighted to cellar it. All the way to China if he could. And put down. It should be put down all right. Made it sound like she was talking about an old dog. A dog'd have to be dying all right before lapping up any of this.

Rita, the daughter of a prospector, had her "aspirations"—he'd known that from the beginning. It was the only reason she'd looked at him in the first place. Though twenty-five years ago her aspirations were simpler and of a variety that Dolby could understand: stockings you threw out when they laddered, new towels and sheets every year, a house with a balcony—not just a porch—a family, and deference from the man.

Pushing two decades her senior, Dolby had met Rita when he was flush with his first big promotional success. It was 1943, and the American war effort was thirsty for oil. Walter Dolby took over a tiny company on the American Stock Exchange, renamed it Sweet Grass Oil, and set about recruiting the tout sheet writers and phone men who would help it take flight. Tired after a day of building his gossamer castle, Dolby was tucking into an onion-smothered steak when he discovered that the name of his waiter with an Adam's apple the size of a grapefruit was Frederick Joseph Rothschild.

Within two days Dolby made the aspiring song-and-dance man, no relation to the fabled financier, a junior partner and formed F. J. Rothschild and Company Investments. He situated the fledgling company in a subterranean office on Park Avenue, across the street from the monied Rothschilds. The phone crews, working two shifts a day, flogged Sweet Grass Oil stock, playing unmercifully on the bogus Rothschild connection. If an investor seemed to have money but was reluctant, Mr. Rothschild himself was brought to the phone to discuss the company's prospects and assure investors that he had his own money at risk. After two months Dolby closed up shop, paid off Frederick Joseph Rothschild, and, one step ahead of the Securities and Exchange Commission, took the train north to Toronto, with $165,000 in his pocket.

And then came Rita. He'd been in the city a week, spending most nights celebrating at Bangers, a bar in the seedy Yonge Street section of

Toronto popular with the prospecting crowd. Tall, with oversized boobs, she inexplicably attached herself to Dolby, to the lewd delight of his cronies. Willowy, except for the boobs, broad-cheeked in a Nordic kind of way, soft in the mouth and hard in the eyes, Rita Mayfield cut quite a figure in the dim cave frequented by small-time money men, prospectors looking for financing in the city, deal makers, and dead-stock sellers. The latter simply bought defunct shares by the pound, then peddled them in places like Topeka, Moose Jaw, Pocatello, and Dubuque. Places where hopelessness could be found in larger than normal measure, providing a fertile audience for those scattering seeds of future promise.

Quicker than he could say "D-cup," the thirty-nine-year-old promoter was married to the blonde, and within days of the Reno nuptials had become the owner of a three-bedroom house in Toronto's Cabbagetown, a neighborhood of strivers near the heart of the prim-minded city. Dolby never learned how old Rita really was—"much, much younger than you, dear"—and it never occurred to him that she might not actually be blond. Nor did he ever discover what attracted her to his troll-like self. He assumed it was the money. But there was always money around if you knew where to look and had boobs that preceded you into the room, money that came wrapped in a far more attractive package than Walter Dolby. Still, he never questioned an unexpected profit on a stock and he never paused more than a moment or two to analyze his good fortune in the form of Rita Mayfield.

✳

On the eve of their wedding, Rita discussed money with Dolby for the first and last time in their marriage. She had him place $75,000 of his Rothschild score in government bonds in her name and exacted monthly housekeeping money of $1,250, rising five percent every year. With her warm belly pressed against him, she made him promise to deposit twenty percent of every successful "business deal" into her account. And finally, as her hand tightly gripped his manhood, she had him swear that he would never ever ask her for any of the money back.

When Beauregard, the second child, came home from the hospital, the sex stopped.

"We're past all that, dear," his still-luscious wife informed him firmly when Dolby felt the appropriate time had elapsed after the birth for him to assert his rights. Dolby could make a penny stock squeal with pleasure or writhe in pain with the subtlest tweak of the market. But he couldn't budge Rita Mayfield. Filled with black impotence, he raged, got drunk, screwed several women, a couple of them at the same time, and camped in Toronto's Downtown Steam for days at a stretch. But he was beat and he knew it. Rita never referred to the matter again and never inquired about how her husband slaked his considerable sexual urges. Every now and then she allowed him to scrub her pillowy breasts through her clothing, but the minute his hard-on pushed out his trousers, she took his hands, kissed his forehead, and said, "Good night, dear."

Over the years, "dear" was summarily informed of many things: his crude conversation in the house would end, and if he couldn't do a better job with his table manners she "would bring someone in to help him." When Tiffany and Beauregard were in their early teens, she informed Dolby that she had purchased another home. He was welcome to stay in this one but he'd have to pay rent.

A month later, after a trip to British Columbia to inspect prospective mining properties, Dolby signed an indefinite lease with the Sylvia Hotel, a 1912 ivy-clad, brick grand dame on English Bay in Vancouver. With a post-card view around every corner and the streets filled with people who all seemed to come from somewhere else, Vancouver beckoned like a second chance. The world junior mining market was increasingly concentrating in the city that was almost garishly beautiful and unnaturally clean to Dolby's eastern eyes.

Walter Dolby always meant to find a mine; his days of rock banging and hanging out with prospectors had prepared him for it. He told himself that the Sweet Grass promotion and others like it were just little deals to give him seed money. In Vancouver he intended to use the money to buy claims and properties, then start putting geologists on the land to look for gold, silver, copper, or zinc. But Vancouver was like an easy girl at a party. You always meant to stay true to your date but . . . Within a year of arriving in Vancouver, Dolby stopped calling himself a prospector—promoting was a whole lot more fun.

Dolby was invited to return home for family occasions three times a year: Thanksgiving, Christmas, and the children's birthdays, which fell on the same summer day. Each stay was to be one week in length, timing agreed upon in advance. However, this visit and the ensuing torture by claret was out of schedule. He and Rita had been married, if you could call it that, for twenty-five years, and Tiffany decided an anniversary celebration was in order.

She phoned the morning after Morty Macklin skipped town.

"Please, please, Daddy, come to Toronto!" she begged in her best little-girl voice, which always melted him. "I ordered four dozen roses for Rita in your name. We've got candles, and pot roast, and those little potatoes. If you're a good boy, I'll let you win at bridge."

"Can't, doll, gotta big deal cookin'."

"Dad! It's your anniversary. Twenty-five years! You've got to come. Can't the deals wait?" She inhaled breathily before adding: "Mom's talking about moving to the coast. It's been a terrible winter here."

Trouble. Tiffany hadn't called Rita "mom" since she was four years old.

"Moving! Moving here!"

"Maybe. Isn't that exciting?"

Since Rita banished him from the marital bed it had never occurred to Dolby to alter the visitation schedules or arrive uninvited. Once Rita said something, that was it. He hadn't wanted to leave in the first place, but now, a dozen and a half years later, Vancouver and the Howe Street exchange were home. He couldn't imagine sharing that with anyone, even Rita. Not that his wife of sorts ever completely left his mind. Even after children, she still had those great boobs, and though he hadn't seen her thighs in over fifteen years, Dolby suspected they'd give to a squeeze just like they did in days gone by. But Rita moving to Vancouver? He'd have to put the kibosh on that.

So here he was, out of schedule, at the table. He'd been in Toronto for two days and Rita hadn't said a single word about any move. Dolby began to wonder if he'd been conned by his daughter.

This visit was risky and that made him even more tense. He liked to keep his finger on a promotion's pulse at all times, yet Toronto was four thousand miles away from Molly Mines. Despite the fallout from Macklin's debunk—precipitated by an FBI investigation that linked him to a well-known mine salter from Nevada—Molly continued to have a puzzling life of its own. It did drop just long enough for Finlayson to recoup the "borrowed" trust account money. But it quickly rose again. While the index was down nearly twenty percent overall, Molly refused to sink, sticking in the $4.50 zone, even threatening the verboten $5 mark. Dolby sold almost his entire holding, trying to dampen the stock's spirits.

Still it didn't go down, and Dolby didn't have enough stock left to keep the pressure on by selling. By going to Toronto he'd broken one of his cardinal rules: never be farther than a short cab ride away from the exchange when a promotion was still in play. But Dolby thought he had things handled.

Using a variety of his accounts under different names, he'd sold 250,000 shares of Molly Mines short, by far the largest short sale in the history of the exchange. That should cool things down a bit. Big short sales were like a bully with a stick, intimidating the stock downward. On rare occasions Dolby shorted a stock but always made sure he owned enough to cover the short if the stock went up instead of down. Short selling without the collateral of stock in hand was extraordinarily dangerous, because the share price could only go down to zero. On the other hand there was, theoretically, no upward limit, hence no limit on the size of the potential loss if he was forced to buy stock in a hot running market to cover the short.

Dolby was confident of his tactics. A few well-placed rumors and a press release or two, combined with the short sale, should take the wind out of the inflating share price. Dolby sold short between $4.25 and $4.65. When he returned from Toronto he expected to start buying back in the $3 range.

Tiffany's voice percolated into his consciousness.

"Huh?"

"Daddy, you weren't listening! You're daydreaming while I'm trying to tell you my good news."

"Yeah, sweetheart, that's great news," he said, scrambling.

"Well, what do you think I should do?"

"Uh, well, I, uh, I'd do it if I was you, doll."

"But which one?"

"Huh?"

A cross look from Rita focused Dolby's attention. "Run that by me again, will ya, doll?"

Tiffany's laugh tinkled merrily. Dolby's pouchy eyes flicked to her and shot open, the bags beneath and the folds above creating a raccoon circle of flesh. The girl had boobs! Boobs like her forkin' mother. Tiffany caught his look and leaned forward on the table, breasts pressed hard against her forearms so they swelled up her chest. Beauregard, her younger brother, had said exactly nine words all dinner long. As they talked, he covered sheets of paper with clever doodles, but he watched the interchange with amusement. Tiffany was such a manipulative whore.

"Okay, here it is again. Merrill Lynch, Pierce, Fenner and Smith are coming to Wharton and they're interviewing. They're only interviewing six people, and I'm one of the six!"

"Hey, great, baby, fork . . . friggin' great." Dolby wondered what in hell was a Merrill whatever. What a stupid name.

"No, you don't understand! Rio Tinto is also coming. My accounting professor put my name forward and they picked my résumé. They want to talk to me too."

Rio Tinto's name woke Dolby up. One of the biggest mining outfits in the whole goddamn world interviewing his little girl.

"Way to go, baby!" Dolby enthused, careful not to let food spray out of his mouth. He'd been warned about that. "What're they interviewin' ya for?"

"Dad, I've almost got a degree in accounting, remember?"

Dolby thought she was taking some kind of administrative course for supervising a typing pool or somesuch. Accounting. Figures. That's why it took three years! He thought about his daughter's boobs. Accounting— what a waste.

"The head of Rio Tinto's accounting department is a woman, the first in the history of the company. She was in *Time* magazine and she wants to interview me!"

"So what's the problem?" he asked, confused.

"Both interviews are at the same time and they can't be moved. Every-one else is slotted in and they're both on campus for just a day. I have to choose. Which one should I take, Daddy?"

Tiffany spoke as if she expected that either job would be hers.

"Take the Mortle Leach one," Dolby responded promptly. "Woman boss, mining—bad combination."

"Would you care for a glass of port in the library, dear," Rita broke in.

"Ya betcha!" Dolby answered enthusiastically. If anything, port was worse than wine.

"And if you put the ashes in the fireplace, you can have a cigar."

"Thank you, Rita," he said happily, this time with authentic emotion. Normally she forbade him from smoking in the house.

The library both intimidated and bemused Dolby. He was surrounded by thousands of books his money had purchased but he couldn't read. Three times since they'd married Rita moved into a larger house with a bet-ter address and a bigger library. Now she lived in a 5,500-square-foot Rosedale ravine-edge mansion with two stone turrets, located just down the street from the president of the Canadian division of Chase Manhattan. The house had maids' quarters, an indoor swimming pool, marble floors, massive mahogany doors, and dark wainscoting everywhere. More forkin' wood than a forkin' forest, Dolby thought as he walked to the library. The books had been purchased by the lineal foot and arranged according to the

Dewey Decimal System, Rita told him. He knew of Huey and Duey, of course, but he'd never heard of any decimal system.

"Perhaps we could play some cards," his wife suggested. Thanks to his memory and his facility with numbers Dolby was a whiz at cards. At Rita's insistence, he'd become a dab hand at bridge in their early years together, but he still preferred the unbridled sneakiness and aggression of hearts, where it was every man for himself, or five-card-stud with its *mano-a-mano* confrontations.

Dolby was just dealing out the first hand when a maid deferentially entered the room.

"Please, marm, there's an urgent phone call for the mister."

"I'm sure you'd like to take that in your den, dear," said Rita, who liked to maintain the fiction that this was still Walter Dolby's home. His "den," a two-story trek from the library, was another book-lined, leather-uphol-stered room that gave Dolby the creeps. The chair creaked alarmingly when he sat down, and the thick velvet curtains made him feel like he was in a funeral parlor.

Dolby's brow furrowed into crevasses as he stumped up the stairs, his feet making no sound in the velvety-plush, forest-green carpet. When he was away, he called his floor trader and his secretary three times a day—just after the opening, at lunch, and just before close. The office never called him. Never. Seven-thirty at night, eastern time. The Vancouver Stock Exchange, which shut down at two-thirty Pacific time, had been closed for two hours. What could be serious enough to warrant a call? Dolby perked up. Maybe another president had died!

When Kennedy was shot in 1962, the VSE, alone among the world's stock exchanges, stayed open at Nathan Wingate's insistence. While the panic-stricken public unloaded everything, Wingate calmly bought. Dolby heard he'd netted over a million as the markets sprang back within days. Dolby himself used the opportunity to take back controlling positions in two of his companies—one a Nova Scotia titanium prospect, the other owning a raft of claims in Mexico.

"Walter, thank God I got you!" Harley Moser, his young accountant-assistant-gofer, sounded as if he was teetering on the edge of hysteria.

"What's the forkin' matter? You swallow a canary or something?"

"It's gone crazy! The market's gone crazy! Molly Mines has gone crazy! I tried to do what you told me but I couldn't stop it . . ." The man ended with what distinctly sounded like a sob.

"The stock's dropping, so what?" growled Dolby. "How much? Did ya start buying back at the price I gave you? It don't matter if it drops more. She'll come back on my buying."

"Walter! You don't understand!" Moser said between sobs. "Molly's gone through the roof!"

At that point Moser broke up and Walter couldn't get another word out of him. Alarmed, he called Gates.

"Brace yourself, Wally. This is bad, very bad."

"How in forkin' hell could the stock go up! I'm in gawdfersakin' Trono fer chrissakes. And I for sure as forkin' hell didn't release any goddamn information."

"Molly went from $5 to $19 during the first hour of trading. Closed at $31.20. I wouldn't be surprised if it opened at $40 tomorrow."

Dolby's voice grew cold. This couldn't be happening. No stock on the VSE did that, not even the real operations. "What in hell?"

"At the open, Wingate crossed an order, a hundred thousand share order at market, and another twenty thousand an hour later. Molly was a rocket after that! Buying came over the phone for the first hour—Los Angeles, Amsterdam, New York. Someone had information. I called all over trying to figure out what info they were buying on." Gates drew a breath.

Dolby boggled. Wingate never bought at market, much less publicly. Canny traders always bought and sold quietly, only alerting the market as to who was behind the moves when their position was solidified and they were set to take advantage of the rise or fall of the stock.

"Huh!" he grunted, at a complete loss for words.

"His company was doing most of the buying."

Dolby could see Wingate's bulk shouldering aside the other floor traders, his booming voice overriding the din. "Anything else?" he asked dully. Nothing in his experience had prepared him for a stock getting so far out of hand.

A long pause. "Word on the street is that Molly hit a motherfucker lode of molybdenum! Wingate apparently got the assay results."

Dolby sucked hard on his cigar. Gates never, ever swore.

"How in forkin' hell did that asshole get *my* assay reports before I did?" Dolby spoke slowly, feeling as if he would explode.

The door opened a crack and Tiffany poked her head in.

"Rita wants to finish the game."

"In a minute!" he barked. The door shut quickly.

"So, what happened?" Dolby asked impatiently.

"Well," Gates sounded amazed in spite of himself. "The darn sample comes up roses. Loaded to the eyeballs with molybdenum. 'Mine it with a number ten shovel' is what Erickson the geologist said. Best I can figure, the geologist thought you'd bury it, so he took the report to Wingate, because Western underwrote the IPO. Of course, maybe Erickson was in cahoots with Wingate all along."

A shudder traveled up Dolby's spine. The shape of things was starting to come clear. "So, shithole Erickson takes the latest assays, the ones I ain't seen, to Nathan Wingate, who then cuts a deal with a major mining company, which tells him to buy up the goddamn stock any way he can? An' before he does this last little forkin' maneuver, he makes sure him and a few favored clients buy into the forkin' thing big time. That about right?"

"That's why your stock was acting up all last week," Gates responded. "Why it wouldn't go down."

There was a long silence. The only way Gates knew Dolby was still on the line was the wet sound of him working the cigar.

"After all these years I found a real forkin' mine and it ruint me," Walter finally said with a gurgle.

"How ruint are you?" Gates asked, unconsciously mimicking Dolby's speech.

"Hunnert percent. I'm up $3.4 million on the promotion right now. I woulda spent seventy-five percent of that bringing the stock back down. But I guess I won't be doin' that now. The shorts are gonna murder me."

"That big short was yours?" Gates asked quietly. A grunt was his only reply.

✳

Dolby easily did the math in his head. Covering the 250,000 short-sold shares at $30, the last trade, would cost a staggering $7.5 million. But from what George said it was likely to open at $40 making the loss $10 million. There was no way he could cover even half of that. He was purely and simply ruined.

"You got anything put away?"

Dolby wondered if Gates was worried about getting hit up for a loan.

"Not nearly enough to make this right."

"What about the house there?" He'd always wondered about Dolby's relationship to the blond beauty, but Dolby never spoke of it.

"Rita owns it."

"Are you clean?"

Gates was asking if Dolby had done anything clearly illegal that could be pinned on him, like taking money out of the company treasury or obviously wash-trading. When someone was down on the market, dirty secrets had a way of getting out.

"Just the usual," Dolby said, referring to the wash-trading every promoter engaged in with his nominee accounts to move the stock up. In the case of Molly he'd needed very little of it, as the stock had its own buoyancy. "I held back a couple of the first drilling reports a few weeks but that's it. You know me, I never monkey with the companies."

"Walter," Gates said quietly, "if I'd known what was going on . . . I would have told you."

"I know, George. I know. Ya got class. Not like some. Not like some."

"Wingate."

"Yah, that forker!" he sputtered angrily. "He din't have to box me like that. Bastard knew I was short. Hell, his company held most of the short! It wouldn't a hurt no one if he'd given me the word. Coulda left me some room to maneuver. That wouldn't a hurt no one."

"What're you going to do?"

"Nuthin'," Dolby answered gloomily. "Suppose I could take outta contract on Wingate." He laughed hollowly. "But I don't got the dough. 'Least not anymore."

Dolby's head felt light as he returned to the library, and his feet seemed to be having trouble finding the carpet. He dropped into his chair at the games table and, without looking any of them in the eye, played eight hands of kill-or-be-killed contract bridge.

"What's wrong, Daddy?" Tiffany asked when Rita left for bed and Beauregard took off with some of his long-haired, coffee-house friends. "They're not hippies," he assured his father with a little smile.

"What makes you think something's wrong?" Dolby growled.

"You're more quiet than usual. Even around Rita you usually have more to say, and you didn't once tease Beau about his art or his friends."

"Aaah, belly's buggin' me, and tonight I gotta sleep in that guestroom bed with all that fluffy shit Rita piles on top!"

"And," Tiffany shook her head, indicating her disbelief, "you're having a little trouble keeping track of the cards. You sluffed the wrong card twice and you finessed when you didn't have to. What gives?"

"Anyone else catch on?"

"No," she said with an edge of criticism. "They live in a different world. They're not like you and me."

"It's nuthin' I can't forkin' handle, kiddo," Dolby said jovially, forgetting his promise not to swear. "Got a bad spell coming is all. Business. No reason to spoil everyone's good time."

65

✷

"Cocksucker!"

Dolby's breath rattled across the room.

"Lousy, stinkin' forker! No good, cheatin' sumbitchin' cocksucker!"

On and on he went until the cursing dried up on his tongue in a mash of incoherency. Harley Moser cowered by the battleship-gray, metal desk Dolby had used since his first VSE company went public. George Gates sat on a cracked wooden bench, his shoulders so slumped he appeared to be almost doubled in half.

Walter Dolby wasn't as clean as he'd thought. He'd left Moser trading authority over $200,000 in his personal account and careful instructions on how to spend it to keep the stock trading smoothly. Moser ran through the $200,000, desperately trying to cover the shorts as the stock shot up and then, on his own initiative, took another $100,000 out of the company treasury when the stock kept rising.

The superintendent of brokers got tipped off and came down hard, threatening to put the young man in jail for withdrawing money from a publicly listed company without the authority of the board of directors. The Royal Canadian Mounted Police fraud squad interrogated the terrified Moser for three hours, making it clear that it was Walter Dolby they really wanted. Even so, Moser didn't give Dolby up. When he returned to Vancouver, Dolby quickly stepped in, telling the RCMP that he had personally ordered the withdrawal. "Look, kid," he told the distraught young man. "A forkin' conviction'd screw ya. I'm already ruint."

Since the VSE opened in 1907, no charge had ever been laid for misuse of company funds. In the old days, the promoters ran the companies and the treasury, and these days the underwriting broker did, in conjunction with the promoter. In most cases the company treasury was just used like another trading account. If he pleaded guilty to the charge, Dolby anticipated he'd get off with a wrist slap and stave off any further investigation—then he could start dealing with his staggering losses on his short sale.

"It is important to send a message to the people who entrust their savings to publicly listed companies that we will stand on guard for them," Gerald Day, the superintendent of brokers, solemnly intoned to the press upon announcing a long list of charges against Dolby, including fraud, theft, and wash-trading.

The wrist slap Dolby expected turned into a mallet blow to the head. Despite the quick guilty plea "to save everyone time and money," an RCMP investigation, which took remarkably little time, came up with proof of wash-trading through the discovery of Dolby's nominee accounts at Western Securities. That information could only have come from Wingate. The VSE chairman immediately pushed through bylaws making the opening of nominee accounts by member firms an infraction meriting suspension from the Exchange.

Dolby began to laugh—low, hard belches of laughter. His ballooning red cheeks and the tears running down his face made him a particularly terrible sight. Neither Gates nor Moser could ever remember him laughing. Dolby had a leering grin, and occasionally a strangled cough of mirth escaped him, but no more. They looked at each other as Dolby roared on.

"Ya gotta say, it's forkin' funny," he said when he finally wound down. "I got a nice little promotion goin' on a piece of forkin' moose pasture with a nice little history of rock bangin' an' even a forkin' mineral show on the site. Everything's as legit as it forkin' gets. We dig a little, drill a little, send out the tout sheets, sell a little stock, move a little equipment around, massage the market, an' just as we're ready to go home on her, we goddamn find some forkin' mineral no one give two shits about ten years ago."

Dolby wiped his eyes and sighed deeply.

"An' here's the real funny part. Everyone forkin' finds out before me, King Stupido!"

"No one could have guessed that Nathan Wingate was going to shaft you like that."

Dolby shook his head vigorously, the wattles of his cheeks making a faint slapping noise.

"Nah! Don't say it, George. I shoulda seen it coming. I got sloppy, overconfident. Left town with a geologist on the site and the stock gettin' hot. Sure, sure I coon't have known there'd be so much molly-forkin'-dumdum in the goddamn ground. But if I'd been here I coulda controlled things. Wingate did what he always does, go for the throat. And I let it happen."

✳

Seven counts of security violations and two counts of fraud and theft netted Dolby twenty-eight months in jail. A week before the conviction he declared bankruptcy, owing more than $5 million.

Newspapers in Toronto, San Francisco, Denver, and New York churned out exposés of the sleazy world of stock promoters concentrated on "the wild, unregulated streets of the world's largest penny-stock market." The duped and swindled appeared like worms after a rain, mournfully detailing their losses. "I am a mining investor," proclaimed a German plunger. "I placed my money in good faith with companies having excellent records of exploration. I fully expected a mine to result." Dolby scoffed loudly when Gates read him the sanctimonious quote.

"Them krauts! Jeeesus!" Dolby pawed at his brow. "The only good kraut was that Count von Schom-whatever. You know the one that got tossed for spying."

Dolby gazed off in the distance as if contemplating the long-dead German. "I don't think that count was a forkin' spy. Whattaya think, George?"

"I don't know, Walter. You never really understand what makes people do things."

"Yah. Yer right on that. I always knew Winbag was an asshole but I didn't peg the pecker for a lying, thievin', backstabbin' jerk-off." Dolby glanced at the magazines and newspaper clippings Gates had in his hand. "More bad news?"

"More of the same, I'm afraid."

Dolby figured prominently in many accounts, which variously dubbed him a "multinational bucket-shop operator" or a "stock-market bottom feeder." Many of the stories were written by journalists he'd hired over the years to create his tout sheets. Somewhere they'd even dug up a widow who'd lost her life savings as a result of Dolby's promotions, and the general tenor was that he and his ilk should be banished from trading everywhere and forever.

A particularly galling story, which referred to Dolby as a "crude scam artist," included a quote from the chairman of the VSE, Nathan Wingate: "If venture capital on this continent is going to grow, we've got to clean out the bad guys, the denizens of the gutter, who give it a bad reputation. There's no place on this exchange for the likes of Walter Dolby."

Just before he was to deliver himself up to the jail, Walter Dolby received a note from Rita. It was terse and to the point:

Walter,

Dear, in light of recent events, you will no longer be returning to Toronto for family get-togethers.

As always, Rita

"Of course, I'm not coming home for forkin' get-togethers," Walter puzzled to George who'd read him the letter. "I'm going to forkin' jail. Don't she realize that?"

"All too well, I'm afraid, Walter," George sighed. "All too well."

✳

"Hi, Daddy."

"Jeeesus, Mary, and Joseph! Whattaya doin' here?"

"Nice to see you too."

Tiffany leaned across the scratched wooden table and dropped an armload of newspapers. Her scalloped neckline gaped slightly, and the tanned flesh swelled out. Those boobs! As fine as her mother's, Walter thought, unable to keep from staring at his daughter's well-presented set.

"I cut out all the stock pages so you could read the numbers and charts. This one's from San Francisco. It covers Denver and Amsterdam as well."

Dolby had been called from his job in the prison tuck shop for an unexpected visitor. Seeing his daughter's round, shining face clutched at him and for one horrified moment he thought he was going to cry. He hadn't seen either of his children since that night in Toronto, nor did he expect to. That was almost a year and a half ago.

"How're you doing, Daddy?" Tiffany's normally sharp, strong voice was low and soft.

"Hey, hey, it ain't so bad. I got off KP real quick an' they pretty much let me go where I want. I guess they figger a fat, old pig like me couldn't escape if they gave me a week's head start."

Tiffany smiled. She wasn't beautiful in the traditional sense. Her round face gave her a bit of a pouty look and her eyes were small, like her father's. But she had great welcoming lips that, when spread in a smile, made her look genuine and open. And her body was tall and elegant, set off by the prow of her breasts. A striking package. Men looked, women remembered.

"What do you do with yourself?" she asked.

"Tradin', tradin'. Like always. Cigs for socks, gum for chocolate. I had the market cornered in cigs from playin' cards, then no one would play me anymore 'cause I won all the time. I was off limits, like some kinda commie. But I'm doin' okay tradin'. Ya know, stuff like that."

Dolby was babbling, which he never did. Tiffany's surprise visit unsettled him. He'd never felt embarrassed or ashamed in his life, but he did now. He was aware of his stained prison-issue garb, his four-day beard, his fatness.

"Great, Daddy, great."

Merrill Lynch, Pierce, Fenner and Smith had hired her and, bowing to her persuasiveness, made her the clerk in the firm's just opened two-person Vancouver office. The junior exchanges (never called penny-stock anymore) were thriving all over North America and ML, P, F and S decided they wanted a piece of the action.

Dolby was happy she'd moved to Vancouver. The feeling surprised him.

"So, they gonna make ya a vice president or somethin'?" he asked her on her second visit.

"The vice presidents of the firm fill an entire page," she scoffed, "and not one of them's a woman. I think I'd have to bang the chairman to even get a sniff of it."

Dolby winced at her language.

"Oh well, itsa good job, ain't it?"

"Sure, but I don't think I'll stay long. I'd like to run my own business."

"Not many women run businesses," Dolby said dubiously. "You'd be better off sticking where you are."

"You were never happy working for someone else," she responded pointedly.

"Yah, but I'm a guy."

"Oh Daddy," Tiffany sighed. "When are you going to catch on? There isn't anything men can do that women can't do just as well. It's almost the seventies. Don't you know about women's liberation?"

"You can pee standing up?" Dolby sniggered.

Ignoring him, Tiffany asked, "Have you heard about the old Morton-Wiles brokerage firm changing hands?"

"Yah, George mentioned somethin' about it. So what?"

"Word is a woman's buying it," she said.

"Never happen. No woman could survive in that shark tank," Dolby said about the owners of the VSE's sixty-two seats. "They'd put her out of business in ten minutes."

"You may be surprised," she said mildly. "Times have changed."

✳

"How'd he seem?" George Gates was folded against the door of the pale-blue Buick.

"Good. Still Daddy and still fat."

Gates laughed.

"But something was weird about him," Tiffany puzzled, hitching up her incredibly short, incredibly tight leather skirt to make it easier to drive the car.

"What kind of weird?"

"I don't know. Something different but I just can't put my finger on it."

The car was pulling out through the gates of the prison's outer yard when Tiffany slammed on the brakes, sending Gates nose-first onto the dashboard.

"I've got it!"

"And I've got a nosebleed," said Gates, touching his tender tip gingerly.

"He didn't swear!"

"Huh?"

"He didn't swear. Not once. Not forkin' once," she said, doing a passable imitation of his favorite word.

"I've known your father a long time and I don't think I've known him to go five minutes without swearing. No, make that five seconds."

"Even when Mom's on the warpath, he can hardly help himself. It was unnatural."

"He has been a bit strange lately," Gates reflected. "He hasn't even been interested in the stock market. Usually he wants every scrap of gossip. Maybe he's sick."

"Never been sick a day in his life," Tiffany responded flatly. "But something's not right. Not one 'forkin'' in thirty minutes. Something's not right."

With six months remaining in Dolby's sentence, Tiffany visited the New Westminster prison fortress several more times. Each time they spoke only briefly about the market or exchange business. Tiffany tried to talk to him about her new job but she could tell Dolby wasn't interested.

✳

Seven days before Dolby was due to be released, Tiffany came swaying through the door marked VISITOR FACILITIES. ALL BAGS MUST BE CHECKED OR YOU WILL RISK PROSECUTION.

"Hi, Daddy, what's the big surprise?"

He called her the night before, demanding she drive to the Fraser Valley jail the next day. She'd been getting more and more worried about him. No swearing, and recently he'd quit smoking. What next, religion? Or was he getting ready to tell her he had a brain tumor? No, he looked as puffed up as a pouter pigeon. No bad news today.

"Siddown," he ordered. "Close your eyes."

When Tiffany opened her eyes, a bespectacled Mr. Toad of Toad Hall sat in front of her—reading a book. *A book.* It took a few moments to take it all in. The toad was her father, Walter Dolby—with a real book, no dirty pictures that she could see, in his lap. He held up his hand, silencing her before theatrically adjusting his glasses.

"In Ontario many of the mines were discovered by itinerant (he pronounced it "iterant") prospectors with no formal training, as opposed to professional geologists." He tilted the glasses forward to catch his daughter's reaction. "That's me all over, iterant."

She was dumbfounded, her smallish eyes filling her face. "How . . . what?" she sputtered.

"When they checked me into this hotel, they gave me a complete medical examination. First time I've ever been looked at by a doctor. And I'm not gonna tell you all that they did," he squirmed uncomfortably on the chair. "I'm a hunnert percent a-OK 'cept I can't see worth a damn. Nearsighted and weak eye-muscles. Din't even know there's muscles in the eye. New glasses, back to school, and now I've read three books," he added proudly.

"Daddy, that's fantastic! All these years! Can you imagine what you might have accomplished if you'd been able to read?"

"Probably something pretty boring," Walter Dolby said after a moment's consideration.

PART XI

Tiffany
Dolby

66

✳

1966

Vancouver Island Airport

Eighteen-year-old Tiffany Dolby adored Vancouver from the moment she stepped on the tarmac of the Sea Island runway. Only in Vancouver, where beauty was in such abundance, could an idyllic island in the mouth of the Fraser River be squandered on an airport. It was one of those sparkling, newborn days unique to the land of Manto and Gitsula. Everything from the mountains to the wide holly and rhododendron hedges stood out like a 3-D comic strip with colors so bright and contrasts so strong they actually hurt the eyes. Vancouver spread out below the frame of the northern mountains and along the Fraser River and the deep bays of the Pacific shore like a barely tolerated guest. In other cities she knew—Toronto, New York, Boston, Miami—the hand of man was so entrenched in the jungle of pavement, parking lots, office towers, and factories, it seemed as if it were always so. Not Vancouver. Nature owned the land and no amount of concrete and glass could overwhelm the raw spirit of mountain, rock, forest, ocean, and river.

Tiffany took a long, hard, gulping breath. The air was so clean and velvety she found herself salivating. Over her shoulder Mount Baker loomed so clearly she half-raised her arm as if to touch it.

"It's all within *my* grasp," she whispered as she walked from the plane to the terminal building. Blocky wedge-heels smacking firmly against the asphalt, she felt excitement growing with every step. Something about this place spoke to her, lodged in her belly, warming her. Her hand went unconsciously to her wide hipster belt and she pressed the buckle into her stomach. The city felt like a great meal, one that left you longing for another mouthful.

Tiffany Dolby had escaped from Toronto and her inane Rosedale girlfriends who talked of nothing but boys, the next school dance, spring break in Florida, and their cottages in the Muskoka Lakes north of the city. Their biggest adventures were Saturday-night safaris downtown to watch the Yorkville hippies smoke pot and chant love songs. Sometimes they ventured farther into the heart of the city and hung out on the sleazy strip along Yonge Street, the boys taking turns at the peep shows, but somehow it all seemed so tame, as if scripted for a movie. There was nothing tame about this city. Tiffany hugged herself, thinking how she ended up here.

As a graduation present, Rita had signed her up for a summer-long European tour chaperoned by a hip, young English teacher who would lecture them about the art and culture of the countries they would visit. Part of the package were weekly prep sessions at different students' homes with slide shows of important sights. Every now and then the teacher threw in a naughty slide of topless women or men in tiny bathing suits on a beach in the south of France. At one session, where the chatter about history and culture started to sound like fingernails screeching on blackboard, Tiffany escaped to the guest washroom with an attached coatroom. She amused herself by pawing through her fellow students' belongings until she happened upon the teacher's jacket and macramé shoulder bag. Inside Tiffany found her ticket to freedom—a bong pipe and a tightly wrapped foil package of hashish.

In mid-June, just before the prom, Tiffany handed the teacher a folder of letters, all addressed to her mother. "I want you to mail these from Europe," she stated. "There's enough for one a week."

"What are you talking about?" the woman frowned. She had been voted the grooviest teacher in the school, but Tiffany was one student who seemed immune to her youthful charisma.

"It's simple," Tiffany said. "I'm not going with you and you're going to cover for me."

"That's silly," the teacher said, aiming for a light tone. "Of course you're going, Tiff, sweetie. Your mother has paid."

"She might not have paid if she'd known about this," Tiffany drawled, handing over another folder, this one full of photographs. Pallor overtook the woman's outdoorsy glow. There were a dozen photos of her opened purse with the pipe clearly visible, and several more of her carrying the purse, looking furtive.

"You little sneak! When did you do this?"

"What does it matter?" Tiffany shrugged.

"What are you going to do?" the woman rallied. "Turn me in? The police will laugh at you!" She opened her purse. "Gosh, officer! I don't know what you're talking about but here's my purse."

"The police won't be necessary," Tiffany responded airily. "The mothers of the girls on the trip ought to be enough. And when I tell them you tried to sell me some you'll never chaperone another trip, and I wouldn't be at all surprised if you lost your job."

✻

Tiffany was charmed by the beautiful, slightly shabby old hotel where her father lived. The beach was steps away, freighters were anchored out in English Bay waiting for a berth in the harbor, with sailboats tacked around them. Walter Dolby's face flushed and drained several times before he managed to speak. Tiffany thought he'd have a heart attack.

"Whatcha doin' here, doll?" he finally managed, pulling a paisley dressing gown with silk trim tightly around him. "You're supposed to be in Europe!"

Tiffany peered past him into the suite, where a tall, thinnish bottle-blonde with overlarge breasts made no attempt to cover her nakedness.

"Let me guess," the woman said brightly. "You're the daughter."

"And you are?" Tiffany asked, trying very hard not to explode with laughter.

"Crystal. The secretary," the woman responded.

"I'm Tiffany," she strode in, holding out her hand. Behind her she could hear Dolby making gulping noises. "Crystal, is it? Isn't that nice— Tiffany and Crystal—we're all precious here, aren't we?"

✻

After a couple of days of seeing the sights—polar bears and timber wolves at the Stanley Park Zoo, the world's greatest view from the Grouse Mountain ski lift, totem poles, the swinging bridge across Capilano Canyon, picturesque Gulf Islands, acres of bold West Coast Indian art—and several dinners at a floating restaurant specializing in crab, clams, and fiddley little things he couldn't even name, Dolby, to their mutual relief, handed Tiffany over to George Gates.

"Keep her busy, will ya?" he begged. "I don't know what to do with her and I can't have her forkin' hangin' around. Shit!"

"Exactly what am I supposed to do with her?"

"You've got two granddaughters, for chrissakes! What do you do with them?"

"Nothing," Gates said simply. "Their mother won't let me near them."

"C'mon, ya gotta forkin' help me out here!"

✳

After following Gates around for a week and helping him assemble his daily news sheet, Tiffany put it to him.

"Dad's not a financier, is he?"

"Oh no, no, no, I wouldn't say that," Gates replied quickly. "He's a financier right enough. He, um, provides financing to get companies going. It's a very important job."

"You know what I mean. He's not like a banker or anything, is he?"

"True, you couldn't call him a banker, but," Gates added quickly, "he has a very important role here in Vancouver."

"He sells stock, doesn't he?" Tiffany said, peering triumphantly out from underneath her heavy bangs. "I guessed that years ago. But he's not a broker. He's more like those carneys at the fairs getting people to throw balls into holes hoping to get the big panda bear."

"That's far, far too simple," Gates said earnestly, though he thought Tiffany came as close to describing what Dolby did as anyone.

"Only everyone knows that some of the balls are too big to go through the holes, but Daddy somehow talks them into playing anyway."

Tiffany kept probing and guessing until Gates finally admitted the obvious. Why Rita insisted on keeping Dolby's profession from his children he had no idea, but now that the story was out he could at least go back to business. It was impossible to do his job without spending hours on the trade floor, on the street, and around the bars frequented by the Howe Street crowd. Tiffany couldn't have had a better guide to the penny-stock world. Though Gates had never been directly involved in a single company, he had been a close observer since his early teens, when he started as a runner and advanced to marking boards on the stock-market floor.

"I'm not smart enough to be a promoter," he told her. "Nor, to tell the truth, brave enough. Not by half. What Walter does takes balls."

Gates, whom she called Uncle George to his secret, reptilian delight, took her to the trading floor to watch the action. It was frenetic; the pushing, shoving, shouting, and furious deal-making. By day's end the floor was knee-deep in crumpled order sheets, and you could smell armpits from one end of the trade room to another. Tiffany loved it all, not just the sheer, testosterone-laced, addictive energy of it, but also the plotting and the gossip that often went long into the night.

It was also the first time she met Nathan Wingate. She watched him cow the other traders when he fired a young runner who'd accidently stepped on his shoe. From the reaction of the traders it was clear that this wasn't a singular event. Later, when Gates introduced her, Wingate pointedly stared at her chest as he patted her shoulder. "It's nice to meet a Dolby who doesn't drool when they talk! Give my best to your father."

"What a jerk! He acts like he owns the whole world."

"Near enough, my dear, near enough," Gates said.

"What's his problem with Dad?"

"Wingate hates Walter because he won't do things his way," George said solemnly. "Since he became the big cheese around here, most of the big initial public offerings go through him, with smaller bits parceled out to other firms. It pisses him off that your father places his underwritings wherever he wants."

"But Dad must make him lots of money, with all the trading he does and the companies he brings to the exchange?"

"True," said Gates, again taken aback at how quickly Tiffany picked up on the workings of the market. Even if another firm did the underwriting, Wingate took up large blocks of it to offer to his own clients, usually a bit below the market. And that generated trading commissions. But the firm that did the initial underwriting got stock options as part of the package, fees from the promoter, plus sales commissions. Missing out on even a little piece of the pie annoyed Wingate.

"Wingate's not Walter's favorite person either," added Gates. "But they need each other. When Walter's got a promotion going, he generates a big chunk of the trading volume."

"Come on, Uncle George," Tiffany tugged at his arm. "Let's hit a few bars and go fish." Gates laughed at her use of his phrase. Whenever anyone asked him what he was doing he inevitably said "fishing"—fishing for rumors, gossip, information, scoops.

"Your father won't be too happy."

"What Daddy doesn't know won't hurt him," she declared.

✳

Tiffany loved Walter's run-down office in a yellow-brick building just down from the VSE on Howe Street—the dented and scratched metal desk, the battered file cabinets, an old Remington on the wall, and even Crystal.

"Your dad's an OK guy," Crystal said, watching Tiffany prowl around one day when Dolby was at the Exchange. "Little shy on manners but . . ."

she shrugged, rolling her Mary Quant–decorated eyes to the ceiling, lower lashes drawn down almost to her cheekbones, "I seen worse."

"Kind of a dumpy little office for a financier," Tiffany observed.

"Yeah, well there's financering and financering, you know."

Crystal picked at her cuticle. She had great difficulty believing this tall, hard-looking girl had any connection to what was hanging between Walter Dolby's legs.

"Say, what's the wife like anyhow?"

Tiffany fixed Crystal with an appraising gaze.

"Trade?"

"For what?"

"You tell me, I tell you."

The kid was a bold one. Crystal had a mind to smack her down. Then again, information was worth something. Every now and then she slid into the leather seats at the Gastown Grill on the waterfront and passed along a snippet or two to a broker or another promoter. Just a small piece over-heard from Dolby's loud conversations in return for a dime pack of hash or a fancy dinner with all the trimmings.

"What do you wanna know?"

"Everything. Anything you can think of—from a woman's perspective, you know. I want to know how this place works."

"Why?"

Tiffany had inherited her father's lack of introspection but this much she knew. "Because it feels right. This," she waved her arm around the office. "That," she pointed toward the Stock Exchange building. "The peo-ple. Everyone's willing to take a chance here. It's like life is just beginning. In the East, seems like everyone is planning their retirement as soon as they graduate from high school."

"Maybe we should go get a drink," Crystal said with a smile. "Walter won't be back for hours."

✳

At the end of her third week in Vancouver, while losing her virginity to a broker she'd met at a downtown bar, Peter something, Tiffany made her first penny-stock buy. It was a bust every which way: she lost every penny of the $400 investment and the broker shot off almost before he started.

"Better to lose four hundred now than ten thousand later," Gates chortled when she told him about the stock, not the other. "You got taken on an end sell. This guy brings in new buyers once the promoter, his own company, and his clients are either out or shorting. It's another way of keeping the market going. Hell, the bad news is usually already published. I put out the release two weeks ago that the company took a "drilling break." That's street talk for nothing showed in the assays and nothing's going to. But most people don't read them, or don't understand. They just rely on their broker to tell them when to buy or sell. He figured you wouldn't be back, so he reeled you in and made a little commission for himself."

Peter sold her a dead stock but gave her a live baby. Hence the emergency call to Dr. Finlayson for what her father thought were women's plumbing problems. While Dolby thought she was having tests at the hospital, the doctor relieved her of the problem.

With only a week left in the summer, Tiffany made her move. Crystal had tipped her off that Dolby was assembling his "bucket brigade"—a dozen odd characters, most of whom he'd known for decades, to man the phone lines in a downtown basement, making calls to "flyers," people who played the junior market.

"Daddy?" she asked one afternoon after shrimp sandwiches at the Dockside Café. The two of them were there with Gates. Dolby had what he always had, three eggs "lookin at ya," hash, extra grease, three sides of bacon, and double toast, which he plastered with Marmite. "I want in."

"Whattya talkin' about?" Dolby demanded.

"I understand you're about to run a market," she said blithely, using the vernacular of the street.

"Whattya mean?" Dolby sputtered, his face developing that ripe-apple hue. "You know, I'm into mortgages and stuff. Boring forkin' money, that's all."

Tiffany leaned over and whispered in his ear, so close the hair on his fleshy lobes tickled her lips.

"That's a load of bullshit. You're a stock promoter. You wouldn't know a mortgage if it up and bit you on the ass."

Dolby shot back in his seat. His hand pawed at the grease on his chin. He hadn't felt so panicked since Rita kicked him out of the house.

"Says who?"

"Crystal, Nathan Wingate, dozens of people," she said. "And oh yes, Uncle George here."

"Unca forkin' George?" Gates looked like he'd swallowed his cigar as Dolby rounded on him.

"Don't be cross with George, Daddy," she admonished her father. "He was just doing what I wanted. Besides, you left me all alone. What was I supposed to do?"

"I was very busy with, uh, business," said Dolby guiltily.

"She's very hard to say no to," Gates said sheepishly.

"Well, I'm forkin' saying no. No, forkin' no. Stock promotion ain't no place for a woman, and besides Rita will kill me if she finds out!"

"That's where you're wrong, Daddy. Rita will never know . . . that is, unless . . ."

"Unless what?" he asked, not liking the nasty emphasis she put on the word.

"Unless I don't get what I want."

"You'd rat me out to your mother?" Dolby asked with disbelief.

"Exactly."

Dolby sagged, caught like a weasel in a trap.

When Tiffany went off to Wharton School of Business in September, she shifted her major from accounting to securities.

67

*

1971

Downtown Vancouver

"What a mess," Gates said, picking his way around the cobwebs linking the mud-green upholstered chairs in the offices of Morton-Wiles Brokerage Inc. Some creature had gnawed most of the cords, chewed the pull ropes on the venetian blinds, and digested, or carted away, most of the pile from the Spanish-style carpet.

"I'm amazed there hasn't been a fire. Look at this!" Gates gingerly held up the cord of an ancient ticker-tape machine, still plugged into the wall and bare right to the wires.

Beaming, Tiffany moved from desk to desk, lifting papers, opening drawers; her swirling, peasant-style midiskirt picked up dust balls as she walked.

"Eeeeew!"

"What!" shouted Gates, his heart whapping painfully. The place gave him the creeps.

"Just a rat," she said a little breathily. "There it is!"

George picked up a piece of debris, threw it at the rat, and knocked over an old turtle-back desk lamp.

"Hard to believe that this was a going concern less than five years ago," Gates said, wheezing from the dust.

"Morton-Wiles Brokerage House, incorporated 1907. Second seat holder on the Vancouver Stock Exchange," Tiffany recited. "Herb Morton, proprietor. No one knows who Wiles was. They made money every year until Morton died, when his son, Mavor, took it over."

"Very good," Gates said. "Now maybe you'll tell me why I'm wading through this garbage?"

"I'm going to buy it!"

"Right, and I'm Frank Sinatra."

"I mean it. I'm going to buy this fucker."

Gates looked up at the tone of her voice.

"I belong here," she said softly. "The market, the street. And this is my ticket."

"Don't you think you're going a bit overboard? You could easily get a job as a broker at one of the firms."

"I don't want a job as a broker!" she responded sharply. "I'd spend my whole life selling stock, getting patted on the head, and never get near the boardroom. I'm only going to get somewhere if I own something, if I call the shots."

"But a whole brokerage firm? If you don't have the bucks and the contacts, the big boys will squash you."

"George!" Tiffany said urgently. "When is an opportunity like this going to come up again? Only two seats have changed hands in the last twelve years. The only reason Morton-Wiles didn't get snapped up is because of the recession. Trading volumes are lower than they've been since the war."

"I am aware of that," Gates responded stiffly.

"Sorry, Uncle George," she smiled. "Of course you are. I'm just excited."

"What does Walter think about it?"

"Haven't told him. And I'm not going to—yet. It'll blow his mind."

"I bet it would. Can't say I'd blame him either. The company hasn't traded a share for five years."

"Yes, but the estate owns the building, and each month it collects seventeen rent checks, regular as clockwork. The estate's still not settled and I understand the heirs are getting tired of fighting each other."

"How did you find out all that?"

"I asked the executor," she smirked. "He came by once to get a signature from the Merrill Lynch manager on the new lease. We got talking and I accidentally allowed him to look at my cleavage, several times. He asked me out for coffee, then dinner . . ."

"And," prompted George.

"He told me lots of stories about the estate and the brats. 'Course, I was giving him a hand job at the time. I doubt he'd ever had one before. He squeaked like a chipmunk." Tiffany punctuated her comments with a pretty fair imitation of the rodent.

Gates's normally gray and scaly face suffused with blood as he desperately struggled with embarrassment and hilarity. Embarrassment won out.

"Goodness knows what I'd find out if I went for a—" Tiffany pursed her pale frosted lips, like fish sucking for air, "job."

Gates, no longer able to stifle himself, roared with laughter. "You're killing me! Stop it or I'm going to blow out my ventricles."

"Now, Uncle George," Tiffany crooned, "can you do me a favor if I do you one?" Gates's moribund crotch twitched. The thought of any female's lips wrapped around his aging member was a jolt. But Walter's daughter? Tiffany laughed again, reading his mind with a knowing female look of appraisal that was ageless.

"Not that kind of favor. Uncle George, you have a very dirty mind. I need to see the accounts. I don't think I'll get that out of the executor—not even if I do give him a blow job."

Gates gave a strangled cough. "Enough already! How the hell am I going to get the accounts?"

"Simple. It's your firm, and your pal," she said, passing him a slip of paper. James Oickle, CPA. His own accountant. Now nearly seventy-five, Oickle played the ponies with Gates at Pacific Downs and poker every other Monday night. Favors went back and forth. A tip here and there. Some clever tax work. An alibi for Oickle's wife after a night with a Richard Street girl.

Tiffany pursed her lips again.

"Okay, okay. I'll see what I can do."

"Uncle George, you're sweet!" Tiffany planted a kiss on Gates's raddled cheek.

As Gates made his way out the door she called to him.

"Get the dirt too!"

"That'll be the first thing I get," Gates said, trying to appear wounded—as if numbers and facts would take precedence over the gossip and tips that had been his livelihood in thirty-two years of publishing *The Street Squabble.*

✳

Three days later they met in George's "editorial offices," a tiny, upholstered corner room of the beautiful, terra-cotta-fronted Carnegie Building, erected in 1901 with $50,000 of Andrew Carnegie's money. Now the grand dowager sat on the pimp-and-junkie-ridden corner of Hastings and Main, its cornerstones as redolent of urine as a lone tree in an urban dog-walk park. It had long ceased to be a library, but Gates, who had wanted to be a novelist in his younger years, still swore he could smell musty leather bindings in its corridors. He set up two card tables for them to work on. Tiffany contributed a copy of the still-unprobated last will and testament.

"How did you manage that?" asked Gates admiringly.

Tiffany pursed her lips like a gaping fish.

"Stop!" Gates held up his hand. "Remember my ventricles."

On a side table was a battered percolator clanking away and a tray of Chinese sweets—coconut-flavored jelly squares and steamed buns filled with cloying lotus paste from Maxim's Bakery around the next corner. George didn't get the name. An aficionado of all manner of Chinese food, he'd been patronizing the bakery for years and he'd never found anyone who worked there who spoke English. In fact he was the only non-Chinese he'd ever seen there. So who or what was Maxim?

Tiffany pored through the books, making notes and grunting softly when she came across something interesting. After he sifted through the will, George sat, smoking and watching. Her concentration was so intense she didn't notice when he periodically got up to refill her coffee cup or headed off to the can.

Finally she looked up.

"What do you think?" Gates croaked, his voice dry from the hours of smoking.

"It looks to me like the toilet's already been flushed on this turd and it's swirling around the rim."

"Hmmph," Gates said. He already knew as much.

"Follow me along and see if I've got this right," she said to his nod. "When the old boy died, the firm was in quite good shape, making a profit in the neighborhood of a hundred thousand per year after all expenses and after whatever he was skimming off the top, bottom, or middle."

"Hey, you're talking about a reputable brokerage firm!" Gates said in mock horror.

"Yeah, yeah," Tiffany chewed the end of her pencil. "When Morton died, the firm had seventy-five grand in the bank, a hundred more in T-bills, and the only debt was thirty thousand on a credit line. Now it's all gone! No business on the books and the only asset is the building and the seat on the Exchange. Worse, my friend the executor has built up nearly fifty grand in debt. The only reason the estate is still solvent is that the company owns the building."

"So far so good."

"Soooo, my little chipmunk friend has been getting fat off the estate for years, and probably plans to settle the debt with the equity in the building when it's sold."

"My, my, a greedy lawyer," Gates said. "Imagine that!"

Tiffany ignored his sarcasm.

"But . . ."

Gates shut his eyes. "I was afraid you were going to say that word."

"With a little leverage I *can* buy this turd."

Tiffany linked her fingers behind her head and stretched back until Gates feared her blouse buttons would pop.

"I can't wait to see Nathan Wingate's face when I tell him he has to put a women's washroom in the boardroom suite."

"Is this about Wingate?" Gates asked, narrowing his eyes. "Because if it is, you're wasting your time. He did the dirty to Walter, sure enough, but this place is all about that. Someone's screwing someone all the time. You can't get back at Nathan Wingate. He's too big."

Tiffany pulled down her embroidered leather bolero, smoothing it with her long fingers. She wasn't about to wait for opportunity, nor would she work her way up; Tiffany intended to snatch what she wanted. Right now. Right here. That was part of the rush, taking what she wanted. She walked to the curved window of Gates's office. The outline of the north-shore mountains had disappeared into the night, leaving the lights of Grouse Mountain's ski hill suspended in blackness, eerily floating high above the earth. Below her, in the illumination of the street, she saw a bone-thin man fumbling to shove money at a hand protruding out of the window of a pickup truck. The hand disappeared, then poked out again with a small tinfoil package. The thin man pocketed it with the care of a collector handling a Fabergé egg.

Wingate was a prize asshole, and the idea of getting back at the man who was responsible for sending her father to jail sizzled inside like the point of a laser beam. But as the years went by, her excitement about smashing through the corridors of the junior stock market overwhelmed her desire for vengeance. Millions were there for the taking by the bold— and she was bold.

In some ways, she was starting to realize, her father had it coming. She would never, ever express that sentiment to Gates, but her old man was a creature of the past. It was clear to her from the hours she'd spent in downtown Vancouver lounges that the junior market was now all about style and glam, not moth-eaten prospectors. The future belonged to those who rewrote the dreams of today into the stories of tomorrow.

"It's not about Wingate," she assured Gates. "But if it grinds him to see Walter Dolby's daughter playing in his backyard then so much the better."

George sniggered. It sounded like a plaster cast being ripped open. "So, what do we do next?"

"We?" she said, arching her eyebrows.

"You can't cut me out now," he bleated. "This is getting interesting."

"All right," she said, feigning reluctance. "You scout around for new business: promoters looking for a home, prospectors looking to get listed, whatever you can find. With your contacts you should be able to scare up something. I want to be able to hit the ground running."

"What are you going to be doing?"

"Selling our new building!"

"Huh? What new building?"

"The Morton-Wiles building. It's pretty much a done deal," she smiled, enjoying Gates's befuddlement. "Yesterday, I met three of the top real estate agents in town. I told them I would soon be getting control of the property and that I'll take $125,000."

"It's gotta be worth $175,000!" George protested. "Maybe more."

"$125,000 cash today is better than $175,000 tomorrow," Tiffany stated flatly.

"Where are you going to get the money?"

"Before Dad went inside he mailed me a thousand street shares of Molly Mines for me and Beau. It was about all he had left. I sold at $39.70."

"And Beau's split?"

Tiffany raised her arms, her bolero riding high up on her bared rib cage. "Oh Beau, well, he wasn't around that day and I haven't had time to ask him. But I will."

While Gates was contemplating this, Tiffany added: "I need more. I'm planning to get most of it from one of Dad's old investors."

"Like who?"

"The good Dr. Finlayson."

"He's got the money, that's for sure," George said. "Walter lost his shirt but most of his people did fine. Finlayson alone made close to a quarter of a million. Your dad told him to sell by $4.50 and, like always, he didn't. This time it paid off, big time. But I warn you: he'll happily gamble away a fortune, but when it comes to lending money Finlayson's so tight he's got a padlock on his ass."

"Don't worry, I know a way to unlock it." Tiffany smiled.

"Of course, that doesn't give me any walking-around money, wardrobe money, car money." Tiffany managed to look genuinely sorry for herself.

She placed her hand on Gates's arm and squeezed rhythmically. "If you think of any way to raise a bit more you'll let me know, won't you?"

"Stop batting your eyes at me," Gates stared at her hand, afraid to touch it. "And don't go offering me anything. I could never look your father in the eye again."

"Sorry," she said with little-girl contriteness.

"Yeah, sure you are. I might have a bit set by if it comes to that," he said, shocking himself as the words came out. Walter Dolby wasn't far off when he joked that George still had his first dime. As soon as he made the offer, he started praying she wouldn't accept. Fronting a little research was one thing but loaning cash money was a whole different can of beans.

※

The first stage worked well enough. The executor accepted Tiffany's offer, or threat. Forty thousand down on a purchase price of $140,000, with principal and interest deferred for twelve months. The mortgage was written up as an unsecured loan, because Tiffany had no intention of hanging on to the building any longer than she had to. There was enough in the deal to satisfy the lawyer. Since he hadn't actually listed it with a real estate agent, he could claim a five percent commission for the building on top of the ten percent he would charge on the whole estate once it was dispersed.

The agents put up a weak fight.

Tiffany dressed for the meeting in a worsted-wool gray pantsuit with a translucent ivory shirt underneath and a wide, dark-red-and-gray men's school tie. The cut of the jacket toned down the thrust of her breasts, and a soft fedora hid her long, pale hair. From the back she looked like a tall, fine-boned man. The only jewelry she wore was a slender gold band around her right ankle and a single tiny hoop in one ear. The jewelry confused both agents, who had offices in the booming gay section of Vancouver's West End. Wearing it in the left ear signified she was a lesbian, and the band on her right ankle indicated she was straight. There were so many pretty people and sexual combinations per square mile on Vancouver's wide, leafy streets that, except for the tag end of hippies remaining, it was necessary to have some kind of code to tell their orientation. But this babe was sending mixed messages.

"There's no money in property these days," one said, trying to beat her down from $125,000.

"Rate of return," crooned Tiffany. "No one speculates on land anymore.

It's all about cash flow and revenue. I have new leases made up with fifteen percent increases, and everyone has agreed to sign."

"Everyone?" Both agents worked the commercial market and both knew how tough it was to raise rents five percent, let alone fifteen, during a recession.

"Sure, half of them are government and the rest are either branches of Toronto companies or importers who can parcel out the increase to a big customer base. And then there's the parking lot." She crossed her legs and paged through a small binder at columns of figures. Both men's eyes went to the band on her ankle, then greedily to each other. Tiffany could have been reading Tarot cards for all they cared.

❋

Two weeks later, Tiffany sat in the same fern-draped bar where she had swung the deal with the two agents. She owned the Morton-Wiles building for exactly three days before flipping it to the agents who turned a quick $12,000 by selling it again. The real estate market was flat, but Tiffany put such a low price on it that the rents did provide a better than ten percent return. A nice holding property until the market turned, which it inevitably would. Three quarters of the money from the sale went to buying the Morton-Wiles firm with its seat on the Exchange. The rest went into the brokerage firm's loss and margin provisions accounts. All members were required to keep a ballast of $25,000. Tiffany still needed operating capital.

She loved the bar, set in the top floor of the recently built Landmark Hotel on Denman Street with a view of Stanley Park and Burrard Inlet. Down on the sidewalk it was all indolence, street musicians, leather shops, basement toke rooms, and cheap jewelry. Up here, obscured by ficus and echeveria, it was all business. She shut her eyes, and over the trickle of water from the fountain she could swear she heard backs being scratched around the bar.

"My dear girl, how lovely to see you again!" A soft voice caressed her.

For a man well over fifty, Dr. Warren Finlayson looked fabulous. With a thirty-two-foot pleasure schooner in a slip at the Vancouver Yacht Club and a nimble laser sailboat for weekend competitions, he had no trouble keeping whipcord lean and maintaining his year-round tan. Rare were the years when serious Vancouver sailors weren't on the water all twelve months.

Tiffany breathed deeply as she accepted his kiss. Canoe cologne with a hint of rum underneath. Nice. Yummy. His wedding band was still in place. She remembered it from many summers ago, when he'd laid her gently back on the examining table in his office and spread her legs to remove the life from her belly.

"I'm so sorry about Walter. Your father was—is—quite a character. We should celebrate people like him in our city. Instead we put them in jail for trying to be a bit entrepreneurial."

Tiffany looked at Finlayson sadly, her false lashes expanding her small-ish eyes. "I told Daddy the penny-stock business was a mean place to be. But he just loved to sell things. He was quite a dreamer, you know."

Finlayson patted her thigh professionally. "But you know, my dear, that is how great countries and great businesses develop. If it weren't for men like your father, searching for the pot of gold, the rest of us would still be in caves."

"Didn't Daddy's dreams ever catch you up?" Tiffany asked.

"Oh no," the doctor lied. "I was tempted. Your father could be quite persuasive. And the 1960s were wonderful to mining interests. I do invest in blue chips, so I follow the majors. But I never had enough of the gambler in me to take a chance on the junior market."

"I guess you could say I'm more of a tangible-assets kind of girl too," Tiffany said grinning.

Assets. It was all about assets. She couldn't understand why women today were so eager to abandon their assets and submerge themselves in a dreary unisex world. The package is the allure, and the brain the trap. She was fortunate, she supposed, to have both.

❉

In the end it didn't take as long as she expected. They fenced with each other pleasurably for a couple of hours with the kind of intelligent, fast-paced repartee that promises the best sex. The end point was known, getting there was the fun. When Tiffany asked him for money, she did it so smoothly he thought he'd misheard. Walter Dolby might be a bit of a gutter fish, but the class in this girl had seemed genuine.

"Do you want to pay now or later?" Tiffany teased.

"I didn't take you for that kind of girl," Finlayson said quickly, trying to make light of her request. He was still sure she was kidding, but it was a strange come-on.

"A business girl? No? Well, perhaps I don't dress the part well enough."

"Not at all." Finlayson admired her knee-high white-leather boots, the scoop-necked, sleeveless, harlequin-patterned dress, and her long, straight hair falling like a shawl over her shoulders. "But let's order dinner."

"All right, I understand the table d'hôte price here is fifty thousand but you can take two days to pay."

Finlayson frowned. "That would be some dinner!" he laughed tinnily. What was going on here?

"A small price to pay for a life these days, don't you think?"

"A life?"

The word was hollow to his ears. Her baby's life. The baby he'd vacuumed from her womb. The bitch was blackmailing him! Nobody blackmailed Dr. Warren Finlayson. The girls of Vancouver's better families came to him from time to time. He helped them out free of charge, to save them from the Hastings Street butchers. Perhaps he got the odd favor in return, a preferential vote on a development application, a driving-under-the-influence infraction overlooked, a zero-interest loan on his latest BMW.

"How dare you!" Finlayson hissed, aware of occupied tables nearby. "Don't you know . . ."

"Who you are?" Tiffany finished. "Oh, yes, absolutely, and that's why I'm here. You have so many accomplishments, board appointments, and titles, I'd need pages just to list them."

She leaned over and kissed his cheek, smelling the sharpness of nervous sweat. Good, she thought, I've got him.

"Then, of course, there's the issue of an underage girl and what else might have happened that day," she smiled. "Did you bill medicare for the consult? I bet you did."

68

✳

George Gates perched on a radiator, his fingers drumming a beat that sounded distinctly like a funeral dirge. Skin hung off his cheekbones like an ill-fitting sheet, and his eyes had more red in them than white. He always looked gloomy, but today he looked both gloomy and jumpy. Tiffany tried to ignore him.

Buying the old Morton-Wiles firm out of the estate went flawlessly, but reviving it proved to be another matter. It had been flat-lining for five years, so there was no current business, accounts receivable, or even client lists. When Mavor Morton died, there were two underwritings in progress, but the promoter, an Australian, had disappeared.

Placing her faith in Uncle George was Tiffany's biggest mistake. An eavesdropper, an observer and analyzer of the market, Gates was an utter failure at drumming up business. There wasn't a company he didn't have an encyclopedic knowledge of, a player he couldn't profile, or a price history he couldn't quote. However, a sales and marketing executive he was not.

But things *were* going to change. Walter Dolby was out. In her desperation, Tiffany transformed him from yesterday's man into their savior. He'd been released from prison two days earlier but had spent the whole time in his old hotel room, reveling in a comfortable bed and room service. He ate and drank so much he came down with a serious case of the runs. Otherwise he'd have been in the office yesterday.

When the knock came, they jumped as if goosed by a cattle prod. Dolby shambled in, looking as disheveled as always. Blinking, he took in his surroundings. With his new glasses Walter Dolby looked less the toad and more an unfortunately featured owl.

"What in forkin' hell ya lookin' at?" he demanded. Tiffany and George smiled broadly, relieved that the profane stump of a man was back to his old self.

"Good to see you too, Dad," Tiffany replied. "We were waiting for you." A week before he'd been released she visited him in prison, triumphantly laying out her conquest of Morton-Wiles. Dolby was flabbergasted to learn that his daughter had become the first woman in North America to own a brokerage firm and a seat on a stock exchange. He said all the right things, but Tiffany left with an uneasy feeling.

Gates clapped his hands and rubbed them vigorously together. "Things'll get moving now!" he exclaimed. "Old promoters never lose their touch, do they, Walter?"

"I dunno," shrugged Dolby. "I ain't old. When I get there I'll tell ya."

Tiffany grabbed a thick pile of folders off the desk and walked briskly over to her father. He marveled anew at her height and elegance. Not for the first time he wondered if Rita had been up to something with someone other than himself. And those tits. He'd been inside nearly three years and in that time he'd seen only four women other than Tiffany—two nurses, a social worker, and the fat, kindly, retired librarian who'd taught him to read. Walking here from his hotel he couldn't take his eyes off legs, boobs, and asses. There was lots of legs to be seen, but either boobs had shrunk since he went inside or women were covering them up, flattening them like they did in the flapper years. But Tiffany let 'em stick out like a pair of torpedoes growing off her chest, like it ought to be, like her mother.

While Dolby contemplated breasts, he vaguely heard Tiffany and Gates bringing him up to date with the zeal of eager schoolkids. Three of his old shells were apparently still in good standing, because the filing fees had been paid every quarter by an old acquaintance of Dolby's who specialized in such things. Tiffany was streaming on about her plans. She had two pitches, one from a young University of Western Washington geologist and another from a seasoned rock banger with a tar-sands play in Alberta. Dolby held out his hand to slow her down. He ostentatiously cleaned his glasses before glancing over the names.

"Hrrumph." Dolby shook his head and laughed. "Old plays. This one's up for a third time," he poked his finger at the tar-sands deal. "And this kid's the son of my *former* forkin' partner on the Sierra Madre mess. Every time the forkin' stock went down a nickel, he peed himself and started throwing paper on the street. Son's probably a pisser like Dad."

Tiffany stared at her father, whose somber expression was in such marked contrast to their elation. "What is it?" she managed, dread filling her stomach. He's dying, she thought, that explains it.

Dolby barely hesitated. "I'm retiring."

"Retiring?" Gates echoed.

"Is it so hard to believe?" Dolby said calmly.

"You're really going to quit?" Tiffany said in disbelief.

"Yup."

Gates stared at his old friend as if seeing him for the first time.

"What're you gonna do for money?" he asked. "Thought you were ruined."

"Ruint enough but I always got a poke hidden," Dolby admitted.

"Don't you want to show Wingate you can still do it?" Tiffany cut in peevishly.

"Is that what this is all about?" Dolby waved his arm around.

"I thought you'd . . ." Tiffany's voice died away as she saw his face.

"That's the worse reason I ever heard for workin' the street. If you went to all this goddamn trouble just so's I could get back at forkin' Winbag, you're nuts!"

Tiffany was stung. "Aren't you pissed at Wingate?" she demanded.

"More grateful than anything."

"Huh?"

"If he hadn't put me in jail, I'd have never learned to read."

"You've become quite the little Pollyanna," Tiffany retorted nastily.

"And if I'da never learnt to read, I wouldna have a chance to get your mother back," Dolby continued mildly.

"Talk about your fucking pipe dreams!" she sneered.

Smiling contentedly, Dolby pulled a sheet of well-thumbed paper out of his jacket pocket and handed it to her.

Dear Walter:

To say that I was astonished to get your long *letter would be the understatement of the year. How wonderful that you learned to read and write while you were away. It is simply the best news I've had in years! Of course I would be happy for you to come for a visit. I've already arranged to have the guest room done over.*

Everything is rather dull now, with Beauregard and Tiffany away. Beauregard is making quite a little business out of the stained-glass company he bought, and Tiffany, well, you know better than I what she is doing. Let me know when you will arrive.

As always, Rita

"It's a start," Dolby admitted. "But at least she's willin' to see me."

✳

"Who's that?" Tiffany asked halfway through her second double Glenfiddich—no ice, no water.

Gates, well into his third Bloody Caesar, looked over to the bar, where a lean man of medium height was deep in conversation with two other men.

"Kirby," he said morosely. "Richard Kirby."

"Broker?"

"Banker. Broker. Candlestick maker," George said. "Bit of a mystery man. Brings deals together. Eastern money, mostly. He's the one who put the package together to buy Wigwam Inn up Indian Arm."

"Looks successful," observed Tiffany.

"He's that all right. I heard a couple of investors are buying a whole mountain right beside Whistler."

"Whistler?" Tiffany asked. "There's nothing there for big money."

"Not yet. They're going to turn it into some kind of Swiss ski village, they say. Bring tourists here by the million—Japanese and German, mainly. He's got Jean-Claude Killy, Parnelli Jones, and old Smokin' Joe as face guys, with a load of Hong Kong money behind them. Supposedly."

"Who's Smokin' Joe?"

"Frazier, Joe Frazier, you know—boxing. The japs love him."

Whistler, an hour and a half from Vancouver, along some of the most treacherous cliff-hanging roads on the continent, used to be a toke-smoking little cluster of alpine houses, a gas station, a grocery store, a burger house, and some of the best vertical drop in the world. It couldn't boast the powder of Sun Valley, the charm of Sugarloaf, or the character of Squaw Valley, but it had the best combination of off-track skiing, glacier runs, snowfields, and wide-open intermediate trails anywhere.

Best of all there weren't any of the annoying environmental restrictions putting the lid on development elsewhere. But it did have problems. It was too craggy and windy for airplane service, and fog made helicopters chancy. Visitors had to come from the airport through a tunnel, across a bridge, into the center of the city, and across another bridge before ending up in the forests of the north-shore mountains and the beginning of the hellish trek up Howe Sound, past logging clear cuts, endless black granite, the community of Squamish, and finally into the tiny village with few beds, bad restaurants, and all that vertical drop.

"Salesman, huh?" Tiffany asked.

"More a deal-maker, I'd say."

"Has to be a salesman," Tiffany said. "Whistler is butt-ugly. If it weren't for the ski hill, you couldn't pay tourists to drive by. All that logging debris and rock everywhere. If he can talk people into imagining a Swiss village there, then he has to be one hell of a salesman."

"Well, he certainly seems to be able to get his hands on money," agreed Gates.

"Know anything else about him?"

"Forty years old. American. Very fit. Very tough. Some kind of military connection in the East, because he speaks Cantonese," Gates recited.

Tiffany looked over at Richard Kirby. From his suntanned chiseled features and erect posture to his immaculate though preppy clothes, the man radiated confidence and competence.

"Do you think a man like that would work for a woman?" she said suddenly.

"I think he'd work for a wombat if the money was right." Gates glanced at Tiffany. "Hey, you can forget it. Why would someone like him work for a failing VSE firm? This guy's a solo flier."

As they talked, Kirby caught her eye. She held his gaze for a moment, but long enough.

"Uncle George," she said briskly, "you look like hell! Go home. Sleep. We'll come up with something tomorrow. Maybe we can get Dad to change his mind."

"Ha!" coughed Gates. "You'd sooner get a turtle to part with its shell. Okay. You're right. Another Caesar and I'd be done."

✳

"Took you long enough," Tiffany said.

"Long enough to what?" Kirby said, sliding into the overstuffed booth seat across from her.

"To satisfy your curiosity."

"Maybe I'm more than just curious."

Kirby studied her face. This was a change. Most men had to hang their eyeballs up by meat hooks to keep them from diving to her chest. Even her father, for God's sake. If Kirby noticed her cleavage under the simple, white, tailored shirt, or her legs under the short, black, flared skirt, he gave no hint.

Kirby and Tiffany talked and drank well into the night. His Virginia roots were still pleasantly evident in the faint round vowels of his conversation. He had an engineering background, she learned, but after his military stint he'd helped a few Hong Kong acquaintances through the ropes of starting up businesses on the West Coast. He came to Seattle to spearhead the buyout of ten small pulp mills in British Columbia and Washington State by a conglomerate of investors.

"And these investors are?" asked Tiffany.

"People with money," smiled Kirby. "There's still more than twenty years before it reverts back to China, but people there plan way in advance. They don't want to be stuck in 1997 with no place to go."

"I don't suppose you're looking for a job?" Tiffany said out of the blue. It didn't come out right. It sounded too flip. Kirby just stared back at her. Ah, what the hell, she thought. No point in bullshitting this guy. She needed him—or someone like him—desperately.

"Look, I've got an empty office, a seat on the Stock Exchange, and sweet diddly else," she confessed. "I need someone who can whip up a sales force and kick-start some deals."

Kirby said nothing for a few minutes. He scanned the room as if waiting for someone to arrive. He was at least a year from approval on his Whistler project, and the pulp-mill buyout was complete. He'd been contemplating taking his Cal 24 sailboat and spending a pleasurable summer cruising the hundreds of islands and bays of the Gulf Islands and the San Juans. But being in the action was always a lot more appealing than play. This might be an entertaining diversion.

"Just how desperate are you?"

"I'll give you a free hand."

"I like it clean. No salary, no contract," Kirby insisted. "I don't want to be tied to you and you don't need to be tied to me. I'll take only what I earn."

Tiffany's eyebrows twitched. Most men would give up a testicle to be tied to her. But she put her annoyance aside.

"I pick my own sales force," he continued. "And I take ten percent off the top from everything they bring in."

"Done!" Tiffany said emphatically. Ten percent of a sales force's commissions could turn out to be a fantastic amount, but right now it represented squat.

"And twenty-five percent of anything I bring in personally."

"That's it?"

"That's enough. I like to be motivated." Kirby had a nice smile, Tiffany thought. His thin lips and a bony face were unrelieved by his long sideburns. All in all a very hard face, but the smile warmed things up.

✳

"You met this guy for an hour in a bar and now he's running the place!" Gates flared the next morning.

"He's not running the place," Tiffany soothed, "he's the sales manager."

"That's my job."

"Uncle George," she said. "You're a shitty sales manager. You know it and I know it. And if Kirby works out you can start doing what you do best."

"That being?" he asked suspiciously.

"Finding things out, schmoozing with the newspaper boys. Why," she said as if she'd thought of the idea then and there, "don't you start a newsletter for our clients. You'd be brilliant at that."

"So what gave you this bright idea?" George said, a little mollified by the flattery.

"He whispered the three magic words in my ear."

Gates groaned. "A marriage proposal?"

Tiffany laughed at him. "People with money."

Even Tiffany was stunned by how quickly Kirby moved. He was in the office the next morning at five A.M. By the end of the month he had enticed eleven salesmen from other firms with a couple-of-percent bonus laid on top of the standard commission. He treated them like a military cadre, organizing them into small teams competing against each other for perks, the favorite being a weekend in a Seattle luxury hotel with an escort service thrown in. But he also dangled tickets to the Rams—flight to Los Angeles included—and the year-end biggie: a leased blood-red Ferrari that would go to the top-grossing salesman.

"You dangled the carrots," said Tiffany one day, looking over the accounts. "How about I show them the stick?"

"Meaning?"

"Every quarter the lowest seller walks the plank."

"Is this what you call the woman's touch?" he said, half mocking, half approving.

Tiffany preened in spite of herself. She found herself eager for his admiration. She'd have to be careful about that.

"I got the idea from Jimmy Pattison, a local car dealer," she said. "The stock market is what Darwin was really talking about when he spoke of survival of the fittest. I don't need losers hanging around. I couldn't hire a cleaning lady two months ago, now I've got brokers phoning daily. If my people don't sell, fuck 'em."

"I like it," he said.

Sales results were tabulated in great secrecy, then prominently posted with some fanfare. Cash bonuses were paid on the spot to the top three on the list, while the poor sap on the bottom slunk out, knowing word would be around the street by happy hour.

Each morning Kirby held a military-style briefing, bringing the crew up to date on any new reports issued, insider-trading volumes, and new listings. He also berated them if underwritings weren't selling well. Within two weeks of his arrival he'd picked up a small underwriting deal with a mining outfit looking for titanium in Nova Scotia. They'd found tremendous mineralization in the sand along the banks of several tidal rivers. But the highest tides in the world there made prospecting difficult. The prospecting company had figured out a way to operate heavy equipment on the sand and get it off quickly when the tides roared in.

"When are you assholes going to get out there and sell some of this!" Kirby roared.

"Jeesus, Richard," complained one salesman. "Titanium, for chris-sakes."

"Yeah," agreed another. "Nobody even knows what it is, and Nova Scotia? Christ, I try to tell people we got a company looking for tit-fucking-anium in Nova Scotia and they just laugh. And we've got the goddamn issue priced at fifty cents—that's way too high."

"Hey, Dick," called out a third. "You 'n Tiff get me a gold or silver property, and I'll sell it so fast your ass hairs'll burn."

Kirby's backhand snapped the man's mouth shut so hard that two teeth cracked. The room of laughing salesmen went silent fast.

"Don't ever call me Dick, shithead."

At the end of the third month, after all the titanium shares had been placed, he hauled a case of champagne into the celebration, accompanied by three high-class Chinese strippers.

"I want them to feel like a team," he explained to Tiffany. "An elite team. You scare the crap out of them, work them hard, then you pat them on the head. It works with dogs too."

Shortly after Kirby came on board, Howard Kinnear, one of the brokers he'd hired away from Wingate, began selling the shares of a newly listed company without disclosing that he was also one of the majority shareholders. He could have carried it off, except he was sloppy and couldn't keep his mouth shut. The superintendent of brokers was still firmly in Wingate's pocket and he wouldn't hesitate to embarrass the firm owned by Walter Dolby's daughter.

The minute Tiffany heard the rumors she summoned the broker into her office.

"I think you're too fucking stupid to live," she said to the tall, tubby man with a vague donnish air about him. What followed was five minutes of prime Dolby-esque invective. Kirby and George, cigar in mouth, sat together on the sofa, drinking coffee and enjoying the show.

"What are you going to do?" the broker finally asked, contrite as a naughty puppy.

"I ought to let Kirby work you over," she said, ready to go on, but beating a cringing dog was not to her taste. "But we're going to help you out."

Tiffany, George, Kirby, and the hapless broker spent the entire night expunging evidence of the illegal trades from the eight trading books of the other salesmen who'd also been selling the shares not knowing their colleague was a majority shareholder. It was tedious work, combing through thousands of entries line by line. The promoter lessened the load somewhat when he told them that he'd funneled all his own trades through just two different accounts.

"You must have a death wish," George said. "Using only two accounts! Don't tell me both accounts were at one firm." The man's expression told him all he needed to know.

"At least we know what we're fucking working with," Tiffany said brightly. "It would be a lot more work if you were smarter and there were more accounts."

In a couple of the books, large sections had to be recopied, with the suspect entries replaced with the accounts Kirby provided. When they found that two of the twelve books were so full of trades in the two accounts that they would have to be recopied in their entirety, Tiffany burned them in a wastebasket.

"The worst we'll get for *losing* the book is a fine, but I don't think it'll ever come to that," Tiffany explained as they retreated from the cloud of smoke. "The Supe won't be able to make heads nor tails of this mess."

After the individual trading books were altered, the master trading book needed to be expunged.

"Is this schmuck worth it?" Gates finally asked.

"Not for a minute," Tiffany responded. "But saving his hide will send a clear message to both brokers and promoters. They can trust us but they'd better deal straight with us."

"Which reminds me," Kirby walked to the door and called in the broker sitting miserably at his desk.

"Tomorrow morning I want the title to your condo. You can lease it back for three months. But then it's mine."

The man's panicked eyes darted from Tiffany to Kirby, then pleadingly to Gates. "Hey, hey! You gotta cut me a bit of slack here. Everyone makes mistakes, right?" The three said nothing. "Look, we're all in this together." Ignoring Tiffany's narrowing eyes, he plowed on. "I mean, I screwed up, I admit, but *you* won't come out lily-white either."

Tiffany shot out of her chair. She was almost as tall as the broker, who stared like a rabbit into her eyes, so thick with liner and mascara he could see only black.

"Is that some kind of a threat, Mr. Dumpling?" she demanded. "Because if it is I've got the number of the Mounties fraud squad and I'm sure they'd be delighted to hear how we caught you red-handed altering the books."

"Don't be ridiculous," he sputtered. "No one would believe you. I saw the three of you do it with my own eyes!"

Kirby walked over, grabbed the broker by the front of his jacket, and smacked him hard. Gates and Tiffany started at the impact.

"You've fucked up and you're going to pay for it. Understand?" The man nodded pathetically, tears streaming down his face.

"You sure taking his condo wasn't going too far?" Tiffany asked after the broker slouched out well past midnight.

"He would have a tough time paying the mortgage sitting in the cooler. He would lose it anyway. From what I've heard, wifey has semipermanent residence in the Winston Hotel, which she manages. She's not that keen to warm the sheets with him, so I doubt she'd be rushing to bail him out if he gets nailed."

"Homeless and jobless," Tiffany said with mock sadness.

"But," Kirby said, holding up a finger, "prisonless. He's a lucky guy. Though he's probably too stupid to know it."

"You like smacking people around?"

"Why do you ask?"

"Just wondering . . ." she let her voice trail off provocatively.

Kirby pulled on his jacket. "I only hit people who deserve it. See you tomorrow."

Tiffany sighed. Talk about obvious. She felt stupid. And rejected.

69

*

1978

English Bay, Vancouver

Opportunities for sex, Tiffany mused as the sun cast its evening magic over the hard glitter of English Bay, abounded if you were a powerful woman in a world of men. But oddly, after some initial sampling, the street's appeal dulled, at least as a hunting ground for men. So she played with Finlayson for a while. The good doctor's pique at being blackmailed evaporated when she collected the money and thanked him with a long kiss full of promises. He was good in bed, gracious and sophisticated. After the doctor came a string of professionals, mostly married. They were enjoyable but ultimately unsatisfying. At some point Tiffany began to scare them. She could never pin it down to a particular moment, physical or otherwise, but she sensed their confidence eroding.

Still, Tiffany's life was a "brilliant landscape," according to *Fortune* magazine. Tiffany had also become a celebrity, not only in Vancouver but across North America. Three international magazine covers and a documentary focusing on her entrepreneurial smarts propelled her to number one on hundreds of reporters' "must quote" lists.

With Kirby gunning the sales staff, Morton-Wiles shot from the basement to the penthouse. Only Western Securities did a bigger volume. The oil embargo that had cast a pall on resources worldwide was long in the past. Even so, Tiffany had begun to think that the venture capital market was far too dependent on oil, metals, and minerals. Vancouver was changing—so should the VSE. Canadians denigrated themselves endlessly as "hewers of wood and drawers of water," but Vancouver was not Canada. Lotus Land, the rest of the country called it, was as different in climate and temperament from elsewhere in the vast nation as Finland was from Chad.

With opposition from Gates, Tiffany took on three underwritings: a salmon fish farm—"fresher and tastier than wild," a postproduction movie facility—"bigger and better than Hollywood," and a boutique cosmetic franchise operation—"the makeup of the stars."

The stories were sexy, with strong print appeal. The two young biology graduates operating the West Coast's first fish farm in a bay along Howe Sound looked rugged and charming next to Tiffany on the front page of the *Sun*'s business section.

Tiffany pulled in a few favors and landed a piece in *Variety*, featuring the postproduction facility. *Eye on Hollywood,* the Los Angeles television show watched by most of North America from 6:30 to 7:00 each night, billboarded an interview with "Mining Superstar Gives the Makeup of the Stars to Women Everywhere."

"What do you think?" Tiffany asked Kirby as they watched the interview together in her office.

"Do you mean what do my investors think?"

"Both."

Kirby scratched his chin. He'd been sailing for two days and hadn't shaved. Tiffany thought he looked incredibly attractive.

"The time-frame's good. You can get these concepts listed and the promotion under way in a lot less time than any mining operation, even if we take a newly explored property and vend it into an existing company. It means I can get my investors in and out quicker. They like that. The downside are the ideas themselves. We have to be careful about that."

"Yeah, I agree. We always have absentminded professors trying to get their latest invention listed. I must turn away a dozen every month."

"If we keep them classy and believable and can show some product, then I think we'll make a killing. The speculators are sick of losing money on mining ventures."

"Wingate refused to take up any part of the three underwritings. That could be a problem. We need the other firms to take some of the action."

"If he starts sucking wind, he'll start selling."

Thanks to the publicity, the IPOs of all three sold out quickly and the stock also rose nicely. Eventually the fish farm went belly up when disease wiped out the fingerlings, and the postproduction company overbuilt its studios without firm Hollywood contracts in hand. But the cosmetics franchise actually showed up in seventeen malls across the United States, posting modest revenue figures—a rare feat for a VSE-listed company.

Nathan Wingate publicly derided the so-called industrial listings as an "impediment" to the VSE's real purpose. At a Tahoe convention of the North American Prospectors and Miners Association he assured the crowd that the VSE would continue to be the center of junior resource financing in the world. Regulations were currently being put in place, he announced, to ensure the fund-raising might of the VSE was not diluted by "oddball promotions" and "snake-oil salesmen."

"I'll give him an impediment right up the kazoo!" raged Tiffany, reading his remarks. "I'd like to slice the bastard's balls right off."

She shook a memo from Wingate in front of Gates's face so furiously she ripped the paper in half. Gates pushed his glasses up his nose and held the two pieces together.

"Quite Machiavellian, isn't he?" Gates peered up at Tiffany, thinking she resembled a magnificent lioness in her anger. "I don't suppose he asked your opinion on this?"

"My opinion?" Tiffany scoffed. "The only *opinion* Nathan Wingate wants to hear from me is my *opinion* that I'd prefer making babies to selling stocks."

The Rules and Regulations Committee, which Wingate chaired, proposed stringent new listing requirements for all non–resource related companies. Owners of founder's shares and the primary underwriting firm would have to post a substantial "listing bond" to cover the first two years such a company was on the VSE board.

"I've got four more underwritings on my desk and not one of the promoters can afford to come up with the bond. They'll just head south and list on the pink sheets. Jesus, I'd love to kill that man!"

Wingate reasoned that the industrials were less stable companies by nature, and if any turned out to be straight scams, the VSE's reputation would suffer.

"I would hate to see the primary purpose of this exchange—raising money for natural-resource ventures—sullied by here-today-gone-tomorrow notions," he wrote in the memo.

Gates said nothing for several minutes.

"You'd like to kill Wingate, but I'm thinking you'd be better off hornswoggling him," he said. "But you'll have to be patient. Not one of your sterling qualities, I might say."

"Hornswoggling?" she said, rolling the word on her tongue.

"Same as cornholing, only harder. Much harder."

Tiffany savored the image. "How?"

"I want you to go to a meeting."

"A meeting?" She hated meetings.

"Just go to the meeting. Then we'll talk."

"What a waste of time," she complained after the meeting of the standing committee governing Rules, Regulations, and Personnel. "The only thing they do is hire low-level staff and some middle management. They only make *recommendations* about who the board hires for the senior positions, and that's it! What's the point?"

"It's a waste of time only if you think in the short term, my dear," Gates answered.

Tiffany fluffed her hair impatiently. Tiring of the long, straight style, which felt too much like the 1960s, she'd had it shorn in a more elegant, Farrah Fawcett do.

"They propose rules like the dirty trick Wingate set up with the industrials. All he needs is a sixty percent majority to pass them. That's how the bastard gets what he wants through: he controls the votes.

"Two can play his game. Especially if you have a friend like this." Gates held up a leather-bound book with old-fashioned lettering on its cover. "Bylaws are a girl's best friend."

"George!"

"Okay, okay. You might be interested in a little detail here on page 237." He began to read: "As the Rules, Regulations, and Personnel Committee is to be responsive to the Exchange on a daily basis, be it resolved that a cochairman shall be appointed to undertake business in the absence of the chairman. The cochairman shall have equal authority and single-signature powers on matters pertaining to personnel and all policy issues arising out of treasury matters."

"But there is no cochair!"

"They stuck this in just after the war, when the chairman had a heart attack. The Exchange shut down for two days, because there was no one to authorize hiring a new board-marker. Wingate took over as chairman in '56 and didn't bother with a co."

"Wingate will never vote for me."

Gates caressed the book. "Doesn't need to. All you need is a nomination and a fifty-one percent majority. Right now your star is rising. Of the sixty-two members of the Exchange, a quarter are scared to death of Wingate, a quarter are pea-green jealous, and the rest support him because he has the power. They'll hedge their bets and vote for you."

✳

"What are you up to, bitch?" Wingate snarled after the meeting installing her as cochair.

"I just wanted to work more closely with you, Nathan," Tiffany said archly.

"Don't give me that bullshit."

"Really, Nathan. Like you, I'm only interested in the good of the Exchange. And I can't think of a better way to serve my fellow members than by assisting you."

"Serving, my ass! The only serving you do is the servicing of whatever stud with money takes your fancy!"

"Careful, Nathan," she said, delicately patting his chest. "At your age too much excitement is bad for the ticker."

Wingate's eyes strained in their sockets as he glared at her.

"You're not going to turn this Exchange into some carnival for selling lipstick and fish!"

"It doesn't make a fuck's worth of difference whether it's gold in the ground or," Tiffany stuck her middle finger into her mouth and pulled it out slowly, "gold on the lips."

Wingate turned on his heel and stomped away.

The boring meetings and endless hours spent vetting tedious amendments paid off unexpectedly when Tiffany spotted a familiar name on the disciplinary panel's list. Howard Kinnear.

"What's this?" she inquired casually.

"Let's see," said the panel's secretary, burrowing into the file. "Here it is. It's a private memo addressed to Mr. Wingate from the superintendent of brokers."

"Hand it over," Tiffany ordered.

"I'm sorry, Miss Dolby," the secretary said prissily. "Mr. Wingate is very particular about his correspondence."

"So am I," Tiffany said harshly, "and I see that the letter is addressed to the chairman of the Rules and Regs Committee. Since I'm *co*chair, that also means me."

The secretary was still reluctant. Wingate's anger was legendary. Tiffany broke the impasse by snatching the letter out of the woman's hand.

"Oh Howard, you sleaze," she whispered to herself.

After two years working in the public relations department of a Denver mining company, Kinnear had ended up back on Howe Street in Vancouver with one of the half dozen new "investment" firms. In a departure from exchange practices, these firms were allowed to operate without a seat on the VSE. They could open accounts, advise clients on investments, and take buy-and-sell orders. But the trades themselves had to be funneled through VSE member firms. Kinnear was listed as an advisor.

"He's got some nerve showing up here again!" said Tiffany that night, after calling Kirby to her condo.

"I doubt nerve's got anything to do with it," said Kirby. "The guy's a jellyfish, but money's money. Some of those boutique traders are doing better than the member firms. No overhead, few staff. They don't take any risks with capital because they don't do any underwriting, and lots of investors think they're cleaner because all they do is sell shares."

"This pindick isn't clean, that's for sure. He's been caught churning, and it looks like he's fishing for a deal with the SoB, but wants to get Wingate on his side first."

Churning—buying and selling stock in a client's account without permission—generated healthy commissions for the salesman. Kinnear had done it fairly cleverly by choosing clients who were already heavy traders. He then bought and sold only a portion of their positions without their knowledge. Unless they pored over their statements, the trading commissions could easily slip past unnoticed.

"What kind of a deal?"

"It says here that he's going to spill information about past illegal practices by a member firm. He's only ever worked for us and Wingate, so who the hell do you think he intends to rat out?"

"Hmmm," Kirby stared over the water. "Dynamite view, isn't it? Wine tastes better when the eyes can drink in something beautiful too." He sipped his '62 Laudun Côtes du Rhône Villages—small sips, each one held against his tongue for a moment.

Tiffany glanced up, surprised at the poetic words.

"What are we going to do about Kinnear?" she demanded. She had come to like her image as a superstar in a world of men, and she didn't want it tarnished even by implication. She recalled another little rule, which Wingate would no doubt enforce—any member under investigation was required to step down from all committees.

"Something will turn up," he assured her, savoring another sip of the wine. "Wingate's touring mine sites in South America for the next ten days. I'm sure it'll be taken care of by then."

Kirby came up behind her. She could smell him—no cologne, only soap and the fresh scent of a man just come in from outdoors. It wouldn't take much—a quarter-turn toward him, a certain way of breathing. He'd get the message. But her mind was filled with Kinnear. She had no intention of just waiting for something to turn up.

✳

The offices of the superintendent of brokers were in a yellowy-gray suite in a squat brick building near the Exchange. A dingy office for Gerald Day, a dingy man. The staff consisted of three "investigators"—ex-policemen, guts spilling over tightly cinched belts—three put-upon compliance clerks, a receptionist, the superintendent himself, and his assistant, a category-two clerk, two rungs up from the bottom of the provincial civil-service hierarchy. It was two o'clock, and the superintendent was out, as usual, on an extended lunch.

Tiffany had long ago realized that the key member of the superintendent's staff was his assistant, Carla Meyers, a massive, grouchy, slovenly woman, to whom everything was an imposition and everyone an imposer. Tiffany was always unfailingly polite to the woman, thanking her for whatever service she performed, but in two years there hadn't been a flicker of change in her sour disposition.

Tiffany brought a draft of recommended rule changes to the superintendent's office. It was official business but could just as easily have been sent by messenger. Meyers morosely accepted the material on behalf of her boss.

"Say, it's past noon!" Tiffany chirped as if the idea had just occurred to her. "I'm starving. Have you eaten? How about a quick bite?"

"Why?" the woman demanded.

"I'm hungry; I hate eating alone."

"It's against the rules," the clerk said.

"Eating?"

"Fraternizing. Staff members are strictly forbidden to socialize with members of the Exchange."

This truly is an unpleasant woman, Tiffany thought. "What's the superintendent doing when he spends all afternoon knocking back gin with Nathan Wingate at the Vancouver Club?" Tiffany laughed.

"He makes the rules," Meyers said bitterly.

"Fuck the rules."

"I can't afford to get fired," Meyers stated bluntly.

"Have you ever been to the Dockside Café?" Tiffany asked, taking the slight equivocation as a sign of softening. "It used to be my father's favorite spot."

"No," the woman said, "but your father used to come into the office. He was very nice. I, uh, was sorry about what happened to him."

"He says it made him a better man. I don't know if it's true but he thinks so, so what does it matter? Come to lunch. Nobody but fishermen go to this place. It'll be our secret. I'm tired of all those Howe Street hangouts, nothing but brokers, promoters, and assholes looking for tips."

"All right," Meyers said slowly. She heaved herself out of her chair and draped a pilled cardigan over her shoulders.

They drove in silence to the Dockside, which appeared tacked onto the end of one of the piers as an afterthought. It was small, immaculately clean, and offered a view of dead fish as they moved from boat hold to packing box. There was every kind of boat tied up at the three piers—two-man trawlers and giant commercial vessels. On the smaller boats the catch was unloaded by hand—one man tossing the fish up from the hold, the other throwing them into coffinlike carts on the dock. When it was full, the fishermen wheeled the catch over to a weigh machine and kibitzed with the scale man, who handed them a chit noting the weight. The commercial boats vacuumed the fish out and blew them into a train of carts waiting alongside.

Meg and Hiram had owned the café since 1941. They bickered gently from dawn to dusk. They wore matching coveralls, and caps so white they shone. With their silver hair and pale faces they looked like elfin ghosts as they scurried from table to table. One or the other hovered over Tiffany the entire time. Without being asked, they served two fat cod, lettuce, and tartar-sauce sandwiches surrounded by crispy, hand-cut fries.

"I used to come here all the time," Tiffany said between bites. "Now I'm too busy but . . . oh, mmm, this is so good!"

"They're very nice to you," Carla said.

"They ought to be," Tiffany said, laughing. "They could have retired long ago from the money they made off of Dad's stock tips. But they say they'd miss the work."

"I'm enjoying this," the clerk said hesitantly.

"I am too!" Tiffany said, surprised that it was true.

For the rest of the lunch they chatted as friends do, about nothing and anything. Though she had an ulterior motive, Tiffany felt more carefree than she had for years, as if she was lunching with an older sister. They agreed to meet again at the same time the following week. As soon as she got back to the office, Tiffany asked Gates for the name of a private detective and ordered a complete workup of her new "friend."

At thirty-seven, Meyers wasn't nearly as old as she looked. Lose a few pounds, Tiffany considered, better clothes, some makeup, who knows? She had a BA in commerce, with honors from the University of British Columbia, the only woman in her graduating class. From there Carla Meyers's life had slid quickly from hopeful to hopeless. Her husband, an alcoholic, had killed himself four years earlier, leaving her with three young children— two in school, the youngest nearing school age. They lived in a three-room flat in New Westminster, an hour's bus ride to work; she couldn't afford a car. Meyers made ends meet on her clerk's salary; she had less than $200 in the bank and no other savings the detective could find. Carla's mother minded the children while she was at work, but the woman was in her late seventies and couldn't manage much longer.

No wonder she's so grouchy. Tiffany put the report down. What a life! What an opportunity! But she'd have to move very, very carefully.

✳

"I'd like to offer you a job," Tiffany said between bites of cod during their second lunch.

"Is that why you've been so friendly?" Meyers narrowed her eyes in suspicion.

"No!" Tiffany lied, crossing her fingers in her lap like a child. "It came to me when I went back to the office last week."

"You found me so charming you decided to hire me?" Meyers said, disbelief heavy in her voice. "Next you'll be hauling out a glass slipper."

"I did enjoy our lunch," Tiffany said, choosing her words, "but that's not why I'm offering you a job. I need help. The details of underwriting are simply getting to be too much for me. Richard Kirby is an amazing salesman but he's not interested in the grunt work of researching new companies, getting the IPOs written up, and making sure those idiot promoters don't get carried away."

Meyers smiled. Much of her job consisted of sharply worded letters to promoters about press releases that veered too far into the realm of fiction.

"And frankly," she added, "I don't trust anyone in my office to be meticulous enough."

"What kind of job?" the woman asked, trying to keep curiosity and longing out of her voice.

Tiffany handed over a business card, printed that morning, which read

"Carla Meyers, Vice President of Underwriting for Morton-Wiles Securities Inc."

"What! Is this a joke? No one hires a clerk-two to be a vice president of anything."

"No one plans to make as much money on underwriting as me. Most firms are still fixated on trading volume—clients in, clients out. And most of them sluff off the job to a broker or office manager. That's why so many IPOs are slow to get to the market. They make so many mistakes the files end up in a security lawyer's office to be sorted out and the lawyers sure as hell aren't going to hurry anything. They get paid by the hour!"

Tiffany leaned in closely enough to see the pores on Meyers's nose. "I need a detail person."

When Tiffany told her the starting salary, precisely two and a half times what she was making with the government, Meyers started crying, sounding like a seal.

"I used to dream about a fairy godmother," she said, blowing her nose.

"This isn't charity," Tiffany said firmly. "I figure with your knowledge of underwriting regulations you'll make me far more than I pay you."

As a nice bonus, the office of the superintendent of brokers won't be half as effective without her. Tiffany hid the thought behind a beaming smile.

70

*

As Tiffany geared her fire-engine red Alfa Romeo Spider around the circular scenic drive in Stanley Park, the wind, brinier than usual, with a strong breeze off the bay, turned her hair into a living thing swirling about her head. She didn't wear a scarf, loving the feel of the wind's strong fingers. She drove quickly, pushing the car well beyond the twenty-five-mile-an-hour speed limit. Normally she avoided scenic routes; today she wanted a little extra time to savor the thrill of triumph.

Tiffany didn't notice the towering Douglas firs encroaching upon the road, their canopies creating a dusky light, though it was only early afternoon. She paid no attention to the grouping of Haida and Kwakiutl totems bordering the commons, the cricket pitch, or the running track of Brockton Oval. As she rounded Lumberman's Arch, a shaft of light lit up the twin peaks of the Lions on the north shore, but she didn't see them. Nor did she waste a glance at Siwash Rock, the curving granite pillar, a phallus shape with a green tuft of bush on top, where Gitsula had washed up so long ago. She didn't hear the shouts of laughter from a volleyball game or a crowd singing happy birthday at Third Beach.

As she screamed around the park for the second time, Tiffany Dolby realized that she was starting to figure out what made her happy. Not a bad thing to discover a few months short of her thirty-first birthday. It really wasn't the money. She had plenty—almost $3 million put away, and the firm throwing off another million a year. Ironically, the Queen of Howe Street, the Princess of Penny Stocks, as the media dubbed her, had every cent of it in banks and utilities. Safe, dividend-producing stuff.

Tiffany Dolby had plenty of money but that wasn't what gave her a chattery feeling of exhilaration that she could only control by breathing shallowly and slowly. It was conquest that filled her up—the thrill of victory after taking a risk. The savoring of success that was sweet but fleeting, like a bite of meringue. Then would come the inevitable hollowness as hunger returned. Surprisingly, the small triumphs were as thrilling as the big ones. Hiring Carla Meyers, for example. One wrong step and Meyers would have gotten her back up. A woman like her moved quickly from annoyance to suspicion. But Tiffany had played it perfectly—friendly but not overly so, just enough to touch the lonely core of the woman.

She actually told Meyers the truth about Kinnear. That too had been a gamble. Meyers could easily have turned on her. Instead she was overwhelmed by Tiffany's candor.

To celebrate her coup, Tiffany decided to drive to Richard Kirby's house high up in the woods of Capilano Canyon. A chilled $250 bottle of Dom Perignon lay nestled in the bucket seat beside her.

Capilano Road followed the canyon as it wound its way to Grouse Mountain, where a gondola ferried skiers up the forested hillside to the runs high above the city. Years went by when the only snow found in Vancouver's winter was at the top of Grouse. Tiffany didn't ski, though half the population of Vancouver seemed to, but she'd been up the mountain many times for parties. Drinking and flirting with the city lights at your feet was like being on holiday in the Caribbean—inhibitions vanished. Sometimes she made the drive just to wring a little performance out of her car, to hear the motor kick back as it ate up the steep and windy road. Most times the little red bomb barely got out of second gear driving about town.

Capilano Road always seemed shrouded in mist, and the thick foliage appeared contorted and spooky. Tiffany had read *Lord of the Rings* as a teenager. She could easily envision hobbits living among the damp rocks and moss-hung trees of the canyon. There was even a popular restaurant there, called the Hobbit House.

Kirby wasn't expecting her. Tiffany pulled in to the crushed-brick driveway, the tires of her car crunching as she turned. There was nothing special about the house, not like Tiffany's forty-second floor, 2,300-square-foot, ultra-trendy West End condo with a 225-degree view of ocean and mountain. She'd bought the unit next door and knocked the walls down, producing a vast open space with three fireplaces and a Carrera marble–topped kitchen of bleached pine, redwood, and steel. She didn't cook much herself, but two or three times a month she called in Umberto Menghi, an Italian expatriate and proprietor of Vancouver's three most popular restaurants, to produce a spectacular dining experience for a dozen or so guests. Menghi was an unattractive man physically, but sexuality radiated from him nonetheless. Every smile bathed the recipient in light. The whole city swooned to be shown to the best tables in his Tuscany-inspired restaurants. Tiffany had never slept with him, but she might.

No one answered her knock, but in the distance, Tiffany heard the rhythmic smack, smack of ax against wood. She made her way down the sloping path around the house to the back garden, her white leather skirt pulling against her legs. Strictly speaking, it could hardly be called a garden—just rock and orange-barked arbutus trees growing at crazy angles. The day had been warm but she shivered in the shadows, her skin already damp from the moisture rising up from the crashing river below.

Tiffany admired the tableau. Back muscles rippled with each decisive stroke, perfect wedges of wood falling to the ground. Kirby wore only scuffed combat boots and shredded denim cutoffs. Steam rose from his bare skin. When he stopped briefly to wipe sweat off his face, he caught her presence out of the corner of his eye. If he was surprised or startled he gave no sign.

"I couldn't wait to give you the news!" Tiffany sang out, feeling briefly silly with her enthusiasm. Kirby eyed the champagne.

"I thought it was worth something special." She held out the bottle like an offering.

Kirby arched an eyebrow.

"The clerk in the superintendent's office," she blurted, unsettled by his lack of response. "The one who caught Kinnear's file. I've hired her to organize our underwritings and she's going to lose the file and tie him up with red tape before she goes."

She was babbling. Kirby frowned.

"Hey! Why the black look? I've just solved a big-time problem."

"We don't need anyone from the superintendent's office snooping around!"

"Snooping! What are you talking about? She's perfect. She eats up details like breakfast cereal. And she's already solved a big fucking problem." What put such a burr up his ass?

Kirby's fury disappeared as if he'd flicked a switch.

"It's a done deal then?"

"Done and done."

"Okay," he said with a shrug. "As long as she doesn't mess with my accounts."

"There would be no reason. I've put her in charge of IPOs and underwriting filings. She won't have anything to do with daily trading."

Kirby took Tiffany's arm and drew her farther along the path to a tiny rock patio, where a coffee cup sat on the arm of a slat-built cottage chair.

"I've some news for you," he said.

He picked up the newspaper from beside the chair and snapped it open.

Howard Kinnear, 39, died early yesterday morning when an early-morning run turned into tragedy. The VSE broker slipped on the treacherous rocks of Lynn Valley Canyon and fell more than 100 feet to his death. It took most of the day to retrieve the body. It was the 11th such fatality in the park since it opened 18 years ago. "He's never gone running in his life before that I know of," his ex-wife commented.

Tiffany didn't know what shocked her more—Kinnear's death just as she'd trumped him or the fact that it happened while he was running.

"Funny how problems take care of themselves," Kirby mused.

As she studied the story, Kirby stepped into her and walked her backward a few feet to the wall of a small shed. Tiffany's eyes locked with his. A powerful musk rose from him, mixing with the cedar and damp, sending little charges chasing through her. She felt his hand move under her skirt to cup her cheeks and tease the crease of her buttocks. He reached back to a knife on his belt and cut off her panties with a quick jerk.

Waves of heat. His cutoffs dropped and Kirby stepped out of them quickly, pulling off his boots at the same time. Most men would have just let their pants fall to their ankles, she thought idly, feeling as if she was standing to one side and watching it all unfold without her participation. He was naked before her but too close to see anything but the hairs of his chest. He lifted her five-feet-eight-inches easily and lowered her down on himself. Tiffany came in that first instant of penetration, her screams echoing through the shrouded canyon below.

✳

Kirby made Blueberry Tea—Amaretto and Grand Marnier combined with tea in a brandy snifter—while Tiffany picked bits of twig, leaves, and wood chips from her hair, the result of a long, vigorous encore. The champagne got kicked down the hill at some point, and when they finished, she laughed as Kirby scampered naked down the slope, futilely trying to retrieve it.

"It really does smell like blueberries, doesn't it?" Tiffany said, appreciating his legs beneath the short kimono. After their first coupling, he'd held her closely as they slumped against the wall of the shed. Not letting go of her, despite postcoital weakness, struck her as incredibly tender and romantic. She giggled at herself. Who would ever accuse Tiffany Dolby of such sentiments?

"I always think of it in the same way as the color green," he said softly. "You take blue and yellow and make something completely different. There isn't a hint of orange or almond flavor when you put Amaretto and Grand Marnier together—just blueberries—a little magic."

There was more to Richard Kirby than Tiffany had thought. Funny how a couple of orgasms changes your perspective. Strike that, a couple of stupendous, earth-shattering orgasms.

"Why do you have such a hard-on for Nathan Wingate?" he asked suddenly.

"You were the one with the hard-on," she grinned, "and I think I see it starting to peek out again."

"I'm serious," he grinned back. "What's the deal with Wingate?"

"It started with him screwing my father, of course. But really it's because he's such a purebred asshole. You know, he told me to keep my tampon in when I tried to make a point at a meeting the other day."

"He's an asshole sure enough," Kirby agreed, "but there's got to be more to it."

"You're right. I want to be number one. Wingate's sixty-five now but I'm sure he'll be running things into his seventies. I don't want to wait that long."

"Number one? You don't need to be number one. Morton-Wiles is the most profitable firm on the Exchange. Feuding with Wingate is bad business. Let's concentrate on what we do best."

Tiffany sidled up to Kirby, loving the lean feel of his body and the smell of dried sweat.

"And what we do best is . . . ?"

Kirby brushed his lips over her hair. "*Underwriting.*" One hand stroked her ass cheeks softly. "And IPOs," the other hand pressed against her crotch. "*Internal Pubic Offerings.*"

"If you keep me busy enough," she panted. "I'll back off old Nate."

"Done," he whispered into her neck.

✳

As Tiffany returned across the Lion's Gate Bridge the next morning, her insides still throbbing pleasantly, she thought about Richard Kirby. Hunger gripped her belly. Once would definitely not be enough. Unfortunately, Kirby was flying out later that day for Hong Kong. She toyed with the idea of joining him. No, she thought, a little breather would give her time to restore her equilibrium, to bring herself under control.

Tiffany wasn't entirely straightforward with Kirby even in the afterglow. She believed that Morty Macklin had become Wingate's Achilles' heel. For some time, she had been monitoring Macklin's promotion of Tintagel Mines, which was exploring for commercial-grade diamonds north of Yellowknife in Canada's Northwest Territories. There had been rumors of diamonds in the North for fifty years but no one had figured out the geology. Late the previous year, when Tintagel was fast running out of money, Macklin had stepped in and bought controlling interest.

For months there was little market interest in the stock. Then the share price started climbing slowly and surely, on the strength of Macklin's own buying, Tiffany guessed, until it was in the $4 range. The market quivered when it was announced that two diamond pipes had been found, the first ever on the North American continent. When those pipes yielded "indicators"—mineralization pointing to the presence of diamonds—the stock went wild, shooting up over $25, followed by a staking rush, as everyone with enough money to charter a plane staked millions of acres of ice and tundra.

On a hunch, she had the detective who'd looked into Carla Meyers sniff around the diamond company. She tromped hard on the accelerator, ignoring the thirty-mile-an-hour limit on the causeway through Stanley Park. The report was waiting on her desk.

"What are you so excited about?" Gates asked later.

Tiffany, elated at what the detective had uncovered, shared the findings with him.

"Who cares," he said. "So what if Macklin's hired a skunky geologist whose last company died under suspicious circumstances?"

Tiffany was irked.

"Releasing this will be like a mosquito buzzing in Macklin's ear. Geologists come and go. It's nothing," Gates added.

"I've got enough to make the stock drop, even just for a day or two. That's all it will take. Macklin'll be pyramiding his margin accounts from the get-go. Wingate will be supporting him, and if I know that greedy old prick, he'll let Macklin go way beyond the margin rules. This is gonna make Wingate very vulnerable."

"You'd better wait until Kirby gets back," Gates said.

"Since when have you given a flying fuck what Kirby thinks," she asked.

"It's just that he might have some of his deep pockets in Tintagel."

"He doesn't," she snapped.

"You know for certain?" Gates knew the deal. Kirby's accounts were private, even from her. Kirby traded daily, tens of thousands of shares, but if he was putting his clients heavily into a company he always told her.

"I don't need to, he'd tell me."

"Sometimes what you don't know can bite you in the ass," Gates said with heavy seriousness.

Gates drew a deep breath followed by a wet cough. "Macklin and Wingate have a lot at stake. Tintagel might be Macklin's ticket to the big time. If this turns into a mine, he'll be a financier, not a promoter."

"It's always going to be a mine," she scoffed. "That's the pitch."

"Sometimes you catch lightning in a bottle," he said mildly. "Remember Molly Mines? It does happen."

"That's one out of a thousand."

"Maybe this is number two."

"You're talking like some goddamn rookie plunger," Tiffany sneered.

"The signs are there," Gates countered. "That land in the Territories is native-owned and they've hired their own geologists to do their own testing. They must think there's something real in the ground. On top of that, De Beers is sniffing around in the background, and they're not fools."

"So what if there is a real fucking mine? I'm sure Macklin's margined to the hilt. And I'm betting Wingate won't have enough in his loss-provision account to cover if the stock drops."

Gates shook his head slowly.

"You don't need this, the firm doesn't need this, and Walter doesn't care. It's crazy."

"Maybe you're getting too old for this," she flared. "Too worn out."

Tiffany felt a twinge of guilt as Gates left without another word.

"He's right, you know."

Tiffany whirled around.

"You were eavesdropping!" she shrilled.

"Hard not to, the way you were yelling," Carla replied blandly.

"Mind your own fucking business!" Tiffany felt like an out-of-control train, unable to stop without running into something. In her heart she also knew Gates was right. Not about her desire to supplant Wingate but about the information. It was damning but not nearly enough to turn away investors what with all the excitement gathering momentum in the North.

"The way I see it, you have the rudiments of a plan but no way to finish it off," Carla continued. "You've got wood but nothing to start a fire with."

"What are you, some kind of a Girl Scout?"

"I'm just the gal with the gasoline," she said as she tossed a fat file folder on the polished redwood surface of Tiffany's desk.

71

Tiffany's eyes widened as she turned over page after page—details going back nearly twenty years, long before SoB Gerald Day's time. It was a catalog of corruption. An intricately constructed recitation of Wingate's back-scratching relationship to whatever SoB was sitting in the chair at the time. She even had details of huge campaign contributions to the man who became the province's solicitor general—the man who appoints the superintendent of brokers.

Individually the dated notations were nothing. Easily explained away by administrative error or bureaucratic backlog. But assembled together they amounted to a cozy and tainted relationship between Wingate and the SoB's office. Tiffany zeroed in on Macklin's name.

"See," Meyers pointed out. "Thirty-two trading infractions quashed. Letters of complaint never followed up. A request by the RCMP for information about his accounts and Wingate's response that Macklin has no accounts with his firm. There's lots of filing delays by the companies he's promoting and each time he gets more time, courtesy of Wingate. And don't you find it suspicious that Macklin hasn't filed an insider trading report in four years?"

"I love it," said Tiffany admiringly. "Why did you do it?"

"Insurance," Carla said bluntly, blushing slightly. "I'm not attractive and I know the superintendent's never liked me. But I was too good to fire. I always thought he'd replace me if he could."

Carla lifted her square, pale face to meet Tiffany's eyes. "Compliance is all I know. Who in Vancouver would hire someone like me after I'd been dumped by the superintendent?"

"You really hate the bastard," Tiffany said approvingly.

"The both of them," Carla said vehemently. "Wingate used to swagger into the office and throw his weight around. Never a please or a thank you. Plenty of times I backdated documents because the superintendent claimed he had the files in hand—'Just slipped my mind,' he'd say. They didn't even trouble themselves to come up with a good lie."

Tiffany patted the file. "This is some kind of insurance."

"I never thought I'd use it for anything but keeping my job," Meyers said. "But after what Wingate pulled with the industrial listings, I kind of thought you might like to see it one day." She pulled at a long, dark mole-hair. Tiffany made a note to suggest she cut the damn thing.

"But what is your plan?" Meyers was saying. "To make any kind of charges stick against the SoB, Wingate, or Macklin is going to take a long time."

"I'm not interested in any charges. I want to use Macklin's M.O. to knock Windbag off his high horse."

"What do you mean?"

"There's a well-established trading pattern here," Tiffany said, almost lecturing. "George pointed it out to me when a high roller tried to open a margin account with us. This is a guy who usually follows Macklin so closely his nose is full of his ass hairs.

"The pattern is this. Macklin creates these margin pyramids to keep the stock supported in all his companies. He does this with individual accounts, as well as accounts from each of the companies. The companies buy stock in each other, all on margin, using their own shares as security. This means he doesn't have to buy and sell stock to himself as much to keep the price up."

"That's the way your father used to do it."

"He called it 'Hungarian magic,'" Tiffany agreed. "Everyone else called it wash-trading. The way Macklin's got it set up is better, much better. He doesn't have to use nearly as much of his own money. That cuts down the risk, and at least on this exchange it's completely legal."

"But what he's really doing is passing the risk onto the brokerage houses," Meyers said, starting to get it.

"Exactly," Tiffany said. "The brokerage houses are essentially keeping Macklin's seven companies flying with credit, through the margin accounts. And when you add in individual investors, it's a shitload of credit."

"And who does eighty percent of the trading in Macklin's companies?" Meyers asked.

"Wingate!" they shouted in unison.

"Tintagel's the big noise in Macklin's stable now, so its stock is being used to create margin accounts for the others."

Meyers nodded. A company or an individual could use fifty percent of the thirty-day average price of a stock as collateral for a margin account. As the value of a company went up, more stock could be purchased on credit.

"So Macklin creates these upside-down pyramids, balanced on the hot company of the day. If that company fails, the pyramid will collapse."

"Like a goddamn house of cards. And here's the point. Once a stock used as collateral falls below a certain point or gets halted, then all margin purchases based on its value get called. That's one rule the VSE really does enforce."

"The Tintagel promotion is too strong for a few street rumors to upset it, right?" Meyers proposed. Tiffany nodded.

"You need to get it halted long enough for people to get panicky and to force Western and the other firms to start calling in margins on the other companies."

"Exactly, and that's where your file comes in."

"The file is good, but I'm not sure Day will see it as dangerous enough to go against Wingate. You'll need control of the superintendent if this is going to work."

"Aarrgghh!" Tiffany grabbed her hair in frustration. "I feel it's all here, in my hand, but I can't quite grasp it. I need one more piece. What exactly does the asshole get for being Wingate's lap dog?"

"Surprisingly little," Meyers replied. "It's really all about socializing with Wingate's cronies and getting to live like you're a hotshot making two hundred thousand a year instead of sixty as a civil servant."

"For instance?"

"For instance he sits in Wingate's private box for every Vancouver Canucks hockey game and flies down to Seattle for Mariner home games. His three children go to a fancy private school too. The tab for that's gotta be half his salary."

"Hmmm."

"I don't know who pays, but I doubt you'll find any money going from Wingate to the superintendent's checking account. Wingate would dummy up a scholarship in someone else's name and then whisper in the right ears to make sure it goes to the right recipient. Something like that."

Tiffany sagged. An hour ago her plan seemed as watertight as the beautiful Salish-made bentwood box George had given her for Christmas last year.

"Of course, there is the matter of the television," Meyers said coyly.

"TV?"

Meyers sat up and pulled her cardigan around herself tightly, not trying to hide her smugness. She enjoyed this—being the center of attention, the favor-granter.

"Two years ago Wingate gave the superintendent a huge home entertainment system. Solid oak. It had one of those new big-screen TVs—thirty-five inches—tape player, stereo, the works." Meyers reached into the lower drawer of her desk. "The delivery man called the office for the super-intendent's home address."

"Oh," Tiffany said, disappointed. "It's just secondhand?"

"I, umm, called the store directly and got a copy of the invoice."

"What does that prove? I bet Day's name was on it."

"Right, but the store mistakenly sent the order form with the invoice," Carla continued. "The invoice says the superintendent bought it, but the order form has Wingate's name as the purchaser, with his signature and credit card imprint. The delivery instructions have Wingate's name on them as the purchaser and Day as recipient, with his home address and telephone number."

"You devious bitch," breathed Tiffany happily. "You've been holding this back."

Meyers smiled like the cat who ate the canary.

✳

Jay Franklin, lead market columnist for the *Vancouver Sun,* was one of the new breed of business reporters. Journalism had suddenly become sexy, with print reporters appearing on television regularly to offer the kind of insights and in-depth analysis the talking heads couldn't possibly provide. Everything was about the inside story, the background, the details, the tell-us-what-it's-like-there-on-the-ground scene-setting. Franklin was hungry for the big exposé, the one that would propel him to national television. He was about the same age as Tiffany—a gaunt, wiry figure with a receding hairline and a long, dark ponytail hanging down his back.

"Let me get this straight," Franklin said, sounding like a hard-boiled detective straight out of a film noir. "You've got the goods on Wingate and Macklin, and you're going to hand them over to me."

"Let's just say I'm public-spirited."

Franklin's eyebrows rose slightly. It was tempting, but Tiffany Dolby made him nervous. She was like a concrete block covered in cream and sugar. If he bit, he might well break his teeth. He'd been burned before. During his first year covering the VSE, he was demoted to the copy desk when a tip blew up in his face. After careful digging he'd discovered that Wingate had set him up. He hadn't forgotten.

"It has to be exclusive," he said. Tiffany saw the words "Business Writer of the Year" scrolling through his mind. "And I need documentation, plenty of it."

"Absolutely," Tiffany said firmly. "I won't give it to anyone else. But you'll have to act fast. The street's like a leaky old sieve. Twenty people probably know what I do but I'm the only one who's put it all together—for now."

"I'll need some time to look over the information."

"Okay, but it's got to run within the week. And no phone calls to either Wingate or Day. You've got to play it my way or someone else gets the story."

It was perfect. Wingate and Macklin would be leaving in a few days for the International Association of Geologists in Las Vegas, the biggest preen-and-brag party of the year. The successful would be holding court, while the losers drank heavily and struggled to keep the desperate look out of their eyes as they sought to attach themselves to hot projects. Usually Wingate and Macklin spent the weekend holed up, incommunicado, with a couple of hookers.

❋

At six o'clock A.M. on Saturday morning Tiffany sat cocooned in her favorite high-back Bertoia birdcage chair, a 1940s marvel of comfort that cradled her body. It would be warm later, but she flipped on the gas fireplace and enjoyed the orange flame surrounded by the rich, pink granite rising to the beams of her ten-foot ceiling. The business section slid out of the paper and presented itself as if summoned.

SCENT OF CORRUPTION FOULS TINTAGEL, blazed from the front page. Halfway down the cutline read, "Macklin Out of Town While Lead Geologist Exposed."

> Despite the best indications in twenty years that the northern mining industry is about to be revitalized, information has come to light that Tintagel may be tainted. Sandy Peterson, the lead geologist . . .

The story cautioned that while Peterson had not been convicted of any offense in his last mining debacle, Morty Macklin showed "poor judgment in retaining an expert with such a cloud over his reputation." Tiffany smiled as she read. She had to hand it to Franklin. He was skilled. He'd woven in hints about an RCMP investigation and insinuated that there were close ties between Wingate and Macklin, which might not pass scrutiny. He implied that the SoB was not on the ball in the enforcement end of things. Right at the end of the story he dropped the bomb that Peterson was once known as Peter Alessandro. He made nothing of the fact but just let the words lie there accusingly.

❋

"Tintagel must be halted."

Tiffany perched on the divan of the superintendent's living room. She'd bearded him in his home at eight A.M. that Sunday, newspaper in hand. The wide shoulders of her polyester pantsuit cut quite a contrast to the unshaven Gerald Day in rumpled pajamas and dressing gown. Tiffany's hair was cut again, this time gamin-style, which set off her cheekbones and made her eyes look bigger. The masculine suit was all the rage, though most women were overwhelmed by huge lapels and wide, cuffed legs. But Tiffany's height allowed her to carry off the look with style.

With her aggressive manner and her penchant for swearing, Walter Dolby's daughter scared the pants off Day. He avoided her whenever possible, shying away from her like a spooky horse from some imagined predator hiding in the bushes.

"Don't be ridiculous. I couldn't possibly do that!"

"You can! And you will!" Tiffany snapped. "Don't you read the fucking papers? It has all the earmarks of a Macklin crash and burn. He's out of town, bad news gets out, stock dives, et cetera, et cetera. How can it be clearer? It's a pattern with the asshole, and on Monday a whole bunch of little guys will see their investments go up in smoke."

"I can't halt a stock just because there's a bit of bad news. If I did, eighty percent of the listed companies would be halted. I need proof of wrongdoing."

"Peterson's or, should I say, Peter Alessandro's presence isn't sufficient?"

"He wasn't charged and his license to trade has been stripped, not his credentials as a geologist."

"If you don't halt the stock and it hits the skids on Monday, after this article, there's a lot of people going to be hurt. Most retail investors will bail. But if you halt it before the open, you'll save them. If Tintagel turns into the real thing, the stock will come back and fast."

"I am not halting a stock just on your say-so, and I think you've got a hell of a nerve making those accusations!"

Tiffany pulled a copy of the invoice and order form from her purse. Anger slowly changed to dismay when Day realized what they were. His face grew sickly when she drew Meyers's file from her briefcase and handed him some of Meyers's notes.

"Where did you get this?" Day's voice was tinny.

"Never mind. Halt the stock or this goes public."

Tiffany held the two pieces of paper out as if they were radioactive. Her pearly nails caught the light as she laid the papers gently in front of the superintendent. "You wouldn't want that, would you?

"Gee, isn't it election year?" she added as an afterthought. "Everyone says we'll have a new government. And, say, isn't your contract up for renewal in ten months?"

Day looked truly sick. Tiffany noted with satisfaction the two red dots burning on his cheeks.

"They'll crucify me," he whispered.

Tiffany waved the invoice, order form, and file. "If you think those two shitbirds'll stick by you, you're nuts. But if you do exactly what I tell you, you'll keep your job and your pension." She paused then added, "Hell, by the time I'm through, you'll be a fucking hero. The man who cleaned up the Exchange."

✳

The superintendent of brokers halted trading in Tintagel Mines just before the bell on Monday morning.

> I have every confidence this office's investigation will result in the resumption of normal trading within a matter of days. However, in light of recent public outcry about the increasing appearance of individuals charged or convicted in other jurisdictions on the Vancouver Stock Exchange, I feel it is my responsibility to fully investigate the matter. (Released 7:30 A.M., SoB.)

As margin calls dominoed into more margin calls, Wingate's six other companies fell off a cliff.

"Fucking bonanza!" Tiffany exploded from her office, startling Meyers and Gates. "It's better than I thought. They went over the edge on this one."

"You going to tell or keep it to yourself?" Gates asked.

"I just heard from our floor trader. He says the spread between bid and ask is getting wider by the minute. There's a hundred sellers for every buyer and all the buyers are tied to Wingate and Macklin."

"Congratulations," Meyers said.

"Wait, it gets better. The trader says word's out that Macklin's margin accounts top $12 million and Wingate's on the hook for most of that."

Gates hooted. "I'm almost starting to feel sorry for the guy." He peered at the ticker tape. "Jesus, Mary, and Joseph. I've never seen anything like this.

"What now?" Gates queried as Tiffany grabbed her coat and headed out the door.

"Hammer another nail in Wingate's coffin," she said smugly. On Friday she'd made a lunch date with Gerald LeFevre, owner of Selkirk Securities.

✴

"I hear you're sucking wind big-time on those margin accounts with Macklin."

"Just over a million," the man lied smoothly. He had a big pain in his gut that no amount of Lomotil could take away.

"I hear different," Tiffany said. "That you couldn't cover all the margins if the superintendent looked at your books."

Her words jabbed his reverie. "What business is that of yours?"

"I'm making it my business."

LeFevre manufactured an entirely unconvincing laugh. "You're into charity now?"

"Let's cut the bullshit, Gerry. You're down over $4 million. You don't have it. And no one's going to give it to you. You're bust."

"Assuming you're right, which you're not, what about it?"

"I'll pay you $1 million now for all the Tintagel shares. That'll take care of your capital problems. And I'll sign a note for another million, payable conditionally in one year."

"Conditionally?" he said carefully, trying not to appear too eager.

"If any word of our deal leaks out, you don't get the extra million."

"Who would I transfer the shares to?"

"No one. This is the second part of the deal. You keep them. When trading starts up, you dump 'em all at once. You'll take a big loss but you've got my million in hand and one to go."

LeFevre said nothing for a few minutes. What Tiffany was proposing was a violation of security regulations. Shares had to be transferred to a new owner within three business days and could not be sold for the benefit of the original holder in the interim. Too bad. Selkirk was hurting and he'd love to wring Morty Macklin's neck. Besides, this mess looked bad for Wingate. If the rumors about the margins he held were true, he was finished. To hell with it.

"OK. But I want the check in banker's draft made to cash."

Tiffany stroked the back of LeFevre's hand playfully.

"You gonna buy a nice, big boat or something? Maybe take a long cruise to Mexico?"

"Just a precaution," he leered at her. "I've already got a big boat. You maybe want to see it?"

Tiffany stood up briskly, handing over the already made-out check.

"Some other time, Gerry. The contract will be there after lunch."

Bitch.

✳

That was Monday at noon. By Monday night both Wingate and Macklin were back in Vancouver. No doubt threatening to fit Day with a pair of concrete shoes, Tiffany thought. On Wednesday morning, as agreed, Gerald Day lifted the trading halt. Immediately Tiffany began selling Tintagel short. This is where she held her breath. If LeFevre double-crossed her or Wingate, and Macklin pulled something out of the hat, it would be she who was ruined. But LeFevre was true to his word. She stayed away from the Exchange, but George reported from the viewing room above the floor. With each phone call Tiffany grew more elated as Wingate's mood ran from raging fury to near hysteria.

On Friday, before the open, Wingate had called an emergency meeting of the board for Monday at six A.M., an hour before the market opened.

"I invoke Section 261.4 of the Exchange bylaws and request leave to operate for sixty days without capital reserves," Wingate spoke in a croaking voice before the board.

Tiffany could barely keep from grinning as she watched her mortally injured foe in his death throes. God, it felt good!

"I also request, as permitted by Section 32.7, a $2.5 million loan for ninety days."

"You must have missed the amendment, Nathan," LeFevre piped up. "We need a sixty percent majority and all signatures of the executive committee."

"What're you talking about?" snapped Wingate, trying to rally.

"Let's see. Yes, here it is, passed two months ago. I guess you were away."

Tiffany was silent. She felt like a young lion who'd overthrown a rival. Suddenly the support of the old lion's pride was with her. Nobody said anything but she could feel it. Wingate's watery eyes turned in her direction. His mouth opened but no words came. The room was quiet as he turned and left.

"Breakfast, anyone?" Tiffany called out. "It's on me. Breakfast at Tiffany's."

"There's no one we'd rather bend the rules for than Mr. Wingate," Tiffany Dolby, interim chairman of the Vancouver Stock Exchange, told this reporter earlier today after the surprise resignation and bankruptcy filing of Nathan Wingate, the longest serving member of the VSE's board of directors. "He devoted years of his life to building the Exchange into what it is today. And I'm sure he would agree that our first job is to protect the public, not one of our own."

✳

72

"I'm brilliant! So goddamn brilliant!" Tiffany hugged herself as she danced around her office, an opened bottle of Dom in her hand. "La, la, la, la boom cha!" Hips gyrating, cheeks glowing, boy-cut hair mussed, Tiffany looked like a teenager who'd just snared Mick Jagger for a boyfriend.

Sipping from her own glass, Meyers wryly watched her reeling about. She sure is gorgeous, she thought. Tiffany hadn't said a word about her own contribution, but Meyers didn't care. Two world-class jerks, Day and Wingate, got what they had coming. She was always uneasy about her position as a vice president—a pretender, an interloper—despite her degree and years of experience. "I deserve it now," she whispered to herself. "I belong right here." Today she'd leave work early and buy a suit. Hell, she might buy two suits, with matching shoes. Then she'd go home and throw out all her cardigans.

Tiffany waltzed past, unable to keep the grin off her face. Even her toenails were chuckling, she was sure. "Wait till Richard hears," she said. "I tried to call him twice on the weekend, but he's in Singapore and checked out of his hotel."

He better not be getting some Oriental tush, she thought. Nah, not a chance, not with me waiting for him. "When's he due back?" Tiffany asked Meyers, though she knew full well.

"Thursday," Meyers said, reaching for the phone as it rang. "That's funny," she said, wrinkling her face. "It's Mr. Kirby on the line now. Sounds like he's in a hurry."

"I'll take it inside." Tiffany tried not to skip into her office. She shut the door and snatched up the phone.

"Richard, I'm so glad you called. I can't wait . . ."

"Come over to the Sylvia, now!" he said hoarsely.

"You're here?"

"Get over here as quick as you can! I'm in suite 206. And don't say anything to anyone!"

"I'll be back at four," Tiffany threw on her coat and dashed for the door.

"Where are you going?" George said to her departing back.

"Back at four!" she sung out.

She settled into the cab and smiled, thinking how romantic it was—Kirby booking a room in Walter Dolby's former haunt. The old dowager was pretty low-class now, with a smoky bar on the main floor and tired decor, but Tiffany had told him about her surprise visit to her father years ago. She was sure that was why he'd booked the room there, instead of inviting her to his house in Capilano Canyon.

At the door to his room Tiffany drew a deep breath. She felt quivery, like a kid. She fluffed her hair and gave thanks for the fabulous, navy-blue, French-made bra and matching panties she'd chosen that morning. You could see her nipples through the sheer fabric and the high-cut panties almost disappeared between her cheeks. Tiffany felt the lace rubbing against her ass. As she raised her hand to knock, the door flew open. Kirby's arms were raised and she flung herself into his embrace.

"You stupid cunt!" he shoved her aside. "Why couldn't you leave well enough alone?"

Tiffany was breathless. Not so much at Kirby's unexpected violence as at the ferocity of his rage.

"Bitch! Bitch! Bitch!" he screamed, driving his fist into the wall. "You've killed me!"

Tiffany stepped back, frightened now. Who was this man? Gone was Kirby's smoothness, his aura of masculine control. Even his voice was different. Kirby sounded like Allegheny Mountain trash, his charming hint-of-the-South accent gone. Spit wet one side of his chin, his chinos were grubby, and his tieless shirt was missing a button. He was also drunk and smelled as if he'd been that way for some time. Tiffany saw the lines in his face, the broken blood vessels, the pouches beneath his eyes, and his pallor. He looks old, she thought, amazed at the transformation.

"She never asked about the dough," Kirby railed on. "Millions and millions of dollars." He turned to her. "Where'd'ya think the fucking money came from?" he screamed.

Blood drained from Tiffany's face so quickly she thought she was going to faint, be sick, or both.

"Your, your investors," she stammered. "You told me . . ."

"*My* investors bought as much as fifty percent of every single IPO and every single fucking new issue. IS THAT NORMAL?" Kirby shouted the words so loudly they seemed to bounce off the walls.

"Didn't you ever wonder why I never tried to buy at the bottom, never held for more than a few months, and always got out, even in the hottest market?"

"You're a smart trader. Not greedy," Tiffany said. "You locked in profits and . . ."

"I was laundering money," he said as if speaking to a child. "I wasn't a smart anything. I didn't have to make money. All I had to do was make sure I didn't lose too much."

His voice dropped so low she could barely hear him. "Funny. It's real fuckin' funny. I told them you'd notice the pattern eventually. I wasn't worried about the Exchange or the SoB—they couldn't spot a pattern in a two-piece jigsaw puzzle. But I was sure you'd catch on within a year or two. I told them I could handle it." He stared at her with a look so hard and hateful she shrank against the wall. "I told them you were a greedy fuckin' broad and as long as I had accounts worth more than forty million you wouldn't give two fuckin' hoots where the money came from. But you fooled me. You're greedy all right, but you're a whole fuckin' hell of a lot stupider than I thought."

"Them?" Tiffany didn't want him to answer.

"Yeah! Them. I shoulda given you a goddamn intelligence test before I took you on."

Some of the blood flooded back. "Took *me* on? I hired you, remember?"

"Don't make me choke on the gratitude." Kirby glared at her. "*I* made *you*. You had nothing but tits. *I* brought the money in. You just came along for the ride."

Kirby staggered slightly. He looked as if he was going to pass out, his face was so gray. "We had Morton fuckin' Wiles in our sights. We were all set to buy it out of the estate, and then this pussy comes along and sucks cock and, bingo, does an end run." He laughed hollowly. "We'd been patiently watching the estate for two fuckin' years and you buy it out from under us."

"Who the hell is 'us'?" Tiffany demanded, calmer now and getting fed up with Kirby's ranting.

"Another funny thing is it turned out better with you owning the joint. We figured five, six years of action, and then gone. I wanted to get out last year, but they wanted to hang on another year and now . . . and now they think I've fucked them. Ain't that the funniest fuckin' thing you ever heard."

"Who the hell are you talking about?" yelled Tiffany. "You sound like you're talking about the mafia."

"If it was the Italians I might have a chance," he laughed hollowly. "They're vicious but you can usually buy your way out of a problem. The Chinese don't just hit you. They pull your guts out inch by inch."

"The Chinese? You mean your Hong Kong clients?" She'd been half joking about the mafia. "If you're talking about Tintagel and Macklin's stable collapsing, you never told me you had money in it," Tiffany accused. She was getting angry. "You always tell me when you're putting clients into a company. I would have told you what was going down."

"You had such a hard-on to prove yourself," he sneered. "You started believing all your own press clippings. Queen of Howe Street. Princess of the Penny Stocks. What a laugh. As soon as I realized you had to *be* that queen, I started moving out. Tintagel was the last investment my clients made and then we were gone. The last thing we wanted was to be moving money through the firm that chaired the fuckin' Exchange!"

"Richard," pleaded Tiffany, trying to push aside the information that he was planning to be out of her life even while he was screwing her. "Who are your investors?"

"The Chinese," he said with a sigh that sounded like the last wheeze of a dying man.

"Chinese?"

"Real hard cases." Kirby now spoke with a resigned air, hysteria apparently over. "They recruited me in Indonesia during my tour. We did some pretty wild stuff over there. Guess that's what caught their attention. As they say, they made me an offer I couldn't refuse. One thing led to another. I got rich and now I'm gonna get dead."

"So you've been laundering Hong Kong money. Great. Fucking great."

"It only looks like Hong Kong money. I learned on my last trip that Vancouver is the origin point. The whole goddamn thing is run right here."

Tiffany brightened. "I know Jake Chong. I could speak to him. Maybe he could help."

"Chong would eat his own rather than deal direct with a cutout like me," Kirby snorted. "I always assumed he was part of it or in charge, but no way he's ever going to invite me to tea."

Jake Chong and his family were major landowners in Vancouver. Their real estate holdings reputedly stretched around the globe, but it was on the West Coast that he'd built his empire on top of that created by his grandfather

Soon Chong. Chong, though retired from everyday business, was one of the most powerful men in the city. He'd endowed chairs at the University of British Columbia and Simon Fraser University, and built hospital wings and a para-Olympic training center. He also took a small, seemingly insignificant heirloom of his grandfather's—a doll-sized, beaded tunic—the earliest example of ancient jade carving ever discovered, and turned it into the centerpiece of a museum of ancient Chinese art. The museum was so extensive and complete that leading Chinese scholars came to Vancouver to learn about their own heritage. It held treasures that made Tutankhamen's seem ordinary in comparison. But at its heart were the simple beads, which dated back over ten thousand years.

A chill, like the cold of a Vancouver winter rain, crept through Tiffany's body. "How heavy were you into Tintagel?"

Kirby heaved a beaten sigh. "Big. We were also in seven of Macklin's other companies you flushed down the toilet. We lost nearly $10 million. You see, it never mattered if we made or lost on any deal." He was talking as if explaining something to a slow child. "I just aimed to get sixty or seventy cents on every dollar. Then the money's clean. But losing $10 million isn't something guys like these will tolerate. They think I screwed them."

"But you can explain, can't you?" The words sounded feeble the moment Tiffany spoke them.

"You don't explain nothin' to these people. They were waiting for me back at the house. I just got away by the skin of my teeth."

Kirby started giggling. "Can't you see the headlines? 'White Man Does Chinese Laundry.'"

He leaped at Tiffany so suddenly, she cried out in alarm. With his hand locked around her wrist in a painful grip, he said, "Get out your checkbook. Your personal checkbook. Write me fifty thousand dollars to cash."

"I'll have to transfer money," she said, scribbling shakily. Kirby pushed the phone at her.

"Tell them to do it within the hour."

Kirby hefted a suitcase by the door, pulled a baseball cap low on his head, and took the check from her. Tiffany's voice sounded like she was speaking through a tin can as she asked the bank to move the money immediately.

"Where are you going?" she asked when she hung up.

"To get good and lost. Somewhere Jake Chong doesn't own one square inch of land."

Without saying a word of good-bye he walked quickly through the door. Tiffany could hear his footsteps on the thin hallway carpet. She had never seen terror on anyone's face before. Now she knew what it looked like.

✳

"We'll have to lay off the rest of the sales staff," Gates said, two months after Richard Kirby disappeared.

"What does it matter?" Tiffany responded listlessly. "There's nothing to sell." She felt sticky, as if she hadn't showered in too long, and her hair lay flat and unstyled.

Three weeks earlier, two Chinese men had arrived to pick up their "reparations," as they quaintly called them. A few nights before that, a voice on the phone, polite but colder than ice, promised she'd be fed to the timber wolves in Stanley Park Zoo if she didn't "settle our claims with dispatch."

Before the men arrived she'd been frightened, but the impact of it only struck her fully when she realized they knew exactly what she had in her personal account, her operating account, and her capital reserves, as well as how much she held in Morton-Wiles's trust account on behalf of clients. They took it all, leaving only bare operating funds. They instructed her to wire the $8.7 million to seventeen different accounts in Aruba, Turks and Caicos, and Fiji. Then they withdrew everything from Kirby's accounts, using his passwords and written instructions under his signature. The signature looked genuine.

Failure has an odor unlike anything else. It's pervasive and clingy, evident to anyone who comes close. Word quickly got around of Morton-Wiles's "troubles" in the wake of Kirby's disappearance. Then more words and whispers about "funny business." Clients left in droves and nobody was interested in bringing any underwriting projects to her.

At the quarterly meeting of the VSE membership, seatholders averted their eyes and broke off conversation when she approached. At the executive meeting to elect Wingate's replacement, her name wasn't even put forward, though as interim chairman she was the heir apparent.

"She could always get by on her back," she heard Gerry LeFevre comment to another member. He'd never get his second million from her, but the million he'd already collected would tide him over until the good times came again.

"I guess I should have known. No one comes by that much money legally."

"We all should have known. Especially me," mourned Gates. "I've heard rumors of money-laundering in the Exchange for years, but no one's ever proven anything. I've got a few friends on the fraud squad and they've always dismissed it as penny-ante mob stuff. Local wise guys, nothing more."

"He built quite a network," Tiffany said wistfully, a small amount of admiration slipping into her voice.

Gates groaned. "Don't even think about it."

"I used to think I could play in the lion cage," admitted Tiffany. "I was so goddamn smart."

"We all thought we were smarter than we were. Kirby too. These people don't tolerate mistakes. And he would have made one sooner or later. You can only control so much, even on the VSE."

Tiffany felt weary and decades older. "Carla took a job in Calgary. For such a fatso she sure moved quickly. What are you going to do now?"

"Right now? Or for the rest of my life, however long that is?"

"Either."

"I've got a little retirement money set aside, and years ago I bought a house on the Sunshine Coast."

The Sunshine Coast, accessible from North Vancouver via ferry, was a hilly, windswept coastline of deep fjords and tiny settlements. Despite its name, the sun was absent far more than it was present. Two logging communities, Gibsons Landing and Sechelt, were the only towns.

"The Sunshine Coast? It's full of hippies and lumbermen."

"I figure I'll fit in just fine."

✳

"Whass this? Some kind of forkin' funeral?" A short, fat man swaddled in expensive clothes boomed out. "I din't come all this forkin' way to attend no forkin' funeral."

"Walter!" George shouted, his first show of animation in two months.

Despite her surprise Tiffany couldn't manage more than a weak smile. "Daddy, what are you doing here?" She hadn't seen him in over a year, and then only for two days in Toronto, where he insisted on telling her about his books and refused to hear a word about the market.

"I come to save yer forkin' asses. Whattya think?"

Tiffany rose and wrapped her long arms around his stubby form. He still smelled of cigars—far better ones than George smoked.

"I'm afraid there's not much here to save."

"Ya got a goddamn phone, doncha?"

"Yes, of course, but . . ."

"Issa start, doll. And here's somethin' else," he said, handing over an envelope.

She recognized her mother's flowing hand. "What's this?" she asked, staring at a check for $250,000.

"Read the letter. Or do you want me to?"

Dearest Tiffany:

Your father and I are very proud of what you've accomplished, though it wouldn't have been the career that either of us would have wished for you. I have made a nice profit on short-term bonds but I can't possibly spend it all. I thought you might need a little help right now.

Love, Rita.

P.S. Try to stop your father from reverting to too many of his old bad habits.

Tiffany felt her throat constrict. She didn't trust herself to speak.

Gates, shedding years, piped up, "You got anything going?"

"'Course I do. Some great forkin' ideas," Dolby tapped his heavy black glasses. "You'd be surprised watchoo find in forkin' books an' newspapers."

"Say, Walter," George drawled. "I thought you would have given up swearing after so many years with Rita."

"Nah," Dolby said. "It's kinda like blue balls, ya know. Gotta let it out or it kills ya. I been saving up for six forkin' years."

Vancouver Sun, March 11, 1993

THE PASSING OF A STOCK PROMOTER

by Jay Franklin

Walter Dolby, the stock promoter's stock promoter died yesterday. Fittingly, the eighty-nine-year-old who was reputed to have run upwards of 125 successful promotions during his long career, succumbed while in the midst of a promotion of Sundees, a cold dessert with a hot topping, which is intended to be sold from specially designed street-corner vending machines. It rose to nearly $4 a share within two months of the IPO, and vending machine giant Opal Foods LV is reportedly considering a buyout.

"It is an exciting concept and an appropriate end for a great man," his daughter, Vancouver Stock Exchange chairperson, Tiffany Dolby, said. "We are looking forward to strong revenue streams in the near future. My father would have been proud of that."

Walter Dolby, dying as he lived, didn't go gently into the night. At 8:13 P.M., he choked to death while eating a 20-ounce sirloin at Hy's Steak House on Davie Street. Bystanders administered CPR but were unable to revive him.

Dolby came out of retirement in 1978 to save the Morton-Wiles Brokerage Inc., owned by his daughter, Tiffany Dolby, from insolvency. The firm was side-swiped by the pyramid trading scandal that brought down Western Securities. Tintagel Mines was implicated in the scandal.

Readers may recall that Dolby's first promotion after he emerged from retirement was Fantastic Fudge, which featured a "miracle plastic milk" ingredient that gave it an indefinite shelf life. It too was to be sold from vending machines. Unfortunately, the machines were too big for small convenience stores and had a tendency to catch fire.

Next came Clear Head, an antihangover pill. When the Health Department questioned the efficacy of the concoction, Walter Dolby remarketed it as Safe-T, an antiflatulent. When that promotion petered out, he sold the remaining product to a salvage broker for cattle feed.

Then there were movies from a vending machine—an idea ahead of its time—but the problems with stocking, credit checks, and movie returns proved insurmountable. Other products included Waft-A-Way, a pocket-sized personal deodorizer; Sculpt-Ur-Self, polyurethane-foam furniture; and NoFat, a zero-calorie dessert. Unfortunately, the latter caused thunderous flatulence. Walter told this writer he briefly considered reviving Safe-T, the antiflatulent, and marketing them together, but even he thought that was too much.

Walter Dolby often said his proudest moment was the day he learned to read. He thanked a spell in the New Westminster federal penitentiary for that. Some might dismiss Walter Dolby as a snake-oil salesman of the old promoter school. But in his career he did locate one of the largest molybdenum mines in the world and he invested in a process to revive water-damaged books. That process saved much of the Queen's library when Windsor Castle caught fire last year.

Tiffany cut the obituary out of the paper and folded it carefully. She tucked it into an inside pocket of her wallet, beside another fraying clipping, dated January 1981.

Richard Kirby, a former employee of Morton-Wiles Brokerage Inc. of Vancouver and a well-known mining financier with dealings in China, was found dead yesterday morning in his Denver apartment. His throat was slashed in what the police are calling a mob hit, though U.S. federal investigators are puzzled about the obvious signs of torture, which are not typical of organized crime.

Kirby, a former intelligence officer . . .

PART XII

Ellie
Nesbitt

73

*

2003

Vancouver's Downtown

Eastside

"Pert," Beauregard Dolby suggested.

"Pert?"

"Covers a lot of bases."

"Pert sounds like a cheerleader, or *Baywatch*. Big breasts and bouncy. That ain't me."

Beauregard, known on the street as Bo Doll, pondered the issue with gravity.

"How about 'perky' then?"

Ellie Nesbitt giggled.

"Now it sounds like I'm a pot of coffee."

"Coffee's good," Beauregard said, shivering in the midwinter chill.

Ellie studied the sheet of paper lying across her knees. EXTRA! EXTRA! MOVIE EXTRAS NEEDED! GREAT WORK! GREAT PAY! MEET THE STARS! TAKE ADVANTAGE OF HOLLYWOOD NORTH'S MOVIE BOOM!

Most applicants are working within seven days, the form promised. On the back was a long list of questions about size (height, bust, shoe, waist), weight, coloring, ethnic influence, languages spoken, personality type, and look, which Ellie took to mean appearance.

"This will really confuse them," Ellie said, writing, "Exotic, Native American, Pert and Perky" in the Look category. "Say, Bo, you ever see a perky Indian?"

"Can't say I have. If I did I might just turn and run. Kind of like coming across a friendly pit bull." He paused. "Perky Indian would be an oxymoron if ever there was one."

"An oxy what?"

"Moron, oxymoron. Two words or ideas that contradict each other. I once tried to teach the concept to my dad. After that he'd call anything he didn't understand 'an oxtail muffin.' Truth is, Dad *was* an oxymoron."

Ellie, with at least half of her blood coming from the Coast Salish, thought of herself as gloomy, but she doubted the EXtra! people would find that description appealing. Her skin was the color of pulled toffee, tending to dark but not quite getting there. Thick eyebrows arched to a smooth, high forehead, framing eyes that were an odd contrast, hazel with the iris almost entirely filling the white, giving her a deerlike look. With the long face and square chin of unknown white ancestors, Ellie looked less Indian than Indonesian.

"Gloomy" was not a word most other people would use to describe Ellie— until her mouth was included in the package. It was wide and generous, thanks to her native forebears, but the corners rarely rose above the horizontal. The Hastings Street glower. It didn't take long for new inhabitants of Vancouver's downtown eastside to acquire the glower if they didn't have it already. Bellies nourished on cheesies, cigarettes, and cheap sherry didn't provide sufficient energy to raise lips in even the semblance of a smile. Children inherited the glower from their parents as they did the shuffling, round-shouldered gait that the white junkie trash of Hastings Street called the Red Rumba.

Ellie and Bo sat companionably on a bench in Oppenheimer Park, an afterthought bit of green on the shoulder of Vancouver's downtown. With Chinatown to the north and west, the railway tracks and Burrard Inlet to the south, and faceless acres of nondescript buildings all around, the area couldn't decide if it was a neighborhood or not. To those who lived there, in the rooming houses, basement squats, shelters, and alleys, it was the place of last resort.

Ellie had lived within four blocks of Oppenheimer Park her entire life, and she often wondered what accident of circumstance had allowed this precious bit of green to survive in the worst area of the Lower Mainland. Though the small park looked like an oasis with a hopeful playground in one corner, her mother, whom Ellie called the Mighty Old One, had refused to let her play there as a child. She'd spun horrific tales of children gobbled up by ogres or falling on discarded needles, which turned them into zombies. The Mighty Old One didn't believe in sparing a child's fears in order to make a point.

A fifteen-minute walk west into the downtown core took you to Holt Renfrew, Tiffany's, and stark boutiques with inventory so minimal browsers could be forgiven for thinking they had stumbled into someone's private walk-in closet. Farther south the much-debated development on the 1986 World Exposition site swarmed over the reclaimed lands, which had once belonged to False Creek. All glass, steel, and aggressive angles, the town houses and condos attracted the young, monied crowd—from the financial and high-tech sectors to the rapidly expanding music, film, and television crowd.

Vancouverites with equal means but the inclination to bicycle to work and eat whole grains gravitated across Burrard Bridge to the leafy streets of Kitsilano, where cedar was preferred over steel, and jogging, not bar hopping, was the exercise of choice.

Occasionally Ellie bused to Kitsilano Beach to stroll the pathways and gawk at toned and bared bodies. Her favorite place was the startling blue expanse of the Kitsilano outdoor pool. Ellie marveled at people who dove in and swam up and down, seemingly for hours. A sign said eleven lengths equaled one mile. A mile—all in the water! She didn't own a bathing suit and she knew she'd drown in seconds if she ever found her way into the water.

Ellie had never exercised in her life, though her lithe body looked as if she did. Her mother resembled a dumpling, with thin legs and arms; a bulging bosom; broad, vein-shot cheekbones; and dark eyes that seemed to absorb suffering the way a black garment does the heat. But somewhere in Ellie's past were long limbs, flat stomachs, narrow hips, and square shoulders. The genes had found their way out in her.

✳

"You taking this to the agency today?" Bo asked, scratching his seven-day beard. Somewhere in his mid-fifties, Bo—cleaned up and shaven—could pass for an absentminded academic. In fact, he did spend his days reading thick books or doodling on bits of paper in the park while sipping from quarts of cheap sherry. When short of cash, he ambled over to the corner of Georgia and Granville and traded literary quotations or sketches for a donation. People who tossed him a few bucks were usually drawn to his dignity, despite his skid-row appearance.

Bo's whippy leanness and carriage owed everything to his tall, graceful mother and nothing to his troll-like father. His sister, Tiffany, had inherited the same build, but she now tended toward the emaciated, with her second facelift and an obsession to keep her breasts jutting well beyond her stomach. What the hell. If it's a skinny, stretched-too-tight, shiny-faced old broad she wanted to be, then let her have it. She had the money, none of which she was willing to share. Bo sighed deeply. When Rita Dolby died five years earlier, he told himself he'd restart his glass business with the inheritance, this time making copies of famous neon artifacts. Vancouver rivaled Las Vegas for the most neon signs until the 1960s, when the city council started tearing down the old works of art, saying they were tawdry eyesores. Now such things were all the rage. But somehow the years since his mother died had disappeared into the bottom of a bottle.

"What's the matter, Bo Doll?" Ellie asked as she finished the form, emphatically marking Yes next to the question "Athletic Ability?" This was kind of fun.

"Nothing. Just thinking about thirst. I s'pose I could go over to the Bluebell and beg a cup of coffee?" He left the comment hanging. Ellie took it as the prelude to a touch.

"Bo!" she warned. They had two unspoken rules between them. He never drank in front of her and he never ever asked for money. That didn't stop the odd hint.

"What?" he said, all innocence. "So why the interest in becoming a movie star?" he added, moving on to a safer subject.

"An extra," she corrected. "I told you already. I signed up for the professional dealer course. It's six weeks and they guarantee you work. I'm going to get out of this city and work the casino ships in the Caribbean."

"Pipe dream, if you ask me."

"And who asked?" Ellie shot back irritably.

Bo had been around since Ellie was born. The Mighty Old One worked for a brief period in Bo's stained-glass workshop and gallery in Gastown before he got so drunk one night he forgot to turn off the propane and the whole building exploded. Everyone took a piece out of Bo, and the taking didn't stop until he and the bottle became permanent bedmates. He shared anything alcoholic he could get his hands on with Ellie's mother in the narrow alleys of Chinatown, where the cops rarely ventured. It was Bo who dragged Ellie's mother off a heating grate in the pouring rain when she had her first diabetic seizure.

"Don't be mad, Ellie-Belly."

"I'm not mad, I just want to get out of here. If I can get a few of these extra jobs, that, plus the money I've got saved from Sparky's, will get me to Reno. I've already paid the deposit."

"How much you got?"

Ellie looked hard at the two men sleeping curled up, like any long-married couple. They were hunched against a totem pole erected to commemorate the numerous First Nations people who died every year on the downtown eastside. She glanced over at the three young people giggling, swaying, and drinking something out of a Frisbee. Farther along, a man leaned against a tree, holding his penis in one hand. He'd been standing that way for ages, willing the urine to flow. Nobody seemed interested in Bo and Ellie's conversation.

"A little over three thousand," she said hesitantly. It went against the grain to tell anyone, even Bo. But Ellie was proud of getting together the money and she hadn't made more than a couple of hundred of it on her back.

"Wow!"

"Yeah, that's what I think. Twenty-five hundred gets me the course. Then I need clothes, a bus ticket to Reno, and a plane ticket for wherever they get me a job. I'm almost there." Ellie's face softened and her lips rose slightly. It was worth a real smile, but she'd wait on that. Too many disappointments had taught her to count on nothing until it was in your hand.

"How much do you think it costs to fly from Reno to the Bahamas?"

"How the hell would I know? I flew here from Toronto thirty years ago. Haven't been on a plane since." Bo stretched his mouth wide in a yawn, basting Ellie with street breath—the fruity essence of bad wine and ketosis from a stomach too long denied food or the odor from a diabetic's breathing out the sugar he could no longer digest. The Mighty Old One, dead of diabetic shock a year and a half before at the age of forty-seven, reeked of it.

"You're really going?" He sounded pathetic, like a lost child.

The white ocean liner floating in Ellie's mind disappeared like a popped balloon. "Yeah, I'm going," she said kindly, "but don't you worry, Bo Doll, I'll be back one day, all married up to some ship's captain and we'll take you on a cruise to Fiji or something."

"I get seasick."

Ellie pulled out a cruise ship brochure she'd been fantasizing with.

"It says right here that even people who get the worst seasickness are OK on these ships."

She rose to her feet, hauling her purse to her shoulder. It was heavy with tips from Sparky's, a rib joint featuring cheap beer and eight thousand square feet of pool tables. Able Morris, the owner, hadn't paid a worker vacation pay in as long as anyone could remember, and he carefully structured shifts so no one worked sufficient hours in any given week to warrant benefits. He also flouted the province's minimum wage. He kept all tips for weekly dispersal, when he paid everyone in cash. Thus no one could prove the weekly envelope was below what the law required, because no one knew the aggregate tips.

"It like fuckink my wife!" he would rail if anyone dared raise the subject of minimum wage. "This damn province wants fuck my wife they make me pay such think! I not let no one fuck my wife and no make me pay what I not wanna pay. You want fuck my wife?" he'd glare at the offender, usually a new employee protesting that their minimum hourly wage plus tips should have produced a pay packet at least fifteen percent larger.

"Sex with Ab's wife'd be kind of like screwing a lizard," shuddered one of the table boys. "An old lizard." From then on Able's wattle-cheeked, pockmarked bride of fifty-two years was secretly referred to as Liz.

✳

Since her mother's death, Ellie's every thought and waking moment had been spent amassing her fortune, her ticket out. She looked at the EXtra! application in her hand. The address was Howe Street, five blocks south of the area once frequented by penny-stock promoters, gold bugs, and geologists. The Vancouver Stock Exchange, amalgamated with the smaller junior stock market in Alberta and the venture exchange in Toronto, didn't exist as a separate entity anymore. The sidewalk boards were long gone and so was the trading floor, as the venture capital market swooped around the globe via the Internet.

"See ya, Bo," Ellie called out.

"Yeah, sure," Bo responded.

Ellie headed for the opening in the chain-link fence around the park. Near it, the totem pole stood oddly. Ignoring the couple sleeping at its base, she glanced at the plaque. She knew it by heart.

TO OUR SISTERS AND BROTHERS WHO HAVE DIED UNNECESSARLY.

"Can't even get the spelling right," Ellie muttered. Spelling had been her strong suit in school.

She stared up at the raven topping the pole. The creature looked disinterested, as did the two wolves beneath it, looking away from each other.

"It won't be long, kids," Ellie whispered. She rubbed her hand over the coppers at the base of the pole for luck. One of the men on the ground pulled a sleeping bag off his face.

"Got some change?" he croaked through cracked lips.

"In your dreams," Ellie said, setting off toward Gastown.

On her way to EXtra! Ellie walked fifteen minutes west through the tourist lures of Gastown, now dead quiet in the aftermath of Christmas as Vancouver braced for the inevitable months of rain. Some winters there was no snow and the temperature rarely went below freezing, but there was rain in the winter, always rain, forty-five inches of it every year, most of it falling between November and March. After years of disrepute, Gastown was spruced up with loft accommodations, where lawyers, stockbrokers, and designers paid extra for pitted-concrete floors, exposed conduits, and rough brick walls with bits of rotting wood showing through open-concept living rooms.

Ellie lengthened her stride just as a dignified-looking, middle-aged black man dressed in a tux moved to intercept her. He positioned himself so that Ellie either had to stop or step over the curb into a large puddle of unknown depth.

"Young lady, you look like a person who might be on the lookout for a fine condominium," he said with an English accent but with the rhythm of the Caribbean in it.

"Yeah right," she said, stuffing the four-color brochure he'd handed her into her pocket and moving to step around him.

"Please, sister," the man said quietly. "You don't go up, I don't get paid."

Ellie looked at him. "Why not?" she said with a burst of unusual spontaneity. What would she lose, having a look? And besides, she wasn't working today and the casting agency was only ten minutes away. She had time and she had money, she thought, smiling to herself. Why not see what her three thousand bucks would buy?

✳

Three stories above the sidewalk there were no walls anywhere, save around the bathrooms, and those didn't even reach the ceiling. Maybe rich people don't make any noise when they do their business, Ellie considered. If they could hear the men in her building let loose in the middle of the night, they'd double-wall these bathrooms floor-to-ceiling.

The real estate agent, in thigh-hugging microfiber and a belly T-shirt under a gauzy top, waltzed Ellie around the room. And it was just one room, all 1,450 square feet of it, if you didn't count the three bathrooms.

"The open-design concept symbolizes Vancouver," the agent caroled. "Did you know *Condé Nast* named Vancouver the World City for the next millennium?"

Ellie wandered around the ice-cold furniture settings. White corduroy, steel-gray, and mint-green oversized chairs. She liked big colors—magenta, royal blue, pumpkin orange—but she would kill for these squishy, enveloping chairs that looked big enough to hide a four-hundred-pound man. The footstool alone would take her entire savings.

"Vancouver's open to the world. Mountain, sky, beach, ocean, everything!" the agent gushed. "Nothing should distract from that openness. So no walls, just pure openness. Like nature itself."

Ellie didn't know anything about nature. Aside from Oppenheimer Park, landscaped with rummies and druggies, it didn't exist in her world.

"See," the agent gestured expansively toward the floor-to-ceiling windows, "nothing to distract.

"Our clients have very busy lives," she lowered her voice, as if confiding. "They need a respite. They need nature."

Enough of the sales pitch. Time to get down to business. Starting at half a million for 550 square feet, she didn't want to waste too much time on *unqualified* browsers. When she'd first started in the business, she chirped to anyone who came in, but her chakra reader said this excessive goodwill was eroding her energy center. Not only that, it was unprofitable.

Unfortunately it wasn't so easy to *qualify* people anymore. While this girl was certainly striking-looking, she was obviously native and dressed like a ragamuffin. She couldn't be a high-class hooker with those dowdy clothes or Someone's Girlfriend—both categories would *qualify.* But maybe she wasn't native. With her long, slightly kinky hair, she might be from somewhere exotic, like Chad; that model Suki came from one of those little countries. She could be a rich daughter of Someone Who Counted. Then again, she could be in the movies. Goldie Hawn and Kurt Russell had stopped by the showroom the previous week. At first she didn't recognize them. Who would, for heaven's sake! They looked like a couple of hoboes, with backpacks, holes in their pants, and layering that went out with the 1970s. And he was so short! But they were most certainly *qualified.*

"What business are you in?" the agent inquired, adjusting her poppy-colored overshirt and smoothing invisible lines in her pubic bone–grazing bell-bottomed pants. A discreet diamond lay at her throat, a present from a developer adept at turning ski areas like Whistler, two hours from Vancouver, into "alpine villages," instant Switzerlands. They'd screwed in the gondola on his last visit.

"Umm, movies." The first thing that came into her head.

"Oh really!" the agent replied brightly. "Are you involved in that new movie studio on Cypress Mountain? I've found homes for several people who are part of that. Partners, of course."

Ellie gazed out of the window at the thick, green blanket of the north shore mountains, cut in slashes almost to the top as far as she could see. Not clear cuts, but developments. I could live here, she thought, surprising herself. I'd paint the walls but I could make a go of it.

"Are you an actor?" the agent probed. "Are you involved in the shoot in Stanley Park?"

"Uh, no, not really."

"A producer, director?" the woman prodded hopefully.

"Kinda," Ellie mumbled. "Producer. I produce."

The woman had her doubts, but what did it cost to be polite? She'd met many producers in the last ten years. Vancouver boasted it was Hollywood North, with Movies of the Week, pilots, feature films, and location specialties overwhelming the streets, making it the second largest movie city in the world next to Hollywood. She couldn't remember any of them wearing Hush Puppies, but there'd been plenty of scruffy hiking boots and safari jackets.

Heart pumping with adrenaline, Ellie dashed down the industrial, rusted-at-the-factory, iron stairs, her Hush Puppies making no sound. By the time she reached the old library on Burrard and Robson, she was laughing to herself. The library was hailed as a monument to midcentury architecture, but to her it was an ugly chunk of concrete, even with the new glass façade and "Virgin Records" dancing across in huge neon letters. She couldn't believe the city left it standing after the books were moved to a new building at the far end of downtown, near the revitalized district of Yaletown. Across from the Canadian Broadcasting Center, the new library was heralded as a monument to 1990s architecture. Yaletown had been an excellent source of vagrant housing until the "latte monsters," as Bo called them, moved in and the pungent smell of urine was replaced by the scents of aromatherapy and java.

Ellie sucked in the cool January air, still exhilarated. Glancing across the street, she spotted her favorite color and crossed over to take a look. In the window of Marco's was a fluffy, deep-hued-raspberry thing—jacket, sweater, shirt, shawl—she wasn't sure but she had to have it or at least look at it. "It'll go great with my shoes," she said aloud.

"*That* is a Lida Biday!" the man/woman in the store sniffed airily to her request. "Only one in the city. What *might* you be thinking of wearing it with?" he/she said as tonelessly as a computer-generated voice. The salesman/woman stared at Ellie's shoes; he/she could spot a light wallet at a hundred paces.

"My, uh, my uh, other shoes." Ellie felt the anger scratching its way up her backbone. Bo called it the righteous anger of the oppressed. "How much is it anyway?"

"$729.99. Why don't you come back with your *other* shoes and try it on some time." The salesperson turned and walked away.

"And fuck you too," Ellie whispered to the twitching hips disappearing behind a floating counter suspended from the ceiling with a massive rusting chain.

74

*

The West Georgia office of EXtra! EXtra! reverberated with barely controlled hysteria.

"What asshole put . . . !"

"Sonofabitch, I'm gonna kill her!"

"Step on it, will ya, Cody!"

"We need seven more!"

"Seven!"

"Seven."

"Where in hell am I gonna find seven Indians?" bemoaned Cody, the casting agent, a crew-cut man in his late thirties, working hard at hanging on to his fading boyishness. "'Scuse me, Miss Politically Correct," he sneered at Jennifer, circumventing a ritual objection, "seven *First Nations People* on Saturday morning?"

"You could try rounding them up on Hastings Street," said a prematurely balding man, who looked vaguely like the beleaguered father in a sitcom.

"Funny, Maurice. Very funny."

"What do *you* want?"

Watching the shouted interchange it took Ellie a moment to realize the last comment had been directed at her. "Well," she started.

"Hey, hey, hey!" Cody interjected. "Angel from heaven, people."

Disconcertingly, everyone lapsed into silence.

"She's an Indian, for chrissakes," whispered Jennifer, a black woman adorned entirely in black, including her lipstick.

"When you wish upon a star," Cody sang off key.

Moving south and west from the downtown eastside, life was supposed to get more civilized. But these people, Ellie thought to herself, could match anyone on the street for crazy.

"I'm applying for a job as an extra," she said haltingly. She willed her mouth to smile confidently.

"Any more like you?" Cody demanded. "You got friends?"

"What?" Ellie was confused by the rapid-fire conversation.

"Sorry, sometimes we get ahead of ourselves." Cody took a theatrical breath. "Let's start from the beginning."

The woman jumped in. "You're an Indian, uh, native First Nations person. Right?"

"Um, yes," Ellie responded uncomfortably. She made it sound like a disease.

"You got papers?"

"Papers?"

Cody gulped down a put-upon breath. "Papers!" he flapped Ellie's application in her face. "Papers! Stature papers. A fucking pedigree."

Miss Politically Correct chimed in, "Status papers, you dolt."

"Get outta my ass, Jennifer. If you'd done your fucking job, I wouldn't have a hundred-pound sparrow pecking my dick off."

"No one said they had to be *real* First Nations." She grabbed a file. "See!" she stabbed her finger at a line, "Type: twenty-eight Native Indians—twelve men, seven children, nine women."

"Well, Madam Sparrow is having the shit fit of the century, because half of them you sent over are Italians, Portuguese, or ski bums with a tan. You even sent a guy over with a turban."

"He promised to take it off," she responded lamely. "He had the look."

"He looked like a man with a turban," Cody scoffed.

Ellie felt as if she had stepped into the middle of a poorly scripted movie with no plot line.

"*Type!*" shrieked Jennifer. "When we did the *Sun Yat-sen Story,* half the goddamn cast was Vietnamese! I didn't see anyone checking ancestry records. I've been in this business for seventeen goddamn years and I've never once had my judgment on matching ethnics challenged. *Not once!*" Jennifer was close enough to Cody to bite him.

Maurice stepped in, arms spread, pushing the two apart.

"Calm down," he soothed. "We've got time to make this right. Tonight and tomorrow they're shooting Act Two, scenes twenty-two through thirty-seven. It's basically Little Sparrow, one old Indian," he looked at the casting list, "and a girl, seventeen to nineteen. We've got the old guy, Alfred George, and he's as Indian as they come."

He turned to look at Ellie. "And if she's the real McCoy," he paused to look at her application, "Ellie Nesbitt here might just do the trick for the girl in the vision."

The three clustered around Ellie, who felt like a mannequin in a store window.

"Good cheeks," observed Jennifer.

"Hair OK, might not need a wig," added Cody.

"The camera'll like her," Jennifer summed up.

"What about the eyes?" Cody said.

"Nice but wrong color, hazel. They have to be dark."

"You wear contacts, honey?" Jennifer chirped sweetly. Ellie shook her head. "No matter, you'll get used to them. Now, tell me. Are you a legitimate Indian, uh, First Nations person?"

In her twenty-three years Ellie had been asked the same thing dozens of times, usually impolitely. Only once did the question have a positive connotation. An enthusiastic elementary school teacher had created a chart detailing the background of every child in her class. She'd been happy at school, even without any close friends, especially when she discovered that if you paid attention to the teachers, they paid attention to you. When it was her turn to state her origin, Ellie piped up with the only thing she knew for sure. She claimed to be a full-blood Hastings Indian.

"Oh my," the teacher said eagerly. "I had no idea there was a tribe by that name. Or is it a band? How interesting! We need to learn much more about First Nations people and their fascinating culture, don't we, class?"

✳

"I am Salish, Coast Salish," Ellie said, eyeing them suspiciously. There were many people who comprised the Salish along the coast—Musqueam and Squamish around Vancouver and Esquimalt, Songhees and Cowichan on Vancouver Island, all bound by language and geography and loosely connected by similarities of culture and tradition. Ellie wasn't sure where she belonged. Depending on which boyfriend she had at the time, her mother would cleave herself to that tribe. After Mary Nesbitt's first diabetic attack, Ellie sat by her bedside in St. Paul's Hospital and listened to her mother rave about her past—great-grandparents Ellie had never met and a people she called the Kahnamut. Ellie took her mother's ranting as seriously as she did her transformation meetings, where she claimed to connect people to their previous selves.

The three beamed.

"Okaaaay!" Cody dug $20 out of his pocket and shoved it at Ellie. "Take this. We'll call a cab. Wardrobe's on site. Two days minimum, maybe three. Two and a quarter a day, more if the shoot goes all night. If you end up with any lines, double that. Get her signed up."

He whirled around and snapped instructions to Jennifer and Maurice. "Jen, you get onto Alfred George. Sweet talk him, if you're capable. He's from Squamish, right? Charter a helicopter and fly him up there. See if he can help you round up six more. Maurice, you get down to the shoot. Little Sparrow likes you. Tell her we're on top of everything. Lay some soothe on the director and producer." Cody drew a breath. "Okay, people, let's go!"

Ellie didn't for an instant consider taking the cab. The call time, Cody told her, was three P.M.. Plenty of time. The fare to the Stanley Park shoot was at least $10. She'd take the bus for $1.25 and pocket the rest. More than $18, what a lucky score.

If she ever stopped to think about it, which she worked hard not to, Ellie might have realized that she was born with a bit of luck. The kind of luck that kept her from sliding from one hit or fix to the next. Ellie had no idea why the bottle, the needle, the paper bag, or the pipe didn't own her, and she didn't consider it luck anyway. When your mother sets the carpet on fire and you burn the soles of your feet escaping the blaze, it isn't considered lucky. When you're six years old and your mother goes out one night then forgets to come back for five days, it isn't considered lucky. When a freeloader pukes his life out all over the mattress on the floor, which serves as your bed, with you in it, it isn't considered lucky. When your mother brings a girlfriend home, passes out, and the slope-assed she-dog decides the eleven-year-old daughter should be initiated, it isn't considered lucky.

The bus accelerating along West Georgia Street toward Stanley Park passed two teenaged girls clasping each other as they walked. They were well-ventilated with multiple piercings, crop tops, ill-fitting baggy jeans, and army boots. The West End, with its back-to-back high-rises and greenery-draped condos, was one of North America's most densely populated neighborhoods. Bound by Stanley Park, English Bay, and Burrard Inlet, it was also home to one of the most concentrated gay and lesbian populations on the continent. Vancouver's style, culture, and politics owed a great deal to their presence.

Ellie figured these two, judging by their expensive clothing and accoutrements, lived in Kitsilano, Point Grey, or West Vancouver, and likely gave their well-off parents night terrors with their outlandish behavior. She shook her head. Half the women on the Hastings corridor slept with each other, as whatever men they had hanging around were shriveled most of the time from booze or drugs. Imagine being rich and choosing to screw your own kind instead of being forced to. Catching Ellie's stare, one girl gave her the finger and the other turned and wiggled her rear end. They thought they were so daring! Ellie would love to drag them down to the sewer-smelling alley behind Princess Street on welfare night. They'd be eaten alive.

The bus turned off West Georgia onto Stanley Park Drive. Joggers, walkers, cyclists, Rollerbladers, and skateboarders navigated around each other on the seawall running close to the road. Everyone was intent on their exercise. Vancouver, called La La Land and Lotus Land, had the reputation of being laid back, with a work ethic far inferior to the more serious cities in the East. But when it came to the pursuit of tight tushes, Vancouverites were as dedicated as missionaries.

The bus chugged toward the eastern end of Stanley Park past the eight Brockton Point totem poles standing like a family at a picnic in the clearing protected by a gentle berm and a pond. Ellie searched the grouping. Kahmi. The name popped into her mind for the first time in years. It was her middle name. On a glorious fall day in Ellie's first-grade year, the Mighty Old One had announced she wasn't going to school. Ellie cried and stormed. She loved the East End school with its little cubbies for shoes and coats and a bit of shelf space with her name on it for her lunch bag, when she had one. There was reading circle at nine-thirty, puzzles at ten, songs at eleven, and lunch precisely at noon. No such precision had ever existed in her life before, and Ellie clung to it fiercely.

But that day they walked all the way to Stanley Park.

"Mommy, my legs are crying," Ellie said an hour into their trek.

"Don't worry, Ellie, honey," Mary Nesbitt crooned, "we'll take the bus back, but I don't got enough for both ways."

"Mommy, Mommy, where we going?"

"Shush, little sister, I will tell you soon."

Just before Hallelujah Point, they cut across the playing field, springy and dewy. Ellie's feet were soaked in minutes. Silently her mother led her to the totem poles. Ellie wanted to look at a thick, heavy pole with a wide-eyed moon-faced figure at the top, which stood off to one side, but her mother pulled her over to the others, clustered together. She pointed to the tallest pole, rising straight and narrow into the gray sky. It seemed impossibly high to Ellie. How did it stand there, all by itself?

"Look at the top," her mother instructed. Ellie craned her neck to see a bird with a large beak and folded wings presiding over five other figures.

"That's you. Kahmi."

"Whass Kahmi?" Ellie lisped.

"Kahmi is the sister of the Thunderbird." Mary pointed to a smaller pole with a powerful bird on the top, its wings opened wide.

"I am Kahmi?"

"Yes, that is your middle name. I give it to you when you was born. Thunderbird rules the sea."

This was the first Ellie'd heard that she had a middle name and the information made her fall silent. They walked to the bus stop and waited nearly an hour for the Stanley Park bus to pick them up, finish the park loop, and drop them off near the glass-clad bank towers in the downtown's center. Neither mother nor daughter said a word the whole time.

Ellie thought of her mother and wondered what she'd say about her being an extra in a movie shot in Stanley Park. Her hand went to her chest and a cheap silverplated locket. Her mother had it all her life but rarely wore it. But Ellie noticed she brought the locket with her and kept it in her pocket when the seekers gathered to hear Mary Nesbitt spin tales of fish walking and rocks talking. Three days before she died of diabetic shock, her mother gave Ellie the locket.

"Something tells me you should wear it," she said. As she leaned over to hook the chain around Ellie's neck, the papery skin of her arms touched her daughter's cheek. It had been a hard six months trying to care for her. Though weakening by the day, she refused to go to the hospital. Ellie never doubted the Mighty Old One would get better. Despite her many vices and faults, there was a power emanating from her mother, a sense of deep reserves. That night was the first time she realized her mother was far from mighty. And, as she gazed into Mary Nesbitt's hard, hurt black eyes, Ellie also realized her mother was far from old. The Mighty Old One. Neither.

Daydreaming, Ellie almost missed her stop at the entrance to Beaver Lake. If it hadn't been for the long line of movie trucks, the bus would have sailed on past. As soon as she got off, she saw a big sign, EXTRAS, with an arrow pointing to a tent. Most of those milling around, drinking juice and eating peanut-butter sandwiches, looked native. They must be ones who'd already passed the star's scrutiny. Some were obvious veterans, having arrived with their own foldout chairs and bags bulging with food, magazines, knitting, and other diversions. Others, like Ellie, were new. They rubbernecked, as people and equipment moved around, tried to listen in on conversations, and stared at everyone who passed, wondering if that person was famous. She heard Pauline Little Sparrow's name mentioned several times.

"Have you seen her?"

"Is she as pretty as they say?"

"I heard she gives everyone these hand-painted T-shirts. Do you think we'll get one?"

An old hand piped up at the back of the tent. He was seventy at least, with a face like a caved-in pumpkin. It was Alfred George. Ellie recognized him, a veteran of every movie shot in the last thirty years that called for a native North American face.

"I been in movies with Harrison Ford, Julia Roberts, Sandra Bullock, Brad Pitt, Jack Nicholson." He listed off the stars' names on his fingers. "An' I din't see one of them the whole time. The on'y two I laid eyes on was Jodie Foster in *Maverick* and Kevin Kline in *Violets are Blue.* So don't count your chickies on seein' Ms. Little Sparrow."

Two people appeared at the entrance to the tent with clipboards and headsets. Virtually everyone got sent away with instructions to return two days later. The veterans shrugged and shouldered their belongings. The rookies didn't trouble to hide their disappointment.

"Nesbitt! Anyone here by that name?

Ellie raised her hand.

"You're in the shore scene, right?"

"I don't know," Ellie shrugged. "They just told me to come here."

The woman pulled off her bright-blue sunglasses, examined Ellie, then studied her clipboard. "Must be. OK, Frank, take her to the set and see when Gordie wants her, will you?"

A golf cart scooped Ellie up and hummed her along the trail leading to Beaver Lake. The real name, Akha-Chu, "little pond," had been forgotten in the years following Warburton Pike's experience in the sweat lodge. From a bird's-eye view, the park, the lake forming an eye, still looked like a dissolute duck with a goiter—Lost Lagoon—and a stogie hanging from its beak— Deadman's Island. The smell from Peter the Whaler's blubber-rendering on the island had long disappeared, as had the stench from the quarantined smallpox victims housed there during the 1880s outbreak. Ellie shuddered as the bus went past it. She remembered her mother's stories about the little island from their totem pole visit. It was a place, she'd said, of terrible secrets.

The cart bumped along the trail. Ellie grabbed the sides to stay in her seat.

"Sorry about that," the driver said. "It was much worse before we got permission to fix it for the vehicles."

There had been the usual coronaries from environmentalists when the producer wanted to widen several trails to accommodate not only the carts but the boom trucks. But films are "nonpolluting" and a "renewable" resource business—at least from the perspective of the air and water, if not the soul. They also equal glamour. Obstacles fall away in the face of glamour. In Vancouver, just about anything the movies wanted they got.

✳

"Yes, but what nation, which tribe? Who are *your* people?"

Ellie couldn't believe that she was standing in the middle of Stanley Park with Pauline Little Sparrow—singer, video artist, actor, businesswoman, clothing designer, and omnivorous collector of native antiquities—your basic all-around super, mega, top-of-the-world star. Her various enterprises grossed $450 million a year. One of her stores, Painted Bird, opened on Granville Street in the city. No tawdry dream-catchers there. Bentwood boxes, carved obsidian bowls, and jade jewelry sold for thousands. And here was Ellie Nesbitt, talking about, of all things, being an Indian.

"Don't be shy," Little Sparrow prompted.

"My grandmother was raised with the Squamish band. My mother as well, before she came downtown."

"Ah, yes, the Squamish, people of the shore and mountain?" Sparrow pressed, her wide, pink lips smiling encouragingly. When Pauline Little Sparrow turned her attention on a person, the intensity was enveloping. Ellie found herself wanting to tell the star everything.

"My mother said we were part of the Kahnamut generations ago," she said hesitantly.

"I don't know that name," Little Sparrow said. "Were they here, on the Lower Mainland?"

"I don't think they exist anymore."

"That's a shame. Ancestors are so important," Little Sparrow said sympathetically.

Ellie was nervous that she would ask for status papers after the fuss at the EXtra! office, but Little Sparrow seemed content with Ellie's appearance and explanation. The fact was she had no status papers, and neither did her mother, like tens of thousands of others without the right percentage of aboriginal blood.

"Pauleeeen! Sweetie! We must along." An impossibly thin Frenchman wiggled his fingers at Little Sparrow. "You do chitty-chatty later, OK, sweetie?" Somehow he managed to smile warmly at the star while scowling at Ellie.

"OK, OK, Hervé!" Little Sparrow snapped. "Get me my ranch manager on the phone. I want to know how those two mares are doing. They've both been waxed up for four days. They should be foaling any second."

Hervé muttered darkly, but not nearly loud enough to be overheard, as he turned away to dial. "Wax! Wax is for the candles. Now I am horse baby-sitter."

"Mares get this yellowy stuff hanging from their teats when they're about to foal," Little Sparrow explained, as if Ellie had asked. "Usually they drop a day or two after, but these two mares are hanging on. It worries me, because they are the only ones I've been able to trace to the Blackfoot Sioux in the Montana area."

"Oh," replied Ellie dumbly.

Recently Little Sparrow had been gathering Paint and Appaloosa horses and ponies from all over North America with a believed connection to long-lost tribal breeding programs. A two-part PBS documentary traced her quest to revitalize the bloodline of the earliest native horses. Her new CD, video, book, calendar—all titled Painted Bird—were breaking every sales record in existence. Ellie liked the CD and bought the calendar with its glorious horses for Bo, who often said if he were born again he'd move to Alberta or Montana and be a cattle rancher. She was pretty sure he traded the calendar for a pack of cigarettes.

A woman hustled up. "Pauline! We got it! Can you believe this! Look at the quality!"

Little Sparrow whirled around, triumph transforming her face. The movie star's personality was like the moths Ellie sometimes saw in Oppenheimer Park. Bluish gray one minute, green the next, and then a change to muddy brown, as the insect flew from tree to bush to grass. Little Sparrow reached out for the blanket the woman clutched in her arms. It was black with a red border set off by pearly buttons sewn close together. In the center was a creature with the head of a frog and arms circling around to end with two whales facing each other, a plume of buttons rising from their blowholes. The figure seemed to move within the confines of its red border. The eyes bore outward, as if fixed on a distant horizon.

"Ohh," Pauline Little Sparrow breathed dreamily. "Perfect, so absolutely perfect." Her voice hardened. "Do we have design rights locked down?"

"Not exactly."

"Not exactly?" Little Sparrow barked. "I can't use it in the film and then license it for my clothing line without the rights. I spent a fortune flying you to the Queen Charlotte Islands. Not to mention the ridiculous cost of bringing the goddamn lawyers up from L.A. Now you tell me you couldn't nail down the design rights!"

The woman desperately searched for the correct response. "The elders agreed to let us use the ceremonial blanket in the film. But they refused to sell the design." She wilted under the heat of Little Sparrow's gaze. "Tried everything. I told them the profits would go to the Sparrow Foundation. I made the lump-sum offer. They took the cash but on the condition we returned the blanket when the movie was finished. Said it had images on it that were important ancestral depictions. They just don't understand business! I told them we couldn't possibly . . ." her voice trailed off as she saw Little Sparrow's reaction.

"Sounds like they understand business just fine," Little Sparrow stroked the iridescent buttons thoughtfully. "Just fine." Her fingers were slender and long, despite her short stature. She was tiny all over, except for amazing eyes, like polished black stones, and a pair of gravity-defying breasts, out of proportion to her slender frame. Though Little Sparrow denied it, there was endless speculation about enhancement, and historians of that sort of thing pointed to her teenaged photo spread in *Playboy,* which showed no hint of her later endowment.

Even standing still and silent, the star radiated energy. Perhaps that's why they all cluster around her like ants on the discarded candy wrappers and fast-food containers littering the streets of her neighborhood, Ellie thought. She too could feel a thrum of excitement. I'm becoming a groupie or something, she teased herself.

Sparrow turned away and sat down on a mossy stump. The pale green-yellow lichen set off the warm brown of her skin and the simple buckskin skirt she wore, decorated only by a line of hand-forged conchos down one side. The long fringe on the skirt draped on the ground. Hervé, envisioning a $6,000 prototype design tossed in the garbage, hustled over and lifted the fringe out of the dirt. Little Sparrow glared. He scurried off. She took a jade medallion from around her neck, held it against her forehead, and closed her eyes. Unconsciously Ellie held her breath. Glancing at the onlookers she realized they were doing the same thing. Sparrow began to sing, or chant, a low mournful sound in a language Ellie didn't recognize.

Most of the group bowed their heads. Some crossed themselves. Others hummed softly along. Only Hervé and the bodyguard kept their eyes on the star. Hervé looked impatient, the bodyguard watchful. Ellie was caught up in the rise and fall of Little Sparrow's throaty tones. Her voice was like liquid chocolate. Goose bumps rose on Ellie's arms and neck. The people, the movie set at the edge of the lake, the octopuslike vehicles and machinery melted into the cedar trees. When Sparrow stopped, Ellie felt a prick of regret and suddenly the noise of a $60 million movie churned back into her consciousness.

"Go back to the elders," Little Sparrow ordered quietly. "Apologize to them for the insensitivity of your approach. Tell them they are right to feel insulted. Tell them, with their permission, I will personally present myself to ask for their forgiveness on Friday. Double the cash offer and cut them in for a twenty percent royalty for any sales with their images. Go as high as thirty percent on the royalty. If they go for it, politely suggest they have their lawyer on hand for a signing."

"They already had a lawyer there," the woman said, understanding lighting up her eyes. "Actually two lawyers, both natives."

Little Sparrow laughed with full-throated exuberance. "Get it now?" she said. "'Don't understand business!'" Another peal of laughter. "Book the chopper for my visit. Make sure it's big enough to hold a camera crew. And get up there as fast as you can."

*

A voice at Ellie's shoulder made her jump.

"Pretty slick, isn't she? Ancillaries like clothing sales, T-shirts, toys can double a movie's net and guess who gets the biggest piece of that? She'll offer them the bigger royalty, but it will be net of costs, costs she controls, of course, so she'll end up getting the rights for what she intended to pay in the first place."

Ellie turned to see an athletic-looking man in his early thirties, black hair cropped short, strong eyebrows running in an almost unbroken line across a square, high forehead, and brown eyes with sun wrinkles extending to the top of his cheekbones. He spoke as if he was picking up a long-running conversation with her. His mouth was so close to her ear, Ellie could feel and smell his breath, which had a cedar undertone. She didn't like his proximity and moved back slightly.

"If there was a title, Queen of First Nations, Ms. Sparrow would buy it," he continued, not seeming to notice Ellie's movement.

"I haven't a clue what you're talking about," Ellie said.

The man kept talking as if they were in a deep discussion.

"If it has aboriginal authenticity, Sparrow buys it. I don't think there's a single piece in her clothing line that sells for under five hundred dollars. Ironic, don't you think? A corporate Indian buying up designs and selling them at a price no native could afford."

Ellie looked at him more closely. He was obviously native. His widely spaced eyes were dark and deep, but his thin lips, long face, and oddly delicate nose made him appear hard and watchful. He was also persistent and creepy.

"Look, I'm just an extra."

"No one is *just* anything."

This guy's quite the preacher, Ellie thought. "Pauline Little Sparrow donates her profits to First Nations people all over the world," she said, giving some of his own back. "The paper said she's going to build two long-houses for Fraser River bands."

"I read that too," the man said. "Great PR. She's a master. And she'll do it too. But the money's tax-deductible, first off. Second, most of it, if not all, is gonna come from corporate sponsors she strong-arms, not to mention three levels of government. I seriously doubt more than a penny out of every dollar spent will come from her."

"What are you doing here, if you've got so much against her?" Ellie was starting to get annoyed.

"Someone has to keep an eye on those who steal our heritage."

"You know what? You got a real holier-than-thou thing going. Work it out on someone else."

The Sparrow coterie was like a wasp nest in August. With Little Sparrow in the center, a swarm bustled on the outskirts, half of them on cell phones or walkie-talkies, the other half trying to gain her attention for a decision, a meeting, a script review.

"You seem to me to be the perfect person to work it out on, as you put it."

"Why me? I just got here, so leave me alone, why don't you?"

"Perhaps you're here for a reason."

"Yeah, a good one. Money. I don't know what's bothering you, but I'm just an extra and she was very nice to me. *I* like her."

"I like her too," he responded. "Actually it's more correct to say I admire her."

Before he could go any further, Pauline Little Sparrow's voice cut through the din of people and equipment. "Mac!" she yelled to the burly bodyguard who was never far. Her face looked magnificent in anger. "What's that asshole doing here? How did he get through security?"

"It's a park, Ms. Sparrow!" the man next to Ellie responded. "A public park. It belongs to everyone. Not just those with money."

"Peeeples! Peeeples!" Hervé shrieked. "We musssss move on. Shooting scene twenty-nine in thirty minutes. Pleeeeeese Pauleeeene! Wardrobe is weeping for you."

Sparrow's glower disappeared, replaced by a girlish giggle. "OK Hervé, don't bust a gusset." She whispered to Mac as she trotted off, "Get rid of the fucker. I don't care how."

✳

75

Ellie was down on her hands and knees, saliva dripping from her mouth like a dog with something stuck in its throat. Bile roiled painfully in her stomach. She'd been raped once, but this was worse, much worse. A shuddering breath wracked her and rare tears joined into drops at the end of her nose.

Gone! Seven dollars short of $3,200. Gone! Ellie stared unseeing at the ancient vinyl flooring, its pattern long-ago worn away. In places, splinters of subfloor showed through. The smell of mold and urine penetrated her sinuses like a stiletto. Panic, anger, and disbelief churned in her gut.

Only thirty minutes earlier she'd returned home from the first day of shooting, two hundred dollars in her pocket, exuberant with possibilities for the future.

She heard Too Tall Frank peeing in the room above her head. He was so tall, and the toilet so close to the ground, it sounded like a hose filling a metal bucket. Ellie thought she'd been one of the lucky ones when she rented her room. Only three in the twelve-unit tenement had toilets. Hers, the one below, and Too Tall Frank's above her. The various shelters, basement hovels, so-called apartments and rooms of her childhood rarely had toilets, let alone full bathrooms. When she heard that the methadone addict who'd been in and out of this room for a year died, she went straight to the owners in Chinatown to rent it. But the toilet proved to be a liability, the wood on the floor had captured years of errant splashings. No matter how much Lysol she used, the smell remained, a constant clinging undertone. Above her the ceiling was stained with decades of toilet overflows in the apartment above.

Thirty-two hundred dollars to take her away. Gone.

Ellie had started hiding money when she was six, the day she found a $5 bill in the street. She'd savored her good fortune, spending hours deciding what to buy—candy, Archie comics, or Barbie's horse, selling for $4.99 in a Pender Street consignment-store window, four blocks from the room where she lived with her mother. That night the Mighty Old One "borrowed" the $5 while Ellie slept. It bought just enough glue to keep her happy for a day or two.

Ellie kept her money in a Ziploc bag wedged into the back of a huge, old, kitchen-type clock that had hung on the wall since she moved in. It looked like one of those clocks you'd see in the popular 50s diners that were everywhere a few years ago. Gone.

"Nooooo!" Ellie pounded the clock with her fist.

"Goddamn it! Who took it! Tell me! Tell me! Tell me!" she screamed, hitting at the clock until the metal edge cut her hand. She staggered to her feet and out into the corridor. Bo would have a kind word, Bo would make her feel better.

"Lemme smell your bitch box, Ellie Yellie," warbled the man who lived in the stairwell.

Ellie ran down the grim hallway past him, pin dots of rage dancing in front of her eyes.

Out in Oppenheimer Park, where a cold winter drizzle was starting up, Bo wasn't on his favorite bench. Half an hour poking into the nooks and crannies around the park didn't turn him up. She was almost across the park, heading back to Hastings Street, when she stopped abruptly. It was obvious. She couldn't find Bo because Bo had taken the money. Who else knew about it? He was gone and he'd stay gone until the money ran out. Why hadn't she figured it out right away?

Ellie laughed, more a whimper.

"Wasso funny?" an unknown voice rasped from the darkness.

"I got the easiest money of my life standing around and listening to the biggest star in the world talk. Easy money for the first time in my life," she spat out bitterly to a figure slouched against a tree. "Then my best friend ripped me off." She felt like she'd swallowed one of those giant gum balls she'd loved as a kid.

"I've had a lifetime of days like that," the voice answered.

"Oh fuck off."

A couple of clean-cut young men were cutting through the park. As they passed, they lifted their heads like predators scenting prey. Ellie had turned a few tricks before her mother died, desperate for extra cash to look after her, and the thought flitted through her mind. No. She hated the pawing, hated the men, hated herself afterward. Briny air from Burrard Inlet mixed with the faint scent of sulphur carried on the westerly breeze from the pulp mills way up Howe Sound toward Whistler. The men veered toward her.

"Little girl, you're looking lost," said one silkily. He stepped closer. "Ahhh, baby, you've been crying? Did that asshole make you cry?" He pointed to the bum.

"Just go away, will you," Ellie responded wearily. There was never any shortage of jerks.

"We'll help you forget your tears," cooed the other.

"C'mon, let's go powwow." The first man reached out and pulled Ellie toward him. The second gripped her other arm and stuck his hand into her shirt.

"Mmmmmm. Nice titties and no bra. We got an easy one here."

Ellie squirmed away, elbowing one and shoving the other. She wasn't panicked. That was one benefit of living in the downtown eastside. You couldn't make it to puberty without some guy with balls bigger than his brain figuring anything with breasts was game for grabbing. Most of the time a few choice words got rid of them.

"Screw off!" Ellie shouted, marching quickly away. "You losers need to travel in packs to get a girl?" she shot over her shoulder.

At the west end of the park an alleyway ran across to Gore Avenue. Locals called it Bang Alley. Why Ellie cut through there she had no idea. Most nights stand-up hookers worked the alley, charging $20 for a hump against the wall next to the Franciscan Sisters of Atonement. Sometimes they worked in a team. Just as the mark was getting his rocks off, the partner ripped off his valuables while his pants were around his ankles. But this night the winter chill and drizzle kept both johns and whores away.

She probably could have outrun them, but when Ellie heard their footsteps she slipped on an oily slick and went down on her knees. They were on her like foxes on an injured rabbit.

"You got a nasty tongue, red bitch!" panted one as he drove his knees into her back, flattening her against the pavement. She felt their hands scrabbling at her, clutching flesh, looking for openings, poking, invading. Ellie was strong, but one was kneeling across her neck. As they turned her over roughly, she lashed out, driving her fist into a throat and landing a kick somewhere soft.

"Fuckin' cunt!" coughed one. "We're gonna hurt you now!"

The men were experienced. They'd underestimated the fight in her at first, but now they systematically worked to hold her still. One pulled her arms over her head and held them tightly. The other used his knees to hold her legs apart and still while he ripped off her skirt. He rubbed his palms over her pubic bone and plunged his thumbs inside her.

"Yummy, yummy."

"Quit fooling around!" the other man urged. "I want a turn!"

The kick to the attacker's head was so perfectly placed it sent him somersaulting off Ellie exactly as if he was executing a gymnastic dismount, except he didn't move when he hit the ground. Barely had the second attacker raised his head when a kick caught him in the kidneys, doubling him over in screaming pain. Ellie couldn't see where the help was coming from and didn't care. Frantically grabbing her purse, she scrambled to her feet and began to run, her skirt falling away as she hit the entrance to the alley.

"Wait! Wait!" a voice called behind her. He was gaining. Ellie ran harder. Dodging a car, which honked at her, followed by the raucous hoots of the passengers inside, she hit the park at full tilt.

"Ellie!" the voice shouted.

She slowed. Ellie?

"Ellie Nesbitt!"

Her rescuer caught her. "Sorry. Didn't mean to scare you," he panted. It was the man from the movie shoot.

Ellie didn't know whether to cry with relief or laugh with astonishment. "What the hell are *you* doing here?" He bent over, breathing heavily, as much from adrenaline as the effort.

"You're welcome," he said. "Did I misinterpret things back there? Was that a date you were on?" The voice wasn't mean, just making a point.

Ellie covered her eyes for a moment. "Oh God! I thought I'd had it."

"Good thing there weren't more of them. I hurt my foot on the first guy."

"Thank you," Ellie said softly, teeth chattering. "No one around here does things like that." She suddenly felt the chill of her legs and rubbed her thighs.

He took off his old leather jacket and wrapped it around her waist. "We should report this."

"What's the point? They were cruisers and they sure won't be hanging around. The police won't give a shit anyway."

"If everyone had that attitude we might as well give up on law and order!" he chastised.

"They gave up on that long ago around here," she countered. "You some kind of spokesman for the cops?"

"No, but I am a lawyer. People have more power than they believe."

"A lawyer!" Ellie looked at him. The Legal Aid lawyers assigned to her mother during various vagrancy stints in the downtown jail wore suits, or gray skirts and pumps. This jean-clad man was nothing like them.

"Let me at least walk you home."

Ellie accepted. Now that it was over, she felt sick and weak. She didn't want to walk along Hastings Street half-clothed and alone. She tied his jacket arms around her waist and fastened the buttons.

"My name's Matthew Beaver."

"Are you really a lawyer?"

"You bet."

"An Indian lawyer. Hmm. You must have a fairy godmother or something."

"Actually I do."

They passed the Hastee Tastee All Night Diner. The menu consisted of yellowing sheets of paper, in English and Chinese, tacked to the walls. TWO EGG, 3 BACON $2.25.

"How about a cup of coffee or something?"

Ellie was suddenly ravenous but still cautious. "How did you find me?" she asked.

"Easy," he smiled. "Got your address from the casting agency. Told them I was your lawyer."

"And why?"

Matthew Beaver flushed. "Well . . ." Suddenly he was every inch the tongue-tied man talking to an attractive woman who interested him. "I . . ."

He seemed so self-assured, it was nice to know he was human, Ellie thought. "I still can't believe you're a lawyer," Ellie let him off the hook.

"You make it sound so unsavory."

"It's just that I'm not used to seeing our kind with jobs."

"'Our kind'? You need to open your eyes, sister," he responded, not unkindly. "'Our kind' are doing plenty of interesting things."

"Yeah, healing circles, dances for tourists, and ticky-tacky crafts," Ellie mocked.

"Nope. Shit-kicking assholes all the way to the Supreme Court as well as shit-kicking a few of them in dark alleys too."

He was handsome in a cold sort of way, Ellie considered. There couldn't be an ounce of extra flesh on the guy. His arms beneath his T-shirt were muscular pipes.

"Tell me about your fairy godmother."

"I grew up in Pemberton, near Whistler. I was like everyone else. Couldn't wait to hit sixteen and drop out of school. Looking back, it seems I spent all my time fighting and drinking. Most of the teachers were white, but I had one from the Squamish band. He called me in one day just before I quit and asked me if I was interested in going to university." Matthew laughed. "He might as well have asked me if I wanted to walk across hot coals! I was going to join my dad cutting in the woods. He made a decent living."

Ellie dug into her chicken burger, which tasted better than anything she had ever eaten. She might order a second.

"Anyway, he kept at me. The summer I turned nineteen, my dad was laid up. Cut himself with the chain saw." Matthew indicated a cut line running about a foot from his knee to upper thigh. "The teacher came to visit and he offered me a deal."

"Why you?"

"You mean why would anyone bother with someone like me?" he asked.

Ellie blushed. Why couldn't she be nice? Even polite conversation brought out the sharp edges in her.

"It's okay. I wondered the same thing. He said if I agreed to go to either the University of British Columbia or Simon Fraser University for four years, I could get all my tuition and living expenses paid, plus guaranteed work every summer at better than minimum wage."

"Jesus!"

"That's what I said. I reminded him of the little problem about high school. I never finished. He said it didn't matter, because there was a special program for First Nations, with upgrading courses part of the first year."

"You got it because you're a reserve Indian, right?" She didn't say it, but everyone she knew resented the red-carpet treatment status Indians got over the mixed bloods or the women who left the reserves and married white or nonstatus. The status rules had changed to be more equitable to women but many were still nonstatus.

"It's not government. There's a foundation set up years ago with all kinds of noble goals for the advancement of the red man—and woman." He saw her disbelief. "I couldn't believe it at first either. I never intended to keep going, but it was easy money for a while."

"What was it like?"

"University?"

"Yeah."

"Like being a dwarf at a giants' convention," he said with a laugh. "But you know what? After a while I really started to like it."

"And you got to be a lawyer after four years?"

"Oh, no, no. I was going to quit several times but this damn teacher, persistent as hell, he said I should go on to something after my undergraduate degree. So I picked the hardest thing I could think of—law. I wrote my law school admission tests sure I was going to flunk. There was no one in the world more surprised than me when I finished in the top quartile."

"What does that mean?" Ellie suddenly felt very stupid. It was a novel emotion, as she considered herself considerably smarter than most she dealt with in life. Of course, that wasn't saying much.

"Top one quarter of all who wrote the test."

"Did you ever find out where the money came from?"

"It really wasn't a secret. The whole thing was set up over a hundred years ago, and today nobody really seems to care about who the money came from. The main point is how it's spent."

"But who set it up?" Ellie pressed, thinking but not saying, Who on earth would bother?

"A white man. A very strange, very rich white man. His name was Warburton Pike."

"Funny name."

"I thought so too. But here's the real funny part. The foundation is administered by the Chong family here in Vancouver. Apparently they've run it from the beginning."

Chong! Jack Chong owned the building where she lived. Ellie had never seen him, of course, but he didn't sound like the sort who'd be handing out any wads of dough to the derelicts along Hastings.

"There's got to be strings attached."

"There is," Matthew replied. "You've got to go to school. If you don't, they cut the money off fast."

"Do you think they'd pay for a casino dealer's course?" Ellie asked, only half kidding.

"Doubt it," he laughed, "but since I graduated I've run into doctors, community development workers, fisheries experts, teachers, a marine biologist, a linguist, and, of course, lawyers. They came from all over British Columbia, from every band and nation you can think of, and all got the same full-meal deal I did. Some went on to graduate school in the U.S. or Europe. They paid for that too. The Chinese administrators call us 'clients,' like a bank would or something. You're assigned a mentor. The teacher was mine."

"Wow." Ellie struggled with the idea of such good fortune.

"I saw a movie where a bunch of young men got everything they wanted—fancy cars, money, girls, until the Devil showed up demanding payback. After I finished law school I waited for someone to put the touch on me. But no one ever did."

"Okay, if you're a big-shot lawyer, how come you're hanging around Stanley Park spying on Pauline Little Sparrow?"

"Is that what it looks like to you?"

Rude again. He seemed like a nice guy. Why couldn't she just go along a little? "It just doesn't seem to be the kind of thing a lawyer would do."

"The park is a place of great power to our people," he said simply.

"Power? Places don't have power."

"This one does," he answered mildly.

"OK, so it has power," she said in a mocking tone. "What's that got to do with Pauline Little Sparrow's movie?"

"Did you notice those vines in the park?" he asked earnestly. "They're pretty, with big, deep-cut leaves, so shiny they look waxed. They start out like little friends."

He drew his fingers through his brush cut and smiled at her. "You find one in your favorite tree and its leaves look real nice against the needles. You admire it and maybe even encourage them with some fertilizer."

Ellie was starting to think this guy wasn't firing on all cylinders. She stole a glance at his face as he talked. Wide and bony face with a strong jaw. A deep widow's-peak marked his forehead. His skin was darker than hers, and he had the strong Siberian features of many West Coast people.

"Then you wake up one morning and the tree is dying," Matthew continued. "The pretty vine has taken its life, strangled its being. You try to prune it back but it's too late."

"I still don't get it."

"Pauline Little Sparrow is one of those vines. She starts out like a friend, a pal to the aboriginal, but in the end she sucks the life out of us. Just like the whites have been doing for hundreds of years."

"You'll never stop the movie shoot," Ellie said firmly. "She's too big for that. Even if you did, how would that help your band or anyone else?"

"Oh, our pint-sized Miss Indian of the World isn't the point here. I'm using her and her movie as a rallying point. To get us going, get us organized."

"To do what?"

"Take back Stanley Park."

Ellie studied his face. His expression was serious, deadly serious. "Get real," she laughed. "It's huge and it's right downtown. It's a goddamn public park. Even if it weren't, it must be worth a gazillion dollars. Nobody's going to give it to a bunch of Indians."

"It's big all right," Matthew agreed. "One of the biggest urban parks in North America. Bigger even than Central Park in New York. It was native land until settlement moved from the Fraser to around Burrard Inlet. Then they started logging it, used it as a cemetery, a quarantine camp, a leper colony, an abattoir—you name it. Then in 1888 they made it a park, and we were gone for good."

"What makes you think you've got a hope of getting it back?" Ellie thought he was a hopeless dreamer, but she liked hearing him talk.

"Maybe there's no hope. But I kind of like David-and-Goliath causes. The problem is we have no evidence of permanent habitation. No big midden, no nice native burial site. That makes it tough."

"And you think the government is just going to up and give it to you?" she mocked. "Maybe you're right. If you ask nicely enough they'll hand it over."

"Take it," he corrected firmly. "Not give it. Take it. And we've done pretty well taking stuff back. The Nisga'a land claims in the north got them nearly eight hundred square miles—there are countries smaller than that. Some years back we took control of twenty-five acres of Ambleside Park, and, of course, the Park Royal Shopping Centre on the North Shore is native-owned."

"You're kidding? Indians own Park Royal."

"Actually, the land. It's managed by the Squamish band that has the reserve on the other side of the bridge."

Ellie smiled.

"What's so funny?"

"I saw that reserve a lot when I was a kid. My mother had a boyfriend there. The usual—wrecked cars, ratty dogs, garbage, unpainted houses. I can't get over them owning the Park Royal with all those fancy stores and BMWs everywhere just spitting distance away."

"Yeah, it's enough to make you believe in God, isn't it?"

Ellie nodded, still trying to picture her mother's boyfriend, with his giant belly and smashed nose, owning a piece of high-priced real estate.

"We also took back the Point Grey golf club near UBC, where the city's millionaires play," Matthew continued softly. "Nobody thought we could do any of that, but we did. Stanley Park's just a slightly bigger challenge."

"I almost believe you," Ellie said, and it was true, she almost did.

76

"Such skin. Such skin," raved Peggy, the makeup girl, a champagne-headed sprite with jet-black roots and a broad, frosted mouth reminiscent of the 70s. "What *do* you put on it?"

Outside of rain and drugstore moisturizer, Ellie didn't put anything on her skin. Though for a time in grade five she had assiduously rubbed lemon on her face after a classmate called her a greasy Indian.

"Not much," she said. "Though I always thought it would be fun to have one of those makeovers—like you see in the magazines."

"Not necessary, I can tell you that. Now I've got to darken you up a bit but you'll look gorgeous on screen. Say, how are your eyes?"

The dark contacts felt like manhole covers under her lids. "They're better now," Ellie lied, not used to people fussing over her. "Thanks for the drops."

"Nada. Nothing. Anything to help." Peggy dabbed, powdered, and patted. Ellie's hair was already done in one long braid festooned with shells that clicked when she walked. She liked the sound. Though the blanket she wore over her shoulders itched, and the moccasins laced halfway up her calves dug into her flesh, she was amazed at how right everything felt.

"Do you do Pauline Little Sparrow's makeup?"

"Gosh no! She's got her own girl who travels with her. I heard she's Aztec or something, with all these secret mud-and-herb treatments. Pauline's going to be selling some of them in her boutiques and I can't wait to get my hands on them. Sometimes I do help with her hair. Isn't she absolutely wonderful? So down to earth. Though her skin's not nearly as nice as yours. Don't ever tell anyone I said that." Peggy never seemed to come up for breath.

"She's probably meditating right now," Peggy looked at her watch. "She gets in touch with her past lives. It renews her, she says, and brings the voices of her people forth," she sighed admiringly. "She has a royal elder from Alaska who leads her in prayer every day. Being an Indian is so cool!" She interrupted herself with a little gasp. "Sorry, we were instructed to say First Nations People."

"Most of us call ourselves Indians," Ellie said. "But you won't find anyone around where I live saying being an Indian is cool."

"Oh it is. And Pauline is going to make being an Indian the thing to be. Just like Iman did for Somalian women. You see, the thing is, Pauline knows how to be where the energy is and how to use it."

"What do you mean?" Ellie wedged in.

"Remember when she released her first CD, *Wilding*? She was like this *sexy tramp*. She was such a babe, an Indian babe. She said all her inspiration came from the gorgeous women of the bayous before the French started filling it up. Remember that song, 'Chitimacha'? It was named after a tribe down there."

Ellie tried out the chorus. "'Chitimacha baby, lady little bit crazy. I'll be your bayou baby, Chitimacha lady.' I thought that was a town or something. It's a great song, kind of sticks in your head."

"Makes me want to go out and buy dangerous underwear . . . wear no underwear at all," she tittered.

Ellie grinned.

"Then," Peggy listed off on her fingers, "she was the *domineering power woman,* an Apache on the warpath. When she had her little girl, she became like those Pueblos, all shawls and blankets and mothering. Right now she's into the ocean and the West Coast and all that gorgeous artwork. She says it all fits together with her past-life stuff, so it's perfect. You know what she said to me the other day?"

Ellie shook her head.

"She said, uh, okay, I'll try to get it just right . . . she said 'It's not who you are but who you were that counts.' Isn't that so wonderfully profound? I'm just so there with all of that."

"You make her sound a little bit, um, phony," Ellie said, Matthew Beaver's words intruding.

"No! Not at all. Never," Peggy protested, genuinely taken aback. "Pauline's totally, a hundred percent sincere. She's the most sincere person I've ever met. I'd never say anything bad about her. She knows in her heart that it's the right thing to be into coastal Indians. You're so lucky to be an Indian," she repeated. "It's so cool."

Later, sitting on a chair waiting for the early twilight to overtake the trees and lend the scene the desired spectral quality, Ellie thought about the woman's words. Lucky to be Indian. The idea that her blood could be an advantage was completely novel. Perhaps if she could sing, dance, act, and open boutiques from Los Angeles to Paris. Huh! During her periodic rides on the wagon, her mother took advantage of her heritage by fortune-telling in dark vaults underneath some of the port-side buildings, in the cellars of taverns along Hastings, and occasionally in rooms jammed with the ill-washed bodies of the hopeless. Ellie often wondered why those people listened to her mother. As far as she could tell, her mother's skill as a seer, if that's what it was, produced nothing but anguish. She remembered women and men weeping, wailing, falling down, and beating themselves as if trying to tear their former lives out of their bodies.

Matthew Beaver drifted into her thoughts. He'd certainly benefited from his heritage. She made a note to ask him again about the foundation and the dealer's course. You never knew.

Ellie had lots of time to think. Mostly what she'd done on her second day as an extra was sit and wait. Surprisingly, Ellie didn't mind the hanging around. The dense growth in this western section of the park made her feel calm and something else. She searched to identify it. Happy, something like happy. The filming spilled out over Stanley Park Drive, on the edge of the park overlooking the ocean and Siwash Rock. Ellie had no idea there was so much to see on the shoreline and hear in the trees around her. Downtown noise was there all the time. You had to work to shut out the sound of vehicles, people, and pain. Here you had to work at it just to hear anything but the birds, water, and wind.

Ellie was starting to think that making a movie was like baking a cake. The Mighty Old One had briefly held a night job in a bakery. As she worked, Ellie slept in a dog basket underneath one of the steel tables. Before she went to sleep she enjoyed watching her mother lay out the ingredients for the three cakes she was responsible for baking. It always amazed her to wake up and discover the boxes, tubs, and jars full of flour, sugar, salt, and egg transformed into deliciously scented crowns of sweetness. What she saw around her in the late-day gloom of Stanley Park's interior was a mishmash of disparate ingredients that somehow would be fashioned into a cake. She relaxed amid the bustle around her as everyone prepared for the scene. For the first time the loss of her money disappeared completely from her mind.

There were only two people in the scene waiting to be shot, Ellie and Pauline Little Sparrow. But Ellie estimated there were forty or fifty others up on the cliff edge and down on the beach manning equipment, conferring in groups, talking on phones or headsets. Below her the director and a large man with an anxious expression walked miles, striding back and forth, checking distance, lighting, and angles.

"Are you nervous?" Hamish Owen, Pauline's acting coach, strolled up. A sixtyish Englishman, he looked and dressed a bit like a character in *Mary Poppins*. "People say I resemble David Niven, but I'm much more masculine," he said when he'd introduced himself earlier in the day.

"I don't understand enough of what's going on to be nervous," Ellie said.

"I haven't understood anything in forty years of acting," Owen said airily. "I just do. That's really the secret."

The movie's plot was fairly simple, as Owen explained it. "It was taken from a long article about West Coast Indian art in the *New Yorker*. Really just a passing mention, a couple of paragraphs about an Indian legend. Someone brought it to Pauline's attention. She bought the rights to the article and voilà, a movie where none existed before."

"A couple of paragraphs? I thought most movies came out of books."

"No, very few really, when you think of all the books that have been written. Truth is, movie folks have dreadful inferiority complexes and they'd much rather construct a film from a drunken gab session or a single sentence than admit they took the idea from a book."

"Really? It's hard to believe this kind of money being spent on a single sentence."

"Oh sure. Gene Roddenberry sold *Star Trek* as 'Wagon Train in Space.' That was a TV series, but you get the idea."

"I love it," Ellie shook her head, smiling. "It seems so, I don't know, so unplanned."

"You're really quite pretty when you smile," Owen said seriously. "You should do that more often, my dear. Unplanned. That's a good word for it. Of course," he continued in a lighter tone, "film people have to be able to sell a movie over and over again to investors, studios, actors, and they can't do that by saying you've got to read this mucking great book. No one reads in the movie business. That's a given. They have to be able to sum up the plot and characters, and pitch it in a sentence, or maybe two."

"Can you do that with this movie? I've only gotten bits and pieces of the story. I guess extras don't really need to know, do they?"

"True enough. If you tell extras too much, they might get it into their heads to act, and that would be a disaster. . . . All right. It's an old myth. I gather there's lots of variations. Sulann—that's Pauline's role—is an Indian maiden who is given as a bride gift to a powerful tribe from across the sea. She spurns the man, embarrasses her parents, and gets beaten by her father who cuts off her fingers. Then she's cast into the ocean by her people but miraculously survives and emerges from the waters on the shore of a land where she starts a new tribe and lives happily ever after."

"That's way more than two sentences," Ellie teased.

"I could probably boil it down to two if I tried. Oh, and I forgot the sacred jewels. Sulann carries them as a gift to the other tribe, but she doesn't know they have special powers. The magic of the jewels creates a new nation out of birds and fish."

"It sounds kind of corny. Pauline Little Sparrow is a big star and all of that, but do you really think white teenagers will come to watch a movie about an Indian?"

"This may be history or myth, but the basics are played out every day all over the world. Teenagers identify with turning against their parents yet triumphing in the end. That's what Hollywood does best. Tell universal stories with lots of goodies like sex, violence, and magic stuck on as decoration. And Pauline sells just as well to the Occidental, the Oriental, and the aboriginal, believe me."

"And I'm supposed to be some kind of vision she sees when she washes up on shore?"

"It'll be quite fantastic when they layer in the special effects," he explained. "You're a vision from a past life, a thunderbird figure who gives her strength, urges her to pull herself out of the water. The scene will have everyone on the edge of their seats. You at the top of the cliff, Pauline struggling to reach you. By the time she reaches you, you'll be gone. But you will have served your purpose and she survives."

Thunderbird. Ellie felt a shiver. Kahmi, her middle name, sister of the thunderbird.

"It sounds like my role is a bit more than just an extra. I thought I was just going to be in crowd scenes. Do they know I've never done any acting?" Ellie tried to keep the anxiety out of her voice.

"Neither have I," Owen chortled. "I've just *appeared* in thirty-eight films. Don't worry, just go along with it and don't ask too many questions. You'll do fine. If you start getting into trouble, I'll be on the set."

As Owen finished talking, a stir ran through the onlookers below. Pauline Little Sparrow had disembarked from her yacht and was carefully let off a small launch at the foot of Siwash Rock. The tide was nearly full, causing the water to lap at the shelflike foot of the rock. Suddenly all was action. It was one thing to keep everybody else waiting, quite another to keep the star waiting.

"Thunderbird! Thunderbird! We're ready for you."

Ellie jumped to her feet as if poked by a cattle prod.

"That's me!" Suddenly she was very nervous. Her breath felt trapped in her chest.

Hamish Owen patted her shoulder. "You'll be marvelous, my dear. You have a luminescent quality, even when you don't smile." He moved off to a position near the upper cameras to watch the effect as Little Sparrow emerged from the water.

Ellie walked over to the area of the cliff above Siwash Rock, the tall spire of battered granite at water's edge. Eons ago the sea had separated it from the land. Cormorants nested on the top, and a couple of scraggling pines clung to the steep sides, just below the pinnacle. The lookout where Ellie stood was disguised to look like boulders instead of a concrete viewing platform. A commemorative plaque was temporarily removed. Below, Pauline Little Sparrow conferred with the director on a cell phone.

All Ellie had to do was stand at the edge of the cliff, gaze out at the mountains and then, when Little Sparrow emerged from the ocean, drop her eyes and bathe the star with a look of compassion. Ellie hadn't mentioned anything to Hamish Owen, but the story sounded familiar to her. The tales her mother wove in all those dark basements melded together in her mind, but this one she remembered because of the gory part where the girl lost her fingers. In her mother's stories, people often lost body parts. Ellie also thought the story was sad. In her heart she believed that if she had a father nothing would ever persuade her to do anything to shame him.

The movie star moved into place, readying herself to slip into the icy waters. Most would have called on a stunt extra, but Little Sparrow insisted on doing it herself. Her body was encased in a microfiber wet suit that fit her skin and curves perfectly, leaving her looking naked on camera. Ellie couldn't see her well, but she seemed to float over the ground. She heard calls from the crew boats and the director onshore, readying everyone for the scene.

At that moment Matthew Beaver materialized, along with a dozen protesters carrying signs. They must have dodged security by coming along the shoreline from Third Beach. On the water a dozen canoes paddled toward Siwash Rock.

THIEF OF STORIES, WHITE REDSKIN, CORPORATE INDIAN, the placards proclaimed.

The protesters chanted words Ellie didn't understand. They didn't look angry, more determined than anything, and Matthew, clearly the leader, seemed disconnected as he directed the singsong refrain to the sky.

"Assholes!" growled one of the crew standing beside Ellie, waiting for the "roll" signal. He was fat and wore a thick belt hung with a cell phone, a pager, and a walkie-talkie, almost at crotch level. His black T-shirt was emblazoned with the airbrushed image of three pintos surging out of a river. On the back were the words "Sparrow Paints." In smaller letters was the phrase "giving back what was." The man spat hard on the ground.

"In New Mexico they name kiddies after her, in Colorado she's an honorary elder, in Washington she's honorary chief so fucking many times over we lost count. In Alaska they create a tribal dance for her ancestors. And the whale the Makah killed, you know that big hoo-ha over the whaling a few years back?"

Ellie shook her head.

"Yeah, well anyway, they put her spirit or something into the whale before they cut it up."

Seeing Ellie's expression, he hastily added, "That was a good thing. But here, in fucking save-the-trees-gimme-my-land-back-only-the-right-Indian-will-do Vancouver, they picket her, for chrissakes! Indians picketing the most famous Indian since Sitting Bull."

"What do they want?" Ellie asked when the man paused for breath. She still thought the idea of taking back Stanley Park was crazy. But after she'd spent some time here, the idea of the park being a place of power no longer seemed quite so bizarre. Her mother certainly thought it was.

"Ahh, they're assholes. They claim she stole their stories for her *Painted Bird* CD and she's stealing another one in this movie. What crap!"

Ellie, watching the Indians below, thought they looked rather dignified. Matthew, despite his jeans and scruffy leather jacket, looked powerful and . . . she searched for the words, in control.

The walkie-talkie crackled.

"Ready for you, kid."

Ellie's heart leaped. She was going to be in a movie with Pauline Little Sparrow! Ellie Nesbitt of the downtown eastside. Ellie Nesbitt. If the

Mighty Old One could see her now. She wondered if her face would actually get on the big screen or would she end up on the cutting-room floor.

"How do I look?" Ellie felt a little silly asking this slob who was sweating heavily despite the wet chill in the air. He studied her carefully, gently readjusted a chain of feathers hanging over her shoulder, and resettled the blanket across her shoulders.

"Sweetheart, you look terrific!"

As Ellie followed the man to her spot, the picketers ratcheted up the volume of their chants. By now, several television crews were on the scene, trying to get shots of the protestors, their numbers swollen by dozens of gawking joggers while reporters argued with the security guards about how close they could get. The whole area was electric with energy.

Ellie felt charged. It was the same way she used to feel when she counted her money. She wouldn't be doing that again for a while. Bo's betrayal seemed far off. Really, the bastard couldn't help himself. She was as mad at herself as she was at him. She should have opened a bank account, like a normal person, instead of hiding it like a skid-row bum stashing a drug cache. Ellie shrugged her shoulders underneath the scratchy blanket; oddly, she did feel pretty and sexy.

Ellie Nesbitt knew she was reasonably good-looking. She'd been fielding catcalls and obscene gestures from drunks and addicts since she was five. But what the hell did good looks do for you when you grew up in the stench of humanity's armpit. She supposed there were worse places in the world—Calcutta, maybe, or those wretched refugee camps that sprang up on the border of every war. Shaking off her blackening thoughts, Ellie was determined to enjoy herself. The money was gone.

After an hour of being positioned here and there and watching the director stride from camera to camera, talking with the operators and the lighting technicians who moved huge lights and giant silver umbrellas around, Ellie finally heard, "Let's roll!" Her heart leaped again. At a signal from the fat man, she raised her arms and moved them back and forth slowly, the blanket flowing like the feathers of a seabird as it fanned its wings to dry. As she did, Pauline Little Sparrow would see her. First she would be fearful and then driven to reach the vision. They rehearsed the scene three times. For each run through, Sparrow's face took on a genuine chilling panic as she first caught sight of Ellie's apparition.

In the distance, there was some pushing as the picketers tried to invade the shot but a dozen off-duty police officers kept them contained.

"And rolling!"

The scene was shot again and again. Ellie felt like a bird raising her arms slowly, feeling the blanket catch the breeze. The waited-for steady drizzle coated her face and left a sheen on her costume. She was lost, the moments absorbing her. Growing up in the nearly treeless center of the city, she'd never really noticed branches and needles before. With each take she studied a different section of the three tallest trees. Cedar? Douglas fir, perhaps? She didn't know, but each one, pushing far into the sky, seemed to have a different personality showing in the angle of limb and trunk. The three trees were a family, the tallest being the father, inclining toward the mother, and in front sprouted junior, a mere seventy feet or so, its limbs thrust outward like a kid catching a ball.

"Cut and cut!"

The walkie-talkie crackled.

The director's assistant hurried over to her, dodging roots and a mud puddle. He looked pissed.

"You're smiling," he snapped. "All through the last scene. Nobody told you to smile."

"Oh, I'm sorry. I just got, uh, kind of lost, you know." Ellie felt her cheeks burning.

"Don't worry about it," he said, softening his tone. "The look's great. You're doing great. Couple more takes and we're done."

Sparrow's concentration was ferocious. Ellie had never seen anything like it. No one approached her or spoke to her during the entire sequence. Again and again she rose from the mucky debris at water's edge, terror stamped indelibly on her face. She had to be freezing but there was no hint of it.

The shoot was almost over when the crowd of protesters, their numbers swelled by casual observers to about a hundred, surged forward, almost breaking through the security cordon. Little Sparrow, her intense concentration finally broken, squared around to face them, Matthew Beaver at the forefront.

The picketers shouted in unison. "Give back our stories!"

Before the guards could react, Sparrow charged forward and straight-armed Matthew with sufficient power in her tiny frame to send him stumbling backward.

"*Your* stories!" she shrieked, water dripping from her. The wind carried her words to Ellie. "And what do you people do with *your* fucking stories? Nothing. *I* make them great! *I* bring them to the world!" Then Sparrow turned her attention to Matthew again. "You pathetic little man. What have *you* ever done for *your* people in your miserable life?"

"Our stories and culture are only products to you," Matt retorted. "Something to buy and sell. To us they're our past and future. You're corrupting them with your greed."

"Don't you dare call me greedy." Hate contorted Little Sparrow's face as her nails raked across Matthew's face, drawing blood.

Matthew grabbed the star's wrist hard enough to make her scream in pain. By then the guards were on them, roughly dragging Matthew away, fending off the other picketers.

"Uh, oh," the fat man said. "Trouble now. This'll be feeding time for the lawyers."

"That man Pauline scratched *is* a lawyer," Ellie said.

"No shit! Must be a loser if he hasn't got anything better to do than be out here protesting."

Ellie was shocked by Pauline Little Sparrow's expression. Previously, even in anger, confidence and control surrounded her, making her seem invincible. But now, as the guards dragged and pushed the protesters back, she looked lost.

A movement on the cliff edge caught Ellie's eye. The camera tipped forward, perilously close to toppling off the cliff. The cameraman jumped back, shouting something incomprehensible. He was followed by several lighting technicians and a sound man. Ellie thought they shouted, "Bear!" and she looked around fearfully. Then she heard it again, "Get clear!"

Perplexed, Ellie swiveled, searching for the fat man; as she did, she slipped on the wet moss beneath her feet. Damn! It was wet and muddy. Wardrobe would probably be angry. Then she felt it—shaking and a faint rumble.

"C'mon, kid, let's beat it!" The fat man ran past, yelling into the walkie-talkie.

"What's wrong?" Ellie asked, scrambling to her feet.

"It's a fucking earthquake," the fat man screamed, not waiting for her. "C'mon, for chrissakes, we've got to get out of here!"

Ellie marveled at how fast he moved. Turning to follow, she stepped out into air.

Vancouver lies along the same fault lines that come ashore at San Francisco and plunge into the dry heart of California. Beneath the date palms of

Indio, Desert Palm, and Quinte runs the ticking bomb of the San Andreas Fault. In Vancouver and all over Vancouver Island, little rumbles occur by the dozen. Few actually feel them, only hearing about the baby temblors on the morning news. Ellie had experienced a couple in her life, but they were little more than the mild vibrations of a truck crossing railroad tracks.

The cliff face peeled away, slowly at first, giving Ellie almost enough time to leap to solid ground. Almost. She flung herself forward, grabbing at the kinnikinnick bushes growing along the edge. They held her long enough. The initial sheer of rock plunged to the seawall below, taking out a camera, a small boom truck, the director's skyjack, and four light stands. That section of the seawall had been closed for the movie. Otherwise joggers, bladers, and cyclists would have been flattened by the debris.

Ducks, cormorants, and seagulls rose in unified protest as rocks cartwheeled into the water. Viewed from above, the reaction of the people below was like a forest blowback, scattering them as if pushed by a powerful wind.

Ellie, clinging desperately to the cliff edge, saw none of it. "Help me!" she called out. The words were no sooner out than she began to lose her hold. The main fall of rock had softened the angle of the cliff. Instead of falling backward into the air and down to the boulder-filled seawall, she slid down the face, the blanket she wore catching and slowing her as she went. Fifty feet later she somersaulted to a stop at the base of the cliff. A hard object dug painfully into her back and she wiggled carefully, testing her limbs, to release the pressure. Small stones rained around her. Her head throbbed and blood trickled into one eye, her palms stung, her nose felt broken, and her knees ached as if someone had been bashing them with a baseball bat. But alive, definitely alive.

Pauline Little Sparrow reached her first. Funny, Ellie thought, drifting in semiconsciousness. Why haven't they whisked her away?

"Oh, you poor thing! Where does it hurt? No! Don't move, honey, wait for the ambulance."

A male voice spoke in her ear. "We're going to get you out of here, kiddo. Hang on."

Kind words floated around her. Little Sparrow's soothing hands stroked her face and dabbed at the blood streaming from her forehead. Everyone else was busy erecting a rough roof in case more rocks fell. Ellie tried to speak. There was something horribly sharp burrowing into her back.

Little Sparrow bent over. "What are you saying?"

"A . . . a rock or something," mumbled Ellie. "In my back. Can you pull it out?"

"I'll try, but stay as still as you can. You might have an injury to your spine."

Little Sparrow slid her hand beneath Ellie.

"Got it. Hang on, it's a piece of wood."

Ellie's head cleared. Everything seemed very bright and sharply focused. The cry of a bird, a crow or raven, pierced the air, sending stablike pains through her temples. She saw a huge black bird circling nearby and willed it to shut up.

"Oh my!"

Ellie slid her eyes over to Little Sparrow, who was holding a small box in her hands. Despite the caked-on mud, an extravagantly carved lid was evident. Pauline pried it open, and out spilled material like a bird's nest and a cascade of small, smooth stones. Some rolled into her lap. Little Sparrow snatched them up furtively, stuffing them back into the box.

"What is it?" asked Ellie.

"Nothing," Little Sparrow said quickly. "Just an old wooden box. The corner was sticking into your back. No wonder that hurt. Does it feel . . ."

Sirens and the whup-whup of a helicopter overwhelmed her words.

Blackness welled up from behind Ellie's eyes. She smiled and sank into it.

77

"The earthquake was good for one thing," Matthew said cheerily.

"Let me guess," responded Ellie, trying not to show how pleased she was by his visit. She'd been in the hospital for three days and there had been an army of reporters—print, radio, and television, plus quite a number of the film crew. But no Matthew. The nurses had been wonderful, guarding her like Little Sparrow's retinue protected her. In some versions of the earthquake story Ellie had been described as Little Sparrow's protégée, then an evening news report called her an unknown First Nations woman from the Hastings Street area of Vancouver.

"They wanted to take that cliff down anyway?" Ellie shifted uncomfortably. Her ribs were killing her, and the scabs on her knees and hands were starting to tighten.

"Well, I don't know about that, but the movie's toast, at least for a while."

"I can't believe a little thing like an earthquake could stop Pauline Little Sparrow."

"Perhaps not, but even the Indian Queen herself can't fight public-safety regulations. The cliff is unstable all the way around to the north side of Stanley Park, so they had to close the road completely and parts of the seawall are washed out around the other side. It's a mess. The amazing thing is you're the only person hurt."

"You sound like a kid at Christmas," Ellie said, peering at him through one eye. The other was still swollen shut.

"You bet. Couldn't be happier. All in all, I consider it a good day's work—protest corporate greed, picket Hollywood North, summon up an earthquake."

"Ohhh," groaned Ellie. "Don't make me laugh. The doctor said that cracked ribs and laughter are worse than childbirth for pain. I believe him."

"I'm not completely kidding about the earthquake," Matthew said pensively. "Three days ago we had a meeting of all the bands interested in trying to get Stanley Park back. It's going to be an entertainment getting everyone to agree. There's ancient rivalries among the tribes that just won't go away. But that's another story. We had the meeting over at the Musqueam tribal office and two elders from a Cowichan band on Vancouver Island came. They claim descent from people who lived in Stanley Park eons ago. They did a dance I'd never seen before. When I asked one of them what it meant, she said it would 'bring forth the spirits of the earth.'

"Hey. I'm just telling you what she said," Matthew shrugged at Ellie's skeptical look. "I've always thought of that stuff as symbolic. After the earthquake I asked the elder about it and she said, 'What did you expect?'"

"I wish you'd warned me," Ellie said lightly. "I could have at least gotten out of the way. Now how am I going to pay for my dealer's course?"

Ellie's brief movie career was over. Her savings were still gone and the dealer's course started in two months. Even if she could go back to work at Sparky's there wasn't enough time to save for the fee.

"Hey there!" a nurse said, poking her head in the door. "You look perkier." Ellie hugged her ribs, holding back laughter.

"What's so funny?" Matthew asked.

"When I applied for the job as an extra I described myself as perky."

"That wouldn't be my first choice."

"Me neither, but I didn't think 'gloomy' would get me a job."

The nurse busied herself taking Ellie's pulse and temperature and checking her bandages. "I almost forgot. Someone dropped this off for you." She handed Ellie an envelope.

In it was a check for $1,500 and a typewritten note from Painted Lady Productions expressing sorrow at her injuries.

"Wow! Will you look at that. All it took was nearly killing myself. I'm almost half there with this," Ellie said happily.

"What's with you and that stupid dealer's course?" Matthew asked.

"Stupid?"

"Look, I'm serious." Putting on earnestness like an overcoat, he was oblivious to Ellie's annoyance. "I can get you a scholarship from the foundation. You're smart. We need people like you."

"Get out," Ellie warded him off with a bandaged hand. "I didn't even finish high school!"

"Neither did I. I told you that before!" Matthew said impatiently. "I've become a mentor, just like my old grade nine teacher. It's part of my responsibility to the foundation to find other candidates."

"All this Indian stuff isn't me," Ellie said firmly. "Besides, I'm not even full-blood, and aside from my mother I haven't the faintest idea who my ancestors are." She set her lips tightly. "When I get out of here, I'm going to Reno."

"You'll never have an opportunity like this again." Matthew wasn't giving up. "I'd love to report to the foundation that I have found a woman like you . . ."

Ellie sat up as best she could. Her Hastings Street con job–spotting radar was pinging rapidly. "Is that what this is all about?" she said harshly. "Filling some kind of quota! Do you get a finder's fee?"

"No! No! I just said it wrong. I didn't mean . . ."

"You said it just right," Ellie interjected. "Now, if you don't mind, I'd like to sleep." She rolled over as best she could and heard him leave quietly. A wave of despondency overtook her. Just for once! Just for once! Can't I be nice and let something go?

✳

Despite the crush of vehicles and trucks at Kitsilano Beach, it wasn't hard to find the Airstream. A forty-foot-long, custom-built gleaming silver bullet sitting by itself, cordoned off with rawhide rope. At each corner of the enclosure tufts of feathers hung, puffing up slightly in the breeze off the water. Near the steps to the trailer a pile of rocks formed a rough sculpture about five feet high—an Inukshuk like those common in the Far North and thought to have been originally direction markers in the featureless terrain. Gastown souvenir stores were full of miniature versions. Ellie looked closer, amazed to discover the rocks were jade of some kind . . . pale-hued and polished, the sculpture caught the light off the water.

Several picketers milled around on the grass verge. Matthew was among them. Ellie peered at him out of the corner of her eye as she passed. He was talking animatedly with a television crew who waved him over to a truck, which he got into and sped off. Ellie took in the bustle. She had been right, after all. The earthquake had barely made Pauline Little Sparrow pause. She simply up and moved everything. Part of the shoot was being done here, the rest at Wreck Beach, a nudist hangout at the foot of the cliffs leading to the UBC Endowment Lands, which encompassed a huge chunk of the proud prow of land separating English Bay from the Fraser River's north fork. The University

of British Columbia occupied the westernmost section, offering students glorious vistas of the Strait of Georgia. On the edge of the campus facing English
Bay stood the UBC Museum of Anthropology, an energetic concrete, wood,
and glass building—a sculpture in itself—housing the world's foremost collection of West Coast native art and artifacts.

When Ellie got out of the hospital that morning, she was surprised and
pleased to find a note from Little Sparrow with her discharge papers asking—no, demanding—that she come for a visit. "*Please come at once!*" the
note finished. "*I have an urgent matter to discuss with you. I will be waiting
for you in my trailer in the parking lot at Kitsilano. Pauline.*"

St. Paul's Hospital, in the heart of downtown, wasn't far from the beach
on the other side of Burrard Bridge. Outside the doors a line of cabs beckoned. "What the hell," muttered Ellie. "I goddamn well deserve it."

The Airstream door opened, and a middle-aged woman with a broad,
flat face and the flattened nose of a South American Indian stood there.

"The shooting has moved to Wreck Beach," she said solemnly.

"Oh," Ellie replied, not sure what to do next. "Well, will you tell Pauline
Little Sparrow that Ellie Nesbitt was here?" She fervently wished she had a
phone number to leave.

"The boat is waiting for you."

The woman leaned out and pointed to a pullout, where a canoe was
resting on the beach with two men standing beside it.

"They will take you."

Ellie stared. "You're kidding, right?"

The woman's face was implacable. Irritated, Ellie stepped down and
walked over to the canoe. She'd looked out at the water; white caps were
forming at the top of eighteen-inch waves.

No way was she getting into a tippy canoe and paddling all the way to
Point Grey. As she neared the canoe, she saw a good-sized launch rolling
slightly at anchor. Well, maybe. Ellie's ribs hurt and her head ached. She wished
she could sink into one of those big squishy chairs she'd seen in the Gastown
loft. That day seemed like a century ago. The paddlers saw her approach and
ran over to take her arm as if she were a frail old lady. Well, maybe.

The launch ran over the wavelets like a fairy dancing on light. Ellie
hardly felt a thing. It took only ten minutes to reach Wreck Beach and the
sixty-foot yacht sitting offshore. Ellie scrambled awkwardly up the ladder,
trying to protect her ribs. Any moment, she was sure, the dream would be
over and she'd wake up listening to Too Tall Frank pissing overhead.

An ancient woman with a deep brown face, shiny and round, waited for her.

"Ellie Nesbitt?"

Ellie nodded, her heart pounding.

"Come."

Ellie stepped over the side, trying not to wince. She entered through the door of the cabin and was instantly disoriented. Her temples throbbed like a bad hangover and she had the urge to sit down before she fell. Not for the first time in the last week Ellie felt as if she was watching a movie of someone else's life. Ellie Nesbitt didn't board private yachts, much less visit movie stars. Yet here she was. From the outside the yacht was a gleaming testimony to wealth. Inside it was like a cave. Blankets covered all the walls, and only thin shafts of light penetrated the side windows and the curving skylights set into the roof. In the shadows Ellie could just make out hides covering the furniture and woven grass rugs on the floors.

The woman put her hand on Ellie's cheek. The touch, intimate and knowing, startled her. She was about to step back when the woman spoke, her words floating over Ellie in a cloud of cloves and cinnamon.

"Welcome, child. Who are you?" The old woman's voice was deep and resonant, somehow commanding.

"Ellie, Ellie Nesbitt."

"I know that, child," she said forcefully. " I say again, who are you?"

Ellie had dodged drunks, users, thieves, and the Chinese and Tamil gangs who descended from time to time looking for an injun bang. She'd survived one rape, a near rape, and now an earthquake. She'd been frightened more times than she could remember but nothing like this. The woman's touch terrified her like the swinging suspension bridge across Capilano Canyon where she'd gone with her grade nine science class. Nothing below but rocks and white-water fury, and only a few boards and a rope to keep her from plunging into it.

"Who are you beneath this pretty skin?" The woman placed her palm against Ellie's stomach, pressing slightly to emphasize her question. For a horrified moment Ellie thought she was going to pee herself. She snatched at the woman's hand and tried to protest, but nothing came out. The woman's eyes, friendly before, shrank to slits.

"Where did the stones come from?" she demanded. "Who give them to you?"

"Stones?" blurted Ellie. "What stones?"

"Stones in box," the woman spoke harshly. "Why you give them to my little sparrow?"

"I didn't give anything to her!" Ellie snapped to hide her fear. This was all getting too weird. This strange woman was sucking something out of her.

She turned to go, pulling away from the woman's unwanted touch. Then the memory pierced her. A box! She'd fallen on a box. The memory was fleeting, a vision of Little Sparrow's hungry face and snatching hands.

"Why you give it?" The voice was almost threatening now. "Stones are out of time, cursed!"

✳

"Thank you for coming," a soft voice rasped out of the darkness—a voice far weaker than the rich, husky tones of the movie star a few days ago. Squinting, Ellie could just make out Pauline Little Sparrow curled up in the corner, shrouded by a distinctive red-and-black Haida blanket.

"Please excuse Malos. She gets a little protective."

Little Sparrow held Ellie with tired eyes. Stripped of makeup, she was still undeniably striking, but the star's personality seemed flattened somehow, like someone just released from jail. You could always tell—their faces were masks, unaccustomed to expression.

"That box I pulled from underneath you. Malos thinks it's making me sick. Silly, isn't it. I'm sure I have the flu. My doctors are too. But Malos says it's the box and the jade beads inside that contain some kind of evil."

"Curse!" Malos emphasized.

"She's right about one thing," Pauline Little Sparrow said, lying back against the arm of the sofa. "I'm cursed by these dreams. Horrible dreams. Birds attacking me, pulling at my clothes, pecking at me—pecking my eyes out. And the noise, I can hear it in my sleep. I'm afraid to go to bed."

Ellie caught the faint sound of Little Sparrow's teeth chattering. She did look ill.

"My bodyguard took the box to a bank vault downtown. But the dreams got even worse! It was like I had a fever but with no temperature." The star seemed on the verge of hysteria but she visibly took hold of herself. "It's like Hitchcock's birds in that horror movie," she said, with an attempt at humor. "If they weren't so real . . ." Her voice faltered.

Ellie heard a growl in the background as Malos cleared her throat. "You must know the thing's purpose. Take care how you possess something, or it possesses you."

"Tell Malos I didn't take it from you," Little Sparrow pleaded like a child.

"It wasn't mine. And I really don't remember much. It was sticking into my back after I fell, and you moved it, and that's it, I guess. I think I saw you open it and there was something inside." It was all foggy and Ellie's head still hurt. Why all this fuss?

"I knew what they were the minute I saw them," Little Sparrow spoke more strongly. "I collect jade. Those stones are jade beads. Very old and for sure Chinese. You can't get that color on the West Coast."

"What do you want me to do?" said Ellie. "The box isn't mine but I'll help if I can." She didn't know what else to say.

"Bring it please, Malos."

A box covered with carvings of fish consuming their own tails sat on the rug in front of the sofa. Malos lifted the lid slowly, as if expecting a monster to leap out. The woman handed it over. Her fingers touched Ellie's and she hung on to the box for a moment. "Who is keeper?" Malos demanded.

"What?" Ellie was perplexed. These people spoke in riddles.

"You take it. Find where it belongs. Leave my little sparrow."

Pauline Little Sparrow knew enough about artifacts not to clean the box. Though obscured with dirt and lichen, which had taken hold in one corner, the strong lines of the face on the lid stood out. Ellie ran her finger over the swollen lips and exaggerated brow. She shivered, but it was a warm, inner thrum of pleasure. The mud was now dry and Ellie had no difficulty removing the top. She stared inside. When she was seven years old Ellie had met her only relative. An aunt. A sister of her mother, who'd married a Yakima and lived on a reserve in Washington. When the woman got off the Greyhound bus in downtown Vancouver, a short distance from Oppenheimer Park, Ellie immediately spotted her own face. She remembered grinning like a jack-o-lantern, as if her recently arrived aunt had lived with her from birth.

Looking at the pale, green stones in the box gave Ellie the same feeling—familiarity, family—a deep knowing as if she'd seen them before. She emptied them into her palm, rolling them back and forth, enjoying their warmth and the clicking sound they made. She didn't know how long she studied them, but when she lifted her head what little light came through the windows had faded and the room was darker than ever.

"Did you ever want to be what you aren't?" Little Sparrow asked.

"Every day of my life," Ellie responded.

"I'm not native," Little Sparrow spoke in a rush. "Never have been. My mother's Puerto Rican, my father's Mexican and white."

In the background, a long, angry hiss escaped from Malos.

"You're the most famous Indian in the world," Ellie protested. "Everyone says you're putting First Nations on the map."

A gurgle of laughter escaped Little Sparrow, like something unpleasant caught in her throat. "I've got the look. I was meant to be aboriginal. I know it! It was a calling. I'm sure of that. Puerto Rican singers are a dime a dozen. You can hardly get into the clubs if you've got a name like Mendoza. But a Native American! That's special. There's Cher with her little bit of red blood, and Buffy Sainte Marie, but they're passé. A *Native,* that's what I had to be."

Malos moved from the back of the cabin, snarling like a dog.

Ellie backed toward the cabin door with the box. It felt like a tiny child cradled against her breast.

"Why are you telling me this?"

"Why not?" hiccuped Little Sparrow, beginning to cry. "You'll never tell. And who in hell would believe you anyway? You're just a kid from the street."

Malos wrapped her arms around Little Sparrow. "Get out!" she spat. "Keep away from my little sparrow."

Ellie stumbled toward the ladder, surprising the men in the launch. Her injuries stabbing at her, she awkwardly descended into the boat.

"We'll take you back?" the kind-faced skipper asked.

Ellie looked numbly to the shoreline. The tide was rising and all the movie equipment was being loaded on boats. In the darkening January light the fast-disappearing sand looked like a dark bruise.

"Take me there!" she said urgently.

"Tide's almost up. There's no way off the beach, except a rickety old staircase." The skipper pointed to the connection to the Spanish Banks, which was nearly underwater. "You don't look so good, lady."

"Take me there! Now!" Ellie shouted. She had to get off this boat. Get away, anywhere, quickly.

The skipper drove the launch right onto the beach, so she wouldn't get her feet wet. But she tripped and her shoes filled with seawater anyway. As they pushed off and began to pull away, Ellie almost called them back as the cold clutched at her. What a stupid idea to be dropped off at Wreck Beach in the middle of winter. Ellie had never been here before, and as the misty air rolled in, she tried to imagine the shore filled with naked bodies. A giggle, half-cough really, overtook her.

"Oh Mama, you must be laughing now," she said aloud.

Ahead of her was a rough staircase. "What the hell. At least I can get out of here."

Holding firmly on to the box, Ellie began to climb. Within minutes, her breath came in short, painful gasps. The stairs were steep, with most of the handrails missing; leaves and moss made the going treacherously slippery. She took ten stairs, then stopped, panting shallowly, trying not to let the air expand her ribs. Ten more, another stop. She could feel her blood pounding at the scars on her palms. Nearly two hundred steps later Ellie came out at a path leading into the woods. She followed it, keeping her head down, so she wouldn't fall on the branches strewn everywhere.

Suddenly the forest gave way to a clearing. Ellie stopped, unable to control her exhilaration at the sight.

The back of the UBC Museum of Anthropology soared—a swooping glass-and-concrete offering to the early evening sky. All around it totem poles stood on scree beds, like arms raised in prayer. Ellie could see past them right into the museum displays blurring the line between in and out. An enormous raven's head looked as if it were going to peck its way out of the glass. She thought of the birds attacking Little Sparrow in her dreams. Right in front of her an old pole, devoid of paint, was topped by a thunderbird.

"Kahmi," she whispered.

Mesmerized by the sight, Ellie didn't immediately notice Matthew Beaver standing by one of the totems. Light from the setting sun highlighted his face as a reporter asked questions. Ellie felt dizzy emotion surge through her—fear, excitement—she didn't know. Matthew spotted her and, bidding the reporter good-bye with a quick handshake, he walked over.

"Hi, Ellie," he said carefully, taking in her wet shoes and distraught demeanor. "I didn't expect to see you here."

Ellie suddenly was at a loss. How to explain the strange feelings coursing through her, the strange events in Little Sparrow's yacht, the hostility of Malos, let alone the box and the stones? She started to laugh.

"What's so funny?"

"Maybe there is something to the Indian spiritual stuff," Ellie said, still laughing. "There was one person in the world I wanted to see. And here you are."

"What's going on?" Matthew asked, happy but baffled.

"I don't know how to explain it," she blurted. "Pauline Little Sparrow asked me to come and she had this box I fell on during the earthquake. They're terrified of it; I mean, really scared to death. The old woman said it's cursed and they just about jumped out of their skins when I opened it. There are these beads and it feels, I don't know, it just feels like I saw them before."

"Whoa!" Matthew put his hand comfortingly on her shoulder. It felt good, very good, wonderful, in fact. "Are you taking some kind of pain medication? You're not making a lot of sense."

"I know," Ellie said, helplessly, "but it happened. When I opened the box, they reacted like I was letting loose some kind of disease. Little Sparrow looked as if she wanted to throw up. But I felt warm all over. Like I did when I was a kid and my mother hugged me."

"Everything's going to be OK," Matthew soothed. Ellie felt her neck hairs rising at being treated like a child, but she bit hard on her tongue. "Let's have a look at this box."

He spent a good ten minutes slowly turning the box in his hands, gently running his finger over the surface, taking care not to dislodge any debris. "It's clearly very old. The carving is primitive. Salish, possibly, but the work is more like the southern Kwakwaka'wakw rather than the tribes of the Lower Mainland." The difficult word rolled easily off his tongue. He grew excited. "I think this is a depiction of the *hamatsa*."

"The what?"

"A cannibal, a birdlike monster who craves human flesh. There's a dance the Kwakwaka'wakw do that explains how he is tamed. I've seen masks and paintings, but no carvings like this."

Again Ellie thought of Little Sparrow's dreams. "How do you know it's old?"

"My university undergrad degree was anthropology," he said. "My summers were spent working right here at the museum. Cataloging all kinds of old stuff. You start to recognize periods. I've never seen carvings quite like this before, but I know they're not recent—definitely not in the last few hundred years. The more recent carvings all up and down the coast have certain similarities—huge eyes, for example. Look here, these eyes are undersized, if anything, relative to the rest of the carving."

"Open it!" commanded Ellie.

Matthew pulled off the lid. Air escaped from him like a puncture.

"This is weird."

"You know what they are?" Ellie asked eagerly. "Tell me you know what they are!"

"I don't know exactly *what* they are, but they look identical to the ones the Chong Museum has displayed. The inscription says something about the oldest example of jade carving known. They're tens of thousands of years old. What I don't know is what they're doing in this Indian box."

He turned to her. "Tell me everything," he said urgently.

Standing there, with the wind pulling at their clothes, she told him all that she could remember of the fall, the box, Little Sparrow snatching it up, the feeling of familiarity when Malos shoved the box at her and told her to take it away. Pieces from her mother's stories flooded back and filled her words. They linked like a jigsaw, finding each other as if only waiting for the right guidance. The shadows had dissolved into evening when she finished, exhausted, throat dry and aching.

"This isn't wood. It's some kind of soft stone—obsidian, probably," Matthew said in awe, studying the box again. "I don't think it would ever have survived so long. It could be thousands of years old."

"It must have been buried in the cliff face somewhere. Maybe at the foot of a tree." Ellie recalled seeing several trees lying on the beach, torn from their rocky bed.

"Were there shells around?" he asked excitedly.

Ellie thought hard, visualizing the scene. "Yes, that's what they were, thousands of them, all over the place."

"You know," Matthew murmured softly, addressing the box, "to tell the truth, I never believed a word of the old stories. Not a word."

He tilted his head, eyes shut, and began to sing, a low croon that rose and fell like gentle waves. Then he began to dance, hopping slowly from one foot to the other, weaving back and forth, shaking his head at the box held out in front of him. It was like the Indian dancing Ellie had occasionally seen on television, but different. The steps were delicate, almost mincing at first, then becoming more powerful. The chant kept pace with his feet. Matthew ended with a great shout that reverberated off the concrete building. A few late visitors hurried away, distancing themselves from his antics. Ellie couldn't help but smile. She wasn't prepared when he suddenly flung his arms around her. They fell to the gravel, Ellie landing heavily on her sore knees.

"I'm sorry, oh Ellie! Shit. What an idiot I am. Here, careful." Matthew helped her up and brushed her off, his hand lingering. "Do you know what this means?"

"I don't have a clue about anything right now. I feel like Alice down the rabbit hole," she said, thinking of one of her favorite childhood books.

"This, my lovely Indian princess, is the first evidence we've ever had that there might be ancient and continuous settlement in Stanley Park." Matthew was fully into his earnest pomposity but Ellie was starting to find it endearing. "No significant midden has ever been uncovered that proved more than seasonal occupation. No burial sites. Nothing. But here, thanks to the earth shaking, might just be evidence. We go to the park board with this and you as witness. Maybe Little Sparrow will even back you up. It'll be great PR for her. They'll be forced to let us dig. The cliff coming away must have exposed a midden, a burial spot, or something."

He brushed the box, then took Ellie's hand. "I want to show you something." He walked to the back door of the museum and unlocked it with a key. "Never got around to giving this back."

Ellie had never been in the museum before. In fact she'd never even been in this part of Vancouver. Matthew guided her through the feast displays, an astonishing carved arch, a massive housefront plate with powerful figures seeming to erupt from it. The objects pulled at her, and she wanted to stop and touch every one, but Matthew tugged her along a lighted corridor into a sizable separate viewing area where a large woodcarving of yellow cedar sat alone under spotlights.

Ellie was speechless. Easily six feet high, the carving was of a giant raven crouching protectively on a clamshell, from which children were pushing their way out. Their round faces were joyous, inquiring, hopeful, as they emerged. The figure was so realistic it seemed to move in front of her.

"It's a Haida myth about the origins of their people. Bill Reid carved it," Matthew breathed deeply.

"It's unbelievably beautiful," Ellie whispered. "I've never seen anything like it."

"We are a great people," Matthew stated. "Some of us have just forgotten."

"You know," Ellie said, "my mother had all these stories about birth and death and reincarnation. I never really paid attention to them. I was always only interested in what was now. She had one story she told me about this tribe, our ancestors, and how they are descended from the tears of a great spirit. She said the tears would bring our people back. When I heard what the movie was about, her words kept coming back to me. I also tried not to think about it, if you know what I mean. It was as if thinking about it made what my mother told me real."

"Do you think it's real now?"

"Real? I don't know. How can people come from clamshells or jade beads or spirit's tears?"

"How can you explain what's in your hand?" he asked softly.

"I can't," she said, cupping the jade beads to her breast.

"Is that real?" he pointed to the carving glowing in front of her.

"It's real," she admitted, starting to believe in spite of herself.

Darkness cocooned the outdoor totem garden when Ellie emerged with Matthew. She felt scoured, like a child after a hot bath and a vigorous soaping.

"What are you going to do?" he asked.

"I used to know. Yesterday I was so sure. Now . . ."

"What about Reno?"

Ellie reached over and took Matthew's hand. "Oh I don't know, maybe I'll go in a century or so."

"It could take a long time, you know."

"What could?"

"The park. Vancouver isn't going to give it up easily."

"Easy? I don't know anything about easy."

Authors' Note

Writing a novel, after eight nonfiction books, is a dream come true. For making that dream possible we must thank Larry Ashmead, Vice President and Executive Editor of HarperCollins in New York. The concept of *Vancouver* was Larry's and so was the inspiration. We hope we've fulfilled your faith in us and thank you forever for the wonderful opportunity.

Krista Stroever, associate editor, HarperCollins New York, was unfailingly supportive and added keen editorial insight throughout. She also demonstrated the patience of Job putting up with our innumerable missed deadlines.

We know that our longtime friend Iris Tupholme, Publisher of HarperCollins Canada, was instrumental at many stages in this book and saw the potential of the idea from the beginning. We are very grateful for her support and look forward to working with all our friends at Harper-Collins.

We are also indebted to our agent, Bruce Westwood, who came through for us at a critical point in our lives. His enthusiasm for the project and his confidence in our making the transition from nonfiction to fiction kept us going.

We never met Olga Gardner Galvin beyond her extraordinarily diligent copy editing work. Thanks for helping make our thoughts clear.

One of the joys of writing *Vancouver* has been the opportunity to take characters from the past—or at least the sense of their characters—and transform them into the individuals on these pages. The idea that late Ice Age Africans were great sailors and travelers who crossed all the way from the African continent to Asia and then eventually to North America via the Bering land bridge is one anthropologists and archaeologists have debated for decades.

Another joy was playing with innumerable "what ifs" in creating the stories. No one really knows if Juan de Fuca found the strait named after him, or if Europeans were attacked and stranded in the Vancouver area so early on. However, we are convinced the sophisticated West Coast native culture has been cross-pollinated from many different sources at a far earlier date than is commonly believed.

All the theories, all the tantalizing possibilities, are wonderful fodder for the novelist. In the end, of course, we have no way of knowing that events happened as we've portrayed them, but . . . they could have.

With any work of historical fiction, the lines between fact and invention are blurred and crossed many times. That's part of the fun. However, we were determined to stay close to the timelines of history as it is known. Similarly, we attempted, as much as possible, to adhere to the known settlement patterns of First Nations People. That said, there is no tribe or people called the Kahnamut, though there are at least two places on the West Coast near Vancouver that bear the name, which, loosely translated, means "welcome."

Three of our characters—Warburton Pike, Konrad von Schaumberg, and Walter Dolby—were, in part, inspired by real people. (All other characters are entirely fictional.) Those familiar with Vancouver history will recognize those three in the characters we created. We elected to keep Pike's name, as we couldn't think of another that so matched the spirit and exploits of this enigmatic individual. More than twenty years ago, historian Patrick Dunae introduced us to Warburton Pike in his excellent book *Gentlemen Emigrants* (Douglas & McIntyre Ltd., Vancouver, 1981), and we fell in love with him on the spot. We recast the real Pike in a slightly different time and took the liberty of creating events of which nothing is known. For instance, we know that Pike did travel around the American West for several years as a young man, but there is no record of his adventures. The real Pike did write two books and undertook numerous hazardous expeditions throughout British Columbia. He also made and lost fortunes and had a penchant for "slumming," as an acquaintance quaintly portrayed his friendship with Indians. We hope our Pike is faithful to the spirit of the man.

Using appropriate language is always difficult when dealing with such a sweep of history. The wonderful resource book *A Stó:lō–Coast Salish Historical Atlas* (Douglas & McIntyre, Vancouver, 2001) was instrumental in helping us with the Halkomelem language common to large numbers of the West Coast First Nations. We also utilized resources from the University of Victoria and University of British Columbia's native studies programs, as well as the excellent material developed by the Museum of Anthropology.

But who knows how or what native people spoke thousands of years ago?

Spelling can drive a writer mad if you are dealing with half a dozen different languages and a few thousand years of history. The great river itself, the Fraser, was originally called Fraser's River but, readers will notice, it changed to simply Fraser River. We elected to use spellings of the day, where comprehensible. Many native words are spelled and accented differently depending on the source. We opted for consistency even though a single place-name like Khwaykhway, a settlement in Stanley Park, can also be found looking like this: Qoiqoi, or this: XwàyXway.

In all, we've thoroughly enjoyed the process. We thank the small army of people from as far away as Shanghai, Mexico, Chicago, and England who willingly answered questions and chased down arcane facts. We particularly thank the many First Nations people from the Squamish, Musqueam, Haida, Stó:lō, Kwakwaka'wakw, Aleut, and Innu who provided information and interpretation.

Many writers and their works were helpful to this book. In the certainty that we will neglect to mention a critical source, we briefly list those authors whose works particularly contributed to the final product. Terry Reksten, George Bowering, Peter C. Newman, Raghu Rai, Khushwant Singh, Bruce Macdonald, Hilary Stewart, Rosemary Neering, Bruce Hutchison, Paul Yee, Diamond Jenness, Ruth Kirk, Brian Fagan, Chuck Davis, Dr. Harjinder Singh Dilgeer, Dr. Awatar Singh Sekhon, and David Chuenyan Lai.

We are also grateful to Peter Griffiths for helping to research so many details about navigation, ships, and Beringia. The work was invaluable. And we apologize to our poor children, Claudia and Quinn, who endured nearly three years of parental neglect, obsession, and fatigue as we struggled to complete the longest book of our careers.